# The
# Midwife

# The Midwife

❖ ❖ ❖ ❖ ❖ ❖ ❖ ❖ ❖ ❖ ❖

A NOVEL BY

## Gay Courter

Boston

HOUGHTON MIFFLIN COMPANY

1981

Epigraph courtesy of Margot Edwards
and Mary Waldorf, from their biography
of childbirth reformer Lester Hazell.

*Library of Congress Cataloging
in Publication Data*
Courter, Gay.
The midwife.
I. Title.
PS3553.086185M5     813'.54     80-26324
ISBN 0-395-29463-0

Printed in the United States of America

P  10 9 8 7 6 5 4 3 2 1

FOR PHILIP,
because he gave me
his most precious gift: time.

*Each child has something to teach us, a message that will help to explain why we are here.*

— from the Talmud

# Acknowledgments

For sharing expertise and giving encouragement, generous assistance, or loving support I thank: A La Veille Russie, Sherrie Allen, Laurie Bloomfield, Sandra Branch, Jem Cohen, Don Cutler, Peggy Drake, Glen Duncan, Margot Edwards, Ann Falbo, Karen Goldstein, Anna Herz, Carl and Loretta Hirsch, Julie Houston, Barbara Katz, Ralph and Muriel Keyes, Stephen and Shari Leviss, Mary Lindsay, Annie Macketon, Esther and Ruth Mandel, Allen Menkin, Lynn Moen, Mount Vernon Public Library, New York Academy of Medicine, New York Historical Society, New York Public Library, New York University Archives, Suzanne Nichols, Rosalind B. Paulson, Mary Pisaniello, Gerald Slaper, Neil Spector, Val Stout, Rita and St. Clair Sullivan, Judy Sutherin, Robert and Donna Wade, Vicki Walton, Warren County Library, Elsie, Leonard, and Robin Weisman, Leah Weisman, Ruth Wilf, Jack Yager, YIVO Institute for Jewish Research, and especially my persevering editor, Daphne Abeel.

# Contents

# BOOK ONE

*Russia*

# I

❖ ❖ ❖ ❖ ❖

# *Victor Golonovin*
## Delivered April 7, 1904

❖ ❖ ❖ ❖ ❖ ❖ ❖ ❖ ❖ ❖

# · 1 ·

HANNAH WAS SEATED ALONE at one of the round tables readied for eight students. "Clang, Clang!" The bells reverberated through the vast dining hall, then ceased. In the brief interlude Hannah caught her breath. "Clang!" There it was: two bells, a break, and one final bell — the call for the "Midwife On Duty." For the first time in Hannah's life that call was for her.

A brief, unfocused glimpse of her reflection in the polished wooden table revealed trembling lips and the excited gleam in her eyes. She took one final sip from her tea glass and willed herself to remain calm.

Hannah Blau had been admitted to the Imperial College of Medicine and Midwifery ten months before, after winning a place among the 2 percent of each class allotted to the Jews by law. In 1903 Hannah was the sole Jewish person admitted to the Midwifery Division in five years. One Jewish woman and four Jewish men were attending the Medical Section. Those five at least had each other on whom to rely, but Hannah was by herself in her class of fifty purebred Russian midwives.

She was a stranger, a foreigner in her own country. Although technically she was as Russian as they, her first language had been Yiddish, and she still spoke theirs with an accent. While she could usually follow academic discussions, the casual social conversations, the jokes, and their idiom further excluded her from the company of these educated women from Moscow and St. Petersburg.

Hannah left her tea glass to the serving girl. No midwife, not even a Jewish one, was expected to handle food or crockery. As Hannah rose from her chair she methodically centered her student's striped apron and snapped the bow at her waist to improve the crispness of her appearance. Her straight black hair was pulled back into the traditional severe bun worn high on their heads by all student midwives. Most of the women in her class did not consider this attractive, but the ebony crown only enhanced Hannah's fine bones and lively green eyes.

With back erect and shoulders squarely set, she was determined to leave the hall looking confident. The experienced midwives took their time. Just as she neared the halfway point to the double doors, someone coughed slightly. Hannah glanced involuntarily toward the sound, and there, in the far-right corner of the room, sat a woman who wore metal-rimmed glasses that were slipping down the bridge of her large nose. Her rounded face, framed in burnished curls, was certainly not handsome, but as she caught Hannah's eye she gave a broad smile and a tilt of her head that unmistakably meant "Good luck to you."

There was no time to dwell on the identity of her mysterious advocate, for as the tower clock chimed quarter past eight in the morning Hannah realized it was her bad luck to be summoned just as a fresh shift was coming on duty. Now members of the teaching staff could hover about criticizing her delivery technique.

Hannah's performance on this first practical test of her career was not entirely within her control. There would be two other factors: the laboring mother and the little stranger she carried. Hannah hoped this would not be the mother's first baby, which, statistically, would indicate a longer, more tedious labor. As her steps quickened down the hall and through the two large West Wing wards on her way to labor and delivery, Hannah allowed herself to imagine her ideal patient: stoical, cooperative, and appreciative, with a quiet demeanor that would demonstrate to any passer-by what excellent care Sister Blau was giving. And the perfect baby, a slim-boned female, would be born pink and have a lusty cry, owing, most certainly, to the fine technique and thoughtful ministrations of the new midwife!

❖　❖　❖

The Imperial College and Lying-In Hospital were housed in a grand palace that had been built for Catherine the Great's son Paul before he became czar in 1796. He was eccentric, tyrannical, unusually ugly, and was strangled by his own officers after only five years on the throne. Thus his name was never associated with the building, which consisted of two wings that formed a horseshoe curve to the east and west. Its massive colonnaded front faced directly on the Voznesenski Prospect, opposite the River Moskva. The large oval courtyard contained gardens, which were still maintained though not kept in the profusion of flowers that would have satisfied an imperial prince of Russia.

A three-storied rotunda formed the heart of the structure. Its first floor, designed as an elegant ballroom, was now the dining hall. The two upper stories contained offices for the administrators and doctors. Balconies of filigreed iron encircled the second and third tiers, and one could step from an office to look down on the dining tables or up at the opaque glass dome divided into eight sections. The rose-veined marble floors and walls absorbed no sound, for they had been designed to be acoustically sympathetic to chamber music recitals. At the points where the eight enormous arches supported the structure, corners were formed. If one person stood directly facing a crevice and spoke to someone standing diagonally opposite, the listener could clearly understand the words spoken fifty feet away. Thus, if a student sat in the wrong nook her most hushed whisper might be heard by a party across the vast room or up several tiers. Indeed this was one place where the walls did have ears, and so the first rule a new entrant learned was "Never discuss private matters in this public place."

The West Wing, which housed the charity wards, was known as the Luisa after the Grand Duchess Luisa Maria Augusta of Baden, who had married Paul's eldest son, Alexander. Here the peasant women of Moscow were cared for by student and professional midwives.

Every Luisa mother filled out two cards, one with the name she wished to use during her stay at the hospital, and another containing her correct identity, which was sealed inside an envelope to be opened only in case of emergency. If a mother had nothing to hide, she would use her real name during convalescence, but if she wished to conceal an indiscretion she knew her secret was safe within the walls of the Luisa. The Imperial Foundling Home was located only a short distance away, and all a mother had to do if she wished to give up her baby was ring a bell outside its gates and a basket would be lowered to receive the infant. Only one question would be asked — "Has the baby been baptized?" — before it would be drawn up five stories and thereafter cared for by the Crown.

The East Wing, called the Catherine for Paul's empress mother, was still furnished with many of the original royal tapestries, canopy beds, ornately carved chairs, and faded, yet elegant, carpeting even in the delivery suites. While the surroundings were appreciated by the noblewomen who gave birth there, the dust catchers contributed to a rate of puerperal infection that was almost twice as great in the Catherine as in the Luisa, where the cold floors and unadorned wooden tables and chairs were much easier to keep clean.

Student midwives, while not expected to straighten their own rooms, were responsible for the thorough scrubbings that preceded every delivery in the Luisa. But the elite clients of the Catherine were delivered by doctors assisted by ignorant peasants with no knowledge of aseptic procedures. Thus the wealthiest, most privileged Russian lady was likely to deliver in a far more germ-filled room than the humblest pauper. Many wives and daughters of the medical staff chose the Luisa because they had heard they would fare better there, although no one had yet correctly surmised the reason.

Luisa babies remained with their mothers, sleeping in little boxed-in shelves attached to the wall near the bed of the mother, who tended and fed her own baby as much as possible, while the

Catherine babies were kept in a central nursery where staff wet nurses suckled more than one infant at a time. Rashes, sores, and contagion of all sorts thus passed quickly from one baby to another. Catherine mothers would remain in this environment for more than a month, while Luisa mothers were released as soon as possible to make room for new cases. Thus their children had less time to contract disease. The official excuse for the difference in mortality and morbidity rates in the two wings was "The noblewomen are more delicate, the peasant women of hardier stock."

❖ ❖ ❖

At the entrance to the birthing corridor Hannah saw her name chalked in on the callboard: "H. Blau, Midwife On Duty." That morning only one expectant mother lay on the thin hair-stuffed mattress upon which she would labor and deliver. She was in her last few hours of hard labor, attended by Sister Kochubey, who looked as though she had been up all night with her recalcitrant patient. Two other women in very early labor were pacing up and down the corridor, silently shuffling close to the walls. Neither looked up when Hannah arrived, and so she surmised they were not her concern.

Hannah turned her attention from them to a frail woman in a black cape and feather hat sitting on a bench and talking quietly with Dr. Speransky. She held her breath as she realized that this fine lady, hardly the peasant she had been expecting, was to be her patient.

"Aha! Madame Golonovin, you see I told you we wouldn't have long to wait. Here comes Sister Blau to attend you. I am certain you will find her very sympathetic." Dr. Speransky's words, cordial to the patient's ears, were condescending enough to remind Hannah that this superior disliked her only Jewish student.

"My pleasure to meet you, Madame." Hannah bowed her head in respect, but curtsy she would not. "May I ask how frequently you are feeling your pains?"

Madame Golonovin paused. Hannah wondered if her accent had confused her or if she had already guessed that Hannah was Jewish.

"I have no pains," she said simply. "It's just that they told me
this was the best time to come, you see . . ."

The doctor interrupted her. "Madame's water broke last night
and we thought she might come in now to save herself an uncomfortable journey, since labor should begin quite soon."

"Yes, that was a good idea," Hannah acquiesced politely.

"Sister, we thought Madame could have this first room, if that is
agreeable to you." They stepped into the Luisa's only remaining
private room, with windows that overlooked the rose gardens. A
large, low canopy bed and the one tapestry that had not been removed made the room infinitely more grand than the other charity
accommodations.

Dr. Speransky was of the same diminutive height as Hannah,
but double her breadth and weight. One direct stare from her
steely grey eyes sent shivers down the spines of all the students,
most particularly Hannah. The doctor lowered her voice to a rasping whisper. "Madame Golonovin is the wife of one of our ministers of state, Sergei Ivanovich Golonovin. He refuses to let a male
Catherine doctor touch his wife, let alone examine or deliver her,
and so we assured him that Madame would receive excellent care
in the Luisa from our wise midwives. Do you understand?"

"Might she accept a blind birth?" Hannah suggested tentatively. This was commonly performed by male doctors, who, for
the sake of their patients' modesty, worked completely by the sense
of touch. The doctor reached under the covers and skirts with only
his hands and did all his examinations and deliveries with his eyes
averted to a point in the distance, a skill much practiced by the
male students, who prided themselves on the sensitivity in their
fingers.

"Impossible!" Dr. Speransky bellowed. "Golonovin cannot believe that any man, even a doctor, wouldn't have unnatural
thoughts for his beloved wife. She will do as well here, we all know
that."

"Yes, of course. I will do my best to make her comfortable,"
Hannah stammered.

"We expect more than your best!" Dr. Speransky hissed. As she
marched from the room her layers of taffeta petticoats sounded like
rushing water.

After the doctor paused to give Madame Golonovin a few comforting words, she disappeared down the center of the corridor. The two laboring women and a passing scrubwoman pressed to the walls to allow her to pass quickly.

Hannah was alone with her patient.

## · 2 ·

AFTER THE BRIEFEST APPRAISAL, the young midwife suspected problems might arise during labor and delivery. Madame Golonovin's height was average, but her skeleton could barely support a full-term pregnancy. The skin stretched tightly over the delicate bones of her pale face where a miniature nose was but a precise chiseled stub in which the large, tensely pinched nostrils seemed curiously out of place. Madame's wide-set brown eyes contemplated Hannah cautiously and her apparent distrust seemed to mask a far deeper fear.

Though anxious to begin the physical exam to see if Madame's pelvic bones would be as narrow and weak as Hannah suspected, she hesitated to touch her patient until Madame was more relaxed. Since it could be a full day before her pains came with any regularity, Hannah thought she should insist her patient rest before her ordeal began in earnest. This noblewoman did not look as though she would have the stamina to withstand a lengthy labor, but if she had borne any previous children there might be hope for more rapid progress; Hannah surmised, though, that anyone as nervous as she seemed to be was probably a first-time mother, or primipara.

Hannah regretted she had no medications with which to ease Madame's suffering. Though the doctors were experimenting with gases and potions, they tested their use in childbirth only when the patient was in such distress that death was probably imminent. In contrast, the midwife's tools were her training in the natural processes of the body, her understanding of the forces that a woman's personality displayed during labor, and a few techniques in applying this knowledge. Hannah's concern was to spare her patient undue agony at all costs.

"Oh, Madame Golonovin!" Hannah pleaded silently. "Please make this labor easy, for your sake as well as mine!"

Instinctively Hannah knew that if she could demonstrate she was not afraid of her charge it would put her in the position of being her momentary equal as well as hint at the intimate level of contact that would be forthcoming. Tentatively she touched Madame Golonovin on the shoulder and found her cloak still wet with the cold Moscow spring rain. Madame turned cautiously.

"Come, let me show you to your room," Hannah said, making an effort to speak in her clearest, softest voice.

But her patient stared over her large mounded belly without moving. "I don't think that is possible. I have, I believe . . ." She stumbled over her words and blushed a mottled crimson from her collar to the soft honey curls that framed her forehead.

Hannah bit her lip. "How stupid of me. Already I have failed her!" she thought to herself, remembering that Madame's bag of waters had broken several hours before.

"Of course, your waters, how distressing for you," Hannah said with sympathy. Then she bent closer to Madame's ear and took one of her velvet-gloved hands into her own small chapped one. "But you must know that while this may never have happened to you before, here it is the most common of occurrences."

Madame smiled slightly and looked directly at Hannah for the first time. "At least my outer skirt is still dry," she whispered.

"I will fix some cloths for you. Just wait one moment."

Hannah returned from the storeroom with a large linen pad and asked Madame to lean against the wall and tilt her hips while the midwife deftly lifted her skirts and fastened the pad in the waistband at the back of her underdrawers, pulled it through her legs, and finished tucking it in front. Then she undid Madame's wet petticoats and gave them to an assistant who was hovering nearby.

"Madame will need these washed immediately," Hannah ordered.

"Yes, Sister, I'll see to it," the young woman replied with deference. Hannah made a mental note to learn the name of the serving girl, who might become useful to her if she wasn't prejudiced against her by the other midwives.

"Now are you more comfortable?" Hannah asked. "We have some waiting to do. Your little one will have to decide whether or not she is coming today."

"Oh, not *she!*" Madame protested gaily. "We are expecting another son!"

Another. Hannah had been wrong in her assumption that this was to be Madame's first child. "You have a boy at home, then?" Hannah asked casually but realized she had made a terrible error as she watched the tears welling up behind Madame's dark eyes. The woman held her breath for a moment.

"There are none at home," she said simply.

Madame Golonovin looked so pale Hannah feared she might faint if she were questioned further.

"You must get settled and I will order tea. That should help you feel much better." Hannah supported Madame's elbow and guided her down the hallway and into her room, which had just received an additional scrubbing. The floor was still damp in spots, so Hannah tightened her grip and steered Madame to the chair by the leaded glass windows.

There was a polite knock on the partially opened door.

"Who is it?" Hannah inquired.

"Irina. I am bringing the tea." The same docile serving girl appeared. As she set the tray on the table by the window, Hannah noted that her face had been hopelessly scarred by the pox and one of her arms was markedly shorter than the other.

Instead of the usual dented brass samovars that circulated throughout the Luisa, tea was presented on an English-style silver service Hannah presumed had been sent over from the Catherine. Slices of a delicate white goat cheese were artfully arranged on a scalloped china plate so that one blossom of the rosebud design was revealed between each piece of cheese. Instead of the usual sour black bread, tiny boulochkee, sweet rolls, were arranged in a neat pyramid. Never in her months of ward service had Hannah seen such a presentation. Even the administrators were not served on silver!

Hannah allowed Irina to pour while she pulled a second chair over to the small wooden table that later would hold the delivery instruments. Irina used her stronger left arm to lift the heavy pot while her withered right hand steadied the china cup. Before Hannah was handed her tea, the door opened slightly to reveal the black frock coat of Dr. Stefan Petrograv, professor of obstetrical practice.

"Sister Blau, may I see you momentarily?"

Of all her professors Petrograv had treated her the most correctly, neither ignoring her nor singling her out for severe questioning. He was a small man, not much over five feet five inches, and since Hannah was not quite five feet herself, she felt more comfortable with him. And she had never feared looking directly into Dr. Petrograv's grey eyes, which reflected understanding even during a critical examination of a student's technique.

"Yes, Doctor, may I help you?" Hannah closed the door quietly behind her after Irina slipped out between them. Dr. Petrograv moved in order to be out of earshot of the midwives hovering in front of the supply table.

"It has been brought to my attention that this is the first patient you are to handle without direct supervision. You may not have realized that you were recommended in this case," he said, and he paused to clear his throat. "Some felt that a senior midwife should have relieved you today, but others agreed that you have the potential to take the case to completion." He waited for Hannah to digest the meaning of his words.

"Did you know that Golonovin is an intimate of Minister Witte's?" he added obliquely and then, stroking his beard between his thumb and forefinger, continued with a warning. "We are standing by, of course, and if there are any difficulties you must not hesitate to summon us for consultation." He removed his wire-rimmed spectacles, folded them neatly, and then rapped them against his open palm to punctuate his words. "Do you have any further questions?"

Hannah struggled to control her voice but it cracked slightly as she answered. "I have just been learning her history and I know her not to be a primipara."

"You must get a full account," Petrograv replied abruptly. "I will be in the Catherine throughout the day, where some very sick babies require observation." Petrograv placed his glasses in his breast pocket and walked away briskly. With admiration Hannah noticed how straight he held his back. As she observed his determined stride, Hannah thought he looked a much taller man.

After the sound of Petrograv's patent leather shoes faded down the marble halls, she was aware of an unnatural silence. Even the laboring woman seemed to hold her moans in check. As she stepped back into Madame Golonovin's room, Hannah tried to assimilate the implications of Petrograv's visit.

His statement about Minister Witte disturbed her. Why had the doctor referred to the one friend the Jews had at Court? It was said that the only reason he stood for moderation in Semitic policies was that his wife had Jewish relations. Even if that were true, Witte had issued edicts liberalizing educational quotas and travel restrictions. He had even spoken against the despicable Plehve, who had found immense popularity among peasants and nobility alike with his frightening solution to the "Jewish Question": one-third must convert, one-third must emigrate, and one-third must be eliminated. Was Petrograv insinuating that an untoward outcome in this case could actually have an effect on political policy?

A groan from her patient brought Hannah sharply back to the present. Madame's hands clutched the arms of her chair and her mouth twisted as she submitted to a wrenching pain.

"You really are going to have your baby today!" Hannah said in her most cheerful voice while observing that Madame's facial muscles had begun to relax.

"It is a remarkable thing that is happening. Do you understand why you are feeling so?"

From her medical bag Hannah pulled a little knitted garment, an absurd multicolored purse with a shirred neck fashioned from scrap yarns. If a drawstring had been added it would have resembled a miniature marketing bag. Though Hannah had not yet shown her creation to the staff, she had used it before to illustrate a point she had been finding difficult to explain even to women who had already given birth.

"Now, imagine this is your uterus."

"My what?"

"Your womb, the little sack that holds your baby. Of course yours is not made of wool, but it does stretch. It started out just this size before you carried the baby, about like a pear, and grew until" — Hannah mirrored the size of Madame's swollen abdomen with her hands — "until it could hold your fully grown baby. And this part is called the cervix, or neck," Hannah said, pointing to the crimped edge, which resembled a ruffled collar. "This is the part that must open all the way so your baby's head will fit through."

Then, wadding up a piece of linen into a ball, Hannah shoved it into the knitted sack and demonstrated how, by pushing on the ball, the neck would slowly dilate. "Watch how the baby's head presses it open until it reaches the widest part of the skull." The ball popped out. "Now your baby is born!"

Madame Golonovin's own uterus chose that moment to demonstrate the force of a contraction, which raised her up in her seat. It passed quickly.

"But, the pain! I can't believe it is as simple as that."

"First you feel the pain as the muscles stretch out, and then it eases off as the muscles relax." Hannah illustrated by pulling the yarn taut and then releasing it back into shape. "Just think of it as a sack opening and a baby slowly slipping out."

"But you are not telling me all of it! You have not explained about the bones that break."

"What bones are those?"

"The ones that must crack to let the baby pass through!"

"No, Madame, you must believe me, that is not what happens," Hannah replied, shaking her head. But Hannah could see that her patient still doubted her words.

The bones! Such a misconception! Yet one that most of the women, peasant and noble alike, seemed to share. As a child Hannah had often heard the ladies' complaints when they were being fitted in Papa's tailor shop. Yet Mama had a different story to tell anyone who would listen.

"It's just something to get through, not so bad; when it's over it's over. It is the only time God rewards you so quickly for your trouble," she'd say, patting the young mothers' protuberant stomachs and smiling so warmly they really wanted to believe her.

When she was almost seven Hannah had had the opportunity to discover the truth. Her mama was expecting her fifth child, though only she and her older brother, Chaim, had thus far survived. The second son, Josef, had succumbed to respiratory infection during his first year. Then, less than two years after Hannah, came another son, who, born prematurely, lived less than a week.

Imagining that babies popped out quite unexpectedly, Hannah would hardly leave her mama's side after Bubbe Schtern, the local midwife, had said the time was drawing near. When her mother's labor began, Hannah had been asleep, waking only when she heard the old midwife arrive. As she peeked into the back bedroom, she was alarmed to see that Mama's eyes were squeezed shut and her limbs were shaking uncontrollably.

"Now, now, don't cry. Bubbe is here and everything will be fine," the old midwife crooned. As soon as she saw the child's wide-eyed stare she added, "Hannahleh, go back to your bed!"

Hannah did as she was told, or pretended to. When no one was looking she slipped behind a drape in the doorway and viewed the proceedings from a small tear in the fabric. She tried to imagine what Mama was suffering but did not feel one bit sorry for her. Mama had lied! It did hurt! Just as all the women said! Hannah listened intently to hear if the bones were cracking. "That will serve her right! She should have told me the truth!"

"Something is wrong!" Mama gasped between pains. "It comes for so long, I push, it slips back. Tell me, what do you see?"

Bubbe Schtern didn't know what to say, for there were many signs of grave difficulty. The child was coming into the world upside-down, in the breech position, but unlike most of these births, the foot had slipped down, as though the baby were testing whether to enter this new world. The child was, in fact, caught with one leg in and one leg out.

"Please, oh please, don't let Mama die!" Hannah prayed silently.

"Ahhhhhhhhhh!" Mama's screams rose from deep down in her chest. "Uggggggghhhh!" she moaned like a hoarse animal, and then "Ahhhhhhhh!" came from her throat higher and higher, ceasing abruptly when Bubbe ended the pulling between her legs. Hannah peeked through the curtain to see a baby half in and half out of her mother's body, its swollen blue foot held in Bubbe's bloody hand.

Then Mama cried out again. Not a scream, but a series of unrelated sounds: huffing, choking, coughing, and intermittent cursing.

When Hannah dared to unclench her eyes she saw her newborn sister lying pale and limp on Mama's abdomen covered with an odd greenish slime. Mama lay back in a faint while Bubbe rubbed and rubbed the child's back, but the baby didn't respond. She slapped at the soles of the baby's feet, flexed her legs and arms, and sprinkled cold water directly on her wrinkled face. "Come on, baby! Come on, baby!"

Finally the child made a sound in her throat, spit up some mucus, and gasped for breath. "Waa, Waa." Her cry was weak but she was alive.

Later, when Mama was asleep, the midwife showed the baby that was to be called Dora to Hannah and her father.

"And her feesela, her foot?" Papa asked. Will she be a cripple?"

"Don't worry, the little bones are soft. I've seen worse turn out perfect. It's just swollen," Bubbe said soothingly. "At worst a slight limp, but . . ."

"But what?" asked Papa gravely.

"I'm not certain, but it was one of the hardest births I've ever seen where the baby . . ." Her voice trailed off uncertainly.

"Kayn ayen hore!" Papa spit to ward off the evil eye. "Ptu, ptu, ptu! Where the baby lived."

A rattling of cups blotted out Hannah's memories.

"Spaseeba, Irina," Hannah said to dismiss the serving girl, who had come to clear the tea tray.

Madame Golonovin cautiously lifted herself out of the chair and came to join Hannah by the window. "Look, the rain has stopped."

"Would you like to see the gardens?"

"Is it possible? I thought I would have to take to bed."

"A walk might be the best thing for you. I believe it helps to move the body around during labor if you feel comfortable."

Hannah placed Madame Golonovin's cloak around her shoulders and wondered if she should get her own. The sky seemed brighter by the minute and there was usually little wind in the courtyard. Better to risk a chill than to abandon her patient.

As Hannah escorted Madame Golonovin out into the hallway she was more amused than threatened by the stares of the staff. Madame, sensing they were doing something out of the ordinary, held her lips slightly curved upward in a mysterious feline smile and nodded with her chin in a regal gesture that bespoke her upbringing. Hannah was pleased by this demonstration of loyalty to her, but when the door was closed Madame lost her composure and glanced about anxiously.

"Oh, look at that!" Madame Golonovin's attention was drawn to the gardener's latest whimsy: topiary ivy formations of cherubs riding unicorns, lions, horses, and large winged beasts. But her interest waned rapidly with the onset of a pain. "Oh! Ah! Here comes another so soon . . ." She held her breath and her face began to redden.

"You must breathe, in and out, in and out, gently, gently, in and out. That's it. When it is over take a good, strong deep breath. Like this!" Hannah sighed a loud demonstration. "Your baby needs you to breathe for him now, so you must not hold your breath." Hannah sat Madame down on a bench by a patch of blooming purple crocuses.

"I don't know why I did that. I'll try the next one your way. Oh, here it is!" This time she calmly breathed through it. Hannah felt pleased that she had already won her patient's trust as well as educated her about her bodily processes. The students often debated how much a woman should be informed. The predominant opinion handed down in the classroom was that the mother should have confidence in her midwife, trusting her as a child trusts the parent. For if a woman knew too much she might ask a difficult question, which might necessitate either a complex, time-consuming answer or, worse, one that might be unpleasant to hear or give. Better to keep her comfortable, keep her happy, and keep her ignorant!

Hannah favored the less popular point of view, one partially espoused by Dr. Petrograv, who taught that pain and fear were somehow linked and the agony was worse when the patient did not understand the powerful forces within her own body. If Madame's labor progressed well, Hannah thought she might have the courage to demonstrate her knitted teaching device and enumerate the benefits of patient education, although her status was still too precarious to allow her the freedom to take a radical position.

"Can you help me? I can't stand up again, I think . . . it's time to return to my room." Madame Golonovin grasped the midwife's forearm as Hannah eased her off the carved stone bench and helped her in the door.

## · 3 ·

AFTER THE FRESH COLD AIR Hannah was hungry, but Madame Golonovin refused any offer of food. She was now in active labor.

Madame was helped to undress to preserve modesty. Hannah's mother had schooled her well in techniques to ensure that the whole skin was never fully exposed. One always kept a bodice or slip loosely draped before adding or removing a layer. Yet Madame Golonovin was less self-conscious than Hannah would have been, accustomed as were women of her station to being tended by servants. When she realized that Madame's vanity had led her to corset herself during her pregnancy, Hannah was dismayed. Deep ridges indented her abdomen and Hannah knew the binding had placed unnatural pressures on the baby. This fashionable practice had disastrous medical implications, as the young ladies with the most envied figures suffered later with compressed and permanently deformed lower rib cages.

Hannah apologized for the coarse hospital gown. "I'm sorry, but we have nothing finer here. Even the Catherine mothers wear these for delivery."

Madame Golonovin didn't respond. She stared at the wall opposite the bed, which was decorated with a golden icon of St. Pantaleon, his head framed in a halo, his body wrapped in a crimson cloak.

"I think you will be more comfortable on your side. Let me try to settle you." In a few seconds she had deftly maneuvered her patient into a hook position so that Madame's right arm curved over her head and her left arm loosely draped along her side, forming the shape of a question mark. Hannah opened Madame's legs gently and tucked a small pillow between her knees. Now Hannah could discreetly examine her from the back.

"I will have to check you, but I'll try to be gentle," Hannah said, slipping her hand between Madame's tense thighs to feel how far the uterus had progressed in opening to release the baby's head. By moving two fingers back and forth one could accurately estimate how much progress had been made. Madame Golonovin bravely resisted calling aloud, but her rasping moan was indication enough that the procedure was unpleasant.

"Now it is done!" Hannah said, removing her hand and wiping it on a clean towel. "I won't have to bother you again for a while. You are doing very well and I am pleased to tell you that this will not go on all day."

"How soon, then?"

"At least the first half, the slowest part, is over. I can't say for sure. It could be a few hours, perhaps less."

Hannah hoped labor would now progress rapidly, for her sake as well as her patient's. Since this was at least a second birth, she might be ready to deliver within two hours, just before late classes were adjourned, so Hannah would not have to perform for an audience that might expect explanations for purposes of instruction.

"Come on, baby, be a good little one and come soon!" Hannah silently prayed. Suddenly, the midwife realized she had never taken her patient's complete history. With the contractions coming so quickly, there was no time to gently ease the information from Madame. She would have to ask direct questions.

Hannah reviewed what she needed to know. Was this the second or third delivery? What happened to the other infants? What other medical problems did she have? Reaching for a box of talcum, she dusted some on her palms, and then lifted Madame's gown to reveal her back and buttocks, which, despite the pregnancy, remained slim and firm. Madame didn't turn her head or react to this intimate intrusion.

"Do you feel your pains here?" Hannah asked, pressing hard at the small of her back.

"Yes, and lower too," Madame whispered, still staring at the icon.

Slowly Hannah moved her hand in a circular fashion, pressing harder into the spine with each counterclockwise turn. Massage techniques were a standard course in the midwifery curriculum. Hannah felt Madame's back tense with the full force of the next contraction.

"Ooooooh, that is where I feel it the most." Hannah pressed harder and Madame's moans became less frantic. "Oooo, aaaah, oooo, aaah." Her sounds echoed the movements of the midwife's hands. As the crest of the pain diminished, Hannah took the opportunity to speak.

"This is your second baby?"

"No, no . . ."

"But not your first?"

"No." Hannah waited, knowing that sometimes silence is the best question.

"My third," Madame whispered.

"And your first was born when?"

"In ninety-nine. Sasha, my Sasha. December. Almost the first child of the new century. Ninety-nine to zero-zero, that is what is on her grave. Zero . . . zero. Nothing! So pretty, so sweet, then a fever . . . nothing."

Another contraction, a hard one. As it passed it left Madame Golonovin's face wet with tears, not so much for the present pain as for the probing into old wounds. Hannah felt cruel but she had to persist.

"Then the second was your son?"

Madame pressed her face into the pillow, which muffled her words. "I could never bring myself to give him a name, but his father had him baptized Ivan Sergeyavich, his own name reversed. Now I don't think we can use the name if this baby is a boy. Can we?"

Hannah replied slowly. "I don't know." Jews never named a

child for a living relative and she was not familiar with Christian customs. "Where was he born?" she asked, to change the subject.

"At home. He was too early, too early. He came quickly and he was so . . . perfect. The doctor said it would be better if I didn't see him again, that there was no hope, he would die, and that it was always worse if a mother saw the face . . . But I heard my baby crying and I screamed until they brought him to me.

"The doctor told the nurse to give me the little ugly thing. Then he left. I'll never forgive him! He did not even sign the certificate. He never came back.

"And the baby was not ugly, he was smooth and creamy. His eyes were open and I was certain he could see me. He was just too small, not even a foot long. His fingers were like tiny twigs without fingernails; his shoulders were like a soft animal's, with downy hairs across his arms and back. Have you ever seen one like that?"

Hannah nodded that she had, but did not speak. She tried to choke back her tears while her patient serenely described the tragedy in a clear, strong voice.

"All that day he lay in my arms. I wouldn't move, I couldn't give him up to anyone, not for a moment. Where would that doctor have put him? What really is merciful or God's will? The priest came and sat with me. He was the only one who didn't think I was insane. He held my hand and placed his other on the baby and then baptized him in my arms. At the end, the baby's breath was so slow; I could see how hard the darling tried. I wished every extra minute for him, every precious second."

She breathed hard through her longest contraction and, when it came to its peak, lost all control and burst into a tragic wail. She sobbed quietly while Hannah washed her face with warm water, and she wept the last tears that were beyond comfort. Hannah pressed against her, staring directly into her eyes, trying to feel with her, to absorb what it must have been like to have held a premature baby, to have watched its little chest rise and sink with the effort of breathing with incomplete lungs. Hannah imagined his tiny ribs pressing through delicate, transparent skin and realized the strain that all creatures make to survive. How could anyone watch a perfect baby, their own freshly born flesh, sink into death before it had a chance for life? In that moment Hannah felt the

most profound respect for this woman, who had refused, against
the best judgment of her medical authority, to give up her baby to
die alone, who held him to her until his last moment of life.


## · 4 ·


AT LAST HANNAH had the information she needed. Fortunately
this pregnancy was full term and Madame was laboring well.

The midwife placed her ear against the swollen abdomen and
discerned a fetal heartbeat that was loud and clear. Then she positioned her hands on the skin and began to palpate the exterior to
reassess the baby's lie, or position. She moved her hands toward
the pubic arch expecting to feel the curve of the baby's head, but it
wasn't there! Her pulse raced. With her skilled hands Hannah
tried every maneuver she had been taught in logical sequence to
determine the angle of the baby's head and back. Something was
very wrong!

Without apology or preparation Hannah began another internal
exam. The neck of Madame Golonovin's uterus was almost completely open — only a slight anterior ridge remained to thin
out — but no part of the baby's body presented itself to press the
cervix open. Hannah reached her free hand over the abdomen and
the combination of the external and internal manipulations indicated that the baby was lying horizontally across the uterus with
the head toward the right and the buttocks to the left. A transverse
position!

Hannah felt beads of sweat forming on her forehead and she
clamped her teeth together to keep her jaw from quivering.
She should have suspected something from the severe back pains!
She should have observed this in the first few minutes of her examination! But she had been so overwhelmed by the status of her patient, so solicitous of her comfort, that she had ignorantly assumed
the baby was in the normal vertex, or head-down, position. She

calmed herself long enough to review the different courses that might remedy the situation. Babies had been known to turn on their own accord within the last hour before delivery — a painful experience for the mother, but one that passed relatively quickly. And there were a few maneuvers that a skilled operator could employ, but Hannah had only read about them. Every delivery she had been permitted to handle under supervision had been a normal presentation, except for one fairly simple frank breech. The problems of the transverse seemed terrifying.

Hannah was at a loss as to how to continue. Should she call for Dr. Petrograv now? He undoubtedly would employ high forceps to bring the baby into position and by doing so would demonstrate Hannah's failure to complete her solo delivery. Worse, she would reveal her incompetence by not having diagnosed the situation from the first. And how would her patient feel after sacrificing some pride to have her baby among the Luisa poor, only to have a distrusted doctor brought in at the last moment against her wishes? Dr. Speranksy would place all the blame on Hannah, rescind her residence permit, expel her. Everyone, perhaps even Minister Witte, would learn of her failure. She would be returned to Odessa in disgrace.

Hannah struggled to remember the lecture on transverse version that Dr. Petrograv had given only a few weeks before. She recalled that the prognosis in such cases depended on the safety and ease with which interventions could be made; the earlier the diagnosis, the better the outlook for both the mother and the baby. Hannah realized she had already failed to prepare properly for this case.

She could attempt the external manipulation, although it rarely worked. Or she could attempt the internal maneuvers she had studied but never tried or even observed, because the doctors were so confident that forceps were the correct solution to these problems. Hannah hated instrument deliveries, not only because they were forbidden to midwives but also because she suspected the doctors used them too frequently and too precipitously. Even Petrograv, with his skill and caution, risked tearing maternal tissues as well as damaging the baby's delicate skull. And the other doctors were worse! They enjoyed comparing their shiny tools, discussing the merits of the different handcrafted leather handles, ordering new velvet-lined storage cases. They used their tools as frequently as possible, if only to justify their expense. Determined not to permit poor Madame to suffer the trauma of the blades or the loss of yet another child, Hannah decided to proceed as best she could.

"Try relaxing your belly wall and take a deep breath," Hannah requested as the next powerful pain subsided. Placing her left hand over the right part of Madame's abdomen, she felt the baby's head. Then she reached across the mound with her other hand to cup what she presumed to be the baby's buttocks. Hannah alternated stroking and pushing the head downward between the next contractions, which came one after another with barely half a minute's rest in between. During the full force of each pain she attempted to retain the small downward gains she had made.

"You are doing very well; now hold your breath once again." Hannah thought she could almost feel the head beginning to slip into the pelvis.

"Excellent, excellent!" Another contraction started abruptly and came to its peak more rapidly than the others, causing Madame to lose the control she had so admirably maintained during the maneuver. Her head lunged backward into the pillow, and as she screamed involuntarily she arched her back away from the midwife's hands, away from the center of her discomfort. This sudden movement jostled the baby, which then slipped inexorably back to its original side-lying position. Hannah gasped at the loss and shuddered with disappointment.

She had made progress with the external pressures. Now if she could only work bimanually, with one hand turning the baby from the inside! Madame Golonovin was sufficiently dilated for the midwife's small arm to reach in, so she could touch the baby even though it was still high in the mother's womb. This would cause the pain Hannah had worked to avoid, but one way or another this baby would have to be born, and the sooner the better for both mother and child! Hannah had another choice to make. She could either reach for a foot in the slightly easier podalic version or attempt to position the head. At this point it was ridiculous to expect success with one or the other, so Hannah decided not to settle on any one course; she would see what part of the infant's anatomy could be found.

Madame sensed the urgency of the problem and tried to cooperate.

"I'm sorry, I must examine you again. I will be touching you inside very deeply, but I'll do it as quickly as possible. It will help if you don't move at all. Try to pant like this: heh, heh . . . heh, heh . . . heh, heh."

Madame obediently imitated the breathing.

"That's it, that's good!" Hannah encouraged.

The midwife reached up deftly and immediately grasped something long and slippery. She pressed it between her fingers. It pulsed with a strong, rapid beat. Alarmed, Hannah let go! She had been holding not the leg she had expected, but the umbilical cord, thus almost causing a dangerous prolapse that would have placed the infant in an even more precarious position. The cord floated up as Hannah reached as high as she dared in a fully conscious woman. Finally she thought she had a foot. Yes! Little toes! A bony ankle!

Madame Golonovin bravely panted, gasped, recovered, and breathed rhythmically again, but she couldn't last much longer. Hannah tried to pull the foot into the pelvis, pushing on the head with her outside hand, but as soon as she applied the slightest traction, the foot slipped from her grasp and retracted back to its obstinate place across the uterus. Hannah removed her arm and wiped her hands on a clean cloth.

"Oh, thank the Lord you are done! It is almost over, isn't it?"

Hannah hadn't the heart or strength to answer, for the process was far from completion. She had lost confidence that she could succeed with internal manipulation. Her arms were too short and the baby was too high, too entrenched to turn! Working blindly, with no real skill or experience, it was wrong to continue. It was a mistake to have avoided consultation for so long. Defeated, Hannah realized she had done all she could. Now it was time for the doctors with their forceps and other devices. Knowing the predicament, Hannah doubted the child could survive the ordeal.

Desperately, she thought of Bubbe Schtern, the old Odessa

midwife with whom she had apprenticed. What would she have done? She didn't even own a set of forceps. Suddenly Hannah remembered! There was another way of turning babies, something so simple that it never appeared in the obstetrical texts! But Hannah would need the assistance of another midwife to attempt it. She looked down at Madame's frail, exhausted body. She was sweating profusely and her gown was soaking wet.

Taking Madame's face in her hands, she said quietly, but firmly, "Look at me!"

Madame Golonovin forced herself to follow the command. Hannah stared into the woman's eyes, dry and reddened, with no tears left to soothe them. As Hannah washed her patient's forehead with a cool cloth, she made her decision. She would take one final chance.

"I'll be back in a moment," she said, covering Madame with a dry sheet. Then she opened the door, turned first to the left and then to the right, searching for a sympathetic face.

## · 5 ·

IN THE BIRTHING CORRIDOR, Sister Kochubey and an assistant were tending to a newborn baby girl.

Sister Anna Persokaya, another student in her division, marched up to her. "Sister Blau, do you require assistance?" she asked.

"I'm looking for one of the regulars scheduled for this shift," Hannah said, for she didn't want this calculating student who had a reputation for bootlicking to interfere with her case. "Weren't you on call all night?" Hannah asked. She remembered overhearing Persokaya brag about how many hours she'd spent attending a dilatory patient just before the duty bells had rung.

"I've been put on special assignment this afternoon, since the others are all required in the Catherine nursery helping to bring down the high fevers."

"Very well, I'll introduce you to Madame Golonovin." Hannah led the way through the door held open by Irina. Once Sister Persokaya was in the private room, Hannah nodded for Irina to close the door, but when she noticed the girl's disappointed frown she changed her mind. "Irina, I'll be needing you as well."

Madame Golonovin could hardly care about a gracious introduction, but the midwives practiced courtesy as a ritual in their training.

"Madame Golonovin, may I introduce Sister Anna Persokaya. She'll be assisting us for a few minutes."

A weak "Spaseeba" was all Madame managed to murmur in gratitude. Finally her twisting and turning had ended and she lay perfectly still without the strength to move or even clench her sore eyes shut.

"But ... I thought ... she was ready to deliver ... What is this?" stammered Sister Persokaya after observing Hannah's exhausted patient.

Hannah shot her a fierce glance.

"What I would like you to do, Sister, is to help me move Madame to a better position, since she doesn't have the energy to turn herself."

Persokaya interpreted this as a request to get the patient down to the foot of the bed into the delivery position.

"No, what I have in mind is ..." Hannah paused. "I want Madame turned completely around ... on her hands and knees."

Sister Persokaya's mouth gaped, her bright blue eyes opened wide, but she checked any further critical comment and said only, "I don't understand how ..."

"First let us just turn her on her side and give her a moment to rest." Hannah went to the head of the bed across from the other midwife and started turning the laboring woman's limp, sagging shoulders toward Persokaya, who supported Madame's head on the left side. Hannah pushed the buttocks, which now lay exposed because Madame's gown parted down the back. Then Hannah rearranged her patient's arms and legs and waited a few minutes for her to recover from the ordeal.

"There, does that feel better? In another moment we are going to move you one last time. I know you are weak, but please try to help us. We'll hold you up; you won't have to use your own strength."

Sister Persokaya bit her lip; her eyes flashed to the left and right. "She is fully dilated, isn't she?"

"That is correct."

"And you plan to deliver her . . . upside-down? I cannot believe it! Who gave you such authority?"

Persokaya had misunderstood the entire situation! Hannah studied her pinched little face, capped with the golden bun that usually gave her an angelic appearance. The groveling mole!

To calm herself she dusted talcum on her hands and began rubbing Madame's back. Round and round, over and over, Hannah rocked at the waist with each rotation of her hand to achieve the maximum pressure. Then she skillfully chose her words, for she wanted her patient to interpret them innocently.

"Now then," she said between clenched teeth, "I see we will be able to manage without you now. Others must need you more than we do at this time."

Sister Persokaya lifted her skirts, twitched her long thin nose into the air, and departed swiftly. Irina, after firmly closing the door, managed a limp shrug with her crippled arm and then, without a word, positioned herself opposite the midwife.

"Now, you push her up onto her arms and I'll support the abdomen."

Their first attempt at the shift was awkward. "Please, no more! Stop it, *please!*" Madame protested.

"I'm truly sorry, but this is absolutely necessary. Now you must try to work with us. We are trying to get you up on your knees. I'll hold you; I won't let you fall."

"But I cannot! Leave me alone! I don't care anymore!"

"You will do exactly as I tell you!" Hannah commanded. "I am responsible for you and your baby and you must do as I say. Now I will count one, two, three, and then we will turn you. Ready? One . . . two . . . three!"

Exerting a last effort from sheer will, Madame managed to help roll herself over to the left and onto her elbows. Irina's left hand pushed Madame by her left shoulder as the serving girl's right one supported the patient's quivering head. Hannah tucked Madame's legs under her massive belly, placing her knees against her chest.

"Now Irina, hold her there! That's right. Madame, you may put your head down; there's no need to hold it up."

Madame Golonovin bowed her head, cradling her tangled hair in her hands. The serving girl, who never before had been permitted to touch a patient, hesitantly allowed her fingers to rest between Madame's shoulders and then, with great sensitivity, gently stroked a tense and tender spot.

The midwife placed her hands around the abdomen for support as well as to check the baby. She was pleased that Sister Persokaya had gone. Childbirth does not usually lend dignity to the female body, and this view brought out the worst. Hannah was glad that Madame did not need to suffer the stares of an unsympathetic colleague.

Relaxing her grasp for a moment, Hannah checked the time on the pocket watch clipped above her breast. Madame had been fully dilated for almost three hours. How much longer did she dare wait before summoning Dr. Petrograv? Five more minutes? She would time it exactly.

Madame Golonovin was supporting her body nicely and seemed more comfortable, since the baby was no longer pressing on every spinal nerve. A gentle rocking motion served to both soothe her and balance her on the bed. Suddenly Madame's head shot up from between her hands. Staring directly into the face of a startled Irina, she shouted, "Dear Lord! My baby ... my baby ... it's ... it's slipping!" She arched her back, not in pain, but from the surprise caused by the child tumbling inside her.

Hannah grabbed at the swollen abdomen to keep Madame from falling and knew immediately what was happening. A large, smooth movement of unknown mass was evident to touch as well as to sight. One moment the bulge was on her left and the next moment it slid downward. The position of the secondary bumps of fetal elbows, knees, heels, and fists changed, and a new set of protrusions appeared on the landscape of her abdominal wall. The midwife reached in, pressing two fingers back and forth along the uppermost reaches of the vaginal vault. Gasping, she withdrew her hand and began to tremble. The head was promptly presenting itself in a perfect position for delivery!

"Turn! Turn her over, Irina. Let's do it!" Hannah crowed in triumph. "Madame, your baby is coming . . . now! Everything is all right!"

Acting instinctively, Irina placed pillows under Madame's head and shoulders and supported her from the back.

"Yes, I feel it!" Madame cried, suddenly no longer exhausted. Her pale lips and cheeks flushed crimson as she clenched her eyes and teeth, tucked her chin to her chest, and pushed. Gasping for breath, she pushed again with every ounce of strength. Again and again she repeated the procedure, her thighs trembling from the pressure.

"That's it . . . that's it. Now wait!"

The baby's head made a slow, constant descent earthward, with Hannah slightly retarding its progress to ease the tension away from the delicate tissues. She could let no harm come to this woman now! The head crowned and the little face pointing downward emerged with a snapping sound. The baby's eyes were pasted shut with white, creamy vernix. The midwife wiped the mucus from its nose, ran her fingers inside its mouth to cleanse the passageway, and before she had its body fully withdrawn the newborn uttered a clear, bell-like cry.

Turning in the precise dance of birth toward the left, Hannah first delivered the upper and then the lower shoulder; and then, after one final push for which no direction was needed, the child was born.

"Here is your son," she said simply as she lifted the perfect male infant in the air before placing him on his mother's chest.

Irina raised Madame's head and shoulders so she could see him still attached to her through the pulsating cord, crying intermittently as he absorbed all the new sensations of living: air rushing into his lungs, the soft afternoon light blinding his vision, the cold of the room a shock compared to the warm world he had left, the strong fingers of the midwife that prevented him from falling.

"He's so beautiful! Look at him turning pink! And he has so much hair!" the new mother said as she reached toward her baby with quivering hands. "He looks like Sergei, just exactly like Sergei when he's hungry!" Madame tilted her head to align her eyes with those of her alert newborn, who blinked and returned his mother's stare. "You are mine, my darling, all mine. Nothing can hurt you now, I promise." Madame's fingertips lightly touched her baby's damp hair and then stroked him completely down the back. Observing the precious moment when infant and mother become acquainted, Hannah felt goose bumps prick her arms, and a shiver of happiness shot up her spine.

"This is odd," Madame murmured, "but I thought I would have a little stranger, and yet somehow I know this one already. It is as though he were always here with me and there was never a time when he didn't exist."

After cutting the cord attached to the still undelivered placenta, Hannah stepped back a few steps to give the new mother and child a modicum of privacy as they shared their first loving moments.

Suddenly the midwife realized she was not alone with her patients and the serving girl. Turning her head toward the doorway, she found it had been opened without her knowledge; and there in the corridor, observing every aspect of the proceedings, were Doctors Speransky and Petrograv, with Sisters Kochubey and Persokaya craning their necks in the background. Quickly Hannah turned her head back toward the delivery bed. Realizing that she had completed the baby's birth expertly, with neither lacerations to the mother nor damage to the infant, Hannah remained calm. If they chose to watch the prosaic aspects of the third-stage placental delivery and immediate aftercare, so be it! Hannah checked her uniform and knew it was hardly rumpled, even after all her exertions.

During her apprenticeship Bubbe Schtern had taught her how to work precisely and cleanly by standing at least eighteen inches from a patient and then extending only the hands and arms. In this way a midwife used a method far more sterile than allowing clothing, which might transmit infection, to touch the body's orifices.

When the large afterbirth slid into the waiting pan, Hannah deftly turned to prevent being even slightly spattered. Then pivoting back, she reached for the fresh linen that she had stacked in readiness and began mopping both Madame and her bedding. Within a few short minutes the delivery was complete, Madame was resting on clean sheets, and her baby was swathed in bands of soft cotton from his neck to his toes.

Ignoring her audience, Hannah continued to palpate Madame's uterus to be certain it was contracting back into position and examined the hardy little boy she cradled in her arms. Irina was sent to dispose of the soiled pans and rags, pushing past the silent staff, who finally dispersed when they realized nothing more of interest was happening.

Hannah sat beside Madame's bed. "May I touch him?" she asked. Now that her job was officially completed, the baby belonged in his mother's charge.

"Of course you may."

"He's the most perfect baby!" Hannah whispered in awe.

"Isn't he wonderful? I feel . . . I feel as though he's my reward, that I won him."

"It was not the easiest of births. I'm only sorry I had to be cruel for a few minutes."

"Not at all . . . I understand now; I did then. You did what you had to do. I have no regrets, only gratitude."

"Have you chosen a name?"

"I want something special for him, something that expresses how I feel about him. Do you know what I was just thinking?"

"What?"

"I'd like to call him Victor, that is, if Sergei agrees, because that is how I feel tonight . . . victorious! Victor Sergeyavich Golonovin. What do you think?"

"That is a wonderful idea! I can just see him now all grown . . . tall and blond."

"Oh, not light like me. His hair should be a fine chestnut color like his father's!" she replied, examining the infant's damp scalp for evidence to support her theory.

All of a sudden the hushed sounds outside the room gave way to a flurry of excited voices. A short, round man with many dimples burst into the room. At first Hannah didn't realize that this was Golonovin himself, for his long waves of reddish brown hair framed a far more youthful face than the stern political figure of her imagination.

"Tatiana, Tatiana! I came as soon as I could. I had just returned from Tsarskoye Selo when Mama told me . . . The horses didn't even have time to be freshened," he blurted. As soon as Hannah stepped back from the bedside, the sight of his wife holding the newborn was revealed. "Oh!" he said, gripping his lapels. "He is born!" Golonovin's eyes widened at the sight of the yawning infant. "It is a boy, isn't it?" he asked more tentatively.

Madame reached her free hand out to her husband and pulled him toward the bed. "Yes, yes! Come see how beautiful he is!"

Trembling from head to toe, Golonovin bent over and stared directly into Victor's eyes, and his son returned the glance without blinking.

Madame uncovered more of Victor's soft face so that her husband could stroke the baby's cheek with his broad stubby finger. Feeling the pressure near his mouth, Victor reached out with the instinct of his species, grasped the protuberance between his lips, and took a strong, healthy suck.

Golonovin startled and gasped, but his finger remained in his hungry son's mouth. Tears welled up in his eyes and he pressed his face away from the onlookers into the neck of his wife, who reached out to stroke his shaking shoulders and cried softly with him. Hannah noticed that real tears had finally come back into Madame's eyes only to be kissed tenderly away by Golonovin.

Closing the door, Hannah knew she was no longer wanted, nor needed.

# · 6 ·

THE OBSERVERS HAD SCATTERED and the noises in the hallway were subdued. Hannah listened and turned toward the sound of footsteps disappearing down the passageway that led to the dining hall. Immediately she recognized the silhouette of Sister Persokaya, who was making a hasty retreat.

Hannah knew that Anna Persokaya had lost esteem in the eyes of the staff while her own success, the first since arriving in Moscow, pounded through her veins and warmed even her eternally

cold extremities. Hannah's face flushed in a happy glow and her
eyes blazed with triumph.

"Sister Blau, will you please join us for a moment?" Dr.
Speransky motioned Hannah toward where she was conferring
with Dr. Petrograv. The administrator's syrup-smooth voice indicated she was addressing her as a peer.

"Hannah, would you tell us more about this case?" Dr. Petrograv asked politely. "We are quite interested to learn the complete
progress of the labor; the delivery we witnessed for ourselves."

Hannah was startled that Petrograv had used her first name and
she wondered if Speransky had noticed the indiscretion. Not even
best friends called each other by their given names in public. Perhaps his use of "Hannah" had been a gentle way of asking for information.

With clinical detail she outlined the course of Madame Golonovin's labor, omitting any mention of her own fears and doubts. "I
had planned to call for your assistance if changing to the full
knees-to-chest position didn't produce the proper result within five
minutes. I was timing the procedure. It did seem to be a chance
worth taking, since there were no risks involved in the maneuver
itself." She watched Petrograv carefully for any signs of disapproval. "Of course, I had every confidence in the success of a forceps delivery, but I felt I owed this patient every opportunity to be
spared any . . . any additional difficulties, since I had ascertained
that this was a most valued child and my overriding concern was to
protect it."

"Very correct," nodded Petrograv. "Yes, your judgment was
very wise. I myself am not certain that forceps could have righted
the situation without some compromise to the baby."

"What interests me, Sister, is why you selected that particular
. . . technique." Speransky paused to clear her throat. "It is not one
that is . . . part of our curriculum, is it?" The doctor was questioning Hannah more politely than she ever had in the past.

"In Odessa I apprenticed with a local midwife who had no instruments and didn't know the modern techniques that we are
taught here at the college, so she had to develop her own practical
solutions. She would say to me, 'If you can't turn the baby, turn
the mother!' This often worked for her, not in every case, but it did

save some babies who otherwise would not have made it. Then again" — Hannah stopped for a moment, remembering her sister Dora's birth — "there were some situations when even her talents were not enough."

"Turn the mother!" Petrograv chuckled. "How clever! We'll have to give the idea some clinical trials. I'll discuss it with Chernyshevsky tomorrow. He'll be difficult to convince, I'm certain of that, but we might at least add it to our repertoire. What harm could be done by trying it for a few minutes before resorting to our more . . . our more elaborate techniques?" Lightly touching Hannah on her shoulder he murmured softly, "Simplify, simplify. Birth is so basic, my dear." Then, turning toward Speransky with his heavy eyelids half closed and his head slightly bowed, he said, "Never be too proud to give thanks that yet another child has survived that short but perilous journey we call birth."

❖ ❖ ❖

Dr. Speransky had left orders for the minister's wife to be moved to one of the Catherine suites, where the elite were attended by the hospital staff as well as their own retainers, usually including a private maid, a nursemaid, and kitchen staff.

Hannah knew it was unsuitable for Madame Golonovin to spend even one night in the Luisa, and yet she worried about sending Victor to the Catherine nursery, where an infection raged so virulently that one infant had already died. If she could persuade Madame to nurse her own baby, Victor would be protected from contamination.

After Golonovin departed, Hannah returned to her patient. Irina had already prepared a white wicker cradle and Victor lay sleeping, covered with the embroidered blanket Madame Golonovin, in happy anticipation, had brought along with her first few belongings. Though still somewhat pale and obviously tired, Madame was already a different woman. Her whole demeanor had changed from that of a frightened, dependent patient to that of the wife of a prominent government official accustomed to running a large household. Although she never implied that the midwife was her inferior, her voice retained an edge that indicated she was now in command and perfectly capable of making her own decisions.

Hannah explained the arrangements for Madame's transfer to the Catherine and then continued urgently, "I cannot recommend that you employ one of the Catherine wet nurses, not at this time. If Victor is cared for in the central nursery or even fed by a woman who tends other babies as well, he might be in jeopardy."

"There is something wrong with the milk?"

"No, not the milk, but the rate of infection has been high. I suggest that we find some way of keeping him isolated from the others for his own safety."

"This sounds serious. What do you suggest?"

"We have been taught about the spread of contagion, and the best way possible to keep him safe would be to allow the fewest number of people to handle him. If you really want to know what I think would be the very best for him . . ."

"Of course I do! You, above all, know what Victor means to us!"

"Then, I think you should — at least for the time you are with us — feed him yourself."

"Feed him myself? How could I? I wouldn't know how, and it is just never done!"

"I would teach you everything you need to know. After all, we have mothers here every day who have never fed a baby. It is not so difficult to learn."

"But . . ." Madame paused to consider the idea. Hannah watched as she studied her son, then glanced down before answering, "Doesn't it hurt to have something tugging at you all day?"

"If that were so, it would be a wonder any mother did it. Some have told me it is very pleasant, and just think of all the extra time you can be alone with Victor."

"It would certainly shock the Court, not to mention my own mother! But I suppose I come as well equipped for the task as anyone!" Madame laughed nervously. "I would have a good excuse not to rush back into our social activities, and since I've waited so long for my son, I don't want to miss any of his growing."

Victor began to stir in his bed and push his tight fists toward his mouth.

"Shall we try now?" Hannah asked. "He looks hungry."

Hannah lifted the infant and pressed him close to her body to keep him feeling snug and comfortable. Victor turned his face toward the midwife's apron, seeming to think she was the one who would feed him.

"Now wait for your mama, you are too impatient!" Hannah admonished softly as she settled him in Madame's arms. When her gown was lifted to expose the left breast, it burst forward, readied by nature for its task. The nipple, a tiny pink bloom through youth and adolescence, had grown wider and darker during pregnancy to prepare it for the baby. The warm brown aureole, studded with a constellation of raised bumps to stimulate the baby's sense of touch and vision, immediately served as a target that attracted Victor's wide-eyed attention. As the nipple brushed his cheek it instantly became erect in readiness for his greedy tongue. Just hours old, he had the perfect sense to open his mouth wide, grasp as much of the ruddy circle as he could, and thrust his tongue to aid the nipple's elongation and flattening on the roof of his mouth.

Madame Golonovin gasped, stiffened, and then relaxed. "He knows just what to do. Isn't he amazing? Who taught you that marvelous trick?" She looked first at Hannah and then, bending her head toward Victor, became engrossed by each nuance of his behavior. Hannah helped settle her back on the pillows and watched the baby relish his first taste of milk. When he was ready for the second breast, Hannah demonstrated a few simple skills: how to place a finger by the nipple to allow the nose to breathe easier, how to break the suction when Madame wanted to remove him from her breast, how to change from one breast to the other, and how to bring up an air bubble. There were some awkward movements, but soon mother and son worked together giving and taking, creating one of nature's most perfect tableaux in the soft fading light of the long birth day.

## · 7 ·

ASSIGNMENTS FOR THE NEXT WEEK placed Hannah in charge of
Madame Golonovin's aftercare, but there was little to do other
than answer questions about feedings, bathe and tend Victor, and
be on call in case a problem developed, because Madame's other
needs were well met by her staff as well as curious Catherine nurses
who were amazed that a lady of her station was nursing her child.
Much to her regret, Hannah was not scheduled into labor and delivery, but she did have more time to review lessons and audit additional lectures, so the extra hours passed quickly. Instead of
rushing through meals, Hannah found herself lingering with the
other students to discuss common cases and concerns. She chatted
amicably in the halls between lectures and on several occasions was
offered tea and bread by a neighboring sister on her floor.

Both delighted and disturbed by her new status, Hannah marveled at how one incident could change attitudes. What if she
erred during another delivery, received a low mark on an exam, or
was guilty of some breach in her conduct or manner? Would she
immediately slip back to her former position? The rank of any
other midwife in training wasn't appreciably altered after the first
practical; respect was gained by the continual exercise of good care,
judgment, and deportment. Thought not indifferent to the whim
of fortune that now placed the balance in her favor, she felt forti-
fied to face her uncertain future with a renewed confidence in her
own abilities.

After checking Victor thoroughly on his fifth postpartum day,
Hannah retired to a small writing table in the Catherine's office to
fill out his records. With pleasure she checked off every item in the
most favorable category. He had steadily gained weight, his head
was rounded and more perfect, and his little arms and legs
plumped quickly from his mother's milk. As Hannah finished

recording his length and head circumference, she was startled as a hand touched her shoulder.

"Sister Blau, may I speak with you, please?" Hannah turned confused toward the unfamiliar voice.

It was the woman whose generous nod and smile had meant so much. Immediate recognition was difficult because her curls, the color of burning wheat, were pinned back in an attempt at neatness. Hannah realized this woman was not a senior midwife, as she did not wear the regulation pinstripe blouse and lace cap. Rather she was dressed in a long brown skirt with a ragged hem and a waist of coarse linen pulled tightly over an unchecked bosom and fastened incongruously by fine pearl buttons, the top two of which were left undone so as not to choke her thick neck. All this disarray was covered somewhat carelessly by her unstarched and stained laboratory smock. Hannah realized her ally must be a full-fledged medical doctor.

Taking her wire-framed spectacles from her pocket and placing them on her nose, she asked, "Now do you remember me?"

"Yes, of course. I knew you without them. You took me by surprise."

"I've been waiting for the right moment to introduce myself. I'm Dr. Rachael Jaffe. Do you have time for tea? My office is right over there." She pointed to a small oaken door under the arch of a stairway.

"Yes, thank you," Hannah replied gratefully. "I was only going to do some reading for a report."

"Are you studying a particular topic?" Dr. Jaffe asked as she led the way into her office.

"I have been asked to present an analysis of the Semmelweis doctrine, comparing the effectiveness of soap and water and chloride of lime."

Dr. Jaffe looked skeptical as she poured tea from her tarnished brass samovar and passed sugar cubes tossed haphazardly on a dusty blue china plate.

Hannah selected two cubes that appeared whiter than the others, slipped them into the full glass of steaming amber liquid, and watched as they spun before slowly dissolving.

"I must admit I knew of your assignment. Petrograv mentioned that he had asked you to do the research at last week's staff meeting. Quite a compliment to you!"

"But you think it might not work, just soap and water?"

"Oh, it would be effective, providing everyone scrubbed long and carefully enough."

Dr. Jaffe spoke comfortably from behind a desk littered with papers, opened texts, correspondence, and mementos. Hannah had been offered the armchair already cluttered by a black and pink flowered shawl, several parcels, and half a loaf of stale black bread. "I'm never in this office long enough to straighten it," Dr. Jaffe apologized. "I have to keep the servants away, as they insist on rearranging my papers and disposing of my little tidbits. If I didn't keep something to eat in here I'd starve, since I rarely waste my time in the dining room," she said as she located a knife with which to cut a salami she pulled from a drawer. "Would you like a piece?" she asked, offering a thick wedge on the end of the knife. "Quite good really, but not enough garlic."

Hannah shook her head. She had pushed the parcels back on the seat and balanced her cooling tea glass on the ragged arm. "I never see you in the Luisa, Doctor. Do you only work over here?"

"I am in charge of the Catherine nursery under Petrograv's benevolent guidance," she answered with mock sincerity. "I am busy here night and day; there are many problems to be solved. You are fortunate that your esteemed patient is breast-feeding her baby; otherwise he would be subject to the capricious whims of our nursery epidemics. I've lost two babies this week already!"

"Two! I heard about only one case. That's why I suggested . . ."

"Just as I thought! You influenced Golonovin's wife to do this!" Dr. Jaffe's voice was so strident that Hannah was certain she was about to be chastised. Then the doctor smiled mischievously.

"You are a very intelligent young woman. I only wish more of them would do the same. But then, Tatiana Golonovin is unusual, don't you agree?"

"Yes, I do. It is a simple thing to have a baby, at least for many women, so they don't appreciate what they receive. But Madame Golonovin is so grateful; she really does want to do the best for Victor."

Dr. Jaffe abruptly changed the subject. "Now, about your Semmelweis studies, I have some notes that might be of use to you, if only I can find them." She rummaged through an enormous stack of material until she found one small card, written in Yiddish rather than Russian. "Now here they are, just a few figures. Let me explain them to you."

"I read Yiddish."

"Yes, of course you do, but these are just raw numbers; you might need me to interpret the data for you," she said briskly before handing over the notes. "It is still difficult to believe most of the medical establishment has taken forty years to begin to accept Semmelweis's work."

After studying the numbers, Hannah replied, "Here's the result from his work in Pest: zero-point-eight-five percent mortality! That was the lowest rate of all and it was achieved under the worst conditions, in a crowded hospital without running water. I know they definitely scrubbed between patients there, and most interestingly, they changed all linens between deliveries. Semmelweis himself was forced to pay the laundry charges until he had proved his case!"

"You are certainly thorough in your work, Sister Blau."

"I want to do my best on this report because so many of the doctors will review it," Hannah added, handing the card back to Dr. Jaffe.

The doctor, who was attempting to rearrange a jumble of papers on her desk, stopped abruptly and stared at Hannah. "I too am Jewish. Most everyone knows it, or knew it, but I think they choose to forget it. It does come up from time to time, but not so often as you might think, and it didn't appreciably hinder my progress through the medical school. And you must be aware that most of the eminent physicians in Europe are Jewish. Do you want to know what else I think?"

"Of course. Just from this meeting, and . . . well . . . the other time, I sense you are interested in what happens to me and now I think I understand why."

"Because you are Jewish? Yes, I'll admit that. And also because I see you suffering with some of the same feelings I had five years

ago. But there is more. I think you have let your background stand
in your way. You have not clearly seen where your talents lie and
what possibilities may be available to you. Do you understand my
meaning?"

"You think I am holding myself back because of our religion,
that I am afraid I cannot succeed here in Moscow because I am
thought to be different, to be less . . . less worthy of respect. Yes, I
did feel that way, but lately I have been doing better now that I
know I can win respect by my actions. Every day I watch for more
opportunities to demonstrate my abilities."

"That's just it. I know you are capable of far more than routine
midwife deliveries. You must continue with your studies and become a doctor. And you are not as far from that goal as it might
seem."

"A doctor! Impossible! I could never have one of the places in
the Medical Section. They admit only three Jews each year and
there is a long waiting list. Besides, I've never excelled in academic
work, because Russian was my second language. I had a good secondary education at the Nikolaevesky Gymnasium, but was denied
admission to the Odessa Technical Institute, so my science preparation is weak. I am really just not a good enough student to study
medicine."

"Nonsense, you are already studying medicine and doing very
well at it. Stop belittling yourself! More than one professor has said
your work is much better than average. With a little help you
could perfect it." Dr. Jaffe paused long enough to catch her breath.
"By the way, I overheard Petrograv himself say that your intuitive
grasp of the birth process was the best he had ever seen in one so
young and inexperienced."

Hannah trembled at her words, for it meant that Petrograv, the
man she most revered, had spoken well of her to others. "I will
think over everything you have said and I would like to thank you
for your confidence," she replied stiffly to mask her confusion.

"Don't take too long to deliberate; you'll have to apply within
the next few weeks. I am certain that with our references admission
will not be a problem."

"But the quotas . . ."

"They might be adjusted. It could be done as a transfer between divisions to avoid government channels."

Just then a Catherine midwife opened the door quickly. "Doctor, I thought I should tell you that Countess Zhukovsky is here with the family physician and they want to have their daughter, the one with jaundice, bled with leeches. What shall I do?"

"I will be there in a moment," she said, pushing her spectacles back over the bridge of her freckled nose, a useless exercise, as they slipped forward immediately. "Sister Blau, let us talk again soon. We are friends, aren't we?"

Before Hannah could answer she dashed out the door. Just as Hannah rose from her chair, Dr. Jaffe's head popped back in the doorway. "Sister, do you know how Semmelweis died?"

"No, I . . ."

"From puerperal fever. What an irony!" she said with a wry smile. "Well, the same thing really. He contaminated an open wound in his hand while dissecting and the infection killed him. There's a lesson for us in that, though I don't know exactly what." Hannah opened her mouth to reply, but before she could speak a word the doctor was gone.

## · 8 ·

As EASTER APPROACHED, the days had become progressively milder, and as the icy patina on walls and ceilings began to disappear Hannah was finally able to appreciate the great beauty of the palace.

She passed through the marble corridor that had once led directly to Prince Paul's private apartments. The hallway itself was more than fifteen feet wide and twenty-five feet high. Huge Corinthian columns, each two feet in diameter, were placed every six feet. They had been carved from a mottled pink marble veined in green, with bases and capitals of a delicate cream.

From the vaulted ceiling hung the seven original crystal chandeliers that gave the hall its poetic name: "the corridor of the seven teardrops." Each fixture was composed of five layers of gold and glass, the bottom of which featured a huge tear-shaped prism more than a foot in length. Since these chandeliers were hung too high to be lit or maintained, they were not equipped for candles. Instead eight-foot-high brass candlesticks were strategically located between the columns to illuminate the path as well as highlight the multifaceted crystals and explode the massive teardrops into a million rainbow fragments. Only enough candles were now lit as were absolutely necessary, and so the full effect was not achieved, but Hannah enjoyed imagining what it would have been like to walk the hallway in its fullest glory a hundred years before, when all this splendor had been arranged to delight one royal gentleman as he journeyed off to bed.

Hannah hurried to her room to be alone. In a few minutes the hall would buzz with the changing ward shifts and she felt the need to maintain her solitude. A week ago she would have dreaded more loneliness, but now she had many new companions with whom to talk and dine and Dr. Jaffe had offered a special friendship. Since her own sisters, Eva and Dora, were too young and immature, she had always lacked this sort of companionship. And Mama? Never were two women further apart in temperament and attitude, and where they were similar they clashed. At one time Hannah had told her father all that was in her heart, but that had been the stuff of little-girl problems. In any case, Papa had died from tuberculosis a few months before she left for Moscow. She knew if he were still alive she would have agreed to attend medical school simply to please him, just to see his eyes twinkle in pride.

Hannah stirred the water in her metal washbasin in a futile attempt to warm it. She undressed to the waist and began to wash her flushed face, her neck, her well-rounded breasts, and under her arms. As she powdered herself dry she pondered what she really wanted. Her goal had always been midwifery; she had never considered medicine. But she suspected it would be a mistake to reject hastily this offering of further education. She would see Dr. Jaffe in a few days, discuss the difficulties, and then perhaps she would have an opportunity to talk about someone who consumed her thoughts. Hannah craved any excuse to hear his name: Petrograv!

And what was it that Dr. Jaffe had said? Hannah strained to recall her exact words: "I overheard Petrograv himself say that your intuitive grasp of the birth process was the best he had ever seen in one so young and inexperienced." "Intuitive"! "The best he had ever seen"! "The best"! "The best . . ."

"So," Hannah thought, "he thinks me 'young and inexperienced'!" At twenty Hannah was older than most of the others in her class. It had taken her an extra year to finish her secondary education. She had worked on her Russian and then it had taken another full year to obtain the necessary permissions to live in Moscow. "Inexperienced"? The records showed she had worked with Bubbe Schtern for almost three years before beginning professional schooling and had attended almost one hundred births before her first classroom lecture.

"Your qualifications were too outstanding to be overlooked" was what Dr. Speransky had said during their first interview. But she had continued, "We shall be the judge of how well you perform to our standards. Moscow is hardly Odessa, and you will be expected to meet every requirement and follow all our rules and regulations to the letter!"

Just to know that Petrograv had spoken about her, and had done so in a manner that indicated respect, made Hannah's spirits soar. She lay down on her bed without completing her toilette. Petrograv was a married man with a young daughter. Hannah had seen her accompanying him in his carriage and remembered her as a beautiful child with long black hair, dressed to perfection in soft leather boots and velvet bows. Once she had seen her in the front vestibule curtsying before Dr. Speransky, who was momentarily charmed by Natalya's pretty pale face and perfect manners.

Even if he did have a family she could still be the doctor's protégée. Petrograv would support her through the difficult studies and she would distinguish herself, make him proud, conceal her

personal feelings so they could work together, so she could have
some time to be alone with him. Pressing herself into the bed with
the pleasure of her reveries, she imagined him introducing her to
visiting medical celebrities. "This is Dr. Blau, who was young and
inexperienced when she came to me from Odessa, but I sensed
that she had an intuitive understanding of the birth process and
encouraged her to go on to become what she is today."

❖  ❖  ❖

The sound of distant voices and closing doors made Hannah realize it was time for the evening meal. As she hurried to change her
apron and redo her hair, she recalled another incident in which
someone important to her had praised her intuition.

How old had she been? Six? Seven? She could visualize Rabbi
Ziskind coming toward her, placing his hands on her head, and
speaking in a voice at once soft and strong.

In the days after Dora's birth the rabbi had become a more frequent visitor because Mama had been reluctant to attend the
neighborhood synagogue. Her excuses were many: no one else
could care for Dora, for she was prone to choke on her food or cry
without apparent cause, and only Mama could comfort her. Yet
there was another reason. Mama didn't want to hear the other
mothers brag about their children of the same age; she hated the
eternal comparisons and questions.

No one understood better than Mama that Dora would never
outgrow her handicaps. She could barely support herself to sit up
at a year; she walked clumsily at two; and at three she still had no
speech except her own call for Mama, which sounded like
"Waaaawaaa."

Rabbi Ziskind had another reason to place the Blau house on his
list of families requiring special attention. From the age of three,
Hannah's brother Chaim had won much praise for his potential as
a Hebrew scholar. Hannah seemed to learn as quickly as Chaim
but was never encouraged, for though there were a dozen Yiddish
words to describe brilliant male students, there were no compara-
ble phrases for a girl's achievements.

As she hurried along to the college dining room, she felt a familiar wave of resentment. No matter how much she accomplished,

she would never be as revered as a boy who studied the Talmud.
Unless . . . she pondered . . . unless she became a doctor.

❖   ❖   ❖

The wind had been blowing grey sheets of moisture across Odessa
Bay that day and the rabbi had arrived dressed in a long black coat
that had dripped all over the front hall, but Mama did not complain. Papa welcomed him, hoping he could convince the rabbi to
join him in a violin duet. Both were accomplished musicians, like
many of Odessa's sons, for the city inexplicably produced more
than its share of prodigies and it was said that a boy began to play
as soon as he could hold a bow.

"Rabbi, I have a Mozart sonata we've never tried."

"I'm sorry, Reb Blau." He always called Papa by that respectful
title. "I didn't bring my instrument today. I have come for your
help with a problem in the congregation."

Mama appeared with little honey cakes no one had seen her
prepare. Somehow she could always produce a treat for a guest.
They were interrupted when a customer rang at the door of the
tailor shop.

"Please excuse me. I'll be back as soon as I can," Papa apologized.

The rabbi turned to Chaim and Hannah. "I hear you are both
good little Jewish children and that you are learning to read and
write. Little Hannah, can you recite your alphabet already?"

Hannah pushed her shoulders back and almost stood on tiptoe
to proudly recite what she had memorized.

"How many little girls could do so well, Rabbi?" Mama
bragged. "It's a shame to neglect the girls' education! You will
have to make them a cheder!"

The progressive rabbi didn't hesitate to agree with her. "Of
course, you are right! But the Torah also reminds us that 'Each
was given a task, for each individual will not find the center of gravity of the universe within himself, but in the whole of which he is
an essential part.' "

As Hannah listened it seemed that the rabbi was cleverly ap-
peasing and also disagreeing with Mama. Then he turned toward
Chaim, who waited passively. "Now you, Chaim, will be a man,

and a man's area is the shul. There you will reign supreme." The rabbi turned his powerful gaze to Hannah, who stood shifting her weight from one foot to the other. "And you, little Hannah, you will be a woman, and your area will be the home, where you will be the absolute ruler, like your mama."

"Rabbi," Mama interrupted. "First you say that a girl should be educated, and then you tell her that her place is only in the home. I never cared much for study and learned only my Yiddish from the melamed's wife; now I regret I cannot read the law for myself."

"Sarah Blau, you are a pious woman. You need do no more to please the Holy One, blessed be He. You keep a kosher home, you follow all the prescribed mitzvahs. You make a happy family. Would you rather have a man's head on a woman's body? This causes great unhappiness, I assure you! So, let your Hannah study, even teach her Hebrew if you wish, but also let her know what it is to be a good Jewish woman and help her gladly accept her responsibilities when the time comes."

The last honey cake was devoured by the rabbi, and as he licked the clinging crumbs from his fingers the children realized there would be no tasty leavings for them. Hannah was annoyed by his unctuous words and angered by his greed. Her sulking did not go unnoticed.

"It would not harm us to try to mend the gulf between our little brothers and sisters," the rabbi said sweetly. "For a long time my own sisters were so different from me that I did not even speak to them in the familiar tense. You see, I was forced to spend almost fifteen hours each day in the cheder and they were really strangers to me!"

"Fifteen hours!" Chaim muttered before Mama shot him a stern glance.

"Now, little children, I have a lesson to teach you. When I return next week I will bring ten kopecks to the one who can say the alef beys back to front the fastest and with the fewest errors."

Back to front! Hannah wondered how hard that could be. She had no trouble memorizing the alphabet the first time, so she would just learn it over again differently. Chaim smiled broadly because he was certain that was an easy way to earn ten kopecks.

With his customary determination Chaim set out to devise a system in which he wrote all the letters on little slips of paper and carried them around to study during a free moment. Within two days he could just shuffle them behind his back as he whispered the letters to himself, pulling a piece of paper forward only if he faltered. When his task was completely finished he continued to work for speed and accuracy.

"You know them already, don't you?" Hannah asked when she noticed the papers had disappeared from his pocket. Chaim answered with only a sly grin calculated to make Hannah furious. He knew full well that she had not yet begun to study.

Since the problem was not particularly difficult, Hannah had decided she would concentrate during one long session at the end of the week. She spent the days in between planning how she would use the money. Oh, the possibilities! Would she prefer several glasses of sweet apple kvass or little flavored ices? Ten kopecks! That was enough to buy a small box of fancy chocolates from Jacob's, the confectioner on the boulevard. Would she rather have assorted creams, or mints, or nut balls, or choose one honey strudel every day for a month?

"The rabbi comes tomorrow," Mama announced as she served a plate of gefilte fish flecked with bright carrots.

"Tomorrow! Not possible, it hasn't been a whole week yet!" Hannah whined.

"It is exactly a week and you haven't done it!" Chaim grinned. "So I will win the kopecks. I knew you wouldn't study. The rabbi was right about girls!" Then he added maliciously, "I am certainly glad I am a boy! Do you know what we are taught to pray every morning, in Hebrew, which you don't understand? Do you know?" he chided.

"Children! Enough!" Papa demanded.

"What do you pray? What is so wonderful about what you say in the morning? What?"

Chaim wasn't naturally cruel and he realized he had gone too far, yet there was no stopping his retaliation even though he knew his words would also hurt Mama. His lips quivered before he said, "We are taught . . . we give thanks that 'Thou has not made us a woman.' "

"Papa, is that true? Do you say the same thing? Every morning? Is it such a terrible thing to be what I am?"

Papa bowed his head; he couldn't answer his daughter. She pushed her chair back and ran from the room before giving vent to her tears.

Everyone had known Hannah wouldn't study! She stopped beside the largest lime tree in the front yard. Still gasping in sorrow and anger, she pulled a few of the last remaining golden leaves from its branches to crush them in her fist. Then she recalled Papa's words to the rabbi when he had agreed to help settle the feud in the congregation. "There is more than one way to solve an issue. Fighting is useless. Every problem has its own solution, but you must search for it."

She grasped the lime tree's thin trunk and spun herself round and round at the end of her outstretched arm, faster and faster until she almost bent the tree toward the ground.

"Hannah! You'll break that tree!" Mama called from the doorway. "Come inside right now!"

Hannah followed obediently. But she had her answer.

"Well, who shall be first?" the rabbi asked, stepping into the front room where the children waited. Hannah prayed the rabbi would be in a good humor. "Chaim, you are the oldest."

Chaim stood in front of the rabbi and quickly and flawlessly recited his alef beys back to front as he had practiced. His parents watched proudly.

"Perfect, I can't imagine a better job! You have a good head and I hope you will put it to great and more difficult tasks with the same fervor. Ten kopecks are a small payment today, but what you learn from the Torah will give you far greater rewards. Remember that!"

"Yes, I will!" chimed the triumphant child.

"Little Hannah, it is your turn."

How Hannah had hated being called "little Hannah," even though the description was apt. Five years younger than her brother, she was less than half his height. Yet her serious face and thick-lashed green eyes made her appear older than six, and everyone remarked on how incongruously her head fit on her petite frame. But Hannah knew there was an advantage to being delicate and hoped it would help her with what she was about to try.

"Maybe I have been unfair . . ." the rabbi said when he noticed Hannah's nervousness. "You are too young for this task after all."

"No, Rabbi, I'll do it for you," Hannah said, managing the faintest smile as she stepped before him. "You said we should learn to say the alef beys from back to front instead of from front to back."

"Yes, that I did."

Hannah spun around, turned her back to the rabbi, and as quickly as she could, recited the alphabet beginning with alef and ending with tof. When she finished she looked at her feet; her face burned hotly as tears pricked her eyes. Surely she would be punished for embarrassing the family! She should never have attempted her stupid trick!

Placing his large warm hands on her shoulders, the rabbi gently turned her around, drew the frightened child toward him, and lifted her chin so she would have to look at him. When Hannah blinked back the stinging tears she saw his face sparkled with pleasure.

"Oh, Hannahleh, I am so happy, you give me such nakhes, for that is exactly what I wanted you to do! I had a lesson in mind, one my own grandfather, the Grand Rabbi of Kherson, taught me when I was about your age, only I, like Chaim, did it the hard way. You did it the clever way. But you both succeeded!"

The family was stunned. Hannah had done it the right way? This was what he had wanted after all? It was the first time Hannah had beaten her brother, and yet she did not feel joyful; her stomach knotted and her legs shook as the rabbi hugged her even more tightly.

"The great Maimonides teaches there are three kinds of perfection. The first is mental perfection, acquired by training. This was exhibited in Chaim's approach to the problem. Then there is the perfection of the imaginative faculty, which you, Hannah, demonstrated by your clever solution to the same task." The rabbi released Hannah and went to stand by her parents. "But, my children, you will each learn from the other. Hannah must study if she is to achieve, and Chaim must free his heart and use his imagination. The spirit must have room to soar!" His voice slowed to punctuate his meaning, as if he were preaching to a whole congregation. "And when you have conquered these, you must strive for a third perfection, a moral perfection, which comes when you are able to ward off every kind of foolish or evil ambition." He paused and then continued sternly, "Did the ten kopecks I offered lead you to think of any foolish ways of spending them? Of course! You are only children. But give some thought to the noble uses of the same kopecks; they might have been given to charity, bought bread for a hungry child or medicine for the sick. Always strive for perfection, for if you can incorporate the three perfections in your daily lives, you will attain true wisdom."

Sitting in the dining hall waiting for the holiday meal to be served, Hannah realized that only one of the perfections had ever come easily: the fresh solution to a problem, the idea that in its originality held the promise of a possibility, such as the one that had worked in the case of Madame Golonovin. She feared she would never achieve the other two goals the rabbi had set before her.

Concentration was still a challenge and her intuition failed to save her from the drudgery of study. It would be far easier to deliver the normal births and turn the more unusual cases over to the doctors than struggle through medical school; yet, in so doing, she would not be perfecting herself, and might always regret this failure.

And the third perfection: the moral perfection! This was her greatest hurdle. She still contemplated only the sweetness of the candy, the pleasure of the kvass. The concept of self-denial eluded her. Perhaps there were those with stronger characters who would naturally give their kopeks to the needy, but Hannah's immediate thought was for her own gratification.

The chapel priest stood in front of the students to lead them in an Easter prayer. To not appear conspicuous Hannah bowed her head, but blotted out the Christian litany with her own silent Hebrew syllables. That night, instead of reciting a simple blessing before a meal, she listened to the voice of Rabbi Ziskind calling to her from the past, exhorting her never to "live with the absence of true knowledge or by the force of animal desires."

The rabbi's admonition made new sense as the old prohibitions clashed with her dreams. This foolishness over Petrograv, this impossibility, was interfering with her good sense. Already Hannah had memorized his every expression, every gesture: the way he held his spectacles, nodded his head; the comb of his hair; the sleepy droop of his heavy-lidded eyes; his full wet mouth framed by a precisely trimmed beard and mustache. She had studied his walk, his posture, the slight differences in his daily dress. She recalled the odor of his woolen waistcoat mingled with antiseptics and a spicy tobacco. To herself she endlessly repeated his name, the one she had never dared speak aloud — "Stefan, Stefan, Stefan" — as she glanced hopefully around the perimeters of the hall, even though she knew Petrograv usually took his meals in his office. Just as well he was not in the room, Hannah thought, for tonight her face might have betrayed every nuance of her feelings.

She stared at her plate, which was now mounded with chopped eggplant, cold chicken, and a small dab of butter for the white rolls baked as an Easter treat. How she would have to struggle to overcome the surge of attraction she felt toward this unattainable man! The feelings could not be denied, but she knew she must control her physical desires. If she could at least contain this raw response, surely she might return to a more sensible attitude toward her studies and her life. Not wishing to spoil all she had achieved, she would have to force herself to suppress this nonsense. Now she knew the meaning of the word *lovesick*. Wasn't it all but a transitory illness from which she would eventually recover? And if it was, why did she desire to prolong the sweet suffering . . . just a while longer?

# · 9 ·

VICTOR GOLONOVIN WAS DISCHARGED on Good Friday, a week earlier than the average Catherine baby, because his father wished to have the family reunited for the holy Russian Orthodox festival.

After waving good-bye to Madame and her son from the main portico, Hannah hurried to dress for the Sabbath. Since arriving in Moscow she had been permitted to leave from Friday sundown to Saturday sundown, not out of personal courtesy so much as for the convenience of having her on duty Sundays when the other students worshipped in the myriad churches that lined the River Moskva.

Deliberately Hannah selected her best costume. Though she could hardly compete with the finery worn by her Moscow cousins, her own wardrobe was beautifully tailored with a special, if traditional, flair. A spring skirt of black peau de soie with a flounce effect and neatly trimmed with three bands of black moiré silk was her immediate choice. Hannah paused before selecting the most elaborate of her dress shirtwaists. Holding it up under her chin, she was pleased that the rose taffeta silk highlighted the slight pink blush in her cheeks. Hannah struggled to close the tiny silk buttons down her back and then tucked the bottom between her petticoats so that the front piece embroidered with flowers lay correctly over her high bustline. Not wanting to hide the whole effect with her heavy fur-lined cloak, she unpacked her spring cape for the first time that season. The black satin bow tied tightly at her throat emphasized her large green eyes and set off the bluish sheen of her immaculate coiffure, the color of soft coal.

Even though she had been active all day on the wards, her hair needed only the slightest smoothing with a moistened finger to be perfect. While the other students had to rearrange their buns several times a day to satisfy Dr. Speransky's standards, Hannah had solved the problem by using six small children's combs, which curved to perfectly fit her narrow head.

The only fault Hannah found with herself was her stature; she was too short to be perfectly proportioned, but that was minimized by garments specially designed by Papa to conceal this flaw. With one final approving glance in the mirror, she rearranged the fillip of lace at her throat, then descended to the front entrance and signed out of the building.

The carriage, sent by Hannah's Moscow relations, was just pulling up to the gate. Feydor, the Polish driver, doffed his cap and helped his passenger into the high seat. The landau's top was folded back to take advantage of the unusually warm afternoon, and Hannah thoroughly enjoyed the twenty-minute trot to 17 Kropotkin Street, conscious of every vehicle that slowed as it came parallel to hers and each pedestrian who turned for a second look as she passed by.

In the nine months since her arrival in Moscow, Hannah had entered only three buildings: the railway station, the college, and the home of her Uncle Velvel and Aunt Toibe Meyerov and their six daughters: Enga, Helga, Marta, Rifka, Reisa, and Lila. Permission for Hannah to study in Moscow had been granted by Mama because there would be family to watch over her, though they were not actually blood relations. Papa's sister, Aunt Sonia, was the widow of Simon Meyerov, and Uncle Velvel was Simon's oldest brother as well as head of that family's importing enterprises.

Hannah had complied with Mama's wishes and had lived with the Meyerovs at first, until the journey between the school and their home became too tedious. Mutually they decided Hannah would stay only the one Sabbath night each week. Although lonely at school, she had also felt alienated by the atmosphere of the Meyerov home, since their ways differed completely from hers in Odessa.

Very few Jews remained in Moscow after the cruel expulsions of 1891. This tight-knit community comprised merchants and craftsmen of the highest guilds who had obtained permits by bribes and influence to live and work in Moscow, yet every legal attempt to congregate publicly was discouraged by the authorities. Once, in the spring of 1896, representatives of the Jewish community petitioned Grand Duke Sergius Alexandrovitch to secure Czar Nicholas's permission to have the synagogue opened at least during the Coronation Days as "a special act of grace, in order that the Jews of Moscow may be given a chance to celebrate the joyful event with due solemnity," but the Grand Duke notified the petitioners through the chief of police that their petition was "an insolent violation of the imperial will" and could not be considered.

The Meyerovs were the leading traders in fine silks, laces, and velvets from France and Belgium. They owned two carriages and maintained a large household staff, which included a private dressmaker who, Aunt Toibe was convinced, was a great savings, since there were seven women continually needing clothing made or refitted. A lovely old mansion, preserved by some miracle at the time of the fire of 1812, had been their home for two decades. When Velvel Meyerov bought the lease-without-deed (because Jews could not technically own property) from the impoverished widow of Count Borsinov, the fine house had not been repaired or redecorated in more than sixty years! The hangings that covered the walls were blackened and faded; the lusters on the chandeliers, discolored by heat and turned into smoky topazes by time, still shook and tinkled when one walked across the room; the solid mahogany furniture, decorated with florid carvings that had lost all their gilt, stood gloomily against the walls. Aunt Toibe had been the first to appreciate the chests of drawers with Chinese incrustations, the tables with intricate little trelliswork ornaments, the rococo porcelains that recalled another age, and she had painstakingly supervised their renovations.

As soon as the carriage drew up in front of the Kropotkin Street residence, Hannah marveled again at how well the house was suited to its inhabitants. The larger wings spread toward the rear, leaving only a discreet yellow stucco façade to face the street.

"Spaseeba, Feydor," Hannah said as she was helped down from the high carriage step. The front door was opened by another retainer, Igor. Bent and grey, Igor, who had been with Velvel's family all his life, now occupied himself with quiet dignity as he guarded the door. He kept the brass polished, the paths swept; and when there were no assigned tasks, he could be heard reading half-aloud from his psalter, or prayer book, the pages of which were now darker than the cover. If one didn't notice the mezuzah encased in a small brass box attached to the front-door molding, which contained the holy Pentateuch of the Jews, no one would think this house anything but a typical Russian residence. Indeed, many of Meyerov's associates were unaware of his religion, since he called himself "Vladimir" in the marketplace because so many had remarked that "Velvel" seemed too "foreign," and Meyerov already was the Russian form of his name.

The sun had not yet set, and Hannah was relieved to arrive for once before the Sabbath had officially begun. During the long winter the crucial hour appeared almost midafternoon, and it had been nearly impossible to leave her duties and arrive at her uncle's on time. A small infraction of the law perhaps, but one that had worried Hannah. Her father had insisted, "Sabbath brings the joy of the future life into our present world; it is a foretaste of what lies ahead for us all," and she wished to honor his memory.

Aunt Toibe was checking the table settings in the darkened family dining room when Hannah entered and kissed her perfunctorily on both cheeks. A cockatoo, a present from another merchant to the little girls, screeched in the back apartments.

"How lovely you look, Hannahleh. Such color I haven't seen all winter! Did Feydor leave the carriage open as I requested?"

"Yes, Aunt, he did. What a difference from the rides a few weeks ago, when I used every robe I could find and still shivered the whole way across Moscow!"

"Is your special patient, the minister's wife, still there?"

"No, Madame Golonovin was discharged today. She wanted to be home for the family Easter."

"Yes, of course. And next week will be Pesah. Will you be permitted to attend the first-night seder?"

"I haven't yet asked, but since things are going well for me, I don't think my request would be refused, unless there are too many patients waiting to deliver."

"So, they are pleased with your work. Well, why shouldn't they be? I always knew you were something special. You'll do just fine, but remember one thing . . ."

"What is that?"

"You are above, not below, them. The goyim always try to make us believe otherwise, but the truth is they are afraid of us. They must make you feel small if they are to feel big. Do you understand?"

Not wishing to argue the point, Hannah nodded slightly. "Where is the service tonight?"

"At Cohen's, across the square. Your uncle will be home shortly. I'll check the kitchen once more and call the girls again." Aunt Toibe marched off to prod her daughters along, for it was almost time to begin the official Sabbath.

All was in readiness. The six Meyerov daughters were urged into the parlor by their mother, who attempted to settle all their arguments while adjusting bows and buttons. Each girl had dressed to outdo the other. Hannah had thought herself quite elegant an hour earlier, but she paled in the light of their colorful silks and velvets trimmed in the most delicate, if gaudy, laces. The long brown tresses of the three youngest were tied in embroidered French ribbons, another popular import in the Meyerov line, while the older ones had worked for hours on elaborate upswept hairstyles. Hannah couldn't imagine why they bothered for a private family meal at which they had no one to impress but each other, yet she caught herself feeling envious of their collectively engaging appearance.

Each cousin had a special quality or outstanding feature: Enga had warm brown eyes and a musical talent; Helga, the most beautiful, was proud of her ripening figure; Marta was gifted with a sharp intelligence and a sensual, if somewhat petulant, expression; Rifka charmed with her lively antics; Reisa's round face was that of an angel; and little Lila, who aspired to join the Imperial Ballet, showed evidence of her artistic potential in every studied movement.

How Aunt Toibe, whose features were angular and sharp, and Uncle Velvel, who was short, round, and balding, could have produced these six beauties was a source of comment in the community. Now as proud parents they faced the serious problem of finding a suitable husband for each of their treasures, since so few eligible Jewish boys were available in Moscow. Already they had begun to make inquiries on behalf of Enga and Helga in Odessa, Vilna, and Kiev, where, because of their handsome dowries, they might find good yeshiva boys. The Meyerovs could only look forward to losing their darlings one by one to strange men in far-away cities, not seeing them from year to year, and most tragically, not having the pleasure of watching their grandchildren grow.

Aunt Toibe, in her Sabbath dress of fine black silk and a double-stranded pearl necklace, performed the ritual of lighting the candles. At the exact moment, give or take but a few seconds, Hannah's mama would be doing the same, as would the female head of every Jewish home in the world, all together, united by tradition. As Aunt Toibe lit the multibranched candlestick, the flames flickered unsteadily, caught, and then firmly gave off their holy light. Moving her arms in a gesture of embrace, Aunt Toibe drew the holiness that rose from the flames and brought it to her.

"Blessed art thou, O Lord our God, King of the Universe, who hast hallowed us by His Commandments and commanded us to kindle the Sabbath light!" she intoned in perfect Hebrew, which, because of her education, she understood as well as spoke. With her eyes still covered, she softly murmured her own prayer, this time in Yiddish. As a child, Hannah had thought only Mama wept during this part of the ceremony, but now she knew that most Jewish women did the same: their heads covered with something — be it a shawl, lace napkin, or elaborate hat — young brides and tired grandmothers, Mama, Aunt Toibe, all of them weeping their grief and gratitude, expressing their hopes and fears. Tears for herself, tears for the family, tears for all Jews everywhere, tears that had been a part of a woman's devotions from time's beginning. As though from afar, she watched her aunt's wet fingers shining in the candlelight. She was as awed by the mystery of the ritual as ever. Yet in her heart she knew she was not wholly commited to the faith.

## · 10 ·

UNCLE VELVEL RETURNED from his prayers dressed in an elegant silk caftan. Momentarily encircled in the haze of the candlelight, he resembled Hannah's papa, except for being shorter and more rotund. Hannah swallowed hard to fight back the swelling loneliness that could overwhelm her when she thought about her father, even though she knew the Sabbath tradition decreed she must try to rejoice and think of the future.

"Gut Shabbes, Papa," the daughters chorused.

"Gut Shabbes, Uncle," Hannah added as they all formed a circle around the long table, in the center of which sat the two brown loaves covered with embroidered lace napkins to match the festive cloth. Uncle Velvel took his place at the head of the table of eight women and began the ritual greeting.

"Peace be unto you, ye ministering angels, messengers of the most high . . ." He turned to the chapter "In Praise of the Virtuous Wife" from the Proverbs of Solomon.

"A woman of worth, who can find her? For her price is far above rubies . . ."

Next he filled the ceremonial silver goblet to the brim with wine, to symbolize abundance, and chanted the Kiddush to consecrate the Sabbath and bless the wine. After taking a taste he handed it first to Aunt Toibe, who passed it around to each of the others to sip. With quiet deliberation Uncle Velvel removed the covering from the breads, lifted each loaf and held them together, then set them down again. Passing the knife over the first, he cut the second in half and gave each of the women a slice. Each broke off a piece, dipped it in salt, and made the blessing for the bread. What Hannah enjoyed was the sameness, the repeated words and gestures that eased her own sense of exile.

Once the traditional prologue was completed, Yelena, the maid, brought in a highly spiced fish and served Uncle Velvel first, in deference to his status. He in turn presented it to his wife as a token of her excellence, in the same manner as Hannah's papa had always done for her mama. Next came the amber chicken broth swimming with fine-cut egg noodles, which was always followed, much to Hannah's amazement, by both a golden roasted chicken and juicy boiled beef to symbolize the plenty available to this house.

"Your chicken is perfect, Aunt Toibe. It falls apart in my mouth. And the soup — oh, how I long for it during the week!" Hannah was careful to comment on each course, since her aunt was personally responsible for every dish and would have been hurt if a fuss weren't made.

"It's a wonder you don't get poisoned with the terrible food they give you. Look how thin you have become! You'll have to let me feed you for a month before we dare send you home!"

"When do you expect to return to Odessa?" inquired Uncle Velvel as he expertly picked the soft meat from the chicken's wing.

"Certainly not before the end of summer. I have at least five months' more work here and there may be some changes . . ."

"Changes? What is the matter?" Aunt Toibe always suspected the worst.

"No, no problem . . ."

"Well, what is it then?" Aunt Toibe was certain Hannah was hiding something.

"It's just that they want me to go for some . . . some advanced study."

"You need extra work, then? You can't finish with the others?"

"I'm sure Hannah is at the top of her class," Velvel said, coming to Hannah's defense, and giving her an opportunity to decide how much she wanted to reveal. As her aunt waited expectantly for an answer there was the unmistakable sound of carriage wheels grinding to a stop outside the house. In response to the three loud rings, Igor stumbled toward the vestibule.

Aunt Toibe clutched at her lace collar and twisted her pearls in fright. "Who could that be at this hour?" she said in a tinny voice. "Velvel, what shall we do?"

Jewish households were never without fear. Powerful Jews like the Meyerovs could usually circumvent the authorities by paying a bribe or publicly denying some aspect of their religion, yet each time they did so they wondered if they would have such good fortune the next time.

"I'll see who it is; don't worry yet," Uncle replied, pushing back his high-backed carved chair. "An important shipment was delayed. I told them to let me know the moment the train arrived," he continued in a low, controlled voice.

Everyone at the table had set her cutlery down and even the giggles of the youngest girls subsided. Hannah heard the visitor's voice, at first polite, then apologetic, and found it familiar and yet out of place. She held her breath to concentrate on the sound . . . Could it be? Her heart skipped a beat.

"The visitor is for Hannah!" exclaimed a much relieved Uncle Velvel.

"My apologies for interrupting your family, Sister Blau," Dr. Petrograv said, refusing to give his hat or cloak to Igor, who waited behind him.

"Welcome to our home," Aunt Toibe said graciously, then made certain that each of her daughters was introduced as well. "And of course, you know Hannah, the niece of Simon, Velvel's departed brother."

"It is an honor to meet the family of one of my students, but now I must leave you to your meal," he said, embarrassed to have arrived at what was obviously not the family's social hour.

"Oh, no, it is you who honor us," Aunt Toibe insisted, "for it is considered a mitzvah, a blessing, if one can feed a stranger on our Sabbath. Also we are in great need of another gentleman at this table, for my dear husband can hardly handle all eight of us by himself!" Aunt Toibe finished with a laugh, which she hoped would ease Dr. Petrograv's discomfort.

"Well, if I can be of assistance, then . . ." He smiled and finally allowed Igor to take his outer garments.

"You can, you can!" Velvel replied as he waved the doctor to a vacant chair opposite Hannah, where Yelena already was setting a place. As soon as he was seated, a steaming plate of soup appeared in front of him.

All her cousins focused their attentions on the doctor. Hannah could tell they were impressed with his sleek figure, immaculately trimmed beard, and aristocratic bearing. But, she wondered, had anyone else noticed how his eyes turned down at the edges, giving them the most gentle of expressions, or the manner in which his heavy lids could at one moment look sleepy and at the next sensual? All the cousins seemed to talk at once. Then they were hushed by their mother.

"You do us an honor, Doctor. We have heard much of you from our niece."

"Actually," Petrograv began, wiping his lips with the hand-embroidered napkin, "I am here not to see Sister Blau, with whom I can confer at the college, but to meet her family and enlist their help. I am only sorry I chose such an inopportune time for a visit."

"You must speak no more of that!" Uncle demanded.

"But how can we be of help to you, Doctor?" Aunt Toibe asked. Her deepest fear was that one of her daughters might become romantically involved with a Gentile, so she had successfully insulated them from any possible contact with Christian boys, insisting they be cloistered at home, tutored by an old rabbi, and chaperoned at all social events. But her independent niece was another problem, and she fretted that the lovely but inexperienced girl might inadvertently attract an inappropriate suitor.

Dr. Petrograv placed his spoon in his bowl. His hands danced in front of him to emphasize his words. "Your niece's abilities have been noticed not only by me, but by the whole teaching staff, who have identified her as one with great potential. We feel she will waste her talents if she proceeds no further than the midwifery diploma she will earn in a few months. Another doctor has already discussed with her the possibility of attending the medical school next term."

"Oh, Hannah!" exclaimed Marta wistfully.

"Congratulations, my dear!" said a proud Uncle Velvel. "We always knew you would do well, but medical school . . . we had no idea it would be possible. After all, so few women are admitted . . . let alone . . ."

"That will not be a problem," Petrograv anticipated. "We have worked out an arrangement for Hannah to transfer between divisions so she won't have to reapply through the quotas. And also — even Sister Blau doesn't know this yet — I have adjusted the requirements she will have to complete as she already has many hours of clinical practice to apply to her degree.

"So why do you need our help?" asked Aunt Toibe again. "Is there some other difficulty?"

"That depends solely on Sister Blau," Petrograv said, leaning across the table to focus his attention on Hannah.

"I am very seriously considering the offer" was all she could respond, since she was more angry with his impertinence than pleased with the attention.

"Considering?" asked her aunt. "What is there to consider?"

"Well, Dr. Jaffe just mentioned it to me a few days ago and I was surprised," Hannah replied. The corners of her eyes twitched imperceptibly. "It wasn't what I had been planning and I am still uncertain whether I am capable . . ."

"Capable? My dear Hannah, you can master any task you undertake!" her uncle confidently replied.

". . . Yes, well . . . maybe it isn't the best thing for me. I had always wanted to be a midwife and . . ."

"How can you say that?" interrupted Marta, who dreamed of a medical career for herself.

"Shhh, Marta, this is not your place!" Aunt Toibe insisted. Marta pulled in her lower lip and scowled back at her mother.

Uncle Velvel spoke more firmly. "How could you discard such an opportunity when so many would give anything to obtain a medical placement?" His thick eyebrows rose to punctuate his remarks.

"And what do you think your papa would have wanted?" Aunt Toibe continued pointing her finger sternly toward Hannah. "Think of the chance, not just for you, but for your whole family. What would this mean to your mama, and Chaim, Aunt Sonia, your little sisters? We would all be so proud of you!"

"I haven't said no," Hannah countered weakly. "It is just that I need more time to think it over." Hannah could see that there was now no way she could decline. She turned her struggle into a silent rebuttal to Petrograv. Why had he never spoken of this to her directly?

"Do you think we will have any more snow this season?" Uncle

Velvel asked to steer the conversation away from Hannah, sensing her acute discomfort.

"I remember many an Easter service attended by sleigh," Petrograv responded. "I would expect at least one or two more disappointing weeks before spring finally settles in to stay."

Helga innocently wondered why he had specialized in obstetrics.

"Why do you think?" he asked, his dark eyes twinkling mischievously.

Helga, who usually had a witty counter, was unable to give a quick response.

"Well then, I'll have to tell you. When I first began my medical studies I found out that I much preferred that which concerned women to that which concerned men!" replied Petrograv flirtatiously.

At this, Aunt Toibe pushed back her chair. "It's time for our zmires!" she interrupted firmly and started for the drawing room. Hannah was so grateful the meal was finally over she was the first one to follow her aunt up the curving stairway, without a backward glance to the doctor.

The completely restored drawing room was by far the most beautiful room in the house. Staring out from ornate gilt frames were portraits of all shapes, periods, ages, and costumes, which held a peculiar fascination for Hannah especially because they were the relics of another family. Aunt Toibe had resisted well-meaning suggestions to store the Borsinov canvases, feeling them entirely appropriate as decoration since they "came with the house."

Dr. Petrograv happily settled himself in the tufted armchair while the Meyerovs gathered in their customary circle to sing the holiday songs. After five or six favorites, Velvel began to test the little ones on Yiddish tongue-twisters. Hannah, still nervous in the doctor's presence, fumbled immediately. Then Petrograv gamely attempted the unfamiliar words.

"Fun Brisk keyn Trisk loyft a pisk . . ." He stumbled. Everyone dissolved into merry laughter when he stammered and tried again. "Ah, I shall have to practice that one, but it will not defeat me!

Sensing the end of the evening had come, he turned toward

Hannah and spoke directly to her for the first time since the meal had ended. "I hope you will discuss all of this with your family. It is too important a decision for a young woman to make herself."

"Of course, Doctor." Hannah started to reply deferentially, until her resentment overcame her good judgment. "But I will make up my own mind about this," she snapped, and then abruptly fell silent.

Petrograv decided not to inflame her further. "You come on duty again tomorrow evening, is that correct?"

"I leave here just after sundown and should be back by seven-thirty."

"I am covering for both Chernyshevsky and Speransky over the weekend, since they both were going to the country for family celebrations. May I save your driver the chore tomorrow and accompany you myself? I always pass by this district, so it would be no imposition."

"That would be very kind," Aunt Toibe replied for her. Hannah was surprised that she didn't seem to disapprove of the doctor as much as she had earlier, until her reason became more evident. "We shall be attending the ballet in the evening and we could all leave at the same time if we didn't have to wait for Hannah's carriage to return."

"I am happy to be of service. Till tomorrow, then. And thank you, Madame Meyerov, for your warm welcome and for including me in your family festivities."

Hannah immediately said her good-nights and went gratefully to the privacy of her own room, where no one could question her further. She looked forward to this one night of the week when she could neither study, for that would have been against the Sabbath rules, nor be disturbed by some problem in the Luisa. Quickly she undressed, splashed some water on her face and hands, and slipped between the large goose-down comforters that puffed around her. At first she tried to banish all worries from her mind and think only of the joys that awaited her in the future, just as the scriptures commanded, but her mind clouded with contradictory thoughts. A few days earlier she had been hungry for a glimpse of the doctor, anxious to hear any words from his lips, even those passed second-hand through Dr. Jaffe. Now he had come to visit her, a fact that, instead of pleasing her, had turned her affectionate feelings into defensiveness. She didn't know if she was truly angry or merely insulted.

What value could she have for that learned and revered doctor? Did he, too, wish for more than a professional friendship? Surely he realized that Hannah's background was such that no illicit romantic encounter would be possible, so he must have been acting truly out of duty to the future of his profession, trying to acquire another competent mind, one he could perhaps help to train and mold according to his conception of modern obstetrical practice.

Hannah turned the possibilities over and over and finally settled on her last conclusion, satisfied that she had not succumbed to the pressures during the evening and had not yet agreed to do what they all wished, because it was better to be certain, to deliberate slowly.

After the quilts and pillows were rearranged to her satisfaction, Hannah lifted the curtain beside her bed. Rain fell in hard, fast sheets; the droplets descending on the window panes glowed like jewels in the amber light cast from the streetlamps. She listened to the clopping of horses' hooves on the uneven cobbles and heard the carriages creak through the night. Even after she closed her eyes, her fantasies did not allow her to sleep: Petrograv talking, laughing, eating, smiling, wiping his chin, blinking his eyes, pressing his finger to his temples, tugging at a slipping stocking. She tried to blot them out by imagining the rain, the night, silver flashes of stars. She curled her body into her favorite position and finally fell into a wonderful dream, not of the doctor, but of Papa sitting beside her in a gaily painted carriage, pulled by a fast white horse, riding out into the countryside on a warm summer's day.

## · 11 ·

AT SUNDOWN THE NEXT DAY it was time for the havdalah, the ritual separation that marked the end of the Sabbath. Uncle Velvel first said a prayer over a goblet of wine, then took a silver box full of aromatic spices from Marta and placed it open on the polished parlor table. Helga solemnly held the special candle of braided wax while her father looked into the wine, then drank it, leaving only enough to quench the candle. Dipping his fingers into the few remaining burgundy drops, he passed them first over his eyes, then behind his ears, and finally he extinguished the flame.

"A gute vokh, a good week," he said to each in turn, and then Aunt Toibe lowered her eyes to give the final prayer, adding a meaningful word for each member of her family. Reaching for Hannah's hand, she said, "Truth is like gold; you must dig deep to find it."

A clatter in the front of the house at precisely seven indicated that Hannah's escort had arrived. When the door was opened a stiff rainy wind was blowing, and Hannah realized that her spring cape afforded little protection from the elements. When Hannah was seated, Dr. Petrograv leaned across her to wave to a delighted Marta. As soon as the door of the enclosed brougham snapped shut, he said, "Your cousin — Marta, I believe — she is very intelligent, isn't she?"

"Yes, she is the best student of them all and I know she would like to study medicine some day, but I don't think her tutor can prepare her to pass the exams with a grade sufficient to win a quota placement."

"Unfortunately you are probably right. What are her prospects, then?"

"For marriage? She will be matched with a student from another city where there are many young men in Jewish schools. My uncle is already looking for husbands for the oldest girls, and since they will all have fine dowries, she should be able to attract, if not a wealthy husband, a brilliant student with a good future. A Jewish boy can best raise himself through learning."

"And why isn't it the same for Jewish girls?" Petrograv asked, smiling at this opportunity to reopen his favorite subject.

"I . . . well . . ." she stammered.

"I hope I didn't offend you yesterday, but I wanted your family to know how pleased we all are with your progress and to understand your potential."

Hannah wanted him to know how angry she felt with his interference, but she couldn't find the words, especially not the polite Russian words, to express her confused feelings.

"Ah, you were upset! I shouldn't have gone to your family without speaking to you first. You are a modern woman, are you not? Believe me, I had no intention of coming at such an awkward time or staying as long as I did."

"No one was upset by your visit and the girls have spoken of nothing else since."

"A very delightful group. Six girls! That must be difficult for your uncle; a man always wishes for one son."

"Do you have a son?" Hannah asked curiously.

"No, just my daughter Natalya, who is four. Have you seen her at the hospital?"

"Yes, I'm certain she'll be a real beauty some day."

"Yes, yes, so like her mother," Petrograv said and sighed.

Hannah drew in a quick breath and her heart stopped beating for a few seconds and then began to pound wildly. She wanted to know more, yet she did not want to hear anything further about Natalya's mother, who was also Petrograv's wife. To change the subject, she said, "Thank you for the ride today. I sometimes feel I am burdening my uncle with my schedule, for they need two carriages when they all must go somewhere together."

"I was happy to have the opportunity to be of service. You are fortunate to have family nearby."

"Yes, Mama wouldn't have permitted me to study in Moscow if they weren't here."

"Your mama was wise. A young woman cannot be left alone in Moscow, especially one who is . . ." His voice trailed off.

To cover the silence Hannah quickly interjected, "The life of my cousins is so different from mine at home. My father was a tailor, like his father before him; and now my mother and aunt — they are both widows — run his shop. I am just the daughter of a simple man, not of a wealthy merchant like my uncle."

"Your background matters not to me or to any others in our profession. Already you have demonstrated that you are a woman with good sense and skilled hands, and through further education you will achieve an important position in life. Now you are at one level, why not reach for an even higher one? Such an opportunity may never come again! I come from a family of wealth, but what would Stefan Petrograv be without the 'Doctor' in front of his name? A bored aristocrat wasting his life away by catering only to his pleasure, instead of a doctor devoted to the welfare of others."

Hannah was finding it impossible to listen conscientiously to his lecture when every bump of the carriage pressed them together. "I don't see it as you do. I think a midwife has an important place, as does the shopgirl or the seamstress in her own way. We can't all be princes or doctors. You wouldn't want to be a 'bored aristocrat,' as you call it, so why would you want to force someone else to spend his or her life doing something not freely chosen?"

"But if you don't try to make the most of what you do have, you waste a gift from God!"

The carriage turned a sharp corner and the doctor was forced to lean across Hannah's lap. Grabbing the leather hand strap by his side of the window with his left hand and gently pushing away from Hannah's thigh with his right, he pulled himself upright once again. During the maneuver Hannah forced herself to stare straight ahead, for if her eyes had met his she would have lost her composure. As it was, she trembled from his touch.

"I'm not disagreeing with you, Doctor, not as it applies to me, just with your general principle." She shook as she spoke.

"I am afraid the weather is still too unpredictable for such a light wrap," he said, lifting the edge of her cloak and rubbing the fabric between his thumb and forefinger. Hannah was grateful that he took her reaction for a chill, for, in truth, she had never felt warmer in her life.

"Here we are now," the doctor said as the carriage pulled into the circular drive at the entrance to the Catherine. "I won't press you again about this, Sister, but if you wish to discuss it further, if you have any questions about what the program will entail, my door is always open." He then stepped down from the carriage and turned to help Hannah. As she took the one long stride toward the ground, the doctor's gaze met hers directly and he stared at her for several seconds before lowering his eyes.

"Yes, Doctor, and thank you for bringing me here," Hannah replied and then walked quickly toward the Luisa wards, hoping that no one else had noticed her arrival, for too much might be made of the innocent ride. Luckily, the halls were darkened and very few people were about on a night when all Moscow was joyously in celebration.

## · 12 ·

AT THE LUISA duty desk Hannah ascertained that no one was in labor, and remarkably enough, calmness also reigned in the newborn areas, so she headed for her rooms to change into her uniform before beginning her evening examinations.

As she ascended the staircase to her quarters, Hannah heard a door opening and peered over the banister in time to see Dr. Jaffe leaving her office.

"Dr. Jaffe! Doctor!" she called down a flight of stairs, but the doctor hadn't heard her name and started across toward the Catherine nursery. "Rachael!" Hannah cried even louder. The doctor turned, startled to hear herself summoned by her first name.

"I'm sorry, I didn't hear you at first, and then, ah, I can't see distances very well," Dr. Jaffe replied, pushing her spectacles into

position. Immediately she noticed Hannah's cape and silk skirt and
switched easily from Russian to Yiddish. "You went home for
Shabbes? I have no one in Moscow so I just try to forget about it
and work straight through, not a bad idea considering how much
there is to do and how little I accomplish."

"But don't you regret it?" Hannah responded, also in Yiddish.

"No, not for myself. My father's family, the Jaffes, are a wide-
spread rabbinic family that traces its roots from Mordecai Jaffe of
Prague back to Samuel ben Elhanan, great-grandson of Rashi the
revered Talmudic commentator. All the men are still very devout;
they study full time while their wives and daughters run the stores
or have professions to support them. Why, in our family the men
don't know one coin from the other!"

"Do they care how you live?"

"I tell them I am very devoted, but what they do not know is
that I worship research, not religion."

Dr. Jaffe centered her glasses on the bridge of her nose and
waited for Hannah's next question.

Hannah leaned forward and spoke quickly. "You are not the
only one trying to persuade me to attend the Medical College."

"Oh?"

"Dr. Petrograv went so far as to visit me at my uncle's house
yesterday to make certain my relatives would side with him . . . and
you. Is this a conspiracy against me?" She finished with a forced
laugh.

"No, a conspiracy *for* you! It is far easier to go on in the same
way, never moving forward. Look at me. I enjoy working with
babies but I know my ultimate challenge lies elsewhere. It might
not be the easiest path for me to take, but who ever promised that
the best rewards in life come as the result of complaisance?"

"I believe Dr. Petrograv used exactly the same argument! You
are right! He is right! My aunt and uncle are right! There is no
reason for me not to try medicine, but I want to arrange it so that I
won't have to enter in midterm. Do you think I can finish all my
practicals and work as a full staff midwife through the summer and
then start in October from the beginning of the curriculum?"

"I don't think you'll have a problem with Speransky. Did you
know that you are following in her footsteps, since she also first be-

came a midwife before being offered a medical placement? Why don't you let her know how much you admire her and ask for some advice along the way?"

"I don't know if I could go that far!" Hannah said, wrinkling her nose.

Hannah noticed the dark look of disapproval that crossed her friend's face. "I didn't mean . . ."

"I was just thinking about something else, someone else who also has trouble bending to authority."

"I have been wondering why you have all taken such an interest in me," Hannah continued, deciding it was safer to bring the subject back to herself. "I do see why you want me to improve myself, since you are a woman and a doctor and Jewish; and my family will be proud if I succeed; but . . . why . . . why is Dr. Petrograv doing so much for me?" Hannah worried that her question revealed too much of her own feeling, so she added lightly, "He certainly gave me a shock yesterday! In the middle of our Shabbes supper — can you imagine?"

"I had a feeling he might do that."

"You did?"

"Don't be angry with me, Hannah. He asked me where you spent your holiday and I thought it would be all right. He means well, and . . ."

"I only hope I can do the job you both have set before me. But beware! Now I will not hesitate to bother either of you for help with my studies, since you are both responsible for my predicament!"

"Anytime! You may even interrupt my research!"

"And Petrograv? May I interrupt him as well?"

"You'll have to ask him about that, but I'm certain that . . ."

"Yes, well . . ." Hannah stammered. She had to ask one more thing, but couldn't find the words. "Perhaps I am just being childish, but . . ."

"What is it?"

"I hope I can trust you . . ."

"Of course you can. When I spoke with Petrograv about you I didn't know you as well, but now we certainly are friends. Is something the matter?"

"I'm not sure, but Petrograv . . . his kindness . . . and his interest in me . . ."

"Exactly what concerns you?"

"He looks at me . . . in a certain way . . . I've never had a man act that way with me!"

"Well, Hannah, it is time you learned how to handle those 'looks'!" Dr. Jaffe leaned back against the wall and placed her hands on her hips. "Surely you know you are a very handsome woman. Now that you have left the protected world of your family you will be receiving many such attentions. Some must be ignored, others encouraged."

"How do I do that?"

"You must learn to give back what you are given."

"I don't understand . . ."

"There is a harmless way of demonstrating that you are a woman, of acknowledging the difference. Hannah, you must learn the art of flirtation!"

"And can you teach me all about it?" Hannah asked, much relieved.

"I suppose I can as well as anyone!" Dr. Jaffe laughed so hard she had to remove her glasses and wipe her eyes. No one would have called her "beautiful," although that was the correct translation of the name Jaffe. Nevertheless, with her height at almost six feet, her sharp wit, and that sunny halo of auburn hair, Rachael could easily unsettle, if not interest, many men.

"Now that you have shared a secret with me, I will seal our friendship with one of my own." She hesitated, then confided, "I am married."

"You . . . you are married!" How could this woman possibly have time in her life for a husband when she so rarely left the hospital grounds?

"Please, you must never mention this. Only a few know that I have a husband and they think he is abroad studying. I will tell you the whole truth. My husband is also a Jewish doctor, but we have kept different names. And he too believes in change, but of a different sort. For some time he has had but one dream: a better Russia with a good life for all her peoples." The doctor's voice became so subdued she needed to bend down to Hannah's level to whisper in her ear.

"Two years ago, one of his friends, in order to save his own neck, implicated many others by giving a list of names to the authorities. At first I hated him for it, but now that I have lived with it for a while I know he is not to blame. If I were chained for months to a wall in the Peter and Paul Fortress, left to rot, to starve, to go mad, I would have done the same."

"Where is he now?"

"Herzog? In a work prison somewhere in the Urals. Since they have no other doctor, he is able to practice medicine. Perhaps they are too pleased with his work and won't let him go for that reason alone!" she added bitterly. "You see how a medical skill can be used anywhere? In the days ahead there will be more need for doctors than midwives, for more will be dying than giving birth, I assure you!"

"When will you be together again?"

"How can I know that? There were never any formal charges; there is no sentence he has to serve. But Hannah, Russia is changing every day, slowly at first, and then ..." Dr. Jaffe's voice had become strident; her eyes blazed brilliantly.

"Isn't it dangerous for us to even talk like this?" Hannah whispered in Yiddish. "I hear the same at home from my own brother and his friends. He belongs to the ... Bund." Hannah could barely release the secret organization's name from her lips, and when she did she looked around furtively to see if someone could have overheard her. The two women had remained standing in the hallway niche under the stairs, and even though no one else had walked past, someone might be standing on the other side of a pillar or silently descending the stairs overhead.

"Is your brother a Zionist or a socialist?" Dr. Jaffe asked.

Hannah whispered, "A socialist, although I think my father was a secret Zionist."

"And what do you believe?"

"Me?" Hannah asked, surprised. She had never thought about joining one faction or the other. As a matter of fact, she hardly thought any of the intrigue worthwhile, for, no matter how much they organized or talked or fought among themselves, in her opinion no one could win against the czar.

Dr. Jaffe recognized Hannah's distress. "Don't worry, I am very discreet. But you are right, we should not talk of this here anymore . . . some other time, then?"

"Yes! I am the senior member on duty tonight and have not made my rounds. At least no Easter babies are expected. Maybe I'll even get to sleep!"

"Until later, then . . ." Dr. Jaffe replied and turned back toward the nursery as Hannah bounded up the stairs two at a time.

· 13 ·

A FEW DAYS AFTER Easter, Hannah received word that she was expected to attend the next staff review. Although other students had been included in the past, this was her first invitation. During the midday meal Hannah watched the senior midwives' table for signs that they were departing for the meeting, and as soon as the first two stood to leave, Hannah followed them up the winding iron stairs to the administrator's office, not unaware that the others were now conscious of her privileged status.

Dr. Speransky had commandeered for herself the most elegant suite in the former palace, with the excuse that she was the one assigned to entertain visiting officials and medical celebrities. Her offices consisted of three connecting rooms, which could be opened to create one large meeting space when necessary. Her private chambers, in the farthest room, featured ten-foot-high windows framed in burnished mahogany with views north and south along the river.

As soon as Hannah entered the doctor's chambers, she was transfixed by the elaborate parquet floor that had been laid during the era of Catherine the Great, when an inexhaustible supply of serfs had labored for months on each room. The parquet consisted of five species of wood inlaid to form squares alternating with octagons. The outlines of the two shapes were first inset with light oak, while the center of each square contained a rich rosy cherry. Highlighting the pattern were flowers set inside each octagon with two petals each of cherry, maple, mahogany, and rosewood in a tumbling pinwheel effect. The middle of each flower contained an additional inlay of four center petals carved from the darkest black walnut and, at its very epicenter, a perfect circle of bleached oak, the size of a fingerprint. Hannah could only guess at the hours of work and the incalculable costs of decorating this one floor, which had been a gift to the ungrateful young prince from his monarch mother.

Everyone stood as Dr. Speransky entered her office, followed by Dr. Jaffe, who was invariably the last to arrive. Both doctors moved to take their places behind the large desk while the four most senior midwives occupied the armchairs tufted in honey-colored Moroccan leather in the first row. Speransky adjusted the green parchment lampshades to suit her eyes and then began to review the week's cases.

"In the Luisa we admitted thirty-seven laboring women, which resulted in thirty-six live births: twenty male, sixteen female. There was one stillborn of approximately thirty weeks' gestation, cause unknown. Two cases required forceps: one primipara whose infant's head did not engage properly, and one frank breech in a multiparous mother with seven previous deliveries. Two cases of infant rashes required isolation. In the postpartum wards we have four maternal infections, one severe with an uncertain outcome. Additionally we report two urinary-tract infections, one breast inflammation, and a leg ulcer." All the statistics had been read in a monotone that betrayed no particular point of view.

Dr. Jaffe stood to present some recent studies on postpartum bladder infections and their management, including recommendations on preventive sanitary procedures, before reading the Catherine statistics in a singsong voice.

"We had fourteen deliveries, with six females and eight males. There were six forceps deliveries, resulting in one intrapartum death. The Catherine had three nursery infections requiring isolation, and I must say the situation for two of these is considered grave. Four cases of maternal infection have been noted, but they are under control."

A long discussion ensued on the causes behind the statistics, and then the interesting cases were reviewed in more detail. Hannah listened with rapt attention, for she was gaining a perspective on the hospital's obstetrical service quite different from the more subjective issues of her own assignments. After Speransky announced some scheduling changes, Hannah thought the meeting would be adjourned, but then the doctor cleared her throat and focused her attention on Hannah.

"On rare occasions our work, which we always strive to perfect, comes to the attention of our official benefactors, who, for the most part, choose to ignore us until they have a personal need for our services. You have all been aware of the confinement of Madame Golonovin, whose son was delivered by Sister Blau. In order to express their gratitude to the Lying-In Hospital and particularly for the kind attention and skill of Sister Blau, Minister Golonovin and Madame Golonovin have given a very generous donation to be used for improvements to the Luisa and the training of new midwives." The doctor paused to allow the others to nod and comment.

To regain their attention, Speransky continued in a louder voice. "While any one of you would have extended the same quality care and courtesy if you had been assigned the case, we still must recognize the work of one, which now brings honor to us all, as well as the much needed roubles!" Speransky attempted a throaty chuckle, but the sound was in such a low octave that the half-empty tea glasses set around the edge of her desk seemed to vibrate.

"Also, I am given to understand that the minister spoke so highly of our services at Court that our annual appropriation will be reviewed and will probably be increased next quarter," interjected Dr. Jaffe.

"As usual, Dr. Jaffe, you know what is happening before anyone else! But I believe that to be a very real possibility. We have been ignored by our protectors for several years and I hope this review will lead to more regular attention to our changing needs."

Sister Kochubey patted Hannah's shoulder and started to whisper a word of praise when Speransky continued.

"One last item I should like to share with all of you. Sister Blau . . ."

Hannah was startled. Speransky waited, and then beckoned her to come to the front of the group.

"This was delivered late yesterday by Golonovin's personal secretary, but I saved it for this meeting," she said as she handed Hannah a large white package tied in an azure grosgrain ribbon.

Hannah quickly untied the bow and lifted the lid off the thin wooden box. Under a small card, penned in the fine hand of Tatiana Golonovin, something inside was wrapped in moiré silk the color of thick cream. Hannah first read the note quickly to herself and then haltingly out loud.

"A token of our gratitude and esteem from Victor Sergeyavich's proud and happy parents." It was signed with a flourish of initials that Hannah held up for everyone to see. Then she reached inside to open the silken covers, which protected a porcelain egg larger than her fist. A second azure ribbon was strung through a hole in the top and bottom of the egg and tied at each end in three traditional loops. One side of the egg featured two hand-painted carnations, one pink and one blue, entwined to symbolize unity or marriage; the other was decorated with an icon of the infant Jesus, under which was written the Cyrillic symbol XB. Hannah rotated the egg once again and saw her own golden initials, HB, under the carnations and was delighted to realize the gift had been made especially for her. Everyone crowded around as Hannah removed it from its box, placing it on its specially crafted four-legged gold stand on Speransky's desk.

"The meeting is over, Sisters. I think our wards may need some staffing now." Speransky had to raise her voice to be heard. "Until next week," she concluded, and the gathering slowly dispersed. Then she lifted Hannah's treasure and gently replaced it in its box. "You mustn't let everyone handle it; the ribbons will soil, and although it appears solid, it is really quite fragile. Things are not always as they first appear, nor are people."

Tucking the covers over the egg, Speransky set the lid in place and returned it to Hannah.

"I've never before received a gift like this from a patient. Is it all right to accept it?"

"Of course we do not encourage gifts and we cannot accept donations of money to individuals, but a token such as this is always permissible, isn't it, Dr. Jaffe?"

Dr. Jaffe nodded her agreement and then gestured for Hannah to leave with her. As soon as they were out of Speransky's earshot, she turned, and said with a certain irony, "Won't your mama be proud of your lovely gift, Hannah!"

"I can't imagine what she would say, so I don't think I will show it to her at all!"

"Well, you can remind her that it is the picture of a Jewish baby!"

"And how would I explain the letters XB? Do you know what they mean exactly?"

"It is the short form of the traditional Easter greeting, 'Christ is risen.' "

"I'm sure of one thing, at least. Madame Golonovin never guessed I was Jewish."

"There, that proves my point once again! No one has to know unless you tell them yourself. Jewishness isn't stamped on your face, so if you don't remind everyone you'll find your life should go easier for you here at the college and in Moscow."

"I am not ashamed of my religion, my family, or who I am! I don't understand how you can feel so differently with your background."

"You will, someday. I don't believe everything I used to when I was your age, and I probably won't always agree with what I am doing now."

"What is that?"

"I'm planning to have my residence papers permanently altered."

"What comes next? Will you take lessons from the priests, wear a cross, hang an icon in your office?"

"Haven't you noticed? I have one already. It was there when I came, so I never bothered to remove it. It's rather beautiful — the halo, the burnished gold . . ."

"That kind of deception may be for you, but I need something to believe in," Hannah answered, raising her voice to defend her position.

"Shhh, don't be so upset! No one is trying to take anything away from you. There is nothing wrong with having different feelings about this, Hannah."

"Of course . . ." Hannah said in a calmer voice, even though her heart was racing. At one moment she found herself profoundly respecting her friend's knowledge and opinions and the next totally confused by her absence of allegiance to what was traditional and familiar. She seemed above deep feelings, appearing not to suffer from her husband's absence nor the alienation from her family. Hannah knew she would never agree with Jaffe's extreme opinions, but she admired her fierce independence.

"Once, when I was a student here, I felt the same as you, I really did," Dr. Jaffe said, touching Hannah's cheek gently for a brief second. "Every waft of incense, every saint and cross reminded me I was a despised outsider."

"And then what happened?"

"Eventually you adjust to the diferences."

Hannah twirled the ribbons that had tied the package in her hand. "Perhaps you are right."

"Just give it more time, you will see!" Dr. Jaffe said, pushing her unruly curls back into place. "Before you put your present away, go show it to Petrograv."

"Do you really think I should?"

"He's in his examining room," the doctor replied, mischieviously tilting her head.

## · 14 ·

IN THE WEEKS that followed Hannah became increasingly dedicated to the idea of becoming a doctor. She alternated her midwifery routine with reading assignments that would bring her to the level of the other entering students. Quite exhausted by the pace she had set herself, she began to look forward to a few weeks of vacation with the Meyerovs at their country home before commencing days of even more intensive study as a medical student.

The July sun glowed a fierce orange light in the evening sky. The Meyerov carriage was late meeting Hannah that day, and she fretted that if it didn't arrive in a few minutes she would miss the candle-lighting ceremonies. As she searched for a sign that it was coming in the distance, she once again was awed by the sight of all the glittering domes that studded the horizon. Within sight of the college were the Novodevichy Convent, the Andronikov Monastery, and the Church of the Zachatievsky, each with its gilded cross competing for space in the sky. The dominant point, however, was the nine onion domes of St. Basil's, each crowned with its own style of crucifix, rising out of the shrouded river mists. The Church of St. Basil's was composed of eight smaller cylindrical churches built around a central structure more than a hundred feet high. Hannah wondered what architectural fantasy organized the polychromed tiling and swirling bricklaying on each chapel tower. One onion shape was scalloped, another formed from bicolored triangles, and still others were built up in a series of cascading arches. St. Basil's reached out to capture even the most dormant imagination, and to Hannah its very existence bespoke a power that was as beguiling as it was frightening.

Feydor arrived just as the sun dipped behind the monastery walls. In order to save time with formalities, Hannah helped herself into the high seat of the open landau behind the driver.

"Why are you so late?"

"I'm sorry, miss, but your uncle kept me occupied until just a few minutes ago. He had many places to go this afternoon, so upset he was!"

"Is something the matter?"

"I don't know, but he was very concerned, I'll tell you that."

A shudder passed through Hannah. Now she was more anxious than ever to join her family. Turning her head back toward the river to ascertain the speed at which they were traveling, she delighted in the rippling reflections of the church spires and wondered if it is not the child in each person who yearns for the comfort of religion and responds to a definitive answer to all questions. Doesn't the church act as the parent with the power of punishment as well as the gift of divine forgiveness? And wasn't it the child inside her, Hannah mused, who clung to religious roots, afraid to break a commandment or be tardy for the Sabbath prayers? Just as she had given up her mama's breast, her rag doll, and left Odessa for Moscow, she felt the time might be drawing near to extricate herself from the religious knots that bound her to the past. Perhaps she would follow Dr. Jaffe after all.

❖ ❖ ❖

During the Sabbath supper, Uncle Velvel listened quietly to the chatter of the eight women. Hannah could see he was worried, but knew it wasn't her place to question him. In any case she was enjoying her participation in her cousins' holiday plans.

"So, Hannah, you are really coming with us!" Marta repeated over and over, not believing that her heroine would be spending the holidays with her.

"Yes, I really will."

"Oh, you'll just love it, I know it!" Marta went on, enthusiastically describing the lakeside family dacha a few miles south of Moscow. "I'll take you out in the boat all by myself. Papa said I could, didn't you?"

Uncle Velvel nodded, but didn't say a word.

"But I don't know how to swim!" Hannah protested.

"How could you live so near the sea and never learn to swim?" Enga asked.

"Mama never thought it proper."

"Oh, that is silly!" cried Helga. "I am the best swimmer in the family, so I'll teach you."

"Wonderful! But remember, I have much studying to do if I am to be ready for the opening of medical school, so I'll need every morning to work."

"I know the perfect place for you to have peace and quiet, Hannah."

"Where's that?"

"My reading place," answered Marta. "It's in the orchard where I have a hammock between two white birches."

"All you ever want to do is read!" whined Lila.

"Did you bring your mama's letter as I asked?" Aunt Toibe interrupted.

"Yes, I did. She understands that it is too long and expensive a journey for me to travel two full days each way and stay for less than three weeks."

"What other news do you hear?"

"Well, maybe you should read it for yourself after dinner."

"Is it so bad you can't tell me now?"

"No, no, it's so good!"

"Tell us, tell us," Lila begged.

"Well . . ." Hannah began cautiously. "Mama has found a possibility, someone you might like for Enga."

"Who is he, what is his name, does he want to come to Moscow?" Helga asked for Enga, who sat blushing and trembling.

"She will be writing more soon. All I know is that he studies to be a cantor."

"Velvel! Mazel tov!" Aunt Toibe cried.

"Don't get too excited. The wedding isn't tomorrow, we'll have to see what happens, you never know . . ." he responded morosely.

"What is the matter with you? A cantor isn't good enough for our daughter?"

"I don't want you to have another disappointment."

"Another? Velvel, what are you saying?"

"I'm sorry, but we won't be able to go to the dacha this year."

"Oh, Papa! Why?" Marta wailed. "It's our house, isn't it? Why can't we go?" She was always the first to complain.

Lila and Reisa hugged each other and began to cry.

"It is a new regulation requiring Jews to remain within the city limits unless they have the proper exemption papers, and these are almost impossible to acquire."

"Isn't there some official, someone we can . . . ?" Aunt Toibe asked before Uncle Velvel cut her off.

"I tried everything. The edict says that a Jew may leave Moscow at any time, but without documents he cannot return." Uncle Velvel placed his head between his hands and rubbed his temples.

Enga and Helga went to stand beside him while Hannah tightly held the moist little hands of Rifka and Reisa.

"It's not fair, it isn't!" Marta stamped her feet and screamed. "What else will they think of next?" she demanded, marching furiously around the room.

"Every year it is one more thing! I don't think I can take it any longer!" Aunt Toibe wailed.

"Toibe, Toibe, what can we do? Think of all we have . . . our health, the children, and business goes well. There's nothing more I can do," he said, turning his palms toward the ceiling.

"We should leave this horrid place!" Reisa whimpered.

"Where would you like to go, little one?" Velvel asked softly. "The shtetl I left in Poland was not a pretty place. Would you rather live in a wooden house with holes in the walls large enough for the snow to drift in? Would you rather walk along boards stretched over muddy streets? I still remember being cold, being hungry. I could not let you suffer so."

"Why not Vienna, Papa?" Marta asked. "I hear it is much more beautiful than Moscow, and you could have your business there."

"Or America!" chimed Lila.

"America? What do you know from America, Lilaleh?" asked her father as he scooped up the five-year-old and patted her on the cheek. "We can still have a holiday!"

"How, Papa? How?" Marta asked petulantly.

"I will close the shop as planned and we'll have adventures every day: picnics by the river, walks through the city. We'll play games, have parties; I'll still read from the storybooks, and we'll give little plays in the evenings and buy special treats."

"And I'll still take off from the hospital and stay here the whole time," added Hannah as she hugged Marta to her.

"Oh, Hannah, that will be fun!" said Reisa optimistically, choosing obedience as a means of attracting attention to herself. "Can we sing our songs now?"

Enga started a Yiddish favorite, her voice quavering at first.

> Sleep, Yankele, my darling little baby,
> Shut your big black eyes.
> A big boy who has all his teeth,
> Ought Mother sing him lullabies?

A big boy growing up a scholar,
And an enterprising merchant yet.
A big boy who will make a nice girl happy,
Ought he to be lying here so wet?

Sleep then, sleep, my groom that is to be,
Right now you're in the cradle, sad but true.
It will cost much toil and many tears,
Before anything becomes of you!

Hannah wondered how Enga felt now that she was about to be
given to a strange man from a faraway place. Her eldest cousin
sang the words with the proper inflections, but the look behind her
eyes spoke more of sad resignation than joyful acceptance.

The plight of the Jews of Moscow had been worsening slowly, but
in recent years the persecutions had multiplied. During the last
days of Alexander III, most of the Jews were expelled to small villages within the Pale of Settlement, and the year 1891 officially
marked the martyrdom of the Moscow community when an imperial ukase decreed the structure of the sealed Grand Synagogue
would be sold to the highest bidder, unless it were converted into a
charitable institution. For more than ten years Velvel Meyerov
had worked with other prominent Jews to obey the law and yet
preserve the holy aspects of the beautiful temple, but one effort
after another was denied. First they had tried a trade school for
Jewish children, then an asylum for orphans of any faith, and most
recently it had been rebuilt to meet the standards for a modern
hospital. That spring, however, the governor general had examined
the alterations and decreed they were not sufficiently extensive to
preclude the building's use ever again as a house of worship, so the
doors were sealed until massive additional changes could be under-
taken — at the expense of the Jewish community.

The Moscovite Jew-haters were plotting to wipe out the last
remnants of the Jews by subjecting them to every religious and ad-
ministrative persecution in the hope that they would finally flee,
one by one, from the precious citadel of Russian Orthodoxy. For
the last few years the worst persecutions were directed against any

Jew who attempted to visit Moscow. Police detectives prowled the streets and railroad stations, seizing any passer-by who happened to exhibit a "Semitic" countenance. The unlucky traveler's papers were then examined, and if his documents did not comply with every technicality of the law he was expelled at once. So anxious were the authorities to rid the city of itinerant Jews, they placed the premium reward for a captured Jew at a price double that for a thief!

Mama Blau had been irate at the tales she heard about the persecution of Jewish travelers and had insisted that Hannah's documents be in scrupulous order before she would allow her to travel to Moscow. When she first applied for the residence permit, Hannah had been told by the authorities that only by listing her occupation as "prostitute" could she, a Jewish woman, have free access to Moscow, with assurances she could attend her studies without being expected to practice that profession. Mama absolutely forbade her compliance with that rule.

Six months had passed before Hannah learned she was eligible for the papers that permitted any doctor or student of medicine to enter the world beyond the Pale. Medicine was the magic word! In fact, the one time the decree against Jewish travel was suspended in Moscow was the week when the International Congress of Medicine held its sessions there, because past street raids on "Jewish types" had caused the government some embarrassment when several European medical celebrities, a great number of whom were indeed Jewish, were arrested. Even before leaving Odessa, Hannah had realized that her medical degree might offer protection beyond the education it represented.

Only four days after her uncle's disappointing news, Hannah was called away from the bedside of a laboring woman to Dr. Speransky's office. It was so unusual to be relieved of duty in the middle of a case, that Hannah was concerned. She no longer feared being called down for an infraction of the rules, so she wondered if there had now been some difficulty with her "guaranteed" acceptance to the Medical Section.

Unexpectedly, Dr. Speransky stood to greet her, then extended her hand, not in friendship but to wave a piece of yellow paper.

"This was delivered a short time ago and I thought I should give it to you at once. It was not sealed, so I took the liberty of reading the message. I'm sorry, Sister, I really am."

"Sorry . . ." Hannah choked. She held the telegram for an interminable moment before reading the first word to catch her eye: the dateline "Odessa." Was it Mama? In the millisecond it took to open the envelope, she visualized Mama prostrate and bleeding in the street. An accident or an incident, that's what they called it when a Jew was murdered! An "incident," something of little consequence! Her eyes clouded so completely she could not read the message clearly at first, and when she read it again it didn't make sense. "It is necessary that you come home at once. Signed, S. Meyerov." It had to have been Mama! Why else would the signature have been Aunt Sonia's? Was the truth so terrible it couldn't even be sent by wire? She double-checked the date. It had been sent the preceding morning, July 17, 1904.

Dr. Speransky broke the ominous silence. "It's from your family, yes?" Hannah nodded dumbly. "Then you must obey it at once. I've already made arrangements for your travel plans."

"I don't understand . . ."

"Don't worry, you'll know the whole story soon enough." Speransky tried to soften her harsh voice to comfort Hannah.

"But why would my aunt send such a message, unless . . . ?" Hannah began to shake uncontrollably. "I'm feeling . . . very strange . . . I can't . . ." was all she managed to say before her legs lost the ability to sustain her weight and folded underneath her. Before she slipped completely to the floor, Dr. Speransky caught Hannah's shoulders in her firm wide hands and lowered her to the cool parquetry. Then she observed Hannah's fluttering pulse. It seemed that Hannah was holding her breath, and then, after gasping for air, her respiration became rapid and shallow.

"Take a deep breath. Now another!" the doctor commanded. "That's right, that's it." Hannah tried to sit herself up, but the moment she raised her head she began to shake and sweat. Speransky pushed her down once again. "You'll be all right soon; it's just the shock."

"But what could it be about?" Hannah asked weakly from her prone position.

"Don't imagine the worst. It is probably only a family crisis too complicated to explain in an expensive wire. Maybe your mother is ill or there is a problem with one of your sisters. Didn't you tell me that one of them isn't quite right? Well, she's apt to have more physical problems than a normal child. We will help you get your things together and get you on the evening train. No point worrying an extra day."

At any other time Hannah would have thought the doctor was anxious for her to go, but now she believed the concern was genuine.

"I'll have the courier dispatch a message to your family in Moscow."

Hannah nodded numbly, allowing the doctor to make all the necessary arrangements for her departure.

"Remember, you don't have to be back until late August; that should be time enough to have a nice visit, settle your affairs. Maybe this is a case where your nursing skills will be put to good use."

"I hope you are right," Hannah responded as she tried to stand upright. Finally she regained her composure by focusing on a distant view of the city outside the window.

"I'm certain you'll be back in time for the next semester," Speransky said with assurance as she guided Hannah toward the stairway. Before she would let Hannah descend, she motioned for an assistant to act as an escort.

"I'm all right now," Hannah protested.

"Just a precaution; the stairs are steep," the doctor urged, patting her once between her shoulders in a gesture more masculine than motherly. "Take care."

"I will," Hannah replied in one long exhaled breath. Then, drawing a deep gulp of air, she whispered, "Thank you for everything . . . all your trouble with me. I'm very grateful."

"We'll see you in August!"

"Yes, of course . . ." Hannah waved.

Yet, with a premonition she had never before felt, Hannah was sure she would never return to Moscow.

# II

❖ ❖ ❖ ❖ ❖

# *Duvid Gimpel*
## Delivered August 18, 1904

❖ ❖ ❖ ❖ ❖ ❖ ❖ ❖ ❖ ❖ ❖ ❖

## · 1 ·

IN ORDER TO CALM her worst fears, Hannah decided to complete ward rounds, even though she was officially off duty. As she stood at the entrance to the Luisa wards, she observed the scene one last time, trying to commit every detail to memory. Row after row of iron beds lined each side of the long room. All but three of the fifty places were filled that day, yet the mood was tranquil as every baby suckled its mother's breast.

Just as she was deciding where to begin, her patient of the morning, who had been delivered by another midwife, was wheeled into the ward and helped onto her postpartum bed. The new mother, Ekatarina Pavolovna, dozed as Hannah lifted her newborn daughter from the little padded shelf beside the bed. Hannah removed the traditional fuzzy pink sweater worn by all Luisa-born girls so she could examine the infant. As Hannah held the tiny garment in her hands she felt ashamed that it and all the standard-issue clothing had to be relinquished before a baby was released, forcing some of the poorest mothers to rewrap their babies in rags on the hospital's doorstep. How many of these unfortunate children lived through their first winter Hannah couldn't guess, but she preferred to believe that "her babies" were the ones who survived.

Then Hannah came to Maria Androvna, the wife of a shop-keeper, whose fourth son she had delivered five days before. A squeaking iron screen was pulled on rusty wheels to the foot of the bed. Its blue paint had almost completely peeled away and the tucked muslin draping was stained and torn. Although the screen served as some protection for her modesty, Maria Androvna still closed her eyes tightly and covered her face with her hands to ease her through the embarrassment of the exam. Hannah checked her temperature rectally. Although some of the midwives took the ax-illary temperature, under the armpit, she was dissatisfied with that method's accuracy and insisted on the more definitive measure-ment to determine early if any infection was setting in.

"Have you any gas? Have you moved your bowels today? Any other pains?"

Maria Androvna whispered a yes or no to each question while Hannah washed her hands in the basin of water mixed with chlo-ride of lime. Next she pulled up her patient's gown and examined the breasts, feeling for any hard spots or any warmth, which might indicate caking or early infection, checked the skin for reddening, and then closely studied each nipple to be certain there were no tiny cracks or fissures.

"Very good," Hannah said, then paused, wondering if she should inform her patient that she would no longer be in her care. No, she decided, it was easier not to say anything.

Moving from bed to bed, she suggested for one mother a hot compress to relieve an engorged breast; for another, whose milk supply seemed inadequate, the midwife left a written request for a pitcher of beer with each meal, the universally accepted method of increasing maternal production. All too soon, Hannah was no longer needed on the ward and reluctantly left to pack for the journey.

What should she take, what should she leave in Moscow? Hannah agonized as she laid out each piece of clothing, every jar, brush, clip, examination paper, note card, stocking, and bodice. When she was finished she heard the door open behind her.

"So, you even pack your pillow, Sister Blau!" Dr. Jaffe looked around and noticed that not a book was left on a shelf nor any linen on the bed. "I hope you will have room for one more small item," she continued, taking her stethoscope from around her neck and placing it across the satchel Hannah struggled to close.

"But this is yours . . ."

"Yes, my husband brought it from Berlin. It's the best design, a Lippauer. You don't have one of your own yet, do you?"

"No, I've been able to use the one in the Luisa."

"That is why you must take this one. I'll be able to get another one day, but I think you will need it sooner than I will."

"Why do you say that?"

"I shall be working within the confines of this hospital, while you . . ." Her voice trailed off, and then, changing her tone, she continued with a positive laugh, "As I have said before, babies are born everywhere, not only in hospitals in Moscow."

Hannah was stunned to realize that Dr. Jaffe also did not expect Hannah to return to her studies. She lifted the beautiful instrument, which the doctor had worn continuously, to examine the shining metal piece more closely. In the past she had admired it, much as a different woman might have coveted another's jewels.

"May I try it?" Hannah asked the doctor solemnly, before putting the earpieces in place. Then she stepped closer to her friend, pressed the binaural disk against her chest, and listened to the strong "lub-dub, lub-dub, lub-dub" of her heart.

"Such a clear sound! This is definitely better than my ear-to-chest technique. I don't know how to thank you," Hannah said, looking up at the doctor's concerned eyes.

Dr. Jaffe thrust a paper into Hannah's free hand and pulled her close. "Memorize this address, then destroy it. You must not carry it with you, do you understand?"

Hannah unfolded the crumpled scrap of paper and read: "Dr. J. S. Bruchermann, 34 Frederrich-Hershen Strasse, Zurich."

"Can you remember it?"

"Yes, I think so. I've become rather good at memorization lately!"

"Don't try to contact me here at the college. But we can stay in touch through Zurich."

"Who is Dr. Bruchermann?"

"That is of no importance; it is just an address. You will always be able to find me if you write there, and through it I will be able to locate you as well." For one moment Dr. Jaffe studied Hannah intently, and then, without a word, turned and left the room.

Hannah suddenly felt abandoned by the doctor's abrupt departure. There was so much more she wanted to say, so little time, and now she was gone! Hannah felt annoyed at herself. She should have sent a message with Rachael for Petrograv, who was giving some French medical students a lecture at the university and was not expected back at the college that day. What thoughts would she have wanted Rachael to convey? Perhaps it was for the best, she consoled herself as she absently stroked the stethoscope. Whatever she had tried to say would certainly have come out wrong, and since she never could have expressed her true feelings, there was no need to say anything at all.

❖  ❖  ❖

At dusk Uncle Velvel arrived with his carriage. Hannah's message to him had been brief, asking only for a ride to the station and requesting he not tell her aunt or cousins, so as to avoid more tears and sad speculations.

Velvel watched as the two satchels, bedding roll, medical box, and book package were loaded. "You are taking everything, then?"

"Yes, I think it for the best."

Every few minutes her uncle's shoulders lifted and fell as he sighed, "Oy, Gottenyu!" Rarely had Hannah seen this kind man without a witty or optimistic word. She felt she must try to be cheerful.

"I'll write as soon as I get there and tell you everything, I promise."

"Of course, of course. Maybe it isn't so bad as we think. Do you have your return ticket?"

"Yes. I don't think Mama expected I would remain as long as I did."

"Let me see it."

Hannah handed over the worn and faded stub that had been packed for almost a year.

"This is still valid, but you mustn't go second class!"

"It was very comfortable, really," Hannah demurred, for indeed second class had the advantage of padded seats, compartments for no more than eight, and a toilet on every car; third class was merely a rattling shell crowded with peasants who fought for the best bench seats as well as the remaining floor spaces. Some of the long-distance trains had an even lower class for the poorest itinerants, who were permitted to ride in the half-filled freight cars. When Hannah had seen them jumping off at stations to relieve themselves beside the platforms, she had been so grateful for the second-class comforts she had never aspired to first class.

"A niece of mine goes home first class!"

"That's very kind ..." Hannah didn't protest, for the idea of sitting upright for at least forty hours did not appeal to her as much as the idea of a quiet compartment that would be made up into soft berths for the night and into a little dayroom in the morning.

After they arrived at the station and the new ticket had been purchased, Uncle Velvel pressed additional coins in her hand.

"This is for the dining car, or if you have a long stop, have a nice meal at a station."

Since her paper money was tucked safely into her undergarments, Hannah placed his gift in the pocket of her skirt.

The porter opened the door to compartment 44 of the International Sleeping Car and helped Hannah up the high step. She stood wordlessly in the doorway as her uncle handed up a basket of food. They stood silently until the porter came down the line to close each outside door in turn. The closer he came, the more agitated her uncle became, and just as he approached number 44, Meyerov signaled the porter to wait while he stopped a platform vendor, gave him a few kopecks, and bought Hannah a peppermint-filled paper cone. The door was shut, but Hannah pulled down the window to take the gift and clasp her uncle's hand. He still said nothing, but his eyes, so brown and deep and somber, clearly conveyed his concern.

The whistle blew, and then in a choking voice he managed to

say, "God will surely help, but until He helps, may God help us!" The train lurched forward a few inches and Velvel released his niece's tight grasp. The sudden movement was enough to destroy Hannah's self-control, and all her feelings surfaced in a flood of tears.

"Good-bye, good-bye, thank you for everything, thank you," she stammered. "I'll be back, very soon, you'll see. Give everyone my love." She choked and sobbed.

The train slowly, laboriously started on its journey. Hannah continued to wave and call to her uncle, even though he no longer heard her. He had turned his back to hide his own tears. Through her watery veil Hannah only saw a bobbing pear shape, slightly bent, becoming smaller and smaller and smaller. And then, when it was too late for Hannah to hear, Velvel spun around and called into the disappearing smoke, "Got zol aykh shoymer un matzil zayn! May God protect and deliver you!"

## · 2 ·

AFTER ALL HER TEARS were spent, Hannah found herself holding a clean, dry handkerchief scented with an unfamiliar perfume. Swallowing hard, she turned away from the window to her left, where a thin young woman sat quietly with her hands folded in her lap. She was dressed in a primly tailored black suit devoid of ornamentation save a watch pinned above her left breast. Her golden hair was pulled into a bun, around which one shimmering braid was tightly wrapped. Her long face was smooth and pale, her nose was broad in the peasant manner, and the expression in her almond eyes reminded Hannah of a startled dove.

"Thank you," Hannah said. "I must look awful!" Hannah felt the loosened combs in her hair and turned toward her reflection in the window to mend the damage. Then she tried to straighten her rumpled skirt by realigning the folds.

"Don't worry, you look fine. Farewells are always sad. Even I want to cry when a train pulls away, though I am not really leaving anyone at all." She smiled to cheer Hannah, who could not help but respond in kind.

"Where are you traveling today?" Hannah asked with the easy familiarity strangers share.

"We're going to Sebastopol and Yalta. And you?"

"Odessa, home to Odessa."

"I would have thought Moscow was your home," she said and then caught herself. "You seemed so sad to leave and . . ."

"I'm . . . I was a medical student, but I've been called home on a family matter."

"I see," her companion replied, tactfully refraining from further questions. "Let me introduce myself. I am Katerina Potyebenya Afanasevich, but please, I am known as Katya to everyone, for that is how my lady calls me."

Her lady? As Hannah mulled the words over she now understood her companion's simple dress.

"You are traveling with your employer now?"

"Yes, she is the Princess Olimpiada, the only daughter of Prince Vasily Yakovlev," she replied. Hannah, who knew almost nothing of the aristocracy, did not recognize the name. To hide her ignorance she turned to the window.

"Tsaritsino," Hannah read aloud as they slowed at the favorite summer resort of Moscovites, with its ruins of one of Catherine's palaces looming gaunt and sinister in the waning light.

As Podolsk, then Serpukhov, and their surrounding forests of white birches, flashed by, her throat constricted, and Hannah became absorbed in thoughts of her first journey past these villages, when the same names seemed to be heralding a new independent life. As each landmark slipped behind her, Hannah felt as though she were gliding backward as well.

Just as a bright full moon began to rise on the pink background of the early evening sky, Katya once again became talkative.

"It is wonderful to be sitting next to a doctor. I must tell my lady about you. She is ill and that is the reason we make this trip. Do you think the mineral springs will help her?"

"What is her problem?"

"She has the rheumatism. This year it is worse than ever before. Do you think you could cure her?"

"I don't think I could be of much help to her, unless she is going to have a baby . . . that's my specialty!"

"Oh, no! The princess isn't even married!" Katya's cheeks reddened and her lips quivered. "She is in pain almost all the time. You would like her; she is brave and wonderful!"

"I am sure that if you speak of her so kindly she must be all you say."

"Then you will see her?"

"If she wishes. But as I said, I doubt there is anything I can do for her."

A clatter arose in the aisle outside the compartment as the porter rapped on the door to call "number 44" to supper.

The dining-car steward made the formal introductions, having taken the names from the porter's list. "Mademoiselle Blau and Mademoiselle Afanasevich, may I introduce you to Monsieur Mendelokov and Monsieur Norbet? I hope you have a pleasant journey." He handed menus around, which, though hand-printed, allowed no choice at all.

The two gentlemen nodded graciously from time to time as they passed condiments, but were completely absorbed discussing sums of money in French, a language Hannah could not understand. The meal, accorded more care in the serving than preparation, began with a hardy schtchee, or cabbage-based soup spiced with black dots of caraway, and ended with a compote of prunes, apricots, and pears that had been stewed in red wine laced with cloves. Inhibited by the distinguished gentlemen, it took all of Hannah's concentration not to say a wrong word or spill her beverage in the rattling car.

After the two gentlemen excused themselves to the smoking car, Katya's face brightened.

"Now we are crossing the River Oka. Do you see Tula in the distance?" She peered down at the river, which looked like a tarnished ribbon in the moonlight, and pointed out the twinkling lights of the city. "Have you ever been there before?"

"No. I've only come this way once, on my way north."

"The city is famous for its cutlery and samovars. But you mustn't eat the caviar there!"

"Why not?"

"There is a story telling how the Tula waiters, when hearing that a train was due, would lick the caviar on the canapés to give it a more appetizing shine! The princess, who believed this tale, always warned me, 'Never eat a caviar sandwich in Tula!' "

Both young women laughed.

"Will you leave the train with me when we stop there?"

"Of course," Hannah replied, grateful for the companionship.

As soon as the train slowed for Tula, they left their tea glasses and made their way to the steps. Katya jumped off before the train had braked completely, and after a moment's hesitation, Hannah did the same. But Hannah's heel had caught for a moment. She stumbled, then fell to the hard pavement.

"Are you all right? I should have waited for the train to stop." Katya helped Hannah to her feet and brushed the dust from her skirt.

"I'm fine, don't worry about me."

Taking Hannah by the hand, Katya led her through the small crowd, which searched expectantly for familiar faces arriving on the Odessa Express.

"Over here," Katya called gaily and pointed to a little stand with a red tiled roof. "Look, aren't they dear?" she asked as she demonstrated the typical Tula articles for sale: small pocket knives, tiny scissors, miniature samovars, and even toy guns representing the munitions industry. "I had always wanted one of these," she said, holding up a little knife, "and I finally bought one for myself on our last trip through Tula about a year ago. I use it all the time."

"They're very nice," Hannah said politely.

"And so reasonable, too. This is only twelve kopecks!" she said, examining one with a black wooden handle.

Although she rarely purchased things of this type for herself, Hannah could see how much Katya wanted her to buy it. Not wishing to insult her new friend, Hannah considered which one she liked best.

"Here's an even prettier one!" Katya called. "It's the same price as the other, but it has a pearl handle."

The intricate details and captivating craftsmanship helped make up her mind. "I'll take it then!" Hannah said, paying for it with the coins Uncle Velvel had given her at the station. She placed the knife in her pocket with the few remaining kopecks just as the train whistle blew its final warning.

The compartment had been made up for the night into four berths, each covered with a green woolen blanket imprinted with the railroad's golden insignia. The two gentlemen had not yet returned from the smoker, giving the women time to get settled.

"I'll have to tend to the princess now. She always needs help washing and undressing."

"Until later," Hannah replied, relieved to be alone.

First she poured water from the pitcher, the handle of which was fastened cleverly by a chain to a hook in the wall to hold it fast as well as permit pouring. After briskly washing her hands and face, Hannah unpinned her watch and clipped it inside her skirt pocket. Then she took out her Tula souvenir, admiring how the shiny blade popped out at the touch of a lever and how neatly it folded back into the pearly pink handle embossed with the words "Made in Tula." Hannah replaced it and counted her coins. After glancing at the untouched food hamper, she realized it would be unnecessary to remove her hidden money during the journey. Hannah unbuttoned her shoes and tucked them under the lower berth, in which she had decided to sleep. Katya would have expected her to have her choice, not realizing how ill at ease Hannah herself felt in first class.

## · 3 ·

THOUGH HANNAH TRIED to read, she couldn't comfortably sit up in the lower berth or focus in the shaking light, so she attempted to fall asleep before her accustomed hour. Every time she closed her eyes a waxen image of her mother flashed in her mind. Could that by why she was going home? Was her mother already dead or dying? Why else would she be called to Odessa?

Odessa . . . Odessa . . . Odessa. The word itself was soft on her lips; she felt it; she smelled its blossoming air, warm and sweet as her mother's skin where it parted between her breasts. She could almost taste the salt air of the Black Sea with its tidy wharves filled with ships from all over the globe. She had never been cold or hungry in Odessa. She envisioned the array of tasty delights Mama prepared to tempt Papa during his last days: crisp sour pickles, creamy kugels made with egg-rich noodles, the tenderest of flanken, chicken soup shimmering with shmaltz. Yet despite all the care and food, Papa had declined. Each morning his face had been visibly thinner, his body wasted to the point where his clothing hung from him like draperies on a pole. She remembered that his racking coughs, the long swallowing gulps for air, were so horrible she had wished she could breathe for him. And when there was nothing more to do but wait for him to die, Hannah remembered her shameful prayer, "Take Mama, not Papa, take Mama instead!"

Visions of her dead mother melted with those of Papa in his last hours, regurgitating black blood past his cracked dry lips and into the bowl Hannah had held to the end. She tried to banish the images by recalling a happier time with Papa: their first train ride together.

During the sixteen hours they had traveled toward the Polish village of Nemirov, Papa had told her about life in the old shtetl where he, his six brothers, and seven sisters had been born. "You know, Hannahleh, we are not really Russians. Nor are we Polish, nor Spanish. We are Jews who still are searching for the perfect land."

"And Russia is not the place?"

"No, little one. Do you know how Poland got its name?"

"No, Papa."

"When the Jews were fleeing Spain, where could they go if not to the east?"

"To the west?"

"But then they would have fallen into the sea! So they wandered for months until they reached a land of many forests and they were very tired. Suddenly a heavenly voice called out to them in Hebrew, 'Pohlin, here you shall rest.' And from that day that land came to be known as Poland! But notice that the voice said this was but a place to rest, not remain forever. Someday, when we have strength, we must move on."

"How did Russia get its name, Papa?"

"I don't know, but it is a good question."

"Why didn't you stay with the others in Nemirov?"

"My papa was a tailor, as were his father and brothers. But Nemirov is not so large that it needs so many tailors, and when times were bad he left his family for Odessa, taking only your Aunt Sonia and me with him."

It was market day when they arrived in Nemirov and Papa enjoyed acting as his daughter's guide to this foreign world.

"Down this lane are our kind of Jews: Krone, the yard-goods dealer; Berish of the soda shop; and Khaytshe, who owns the kerosene store that never closes.

"And here is the shul where your grandparents were married. Now look over there," he said, pointing to a mound of earth surrounded by a high fence. "This is the bride and groom's grave. Do you know who Chmielnicki was?"

Hannah nodded, for Mama had cursed him along with all the other Hamans of the past.

"Then you know how he and his hordes overran all of Podolia, wiping out whole shtetls during the middle sixteen hundreds. In one of the raids, right here in Nemirov, a bride and groom who were standing under the marriage khupe in this very courtyard were murdered together. Since then it is the custom for every bride and groom, before being led under the canopy with their parents, to circle the grave seven times. Look, you can still see part of the inscription: 'Beloved children, dearest bride and groom, only your bodies are separate, your souls are united forever!' "

"Why does this always happen to Jews, Papa? And why must we always move from one place to the other? And why are we forced to stay within the Pale?"

"Everyone has always been afraid of the Jews."

"But we harm no one!"

"Yes, but no matter how many of us they manage to kill or persecute, we persist. They cannot destroy us and they hate us for that alone."

"Why is that so?"

"First, we have a common language: the Yiddish. Now that may not seem so important to you, but wherever a Jew goes in the world he can find another Jew who will understand him. And second, though we Jews are a weak and harmless people without armies we survive because of our 'Covenant with God,' which says . . ."

"I know," Hannah interrupted. "But if we are the Chosen Ones, why are we now forced to live in the Pale?"

"Hannah, this is but a transitory problem. Even the laws are called the 'temporary rules.' The restrictions to the Pale, although they began in the late seventeen hundreds, have only been severe since eighteen eighty-two, just before you were born. Now that seems like a long time to you because you have known nothing else, but it is only fifteen years, a very short time in the history of the Jews and one that should pass quickly by."

"But Mama doesn't think so. She says it will get worse and worse!"

"So you don't want to listen to what your papa says?"

"I just don't like knowing that there are places I cannot visit because of who I am."

❖  ❖  ❖

Hannah's musings were interrupted as the two gentlemen began to settle into the compartment for the night, whispering so as not to wake her, but their coughs and other noises were an embarrassment to her. Hannah had always despised sleeping among strangers. Again she remembered the four nights in Nemirov when she had been forced to share a thin quilt and scratchy straw mattress with her cousin Itke, both whose name and person she found most unpleasant. Itke's mother, Aunt Maida, was a widow who worked as a bathhouse attendant, cutting toenails and helping women at their mikva, or ritual bath. The other aunts also worked to support their families: one as a syrup maker, one as a kosher-chicken seller, and the last as a knitter of coarse socks and scarves. But the one person in her Nemirov family who impressed Hannah the most was the youngest of Itke's nine brothers and sisters, eighteen-month-old Avrom, a chunky, wide-eyed cherub totally devoid of hair, who ran instead of walked, jumped instead of standing still. Since he was one of only two boys in the family, he was much cherished by his sisters, who doted on his every whim and spoiled him terribly. Perhaps they did so even more because he was crippled.

When Hannah first noticed the defect, a clump of scar tissue where a normal thumb had obviously once been, she had asked "What happened to him?" imagining some kind of hideous accident.

"I cut it off," Aunt Maida had responded without sentiment.

Horrified and choking with rage, Hannah ran to ask Papa. "What kind of monster could do such a thing to a child, her own baby? Why don't we take him away from them before they kill him bit by bit?"

"It was the boolegh, the terror," he tried to explain. "It all began with Czar Nicholas I, who decided that the Jews must serve in his army. Not just the regular time, mind you, but twenty-five years. First they started recruiting boys who were just twelve, boys who had not yet made their bar mitzvah, so they might better be converted to the Christian ways. Then they made the draft quota higher for us than the peasants: one Jewish boy for every thousand Jews. Since the rich ones could pay off the kahal, the community council, the sons of the poor were sent in their places. Only the lame were ever spared.

"Maida remembers well how the kahal punished our family because one member had a personal gripe against my father, and so they drafted my brothers Benyomen and Kiva and Faybush. Only Faybush has ever returned, and he has been a little meshugge ever since."

"What happened to the others?"

"They starved, or succumbed to wounds or consumption. Or worse, they were driven away from the old beliefs and live like heathens, afraid to return home again. That's another reason my papa took me to Odessa when he did, to protect me from this local kahal, figuring, correctly, that another would be more fair when they learned he had already given three sons to the czar."

"But why hurt a baby?"

"Your Aunt Maida's first son, Mendele, was spared conscription, but it cost all the family's savings to pay for another, poorer boy to take his place. By cutting off his thumb, his mother made the little boy useless for the military because he cannot pull the trigger of a gun. He is so young he'll never know — well, hardly know — what he has missed. Is it so terrible? A mother protecting her son's life like that? Hannah, there are worse things, though I pray you won't live to learn about them."

Hannah listened, but could not accept her father's calm reasoning. It was a terrible, impossible thing to have done! She would see to it that her children would be safe from the armies of the czars, safe from the Cossacks, safe from the Jew-haters of the world! And if she couldn't protect them in Russia, she would take them elsewhere, somewhere far away. If the sight of baby Avrom's damaged hand was a frightening specter of past horrors, it could become a symbol for the future as well.

## · 4 ·

As THE TRAIN WHISTLED and braked during the approach to Orel, a provincial capital and major crossroads for railway transfers, Hannah gave up the futile effort to sleep and stared out toward the blinking platform lights. It was clear that the three others in her compartment had traveled more widely than she, for they seemed inured to the commotion until an officer opened the sliding compartment door and announced, "Police inspection!"

Katya awoke with a start, her head bumping the ceiling. After rubbing the spot, she reached under her pillow, where she kept the small satchel that contained her papers. The bored police officer reviewed her documents briefly and, seeing she was in service to the princess, handed them back without comment. A second officer studied the papers of the two business associates while they watched dispassionately as each page was scrutinized.

Unfortunately Hannah had packed her papers at the bottom of her largest bag, thinking they would be safest among her clothing. It took her some moments to pull out the heavy case, as it had been wedged down when the seats had been converted to berths. The official demonstrated his impatience by tapping his foot. After handing her leather packet over, Hannah nervously watched the precision with which he flicked it open.

"Jewess! This says you're a Jewess!" he shouted so loudly all four passengers flinched inadvertently.

"You came on board in Moscow?" he asked accusingly.

Hannah barely managed to answer. "Yes . . . I did."

"Where is your permit of residency?"

"It's there, sir. The one with the red seal." Her voice began to crack.

"I see. You claim to be a medical student. Does she look like one to you?" he asked his fellow officer.

"We can easily check into that," the second replied curtly and motioned toward the passageway. When he blew his whistle, a third officer appeared, and in another moment the car's porter came running as well.

"Do you know that you have permitted a Jewess in a first-class compartment?"

"No, no, sir, I didn't," the porter meekly replied. "I have been the victim of a deception!"

Katya slipped down beside Hannah and pressed her hand. "That's not true," Hannah whispered. "There is no rule about Jews in first class. I paid my full fare!"

"Shhhhhh!" Katya warned, stepping back from her friend as the officer backed into the room again.

"What are you standing there for? Get her out of here and put her where she belongs!" the officer demanded. "She is tainting the good name of the railroad and contaminating these gentlepeople. Why, here she slept, directly beneath the princess's lady in waiting," he exaggerated. "How do you know she isn't another of those rebel conspirators who will stop at nothing until the whole monarchy, the whole Russian way of life is destroyed. Is that what you want?"

"N-n-n-no . . . no . . . of course not!" the porter stammered.

"Who knows when they will strike again? Another explosion, like the one in Petersburg last week, could happen anytime."

Hannah had watched, trembling with fear, but the absurdity of his accusations gave her new strength. "That's not true. I paid the full fare, so I have as much right as . . ."

"Right! I have as much right!" The officer mocked the girl's high-pitched defiance. "You have no rights! You have entered this train illegally and are now under suspicion for conspiracy."

"I have done nothing wrong!"

"Yes, yes, my dear. They all say that . . . at first." Turning to the porter, he lowered his voice for effect. "Get her out of here! I will investigate the case personally."

Katya watched in horror, hand to her mouth, as the second officer and the porter grabbed her new friend and started to push Hannah into the passageway. Noticing Hannah's bare feet, Katya bent down and, with the certainty of one who had often helped dress another, placed Hannah's shoes loosely on her feet.

Curious passengers poked their heads into the corridor when they heard Hannah being dragged past their doors. She refused to go in silence and screamed, "No, no! You have no right, I have done nothing wrong," until the officer managed to adjust his hold so that one hand firmly covered her mouth. Still Hannah continued to struggle, but as she was dragged back, car after car, to the bowels of the train, her body became more limp, more compliant, and she discovered that if she walked quietly the guard relaxed the iron grip that burned her arms.

"So, you will be reasonable?" he asked.

Hannah nodded numbly. She knew she could not fight him, the other guards, the imperial government, the czar. The train lurched to one side as it rounded a tight turn and Hannah fell away.

"Easy now!" he said, pulling her to him by one of her breasts.

She flinched but said nothing. Without possession of her papers she was nothing . . . worse than a criminal . . . a nonperson. She wondered when, or if, she would retrieve her precious documents.

Unable to bear such speculation, Hannah repeated a litany to herself, "At least I have my shoes, I have my shoes, at least I have my shoes."

❖   ❖   ❖

Twelve cars removed from the world of green velvet padded seats, Hannah was thrust into a stinking boxcar filled with living human bodies who showed not a glimmer of interest as the guard pushed her into their midst and bolted the door between the cars behind her. The odor made her gag, and she pressed her nostrils to blot out the nauseating evidence of too many people and no sanitary facilities.

The car was dark except for two small lanterns, one at either end, which cast their eerie illumination over more than fifty peasants who sprawled on the floor and perched on the crating. In the flickering light, faces loomed at her: cadaverous eyes, gaunt chins, toothless grins, hairy heads, shrouded silhouettes. All leaning, glaring, menacing. The only sounds were the occasional crying of a baby, a choking cough, a repulsive spitting.

Searching for a means of escape, she considered jumping off at the next station. But she knew she wouldn't get far without her papers. She didn't have her baggage or food hamper and her only accessible money was the few kopecks left over from her purchase in Tula, and though the paper notes were still tucked into different parts of her underclothing, they could not be extracted in public. If only she had not foolishly wasted her coins on a souvenir!

Noticing a bucket in the center of the car, she decided she could have some water, but then thought it would be better to control herself than to tempt dysentery under these conditions. As she began to perspire, Hannah licked the salt from her upper lip, craving a drink even more now that she denied herself one.

Unable to steady herself standing upright any longer, she sat near the door she had entered and tried not to close her eyes, thinking she had to stay alert, to watch everyone, for if she slept she might be robbed, and then she would have nothing. She leaned back for a moment against a bundle. It stirred. Hannah jumped in fright and stared into the watery eyes of an old woman who coughed a few times and resumed her hunched position. Hannah inched away from her, drew her knees up to her chest, and hugged them for support.

Now she tried with all her might to think of something pleasant, someone she cared about. Her thoughts drifted back to her first meeting with Lazar.

❖ ❖ ❖

Lazar Sokolovsky had been no more than another in a long line of shy yeshiva students welcomed into the Blau household to "eat days" twice a week. The family considered it a blessing to feed a gifted boy who had traveled far from his provincial Kishinev family to study the Talmud with the finest minds of Bessarabia. Even Papa Blau had heard of the boy's uncle, Ben Ezra, the Grand Rabbi of Ritznia who, though blind from early childhood, had learned his Talmud by memory and, having no sons of his own, had selected his nephew as his successor.

"Did you know that this is the first family to give me breakfast as well as the evening meal?" Lazar had told Mama Blau by way of a compliment.

"What kind of Jewish people are they to eat and not feed a boy?" Mama berated.

"No, you don't understand; food isn't that important to me. I could spend more if I wanted, for I have few expenditures other than the bathhouse every Friday, though once in a while I do succumb to something extravagant."

"Ah, I suppose it is something sweet: candy or cakes," Hannah guessed. It had been the first time she had the courage to speak directly to the handsome young student.

He went on without turning in her direction. "Not at all. Several weeks ago I was seized with a strong desire to buy a pretty little book, so I lived for a couple of days on dry bread, begrudging myself even a kopeck's worth of herring until I saved enough to have it. Would you like to see it?"

"Oh, yes!" Hannah cried involuntarily, wondering what book could have inspired him so much that he would go hungry to have it. This time, Lazar looked directly at her. His pale blue eyes filled with light from the window and sparkled like sunshine on the Black Sea.

Hannah fondled the book's soft leather cover, then thumbed through the tissue-thin pages that were painted red along the sides. "It's the loveliest book I've ever seen!" she murmured.

"I was like this even as a child," Lazar continued. "Books were more important to me than food or sleep or anything. One time, when I was only ten, I traded a fine vintage wine for a small half-torn book written in Russian, which contained a Yiddish translation of the text. Do you now how much better I felt when I could finally read Russian? For the first time I felt I belonged in my own country!"

"Yes, I was the same way!" Hannah said, thrilled that she understood what had motivated him.

A few weeks after Lazar had arrived in Odessa burdened with the full trappings of the traditional scholar, he cut his payess, or earlocks. Next his beard was trimmed by inches until he shaved even the mustache. He exchanged the heavy black frock coat and beaked hat of the shtetl for the informal garb of a university student: striped linen shirts worn open at the neck, high leather boots, loose blouson pants.

The more Lazar changed, the more Hannah became aware of her physical attraction to him. The first time he appeared with his shaved face naked of all hair she was momentarily shocked, as though he had exposed a private part of his anatomy.

Soon both Lazar and Hannah's brother Chaim enrolled in courses at the university. Sometimes days would go by without an appearance by either one, but Mama wasn't worried because she thought they still spent their nights at the synagogue, though Hannah was not so naive.

To discover what had captured their attention, she searched for clues in the books piled in Chaim's room. Burying the religious works were freshly dusted tomes by Hegel, Kant, Marx, Carlyle, and Engels. Smaller tracts such as *What Is to Be Done?* by Vladimir Ulyanov, who became better known when he went by the name of Lenin, were side by side with obscure works such as Zhitlovsky's *A Jew Is a Jew* and other radical publications.

Then there were scraps of writing in Lazar's own hand. "We must organize to fight the great Russian bear. Now he lies dormant in his winter sleep, sucking his paws in the dense forest as he waits for spring. But beware, when the rivers melt he will awake to stalk his prey once again!" Although it was only standard political fare, Hannah was thrilled to read something written by someone she knew.

It was clear that Lazar's interests were primarily intellectual, and unless she could appeal to him on that level, he might never give her a second glance. Not daring to enter the political discussions because she had no debating skills or understanding of the basic concepts, she prepared herself for discussions of literature by reading the short stories of Isaac Meir Dick, everything by Shomer, whose novels criticized the most terrible conditions of the time, and the satirical works of Mendele Mokher Sforim, whose characters so resembled her own Nemirov relations. But it was not until she discovered the poet Chaim Nachman Bialik that she felt ready to approach Lazar.

She waited for an evening when Chaim would not be home, and then was patient until Mama busied herself with the little girls' bedtime. Finally she was alone with Lazar by the warmth of the kitchen stove. Hannah pushed the last piece of almond cake toward him before asking tentatively, "Do you know the poems of Bialik?"

"Bialik! But of course I do! The question is, How did you?"

"I found a book, a small publication, in Chaim's room one day when I needed something to read . . . and now, well, I am just in love with the poems."

"My favorite is the one called 'Queen Sabbath.' Do you know it?" Lazar asked.

With her excellent memory Hannah easily quoted: "The sun in the treetops is no longer seen./Come forth, we will speed our Sabbath, the Queen./Know that for six days we wait you, our sure one!/Go thou in peace, our good and pure one!" She recited carefully, without much emotion, wishing to be precise in the wording, but she continued with more feeling when Lazar joined in, his face beaming in the joy of the shared stanza. "Thus for the coming

Sabbath,/Thus for the coming Sabbath!/Pass forth in peace, ye angels of peace!"

"So," Lazar said, tilting back in his chair and sighing with pleasure. "I thought you only read romantic Yiddish novels. Modern poetry might put ideas into your head!"

"What do you mean by that?" Hannah asked abruptly, angered by the insinuation that she would be expected to read only the simplest form of literature and embarrassed because the truth was she enjoyed novels the most.

"Have you read Bialik's newest work? It was published last month in the *Yiddish Daily Journal* and I don't think it is in any collection yet."

"No, I didn't see it," Hannah lied, for she had clipped and saved it among her school papers.

"I would like to read it to you, but not yet."

"Why?"

"Because I would like to wait until you've met Bialik himself."

"Bialik! Really? How could I do that?"

"He comes to a café near the university. I've spoken to him many times; he's very pleasant. Once he asked me if I wanted to be a writer."

"What did you tell him?" Hannah asked.

"I said that I already was a writer."

"Lazar, how could you say such a thing?"

"Because it's true. You didn't know that did you, Hannah?"

"How should I know what you do? You only told us you were a yeshiva boy!"

"I write things of a political nature as well as some poetry, not that Bialik can expect any competition from me!"

"I'd love to see some of your poems."

"Someday I'll show you something I've written, but it is difficult for me to let anyone read my work, unless I use my pen name and they don't know I wrote it."

From that time on Hannah kept a copy of Bialik's "Garden Rail" poem close by until she had it memorized completely.

In her daydreams, Hannah never tired of believing that Lazar would one day recite it with her, then take her into his arms, press her to his chest where she would hear the fast beating of his heart, and then . . .

❖ ❖ ❖

As the train rolled on, she tried to recall when it was that Lazar had ceased to be as frequent a visitor in her home.

Something had happened. She remembered he had kept his promise to take her to meet Bialik, but the poet had not appeared that afternoon and he never invited her back to the café. If he had come to the house again it was only long enough to meet briefly with Chaim. He apparently had no time to discuss poetry or even partake of Mama's meals. When Hannah dared to ask Chaim if Lazar still liked her, her brother speculated that some members of the Sokolovsky family might have been murdered in the Kishinev pogroms. No one had the courage to ask Lazar directly if anyone he knew had been harmed. They waited for a sign that Lazar was in mourning. Since they found none and since Lazar himself never mentioned it, Hannah guessed that at least his immediate family had been spared.

While the family sat in mourning for Papa Blau, Lazar had made the appropriate duty calls, joined Chaim in prayers, and vanished once again.

On the night before her departure for Moscow, Lazar had brought her a farewell gift, a leather-bound journal. "It's for taking notes, or writing poems, or whatever . . ." he had said.

"I don't write poems," Hannah said as she stroked a crisp blank page.

"Do you still read Bialik?"

"Sometimes."

"I was supposed to read one to you, do you remember?"

"You thought me too young!"

"Not really . . . I'm sorry I never did give it to you."

"I found it myself; you knew I would."

"I suppose . . . but I'm glad you did. You liked it?"

"It's my favorite. I know it by heart."

"And so do I. Hannah, when you leave for Moscow and when you are there . . ." He stopped to reconsider before he went on.

"Will you think of me when you say Bialik's words to yourself?"

"I will. I always do," Hannah replied, trembling.

Lazar dropped all pretense, reached for her hand, and pressed it tightly between both of his palms. "I'm sorry you are leaving. I don't want you to go. Somehow I always thought you'd be here, waiting for me to come to dinner, to talk. I never realized you'd be the one to leave."

"I want you to promise me one thing only." Hannah's voice quavered.

"What is it?" Lazar asked, his lips tight in anticipation.

"When I come back, will you read me your poems?"

"By then, Hannah, you should be old enough, even for my poems!"

## · 5 ·

THE LONG NIGHT ENDED and a new day's arrival was heralded by pink rays of dawn piercing cracks in the boxcar wall. As the light became brighter, the train slowed for a stop at Belgorod. Motionless bodies began to stir at the welcome bumping and scraping sound of the huge outside door sliding open. As soon as a gust of fresh air filled the car Hannah breathed deeply. In a few seconds everyone pressed forward to be first out on the platform.

A guard barred their way. "Stay in your places! They have forbidden fourth-class passengers to soil their platform here. Anyone who disobeys will not be permitted back on the train and will be under the jurisdiction of the local authorities. Stand back or we shall be forced to shut the door as well."

Men raised their fists and cursed the guard, women cried out, babies screamed as they sensed their mothers' anguish. No one was more disappointed than Hannah, who had thought she would be able to visit the rest facilities in the station, as her stylish traveling clothes might have at least won her access to a second-class waiting room. How much longer could she wait before being forced to urinate on the straw? Since she could never lift her skirts in public, her bladder would surely burst!

Vendors appeared selling cheeses, sausages, breads, and fresh fruit. The dining car, the gold-rimmed china plates, the delightful Katya, all seemed part of another world, another time. She watched the peasants bartering for their breakfast, fighting for the freshest loaf, the longest salami, but decided to hoard her remaining coins for a few more hours. As soon as the heavy door clanged shut and the boxcar came alive with groups sharing their meager meals, Hannah thought of a way she could have discreetly extracted a bill from her hem and regretted her decision to buy nothing at the station.

In a far corner two men amicably shared a long sausage, one cutting off hunks with his knife and offering it to the other on the tip of the blade. Suddenly the train swerved as it pulled out of the station, knocking one of the men into the other. The knife blade barely grazed an arm, but it drew blood to the surface in a thin, angry red line.

"Are you trying to kill me, you idiot? Why can't you be more careful?"

"What did you say? I offer to share my food and you accuse me of trying to kill you! What kind of an ungrateful bastard are you?"

With those words, the injured man began to pummel the other. They were two caged animals releasing their frustrations on each other, and at the same time aware of the spectacle they were creating for the rest of the travel-weary group.

It was over as suddenly as it had begun. Curiously, the two men seemed refreshed by the violent episode. Then, as though they had created a spark that blew out of control, another confrontation ignited on the other side of the car where a stout peasant with a shattered nose began to pound his wife. As the man's massive fists crashed into her flesh, first on her arm, then in her jaw, and finally in the soft places on her belly and between her legs, she groaned and doubled over. This incident aroused more interest in the group at large, and several men even put down their food to watch, their eyes growing bright with excitement.

Now the man with the sausage stood up, his eyes darting wildly back and forth. He held up the meat and then dangled it obscenely, making lewd comments in his low Russian dialect. Continuing to bait the group, he waited for someone to become aroused; but since he was obviously the most aggressive and powerful of the men, there were no takers. Hannah thought he might be some kind of laborer. His brown muscles rippled out from the tight short sleeves of his grimy linen shirt, which was unbuttoned at the side of his neck to reveal a chest covered with matted black hair. His striped suspenders held up a loose and tattered pair of pants. The face was that of a brute.

"Grigor, you are going too far," called his companion in a friendly voice, hoping to make peace.

"Oh, shut up, you crazy stupid ass! It's about time we had some fun in this stinking place!"

The excited man's roving eyes alighted upon an old man crouched in a far corner behind some sacks of grain. As soon as Grigor focused his eyes on the bent figure, the old man seemed momentarily illuminated by the attention. The old man slowly raised his face to the group, then shielded his eyes from a crack of sunlight that flashed across his face. On his head he wore a streimel, the flat hat trimmed with fur traditionally worn by Galician Jews, and from under his caftan the fringes of his prayer shawl were evident. His eyes were well lined, but unlike the sad old men who finished their days on the seaside benches of Odessa, his wrinkles all curved upward, so that his face, even now so concerned and serious, had the constant appearance of amusement and delight. Hannah thought he must have been someone's beloved zeyde, or grandfather, perhaps on his way now to visit his children in a distant city. Probably he traveled this class to avoid being conspicuous, to stay out of trouble, as well as to save a few kopecks.

"Look!" pointed Grigor with his stubby dark finger. "Look at the old zhid. He's one of the bastards who suck the blood from our children for his feast days. What is the imperial government coming to? They protect the zhids, and where does that leave us?"

"Yes! Remember what happened in Petersburg just last week?" shouted his compatriot, who stood up self-righteously. When he turned his face toward Hannah she could see a long scar across his trunklike neck.

He stepped across some peasants and kicked a sack aside, pausing as the grain spilled at his feet. "Hey, Grigor, throw me that sausage," he said, standing menacingly over the old man. He caught the sausage in midair, cut off a piece, and with mock politeness, said, "Old man, you, you dirty zhid, won't you take some breakfast with me?"

The zeyde turned his head to the side as the meat was pressed under his nose.

"What's the matter? Isn't this good enough for you?"

The zeyde said nothing, but Hannah noticed his hand quietly reaching under his coat to touch the fringes of his prayer shawl. His mouth moved softly, but no sound came from his lips as he silently invoked protection with holy words.

Sick with horror, Hannah watched, riveted to the sight, unable to move or protest. Two other men moved beside "Scarneck" while Grigor stood close by to urge them on. Holding the old Jew down, they forced open his fragile jaw and shoved the sausage hunk down his throat. He choked and gagged, but still didn't raise his arms to defend himself. A moment later he heaved his chest and the sausage spun toward the wall.

The others — men, women, children, everyone, it seemed, but Hannah — joined in, shouting "Kill the zhid, kill the zhid! Get him! Get him!" Now they had a target for all their fears and hostilities. The din finally attracted two of the train's guards. As soon as Hannah heard the heavy metal door between the cars being unlocked, she was relieved.

"What is going on here?" the tallest one, with brass buttons and official epaulettes, shouted above the roar.

"It's nothing," squealed an old hag. "Just another Jew who won't cooperate with us."

"Oh, I see. Well . . . I'll watch for a while, but I won't have to make a report if it's only a Jew."

The second officer, in a plain grey uniform, unlocked the outside door and slid it open a few feet to allow more light on the spectacle. Hannah's heart hammered in her head, but it did not block out the sound of the yelling, the pounding of the fists, the cracking of bones, human bones, breaking. The old man said nothing during the brutal kicks and punches. When there was a lull she half opened her eyes, but saw only a ring of husky figures crouched in a circle. The shadows on the wall revealed their heaving arms and bobbing heads involved in some maniacal dance. Then they paused to lift the old Jew to his feet.

Still taunting with the sausage, they asked, "Now will you eat it? Come on, don't be a crazy old jerk! What harm in a little meat? You think you are so much better than the rest of us?"

"They put a curse on my baby, he died of the pox!" shouted one woman excited by the sight of blood pouring from the old man's mouth, carrying with it ivory shards of broken teeth.

"And last year they killed my horse!"

"They ruined my business, stole all the best merchandise!"

The old man staggered away from the knife, which was now bare of the forbidden pork but threatened his neck and upper chest. He held his right hand across his mouth, and although his left hand dangled from a broken elbow joint, it still held his fur hat as he staggered toward the partially opened door through a path opened up by the peasants. The guard in the grey uniform stood with one arm protectively braced across .he opening. Outside, the Ukrainian countryside flashed by in small rectangular patches — fields of grain, a few fences, a whitewashed hut, a streak of sunlight, an orchard, a babushkaed peasant standing in her garden waving at the train. But as the wind whistled through the boxcar and billowed Hannah's skirt, it brought no welcome breath of fresh air. Only the sharp iron scent of hot fresh blood, the odor she knew so well from the hospital as the smell of birth, now reeked of cruelty and death.

It was over in a moment. First the guard at the door raised his free arm to keep the Jew away from the opening. Then, changing his mind, he removed the outstretched support and simultaneously stepped aside, leaving the abyss unguarded. Perhaps the zeyde could have caught himself and lurched back into the crowd, but Hannah thought that in the millisecond between life and death he had chosen to tumble from that smouldering Hades into the fresh summer's day, where a better end, or at least a quicker one, greeted him.

The guard leaned out the door to check where the body landed and then, without a word, closed and relocked it with an official click. The crowd, showing visible relief, sighed in unison before attempting to settle back into their individual lairs. Only Grigor was apparently not yet satisfied, as he had played but a minor role in overseeing this horrible incident, which Hannah could only call murder. He sauntered over to the water pail, dipped the ladle, and gulped three large swallows.

Wiping his mouth on his sleeve, he turned to the brass-buttoned guard. "Well, that was no loss, was it?"

"It's of no importance," he said, laughing. "Stempakov, come here!" His underling snapped to attention. "I had better return to my post in Car Three, but you stay here for a while . . . ah . . . until this place is cleaned up. We can't have it looking like this when we arrive in Kharkov. There might be an inspection."

Hannah raised her eyes for a good look at Stempakov. It was he who had reviewed her papers and had brought her there in the first place.

"So, that was a little fun," remarked Grigor as he picked up the bit of sausage the old Jew had spit out, plopped it into his mouth, and swallowed it whole without chewing. He gave a belch and continued, "I suppose the rest of this trip will be quite boring . . . unless someone else has an idea?" He paused.

"You know," Stempakov suggested, "there is another Jew in this car." Stempakov began to chuckle. "And it's quite a different matter altogether." He took a step toward Hannah. Instead of quivering or restraining herself as had the old Jew, she stood up, backed toward the wall, and began to scream.

"This is definitely my kind of problem!" Grigor announced. With obvious delight he tucked his knife into the sleeve of his shirt and moved toward Hannah while Stempakov approached her from the other side.

"No! No!" Hannah cried as she felt a hand roughly cupping her breast. Someone grabbed her from the side and pulled her back by the roots of her hair. She clenched her eyes shut as she felt herself slipping to the floor. Something warm and wet hit her on the chin. Squinting, she realized Scarneck had spit on her. She reached to push at his face, intending to gouge at his eyes, but her arm was jerked behind her head and a stab of pain shot down her arm and across her side. Her head landed on the hard floor once, then twice. Was it from the train's movement or was someone trying to knock her senseless? Everything was a blur of voices, laughter, rough words. Her skirts were torn away. She had many light layers and long underdrawers that were tightly tied at her waist. Feeling a cold blade on her thigh beginning to rip the delicate fabric, she knew it must be a knife. A knife! She remembered her Tula knife. Reaching down with her injured arm, she found it in her pocket and slipped it into her hand. The little catch gave way instantly and the blade sprang open. With one smooth gesture, she pulled it out and stabbed wildly.

She heard a loud curse, some garbled Russian orders, and then she felt herself being dragged past a windy space as they crossed between the moving cars. She wouldn't go quietly. "No! You can't do this! Help!" A firm hand clamped over her mouth. She bit into it deeply again and again, but the hard calloused palm didn't flinch.

· **6** ·

TWO CONCERNED FACES hovered over Hannah. A warm cloth wiped her face. Her shoes and stockings were slipped from her feet. Gently someone stroked her legs with a towel.

"You are all right now, everything is over. It's me — Katya." Hannah forced her eyes to focus.

"You are in my lady's private suite. No one will hurt you now."

Again she opened her eyes and noticed another woman folding her soiled garments. Katya stood beside Hannah and eased her arms into a red silk lounging robe.

"And you are the Princess Olimpiada?" Hannah asked.

"Yes. You are safe here with me," said an aristocratic voice.

"How did you find me?"

"Katya had told me all about you. I had asked her to bring you to me this morning, hoping you might give me some advice on my condition."

"If I had only known what might happen, I would have told the princess last night . . ." Katya interrupted.

"She didn't wish to wake me after my medications. This morning as soon as I heard I summoned the porter, but he said he didn't have the authority and so he sent for the officer in charge."

"The officer didn't dare argue with the princess, of course, but when he found you . . ."

"Yes, well, you know what was happening, don't you, my dear? We don't have to dwell on it any longer. But he did have a time stopping those beasts."

"And you didn't realize you were being rescued, did you?" Katya asked. "You apparently protested all the way here!"

"We admire your spirit. Anyone else might have just let it happen!"

"Do you know all the trouble you caused?"

"What do you mean?" Hannah asked, genuinely confused.

"The knife, the Tula knife I convinced you to buy! You managed to get it out. You stabbed one of them in the stomach and leg, another in the face: they say his nose is ripped. Even the guard who saved you has a bandaged hand from your bites and a small wound on his neck."

"I didn't know. I'm sorry, I didn't want to hurt anyone."

"Sorry!" cried the princess. "You were magnificent. That will teach them to trouble a woman again!"

Hannah stared at the mound of soiled clothes, saw her stained and torn undergarments on top of the pile. "I should have let them kill me."

"Oh, Hannah!" Katya wailed. She took her friend's hands in hers and pressed her face close to make Hannah believe her sincerity. "No, no, it didn't happen. They bruised you, yes! Your head is swelling, your arm is sore, your hands are scraped, but nothing else. Believe me!"

"How can you say that? My clothes . . . they are ruined."

"They were only ripped at the knee. I took them off myself. No one got near you."

"That is the truth! Praise to God!" the princess persisted. "My valet is bringing your luggage in here. After you wash and change you'll join me for a light lunch and we can become acquainted in a more . . . proper manner." She departed for the adjoining sitting room while Katya helped her friend to the chamber pot behind a silken screen emblazoned with a Chinese dragon. After washing and examining herself Hannah was finally convinced she had not been raped. She seated herself on the porcelain commode decorated with yellow roses and swirling vines, placed her sore head between her hands, and allowed the burning tears to rush between her fingers. Then she rewashed her face, arranged her hair, and finished dressing.

The heel on her left shoe was so smashed she padded to lunch in her stocking feet.

"I'm sorry about this," she apologized.

"You must have broken the heel when you were dragged between the cars," the princess replied.

Katya helped button Hannah into a pair of handsome kid dress boots. They fit perfectly.

"You must have them," the princess urged. "I rarely wear high shoes. They hurt my feet too much."

The princess's "light lunch" was served and Hannah contemplated the assortment of delicacies greedily. As she ate, she studied her benefactor.

Princess Olimpiada Yakovlev was not the wizened dowager of Hannah's imagination. She said she was the same age as Hannah, although she appeared much older because rheumatoid arthritis had ravaged her youthful body. Her affliction was visible in her once delicate hands: the knuckles were enlarged and slightly off center. She held them with great tension and, even when she relaxed, they froze into a clawlike form.

"Usually I am better this time of year, but Moscow has had so much rain this spring! My father wanted me to go to Sebastopol and Yalta for the cure, and I must say my bones crave some sun!"

"So, you will change to the Southern Express in Lozovaya?" Hannah tried to ask casually.

The princess immediately sensed her concern. "No, I've decided to go to Odessa first, then on to Sebastopol by boat. I haven't been to Odessa since I was a child. We always used to stay at that lovely hotel above the harbor, the Richelieu. Do you know it?"

"Yes, I know where it is," Hannah replied. Jews never dined there.

"I am so impressed to know a doctor, a doctor who is a woman my age!" the princess said.

"Not exactly a doctor, Princess." Hannah launched into the story of her education, and the reason for her journey back to Odessa.

Thus the balance of Hannah's journey was made in great comfort and freedom from anxiety. Even Hannah's folder of papers had been returned intact. A liveried waiter answered every summons, and although Hannah could never think of anything she wanted, the princess required all manner of treats. At Nikolayev Station Katya was sent to purchase a surprise: hollowed-out lemons packed with citrus ice.

As the train slowed for the outskirts of Odessa, Hannah and the princess remained seated while the valet and porters arranged their luggage in a neat group by the outside doors. Purposely turning away from the bustle on the platform as the most anxious passengers rushed to disembark, Hannah kept up a light conversation on the sights of Odessa. She did not want ever again to set eyes on the peasants, but a sudden whistle from a departing train startled her for a moment and she involuntarily glanced out to see from where it had come.

In the thinning crowd she saw him, hanging back trying to be inconspicuous, yet searching every stairway.

"Someone has come to meet me."

"Oh, how nice for you!" the princess replied, though her disappointment was evident.

"How can I ever repay you for everything?"

"No payment is necessary or expected. We must help each other through life as best as we can. Then in turn someone else, someone unexpected, will require your help and you will give it to them. My father, Prince Vasily, taught me that life is not a direct exchange back and forth, but circular. One takes from the right and gives to the left. Eventually it all balances out. But, Hannah, will you please visit me at the Richelieu? I have no friends in Odessa." She sounded more lonely than polite.

"I'll come as soon as I can."

"I wish you every good thing in the world, Hannah — I mean, Dr. Blau," Katya said, politely shaking Hannah's hand on the platform. "I hope we will see you again."

"Of course you will." Hannah turned quickly and found herself face to face with Lazar.

"I knew you would come today," he said simply. "Let's get away from here as quickly as possible."

"You don't know how happy I am to see you!" Hannah said with relief.

"I hope you had a pleasant journey" was all he replied in a flat, unemotional response that dampened Hannah's exhilaration at their reunion. As she followed him up the stairs to the street, Hannah wondered how much she dared tell him about her adventure.

As soon as they were at the carriage dock she demanded, "Tell me what has happened!"

"Not here!" Lazar replied sternly. "Wait until we're home. Your mother will tell you everything."

"Then Mama is all right?" Hannah said in relief.

"Yes, of course. What did you think?" he snapped, not understanding her concern.

"I don't know what this is all about!"

Lazar became even more abrupt. He steered her to a shabby vehicle that was driven by an old Jew from the market district. "Not now!" When the luggage was loaded and the carriage lurched on its way, Lazar responded to the hurt and confusion in her face. Placing his arm around her shoulders, he pulled Hannah toward him. "You don't know how happy I am to have you home again!"

Hannah's jaw quivered. She pressed her lips together for control and turned from Lazar. There was nothing to say if he wouldn't answer her most burning questions. She watched the passing scene, every view a joyful reminder that her nightmare journey was over. The lime trees had blossomed and now contained miniature fruit, the white acacias wafted their heavy perfume into the early evening air, and the mimosa leaves curled for the night.

Lazar held Hannah's hand, squeezing it every few moments. Turning toward her a dozen times, he tried to catch her glance, but she was too tired and anxious to respond to him. As they neared her home, she could only wonder at the disaster that had so destroyed her plans.

## · 7 ·

"So, HANNAH, YOU DID take the first train. We weren't certain you would!"

"Why do you say that, Mama?" Hannah asked anxiously as she stood inside the front door.

"You didn't show any interest in us until we were forced to summon you!"

"Mama, please . . ." Hannah said. "I missed you very much," she added, trying to evoke a warm response from her mother.

"So you didn't forget us completely?" Mama replied in her sulkiest voice. Mama stood with her plump hands akimbo on her wide hips. Hannah noticed she had gained even more weight, now appearing almost as broad as she was high.

"You know how long a journey it is for just a short visit, but I am happy to be home now that you need me. I still don't even know why I'm here. Lazar wouldn't tell me anything," she continued, looking around for Lazar. "Where is he now?"

"He is not here. It took courage just for him to meet you."

"Is he in trouble?"

"Hannah!" Mama said in exasperation. Then, as she studied her daughter's puzzled expression, she sighed, lowered herself onto the edge of the sofa, and continued, "It's Chaim. He's been . . . he's been . . ." She kept wringing her hands, as though the activity would wrest the difficult words from her throat. "Arrested!" she finally whispered. "In Petersburg, last week. We don't know what has happened to him."

"Arrested!" Hannah shouted and looked about frantically. "I don't believe you. It must be a mistake."

"Hush!"

"But what has he done? Why was he there?"

"How is a mother to know what her children are doing? They tell me nothing! I thought he was going to Vilna for the Bund. He could never have gotten a permit for Petersburg with the way it goes these days, so if he really was there, he entered illegally. Whatever else he did, he broke the law by leaving the Pale without permission."

"Why would he take such a risk?"

"Who knows? I only pray he was not involved in the trouble there . . ."

"I heard about something. What happened?"

"What happened? If I weren't so worried about your brother it would be a wonderful thing! Plehve, the monster, was murdered. May his name be blotted out! He was a man with a thousand enemies. I could have torn his eyes out myself for all the wickedness he has done. Kishinev was all his work! He gives the permission for every pogrom! But it will not end with him. His successor will continue his work and will find the same bitter end, and the one after him as well. Mark my words."

"But Chaim — how was he involved? He's not an assassin. How do you even know he was arrested?"

"Lazar knows. He has ways of obtaining information."

"Has anyone contacted you?"

"No."

"Then this could be a mistake?"

"That's what I keep telling myself. Chaim may be in Vilna after all, but I think Lazar knows from where he speaks. In fact, I don't think he has dared reveal everything, at least not to me."

"What exactly do you know?"

Mama pulled the crumpled front page of a newspaper from a pocket under her apron. It was from a St. Petersburg paper dated July 16, 1904, and was banded by a thick black border. A portrait of Plehve, the minister of the interior, was at the top left. His heavy, bland Germanic face with thick eyebrows and pince-nez stared out accusingly over the bold-typeface account of his death.

Hannah read aloud: "The hideous assassination of our beloved minister took place on the crowded Isamilovsky Prospect across from the Warsaw Hotel. The bomb was thrown into the armored carriage by an unknown terrorist, who was critically wounded by the explosion but is still alive." Hannah paled. "Chaim! Wounded! Oh, Mama!"

"No, no. We don't think Chaim threw the bomb. We would have heard by now if he was the one. Lazar knows the name of the culprit . . . a railway porter who called himself Jacob but was really a Yegor Sazonov. Not even a Jewish boy! He only wanted the authorities to think he was Jewish. Now isn't that a terrible business? Even the revolutionaries make the Jews suffer, for there will be reprisals after this!"

Suddenly it made sense . . . the boxcar, "trouble in Petersburg," the rationale for the old zeyde's murder!

"I can't imagine him in this kind of predicament. Politics, yes, but he was always reading books, talking, arguing . . . how could he go from that to . . . this . . . this . . . violence?"

"The world is crazy, meshugge. Even if he did nothing, even if he was just arrested because he didn't have the right papers and was in Petersburg on the wrong day, even if he is just safe and hiding until the trouble blows over, our whole family is jeopardized."

"Why? What did we do?"

"Word travels faster than fire. That's why Lazar can't be seen here associating with the 'revolutionary's' people. We had to get you away from Moscow before the authorities there discovered who you were."

"Has this affected the business?"

"Orders have stopped almost completely; no one will come for fittings; and those who still owe us will never come around to pay their bills now that they have such a convenient excuse." She went to the window and tore back the curtain. "Just look for yourself. See how everyone stays on the other side."

"Mama, that can't be true!"

"Walk outside. Then watch our 'friends' retreat without so much as a hello. Only the family will stand with us now."

"Do we have enough money?"

"For a month, maybe more if we are careful. After that I don't know what we will do!" Mama sat down and rubbed her cheek in resignation. It was plain to Hannah that this was not the usually contentious woman who relished a fight and loved to laugh about it later. Her tightly curled hair fell into frizzy strands and her apron, usually immaculate, showed moist stains from the sweat of her hands. This general disarray of a normally fastidious woman brought her more sympathy from Hannah than all her words.

"I suppose I will have to remain with you in Odessa," Hannah said quietly. At first she felt a pang of regret and then added with genuine anticipation, "Do you think Bubbe will allow me to assist her again or even take over some of her cases?"

"We've already discussed it. Bubbe can hardly see anymore; everything is just blurs and shadows. I don't know how she has gone on as long as she has. So disappointed she was when she heard you were staying for medical school. I don't think she expected you would ever settle back at home."

"If everyone is avoiding us, how will they feel about me delivering their babies?"

"Bubbe says there is no political talk once a woman is confined. They just want someone to help them."

"I hope she's right."

"Who knows? In a few months maybe you can help restore our good name!"

"I'll try to do that," Hannah replied flatly.

Although Hannah was looking forward to working with Bubbe, she felt a growing irritation when she realized the decision had not been hers. Mama continued to break in on her thoughts.

"The first thing you'll do is get more information about Chaim."

"How do you expect me to do that?"

"Lazar will trust you with more of the details."

"Why should he tell me anything he wouldn't tell you?"

"Don't argue with me. You can go places, hear things, do things that I can't."

"What places?" Hannah asked with a false innocence.

"We'll wait a few more days, let everything quiet down, give Lazar more time to ask around. That boy was so anxious for you to get home, he'll tell you anything!"

Hannah realized she could not hide all her feelings. "Of course, Mama. I'd love to see him. There's so much for me to tell him about Moscow."

"Good! You'll visit with family for a few days. At least we are still welcome in the homes of our relations. You'll rest, eat well, and then you'll go to Lazar."

Struggling mightily to restrain her anger and resentment, Hannah felt her temples pound with rage as Mama laid out her plans. She had been told to eat and rest, to visit her relatives. Everyone assumed she would forget her medical studies and begin her career as an Odessan midwife, handing her earnings over to support the family. And what else had been decreed? Had Mama ordered the matchmaker to find a suitable husband? Had she started on the trousseau? Perhaps she had already selected the names of her children.

After a year of living independently and succeeding with her own decisions, Hannah bristled at this interference. Her tendency had always been to say "black" to Mama's every "white," no matter how she really felt. Now some germ of maturity materialized to curb an immediately negative response. Hannah would force herself to behave dutifully while slowly extricating herself from the maternal demands.

"That's an excellent plan, Mama," Hannah forced herself to reply cheerfully. "And, Mama, how good it will be to eat at your table again," she added. But that, at least, was the truth.

The sour mood quickly changed when Hannah's two sisters arrived, followed by Aunt Sonia, who had been keeping them at bay while Mama broke the news.

At fifteen Dora had the figure of a woman, but her behavior was that of a much younger child. If her gravy spilled on her vegetables or a spoon slipped from her clumsy hand, she might hurl her dish across the room and cry uncontrollably. She had not learned to read or write more than a few words but was remarkably thorough about the tasks she did undertake, spending an hour or more to scrub every burnt particle from a baking pan. She was slow. Her gait was hesitant, her speech slurred, and she was known to stammer if she needed to express more than the simplest thought. But her face was not unpleasant. She had beautiful thick hair, which was combed with a middle part and braided so she could mind it herself. Fortuitously she had inherited Mama's dark eyes and Papa's thin nose and chiseled chin. Her figure, with a high, full bust and matching wide hips, was extremely flattering to the youthful girl, though she threatened to turn zaftig like Mama. Dora's most unattractive feature, her full lips, seemed more noticeable because her expressions were rarely animated.

"Oh, Hannah, I missed you so much!" Dora cried, throwing her arms around her sister and hugging her so hard it took away her breath.

"I missed you too, Dora. I really did," Hannah said just as Eva pushed herself into the same embrace. "Come, Eva, sit still for a minute and tell me about school. What have you learned?"

As her youngest sister chattered on about her courses and professors, Hannah half listened, for she was distracted by her little sister's physical development. Unfortunately, Eva was ugly. The family had hoped this was just an awkward stage that, when she reached puberty, would develop into a more pleasant physiognomy. At thirteen she was still young for her age. Her breasts were not developed, but her skin was erupting with an abnormal number of crusting protuberances. She also had a full head of dark hair, but it lacked the luster of her other sisters' and was studded with white flaking granules that spattered her blue shirtwaist. Although Eva had also inherited Mama's dark eyes, they were encased in small sockets and functioned poorly, causing a perpetual squint. Luckily, she did not seem to gain weight easily so her thin body, which at that age appeared unhealthy, had some potential as she neared maturity. And, thankfully, her mind was sound and she had a clear, practical head. Although she had missed an education at Papa's knee, she had already mastered Yiddish, Hebrew, and the Russian of the marketplace. In the last year she had won acceptance to the best gymnasium and seemed to be doing well there.

"Wait till you see my pillow lace!" she boasted. "I've completed all of Aunt Sonia's patterns and the Meyerovs are sending me new ones."

"Not till after Hannah has her meal! Come, come, all is ready!" Aunt Sonia insisted. As she led them toward the kitchen she whispered to Hannah, "Your mama goes about worrying and crying day after day. That is her way, but mine is to work even harder. So I decided to cook, and all week that is what I have done." She finished with a flourish of her hand toward the kitchen.

Hannah's eyes feasted on an array of her favorite dishes. Two kinds of noodle pudding, one stuffed with apples and almonds and one prepared with poppy seeds, were placed on either end of the table. There were holibtses, chopped-beef-filled cabbage rolls; a steaming tureen of beet borsht; a pot roast surrounded by browned potatoes, carrots, and turnips; even stuffed fish shimmering in gravy. A freshly baked challeh graced the center, though it wasn't Sabbath. On the side table rested a dome of teyglakh dripping with honey syrup; apricot tarts; and a fresh watermelon compote.

"Come, sit down! You can't eat with your eyes!" Mama said, laughing. But as Hannah moved to take her place across from her sisters, she watched Mama's expression turn to a deep frown. "Hannah! Where did you get those shoes?"

"They were a gift from a kind woman I met on the train. You see, I had an accident . . ."

"You were hurt?"

"Only a few bruises when I fell. My heel caught on the train platform and broke. And my clothes became filthy."

"What did you do?" asked Eva.

"I had met a girl in my compartment, a servant to Princess Olimpiada. She took me to her lady's private quarters and they helped me wash and change."

"A princess?" Dora was impressed.

"Yes. She is my age, but the poor thing has the rheumatism. She's on her way south for the cure. She insisted I spend the rest of the journey with her, and she loaned me these shoes."

"You must return them, of course!" Mama instructed.

"Yes, you are right. She'll be at the Richelieu for a few days. But I must attend to our family matters first."

"Very true, and the first matter of business will be to have one bite of everything I prepared!" Aunt Sonia demanded with a laugh calculated to lighten the mood.

## · 8 ·

THE CAFÉ BESSARABIA was located on a narrow back street near the university. Even though she had been there only once, the day Lazar had brought her to meet the poet Bialik, Hannah managed to find her way through the winding streets in the old section of the city. She arrived just about three o'clock, when she surmised the students would be occupying themselves at the café between the classroom and supper hours.

Chaim had deplored wasted study hours, yet he could be found sipping Turkish coffee from a tiny gold-banded cup as often as Lazar and the others. True, he usually made an attempt to study a text while the others chattered, but whether he absorbed much learning in the smoke-filled atmosphere was doubtful, although he earned himself the nickname Ostrich for his efforts.

When Hannah entered the side door of the café, her heart leapt when she saw someone whose dark ringlets and broad, square shoulders resembled her brother's. But one look at the snub-nosed profile that emerged from the grey whirls of smoke proved he was not Chaim. Nor was Lazar in the noisy crowd.

Feeling apart and alone, she retreated slowly toward a second, smaller room. In her tailored skirt and lace-trimmed shirtwaist she knew she must have appeared a misfit, for the other women wore soft clothing: peasant blouses, patterned skirts, and drab shawls. Hannah's hair was pulled tight in her midwife's bun, while they favored loose styles with natural curls that fell in tangled tendrils or schoolgirl braids. A few permitted their straight locks to cascade unbound by pins or combs. Heads lifted, paused, and looked away as she passed by each table. No one recognized her as Chaim's sister; no one welcomed her to join their cluster. Finally she decided she would feel less awkward waiting at one of the outdoor tables that catered to an older, more artistic group, many of whom sat alone reading papers and foreign books. Just as she was about to take a seat at a vacant corner table, a young woman hurried by, stopped, then turned back to Hannah.

"You are Chaim Blau's sister! Am I right?" she blurted.

"Yes, how did you know?"

"I have an excellent memory . . . for faces, that is. And you are a medical student!"

"That is remarkable," Hannah replied cautiously.

"I'm Vera, Vera Goldfarb. I study languages and do translations. I knew your brother very well, until . . . He used to be in several of my classes," she said, faltering, and then recovered by asking, "Who are you looking for? I know almost all the regulars."

"Lazar Sokolovsky. He wasn't really expecting me; I just thought he'd be here."

"He usually is, but he'll be in later than usual today. He is finishing an important assignment. Come, I'll introduce you around while we wait."

Vera ushered Hannah to a crowded table in the corner of the first section. Although there was hardly room for two more, they squeezed together on the benches. Hannah was pressed between Vera and a thin, sallow man who stared straight ahead even though they made contact at thigh, buttocks, and shoulders.

Vera moved cups, glasses, and Chopin beer corks, wrinkled her nose at the mess, and boldly summoned the waiter. "Hey! This table needs cleaning! And we're thirsty here!"

"What do you want?" the waiter, a student himself, asked in a sleepy voice.

"The usual for me, and my friend will have . . ." She waited for Hannah. "Do you drink beer?"

"Yes," she lied. "But I'd prefer tea now."

"Of course," Vera replied with a knowing grin. "Anyone else?"

The others stirred themselves and ordered additional beers and coffees.

Vera introduced Hannah to her companions. "This is Chaim Blau's sister. You remember him, don't you?" she said with an edge to her voice.

"Shall we just call you Blau?" one of the students asked in a teasing tone.

"It's Hannah," she replied softly.

"Of course, Hannah! I've heard about you!"

Hannah blanched, wondering what he meant.

"Blau's sister, eh?" responded the thin man at her side. "What's become of him, anyway?"

"This is not the time to discuss that," a large, bearded man across from her gruffly interrupted.

"Now, gentlemen, let me at least introduce everyone before we involve our guest in one of our quarrels." Vera enunciated every syllable for effect. "On your left, Hannah, is Boris Slavinsky. He's from Grodno. Don't let his face depress you; he's a typical morose Litvak. Next to him is Gnessa Weiskoft." Vera pointed to a delicate woman who napped with her head cradled in her arms. "Oh, don't worry, she's not drunk. She was up all night helping your friend Sokolovsky with the presses. And next to her we have Hershel Makunin, revolutionary and poet . . . Did I place those in the right order?"

The bearded man grunted. "As you wish, I do not care for labels myself."

"Maybe I should have said 'revolutionary, poet, and father-to-be,'" Vera responded acidly. "You should take more of an interest in our visitor. I believe she is a midwife and might be of service to you in the near future."

Makunin's response was an audible belch. Vera grimaced, but softened when he offered her a pink-edged cigarette as a gesture of reconciliation. "Have one, Goldfarb, it might help warm you. Your voice sounds very chilly."

Vera accepted his offering, fumbled with matches for a moment, and then settled into her smoke. Fresh drinks were served and Hannah was content to occupy herself with the sugar and glass to avoid making conversation.

As she imagined her brother in their midst, she was repelled by the thought that these abrasive people had inspired him. Why had he become so involved in Der Bund, or The League? Why did he believe that this secret group of consolidated workingmen who demanded a national Jewish autonomy would ever succeed in anything against the organized policies of the Court? Though the proposals her brother had drafted to gain recognition of the Yiddish language were probably useless, Chaim had zealously worked to the point where he had been elected as a delegate to conventions in Vilna and Kovno. No wonder he was in a predicament, she thought, for these purported friends were obviously troublemakers.

Lazar, more than Chaim, had hinted at their way of life, especially admiring the spirit of the "new women" who freely chose their own paths, refusing to subjugate themselves to the old traditions. Although impressed with the respect he had shown for the rights of women, Hannah had chosen to argue with him.

"There is one difference between us which will make you and me unequal forever," she had challenged.

"And what is that?"

"A man will never be a mother!"

"The revolution needs babies!" he had countered. "In the new society our children will be trained in free thought from birth instead of ritually enslaved by a religion that divides men from women. Together we will share the work of the revolution; together we will reap its rewards."

Rather than press her point, Hannah had dwelled silently on his definition of "our children." Had he meant the all-encompassing children of the revolution or, more specifically, the children they might together bear someday? But she had not dared ask him to explain.

As Hannah observed Vera and Gnessa, she wondered how dedicated they were to the revolution. In one of Chaim's pamphlets she had read about the Am Olam movement. Could these women be part of the same communistic group, sharing wages, food, clothing, and living space; sleeping next to these men as sisters; living without any notion of personal property; attempting to become symbols of the new order to which they aspired? Hannah dismissed the idea as preposterous. How could this humorless bunch live in platonic harmony or work toward a common goal?

Gnessa, who had not wakened fully, gave the appearance of being not only unkempt but unclean as well. Grime was lodged under her fingernails, her uncombed hair was dull and greasy, and her breath, even from across the table, was unbearably sour. Vera, on the other hand, was a curious amalgam of purpose and femininity. Her hair, the color of tarnished copper, was pulled back and rolled to frame her face, then braided and wrapped around her head to emphasize its luxurious fullness. Although her nose formed an angled line in the center of her face, its length was well balanced by a prominent chin. Her eyes were blessed with a blue grey tint that perfectly complemented both her ivory skin and metallic hair, and her full red mouth was only slightly marred by the discolorations on her front teeth. To Hannah, everything about Vera seemed studied, somehow false: the gestures with her tapered fingers, the nodding of her swanlike neck, the poses and expressions she affected. Without knowing exactly why, Hannah was certain she disliked this poseur intensely.

No one spoke to Hannah and she longed to be the first with some brilliant question or witty remark to lighten the oppressive mood. The long silence persisted.

She reached for her glass. Suddenly, like a bird of prey who waits for a movement from her victim before pouncing, Vera began to address the group excitedly. "Hannah knew Sokolovsky before she went away," she began, and waited a second to judge the effect of her words. "He boarded with her family . . . before we met." Again Vera paused to observe Hannah's reaction. Though Hannah tried to remain calm, her glass began to shake in her hand. "Hannah . . . if you hadn't left for Moscow, well, it might have been different for you, for both of us."

Hannah felt as though someone had struck her. Just then a loud confrontation broke out across the room, diverting attention away from her mute embarrassment.

"What a political innocent you are!" yelled a thin, mustached man. "It's your kind who create these problems and then slink away instead of cleaning up the mess."

His companion, noteworthy for his shaggy blond beard, refused to rise to this provocation and motioned for his adversary to be calm.

"Don't try to mollify me, Rechtman! Do you expect to take every Jew to this promised land of Zion? What will become of those who remain behind — the ones who don't choose to leave or cannot?"

The man addressed as Rechtman mumbled a few words of disgust, reached for some books on the bench, and made ready to leave. This further aroused his opponent, who pushed him back in his seat.

"Not everyone has a rich merchant father who will pay his fare. What do you say to hunger, to illness, to the myriad miseries of our people? What do you say to . . . to . . ."

"Here we have an interesting example of two points of view, handled indiscreetly and with childish displays of emotion; nevertheless, a good lesson to illustrate the basic ideological factions represented here today." Hershel Makunin pontificated for Hannah's benefit. "On one hand I give you Jakovoitch, the hirsute lad with the purple face who espouses the doctrines of the typical social democrat. While he claims to be a devoted Bundist, he speaks for the worker — not every worker, mind you, only those who are Jewish as well. On the other hand, Rechtman is an equally ardent Zionist who sees the remedy for every Jew to be the same: a refuge in a homeland of his own."

"*His* own is exactly it!" Vera exclaimed. "At least the socialists admit that women have rights. The Zionists are so orthodox they haven't yet realized they are working for only one-half of humanity."

"That's very simplistic thinking, my dear, but I'll let it pass," Makunin countered and then smoothed a ruffled eyebrow with one finger.

"You theoreticians will lose in the end," Gnessa said as she rubbed her tired eyes. "It is not the language of the leaders that matters, it's the language of the workers!"

"But Gnessa," Vera replied, "all the true socialists are ignoring the Bund because there is no place for a separate nationalistic organization."

The attention of the room was directed toward Hannah's table, now that Rechtman and Jakovoitch had stopped shouting.

Vera was enjoying center stage. Without lowering her voice, she continued, "Makunin is a very devoted Zionist, Hannah, if you didn't already guess."

"And you are a socialist who does not believe in the Bund?" Hannah asked in a whisper. Knowing Lazar's dedication to that very cause, Hannah was testing the woman's emotional and political allegiance.

Vera blanched. "I . . . I believe that the Bund is a useful vehicle, but it will not truly effect the great changes we fervently desire. Today it may raise the status of the Jewish population as a whole in the matter of civic rights and cultural interests . . . to whatever extent they go hand in hand with socialist interests."

"Notice how Goldfarb bends with the wind, but one of these days she will see the truth and become a Zionist!" Makunin again stroked his eyebrow in a saucy, self-righteous gesture designed to incite Vera further. Then, turning to Hannah, he added, "Little sister, I'll tell you a secret about these Bundists. They are really all Zionists who are simply afraid of becoming seasick!"

"That's completely unfair, Makunin!" a new voice countered. "A poor joke when you know that the Jewish socialists pay the highest toll of sacrifice to the Russian bastards, for when they are caught they are punished for their politics as well as their religion. It takes far more courage to be a good Bundist than to plan a cruise across the world to a supposedly safer land!" Lazar, who had entered through the back door and had been observing the debate from the shadows, finished by placing his hands on Vera's shoulder.

Looking up with obvious admiration, Vera savored Lazar's defense. "Well said!" She gave to Makunin a contemptuous sneer before craning her neck back to smile at her protector. "Did you finish the job?"

"Yes, finally. Everything goes as planned."

"Look who I rescued for you!" Vera nodded toward Hannah. "But I'm afraid we haven't been good company."

"I'm sure you've had your usual squabbles," Lazar muttered.

"Without which there would be no change," sighed Gnessa.

"Hannah, you have probably had enough of the stale air in this room," Lazar said in a fresh voice. "Why don't you come outside with me for a while. I have something to discuss with you."

"Of course," Hannah replied in relief. As she tried to squeeze out from behind the crowded table, she stepped on Vera's outstretched foot.

"Clumsy!" Vera complained loudly enough for Lazar to hear. He turned toward her, frowned visibly, and then placed his arm around Hannah's shoulders as he led her to the street door, glancing back to be certain Vera caught his meaning.

## · 9 ·

FOLLOWING LAZAR, Hannah made her way down the narrow passage between the old stone buildings. Taller than most of his associates, he had developed a forward thrust of his sinuous neck. His muscular legs rippled beneath his tight sailor pants. His earlocks had long ago been shorn, but Lazar's thick straight hair, the color of the sun-baked grasses of the Ukrainian steppes, was still worn long in the student manner. Although she had always been attracted to this dazzling and brilliant student, Hannah was never more impressed than at that moment, when Lazar tossed his head like a stallion rearranging his mane.

Hannah feared she had little to offer him compared with Vera, who understood his political goals, was more at ease in his society, and lived more boldly than Hannah yet dared. Surely he had found Vera's careless yet feminine attire, her vivid complexion, and her vibrant voice more stimulating than Hannah's own pale face and subdued manner. As they approached a courtyard bathed in shafts of light at the end of the musty passageway, Hannah resigned herself to the fact that, no matter how she tried, she would never be able to compete with Vera. Probably she and Lazar had already slept together and were united with a very private sort of understanding.

"No one should bother us here," Lazar said as he pointed to a niche in a crumbling wall and maneuvered Hannah so her back was pressed to the damp stones. "If I stand like this, anyone who sees us will take us for lovers and hurry by." To further the illusion, Lazar positioned his head at the level of Hannah's.

With a start she remembered her brother. "Please, tell me what you know about Chaim!" Hannah felt her body become rigid in preparation.

"You came for the truth and now you will have it!" Lazar said resolutely. "Do you understand?"

Hannah nodded numbly.

"This is what we know," Lazar continued. "Chaim was arrested in Petersburg the evening after the assassination. The culprit who threw the bomb was definitely Sazonov. He is being kept alive until the authorities are able to extract all the information they need."

"Oh, my god!" Hannah wailed. "He's giving names?"

"How else did they know exactly where Chaim was hiding?"

"So, he really was in Petersburg!"

"Yes, doing some . . . some advanced studies at the Technological Institute before they brought him in for questioning."

"Questioning!"

"There have been no charges; there is no evidence. All they know is that Chaim is a Jew, a Jew in Petersburg without valid papers at the exact time of Plehve's murder."

"Is that enough?"

"They got his name from a reliable source, if you call Sazonov reliable. They say he has already implicated his dearest friend, Dulebov."

"Don't those people have any kind of code?"

"I don't know, there comes a point . . . I have thought about what I might have been forced to say."

"No! No!" Hannah clutched at Lazar's shirt and cried, "You wouldn't have, you couldn't have." Lazar held her hands firmly, waiting for her to calm herself.

"I might have done the same, Hannah. I want you to know that. Because if you understand that, you will see that Chaim is nothing to Sazonov and his friends. To them he is just another expendable part of the anarchist machine." Lazar held Hannah more tightly and gently stroked her shoulder. "At least fifteen others have already been arrested, and more will be found."

"If Chaim is arrested, if there are no charges, how can he be freed?"

To comfort her Lazar smoothed Hannah's hair with his fingertips, sending a current of desire through her body that obliterated her concern.

Her nipples stiffened. In an attempt at modesty, Hannah pressed herself back toward the stone wall. "Yes, you are right," she said aloud, thinking that Lazar could have betrayed Chaim, just as she was doing at that very moment by placing her own romantic feelings before her brother's life.

"There are still things we can do," Lazar continued.

"What, then?"

"First we must wait, take everything slowly, find out what we can."

"Do you know any more now?"

"Yes. The last we heard he was in the Kresty, a large, recently modernized prison overlooking the Neva. They say it is an improvement over the old Peter and Paul Fortress ..."

"Will there be a trial?"

"I doubt it. There is no evidence to support a case, so they'll probably ship him to an exile prison somewhere in the East."

"Siberia?"

"Or Turkistan. But there are enough members of the Terrorist Brigade scattered throughout these places to advise us when he arrives. If nothing else, we are able to get information."

"Why won't we hear directly from Chaim?"

"Eventually we will. He'll learn the tricks involved in sending messages, and later you might apply for permission to communicate once or twice a year."

"Once or twice a year! What are you saying? He is as good as being dead and buried!"

Lazar held Hannah's face in his hands and forced her to look into his eyes. "Chaim is not dead!" he said sternly. "We can't stop thinking about him or working for him for one single day!"

"Ha! Tell that to those purported friends of yours and his!" Hannah gestured toward the café. "To them he is as good as dead!"

"Don't be too harsh. Remember, I said there would be others ... They worry for themselves, other friends. Don't judge what they are thinking and feeling."

"There must be something more I can do!"

"Everything possible is already being done."

"And what do I say to Mama? She will go crazy with this."

"Help her. Stay at home, be with her, and whatever happens, I promise to bring you the truth."

"You expect something worse?"

"I don't think anything will change for some time."

"I know of someone else in a work camp, a doctor. His wife waits courageously. He writes that it isn't so terrible because he can still take care of patients. Remember Chaim's technique of manipulating to get his way?"

"I'm happy you are thinking so positively."

Hannah's voice became hoarse. "To think of him starving, alone in a dark cell, chained to a wall, or . . ."

"Hannah, that's enough!"

"I can't help it." She began to sob.

"I know, I know." Lazar's voice sounded as if gravel were caught in his throat. Resting his chin on the top of her head, he gently moved his lips. "Chaim would be proud of you. I am too. You've changed."

"How?"

"You're not as young, I suppose. Which makes me very happy, for now I need you more than ever." Lazar stepped back and cocked his head to one side, giving Hannah an appealing smile. "Won't you help me?"

"You know I will."

"I knew I could count on you . . . for everything."

"Is there something I could do now?" Hannah was ready to press her body against his to give the token of affection he was requesting.

"Just an errand. I need some papers delivered across the city, near your district, and I won't have time today to go there myself."

"Of course!" Hannah said with mock brightness in her voice, still eager to please him even though she was momentarily disappointed that his request wasn't for the affection she yearned to demonstrate.

"I'll have Gnessa take you to the place where the bundle is waiting. It's down an unmarked alley and I wouldn't want you to get lost. Do you have your documents with you?"

"Yes. I carry them all the time."

"Are your medical papers with them?"

"Yes, but why?"

"Just a precaution. If you should be detained . . . It won't happen, of course, but we must always have a contingency plan . . ."

"I don't understand."

"Don't worry, but in case you are stopped, show them your papers and explain you are going to a confinement. Makunin expects a child soon. His woman, she's called Martina, lives at five-two-three Zhulevsky, near the Science Institute."

Realizing she was being entrusted with an opportunity to further earn Lazar's trust, she didn't object to the mission. When they returned to the café, only Vera and a music student remained.

"Take Hannah to Prozka Street," he demanded in the voice of a commanding officer. "She'll never find it on her own."

Suspicion and jealousy were revealed by the set of Vera's mouth and her hostile stare.

To ensure her cooperation, Lazar softened his voice. "Vera, won't you help me?"

Hannah recognized the exact words and tone he had used with her a few moments earlier and thought that Lazar had learned much during his association with her brother. Unable to refuse, Vera stood up, finished her beer in one long swallow, and headed toward the door. Lazar reached to touch her buttocks in a familiar gesture, but she skillfully sidestepped his advance and marched resolutely toward the street.

## · 10 ·

HANNAH FOLLOWED VERA wordlessly through the university quarter, making more than two dozen turns through the damp cobbled streets. Arriving at one of the shabbier courtyards where crisscrossed lines were hung with shirts and bed linens, Vera stopped, looked around to see if they had been followed, then pushed aside two galvanized washtubs before pounding a battered wooden door.

"You have some laundry?" called a timid voice from within.

"No, you have an order ready for me."

"What is the name?" asked the woman, tentatively opening the door a crack.

"Vronsky."

"Vronsky?" Hannah asked in surprise.

"Hush!" Vera demanded.

The anemic young washing woman, with one child poking between her legs and a baby supported on her hip, opened the door further to study the two women before backing inside and bolting the door. In a few minutes the door reopened and only a masculine arm appeared with first one, then two large bundles wrapped in brown laundry paper and tied with a thin loop of coarse string. After setting them on the stoop, the arm withdrew.

Hannah stared in disbelief. She had expected one small package she could tuck under her arm, but each of these was the size of a large market basket. She tried to lift one, then set it down with a thud.

"This is impossible!" she protested. "How can I carry these to the trolley, through the change at Nezhdanov, across Kirov Square, and over to the Old Bazaar? I can barely manage one."

"You can't leave them here!" Vera hissed. "Lazar is counting on you . . ." She finished with a self-satisfied set of her mouth.

Hannah positioned herself between the two packages, lifted them in tandem, and took a few hesitant steps. She found that if she walked with a rhythmic, slow gait she could carry them about twenty paces before needing a rest.

"Is there a trolley stop nearer than the University Line?"

"Very close, follow me," Vera replied.

Hannah trudged behind her guide, resenting Vera more deeply because she hadn't offered any assistance. In just two short turns they were out on a major boulevard and Hannah was relieved to recognize the street. When she reached the curb of the trolley stop she lowered her arms and placed the packages on the ground. Her neck was stretched and taut, her shoulders ached already, and deep red grooves lined her hands. As she rubbed them together in an attempt to bring circulation into her sore palms, she looked for Vera, who already had disappeared.

The trolley arrived in a few minutes, and just as she was about to attempt lifting her burdens onto the car, a derbied gentleman took them from her. "May I be of service?" he asked in an unctuous voice. After handing the packages up and then helping Hannah to a seat by the door, he continued, "What in the world are you carrying, dear miss? Bricks?"

"Oh, how did you guess?" Hannah replied as lightly as possible. "Very strong ones. I'm building a house." At first she was pleased to have thought of a clever reply, but then she regretted opening a conversation that might necessitate further explanations. "Thank you," she added more formally, then, nodding demurely, made a quarter turn in her seat.

The setting sun cast a pale amber light on the shops as the trolley clicked its way across the city. As they left the commercial district, more and more passengers disembarked and fewer came aboard, so by the time they reached Kirov Square Hannah was the only one making the transfer. When she slid each package down, one at a time, the thin string felt loose. Hannah hoped it would hold as she began to make her way across the almost deserted square.

The merchant families who made their homes in the pastel dwellings that encircled the desirable residential area were all indoors. Lights flickered from almost every window to cast long brown shadows across the lawns. The park's crosswalks were lit by gas lights, so Hannah could see her way down the pebbled paths crisscrossing the square. A coffee vendor wheeling his cart with its brass spigots and fancy painted wheels home for the night was the last soul remaining after a busy afternoon in the park, not counting the few gluttonous birds that still pecked at the leftover crumbs near the iron benches.

Pausing at the first gas lamp, Hannah took a deep breath and steadied the parcels before selecting the shortest diagonal path. Determined not to stop, she completed more than a third of the distance before again resting. To loosen her tight muscles she swung her sore arms back and forth, pressed her head toward her back, pumped her shoulders up and down, and took some purposeful long deep breaths.

The night was oppressively still. Hannah strained to hear any familiar sound that might calm her racing heart. The static whine of the disappearing trolley had been replaced by the distant creaking of the vendor's wooden wheels. A few hooves clicked on the pavement, then passed around a far corner. What else could she hear? Some faint laughter from a nearby house, the closing of a door, the rattle of some pans in a basement kitchen? With a renewed sense of fright she realized these were the sounds of people too far away to be of help to her.

It was an unfortunate hour to catch a connecting trolley, for if one had just left she might have to wait an hour for the next. She selected a distant tree as a goal and continued with long, determined strides, passing the Kirov Bandstand, where she and her family had attended many a Sunday concert. Papa had always chosen a seat at the far end of a row to allow Hannah and Chaim the freedom to move about and stretch their legs. "Chaim! Papa! Do it for them, carry the packages for them," she thought. "For Papa, for Chaim . . . but not for Lazar!" In an instant the fuel that fired her devotion to her family turned to smouldering anger at the man who played with her feelings. How many other women had Lazar used as pawns?

All of a sudden she heard footsteps approaching. As she glanced briefly over her shoulder she saw two uniformed men gaining on her with their faster stride. Suddenly she no longer felt the weight of her load. Swiftly she passed the tree she had designated as a stopping point, but the sound of feet marching was right behind her. She counted off her paces: one and two, one and two! Get to the trolley, pray that it comes. She slowed slightly, and in a second the two men were even with her, one coming around to her left, the other to her right. In one mirrored movement each man grasped a bundle and removed it from Hannah's grasp.

"Who gave you such a load to carry? Someone without pity, I can see that," said the tall officer with a curlicue mustache, who was on her right.

The one on her left doffed a cap with a shining emblem on the brim. "At least we can help you to the trolley platform?"

"Yes ..." Hannah cleared her throat, which was swimming with sour mucus. "Thank you," she finished, hoping her choking voice wouldn't betray her.

"Let's hurry, though. The seven o'clock should be here soon, although I wouldn't mind waiting for the eight o'clock!"

"Nor would I!" his partner agreed.

Hannah's eyes opened wide in disbelief when she realized they appeared to be flirting with her. Were they truly trying to be of service or was this a ruse to find out what the packages contained? As she kept up with their steady march she decided they were just taking their time, toying with her, knowing full well she could not evade the two of them.

"What is in these ... ah ... little boxes, miss?" asked the shorter of the two.

"Some bricks." The line she had used earlier was advantageous once more.

"So you are a builder?" He chuckled.

Hannah observed him carefully and decided, from his manner and the amount of gold braid, that he was the superior officer.

"Yes, can't you tell? And you must be a sailor. I recognized the uniform."

"What an intelligent woman!" He winked to his associate. "Here comes the trolley. Pity it's on time."

Now Hannah would find out the extent of her predicament. If they were just flirting they would leave her now; otherwise she would be arrested. As they began to lift her packages on to the open side of the combination car, Hannah felt an enormous relief. The one with the mustache took Hannah's ticket directly to the conductor while the other settled her in her seat.

"Where do you go now, miss?"

"Melnitsky Square."

"A long walk from the end of this line. Ivan Pavelovisch, don't you think the least we can do is help the lady all the way to her destination? Who knows what she might encounter tonight?"

As the trolley jerked forward Hannah was still not convinced she was completely safe. Yet the officers seemed so relaxed and jovial she forced herself to bury her suspicions.

When the three approached the square across from Hannah's home, she saw from the way the window curtain was parted that Mama was watching for her. As the group approached the doorway Hannah knew she must send them away as quickly as possible.

"My dear friends," she said jokingly, "I thank you on behalf of the bricklayers of Odessa."

Hannah pushed the door open and fell into Mama's outstretched arms.

"Hannah! What is the meaning of this? What do you have there? Answer me at once! I send you on a simple errand and you come home hours late, escorted by two of the czar's police. What am I to think? Hannah! Why are you laughing!" Mama reached over and shook her daughter firmly. "Have you gone crazy? Have you lost your mind?"

## · 11 ·

ALTHOUGH THE POLICE ESCORT was difficult to explain, Hannah convinced Mama that she was not in any trouble. As soon as possible Hannah quickly stored the packages under her bed, explaining they contained books for her studies.

More difficult was the task of conveying the news about Chaim, which Hannah couched in less direct terms than had Lazar.

"We can always hope that there might be a sudden thaw in government policies ... or a change of ministers ..." Aunt Sonia muttered, nervously twisting strands of her greying hair.

"He's gone forever!" Mama grieved.

"Don't say that, Mama. Lazar may have some more news soon."

"More like that I don't want to hear! Hannah, you must not go to the university quarter again!"

"It was you who insisted I go in the first place!"

"It's too dangerous."

"But I was thinking of attending some classes at the medical school . . ."

"That I forbid! Absolutely. I have enough to worry about. Better you should not associate with those so-called friends! And I'll need your help here."

"You never have before!"

"Sonia must go for work. Uncle Leyb will take her into the store. We don't have enough orders to support us now."

"But my education, my work . . ."

"Bubbe has many babies for you. Stay at home so she can reach you. She's counting on you."

Controlling an urge to lash out in defiance, Hannah merely nodded. Mama had shown a brilliant gift for organizing everything, as well as foreseeing the future, and it sometimes galled Hannah to remember how many times her mother's predictions had proved true. Even in unimportant matters, Mama always had to be right and would fight over the most insignificant details. If all else failed, she could usually obtain a surrender by wearing down the enemy with persistence. Papa had mastered fielding her temper and it was rare for them to have harsh words, yet Papa would slyly get his way in the end. Chaim had inherited this talent for deception, while Hannah had not.

"Let Mama think she's won; then you can do what you wish," Chaim once explained.

Hannah's boredom at home ended finally a few days later, when Bubbe Schtern requested her assistance in delivering Zelda Gimpel, the eldest daughter of an old patient. Bubbe had brought Zelda, as well as her nine brothers and sisters, into the world.

Together they waited through the long hours of labor, sharing birthing stories. Hannah especially enjoyed telling about Madame Golonovin!

"I had one like that, in eighteen eighty-nine, upstairs above the bakery at Chumka Street. It was the third daughter of the Lochov family . . ." Bubbe recalled. Her memory for details was amazing, and Hannah realized she had built her career on the meticulous base of knowledge she gained from each delivery.

Hannah watched the old midwife as she spoke. Her hands were twisted by rheumatism; her spine, which never had been straight, now curved like a bow; and her thin grey hair could barely cover large shiny patches of skin on her mottled scalp. Her glaucoma had progressed so rapidly she had lost her confidence in handling by herself any untoward event during a delivery.

"Maybe you should go home and rest, Bubbe. This may take quite a while."

"No, no, I'll stay with you."

"You don't trust me?" Hannah teased.

"You may be ready, Hannahleh, but your old Bubbe isn't. Maybe there are one or two little things I could show you?"

As Bubbe tended the laboring Zelda, Hannah relearned her special measures for comfort: hot compresses for the lower back, a massage with the heel of the hand during the hardest part of every contraction, slow downward manipulations of the thigh muscles to ease tension and aid relaxation, not to mention the soft Yiddish phrases that mothered the mother-to-be.

"Until the child is born, the mother is the baby. Do for her as you will the infant," Bubbe crooned.

Bubbe offered more than medical knowledge. As a simple, compassionate birth attendant she had helped hundreds of expectant mothers overcome their fears; and although she brought little scientific training to the bedside, all her babies were brought into a spiritually safe world because every ritual was meticulously followed.

"Hannah, you must teach about the Watch Night," Bubbe instructed. This was the treacherous time during the eight days after a birth when Lilith was said to steal newborns from their mothers. "Like a cuckoo bird she arrives to either exchange a child for one of the demons or, worse, to kill the baby outright. So you must post a Hebrew sign on the wall outside the birth house. I'll show you how to write the characters for 'Lilith and her band — keep out!' "

"Do you always do this?"

"Just as you evaluate how it will go in the labor bed, so you must determine how observant is the family, how much will please them. But there are some things you must never forget to do."

"What are those?"

"You must bury the umbilical cord and placenta where no spirits can reach them. And don't forget to place a curtain around the mother's bed and make certain the baby also lies within."

Hannah winced. "And I must pin on the pieces of paper!" She referred to the psalms that were hung around the mother's bed.

"You do not believe in the evil eye?" Bubbe asked, recognizing the signs of modern rebellion in her young associate.

"But you cannot prove . . ."

"Proof she asks! If you had seen everything I have, if you had lived as long as I, you would believe! How many babies are lost in the first week? Even in your fancy place in Moscow? No one must look at the baby except the father, mother, and midwife during that time, and when they do they must follow the rules. Teach them not to praise the child aloud, not to even think of the child's beauty. Tie a red ribbon around the baby's arm and have the girl's ears pierced so she can wear turquoise as soon as possible."

Hannah listened and did not argue. When she had her own midwifery service she knew she would not be constrained by the precepts of ancestral superstitions, but would provide sensible maternity care with gentle hands and a warm heart.

Reaching up to twist her own gold earrings, Hannah asked, "Did you pierce my ears?"

"Of course I did! How well I remember your birth. It was the fourth day of Tishrey. An old lady yet remembers the date! You had lots of dark hair and as soon as you were almost completely born you called out once — not a cry, more like the mewing of a cat. Then you were silent. You looked right into your mama's eyes and cooed like a dove.

"Then I asked what you would be called and your mama said, 'Hannah for my mother's mother and Leah for Itsik's mother,' and I wrote the Hebrew letters of your name in my birth book. Then do you know what I said? 'Hannah Leah Blau! Such a song! Perfect for a baby who finds this world so pleasant she doesn't even cry when she's born.' Next I wrapped you in swaddling bands from your shoulders down to your little feet and covered your head with the white cap your Aunt Sonia embroidered, and your mama whispered to you, 'Hannah Leah, may you always find it so.'"

The old midwife's eyes were moist with tears. "Hannah Leah, so far, has it been so bad?"

Hannah reached over and kissed Bubbe and hugged her close. "For the most part it goes well, Bubbe. I am glad to be here."

The two women had little time left to indulge in their sentimentality, for the change in their patient's breathing to a fast pant signaled she was ready to give birth. Hannah positioned herself to deliver Zelda Gimpel's first child, while Bubbe chanted the prayers and repeated the familiar phrases. With supple hands Hannah gently eased the almost completely bald baby from between his mother's legs and, holding the warm fresh bundle in her arms, thought, as she did each time, that this was the most beautiful baby ever born.

❖   ❖   ❖

After the sixteen hours of waiting and work to help bring Duvid Gimpel into the world, Hannah gratefully slid into her bed just as the sun was rising over Odessa Bay. She had just slipped into the first heavy sleep she had enjoyed in many weeks when she was called by a distant voice.

"Wake up, Hannah! Wake up!"

Hannah blinked and saw that Aunt Sonia was shaking her shoulder. One glance at the sun's height outside her window indicated that it was past noon.

"I didn't mean to sleep so long."

"I would like you to sleep even later, but there is a message we thought you would want to see right away."

"Another baby on its way? And I thought I would have nothing to do here!"

"No, not a baby."

"Chaim!"

"It was addressed to you, and your mama thought you had better open it first. We are all so anxious to know . . ."

Hannah sat upright in expectation of good news as Aunt Sonia handed her the envelope, which bore a raised imprint of the Hotel Richelieu. "This must be from the Princess Olimpiada. You remember, Auntie, the one who loaned me her shoes on the train. I've neglected to return them."

"I should have thought . . ." she replied forlornly.

"We had no reason to expect word so soon. We must wait . . ." Hannah said with disappointment.

But that feeling did not last long as Hannah read the brief note written in an obviously masculine hand. Her eyes widened and her body shuddered involuntarily.

"Is something the matter?"

"No . . . no . . ." Hannah said, folding the letter while she searched for an answer. "She is leaving Odessa soon and wishes to see me, she . . ." Hannah groped for words, lies, anything to cover the feelings of hope and anticipation that threatened to overwhelm her. "I'm sorry it wasn't what you hoped, Auntie, but thank you for waking me."

"I'll make you some hot tea and an egg; then you must tell me about last night."

"Last night?" For a moment Hannah wondered what she was talking about. "Oh, the baby, yes. She had a lovely little boy; he's called Duvid, Duvid Gimpel."

Her aunt left not a moment too soon, for Hannah could no longer have explained her uncontrollable reaction to the letter. Perspiration soaked her thin gown. She placed her head between her shaking legs until she felt her heartbeat and respiration were under control. Then she permitted herself to reread the note.

"Dear Sister Blau, I am in Odessa for a lecture and would be honored if you could meet with me before my return to Moscow in three days. With best wishes for your good health, I remain, Stefan Petrograv."

## · 12 ·

As HANNAH PREPARED to meet Dr. Petrograv, she knew there was no possibility of telling Mama the truth, since she had been forbidden to have any further communication with the Imperial College.

"But, Mama," Hannah had protested. "I must at least advise them I won't be returning!"

"When you don't appear for your classes, they'll know soon enough!"

"I have friends who will worry. And the administrators will be angry if I don't give them the courtesy of a written explanation. What if I decide to continue my work someday?"

Mama threw her hands above her head. "Hannah, you are a dreamer!"

"I just want to be certain that the doors remain open to me, just in case I should choose to pass through them someday."

"This is a family matter now, Hannah," Mama said, placing her hands on her hips. "You'll do just as I say!"

With reluctance Hannah had deferred to her mother's demands. But she could hardly relinquish this opportunity to see Petrograv one last time. As Hannah stepped out onto the sunlit square she hardly felt a single pang at being devious to gain her freedom.

Dr. Petrograv had arrived at an inopportune time to convince her to leave Odessa, for at that moment Hannah felt content to be a midwife serving the women of her own community. Petrograv meant Moscow, and Moscow conjured up images of icy winds raging up from the River Moskva, the bleak months of cold and isolation, the wretched anti-Semitism. As Hannah rejected these depressing images, her romantic vision of the doctor faded and she reveled in the warmth of another perfect Odessan day.

Odessa's situation was unique. The city curved like an amphitheater along the coast of the Black Sea at a point where the high Ukrainian steppe abruptly halted 150 feet above sea level. While the commercial and residential neighborhoods were in the heights, the port and beaches plunged dramatically below. This curious topography created beautiful vistas from most parts of the city. Because warm land currents formed a protective veil on winter evenings, the port rarely froze for more than a few weeks of the year and the surrounding bay was hardly ever closed to worldwide commerce. With sea breezes relieving the hot summer days, the city was able to boast the most agreeable climate in Russia.

It was also a very beautiful city. It had been designed only a hundred years earlier by the duc de Richelieu to have a regular plan of shaded boulevards crossing each other at right angles so that each section created a plaza or square with a magnificent view of the sea. Richelieu, in his role as the city's first governor, had ordered every new housebuilder to plant flowering trees and vines; and this procedure was still being carried out by tradition, not decree.

Though second in size to Warsaw in its Jewish population, Odessa was unquestionably the more important cultural center, producing an uncommon number of romantic writers, celebrated artists, and gifted string players and pianists. Yet Odessa had a flaw. For all its music and culture, its citizens were not a refined lot, not even the Jews, some of whom inhabited the notorious Moldavanka district, where thieves and whores lived among the poorest of the poor to form an underworld more picturesque than sinister.

Perhaps it was the mild climate that tempered the spirit of Odessa's bureaucrats, who tended to leave their Jews alone. Or it might have been more than simple charity, for there were too many affluent, educated, and politically organized Jews to control with brute force. Of the 450,000 Odessans in 1901, almost one-third were Jews. There were more than forty synagogues, including one in the oldest section of the city that served the rare Karaite sect. Even though they couldn't combat imperial policy, Odessa's Jews were prominent members of the community.

"If all the Jews of Russia could live in Odessa!" had been Papa Blau's favorite exclamation.

Mama would shrug and say, "Don't let the heat bake your brains, Itsik. A Jew must beware in Odessa as in Warsaw, Minsk, or Moscow."

"Sarah, you worry all the time." Papa would pat her gently. "Nothing has happened since eighty-one, almost twenty years ago."

"Twenty years! Twenty years is nothing! A drop in the bucket! A thimbleful! It will happen over and over again. How much time has there ever been between the monsters? Chmielnicki! Torquemada! Pobyedonostsev! Ignatiev! Plehve!" She spit out the hated names. "Ten years, twenty, a hundred? I watch over my shoulder as every Jew must, even if he lives in your blessed Odessa. Unlike you scholars and dreamers, I am ready!"

The rest of the family refused to share her fears, made no plans, and enjoyed the beauties of their city.

❖  ❖  ❖

As Hannah waited before crossing the Kosswenn Boulevard, several carriages passed near the curb, spattering water on her feet. She stared down to survey the damage to her skirt or petticoats and remembered with chagrin that she had worn the princess's boots because they were the perfect match to her best grey cotton walking skirt and shirtwaist trimmed with an ingenious openwork embroidery, which revealed nothing yet hinted at everything. The whole costume was accented by a frosting of Valenciennes lace from the Meyerovs' private stock, a touch that Hannah felt made her the equal of any lady on the promenade.

Too anxious to wait for the local trolley, she decided to save time by walking a few blocks to the number 5 express and then transferring once in the business district. The number 5 route had been the first trolley line to be electrified in all of Russia. Hannah remembered her childhood excursions to the seaside on the old, tedious, unreliable horse-drawn conckas. Pulling a horsecar packed with people, some still holding the side of the platform as it lurched away, had not been an easy job, even for the best horses. Stopping on a hill was even more treacherous, and as a child, Hannah had been frightened of any route that included a downhill run, for the driver had to know just when to help the horses by winding up the brake chain. Then, to start again, he would have to release the brake at just the exact moment when the horses lunged forward, for if he unwound it too soon the horses would be dragged backward and might kick and protest.

By the time Hannah was traveling the trolley lines to her secondary school, the cars had been converted to steam, which seemed a happy solution to skittish horses but brought another set of problems: the noise from the rods that connected the wheels, puffs of steam and smoke, and the ever-present danger from exploding boilers. How thankful everyone was to now have the safe, reliable electric trolleys that worked under all weather conditions.

At Ickatcriniskaia Hannah transferred to a number 6 for the northern ride up the 500-yard-long Nikolyevsky Boulevard to the port, handing the conductor her card punched at the picture of the lady with a Gainsborough hat. The transfer card, covered with sketches of men with different shaped whiskers, women in various styled hats or accompanied by children, and schoolboys with books under their arms, read: "Picture punched indicates type of passenger." Hannah loved these curious details.

In a few minutes the trolley's fast humming became a slow whine as it jerked toward the last stop. When Hannah alighted opposite Richelieu's monument, turned right, and made her way toward the hotel that bore his illustrious name, she wasn't certain which she feared more: seeing Dr. Petrograv or confronting the desk clerk in the lobby. What kind of icy stare might she receive when asked to identify herself? "Blau" was a common Jewish name, originating with the Germanic Jews who settled in Poland and Russia during the migrations of the seventeenth century. Catching a glimpse of herself in the polished plate door, Hannah realized she looked as fashionable as anyone she had seen that day, and so, with a deep breath to give her confidence, she entered Odessa's grandest hotel.

Built in the Italian baroque style by Rastrelli, the Italian count who was one of Catherine the Great's most productive court architects, the Richelieu had first been one of the seaside palaces of the Razamovskys, the same family who lent their name to the boulevard in the Jewish merchant quarter of the city. The building's wine red façade was relieved by slender columns, those certain hallmarks, trim and elegant, of imperial Russia.

When Hannah entered the marble lobby, she noticed an immediate drop in temperature. Thick green rugs floated like islands in a shimmering alabaster sea. Guests mingled in small clusters speaking French in hushed tones. Realizing she understood not one refined syllable, Hannah shuddered visibly as she approached the great mahogany desk carved in rosettes and ribbons. The clerk, wearing black tie, which further offset his pallid skin and lackluster expression, came to life, his head jerking to the left in anticipation of a request.

Hannah mouthed only the words "Dr. Stefan Petrograv?" with a slight question mark in her voice.

The clerk's head snapped forward in a nod and he mechanically produced an envelope matching the one she had received that morning. "Pour vous, mademoiselle." As soon as Hannah clasped the letter in her hand, he gestured toward a sculptured divan covered in velour. To avoid having to speak, Hannah immediately took her seat and tried not to appear anxious as she removed the letter from its folder.

"Dear Sister Blau, Thank you for coming so promptly. I will be returning at three this afternoon and hope you will do me the honor of joining me for tea if the wait is not too inconvenient. Stefan B. Petrograv."

Hannah was not as interested in the content as in the slightly different signature. Consumed by curiosity, she wondered what the middle initial stood for. Of course it was related to his father's name, but was it Borionovich, or Bogdanovich, or . . . ? Perhaps she could ask him if an opportunity arose.

As Hannah looked up she thought she saw the desk clerk avert his eyes. With more than an hour to wait, Hannah did not want to endure his critical eye, nor did she wish the doctor to discover her waiting like an obedient puppy. An invigorating walk would be just the thing! For, whatever Petrograv had in mind, Hannah knew she would need her strength.

# · 13 ·

PROCEEDING NORTH, away from the matrix of activity around the hotel and cafés overlooking the new port, Hannah briskly strolled toward the older Port of Charbon and the Practical Port, where golden grain from the Ukraine was loaded on vessels from all over the globe.

The pace she set herself had been determined by a need to still her anxiety, but it was much too rapid considering the midday sun. Every other woman on the promenade had sensibly brought a parasol for protection, but Hannah had always disdained them as more ornamental than useful. Feeling dizzy, Hannah paused to rest on an unoccupied iron filigreed bench across from the Glass Pavilion. Her view was of the Perssip bathing beach, where her family had often come for walks but never to swim. Swimming was not considered a suitable pastime in Jewish families.

"You could catch diseases from public waters," Mama had chided. Yet Hannah suspected the real cause of the prohibition was the necessary exposure of flesh, even in the most discreet bathing costumes.

As Hannah observed the bathers she divided them into groups as to how they approached the undulations of the waves. There were adventurous swimmers, timid waders, and those who waited for the crest of the wave. Hannah wondered which group she might join were she ever to try the sea. The timid waders who leapt back with high shrieks if their skirts became the least bit damp? Never! Nor could she imagine waiting at the breaking point to decide at the very last second whether to allow the surge of water to crash upon her back or to dive directly under its powerful curving force, though that would have been Chaim's course.

The rhythm of the sea . . . so similar to the rising and falling contractions in the laboring woman. Hannah concentrated and tried to compare the bathers at the scalloped shoreline with the manner in which women confronted their travail. As she strained to organize her thoughts, Hannah saw the analogy as a clue she might utilize in her work. If a person could be taught to swim, could she not also be taught to labor? Since a woman is not born with all the knowledge she will need — she must learn to speak, to read, to ride a horse, to swim — might she not also need lessons in giving birth? But, Hannah argued with herself, a woman is born knowing how to eat, excrete, sleep. She will turn over, crawl, walk, grow, and eventually conceive without the benefits of education; and so she probably should be able to give birth without instruction. The sounds of the surf roared in her ears, the salty scent of the sea stung her nostrils, and as she took long, deep breaths, she realized that these thoughts were too complex for a mind already muddled by anticipation and anxiety.

Yet Hannah felt a new sense of determination. Someday she would try everything: she would join the bathers at the water's edge, feel the tug and pull of the waves upon her body, discover new techniques to help women giving birth, and make all her own choices.

Her musings were interrupted. She looked up to see the glare of the sun temporarily blocked by a quick-stepping figure moving closer. Dr. Petrograv came toward her. His strides were long, fast, and firm, and in a few seconds he stood before Hannah and took both her hands in his.

"Sister Blau!" His first words were warm and welcoming. He looked more elegant than Hannah had remembered in his grey pinstripe summer coat, crisp wing-cut collar, and four-in-hand neckpiece. He even wore the black-banded straw hat every society gentleman was sporting that season.

"Dr. Petrograv," Hannah said as she tried to meet his gaze directly. "You look very well," she murmured and then averted her eyes. "Are you here on holiday or business?"

"Neither ... exactly." He continued to stare, his dark eyes burning like coals on a hearth.

"Have you ever been to Odessa?" Hannah asked, searching for a topic of conversation.

"No, I haven't. I am quite taken by its beauty ..." He tilted his head again to make eye contact with Hannah. "And its charms." Turning slightly, he offered Hannah his arm. "Shall we take our tea at the Richelieu or would you prefer the café just beyond?"

"The café, please. It's too lovely to go indoors. But since I am so thirsty, you will have to order two pots!" Hannah continued nervously.

"I'm sure we can manage that," he smiled, and they glided together down the shaded side of the promenade.

Appalled by the silence between them, Hannah attempted to begin a kind of tourist's guide. "Have you seen the statue of Pushkin at the far end of the boulevard?"

"Yes, during my stroll this morning. The Odessans seem very

proud of him; so many streets and buildings are dotted with his name."

"I think it's a silly affectation myself. After all, Pushkin only lived here two years, when he was in exile."

"You seem to know quite a bit about Pushkin. I would have thought your head was filled with science, as mine was at your age."

Again an uneasy silence welled up between them. "Do you know the story of why Pushkin was exiled and then left Odessa so soon?" Hannah rattled on quickly.

"I don't recall it."

"Pushkin was exiled from Petersburg when his *Ode to Liberty* was brought to the attention of the governor. First he was sent to serve in the Caucasus Mountains with a General Rayevsky, but he brought more trouble to himself there by mixing with secret societies. Then he came to Odessa in the service of Count Vorontosov, who sympathized with his plight," she rambled on without a pause. "Now the count didn't seem to mind his politics, but when he discovered one of Pushkin's letters espousing atheism, that was too much, so he demanded that Pushkin, the sinner, leave his employ."

"What did he write while living here?"

"Not very much. It wasn't until a few years after his departure that he finished *Boris Godunov* and my favorite, *Eugene Onegin*."

"You are a romantic!" Petrograv chuckled softly in his throat. "Didn't Pushkin die very young?"

"He wasn't yet thirty-nine. My father used to say we were cheated out of his greatest works by his own folly." .

"He was killed in that ridiculous duel with someone's husband. Who was it?"

"Pushkin's wife's sister's . . . or was it his brother's wife's . . . ?" Hannah laughed.

"Your papa was right, it was a great loss to literature. I understand what it is like to watch someone waste his life, by illness, death, neglect of talent . . ." He continued meaningfully, changing suddenly to add, "Why, Pushkin was just eight years older than I am! A true tragedy!"

Immediately Hannah did some simple arithmetic to determine

that the doctor was thirty-one, exactly ten years older than she. How pleased she was to know another personal fact! Arriving at the Café Franconi, Hannah observed the doctor's appearance and tried to decide if he looked younger or older than his age. The waiter appeared, wearing white summer livery, and led them to a table surrounded by four bent-wire chairs.

"We'd like two complete teas, and we'd like two separate pots," Petrograv said gravely. The waiter's stony countenance did not register any surprise.

"I wasn't serious!" Hannah exclaimed as soon as the waiter had left.

"Oh?" the doctor asked, raising one eyebrow. "I take everything you say most seriously, little sister."

"Then you mustn't. I say silly things all the time!"

"I took you for a very sedate and earnest young student."

"I was, or at least I made an attempt to be."

"You were?" his concern deepened his voice. "And not now? You no longer consider yourself a student?"

"Not exactly . . ."

"You aren't returning to Moscow to continue your studies?"

"No, I'm afraid I cannot."

"Sister Blau," he continued, so severely Hannah wished he would use the affectionate "little sister" again. "Now the time has come to unravel this mystery. I was greatly concerned when you disappeared, overnight, without a word. I was told only that there were some family problems. I hope they are not continuing."

"They are."

"What is happening? Can't you tell me?"

"No." Hannah hesitated because of Mama's prohibitions. "It's too complicated and . . ."

"You don't feel you can trust me?" Petrograv asked, again raising his left eyebrow higher than the right.

"I do trust you, it's just . . ." Not able to avoid his questions, Hannah decided to hint at the problem without explaining the specifics. "My brother has become involved in political matters. Mama feels I might be in some jeopardy in Moscow and also she needs my help supporting the family. Only last night I delivered my first Odessan baby."

"Congratulations! Did it go well?"

"Yes, but the case was not particularly interesting from a pathological point of view."

"I'm more interested in you, Hannah. I am disturbed to think that all your plans for a medical education have been altered by this . . . difficulty."

"Doctor, with respect, I must remind you that they were not my plans. They were yours and Dr. Jaffe's, and I don't know who else's; and while I am sorry to disappoint all of you, I am actually embarking on the career I always wanted."

"But don't you see you could be so much more?"

"Perhaps in another time or place. Right now I am needed here. I won't be returning to Moscow," Hannah said with a finality that surprised even her. Trying to change the subject, she asked, "Can you tell me what your lecture topic will be? Has it something more to do with your sepsis studies? Or have you finished your work here already?"

"It has hardly begun. I arrived only last evening."

"I am pleased!" Hannah said sincerely. "I have always learned so much from you and I would enjoy hearing you speak again. Will you be addressing the faculty of medicine?"

"I have no plans to be at the university."

"Oh, then you are giving a private lecture?"

"Yes, very." Hannah waited for him to explain, but he sat passively. His eyes darkened but gave no clue to his meaning.

"Then I will be disappointed I won't be able to hear you one last time."

The doctor opened his mouth to reply, but closed it suddenly as the waiter interrupted with their pots of tea, a plate of open sandwiches decorated with slivers of cucumber, dollops of sour cream, and florets of fresh butter. A second two-tiered platter contained a rainbow of iced tea cakes, which were already softening under the heat of the afternoon sun. When the waiter reached to pour from the first brass samovar, Petrograv waved him away, indicating he himself would do the honors. He grasped the wooden handle, but

did not turn the spigot. Instead, he leaned toward his companion
and seized her hand.

"Hannah! I have journeyed for only one reason. I came to find
you and beg you to return to Moscow with me."

"But the lecture . . . you said . . ." She trembled in voice and
body.

"Ah, the lecture! Are you ready for it now? Then I will begin.
Mademoiselle Blau, I would like to ask you to return with me to
Moscow to continue your medical education as planned and also
to consent to become my wife."

Hannah snatched her hand from the doctor's grasp and clutched
the silken fabric nearest her heart. With the other hand she held
the canvas seat of her chair.

"Hannah! Are you all right?" Petrograv asked with alarm. Remembering the samovar still in his other hand, he poured an unsteady stream into her glass and passed it to her, indicating with a
nod of his head for her to sip slowly before replying. Hannah tried
to comply, but the tea was too hot to swallow.

"I don't understand! How can you say such things to me? You
hardly know me!"

"That is not true, my dear. We have worked together for almost
a year; we have spent many hours in each other's company. I have
known many midwifery students and I can judge, if only by comparison, how unique you are. I thought you both respected and
liked me."

"I do, but what you propose is impossible!"

"Why do you say that? I have much to offer and I would like to
give you everything you desire. If you would only permit me a
chance to explain how I feel . . ."

"How can you explain?" Hannah cried in a mixture of surprise and confusion. "You are already married, you have a child,
you . . ."

"Oh, dear heaven! Is it possible that you do not know? No one
has told you about my wife?"

"No, but I've seen your little daughter and assumed she had a
mother as well as a father."

"Natalya has only me. She never knew her mother, who died

from childbed fever, the very disease I have waged war against ever since."

"I never knew . . . Oh, I'm so sorry. The others did not talk with me; they barely accepted me professionally, never as a friend. I never thought to question, to inquire; how stupid of me!"

"Not at all, it was I who made the assumptions."

Hannah's breath came in short little bursts. Her mouth felt as though it were filled with sand and she reached to sip some tea to clear it before she could speak. "Forgive me, Dr. Petrograv. I was so unprepared, there is nothing I can say to express how I really feel."

Hannah saw him swallow painfully. "It seems that I have not completely mistaken your feelings for me?"

"Not completely," she said, allowing herself the blush that went with such an admission. "I never guessed you would want me to . . . we hardly know each other . . . and . . ."

"You must forgive me for being so impulsive. I have been that way ever since I was a boy. Like the majority of children I have known who were brought up in solitude, I fling myself on everyone's neck, and yet I do so with sincerity. My father always said I should be courteous to all and intimate with no one. Since I knew him to be a very miserable man, I rebelled and, as a consequence, seemed to put my trust in everyone and seek theirs in return."

"I do trust you, Doctor. It was foolish of me not to explain more fully about my brother, but I am more dutiful than you, perhaps, and only followed my mother's instructions."

"Do you always obey your mother?"

"Not always," she said, reddening slightly again. "Are you still interested in my brother's story?"

"No, I'm not very interested in either your brother or mother," Petrograv responded.

"I think you had better be more interested in him, my family, and my background if we are to begin to discuss any future we might have together. Suddenly I find I am very interested in yours. You say you were brought up in solitude?"

Petrograv took her question as a positive sign, and it was with a new sense of purpose that he launched into his story. "Yes, I was the only child of Count Boris Fedorovich Petrograv, and my parents worried endlessly after me, as I was their only heir. You can't imagine such protection! Even at the university, my old tutor still followed me everywhere under orders from the count. At the completion of my medical studies I married the wife my family selected. Natalya's mother was my mother's distant cousin. Although I did not choose her, I did learn to care for her very much, but never in the same way as it would have been if the decision had been my own."

As he spoke, Hannah began to understand why he wanted her. At his advanced age he was finally ready to defy the strict conventions of his family.

"I can't see how your family would ever approve of me to take your wife's place."

"It is no longer their business to approve."

"From what you have said, and what I know of my own, they will make it so."

"I no longer depend on them, if that is your meaning. I have my own income and additional monies from my wife's estate. My daughter has her own settlement, and I receive a professional salary as well," he replied petulantly.

"That is not the concern I have," Hannah added as forcefully as possible, realizing she had mistakenly entered this line of conversation. She would have to avoid such discussions until the basic issue of her feelings for the doctor were settled.

"I know you are worried about your religion; my family, my associates are all very enlightened," he continued, then fell silent.

They reached for their tea glasses at the same instant and sipped slowly. Studying his face Hannah wondered why she had never before noticed the mole above his right eyebrow. He lowered his glass first, pressed a snowy napkin to his mouth, and when it was blotted, he removed the cloth to reveal lips pink and soft in comparison with the dark bristles of his beard and mustache. Hannah replaced her glass and fumbled to find her napkin, which had slipped from her lap. Suddenly they were interrupted in their courtship ritual by a woman whose high, familiar voice called to Hannah.

"Dr. Blau! You've come to see us at last!"

Hannah looked up, but did not recognize the face at first because the sun was directly at her back and the woman's features blurred in the orange haze.

"The princess has asked for you many times these last few days, but I didn't know where to find you," Katya said quickly.

"I am sorry I didn't come sooner, but there were family problems and . . ."

"No need to apologize, just so you are here now when we need you the most."

Petrograv politely cleared his throat and Hannah introduced him.

"Ah yes, the Yakovlev family. My father knows the prince. I am certain of that."

"You are a doctor also? How fortunate!" Katya responded. "The princess is very ill now. I don't know what to do; the pains are the most terrible I can remember."

"What exactly is the problem?" Petrograv asked curiously.

Hannah related what little she knew about the illness.

"Who treats her in Moscow?" Petrograv asked Katya.

"Menikov and Falbonovich," the servant responded, leaning on the marble table to steady herself.

Petrograv, who had remained standing after greeting the woman, lowered Katya into his chair. "This must be a difficult time for you, my dear."

"I haven't slept for two nights. I've done everything I've been taught, but the pain is so terrible that no position helps. I think I'll go mad if I must listen to her suffer one more night."

"Sister Blau, we must go to the princess at once!" Petrograv demanded and summoned the waiter to pay his bill. "What has she been given for pain and fever?"

"Mineral waters and the electrical medication," Katya replied.

"Electrical medication!" Petrograv exploded. "What kind of quackery is this?"

"Well, sir, it's not a shock," Katya replied in a timid voice. "It's a process that takes regular medicine and makes it act better in the stomach by producing a nervous force to bring the healing to the parts of the body that need it the most. Oh, I don't know how to properly explain it, but her doctor claims it has worked miracles."

"Ridiculous!" scoffed Petrograv. "I'll go for some things from my room; then we'll see what is to be done."

❖   ❖   ❖

The royal suite was the largest and most elaborate the Richelieu had to offer. Reclining on the wide canopied bed, her swollen extremities propped with cushions, the princess was a shadow of the brave companion Hannah had met on the train. Her waxen face was fused into a permanent mask of pain. And one could hardly distinguish her from the linens. Everything was white: her morning dress, her cap, the pillows, the lacy covers. Each intake and outlet of air was so excruciating she seemed scarcely able to breathe. The only sound in the room, which accompanied her labored respirations, was the English table clock. Its measured "tick-tock, tick-tock" marked off the minutes of respite between her mounting moments of agony. As Hannah approached the bed, the princess's feverish eyes flickered with recognition, but she said nothing.

"I've brought Dr. Petrograv. He's also from Moscow; maybe he'll be able to help," Hannah whispered.

Petrograv leaned over the princess and lifted her gown, noting the distention of her knees, ankles, and feet. Then he examined the wrists, elbows, and joints of her hands with the utmost care. The worst swelling, hallmarked by red circles, appeared on her hands and feet. The right hand in particular was grossly enlarged and so tender that the merest touch made her cry out in pain. Dr. Petrograv checked her tongue, noted that it was coated, and asked Katya about her digestion.

"She has no appetite at all, Doctor," Katya answered softly.

"And her bowels?"

"Very hard, sir, as usual during an attack."

"Her fever? Has it been this high for many hours?"

"All night, and most of yesterday," replied Katya, handing him a towel to wipe the princess's brow. The room was so filled with the acid smell of perspiration that even the scent of the fresh Odessan lilies standing in large ormolu vases on each bedside table could not combat it.

"She was doing so well," Katya continued. "The first few days the warmth of the sea air seemed to help and then this ... the worst I can remember since we were children."

"I thought it was cold weather that triggered these attacks." Hannah questioned Petrograv in a professional voice.

"That is a frequent supposition. We once thought that rheumatism was occasioned by a suppression of the functions of the skin attributed to the action of cold upon the surface of the body. Now we know that any change of climate, to cold or even warmth, can be the exciting cause. This is a disease of the blood that prevails most extensively in the regions that are the most changeable. A place such as Moscow is one of the most terrible. But once she makes her adjustment to the South, the symptoms should ease voluntarily. Until then she deserves some relief from her distress. I'll give you a formula for the chemist."

"I'll call the valet," Katya said. "He can have it filled immediately."

"Write this down, Sister," Petrograv ordered, reverting to hospital procedure. "I'd like the following mixture: acetate of potash, one ounce; fluid extract of black cohosh, one ounce; fluid extract of hemlock, two drams; simple syrup, six ounces, made up to be served in a teaspoonful dose, three times a day, in alternation with the Golden Elixir I've brought with me. In a few days she will be ready to resume the use of alkaline and vapor baths."

The princess looked up gratefully and then closed her swollen eyes while Petrograv explained the dosages to Katya and left her with a bottle of the Golden Elixir. "I will return this evening to check on your mistress, but if she worsens, don't hesitate to send for me. I am staying on the third floor of this same hotel."

"Thank you, Doctor. You will never know how grateful we are to you!" Katya said with tears in her eyes.

"As soon as she's had her medication, I order you to get some rest. You'll do your lady no service if you become ill."

"Yes, sir, I will," Katya replied, closing the heavy paneled door to the suite.

As Hannah and the doctor waited for the lift to arrive, she asked curiously, "What is this 'Golden Elixir'? I've not heard of it before."

"It's my own combination for an effective pain reliever, but one that should never be used without real cause. It contains a few drops of laudanum, a drop of chloral, essence of peppermint, and a little brandy, all combined in a palatable orange flower-water solution."

"A powerful potion, indeed! Have you thought of distributing it yourself?"

"I hope you are not serious," he answered in a voice edged with a mock chill. "A man of my position could never trade in patent medicines."

The lift arrived, and as they stepped into the beveled-glass and mahogany interior, Petrograv told the operator, "Lobby, please." Then, looking down at the large medical bag he carried, he changed his request. "Pardon, I'll need to stop at the third floor to put this away."

Hannah wondered if she should continue to the lobby, but when the door was opened, the operator fully expected Hannah to alight with the doctor and she did so to avoid a fuss. "After I put this in my room, we can continue our tour of your fine city. I would like to walk down the Boffo steps to the customs house, and if we have time, I'd like you to show me the new opera house."

Hannah felt only the slightest reluctance as she walked into his apartments. The rooms overlooked the busy harbor, a less expensive and noisier location than the princess's royal suite. The doctor went to put his bag away in his sleeping room while Hannah stood at the window amazed at the view, which was centered over the magnificent steps leading down to the quay. Although she tried to assume a relaxed pose, she felt her body stiffening.

"Did you know that Boffo intended the Odessa steps to be the main entrance to the city and had planned one of those triumphal arches for the top of the staircase? For some reason it was never built . . ." She kept her face turned away as she heard the doctor's muffled step on the pale Oriental carpet slipping closer to the window.

"Very interesting," he said, leaning toward Hannah and very gently placing the palm of his hand in the small of her back. Concentrating on the harbor view, she deliberately forced herself not to move or flinch.

"There are one hundred ninety-two steps. I used to count them when I was little. They look even longer, don't you think? Boffo built them narrower at the top than at the bottom to create the illusion of greater length."

"Very clever, those Italians," Petrograv whispered close to her ear while exerting a firmer pressure on her spine. Any resource of reserve in the young midwife melted at that one gesture, and her involuntary shiver was the signal he needed to clasp her toward him, pressing her high, firm bosom to his chest. Only a few inches taller than Hannah, Petrograv brushed his mouth across hers without great effort. He didn't press his lips to form a kiss, but this more delicate intimacy was just as stimulating. Hannah could neither decide on a correct response to his advance nor form the right words of protest.

Backing away slightly, she took a deep breath, which allowed some color to flow back into her face before she said, "I don't know if I can be what you want or do as you wish."

"I know, little sister, I know. If I cannot convince you with words perhaps this will help you discover what is in your mind," he finished, firmly centering his lips on Hannah's and kissing her deeply. Then, keeping his face only inches from hers, he continued, "Are you considering my proposal? I must know that at least."

"I never thought . . ."

"You feel this is wrong, don't you?"

Hannah nodded mutely and risked meeting his gaze for the first time.

"My wife's death taught me an important lesson, one that sent me rushing to find you again before you slipped out of my life."

"What lesson is that?" Hannah asked gently.

"There is one sin that every one of us unknowingly commits. It is not the loving of another, nor the carnal act that demonstrates and fortifies that love. It is the abuse of youth and vitality. It's not using God's precious gift of time and energy. Remember Pushkin! He ruined his life in the prime of his creativity by drinking, dueling, mixing himself in ridiculous political affairs when he could have done so much more!

"And your friend, the princess," he continued. "What would she give to lead a normal life? Hers has been the cruelest of fates;

her youth is a wasted wreckage of disease and pain. We have our health, at least for the present. We have the time. We have each other. Today we must use these gifts, share them with each other, before we are forced to surrender to the darker side of our existence. I have already made that mistake once and vowed not to do so again. Now I need your help to keep that promise to myself."

"But surely you have led an admirable life?"

"So it seems to you, but I have wasted so much. I thought my study and career should come first, that I would have many years to enjoy my young wife and child. When I finally learned how deeply I did care for her, she was taken from me. I won't, I can't, let it happen again!" he finished fiercely, his teeth clenched and eyes set on some far-off point. Then he grasped at Hannah roughly, held both her forearms in his tight grip, and pleaded, "I thought I had found happiness again when I came to know you. I thought I would have time to court you properly, and just as everything was going according to my hopes, you were taken from me!"

"So you decided to come after me?"

"I cannot waste another chance for happiness!"

"You really think I am the one who can do this for you?"

"Yes, if you will only try. And I'd like to presume I could do the same for you. Hannah, dearest Hannah, do I have a chance?"

Because Petrograv appeared even more vulnerable than she, because he spoke to a chord in her own aching heart, Hannah wanted to reach out to him, to wrap her arms around him and agree to love him as he wished. Yet words would not come; her arms fell to her sides like leaden weights. Instead of releasing Hannah, the doctor drew her even closer to him, and during his second full kiss she reeled in the aura of his embrace, breathing deeply his scent composed of a spicy mixture of fine tobacco, hair oils, and a peculiar, not totally unpleasant, odor all his own.

Still uncertain of her own feelings, Hannah wondered how she could muster the strength needed to refuse him. He had traveled so far just for her; he had suffered through a tragic marriage; and now he looked to her for his future happiness. And why would she even consider a refusal when she had felt similarly for many months? Wasn't this the answer to her dreams? Was she not, more than anything, grateful that he returned her respect and devotion?

Hannah's silence, coupled with a lack of resistance, encouraged Petrograv to believe he could go further. Releasing her for an instant, he reached around the edge of the window frame where the silken cords of the draperies hung from a track. With one defiant snap, he closed out the rest of the world.

## · 14 ·

HIS HANDS PLACED FIRMLY on both her shoulders, Petrograv steered Hannah to the slipper-shaped divan on the other side of his sitting room. She could neither walk nor seat herself, so he guided her in all movements. He unpinned her hair, which cascaded like a reluctant waterfall toward her waist, and then, without the slightest protest, Hannah allowed him to unfasten each of the twelve silk-covered buttons that formed a straight line down her back.

He whispered, he coaxed with his hands, caressing her neck and bodice. Each time she attempted to summon her reasoning self, his kisses blocked its emergence. Hannah was more curious than afraid. To know what would happen, to understand the budding feelings, to meet the wave full force, to know its power — and for once, to let it take her where it would — was all she desired. Later there would be time to sort it all out, later she would analyze and understand . . .

After the doctor had removed Hannah's blouse he began to undo the snaps on the princess's boots, caressing first the fine leather sole and then the foot that emerged from within. Hannah smiled at the fortune to have such lovely shoes instead of her own battered pair, and momentarily thought about her excuse for not returning the boots when she saw Mama that evening.

Standing in her underclothes, she felt no shame, even though the doctor stared with unabashed approval. But when he began to undress himself, Hannah turned her head. It took him some time to remove, fold, and place each item on a neat pile at the end of the divan. Finally he took her hand and led her to the sleeping room, where he pulled back the azure silk coverlet, the color of an undulating sea, and gestured for Hannah to sit down. She tried not to watch as he undid his final garment, but dared a direct stare before he slipped between the sheets. One short glimpse, one view of the man without his conventional drapes, one brief moment, and everything changed.

On the inhalation of a breath Hannah had been in wide-eyed anticipation, but with the next exhalation she felt a peculiar admixture of fright and revulsion.

"I won't hurt you, little Hannah, I promise."

"No, I can't! Please! I don't want to!" she protested, moving away from his outstretched arms.

"Oh, darling girl! I need you so much!" he begged and pulled her forcefully toward him.

Hannah knew enough to realize she had waited too long to disappoint him. Let it be over soon, she prayed as she closed her eyes against him. Perhaps in her own dark world she could still summon some of her old reveries, might remember him as the professor she worshipped — anything to get her through the next few minutes. The sensations he pressed upon her were unsettling, but not as painful as she had feared. It was abrasive, yet not agonizing. Her body seemed to belong in another time; he rose and fell upon another woman, in some other place. Blissfully for him, he seemed unaware that nothing was really happening between them, that he was only doing something to her, not with her.

Her position was so incongruous Hannah wondered how she could rearrange herself to prevent her legs from aching. And wasn't there something she was supposed to be doing? She tried to wrap her arms around his body, but found herself aware of how poorly the doctor compared with Lazar, whose broad chest Hannah could hardly reach around. Lazar, whose height rising above her meant strength and pride; Lazar, whose hair was the color of sunlit sand; Lazar, who compelled her with one glance of his vivid blue eyes. The doctor had presented a deceptive figure lecturing from a podium; he had cut a fine form striding the halls of the hospital; but here, with every inch of him pressed into her, Hannah found the reality a weak excuse for a man.

Opening her eyes, Hannah stared into his face. Petrograv's eyelids were clenched with concentration and his mouth twisted in an angry, rather than tender, expression. His teeth were discolored and saliva slipped down his beard. Hannah did not so much regret the act in which she was engaged as the impossible choice she had made. In a few seconds the doctor emitted his final groans, shuddered, and collapsed his full weight on Hannah's naked body.

His immediate reaction was apologetic. "I didn't hurt you, did I, little sparrow?" he said self-consciously. Then, solicitous of her comfort, he set about to rearrange the covers.

"No, no," Hannah answered flatly.

He kissed her forehead and then raised himself on one elbow. "You didn't cry out, so I thought it was easy for you. Was I mistaken, dear one?" he asked, finally aware that she had not responded with enthusiasm.

"It's all right, really," Hannah said, unwilling to admit the ache she felt between her thighs.

"A woman never enjoys it fully at first, my angel. It's something that must be learned. Next time it will be better for you. Don't concern yourself with it now. Just let me hold you."

Turning away from his outstretched arms, Hannah only wondered how quickly she could leave. Everything he said made her feel worse, each obsequious endearment pushed her further apart from him, every word made him seem more ridiculous. He lay quietly beside her for a moment, then reached for his tobacco and pipe.

Hannah's thoughts turned to a concern about her appearance. Without brushes and combs she would never get her hair styled correctly, and she observed ruefully that while his clothes had been folded hers were severely creased because he had merely dropped them on the floor.

The light from under the draperies was becoming so dim she could hardly see into the other room. "It must be getting very late!" Hannah said, sitting up with a start. The nipples of her exposed breasts saluted the change in temperature. Petrograv noticed, turned toward her, and started to touch them, but suddenly withdrew his hand as though he were reaching into a burning fire.

He pressed the coverlet into her hands, and she thankfully wrapped it around herself.

"When you are ready I'll escort you home."

"That would be impossible! Mama doesn't even know I am with you."

"What did you tell her, then?"

"I knew the princess had been at the hotel and I was supposed to see her before she left . . . so . . . I told her that. How could I ever have explained you to them? Can't you see we could never be together? I was foolish to even consider anything, so stupid to let myself believe . . ." Hannah choked back her tears.

"But we have been together, we can still, if you'll only let me . . . I can help you . . . we will find a way . . ." Petrograv stammered. Then he stood, walked toward Hannah, and tried to comfort her by burying his face in her neck. In his attempt to touch her the coverlet fell to the floor and she shrank away.

There he stood: naked, limp. She found him utterly foolish. Never again could she see him as her esteemed professor.

❖   ❖   ❖

After working to perfect her appearance, Hannah saw no evidence of her folly betrayed in the mirror, although she worried that some indefinable odor, unusual crease, or unfastened wisp of hair might give her away. As they made their way through the lobby to the promenade, discreetly maintaining a respectful distance, she asked, "Will you look in on the princess tonight?"

"I'll reevaluate the medication if her fever is not down in a few hours. But I think the crisis is almost over."

"I am very concerned about her welfare. I owe much to the princess."

"How can that be?" Petrograv raised his eyebrow in his familiar gesture of surprise.

"It's a long story. And not important now."

Petrograv did not question further. Even though he was curious, his own good sense reminded him not to press her. As they walked the short blocks to the trolley stop, Hannah was too lost in her own self-recriminating thoughts to be sensitive to her companion's emotions. Without warning he stopped, spun her around to face him, and haltingly pleaded, "Hannah, do you think you can ever forgive me?"

"There is nothing to forgive," Hannah replied, stepping back into stride.

"I know that is not what you wanted. I thought only of myself, and now I don't know how to make it better for you," he continued, stopping her once again.

Aware of the strangers who ringed the hotel in the early evening, Hannah insisted they continue. "Doctor, please, my family will worry that I am out so late."

"I am sorry," he replied, relinquishing his grasp once again. "If only I had stopped when you asked me to!" He bowed his head.

"I didn't know what I wanted," Hannah sighed. "You sensed that, so you . . ."

". . . took advantage of your indecision, your inexperience," he continued in the same self-deprecating tone. "You must understand my problem. I knew what I wanted and I was so terribly afraid I would never have it unless . . . unless I took it. I should have remembered that happiness can neither be purchased nor stolen."

"I am very confused by all that has happened."

"Then let us speak no more about it tonight, except. . ."

"What?"

"I have one more humble request . . ."

"Yes, Doctor?"

"Could you . . . could you call me Stefan?" He punctuated his words with a smile.

Hannah lowered her eyes but did not respond.

"Will you see me again tomorrow morning, then?" he pleaded.

"Not tomorrow," Hannah answered, trying to dodge the next awkward question.

"But you must! I return to Moscow on Monday. We must have time . . ."

"Tomorrow is the eve of Sabbath; they will need me for the preparations . . ."

"Then the day after?"

"That is our Sabbath day and I am not permitted to ride the trolley or to leave my family."

"When will I see you again?"

"Since you are staying through Sunday, we'll discuss your plans then."

Petrograv's face beamed in anticipation. Hannah had done well to use the word *plans*, for this gave him the hope he needed as well as giving her time to decide how to extricate herself from the association without undue pain to either party. When the trolley clanged to warn of its departure Hannah was several yards away. She signaled for the driver to wait and ran the last few feet. Petrograv helped her mount the steps to the outside deck and waved as the trolley made its turnaround and headed back down the boulevard, its brass bell reflecting the burning glow of the suddenly setting sun.

As soon as the hotel was out of sight, Hannah relaxed in the motion of the trolley car. Mesmerized, she observed how the little park in the middle of the boulevard reflected the pale pink from the glowing sky.

Was there any possibility of an association with the Christian doctor? Her family, especially Mama, would never accept him. But Hannah could not blame her rejection of him on others, for in her heart she realized she did not want him. Though she was concerned about her own cold response, she instinctively felt that it had not been entirely her fault, because the man who could awaken her sexually was not Stefan Petrograv.

## · 15 ·

ARRIVING HOME well after dark, Hannah prepared to defend herself. She felt some shame at what she had done, but this was overshadowed by a feeling of emptiness and disappointment.

"Hannah, we were beginning to worry," Aunt Sonia greeted her warmly.

"I am sorry to be late," she said to Mama, who, she thought, sensed something.

"Your nose is all red, Hannah! You should have worn a hat with a wider brim!"

"Oh, Mama." Hannah laughed in relief. "The sun is very healthy."

"It's your complexion," Mama continued absentmindedly. "Come into the kitchen. One of your new friends has been waiting for you."

Entering the back room, she was greeted by the smell of simmering barley soup. Hannah didn't immediately recognize the modestly dressed young woman, who munched on one of Mama's garlic pickles, until she turned and revealed that she was none other than Vera Goldfarb.

"There you are." Vera spoke in a soft tone. "I was going to leave in a few minutes; my family doesn't allow me out in the evenings alone."

Not only had her voice changed from the strident, argumentative one she used before, but her whole manner was more genteel. With her hair pinned tightly back into a high chignon, and wearing a trim summer suit with a fitted jacket that allowed only a discreet amount of thin batiste and lace to be revealed at the neck and cuffs, this stylish young woman was hardly the same person Hannah had encountered in the café.

"I am so glad you could come." Hannah's voice was civil.

"And how was your princess?" Mama asked, emphasizing the word *princess* to see what effect it had on Vera. Vera's expression did not disappoint.

"Not at all well, Mama. She was having one of her attacks of rheumatism and I stayed to help nurse her. Also, I was fortunate in finding a doctor I knew from Moscow staying at the same hotel, and he agreed to attend to her." Hannah was pleased with her story.

"That was a coincidence, wasn't it?" exclaimed Aunt Sonia.

Avoiding any further explanations, Hannah directed her remarks to Vera. "Such a sad case! She is just the same age as we are. If you could see those horrible swollen joints, and the pain she endures daily!"

"When you speak like that I can see why you selected midwifery," Vera replied with a sincerity even Hannah found convincing. "It must be wonderful to have people who need you so much and then be able to help them."

Noticing that her friend's mannered pleasantries could not cover a repetitive nervous gesture of pulling the lace on her cuff, Hannah thought it was time to determine the real reason for her visit.

"Come upstairs before you go, Vera, and I'll show you those medical texts I told you about. I'll happily lend any of them to you if you are still considering midwifery or nursing." Hannah tossed her head, pleased she had woven Vera's words into another convincing scenario.

"I would like that very much." Vera immediately perceived Hannah's meaning and followed Hannah up the narrow stairway behind the kitchen stove to Hannah's temporary quarters in Chaim's room. As soon as the two women were alone, Vera's voice lowered and darkened.

"What happened to you? No one ever thought you would be so irresponsible!"

"Irresponsible!" Hannah was indignant. She knew she had to be firm or Vera would try to insinuate that she had been completely in the wrong.

Vera backed off for a moment and added softly, "We were very worried."

"I should think so!"

"I told Lazar . . . I thought you wouldn't . . . I mean . . ." She stumbled, realizing it was bad form to have mentioned Lazar at that moment. "I had every confidence in you, but I couldn't explain what you had done, so I came here to find out . . ." she blindly continued, expecting Hannah to defend herself.

Hannah refrained from arguing while she considered where she stood. She decided to tell Vera the whole tale factually. When she came to the part about the flirting policemen, she exaggerated to demonstrate the effectiveness of her womanly charms, and then showed Vera that the bundles were stashed under her bed.

"Why didn't you contact us?" Vera asked.

"Mama didn't want me going back to the university quarter again, and I had to see the princess and there was a baby to deliver."

"A baby! I really am interested in midwifery. There is a class in Odessa I could take. Would you recommend it?"

"I heard there was a new program. Just my luck, after I freeze to death in Moscow!"

"To me Moscow sounds very exciting. You made so many friends there! A doctor! A princess!"

"The doctor really came to Odessa to see me again, but I didn't dare tell Mama about that," Hannah admitted.

"Why? Is he not Jewish?" Vera asked, forgetting to close her mouth when she finished her question.

"No, he's not. Also, he's older than I am. A widower. With a young child."

"How did you come to know him?" Vera's pupils widened in anticipation.

"He was my professor, the one who suggested I apply to the Medical College. He's a very brilliant man . . . He taught me so much . . ." she finished. To fill the thick silence, Hannah continued stupidly, "Tonight he asked me to return to Moscow with him, to continue my education, and . . . to marry him! But how can I with the way things are here?"

"Oh, Hannah!" Vera cried in a voice that spoke of the victory she thought she had won.

"You'll keep my secret? Please! I haven't made my decision yet."

"Of course! Who would I tell?" she asked, even though both knew the first person who would be most interested.

Hannah only nodded.

"I don't know what I would do if I were you," Vera continued sympathetically. Then in a girlish afterthought she burst out, "Tell me, is he very handsome?"

"I did think so . . . I mean, he is," Hannah answered awkwardly. The more she talked about Petrograv, the less he seemed to mean to her and the more remote he became. Hannah had only fueled the conversation to tantalize Vera, yet as she revealed her private illusions they shattered in the sharing. Perhaps there was something wrong with her, Hannah worried, her head pounding in confusion. After her return to Odessa Lazar had disappointed her and now Petrograv, whom she had idolized, was impossibly flawed in reality.

As Vera prepared to leave, Hannah regretted having revealed her relationship with Petrograv. But she talked pleasantly with Vera by the doorway.

"I'll tell Lazar you still have the packages and let him decide what to do" were Vera's last words.

Vera's shadow grew thinner and thinner in the pale circle of lamplight. As Hannah watched, a shiver ran down her spine. She should never have trusted her! The spider had set the trap and the fly had blissfully ignored the warning signs: the telltale sweetness, the tightly woven web. Desperately she tried to recall every word she had uttered, every gesture she had made, as she struggled to convince herself that her faith had been well placed and Vera had offered genuine friendship. But Hannah could not shake the inexorable feeling that she had made a terrible mistake.

# III

❖ ❖ ❖ ❖ ❖

# *Abraham Meyerov*
## Delivered August 22, 1904

❖ ❖ ❖ ❖ ❖ ❖ ❖ ❖ ❖ ❖ ❖ ❖

· 1 ·

T HE FOLLOWING SABBATH DAY was one of the longest of the summer and it seemed interminable.

There were no men to welcome home from shul, no father or brother to read the male parts of the prayers. The house contained only five sullen women, bored with the routine of caring just for themselves, each involved in her own irritable thoughts as they finished their cold meal and sipped their lukewarm tea. Dora scratched at one of the prickly rashes that befell her during the humid season, while Eva, ever restless, paced around the room clicking her heels in an unnerving rhythm.

"That noise is making me crazy!" Mama complained.

"Can't we do something?" Eva whined, rushing to the west-facing window as though she expected to see the sun finally drop like a stone.

"Go for a walk with Hannah, but I am too hot to move," she replied, fanning herself.

"Hannah, please, please ..." Eva implored with an expression more manipulative than sincere.

"Ask Aunt Sonia," her sister replied.

"But you know she's asleep!" Eva sniffed.

"Hannah, you should go out. If you sit all day you'll get a head-ache," Mama said.

"I already have a headache!" Hannah retorted, and indeed all her worries had produced an aching sensation on the right side of her temple. "If you want to avoid headaches, why don't you go out? They're your children, not mine!" Immediately Hannah re-gretted her harshness. "I'm sorry, Mama, the heat is bothering me too. Just let me take some headache powders and change my skirt. We'll walk toward the Botanical Gardens."

Eva nodded solemnly while Dora responded with glee, "Hurray! Hurray! We're going to the gardens, we're going to the gardens!"

"Good, good," Mama muttered. "Now go outside and sit on the steps before you wake your aunt."

Hannah prepared herself and then, coming back through the front room, paused as she watched Mama sitting alone in the dark-ened room, her mouth moving but expelling almost no sound at all. At first Hannah thought she was in prayer, and then realized her mother was not talking to a private God but discussing her problems with her deceased husband. Hannah strained to hear the phrases. "So why is Hannah acting so? Did I do right? What would you say to that? Tell me, do you know about Chaim?"

Tears stung Hannah's eyes as she realized how often she had done much the same. And yet lately she had been ashamed to summon Papa, even in her imagination.

"Hannah, there's someone here for you!" Eva burst through the door and shouted, startling both women inside. "He's come from Zalman's."

Mama jumped in alarm and went to the door. "From Zalman's? On Shabbes?"

At the curb she saw a double landau pulled by an immaculate white horse. The driver was one of the Zalmans' Shabbes goyim, a Christian servant who ran errands, lit fires, and prepared meals for an observant family.

"Pardon, is this the home of the midwife Hannah Blau?"

"Yes, I am the midwife," Hannah said, stepping in front of the other women.

"I have been asked to especially apologize for breaking your rest, but we have true need of your service." He spoke slowly in case she did not understand his Russian.

Hannah looked to Mama for the final approval. "You must go, Hannah," she said. "A baby is reason enough!"

"I'll just get my things," Hannah responded.

Mama followed her inside. "Asher Zalman's called for you! What a chance! Do you think it's their little golden-haired daughter? I sewed for some of her wedding guests last year. Or perhaps. . ."

"Mama, I'll tell you all about it later," Hannah said as she was helped into the carriage and nodded for the driver to be off.

❖   ❖   ❖

Yacob Zalman had done well as a wheat broker, and then his son, Asher, parlayed the family's capital into a fortune by a seemingly magical ability to control shares on the Odessa Exchange. Papa Blau had attended the yeshiva with the younger Zalman and had continued the friendship.

As a money speculator, Zalman bought and sold roubles, which were backed by gold, against the British pounds in sterling. He was the master of the stallage, an operation by which the speculator sells and buys the money of one country against that of another in the hope that by the time the sale or purchase is completed the prices will rise or fall so he makes a profit. Many smaller merchants, including Papa Blau, were tempted to "do a Zalman." If Zalman feared he might have made a bad guess, he would hedge by telling his broker to sell some roubles for him at the low price, so, if they later went down, he had cut his losses or managed to squeeze a small profit from the deal, depending whether the difference came out in favor of or against him. Too often amateur speculators would panic too soon or wait too long, losing all their savings; but Zalman had an uncanny sense of which way the wind was blowing that others envied and feared. Though Papa Blau had made a small sum by emulating Zalman, Mama had heard too many stories of bankrupt families, and eventually forbade him to take any more risks.

As she arrived at the imposing foyer of the Zalmans' great stone house, Hannah realized she could gain introduction to the finest Jewish families in Odessa after this delivery. Immediately she was ushered into the family parlor, where the Zalman women were waiting out the Sabbath. Madame Zalman, a tiny frail woman draped in layers of thin brown silk, rose and led Hannah to the hallway before speaking in a voice edged with a lisp.

"We are so sorry to break your Sabbath. I thought Olga could wait a few more hours, but then I was told there was some difficulty and I didn't want the poor thing to suffer any more than she must. I myself have had eleven children, and even though she did wrong, I must do my best for her."

Hannah nodded automatically. Madame Zalman led the way up three flights of marble stairs to the servants' quarters under the eaves. A series of low moans rose from the room where Hannah was obviously expected.

"Do whatever you think is best. My housekeeper, Antonia, will bring you anything you require. You come with the best recommendations, and even in this case, we are happy to pay your full fee," she said and sighed. The weight of her holiday pearls, at least seven enormous strands, seemed to make her breathing more difficult as she descended the stairs. Clearly, the expectant mother was not a member of the family, Hannah thought with disappointment.

Antonia sternly guarded the door to a small, stark room. It was furnished only with a short metal bed and an unfinished wood stand supporting a chipped enamel basin with a yellow ring above the water line. Two hooks on the wall held an apron and a change of clothing. A single pair of worn black shoes was on the floor. Olga lay flat on her back without so much as a pillow to support her head. Antonia observed her suffering but did nothing to offer comfort, seeming, in her silent stance, to be contemptuous of her charge's condition.

"I am your midwife. My name is Sister Blau," Hannah said slowly in Russian.

"She's just a Polish girl who helps in the kitchen," Antonia said with an unpleasant grimace. "She won't understand your words." But the girl's expression indicated she comprehended everything.

As Hannah reached for her stethoscope, she had a fleeting image of the metal prongs encircling Dr. Jaffe's neck. Then, lifting Olga's coarse chemise to bare her swollen abdomen, the midwife placed the bell of the instrument just below the navel and listened for the familiar fast twittering of the fetal heart. Hearing nothing, Hannah decided the baby's head might already be firmly engaged in the pelvis, so she lowered the bell to a point just above the pubic line. Still nothing was heard but the "voos, voos, voos" of blood rushing through the placenta. Fearful that it might be a breech or transverse lie, Hannah pressed the stethoscope to the upper abdomen, just below Olga's pendulous breasts, but the only noises were those present in any woman, pregnant or not.

The midwife began to move the instrument around, leaving little circles imprinted on the distended landscape. She pressed as hard as she dared to get a better connection; she listened intently, stopping her own breathing to concentrate. Nothing, she heard nothing!

The girl, who could not have been more than sixteen years old, waited for Hannah to say something. And when she did not, Olga's eyes widened with both the force of the pain and the knowledge that had been transmitted from the midwife's glance. Hannah removed the earpieces and reached for her patient's hand.

"No!" she cried. "No! No ... No ... Nooooo!" In the middle of the contraction, Olga attempted to pull herself up by grasping Hannah's wrist, but fell back, leaving clawlike scratches on the midwife's forearm.

Antonia bent over Olga and shouted, "What's the matter with you?"

"I think ..." Hannah whispered, "... the baby has died already. I do not hear its heart beating."

Antonia pointed to the stethoscope. "What did you do to her with that thing?"

"What did I do?" Hannah asked incredulously. "This baby was gone long before I got here. You called for me too late!"

"Do you still need me?" the housekeeper asked, anxious to leave the scene.

"Not at all."

"Then I had better inform Madame Zalman of these events. Yet, it is for the best, don't you think? A child without a father? It would not have been any good. This must be a sign for Olga. I will go and light a candle for her," she said, bowing as she retreated from the room.

The mystery was solved after a brief internal examination. The membranes had ruptured and a prolapsed loop of umbilical cord hung down through the opening in the almost totally dilated cervix. Each contraction resulted in a deprivation of vital nutrients to the baby, and the infant had expired after the continual assaults to the soft blood vessels caused compression and asphyxia.

Why this baby and not another? Hannah pondered this question as she waited out the sad hours necessary to deliver the perfectly formed stillborn girl child. Olga bore the rest of her labor in stoic silence, succumbing to one more outburst of tears and screams when the midwife handed her the wrapped little child for a farewell kiss. Antonia arrived with a small box lined with white velvet to hold the dead infant and gave the midwife an envelope with her payment enclosed. Not knowing for the moment how to refuse it, Hannah tucked it in her apron.

After completing her postpartum check, Hannah spoke to Olga quietly. "Someday you will have another baby, a strong healthy one. And after that, all the children you would ever want. This was an accident; it happens, no one is certain why."

Olga nodded sadly. "It will not go like this again?"

The odds of a recurrence were so small Hannah was able to answer with sincerity. "No, never again."

"Thank you for all you did for me." Olga surprised Hannah by speaking in clumsy Yiddish, which she had picked up in the Zalman house. Then she turned away from Hannah and closed her eyes.

Taking the envelope from her pocket, Hannah placed it beside Olga's pillow, guessing the servant girl needed the roubles far more than she did.

· 2 ·

HANNAH HAD ARRANGED to meet Petrograv in the most public of places, the Old Bazaar.

Waiting for him at the trolley stop, she knew instinctively that she had made a prudent decision. As always on Sunday, the bazaar was teeming with merchants hawking every kind of ware from tin pans to rags, gypsy jewelry to carved musical instruments. It featured foods from meat pies to ice cones and fried potato dumplings. This was the Jewish marketplace and Hannah wanted the doctor to see her in her own environment.

The doctor jumped off the trolley before it came to a full stop at the platform, and he rushed to greet Hannah. She kept him at arm's length and he fell upon her fingers, kissing them as passionately as he dared in public.

"Good morning, Hannah. I've just checked the princess; her fever has completely subsided. I hope you didn't wait very long."

"Just a few moments. I thought I would be the one who would be late. I had another delivery last night."

"The mothers of Odessa will keep you very busy, if you let them," he said, offering his arm for a stroll. "You are looking very lovely this morning," he observed.

She wore a white silk waist with a minimum of open embroidery, buttoned securely in the front, and her hair was pinned back as severely as possible. The doctor, however, had taken a different tack, selecting his softest cashmere suit cut in the French sack style, a classic derby instead of the straw hat, and to Hannah's surprise, he carried a cane, which added to the elegant effect.

"I hope all my cases are not like that one."

"You had some difficulties?"

Hannah was relieved to launch into a description of Olga's stillbirth. She finished the tale by adding "I only wish they had called me sooner."

"The prolapse is a condition of the gravest nature. If you had found the baby alive and experiencing great distress, you would have had some difficult decisions to make."

"What would you have done?"

"To be truthful, I have lost almost every one of these infants after hours of work and effort, not to mention the additional agony I induce during my attempts. But lately I have had some success with positioning."

"Would you please explain it to me?"

Petrograv seemed somewhat reluctant to slip back into his professorial role. "If you like."

They began their tour of the marketplace by strolling the intersecting boulevards that formed the perimeters of a square and were known as the four B's of the bazaar. First they turned north on Baspensky, passing the stalls that displayed leather goods, ironware, and textiles. Then they turned east on Botchaidainaioutskaia, where flour and spices, fruits and meats were sold by women vendors wearing bright babushkas. At the corner where they turned south onto Bolgarskaia was the pharmacy, with its large black sign and strong odors of medicine. As they approached Bazarney, the southernmost street, Hannah said, "There's nothing like the Café Franconi, but I know which vendor sells the best apple kvass, made with pure sugar, not saccharin."

"Is there anywhere we could get some bread or cake as well?"

"Next door they make little strudels filled with crushed almonds, apricots, or prunes. Take your pick!"

While they ate and drank, Petrograv explained his treatment for prolapse. The conversation was blessedly factual.

Hannah's thoughts drifted back to Olga's plight the day before. "I understand that you prefer reposition for a primipara and version for the multipara, but what if the child is in very bad condition?"

"Hannah, you know we cannot save every baby in the world. Sometimes, as you found out yesterday, all our techniques may be useless. That is the lure of our profession, isn't it? Every pregnant woman carries a secret that will only be divulged at birth. Just when I am completely confident, a case challenges all my skills and humbles me once again. As birth attendants, the mystery is ours to unravel and our reward is the joy of receiving into our hands a newly born human baby, more often than not a perfect healthy baby. You must not let the accidents of birth, cases such as you had yesterday, frighten you. The odds for them are but one in four hundred. The amazing fact is that so many babies are born without incident, considering all we know that could go wrong."

"I remember when I first attended births there was only one question in my mind: would it be a boy or a girl? Now that I know the possibilities, I question every phase of labor, every deviation. Sometimes I think my education has only taught me how little I know. I only hope I will be equal to the task."

"It would be to my advantage to say that you are not. But Hannah, you are. I could teach you more. You could learn to use forceps, to perform destructive operations on the fetus, to practice abdominal surgical techniques; but you are already well equipped to handle almost any birth you are likely to encounter."

Wishing more privacy, he steered Hannah toward the shaded awning in back of a dairy cart. He placed his hands on Hannah's shoulders. "I know you won't be returning to Moscow with me. In my heart I have guessed what you have to say to me, and as a last gesture of respect, I wish to spare you the telling of it."

Hannah was stunned by the sensitivity his words demonstrated, something he had acutely lacked during their most intimate moments.

Just then a group of strolling musicians, the klezmorim, began to play, droning a gypsy melody in a minor key. Petrograv pressed his finger to her lips to silence her and drew her close for an instant. His thoughtfulness had an effect on Hannah that she would never have suspected. Instead of making the parting easier, it had made it more difficult.

When the song ended Hannah summoned the precise words to convey her meaning. "You must see, dear Professor, I cannot easily leave my family. Sometimes I wish I did not feel this way, for I am bound so tightly I fear I will smother from the constriction. Yet I desire only to loosen the cords, not cut them completely."

"Are we so far apart? After the czar's edict of August eleventh, your position should improve. Jews will have more rights; you won't feel so much the outsider."

"What edict is this?"

"It was issued ten days ago. Surely you have heard about it. On the occasion of the birth of his first son, Nicholas issued the Alexis Doctrine, granting favors and privileges to the Jewish population. It should hold up for years as a document of great foresight and compassion."

"That nonsense!" Hannah said with impatient contempt. "You think that will mean anything to the Jews? It's a joke, and a sad one at that if it convinced someone as learned as you, Doctor. All it did was introduce, pending the general revision of legislation affecting Jews, several amendments concerning the rights of residence. These are trifles!" She pushed away in irritation.

"I thought . . ." Petrograv's surprise registered in a hoarse whisper.

"You believed the propaganda, but the Jews of this community look upon these gifts as a momentary whim."

"You are too cynical, Hannah. Have you no faith in the future?"

Just then they heard a strange commotion at the far side of the market square. A general panic swept the air; horses whinnied and shook their wagons. A young peddler of matches and shoe polish ran diagonally away from the ruckus.

"What's happening?" Hannah called as he dashed past, matches flying in all directions.

"Pogrom! Pogrom!" he shouted as he ran to hide in the Old Quarter.

"We don't have pogroms in Odessa!" she said with disbelief. "Maybe in Kishinev, but not here!" Her denial was interrupted by Petrograv, who pushed her behind the dairy wagon and pressed her down.

From under the roughhewn wagon Hannah observed more than a dozen horses, so well matched they must have belonged to the mounted police, ride into place and stand in formation. They now ringed the whole center of the bazaar.

"We are on the outside of their circle," Petrograv whispered close to Hannah's ear. "Now listen to me. I want you to back away slowly and then cross the street behind us. Keep low and follow me into one of the buildings. Now take my hand and keep down!" He led her under a few wagons. When they were well behind the main merchants' area Petrograv pulled her quickly across the deserted cobbled street and into the doorway of the first building they reached. Hannah attempted to turn around to see what was happening, but he pushed her roughly up four flights of stairs until they were in the washing attic of the residential building.

There were no windows on the top story, only a series of open arches that were too high for a view. Petrograv dragged a wooden crate to the wall and together they stood on it and peered down at the scene below.

# · 3 ·

THIRTY OR FORTY Russian reservists marched into the square. The police, watching from the side in orderly parade, made no immediate attempt to stop the bloodshed and looting.

The soldiers, who were clearly drunk, pulled several old Jews down from their carts and bludgeoned them mercilessly. Hannah saw a woman being dragged behind a horse across the rough cobbles. Looters began by taking the best furs and trinkets before setting fire to the stalls. Because the action took place several blocks away, Hannah and the doctor were spared a close view of most of the violence.

But then, just across from their building, three reservists, their hands filled with booty, spied a chair peddler who hid frightened and immobile under the dairy wagon that had provided Hannah brief refuge. They taunted him to come out and, when he refused, dropped their bundles and went after him, clawing and barking like a pack of wild dogs. They had him by his beard, and then, in a concerted effort, they counted: "One, two, three . . . . pulllll!"

"We must do something . . ." Hannah buried her face in Petrograv's shoulder.

"Do you think those madmen would stop to listen to my words?"

"No, but . . ."

"I feel as helpless as you," he said, wiping at the tears building up behind his heavy-lidded eyes.

Hearing a new sound, Hannah asked, "What's that?"

Hannah and Petrograv leapt back to their perch and watched as five or six dozen men, brandishing clubs and sabers, rushed at the reservists from every direction. The police still took no action.

This new group seemed more organized. Each wore a red rag tied to his left forearm. At first Hannah thought they might be coming to the aid of their exhausted comrades, but soon it was clear that each small band had come to defend one portion of the square, attacking the reservists with shouts, pummels, and curses. The reservists were no match for these sober reinforcements, and grabbing whatever they could steal, they ran from the marketplace without fighting back. The police captain, satisfied that the incident had been ended without his men having to either soil their hands or tire their horses, ordered his men back to barracks. Within moments the pogrom was over. Most of the avengers seemed to have vanished.

Finally Hannah and the doctor felt it was safe to aid the wounded. First they carried the chair peddler to the nearest well pump, where they washed and wrapped his swollen face with linen from the attic. Then other victims came and waited for their wounds to be cleansed and bandaged. Considering the amount of blood and anguish, the actual injuries were not as great as Hannah had feared.

"How many are dead?" Petrograv asked a sturdy lad who carried the wounded from the makeshift clinic to rest in carts.

"I haven't heard of one yet."

"What about the woman who was dragged?"

"She is still unconscious, but breathing."

"Have her brought here at once!" Petrograv ordered.

"Very clever," muttered a toothless old woman who had run the largest goose-down concession. "They are required to report only death statistics to the government. If they don't manage to murder anyone, the whole day will go unrecorded, unremembered!" she said, and spat in the street in disgust.

Hannah worked alongside Petrograv for two hours. The doctor took a final strip of clean cloth, soaked it in water, and began to wipe the blood and grime from her tired face.

As he turned away to rinse out the cloth, someone tapped Hannah's shoulder and she jumped in fright.

"Hannah, what are you doing here?"

"Lazar! What are *you?*" she asked before she noticed a strip of red cloth tucked into his hip pocket.

"Were you hurt?" he asked, surveying her filthy clothing. "Is anyone else in the family here?"

"No, I came alone ... I mean ... I was with a friend, Dr. Petrograv." She indicated the doctor, who had stopped his ablutions to observe who was questioning her.

"I know all about your 'friend'!" Lazar snorted.

How quickly Vera had betrayed her confidence! "Really?"

"Then it is true?" Lazar asked more softly.

"How should I know what you think is true?"

Petrograv's attention was momentarily diverted by a hysterical girl.

Lazar pointed as he ministered to the child. "That you and he ... that you are going back to Moscow with him and ..."

"I'm not going back to Moscow, not now, nor ever," she answered simply.

"I was told ..."

"I don't know what you have been told, but I am telling you that I am remaining in Odessa."

As she turned away from Lazar, Petrograv came toward her. "Sister Blau, our work is finished here. Now I must get you home safely to your family before they hear what has happened here today and become worried."

"That is not necessary," Lazar interrupted. "I will see Hannah home and explain everything," he continued in Russian.

"Who is this?" Petrograv asked suspiciously.

"Dr. Petrograv, may I introduce Lazar Sokolovsky, a close friend of my brother's. I think it might be better if he took me home.

Mama would be more alarmed to see me with someone she doesn't know."

"If that is what you think is best. I take the express back to Moscow this evening."

"Tonight?" Hannah asked in surprise.

"There is no reason to remain longer, but I leave your city with many memories," he said, with no hint of meaning in his flat voice.

"Come, Hannah," Lazar said. "We should go now."

Nodding numbly, she followed him, turning but once to give the doctor one last wave and call, "Say good-bye to the princess for me, won't you?"

Lazar lifted her onto the seat of a tin-peddler's wagon.

"Whose cart is this?" she asked.

"Grisha's. He'll know I've taken it," Lazar answered and snapped the reins. The old mare began to lumber off in her version of a quick trot.

Suddenly, Hannah looked back to memorize the rigidly controlled expression on Petrograv's face. As she turned the corner, his forlorn figure was blocked from her sight. She doubted she would ever see him again.

## · 4 ·

HANNAH PULLED AN END of the red armband that poked from Lazar's hip pocket.

"You were one of them, weren't you?"

"The Defense League? Yes, I was."

"The police were everywhere; you all could have been shot!"

"Ha! The police were happy to have us finish their job. Now the officials can wash their hands of every responsibility."

"How did you all disappear so quickly? One minute there must have been a hundred of you, the next you were gone."

"It is part of our plan. First we dispose of our weapons, then put on our disguises: false beards, extra shirts, and such. We can join a family at supper, a merchant in his storeroom, or just blend into the crowd. Some of our boys, like Grisha, dabbed themselves with blood and lay moaning in the gutter, all the time alert and ready to defend if necessary."

"So this is how you spend your time, training actors?"

"You may call it that. We go from neighborhood to neighborhood to recruit volunteers. We conduct secret meetings, write and distribute our leaflets. Already we have signal stations to alert us at the first sign of trouble."

"Don't the observant object to your actions?"

"We can read the scriptures back to them. There are many passages that uphold our militant point of view."

"Such as?"

"There's this one." He recited in Hebrew: " 'Cure ye Meroz, said the angel of the Lord. Cure ye bitterly the inhabitants thereof, because they came not to the help of the Lord, to the help of the Lord against the mighty.' "

"I am so afraid for you, Lazar. Isn't there another solution?"

"There is no other! We shall not be led to slaughter like those in villages such as Kishinev!" Lazar was strangely silent for a moment. He then pulled a pamphlet from a familiar bundle under the seat of the cart. "Here, look at this."

"That is like the ones I carried for you!"

"Yes, it was written by one of our members, Simeon Frug. It is my mission to disseminate it to every Jew in Bessarabia."

As Hannah stared at the words, Lazar allowed the reins to slip from his hands and he embraced her. "You can't imagine how I felt when I saw you, your skirt all bloodied. I feared they had . . . hurt you, and I thought: if anyone has harmed my Hannah, I'll kill them! Don't you yet know that you mean everything to me? I had always thought we had an understanding, and then when that doctor came, when I heard about you and him . . ."

"What kind of an understanding?" she demanded, not returning his affectionate gesture.

"That you and I . . . I always believed that when you returned home . . . when I finished my work . . ."

"Your work will never be finished! I also thought we were together a long time ago, but once I came home you proved you had no interest in my feelings or safety!"

"That's not true!"

"No? You are accustomed to friends who will do anything to stay by your side."

"Do you mean . . . ?"

"How else could you have learned about the professor? What craziness did she fill your head with?"

"Just that you and he . . . that you were going to run away with him and go back to Moscow."

"Lies, all lies!" Hannah denied everything. "She would say anything to keep you for herself."

"You are jealous?"

"Jealous!" she screamed, enraged.

"I will freely admit I didn't wish you to go with that man, but Vera means nothing to me. Oh, she's intelligent, devoted to the cause, we all relied on her; but I have no special feelings for her, I never did." Lazar lifted Hannah's unresisting hands to his mouth and kissed her fingers.

"Lazar, may I ask you something?" Hannah asked softly.

He looked at her shyly. "Yes, of course."

"Where are we going? This is not the way to the Razamovsca."

"You are right! The horse always follows the same path home from the market."

"Where is the stable?"

"Around the corner from my lodgings. I want to show you what I am doing, to let you discover for yourself the importance of my work, and besides, if you don't wash yourself your mama will lose her mind at the sight of you."

Hannah looked down at her stained skirt and did not protest.

Lazar made no apologies as he led Hannah down the wooden stairs into his airless basement rooms. "This is where I work and live."

Hannah had no comment on the sparse and filthy quarters furnished only with two straw mattresses covered with a faded spread woven in shades of blue and burgundy. There was a large table strewn with books, pens, and papers; two kerosene lanterns; and a basket into which both clean and dirty clothing had been tossed. The floor was littered with stacks of books and pamphlets, plates with molding pieces of bread and herring, and empty bottles that had once contained Chopin beer and Bessarabian wine.

At the far end of the room hung an Oriental rug, which Lazar pulled aside. Gesturing to Hannah, he showed her how to pass through a thin door cut between the studs of the building and led her down a darkened staircase to an even larger room. "Here are the tools of my trade," he said, proudly pointing out two printing presses, rolls of inexpensive rag paper, and vats of ink. A simple folding machine had been crudely nailed together, and partially folded tracts lay stacked in front of it.

"This is where we prepare the food that feeds the Bund. Here is also where we store our plans, lists, maps. It is the heart of the Defense League."

Hannah picked up one set of proofs: "To Haman," a diatribe against Plehve. "You needn't finish printing this one!"

"No, that job is complete."

"At a very great cost, don't you think?"

"Everything worthwhile has its price."

Hannah felt her stomach turn at his indifference. "Doesn't my brother mean anything to you?"

"Hannah, he is my brother too."

"Then why don't you do something for him? Where is he now?"

"We are almost certain he is in the Urals, and if we are right, the camp to which he has been assigned is a good omen. There might be a chance of a reprieve or even escape."

"Oh, Lazar, when will you be sensible? Do you think Plehve's successor will let those he believes to be assassins out of prison ... ever?"

"I don't know. They say that when Svyatopolk-Mirski was governor general of Vilna he displayed comparative leniency toward the Jews. In his first speech he claimed he would be guided by justice and kindness to all peoples."

"How can you believe such words?"

"I think I know more about propaganda than you do!"

Hannah walked around the room, far more tidy than his living quarters, and handled some of the publications, noting that many were written by the same Mikael Vronsky.

"Who is this Vronsky? The name is familiar but I don't recall ever reading his work."

Lazar strutted a bit as he said, "Vronsky is my pen name. I'm becoming so popular even the authorities are eager for my work."

"Oh, Lazar! If you aren't careful you also will end up in prison, or worse."

"Surely you now realize the importance of my work."

"I have always hated politics; I resented what happened to Chaim because he brought it on himself. But today, for the first time, I do see the practical side of all those endless arguments."

"This is what I have been waiting for!" Lazar pulled Hannah to him, reached down, and pushed her hair from her face so he could gaze into her startled green eyes. "Now that you understand what I am doing you will join me in the cause!"

"I don't understand it completely. I don't know what to think . . ."

"Then you had better not think." He kissed her forehead, her eyes, then stopped. "Do you know what it means to me to have you here with me, finally? To have you alone after all I have suffered these last few days?"

"Why have you suffered?"

"After what I heard, I was certain you were lost to me! I know I haven't had time to be with you, but the danger has been mounting. I'll make it up to you, I promise!"

Without another thought, she began to caress his muscular arms and willingly nestled against his solid chest. Lazar easily lifted Hannah and, cradling her like a baby, carried her up the stairs, through the secret door, and back to his sleeping area.

"You must take off your clothes and wash them in cold water," he whispered as he undressed her. As each piece of clothing fell to the floor, he stroked the skin underneath with surprising gentleness, considering the roughness of his hands. Hannah compared him to Petrograv, whose fingertips were more smooth, but whose touch was less gentle. Lazar lingered: smelling, tasting, kissing every surface of her unresisting body. Only a last vestige of modesty prevented her from begging him to take her more quickly as she arched toward him.

When he finally removed his own clothes and lay next to her he continued to kiss her until she entwined her legs around his back and gave herself to him. He did not pierce her in the abrupt way that Petrograv had. Instead his motions were slow and deliberate, and he was ever watchful of her response. From time to time he held himself back, lifting himself on stiff arms as he surveyed Hannah's radiant face. Waiting, waiting, interminable seconds until she willingly drew him deeper inside her.

At first she was unsure of where her own thrusts would lead until a small spark flared out, caught, and burned. Lazar reacted to the tightness of her straining muscles by stroking her neck and cheeks with his lips while maintaining the steady rhythm that Hannah seemed to crave.

Without knowing why, she cried out, then froze as she worked to make sense of the pulsations she had never known before. Although he tried to halt with her, Lazar could not. He trembled like a branch in the wind.

So, there was nothing wrong with her after all. Hannah smiled inwardly and allowed herself to stare directly at Lazar. One look at his eyes, the color of the sea in summer, convinced her that he too had found it very special.

Lazar hopped around the room happily naked. "Let's get you home before your mama sends out her own defense group!" he said as he picked up Hannah's bodice, skirt, and waist before dusting them off and then dabbing at the stains with water.

"You are making it worse! Let me!" Holding the fabric of her skirt taut over the basin, Hannah instructed him to pour a thin stream of water from several inches above in order to push the stain through the stretched pores of the cloth. Then, rubbing it with a clean rag, she removed all but the dark ring at the edge of each circle.

"That should be less noticeable," Hannah said, letting the outer garments dry for a few moments while Lazar helped her button her underclothes.

"Here's your other stocking. May I put it on you myself?"

"You make me feel like a little girl who cannot dress herself."

"You are my baby to take care of from now on," he replied, kissing the nape of her neck and then cuddling her in the curve of his lap.

"I'm a big girl now," she said, pushing him away.

"I can't deny that!" he said with a glint in his eyes. "After today, no one can call you a little girl again."

As he began to dress himself, Hannah was certain that he did not suspect there had been someone before him. Vera may have guessed, but she had not known for sure. Her secret was safe.

Suddenly they were startled by a loud, constant pounding at the door.

"Who could that be?" Lazar asked with alarm.

"Lazar, Lazar, let me in! Let me in!" shouted a loud female voice.

Recognizing it at once, Hannah cried, "It's Vera Goldfarb! She can't see me here!" Hannah grabbed her waist and rushed to fasten it behind her back.

"Let me in! Lazar, we need you! Lazar, are you there?"

"I can't leave her screaming on the street; she'll draw too much attention."

"Oh, no," Hannah moaned, slinking back into the corner, her skirt held up before her in self-protection.

Lazar unbolted the door and Vera tumbled into the room, disheveled and perspiring.

"I've told you never to come here unescorted. You know where to leave a message if you need me."

"There wasn't time. Everyone has been looking for you. It's happened, it's happened again!"

"What do you mean?" Lazar demanded, aware that something must have caused her terrified stare.

Vera did not answer. Her eyes swept the darkened room and rested on Hannah. Her mouth dropped open as she backed away from Lazar until she touched the far wall. She looked from his bare chest to Hannah, who was buttoning the high collar on her blouse, saying nothing. Vera's face froze into a grimace of shock and hate.

"Enough of that, Vera. Tell me why you are here, at once!"

Vera refused to answer. Losing his patience, Lazar took three large strides and stood directly in front of her and began to shake her. Her head knocked against the wall with each shove.

"Lazar! Don't hurt her! Can't you see something has upset her?" Hannah shouted. Pushing Lazar aside, Hannah spoke directly to Vera. "No one wanted to hurt you. We'll talk again, but now, for God's sake, Vera, give us your news."

Vera had slumped to the floor and begun to weep violently. Bewildered by the cause of this unbearable sadness, Hannah asked again. "Tell us what this is about."

"There's been another pogrom," she managed to say, though her hands covered her face. "We thought the one in the Old Bazaar was over, but it was only a ruse. With our self-defense groups mobilized, no one was left to help where it was needed the most."

"Another pogrom . . . where? Vera, tell me!" Lazar began to sweat profusely.

"It's, it's at the Razamovsca." Vera choked at the words. She stared at Hannah. "All the stores, looted, burned, and . . . Oh, God! I cannot tell you everything."

"Vera, you must," Lazar said steadily. "I'll ask you some questions and you just answer them. All right?"

Vera nodded.

Lazar began to exact the terrible information. "Have the self-defense units been mobilized?"

"Yes, no, well . . . some were, but they came too late. Most of the captains were down in the taverns near the bazaar, celebrating their victory. We were so unprepared, no one was ready for this."

"Is it still going on?"

"I think not. It must have begun about the same time as the one at the bazaar, maybe a half-hour later. But they were sober, very organized, and there were no police. They had a leader giving orders."

"Who were they? More reservists?"

"Some. But mostly they were a specially trained group of Cossacks who knew what they were about. They went from house to house, selected the best merchandise for their carts, then . . . then they burned everything behind them."

Hannah brought her right hand to her throat. "Burned everything?" The words repeated in her head over and over. Burned everything, Razamovsca, Mama. It couldn't be! Not after today, not in the hour of her greatest happiness. It was impossible!

"You are lying! You are doing this because you can't get Lazar for yourself! How could anyone say such things to hurt another! May you go blind and lame!" She tore at Vera's face with her nails.

"It's true, it's true, my God, it's true!" Vera sobbed, hardly resisting the attack. "I saw it all."

Lazar positioned himself between the two women and said calmly, "If this is true, there will be much for us to do. Now, Vera, you tell us the rest. Hannah, be still!" Lazar pressed her shoulder firmly. "The squares around the Razamovsca: Glinka, Melnitsky, Masterskaia?" Lazar continued.

"I'm not certain exactly what streets were spared. Hannah, I'm sorry, but it's true."

"But not every square? They can't have hit every house on every street."

"Not every one, except on the Razamovsca. That is finished!"

"Were they dressed in black?" Lazar asked.

"Yes, and they carried signs saying 'Down with the zhids, wherefrom all misfortunes flow' and 'Kill the traitors!' "

"It must be the Katzaps; we've heard about them."

"Was anyone killed?" Hannah asked weakly. "In the market there were no casualties, only wounded. Perhaps they had the same instructions?"

"Wounded? I think they were ordered to leave no one alive!"

At that pronouncement, Hannah lost all her self-control. She swayed into Lazar's arms. While he attempted to calm her, Vera began to beat her fists against the wall to vent her frustration and anger.

The opened door was a signal to others who looked to Lazar as their leader, and soon his compatriots flowed in, each with his own terrible tale of brutality.

"They beat me in the street, but I rolled to the gutter and dipped my head in a pool of water," wailed one student whom Hannah recognized as Rechtman from the café. "The water revived me, but I lay as still as possible so they wouldn't come back to me. When the noise in that section ceased, when all I could hear were the moans of the other victims, I dared to stand. As long as I live I shall never forget that sight.

"And the women . . ." He babbled uncontrollably. "One gymnasium pupil who saw his mother attacked by these fiends threw himself upon them. He saved her honor at the cost of his life."

"What happened to him?" Hannah was mesmerized by the horrible details.

"He was killed and his mother's eyes were put out. Then the drunken hordes broke into the synagogue, the small one behind Semyonovka, got hold of the Torah scrolls, tore them to shreds, trampled them. The old beadle who tried to shield the ark with his body was knifed and left to die."

"Didn't anybody try to stop it?" Lazar demanded.

"No!" Rechtman rasped. "Do you know what I saw? Police, even gentlemen, indifferent to the terrible deeds."

"That's not possible . . ." Hannah protested.

"No? Some say they saw Von Raaben, our esteemed governor of Bessarabia, being begged by a delegation of Jews. He was heard to say he could do nothing until he had instructions from Petersburg!"

"Enough! Enough!" shouted Lazar. "No more!" He pointed to Vera and Hannah, who both put their hands over their ears.

"All our work, our organization, useless." Rechtman held his palms outstretched.

Lazar clasped Rechtman's hands between his own. "We must see who is alive."

"Mama . . . the girls, my aunt . . . Lazar, I must know," Hannah sobbed.

"How many here are able to work with me?" Lazar took command. "Let's get our wagons, carts, blankets, rags, whatever. We'll do what we can. Vera, if anyone is lost or seriously injured have them brought to the Guild Synagogue. Can you arrange that?"

"Yes, I want to do *something*." The girl looked crushed.

"Good. Now Hannah, let's go home. I promised to take you home."

# · 5 ·

THERE WAS A FULL MOON that night. An acrid column of smoke rose in a visible sentinel from the western sector of the city.

"Thank God Papa is not alive to see this!" Hannah's voice was steady.

Though Lazar steered the cart around back streets to avoid the smouldering Razamovsca and approached Melnitsky Square from the opposite side, he could not escape evidence of the pogrom. They saw faces hollowed-eyed with fear and smelled the odor of charred bodies.

As they rounded the corner before the Blau house, Hannah gripped Lazar's arm. "If only someone has been spared, if only they could by some miracle still be alive . . ."

The gas lamps were still lit. Not a single house was burning. In front of the house on the corner of Melnitsky and the Razamovsca lay a twisted iron bedstead, pieces of wooden chairs, broken bags of flour and grain, and a crushed wire birdcage. Number 44 was dark. The parlor and shop windows were broken. Hannah recognized the furnishings, which were strewn around the lime tree like unwanted playthings. The velvet sofa had been brutally disemboweled, its horsehair stuffing blowing in the evening breeze. A great mess of kitchen garbage defiled the front steps, which were usually so immaculate from Mama's scrubbing; and worse, Papa's treasured Austrian sewing machine had been tossed through the shop window and lay like a corpse on the pavement.

Bending to touch the dangling treadle, Hannah sobbed, "It's over, they're all gone."

"They might have escaped." Lazar lifted Hannah to her feet and helped her walk to the door.

Before pushing it open, they listened. "I don't hear anything! Not even one has survived!"

At first they were accosted by a penetrating smell of vomit and feces that soured the once spotless home. Hannah coughed and choked while Lazar lit a parlor lamp. In the eerie light she saw torn coverlets with their costly down scattered everywhere. Hannah lifted each, searching for bodies.

"Where are they?"

"Since there hasn't been time to take anyone away, they must still be alive."

"How can you think that? . . . after this!" Hannah held up a quilt stiff with clots of blood.

"Hush!" Lazar commanded as he put his ear to a wall in the kitchen.

"What is it?"

"Shhhh!" He listened again. "I think I hear something!"

"The basement!" Hannah pointed to the door that led down to the fruit cellar, where Papa had kept pickles floating in brine, crocks filled with his own plum wine, baskets of potatoes and apples.

"But it is still locked from this side!" Lazar pointed to the board that lay across two wooden L's to hold the old warped door shut and prevent the damp basement air from chilling the kitchen. When he attempted to pull it away, it wouldn't budge.

"The bolt is hammered in!" Hannah exclaimed.

Lazar felt around the edge of the door until he found the true latch, but it was locked from the inside.

"Mama! Mama! It's Hannah. It's me!" she screamed and beat on the door. "Are you down there? Answer!"

"Hannah? Hannah? Are you there? Thank you, our Father in Heaven, for protecting and delivering you to us!"

"Is it over?" Aunt Sonia cried.

"Let me out of here, Mama," sobbed Eva. "Let me out!"

In a moment the door swung open from the inside, knocking Lazar in the jaw. The children blinked in the moonlight that streamed into the kitchen window. Mama clutched Hannah and held her close. "I told you this was coming! It was my preparations for just this day that kept us all safe. Have you eaten, Lazar? Hannah? I had enough food in the basement to live for days."

"Mama ... no ... we aren't hungry ..." Hannah realized Mama was oblivious to the extent of the pogrom. "I don't understand what happened here." She gestured to the destruction in the house.

"I always knew this was coming. I had a plan," Mama explained.

"I don't know how she did it," Aunt Sonia continued. "Your mama was like a madwoman, ripping at the furniture, tearing at the bedding with her chicken knife."

"And I missed it all!" complained Eva. "I had to bring the food and blankets and clothes and stay down there with Dora. And Dora kept screaming, until Mama brought the tea."

"The tea?" Hannah asked.

"I saved some laudanum for this. I gave it to Sonia and the girls so I could finish the job!"

"Mama!" Even Hannah was shocked at the depth of her premeditation.

Now Mama relished the telling. "First I killed the chickens, the ones you always said were so foolish to keep because they never laid enough to pay for their feed. Finally they earned their keep! I used their blood, everywhere, then hid their bodies in the cellar. When the shouts got closer I made my own pogrom: tore up our quilts, broke the lamps, whatever I could imagine the bastards doing. I never planned to throw out Papa's machine, the finest in Odessa. But I tried to think like a pogromchik who would see it, try to carry it with him ... it would be too heavy ... he would become angry that he couldn't have it ... so he wouldn't want the Jew to have it either ... out the window with it! You think that was easy to do?

"Then I made my combination: pickle juice, buttermilk, stale bread, meat scraps, which I poured onto the steps and into the front room."

"But why would you do something like that?" Lazar asked, incredulous as he realized the extent of Mama's foresight.

"I thought about it for a long time, even after the cellar door was ready. If you were a ruffian, even a Cossack, you might need to drink a little too much before you could really work up enough . . . I don't know, but whatever it takes to do such things. And then, after you did what it was that they do, after you stumbled out of the house, might you not be sick with yourself or at what you had seen and done?"

"Will you join our self-defense group?" Lazar said, kissing Mama. "You certainly might teach us a thing or two!"

"Tell me now, were many families hurt?"

"Mama Blau," Lazar began with respect. "I don't know what to say."

Mama removed her soiled apron and rolled it like a sausage. "How bad can it be?"

"The Razamovsca is gone . . . burned to the ground." Lazar began slowly.

"Is the midwife here?" came the shout of a boy who stumbled into the parlor. They recognized him as a clerk from Leyb Meyerov's store.

"R-R-Rayzel . . . her b-b-baby . . ."

"It's Cousin Rayzel's baby they want me for!" Hannah gasped. "Bubbe told me about her, but she's not due this soon. Lazar, can you take me to her? I'll get my instruments."

"Where to?" Lazar asked the boy.

"The Guild Synagogue. It's like a hospital now."

They took the fastest route up the Razamovsca, where hysterical families moved from corner to corner identifying and claiming the victims. Lazar counted shrouds.

"Must you make it more horrible than it is?" Hannah asked.

"Yes! I plan to gather every name, list every wound, every indignity. I won't let them forget!"

❖  ❖  ❖

No expense had been spared by the elite merchants who had constructed the Guild Synagogue forty years earlier. The elaborately carved and tiled façade featured two enormous pillars, each topped with a bronze Star of David.

Hannah was led into the vestibule. Beneath the steps leading up to the women's gallery, Leyb Meyerov rocked and prayed over his

young daughter-in-law whose head was swathed in a thick cushion
of bandages. Blood still oozed from her battered skull and formed
red rivulets in the grouting between the enameled floor tiles.

"Gilda, Gilda, what should I do?" Meyerov called out to someone who obviously wasn't there.

Kneeling beside him, a plump woman, with breasts as broad as a
shelf, prayed aloud.

"Who is that?" Hannah whispered from the doorway.

"My mother, Sussa-Henna," the boy answered.

"Go to her." Lazar pushed Hannah toward the prostrate girl.

"Don't leave me here alone!"

"Hannah, my first obligation is to you, now and always. But I
cannot help that girl. I must find out more about this, help bring
in the wounded!"

"Please don't do anything foolish. And come back for me."

Hannah knelt on the mosaic floor beside the dying girl.

"I am Hannah Blau, Sonia's niece. I've come to help Rayzel."

Leyb Meyerov, Hannah's uncle by marriage, did not acknowledge her, but Sussa-Henna said, "Rayzel is like my own daughter;
we have lived in the same courtyard since she was born. She and
Abraham were married less than a year."

Hannah felt Rayzel's pulse, which fluttered intermittently like a
bird's soft wings. She gently turned the girl's head and noticed a
large concave area and something sharp, probably bone, protruding in two places beneath the wrappings. Placing her hand over
Rayzel's mouth to monitor her respiration, she asked, "Do you
know what happened?"

"The worst thing in the world! How can I say it?"

"I must know, if I am to help."

"I saw it all . . ." she said, and then, between her tears and
curses, told the tale. "We were baking cakes, a party for Abraham
we were going to have. Today he would have been seventeen. Born
and died on the same date!" she wailed. "They came after Rayzel;
one of them had a large knife. First Abraham tried to beat them
off, but what could he do? A soldier he's not! They cut him in
slices like a roast; you wouldn't know him if you saw the body . . .
Then they tried to have their way with her, but she was so big with

child they couldn't manage it, so they held her and forced her to watch while they raped her mother-in-law. But Rayzel closed her eyes! They ordered her to open them, and when she wouldn't, they rammed her head into the wall, over and over, until she collapsed."

"And what happened to Aunt Gilda?"

"When they were done with her . . . kkkkkluch." She made an ugly sound and graphically drew her hand across her throat.

"And you? Where were you?" Hannah accused the poor woman.

"I was there; others were too. They went right by; someone else caught their attention. I don't know why!"

Shaking from the impact of these details, Hannah tried to control herself by focusing on the patient. As she lifted Rayzel's tissue-thin eyelids, the pupils did not react to the light. Hannah removed her stethoscope from her case and listened. "The baby . . . is it alive?" Sussa-Henna asked.

"Yes, yes, it is." Hannah sighed with relief when she heard the faint beat of fetal life. "The baby is alive, Uncle Leyb."

"Do you hear that, Gilda?" he spoke as though his wife were still beside him. "The baby will be fine."

Listening more carefully, Hannah counted seventy-five heartbeats the first minute, then eight-five, and back to eighty. The normal fetal heart rate should range between 120 and 160 beats per minute. The baby was surviving, but just barely.

As discreetly as possible, the midwife checked the girl vaginally to see if there were any signs of labor having begun, but her cervix was as tightly closed as would be expected at that time in her pregnancy. Taking a cloth tape, Hannah measured the size of her abdomen from the top of her pubis to the highest part of her uterine wall and made some calculations. The baby was not expected for at least another month. Then she palpated the uterus to ascertain the position and approximate size of the baby. Hannah double-checked her estimates.

"This baby is already four or maybe five pounds."

"Could it live on its own now?" asked Sussa-Henna.

"I believe it would have a chance."

"What are you going to do?"

"I don't know." Hannah watched Leyb Meyerov, who still had not acknowledged her presence but who, Hannah was certain, had been listening to every word.

"Uncle!" Hannah said loudly, as though he were hard of hearing. "Uncle, do you want this child?"

"Gilda says to tell you that we must save the candlesticks and the baby. That's all that's left," Meyerov answered obliquely.

"You have other children . . ."

Sussa-Henna shook her head and held her hand over Hannah's mouth to prevent her from saying too much.

"All of them?" Hannah pushed the plump fingers away.

Her fleshy face, soft as fresh dough, trembled in response. "If this baby is a boy, it is the last of all the Meyerovs. The brother in Moscow has only girls."

"I don't know if I can do it."

"You don't know how?"

"I know the technique, but the baby is so weak. It might not last much longer . . . and . . . I would have to take the baby now if it is to have any chance at all."

"Before the mother is gone? Is that permitted?" asked Sussa-Henna.

"I don't know."

"Stay with them. I'll find someone who will know what is right."

In a few minutes Sussa-Henna returned with Reb Herska Itche, the head of the local yeshiva, teacher to both Chaim and Lazar, and the new Polish rabbi, Reb Shmuel Baltermantzer.

"She will not live through the night," Itche decreed, cracking his knuckles.

"Do we know for sure?" asked the Polish rabbi, who was revered for his impatience with shallow interpretations and superficial explanations of the Talmud. Then he questioned Hannah as to the condition of the mother and baby, pressing for every detail. "So you are certain that this child will die before the mother?"

"Unless there is a miracle."

"And the mother, could she survive this wound?"

"Look for yourself, Rabbi." Hannah rotated Rayzel's skull to reveal the pulpy hollow area that had totally absorbed the bandages.

The learned men whispered among themselves. Finally, the Polish rabbi addressed Meyerov. "The law is very clear on one point: we must never take the mother to spare the child. But now we are convinced the mother, may she be forever blessed, will surely die. So the question is this: shall we take her baby before she is gone? No doubt it would be best to wait, but in this case we will also lose the baby."

"And so we turn to the commentaries that refer back to the time of Maimonides," continued Reb Itche. "The subsequent law is based on a criminal who was sentenced to die in the last month before her child would be born. So that the baby would not be punished for the sins of its mother, it was taken from her just before the execution commenced. Since that time, the rule has been that if death for the mother is certain, and if there is a reasonable expectation that the child might live, it is permissible to do whatever is necessary to bring the baby promptly forth."

"Do you understand, Reb Meyerov?" asked the Polish rabbi. Meyerov nodded that he did.

"You have lost much today," the rabbi continued. "This baby may be all you have left, but you must answer this one question: If this poor girl were your own daughter, would you want the baby taken from her body?"

"How can you ask such a thing?" Hannah was shocked.

"Hush!" demanded Sussa-Henna. "It's not for a woman to decide!"

Anger flushed Hannah's face.

After much hesitation Meyerov began to speak. "I have thought . . . I asked Gilda what she would want . . ."

"Gilda is dead, dear friend," the rabbi said firmly. "You must decide alone, for you will be the one to most regret this act if the baby doesn't survive."

"Yes, I know, and I also know that life must have a chance; even the tiniest spark might become a flame. For the sake of all who have perished, and for mine as well" — he turned from the rabbi and looked across Rayzel's limp form to Hannah — "do what you must."

## · 6 ·

THE MEN WERE BANISHED to their prayers while Hannah made the preparations for surgery, regretting that her only experiences with the knife had been during dissection.

Every decision she would make would be based on doing her best for the child. The mother could feel no pain, for all the prodding and probing had not disturbed her. Sussa-Henna brought a basin of hot water and a pitcher of cold. Hannah washed herself fastidiously and ordered the woman to do the same. Then she washed Rayzel's hard abdomen and draped clean sheets around her, covering even the mother's wounded head.

"Do you know how to make wrappings for an infant?"

"Yes, I've had seven of my own."

"Then do that. You'll take the baby from me. Place the cleanest cloth in the center and cover it with a sheet for now."

Not having a proper set of surgical instruments at her disposal, the midwife had to make do with a standard delivery kit. Slowly she unwrapped her boiled instruments from their sterile packs and laid them on a towel in the order she thought she would need them. She lifted the cutting tool and set it down again. She was not ready, not yet ready.

"Shouldn't something be said?" she asked Sussa-Henna.

"Boruch ato adonoy elohenu melech ha'olom," Sussa-Henna prayed. "Blessed art thou, O Lord our God, King of the Universe, who giveth life and healeth the sick."

Then conceding to the ancient rituals that might still have some validity, Hannah untied all the knots in Rayzel's clothing to permit an easy birth and drew with her finger, because she had no chalk, an imaginary circle around the mother.

There was no more time. Hannah lifted the scalpel and steadied herself. The first cut was a razor-thin line to open the belly wall.

Detached, Hannah watched a thin river of red form and followed the vivid drops down the arch of Rayzel's white hips. Forcing herself to concentrate on the task, Hannah reached for her scissors and cut from the pubic bone up eight inches to the left of the navel, through the thin layer of glistening fat, until she felt resistance. Pausing, she soaked up some of the blood with boiled rags to clear her view. Then, slowly, she revealed the transparent peritoneum and observed the pale pink womb with loops of intestine draped over it.

Now she had to decide where to cut to best protect the child living within. She stroked the uterus looking for the precise spot to insert the scalpel. Placing her thumb on the surface of the swollen balloon, she pressed inward. "No baby here!" she said aloud just before puncturing it. A bloody geyser of fluid shot into the air and showered her and Sussa-Henna, who gasped in surprise.

"That's normal," Hannah explained. Then, cutting between two fingers to steady her scissors, she enlarged the uterine cut at the top of the womb and worked downward until she found a leg, which she grabbed tightly and lifted into the air. Foot, ankle, cord, belly, shoulders, and head were born. A tiny boy, the last hope of the Meyerovs, lay limp on his dying mother's abdomen. Before tying the cord, Hannah again raised him aloft and, supporting his head, listened for him to cry, but the only sound was a wet gurgle. Holding him upside down, she stroked his neck downward to clear his windpipe. He gasped and shuddered. Then she inserted a thin tube, sucked fluid from his mouth, and spit it to the side in the rhythm of a train starting down its track; "Pssht . . . pssht . . . pssht . . ." Finally, she reached in with her forefinger and wiped the mucus off his palate. A weak but genuine cry issued forth. "That's a good baby, good baby. Come now, baby, do it again." The baby's cry sputtered and stopped. Hannah sprinkled cold water from the pitcher across his face. He wrinkled and grimaced, then gave a more passable screech. "Take the baby, wrap him warmly," she said after cutting the cord and wiping his face.

"Will he live?"

"I don't know, but if we can keep him breathing till morning he'll have an excellent chance."

As Sussa-Henna tended the child, Hannah observed his tight

fists and hardy appearance. Then she turned back to his mother and wondered what kind of repair she should do. Even Rayzel's faint attempts at breathing had ceased. Over and over again Hannah felt for a pulse, but her cousin was clearly gone. As soon as she realized what she had done, she turned the scissors, still in her hand from cutting the baby's umbilicus, toward herself and rended her clothing in the traditional keriah, putting the mark of the broken heart on her outer garments.

"I've killed her! Forgive me!" she said with a convulsive shudder. "Blessed are You, Lord our God, King of the Universe, the true Judge."

And then, as a final service to the woman who would never know she had given birth, the midwife bound up the leaking abdomen.

No one could be found to carry away the body, so Sussa-Henna, out of respect for the deceased, remained with the corpse. One by one, other bodies were brought to the vestibule, and soon all the psalms and sobs mingled in one grieving voice and echoed through the streets as though the wind itself sighed the eternal syllables. "Yisgadal v'yiskadash shmey rabo." The words exhorted the living to have faith in God and his plan for human life. But there was little comfort even in prayer on Odessa's bleakest night.

· 7 ·

THE BABY, who was born on the same date his father had both been born and died, could have no other name but Abraham.

As soon as Lazar returned, Hannah wrapped the newborn against the night air and together they carried him home. For the first night of his life, when by rights he should have slept in the arms of his mother, the infant Abraham was tucked in beside the midwife so she could warm, comfort, and observe him.

In the morning she had Aunt Sonia combine a formula of boiled milk and honey and tried to feed Abraham with an eyedropper every two hours. But the infant choked and sputtered, not absorbing more than an ounce of the liquid.

"The baby must be nursed! If only I could will my own dry breasts to sustain him!" Hannah sighed.

"With all the confusion, how will we ever find a wet nurse?" Sonia asked.

An idea came to Hannah, and for a few moments she was angry at herself for not thinking of it sooner. "Go to Asher Zalman's and ask for Olga, the servant whose stillborn baby I delivered. No matter what she says, bring her to me," she ordered.

"Will she still have any milk?" her aunt questioned.

"I know some tricks to make it flow."

And so Olga was brought to her, protesting that her breasts were empty.

"How much did Zalman pay you a month?" Hannah asked the confused servant girl.

"Five roubles."

"Then we will pay you fifteen. All you will do is feed this infant and follow my instructions for his care. You may sleep whenever you wish and may eat whatever you like. You will live as a member of this family. Will you try it, then?"

Olga grinned and nodded, not believing her good fortune.

Hannah settled the servant in Aunt Sonia's bed behind the kitchen. The house was once again orderly and clean. Then she requested that a tray be brought with a large pitcher of beer and any delicacy Olga desired. She unbuttoned the girl's embroidered linen blouse to fully expose her large, globular breasts and then placed hot compresses over the generous flat expanse above the cleavage. "Drink this," she said, pouring the first glass of beer. "And a second," she coaxed. "Your breasts are filling with milk!" Hannah encouraged, stroking the spongy masses around and around, kneading the nipple area until it blossomed into a pointed little peak before she brought Abraham to be fed. His mouth opened like an unfolding rosebud, but the nipple slipped from his weak grasp. He cried in frustration.

Olga sighed. "He knows I am not his mother."

"No, he wants you too much. See how he's trying again."

At the third attempt he held on and began to suck.

"He likes me!" Olga stammered with pleasure. "He likes it!"

Hannah sat beside Olga, supporting the baby with her right arm while stroking and massaging Olga's breast with her left. Through the whole nursing, she crooned to the baby to keep him sucking, even propping up his chin with her thumb when it looked as though he might release the nipple.

"The more he sucks, the faster you will make the milk," she continued to reassure Olga. "So you must give him your breast the moment he wants it and let him have it as long as he wants. Do you think you can do that?"

"Oh, yes, I don't mind this at all."

"Then can I do anything for you?"

"Could I have a little more to eat?"

"What would you like?"

"Everything!" she said happily, a lacy blush masking her plump cheeks.

"Of course," Hannah replied, noticing with great satisfaction that Abraham was still nursing vigorously.

Not a mirror remained uncovered in all of Jewish Odessa. Almost every family had lost at least one member, and in some not a soul survived to carry on the family line. There were shortages of caskets, medical personnel, and bandages. Even the traditional foods of mourning — hard-boiled eggs, bagels, peas, and lentils, all round in shape to symbolize the circular nature of life — were scarce. Members of the community burial societies worked without cessation, and prayers beginning "Lord who is full of mercy . . ." were recited from dawn to dusk. Hardly enough friends of the deceased could be united to carry coffins or women found to prepare the Seudah Havraah, the meal of consolation. On each block a communal minyan was formed twice a day so that ten men could be gathered for the ritual prayers, after which they traded tales of both tragic and fortuitous coincidence.

Abraham brought life into a stunned family. The constant demands of the newborn diverted their attention from the horrors that surrounded them. He provided a reason for everyone's existence, particularly Leyb Meyerov, who, after losing his wife and four children, now lived in Mama's room, while Mama shared the spare room with Aunt Sonia and Dora. Eva slept with Hannah so that Olga and the infant could have the back bedroom. But, in fact, none of them stayed in their own rooms at night, wandering about instead to check on the child, starting at every sound from the street, rushing to comfort one another when the anguish became too much to bear alone.

Abraham could not be permitted to cry. If he wasn't being nursed at Olga's ample breast, he was carried and sung to by one of the family. At the first sign of any discomfort, three women would appear, ready to fight for the honor of his care, and more often than not, Aunt Sonia won the race to his cradle, where she would rub his back and sing a lullaby. While the song might put the baby to sleep, it tore the heart of all else who listened because it reminded them acutely of Sonia's barrenness, a state she had borne nobly for more than forty years.

❖    ❖    ❖

Lazar kept his promise and became the keeper of the grim statistics. Jewish Odessa, at his count, had lost more than 300 people. There were 2600 crippled, among them many who had gone mad from the horrors. The posters, printed in his cellar, called it "The Pogrom of the Century!" They listed the names of 145 widows and 930 orphans and guessed that more than 40,000 had been materially wounded.

The numbers meant nothing to Hannah. Nor could she grieve for everyone they knew who had been lost. Instead she focused her prayers on all the Meyerovs and their closest neighbors. She especially mourned and could not forgive the senseless loss of the woman who had inspired her: Bubbe Schtern.

In the Blau house it was not difficult to follow the commandments which decreed that all must either sit on the floor or on boxes during the seven days of mourning, since most of their furnishings had been destroyed. Lazar came daily, attempting each time to bring a few men to help form the minyan. On the sixth day after the pogrom, he brought a stranger for the evening prayers.

"This is my Uncle Moishe from Kishinev. He is my only surviving relative. See his cart outside?" He pointed to a high wooden affair filled with the largest barrels Hannah had ever seen. "He sells his sparkling wine to the bottling plants."

Uncle Moishe was a short, round little man with a pleasing face. His hands demonstrated that he worked the land, but he had the countenance of an angel. When he prayed with the men, everyone stopped to hear his clear tenor voice and later hung on the tales he told of Lazar as a youth, the beauty of the vineyard, and the trials of the rural Jews.

"I was in a neighboring town when we heard of the pogrom," he said, referring to the horrors the year before in Kishinev. "On the way to help my family and fellow Jews, we were met by a crowd of peasants and workingmen who had been aroused by a rumor that we were slaughterers marching to exterminate their village. A mob fell upon us, and killed about ten of us while the rest were beaten with hatchets and clubs. I was roped and dragged to the priest. He begged that I should be left alone, but the Katzaps made fun of him, pulled me out again, and started to beat me. The policemen began to tell them that they would answer for hurting me. 'Well,' said their leader, 'if that is the case, we will let him go. But before we do, that hound of a Jew must have a look at his fellow zhids.' So I was forced to behold the dead bodies of my comrades, and no matter how long I may live, I shall never forget that sight . . ."

"That is the reason for our self-defense groups, Uncle. Here in Odessa we are organizing. Next time . . ."

"Next time? Don't be a fool! Those involved in self-defense are punished the worst of all. You are so few, they are so many."

"So, how long will you be in Odessa, Reb Sokolovsky?" Leyb Meyerov asked to avoid an argument.

"Every year at this time I bring my wine to the three main bottlers here and each offers me the same price for a cask. There is no bargaining with these goyim who, among themselves, fix a price, exactly the same figure to the kopeck! This year I have a better plan!"

"You've chosen a poor time to try to outsmart the goyim," responded Meyerov.

"Ah, but you see, I will not even go to the bottlers. After all, what do they do? They fill the bottles and sell them again, making three times in profit. Already I have been to two tavern owners who say they will buy from me directly. My price is less than they usually pay and more than twice what the bottlers will do for me. A curse on those middlemen! They've worked me over one year too many!"

"You will go home a rich man, Uncle!" Lazar said proudly.

"Who is going home?"

"You are staying in Odessa?" Lazar sounded worried, as though his uncle's presence might hamper his revolutionary or romantic activities.

"Odessa! Never! You haven't had enough of Odessa yet? What is left here for you? What is left for me in Kishinev? I've lived through enough nightmares."

"Where will you go?" Eva asked.

"Guess, little one, guess!"

"America!" shouted Eva. "You're going to America!"

"May I go too?" asked Dora.

"Why not?" replied Moishe.

# · 8 ·

IN THE MONTHS to follow, each one claimed he or she had made the decision. Of course, all acknowledged that Moishe started them talking, planning, considering, but who was it who agreed first? Even Lazar would, many years later, attempt to take the credit, but at first no one and then everyone decided to leave Russia.

Not for twenty years, not since the pogroms of the 1880s, had America looked so promising. Russia was home, Russia they knew, but another land — who could tell what fortunes or miseries it held?

They talked. They considered. They argued. How to proceed with life in a land that clearly rejected them? How to walk the same streets without remembering? How to overcome the irrevocable loss? How to make a new life without the old friends? Should they rebuild or rebel? Should they remain or follow the tide that had gone before them, choosing exodus instead of reconstruction?

They compared every story they had heard, every periodical they had read. Mama Blau had an entire box filled with steamship pamphlets shamelessly touting the Golden Land where all men were equal under the law, where workers were paid their true worth and held in the highest esteem. Aunt Sonia had lists of families with relatives in America and quoted from their letters that spoke of opportunity but also described perilous journeys across the sea and less than savory conditions ashore.

On the other hand, Lazar referred to the *Russky Evrei*, a Russian weekly edited by Jews, which exclaimed: "By supporting mass emigration the Jews would be playing into the hands of their enemies, who hope they will flee from the field of battle."

"Don't you see?" Mama argued. "It will never change here!"

"Sarah, I know you are right," Uncle Leyb said, wiping his balding forehead to ease an eternal ache, "but I hear it is a corrupt land where the Sabbath is not Sabbath. Is it any wonder they say that when pious Jews leave Russia their final prayer is: 'And now, good-bye, O Lord; I am going to America.'"

"But Leyb," Aunt Sonia protested. "How can that be so? The letters I read tell a different tale, of yeshivas and synagogues, Jewish societies of all kinds. It's where all the great scholars are going. Will they not at least have kosher homes? Won't they observe the laws?"

"Yes, yes, I suppose you are right," he agreed.

"And Leyb" — Mama pushed another word in — "what about Abraham? If we raise him in the Pale what will become of him? Will he survive the next pogrom, or the one after that, only to be caught by the khapers and sent to the military before his bar mitzvah? Or if you buy his way out of that, will you also be able to send him to school, purchase a home for him, leave him your property? Maybe America will be better for him — worse for you, but better for him."

"Just look to his name for the answer," Hannah said with a sudden sense of revelation. "Abraham! What does that mean?"

"Abraham, the bearer of the promise!" Mama exclaimed.

"The seed of the promised land!" added Aunt Sonia. "Of course! Abraham offers us the promise of a new life. He has been spared by the Holy One for a reason, to convince us all to leave for the new promised land," she said with an unusual degree of fervor.

Uncle Leyb twisted in his seat. "How can I take a motherless boy to America?"

"In thirty days you can remarry. You aren't too old to be the papa." Mama tried to flatter him, for Leyb now looked ten years older than he really was.

"Take a wife? After Gilda? How can you even say such a thing?"

"Not a wife for you as much as a mother for your grandson. You think you can raise him yourself? What do you know from babies?"

"I know from babies," Aunt Sonia said in a voice so weak it was hard to believe she had spoken. But her quiet words rang out like a chime and everyone in the crowded room fell silent.

"And so you do!" agreed Hannah. "You've helped raise all of us, you've been our second mama." Hannah ran to her aunt, who was also the widow of Leyb's older brother, and hugged her.

Uncle Leyb appeared so startled by the idea that Lazar chose words he knew the religious man would appreciate. "What a mitzvah, what a good deed you would do! Remember what it says in Deuteronomy about the regulations for marriage? Is it not written that if a brother dies and leaves no child his wife should not marry a stranger, but should marry the living brother?"

"Yes, and do you recall the rest?" asked Uncle Moishe. "That if the brother's wife comes to him and he refuses, she should take the shoe from his foot and spit in his face!"

"Would you do that to me, Sonia?" Leyb asked with tears of mirth and pity filling his eyes.

"I would not!" she answered and turned her head aside to hide her great rush of emotion.

❖ ❖ ❖

Money! Tickets! Routes! Decisions! What to sell, what to pack! Leyb Meyerov had lost his store and its stock, his family and his home, but not his whole fortune. When it was all counted out there was enough for everyone to leave together. No one would have to be sent for later. Because Aunt Sonia was to marry Leyb, everyone felt she was reclaiming the inheritance that would have been hers had Simon lived, and as Papa's sister, she was correctly assuming the responsibility for her brother's widow and children.

Soon all decisions were determined by what would be best for baby Abraham. While a crossing via Odessa was longer and more costly by almost double, it afforded only one adjustment for the frail newborn. Most of the departing hordes passed through Brody, which had set up systematic depots to handle the crush of emigration, but word had it that weeks could be spent in unhealthy conditions in the Galician town, then again in the German ports. Even though they could expect to spend more weeks at sea on the Odessa route, they might very well arrive in America before their fellows who went by rail to Germany. Also the cost of the steamship could be precisely calculated, but who would know what bribes might be needed at the border, on the train, and in the feared quarantine in Hamburg?

Documents, passports, exit permits, tax stamps all had to be obtained in the weeks that followed. Moishe, the vintner, remained in his nephew's rooms when he too was not involved in the tedious task of preparations for departure, and this made it difficult for Hannah and Lazar to meet. But opportunities presented themselves here and there, since the Blaus were much too distracted by Abraham and America to worry about where Hannah went or what she did.

Lazar seemed almost too preoccupied with the political ramifications of the pogrom to find time to be alone with Hannah. If anyone initiated their private moments together, she did. Each time they were intimate she thought she had made a new discovery, found a better way to embrace him, experienced a more pleasurable feeling. Though Lazar was outwardly attentive and loving, she sensed that a part of him was not fully there for her; and since he would not be drawn into her plans for the journey or their future together, Hannah lived with a series of tentative assumptions.

Finally she steeled herself to ask him directly. "Lazar, are you having trouble getting your papers?"

"What papers?" He feigned ignorance.

"Your exit permits? Your visas? Your residence papers?"

He forced her to press the question. "Why do I need those?"

"Then you aren't coming with us?"

"How can I leave Russia, my work? I'll come later, in a few months . . ."

"If you don't come with us now, you'll never leave."

"I have a duty to more than just your family, Hannah. And what about Chaim? Don't you want me to stay until we know more about him?"

"That is unfair! You know the greatest pain we all feel is leaving him behind. But what can we do? He may be dead already."

"Then if that is your greatest regret, you need not worry about me."

"Lazar, I didn't say that at all."

It was useless to fight him. He was a master of argument and Hannah felt an incompetent contender in this war of words.

❖ ❖ ❖

All of Hannah's books had been packed or given away, except one: *The Matron's Manual of Midwifery*. Again and again she studied the engraved frontispiece, a drawing of Eve with a babe at her breast, and read the caption, "And Adam knew Eve, his wife, and she conceived and bore Cain." Then the book fell open to the chapter she was rereading for the hundredth time: "Signs of Pregnancy." Over and over she searched anxiously through the text for an explanation that would deny what she feared, but one could not be found. Though impossible to contemplate, it seemed she was pregnant. Nor could she determine, as she repeatedly counted days on the calendar backward and forward, if Lazar or Petrograv was the father. What did it matter in the end? Now that she could never return to Moscow, she no longer had any choice, and neither did Lazar. No matter what he said they would have to go to America together.

❖ ❖ ❖

Though Hannah had prepared a rational approach to Lazar, it was difficult for her to control her confused emotions. She willed herself to remain calm as she presented the facts.

"How do you know for certain that this is so?" he asked after he was confronted with her news while walking toward the Botanical Gardens.

"No one knows that until the baby is born, but there are certain signs that cannot be disputed."

"And which do you claim to have?"

"There are two kinds, the formal and the informal. Neither is more accurate than the other." Hannah stopped and leaned against a lamppost.

"Can't you know definitely?"

"My menses have not arrived. Some women are always irregular, although that is not the case with me. It could be caused by changes in climate, such as my move south, or illness, or a great disturbance of one kind or another."

"You have experienced all of these . . . Chaim's arrest, the pogroms!" He raised his voice loud enough to attract attention.

"That is possible, Lazar." Hannah whispered by way of an admonishment. "But there are other indications, such as changes in my digestion. You know I have been having problems keeping my food down . . ."

"Yes, but you haven't been well since the pogroms. That is natural considering everything," Lazar interrupted.

"I agree. There are also nervous derangements: ill-tempered moments, weeping without cause, insomnia. I have suffered all of these."

"Yet with reason, as I have mentioned."

"There are other physical signs only I would have noticed. My throat is always dry, there is a numbness in my hands and feet, a sudden sinking at the heart. And I have one of the most common hallmarks: an increase in the size of the neck. Haven't you noticed how tight my collars appear?" Hannah tried to stick her forefinger down the hollow at the base of her throat to demonstrate her words. "Some women can, by always keeping the measure of their necks, tell they are pregnant within a few days. It has to do with a sympathetic connection between the uterine organs and large nerves in the neck."

"Now that you mention that, Hannah, I think you are right,"

Lazar said, placing his wide hands around Hannah's slender neck. "You really believe that is what it means?"

"It is what I was taught."

"Then we have no choice. I cannot send you and my child to America without me. Even in the Golden Land there must be some oppression to fight, some workingmen's group to join. We must go and see your mama!"

"Lazar, I can't possibly tell her!"

"You cannot tell her that a match has been made? Does she not want another son? Do you think Uncle Moishe has any champagne left for a wedding?" Lazar said, breaking into a joyful smile.

"He was saving us a barrel, didn't you know?" Hannah smiled, unfastening yet another collar button, for her neckline had, almost instantly, become unbearably tight.

# BOOK TWO

❖ ❖ ❖ ❖ ❖ ❖ ❖ ❖ ❖ ❖ ❖

# Between
# Two Worlds

# I

❖ ❖ ❖ ❖ ❖

# *Geitel Belinsky*
## Delivered October 31, 1904

❖ ❖ ❖ ❖ ❖ ❖ ❖ ❖ ❖ ❖ ❖ ❖

## · 1 ·

O LGA HAD SENSED her importance in the family immediately. Outwardly she deferred to them, yet she did not hesitate to select the juiciest slice of meat, the largest potato, the first piece of cake. Hadn't they told her she must eat? Wasn't it her body that sustained their most precious possession?

Because she sat silent as she nursed Abraham, the family conversed as if she were not there, often forgetting her comprehension of their language far exceeded her ability to speak it. Long before she was told, she had guessed about America, but the Blaus did not know this.

"Someone will have to explain it to her," Hannah had said as she grated potatoes, her knuckles white with the effort.

Mama tossed some flour into the bowl Hannah was using and kneaded the potato mixture with her fingers. "She'll know soon enough."

Hannah continued, "We can't just assume she'll come with us. We don't own her."

Aunt Sonia, who was unpacking a blanket chest in the bedroom behind the kitchen, heard the familiar dispute aired again. She looked over to the bed where Olga lay on her side giving her left breast to Abraham. As the baby's belly became filled with warm fluid, his body uncurled like a flower opening to the sun and his sleepy face beamed in satisfaction. Olga's breathing slowed in concert with his as she drifted asleep. Aunt Sonia decided it was time. To gain the girl's attention, Aunt Sonia shook out an embroidered silk comforter and pretended to examine it. "I think this is worth mending and taking to America," she said slowly in Russian.

Olga's eyes fluttered open.

Looking down at the beautiful spread, Aunt Sonia continued. "Do you like this one with the flowers and butterflies? You could have it for your own, if you come with us."

Olga's response was immediate. "I will not go!"

"But why?" she asked gently. "You'll have a good life; we'll take care of you."

Olga pouted. "I want to go home."

"To Lodz? But what is there for you?"

Unaware of the conflict, Abraham had fallen into a deep sleep at the uncovered breast. Olga handed the baby to Aunt Sonia and spoke simply but forcefully. "I want to go home."

Aunt Sonia smoothed the baby's hair over his damp forehead and rocked him. "You miss your mother, is that it?"

Olga buttoned her blouse and answered, "No, she is dead."

"Your father?"

"I did not know him."

"Then why do you refuse us?" Aunt Sonia's voice rose in a mixture of anger and confusion. "How can you leave our baby?"

"I want to go home."

Aunt Sonia rubbed her brow and shook her head at the girl's stubborn replies.

"I don't kow what we will do, then!" she cried, so loud that Hannah rushed from the kitchen.

"What's wrong?" Hannah asked, looking at the baby. "Is it Abie?"

Aunt Sonia's face pinched into anxious lines. "Olga refuses to come to America! Any other Polish servant would envy the chance! Why does she refuse us this one small thing?"

Hannah noticed the firm set of the girl's mouth. "She must have a reason."

"How will our baby survive?"

Placing her hand on her aunt's shoulder, Hannah said in a comforting voice, "Go to the pharmacy and buy a glass nurser with the longest teat you can find. Then see if you can get any fresh goat's milk."

When her aunt returned Hannah demonstrated how to prepare formula from boiled milk, honey, and water. At the next feeding she sat with the squirming baby and tried to introduce the black rubber nipple into his mouth. Angrily he protested its approach, and with all the strength he could muster in his tiny fist he knocked the bottle away.

"Bring the honey!" Hannah called to Aunt Sonia. After coating her forefinger with the sticky syrup, she inserted it into the baby's tense mouth. He sucked eagerly until the sweetness was exhausted, but when she substituted the hated bottle for her finger he screamed as though he had been beaten.

Aunt Sonia wailed, "It's no use!"

"Let him have Olga for now. We'll try again when he's not so anxious."

But Abraham knew what he wanted. He wanted Olga. He wanted her soft breast, the nipple he had trained to deliver his nourishment in just the right amounts, the milk that was always the correct temperature and came from a woman whose smell, whose touch, whose love he trusted implicitly. And, as Olga knew so well, he preferred her to the three other substitute mothers who wished to claim him as their own. Even though the bottle and nipple were reintroduced every day, Abraham was adamant — only Olga would suit. Hannah inquired for another wet nurse, but during those difficult and confusing days none could be found.

When Uncle Leyb and Uncle Moishe returned one evening from prayers, their tallis shawls peeking beneath their caftans, they were greeted by Hannah, Aunt Sonia, and Mama loudly debating what would be best for the child. "You have tried everything?" Uncle Leyb asked in Hebrew.

Aunt Sonia's face twitched like a nervous squirrel. "Yes, she refuses, but she won't say why. She has no family to speak of, no prospects here. Why in the world won't she agree?"

"I think I know." Everyone turned toward Lazar's uncle. Moishe now took almost every meal with them and, in return, spent his time making arrangements, procuring documents, and advising on travel plans.

"What is it?" Mama Blau demanded. "What have you discovered about our little milk factory?"

Hannah chafed at the insult. "Mama!"

Mama shrugged her shoulders. "She's just so . . . so stubborn!"

"Uncle" — Hannah included Lazar's relative by using the honorary title for the first time — "what do you think?"

Moishe tugged on his grizzled beard as he answered. "I can't imagine why you have not guessed. After all, this young girl recently gave birth to a child of her own, did she not?"

Suddenly Hannah understood. "Of course!"

"Who do you think the father was?" Mama asked. "Some boy from Lodz?" she said, spitting out the word in the Polish manner so it sounded like "Wootch."

"I thought she had been in Odessa for more than a year, so I hardly think it could be someone from there," Hannah replied.

"How could she have an opportunity at Zalman's unless she met another servant, a Shabbes goy, or . . . ?" Mama's unfinished thought died on her lips. Whoever he was, Olga still felt more loyal to him than to the baby she nourished.

"If she will not be convinced, she leaves us no other choice," Uncle Moishe said darkly.

Aunt Sonia dabbed her wet cheeks with a corner of her apron. "But what can we do?"

"Her papers are in order. They required far less work than ours, since she is not burdened with the status of 'Jew.' Tell her nothing, be kind to her, and leave the rest to me."

"But, Uncle, what are you planning?"

"To bring Olga with us to America." And that was all he would say.

## · 2 ·

WAS IT RIGHT for them to take Olga's destiny into their hands? Hannah considered both sides of the question. After all, what future did Olga really have in Russia? Once her breasts began to cake with useless milk, she would return to being the lowest of servants.

Yet no one felt more strongly about self-determination than Hannah did, and so she deeply believed that Olga should be allowed the final choice. Hannah was pleased that, for the most part, she had been able to make her own decisions. Papa had been the one to encourage her the most. "There are things we owe to God, and things we owe ourselves," he had told her. First you must be a good Jewish woman, then you must find something to do for yourself. And if you want to be a baby catcher, be the best one there is!"

Those who had tried to make her into a doctor had been thwarted by circumstance. And even though she had resented leaving Moscow before she had been ready, Hannah was grateful that this had enabled her to keep her cherished status of midwife, the one decision for which she gladly accepted total responsibility. And now everyone thought she was so fortunate to have chosen her own bridegroom. If they only knew the truth.

Still, Mama didn't hesitate to brag that her eldest hadn't needed a shadchen to make the perfect match with an appropriate and scholarly boy. "We've saved two fees!" Mama began to sing as she rummaged in the tailor shop for trimmings for the wedding and traveling clothes for both brides.

"What about this English torchon lace?" Aunt Sonia asked, holding up a four-inch-wide piece with a pearled edge.

"Place it next to your neck," Mama said. Then, wrinkling her face, she said, "It's too young for you, Sonia; leave it for Hannah."

Sonia dropped it as though she had been burned, but her sister-in-law was insensitive of the hurt she had caused and went on, "You know what they say? The young marry because they are hot, the old because they are cold!"

Aunt Sonia's small ferret eyes danced back and forth. "Is that why you married my brother?"

"Not all of us are so lucky to choose who we wed. Not that mine was exactly a funeral with music!" she said before unwrapping another trimming package to see what was inside. "Look, here's a white cambric with a nice leaf pattern that would match your dress!"

Sonia wrapped it around her wrist and preened. "That's perfect!"

"Hannah!" Mama called into the front room. "Come see what we've found for you."

Mama encircled her daughter's waist with a satin bow while Aunt Sonia displayed the trimmings.

"Pick the ones you like best; it doesn't really matter to me. There's only one thing I care about," Sonia declared.

"What's that?" Hannah asked as she compared the cambric and torchon lace.

"I don't want to be married the same time, or day, or place as Hannah."

"But, Sonia, why?" Mama asked. "Wouldn't that be for the best considering everything?" she said, punctuating the last word to mean not only the pogrom but also the fact that Sonia's wedding was a matter of convenience, not romance.

"Hannah should have her own day, as I did many years ago when I married Simon. I asked Leyb and he agreed, for according to the Shulkhan Arukh one joy should not be made to interfere with another."

Hannah handed the laces back to Mama. "Whatever she wants is fine with me, but I like the cambric best. It's plainer, more suitable I think."

"Fine, I'll take the torchon," Aunt Sonia said, delighted to have her first choice. Then her voiced quavered. "Also, I want mine on a Tuesday. My first wedding was on a Monday. Even I should have known that was unlucky."

"Why is that?" Hannah asked.

"Because when God was creating the world, at the end of the third day He said twice, 'It is well.' But on Monday He did not say it even once," responded Mama.

Hannah sighed. "You believe that could make a difference?"

Aunt Sonia nodded. "I didn't when I was younger, but my first marriage lasted such a short time, who knows?"

"Then you shall have whatever you want," Hannah said graciously. "When shall it be?"

"The first Tuesday after the High Holy Days."

Mama did some quick calculations. "But then if Hannah is to have a lucky Tuesday as well, she cannot be married until the twenty-seventh, the night before we sail!"

"I don't mind," Hannah said, ready to agree to anything that would lead to wedlock and legitimacy.

At six each evening Lazar appeared for supper and then to take Hannah for a brief stroll around Melnitsky Square before returning to his rooms near the university.

"Did you know that Mama and Aunt Sonia have arranged for our marriage the night before we sail?" Hannah said as soon as they were alone that evening.

"Good, good," he said absent-mindedly.

"Don't you care?"

"Not about the time or place."

Hannah stopped, but Lazar kept on walking. He was almost a block ahead of her before he turned around. Instead of returning for her he waited until she approached him. "Is something wrong?" he asked.

"They say we are fortunate to have chosen each other. Sometimes I wonder if we are meant to make those decisions."

Pretending to be a puppet, Lazar jerked his arms and head. "Marry blindly and your wife will lead you by the nose; marry by choice and she keeps you on your toes!"

Laughing, Hannah cut the imaginary strings that held his arms, and he stumbled against her. "Can't you be serious about this?" she asked.

"There is too much else to worry me. At least when we are together I am happy."

"That is all I can hope for." Hannah's voice was sober. Changing the subject, she continued, "Sonia is acting like a real bride!"

"Well, she is one, isn't she?"

"Yes, but did you now that she is having her hair cut? She never wore a shaytl before, but because Leyb's first wife did, she's going to get a wig."

"Don't you dare cut off your hair!" Lazar warned Hannah.

"Of course I wouldn't do that, but they have been trying to get me to the ritual baths. I went with my aunt just to see what they did. What nonsense! Doesn't Sonia see how ridiculous it is? She is behaving as though this marriage will lead to something wonderful."

Lazar was amused by Hannah's puritan stance. "And why shouldn't it?"

"They are only marrying for the baby, not for each other."

Lazar laughed aloud. "You are a fine one to mention that!"

For a moment a frown crossed Hannah's face until she realized Lazar was not angry with her. "It's different with us."

"Is it?" He raised his eyebrows. "There is no reason, after a time, why they shouldn't have a real marriage. Your uncle will get lonely and your aunt, once freed from that terrible widow's posture, will show her charms. Whatever happened to her first husband?"

"Simon? He had been so ill even before their marriage, she had not wanted him, but obeyed her family's orders. When she first saw him she told her father, 'He looks as pale as death,' then wondered if she hadn't put a curse on him."

"And afterward did they get along with each other?"

"She had many comforts, but not much else."

"And no children?"

"No, along with his diesase he had a problem. Most of the time he couldn't, he didn't wish to . . ."

"Our problem is just the opposite!" Lazar rubbed up against her hip to prove his point.

Hannah pulled him by the hand to lead him back home. "No more of that until . . ."

"And why not? What could happen?"

"We should wait . . ."

"Hannah! You can't leave me to suffer for seventeen more days!"

"You are counting?"

"Of course, every day, every second."

"Oh, Lazar!" she said, flinging her arms around his neck. "I'll come to your rooms tomorrow morning. After all, you need help packing your things, don't you?"

"Tomorrow, then." He smiled so broadly he bared his square teeth. "But there will be other times for packing," he answered gently. "Plenty of time for that."

## · 3 ·

BECAUSE AUNT SONIA and Uncle Leyb were both widowed, they were married in the besmedresh, or study hall, instead of the main part of the sanctuary. The dim room was lit only by one window opposite the ark and the candlesticks set in front of the bride and groom.

Hannah held Abraham while the simplest of marriage ceremonies was performed by Rabbi Ziskind. In an attempt to keep the baby from crying aloud, she stroked the infant, whispered nonsense words, and played with his delicate fingers and toes, paying little attention to the betrothal benedictions. Instead she studied the dimpled hand clutching her forefinger and marveled at its perfection. Then with a start she remembered another baby: Avrom! Why, even the name was almost the same! Avrom with the severed thumb, the disfigurement that had saved him from the terrors of maturing in Russia. Remembering the promise she had made to herself years before in Nemirov, Hannah realized that almost in spite of herself she was keeping it by carrying her own unborn child across the ocean. As the ceremony ended with the solemn words,

"Behold, thou art consecrated unto me, according to the Law of Moses and Israel," a triumphant feeling welled up inside her and gave her a fresh certainty about the future.

❖ ❖ ❖

A week later, on the morning of her own wedding day, Hannah refused breakfast.

"Is something the matter?" Mama asked.

"Lazar and I decided we would keep to the traditions and fast before the ceremony."

"You didn't go to the mikva, you didn't cut your hair, and your Lazar only answered the call to read the Torah on Sabbath because there was no way he could refuse! I'm not complaining — you do what you want to prepare for your marriage — but why do you choose fasting? Do you have so many sins that need to be forgiven?" Mama baited Hannah.

"No, not many, but in case . . ." Hannah replied with a convincing laugh. The truth was she was feeling queasy.

"It's your day, you do as you wish," Mama said flatly. "Do you have everything ready? All our boxes to be stored in the hold of the ship must be at the wharf at noon. Anything you can carry yourself may be brought aboard tomorrow." She stopped at a sound outside the door. "There's Sonia's carriage now."

Aunt Sonia bustled into the room carrying a large round wooden box. "Here comes the bride!" Mama laughed as she opened the door. "Do you have everything ready?"

"Yes, my husband has already taken everything down to the ship," she answered, with an unmistakable emphasis on *husband*. "He wants to personally see it aboard. The papers are all in order; we each have our own little packet with our names imprinted! And, Hannah, here are some gifts from us to you." She opened the box and placed on the table a pair of brass candlesticks of simple design but unusually fine quality, a heavy mortar and pestle, and a matching set of three kitchen knives. Aunt Sonia whispered, "They belonged to Abie's mother. I want you to have them!"

"They've hardly been used," Mama remarked before she realized what her words meant.

"Thank you very much; they'll be the first things for our new home," Hannah said politely.

Perhaps it was only the dark wig that covered Aunt Sonia's silver-streaked hair, but Hannah was certain she looked years younger and wondered if their marriage had already included some intimacy. They had, since their wedding night, slept in a small room over Leyb's old yard-goods shop, even though it was furnished with the sad remains that had survived the pogrom and fire.

"Where are you and Lazar staying tonight? With the rest of us at Rabbi Ziskind's?"

"No, no," Hannah said nervously. "Moishe has had difficulty with Lazar's papers. There is one official stamp he cannot get."

"So what is one after the hundreds we have already?"

"It is the conscription waiver; they look for it first."

"Isn't there some way, for a fee perhaps?" Aunt Sonia suggested. "We had some trouble with the baby's documents, but now everything is approved. It was just more expensive."

"Believe me, everything has been tried."

Mama clutched the fabric above her bosom. "What are you saying?"

Hannah swallowed and hoped she could speak in a calm voice, for although Lazar had assured her his plan would work, she lived in terror of it failing. "Lazar has arranged to board the boat later this evening, after . . . after the wedding. He will hide himself with the cargo until we have sailed."

"Why didn't you tell us before this? We could have changed your wedding date. Now you will not have your night together."

"I just found out yesterday. We thought a certain official was going to help, but then he disappointed us." Hannah tried to sound nonchalant. "What is one night?"

Mama shook her head. "Have you ever seen a less anxious one, Sonia? Even you were more . . ."

Aunt Sonia seemed not to hear. "Hannah is being very sensible not to cry about something she cannot change. After all, it is only a matter of a few hours. Lazar will be able to take care of himself. I am more worried about . . ." She tossed her head in the direction of Olga's room.

"Shhhh!" Mama put her finger to her lips. "Don't you know better yet?" she continued in Hebrew.

"Do you know what is planned? Moishe tells me nothing."

"He showed me the girl's papers; they are in order."

"But she thinks she is going back to Zalman's. She said their driver came for her things."

"It's good she believes that," Hannah said. "I've even been teaching her how she can dry up her milk."

"Are you certain she doesn't suspect?" doubted Aunt Sonia.

"Not a thing! Every hour she kisses the baby good-bye and weeps into his blankets," Mama answered.

"But how . . . ?" Aunt Sonia stopped as Olga, plumper than ever, appeared in the doorway to see if a meal was ready yet.

"Sit, sit, Olga, taste some of my wedding treats." Hannah pulled out a chair for the apple-cheeked wet nurse. "Tonight you will dance with us, won't you?"

Olga nodded in agreement before stuffing her mouth with nuts and apricots.

## · 4 ·

"MAZEL TOV! MAZEL TOV!" The words resounded in the synagogue after Lazar stamped the traditional wine glass at the conclusion of the ceremony. Then, with Mama on one side and Uncle Moishe on the other, the bride and groom were led away from the congratulatory throng to a small room outside the sanctuary where they were given bread, wine, and fruit with which to break their fast in privacy. Their solitude was guarded by two witnesses outside the door that led to the hall where the festivities would be held.

"I'm starving!" were Lazar's first words to his bride.

"Maybe that's why I feel so . . . I don't know."

Lazar handed her a wine goblet. "You look very pale."

She sipped while he cut the bread for them both. Keeping their distance from each other, they hastened to chew a few pieces.

Hannah surveyed the confining room. "What are we supposed to do in here?"

"What do you think?"

"Here? With everyone we know waiting in the next room? There isn't even a place to lie down!"

"So now you are getting particular about where and when, my little wife!"

Hannah couldn't resist smiling at his new name for her. "Just as long as you don't start calling me 'little mother' too soon."

"Who's to know?" Lazar took her in his arms and kissed her face and neck, and bent his knees to kiss her breasts. "Who's to care?"

"Lazar! Do you really plan to . . . ?"

"No, no. We remain here a few minutes while the guests go to the hall and prepare for us. Maybe long ago our grandparents used a room such as this one as it was intended, but I think the true reason that the newlyweds were cloistered together was that it was usually the first time the bride had a really good look at her groom."

"Can you imagine marrying a total stranger?"

"My mother said that she only saw my father from a distance as he was led into the town before the ceremony, and they had a good life together."

For a moment Hannah was startled by his words. It was the first time in many months she had heard Lazar refer to his parents.

He looked pensive for a moment. "Are you certain you are ready to leave? There is no one you will miss?" Lazar asked.

Hannah gestured toward the banquet room. "No one out there. Chaim doesn't even know where we are going, does he?"

"No, I arranged for him to find out after we sail. You understand that it would have been too great a risk to send the message first?"

Hannah nodded that she did.

"Then come, little wife, or our witnesses will start telling tales on us."

As Lazar led Hannah through the door, they were greeted by musicians sounding the fiddle, flute, horn, bass, viola, and drum. Around the room they marched to the music, displaying themselves to their family and guests.

Lazar was led to the head of the men's table to give the groom's speech, or droshe.

After reciting a bit of the Torah, he launched into an appropriate commentary on marriage, but was rudely interrupted by Abraham's lusty wails. Aunt Sonia was once again attempting to bottle-feed him, but he stubbornly refused the rubber teat. Finally Olga was summoned from her chair at the end of the bride's table, but not before all attention had been diverted from Lazar. Shaking his head in amusement, he raised his hands to give the blessing for the bread and then reached out with the signal to let the dinner progress.

❖  ❖  ❖

The traditional "golden soup" was served first to Hannah and then to all the wedding guests. But after a taste she placed the spoon beside her plate, for the flavor turned sour in her mouth. All of a sudden her head began to pound and a circular pain developed under her breastbone. No one seemed to notice her distress, and her bowl was replaced with tender flakes of boiled chicken, freshly grated horseradish, and a large slice of bread cut from her wedding loaf. This time she didn't even try to eat; the mere sight of the lifeless meat decorated with the weeping juice from the beet-red condiment made her stomach dance. But she was forced to sip from her wine goblet as the appropriate toasts were made.

Wine had never before made her ill, but perhaps it was because the sweet drink was the first thing to break her prenuptial fast, or because of her condition. Whatever the reason, Hannah prayed only that she would be able to last through the dinner without announcing her illness. She glanced over to the groom's table. Immune to her nauseous plight, Lazar joked with the men and heartily ate each dish, commenting loudly on its tastiness so that its preparer would be flattered.

After the rabbi's wife filled his plate with a third helping of prune and carrot tsimmes, she noticed Hannah had not finished her first. "What is the matter? Your husband says I must give you my recipe, but you seem not to like it at all!"

"No, I do, it's just . . ."

Loud enough for most everyone to hear, the rabbi's wife continued, "A real bride she is! She cannot eat a morsel! Didn't your mama tell you anything?"

All the women around the table laughed in one explosive burst.

"No, it's not that," Hannah protested weakly.

Aunt Sonia placed her arm around her niece's shoulder. "I never would have thought that you of all girls, with your education, would act so!"

"What does she know from the beginning? She only knows how to take care of the result!" cried Yetta Syrkin, one of Papa's oldest customers.

Again the women laughed, this time sympathetically, but the sound buffeted Hannah's aching head.

"Hush! Shhhhh!" called Eva, sensitive to her sister's troubles even though she did not know what had caused them. "Look, the badchen is ready!"

Despite their sorrow, Uncle Leyb had wanted Hannah to have a traditionally joyous party and had hired Beryl, the best storyteller in Odessa. He was known to be able to elicit tears as quickly as laughter. When there were no weddings at which to perform, he was also the undertaker. With a reference to his other profession he began his speech.

"You haven't seen me yet at a wedding? Maybe you know me better in another capacity? Tonight I will make you laugh as you never have before, and if you die, I will promise you another good job, for not one that I have buried has yet come back!

"I must first be serious or I only get half my fee. So let me say this, dear Hannah, dear Lazar: a man is like a flower of the field, today he flourishes and grows, tomorrow there is no trace of him. Do not waste a moment or you will live to regret it. Oh, and speaking of philosophy . . ." Beryl's face metamorphosed from the serious to the comic. "Do you know about Bernstein and Levy? They were sitting over their tea and saying nothing. At last Bernstein broke the silence. 'You know, Levy,' he said, 'life is like a glass of tea.'

" 'Life is like a glass of tea? Why?' asked Levy.

" 'How should I know?' replied Bernstein. 'Am I a philosopher?' "

The guests roared, but Hannah was preoccupied by the dizziness that threatened to overwhelm her.

"Now for our lovely bride I have a special story." All eyes focused on Hannah, and she did her best to force a smile toward the jester.

"Levine's daughter was married, and in due course the midwife was called to her home. There she lay moaning, 'Dear God, please help me!'

" 'Quick, quick!' Levine called in alarm to the midwife. 'My daughter's giving birth!'

"The midwife shook her head indifferently. 'Not yet, not yet.'

"An hour later she clutched the midwife's hand and wailed, 'Save me, dear bubbe, save me!'

" 'Midwife, my daughter's giving birth!' Levine cried, wringing his hands frantically.

" 'Not yet,' replied the bored midwife.

"A few minutes later a shriek ran through the house. 'Gevald! I want my mama!' cried the daughter.

" 'Now she's ready!' said the midwife to Levine and hurried to the daughter's room."

The room bubbled with laughter. "Of course!" Aunt Sonia said to prove she understood the joke. "A girl calls for her mama when she really needs help, doesn't she?"

After trying out his best stories, even the old favorites about the wise men of Chelm, the storyteller saw that the guests were tiring. He began to stamp his feet to alert the musicians to play.

As soon as Uncle Moishe pulled Lazar out onto the floor, the musicians changed to the flash tants. Placing a bottle on his head, Lazar looked toward the tin ceiling in an imprecation for help and then slowly held his arms above his head for equilibrium. Cautiously he raised a foot, then placed it down and lifted the other just as carefully. His brow wrinkled in concentration and everyone laughed at the tight expression on his face. The music swirled faster and faster, the company clapped in time, and his friends called out "More! More! More!" and "Steady! Steady! Steady!" in en-

couragement. Since he was doing so well, Lazar was expected to try
some tricks: leg lifts, hand clapping, stomping and kicking his legs
like a Cossack, until the bottle finally crashed to the floor. Other
men were called to the center to try their luck, and surprising everyone, Leyb Meyerov was the winner. Aunt Sonia broke out in
delighted applause.

Next the musicians began the mekhutonim tants, in which the
relatives of the bride and groom were expected to perform. Eva,
Dora, Mama, Aunt Sonia, and Uncle Leyb rose to stand for the
bride, while Uncle Moishe corralled an equal number of friends to
serve for the groom. The fiddlers began the mournful song "Hair
Nor Du, Sheyne Maydeleh" and acted out the roles in a pantomime so tender that it brought tears to the eyes of the guests
caught up in the meaning of the words.

> Just tell me, pretty maid,
> What will you do
> In such a far-off place?

> I will walk through the streets
> And will cry: "I wash clothes!"
> So that you and I will together be,

> Just tell me, pretty maid,
> What will your coverlet be
> In such a far-off place?

> The dew of heaven will cover me,
> The birds' singing will waken me,
> So that you and I together will be!

Grateful that she only had to observe and applaud, Hannah almost enjoyed the spectacle performed in her honor, but each time
a bright candle flickered in front of her eyes, or someone laughed
too loudly, or she smelled a freshly sliced piece of roast, she feared
she might disgrace herself by becoming sick at her own wedding.

Finally the moment Hannah dreaded most had come. Lazar
waved a handkerchief and called Hannah for the kosher tants, the
only dance done between the men and women. Since touching
hands in public was traditionally forbidden, even to the young
couple, the partners were given the corners of a handkerchief to

hold between them. As Hannah stood the room reeled. Lazar reached to steady her and the music began.

For a moment she was caught up in the rhythm and the clapping, the cheers and good wishes that filled the room. The beat got louder and stronger; the room shook with the laughter and stamping; the lights that hung from the ceiling swayed so hard Hannah thought they might fall. She concentrated on Lazar as he pulled her to right and to left with a mere twist of the handkerchief that flicked like a sail in the wind.

Please, let the song end, she prayed, but in defiance of her wishes, it seemed only to get faster and louder. She stared at Lazar: his blue eyes flashed like brilliant jewels, his chest heaved with the work and pleasure of the moment, and the front of his caftan was stained dark from the sweat of exertion. She lowered her gaze toward his feet and marveled at the precision of his steps, each one in perfect time to the music. She stumbled and faltered, but no one seemed to notice. Sensing something, Lazar pulled the handkerchief taut and stepped closer. And then she fell toward him, flinging her arms about his waist to keep from slipping to the floor. The spectators gasped. Mama rose and ran to her daughter, and together groom and mother carried her outside for air.

Mama fanned Hannah while Lazar supported her weight. "What is the matter?" Mama asked. "You haven't looked right all evening."

"I never should have fasted so long," Hannah whispered after she was propped up against the wall.

Mama felt her daughter's forehead with her lips. "I told you not to be so foolish!"

"You'll have to take care of her now," Lazar whispered to Mama Blau. "It's time for me to go!"

Hannah's breathing became fast and irregular. "But our wedding isn't over . . ."

"I must get aboard before the dawn and I haven't yet collected my belongings and taken them to the wharf."

"You could have done that before!"

Mama pressed her face in front of her daughter. "You'll see him as soon as we sail."

"Mama! Please!"

With a flutter of his eyelids Lazar signaled that he also wanted a moment alone with Hannah. Mama understood.

As soon as her mother stepped back into the festivities Lazar pulled Hannah close, covering her face with kisses.

"So they take your troubles for a frightened, inexperienced bride? Wait till I have you now that you are properly mine! I'll give you something to worry about!"

"Lazar!" Hannah pushed him away in mock protest.

"I love you!" For the first time he used the words Hannah had long hungered to hear. Then, giving her one last embrace, he turned resolutely toward the street.

"Lazar!" Hannah called in a choking voice as his hand slipped from her grasp.

"Wait for me on deck after we sail," he called back in the dark.

"Be careful . . ." she whispered to no one at all.

## · 5 ·

NO ONE SEEMED to miss the presence of the groom, except Hannah. When she returned to her place at the head of the table, she found that the pain had focused on the right side of her head and if she pressed three fingers into the spot the nauseating pulsations would subside. Suddenly her body craved nourishment almost as a replacement for her missing husband, and so she made an effort to swallow some bread and taste a honey-rice custard.

The songs and festivities continued. Hannah laughed and clapped when necessary and watched as the dancing became more frantic and less skilled.

While Abraham slept, immune to the din, his wet nurse was being entertained and indulged by Uncle Moishe, who made certain her glass and plate were never empty. Every once in a while, when her drinking would seem to falter, Moishe would walk her outside to refresh her, then would cajole her to have another glass of his famous champagne.

By midnight Olga's face and uncovered arms blossomed with splotches, and her eyes and nose watered so freely that Uncle Moishe was kept busy wiping her face with his kerchief. Oblivious to other aspects of the party, even to her infant charge, she indulged fully in the food and wine, believing that she never again would have an opportunity to have as much as she wished.

Along with the more inebriated guests, Hannah napped with her head between her hands on the supper table. At dawn the musicians began in earnest to wake everyone and lead them in a procession through the vacant streets. Out of the morning mist two hired carriages appeared. As they wound their way toward the port, Hannah tightly held the hands of her sisters, who strained for one last look at the Odessa they knew: the house on Melnitsky Square, the ruined Razamovsca, the faces of their friends and neighbors. Only Mama stared straight ahead.

The last to enter the emigration hall at the Port of Charbon was Uncle Moishe, supporting an exhausted and intoxicated Olga, who intermittently sighed and sobbed. Hannah was relieved to notice how many of the other emigrants were similarly distraught. Children cried in fear, women wept into their skirts, so Olga's distress did not attract much notice. In order to comfort the wet nurse, Hannah made one attempt to stroke her shoulders and whisper appropriate concern.

Uncle Moishe hissed his disapproval. "Shhhh! Leave us!"

"But why?" Hannah questioned.

"I want them to think she is with me."

"Oh!" Hannah replied, stepping back to the area in which Mama and her sisters were seated near the large arched window that peered out on the frantic dockside activity.

The sun rose higher in the sky before the officials arrived to check documents. A table was set up at the front of the high-ceilinged hall and two men took their places with stamps and papers, while a third read from the ship's manifest. As each family group was called, they approached the impassive faces behind the table, stood with feet slightly apart, and gazed down at the floor, answering yes or no to a long list of questions. The steamship company had to be thorough, for if any of their passengers failed inspection in New York they would be sent back at the line's expense.

As Hannah surveyed the room she noticed that the crowd was not an impoverished one. Indeed, those emigrants able to afford this long sea voyage had paid quite a price for the convenience. But there was also something strange about the mix of ages. There were children, young women Hannah's age, couples with babies, and many Mama's age and older. There were bar mitzvah boys and young fathers, but not one male Lazar's age. So it was true! They would not allow out of the country any Jewish man who could be conscripted.

The Meyerov baby was checked several times, but was given a health approval the third time around. Impatiently Hannah waited while Uncle Moishe and Olga were processed. Finally the Blaus were called and all four of them stood in front of the White Star Line's table. Hannah handed the first gentleman her ticket voucher, which he stamped. The second man, a professorial type wearing a monocle and frock coat, asked three questions. "Your name?"

"Hannah Blau Sokolovsky."

"Place and date of birth?"

"Odessa, fourth of October, 1883."

"Have you been vaccinated?"

"Yes," she said, rolling up her sleeve as the others had done.

Evidently she passed, for she was handed her inspection card, number 48885, with the large red letters JJ stamped in the center, and directed out the doors leading to the wharf.

She stood in line only a few places behind Uncle Moishe, who pushed Olga toward the gangplank where a sailor was collecting a departure tax before allowing anyone to board. After paying, Uncle Moishe prodded Olga to go aboard, but she refused to take another step. Uncle Moishe spoke firmly and lovingly, like any husband to a young wife who feared the great upheaval of travel.

"They always calm down after the boat sails," an officer said sympathetically.

Too physically ill from her revelries to defend herself, Olga wept and allowed Hannah and Moishe to push her aboard, mumbling "Misha, Misha, Misha!" all the way to the deck.

❖ ❖ ❖

Steerage on the S.S. *Haverford* consisted of ten large rooms. Hannah was directed to the last, JJ, which matched her inspection card. Wooden bunks wide enough for three people were built in three tiers around the room. Tables for meals lined the center of the steerage hall and sanitary facilities were placed at each end. Two narrow stairways leading to the deck were marked with arrows, one pointing up and the other down.

Mama moved and sorted bundles, unpacked some possessions, stowed others in so efficient a manner that one would have thought she had traveled by ship many times before. Hannah tried to comfort Olga, who was becoming hysterical.

Mama pulled Hannah away. "Leave her be; she'll get over it soon enough."

"I hope we haven't done something terribly wrong!"

"What's done is done," Mama said, clicking her tongue. "Let me show you what I have arranged for us."

With a final pat on Olga's golden braid, Hannah followed her mother across the hall.

"Your sisters and I will sleep together in the top berth. You and . . . you and Lazar will sleep below us . . . no need to share your bed!" she laughed. When Hannah didn't respond she said more softly, "Do you know so little that you are still afraid?"

"It's not that, Mama." Hannah didn't continue.

"I don't know about you modern girls, but in the old days it was worse. I didn't even know your papa when we wed, and look, it turned out fine. Yours is a love match with your mama's approval. No one could have asked for more than that!"

"Yes, Mama."

"Is there anything you want to know?"

"No, Mama."

Mama removed the lid from a bulging straw container. "Your things are in this basket," she continued, having satisfied her maternal duty. "And everything else, including our kosher food, is in mine. The valuables — the candlesticks, the brass — are all in the hold of the ship."

"Where will Aunt Sonia and Uncle Leyb be?"

"Right below you. I gave them the bottom so Sonia can get out to tend the baby or bring him over to Olga, who is sharing with the daughters of a family from Lvov. They seem all right, for Galitzianers, that is. And Lazar's uncle will be across the way with their sons."

"You've planned everything very well, Mama! And in such a short time!"

"Haven't I, though?" her mother agreed.

## · 6 ·

THEY WERE ALLOWED to remain on deck as the boat brought up anchor and sailed from the port. Hannah had never before seen Odessa from that perspective: the neat little houses along the quay receding from view, the quarantine port curving out to sea like a giant question mark. Before they rounded the bend she was able to catch one last glimpse of the promenade, the Glass Pavilion, and the Hotel Richelieu. As Odessa sparkled in the midday sun more than thirty church bells in the city rang their two o'clock knell. And when the last peal had died in the soft wind, Hannah felt she could finally look out to the open sea and the future.

It surprised her that Mama, who had instigated the mass migration of her clan, was the one who could not let go. She sobbed at the rail, grieving not for the city nor her past life in Russia. Only one name was on her lips: "Chaim! My son! Chaim!"

Eva placed her hand on her mother's heaving shoulders. "Mama, don't cry!"

"It's as though we've closed the lid on his coffin!" Mama screamed. "We've condemned him to death!"

Hannah's voice rose in anger. "Lazar has ways of keeping in contact with him!"

"Lazar and his 'ways'! Why is he escaping to America while Chaim is imprisoned?"

Though Hannah thought about the baby, she remained silent.

❖  ❖  ❖

The only meal served by the shipping line that night was a thin soup and a piece of overripe melon. The strictly kosher passengers ate what they had brought, but Mama, more pragmatic than most, could see no harm in the soup.

"They'd never put any meat in it anyway!" she said, passing out tin bowls and spoons.

Dora was full of complaints. "It's so hot in here! The melon tastes like garbage!" She held her nose. "Everyone stinks like dirty socks!"

It was true. Very little air circulated in steerage, and the room reeked from unwashed bodies, garlic, herring, salami, and tobacco smoke. The noise of frantic children, praying men, sobbing women competed with the clatter of the engine and the slopping water in the bilges.

As soon as she had finished her meal Hannah said, "I told Lazar I'd meet him on deck," and climbed the slippery stairway leading to the small section of the deck permitted to steerage passengers.

The sun had already set and a thin moon rose in the somber sky. Hannah wrapped herself in her flowered shawl to keep out the damp evening air and leaned against one of the large brass horns that fed air down to the lower decks. Only a few men were on deck, smoking cigars and talking seriously. The sailors responsible for the group relaxed beside the flags at the stern, although in the crush of departure they had scolded anyone who pulled on ropes or leaned against the rail.

Hannah waited expectantly, hoping Lazar would appear any moment. She walked from one side of the deck to the other, watching each doorway, for she did not know which stairway led to the cargo area. Had he found the hold unbearable during the heat of the day? How had he slept last night? Was he as anxious as she for their reunion?

The boat rocked gently, creating a pleasant sensation that stilled her anxiety. Waltz music rose from the upper decks. The first stars blazed out from the darkening sky, the only illumination in the whole world. The sea was an eternal blackness in all directions. Floating forever, she was part of an endless night, a timeless journey. The feeling of being in a place unlike any other excited her. The fresh pungent air stimulated her and she wondered if she had ever before felt so alive.

All her previous concerns belonged to the past. The book was forever closed on Russia, Petrograv, her medical education, even her love for her father and brother. Silently she listed her grievances against herself: fights with Mama, impatience with her sisters, laziness regarding study, lapses in religious feeling and practice, self-absorption with Lazar, and before him . . .

The doctor had never truly existed, she reminded herself. There was only Lazar, her husband, the baby's father. Surely he was the one! How was it that a tiny seed could grow to be a person? Any doubts about God vanished at the contemplation of His most miraculous feat: the creation of life. God was the ultimate father and he would see to it that the baby was Lazar's. Hannah comforted herself with the belief that Lazar must surely be the father of her child.

❖  ❖  ❖

Crouched beside a lifeboat, lulled by the sound of the lines slapping the mast, the splashing of the water against the bulwark, the song of the wind stirring the sea, Hannah slept with her head cradled in her arms. Startled by a hand on her shoulder, she awoke crying "Lazar!" But instead of her new husband, her eyes encountered a sailor who commanded her in German to go below decks.

Hannah shook her head to indicate the importance of her vigil. "No, no! I must wait here!"

Just as adamantly he pointed to the descending stairway. When she again refused, another sailor came and took her arm and led her firmly down to steerage. Everyone in that fetid room was asleep. She stumbled to her bunk and cried into the sack that contained her featherbed.

Where was he? Her fantasies began to frighten her. He was not aboard the ship. He had never intended to come to America! Where was he now? Probably celebrating his freedom with his friends: Makunin, Slavinsky, Rechtman, Gnessa, and . . . and Vera! So in the end Vera had been the triumphant one! Perhaps she had even supported the marriage ruse, knowing that a Jewish ceremony was not binding under Russian law. After all, Lazar had not given a straw for his religion in many years.

And his baby! Now it was hers alone. How would she ever explain its presence when there hadn't been time after the wedding to make a baby? Everyone would know; Mama would know. Her sin would be with her always; the child would suffer its whole life the stigma of being a bastard.

Hannah staggered out of her bunk and back up the stairway. The sailor barred her way until she indicated that she was about to be sick. Hannah felt a bitterness rising in her throat and a loathing that could not be swept away as she leaned heaving over the rail.

Unless . . . For once she stood in complete control of her future. She could jump and no one would really know what happened. It could be an accident, just another tragic accident. She stared at the waves that lapped like tongues at the stern of the boat. It would not take long. She'd float with the tide, away, away, down and down, then it would be over. Footsteps sounded behind her and then disappeared to her right. She waited. It was quiet. Now she would do it . . . now . . .

But the interruption had broken the momentum. Hannah stumbled from the rail. Tomorrow, I can always do it tomorrow, tomorrow. The word was a comfort as the thick smells of steerage surrounded her. "Tomorrow," she whispered to herself as she once again crept into her berth, "tomorrow."

# · 7 ·

A WHISTLING SOUND. A familiar tune. Close to her ear. Hannah remembered it as one of the songs from her wedding:

> The dew of heaven will cover me,
> The birds' singing will waken me,
> So that you and I together will be!

A hand stroked her damp hair. She turned toward the slightly parted muslin curtain, which framed an unkempt head and a frizzy beard.

"Lazar!" she gasped. "Where were you? What happened? I thought . . ."

"What did you think, darling girl?"

"I . . . I worried . . ."

"No matter. You cannot know how it was down there . . . rats and pests. I must find somewhere to have a proper wash or you will never let me into your bed."

"What took you so long? I waited on deck half the night, until they forced me to return to steerage."

"Remind me to never again pay someone in full before the job is done! The sailor drank away his profits on shore and then claimed he completely forgot about me until this morning. I had some water, some bread and herring, but I couldn't have lasted in that heat another day."

"How horrible for you! Weren't you frightened?"

He stroked her head to soothe her. "More lonely for you than afraid," he said softly, "and worried that you might not understand."

"You are here; that's all that matters."

"Come up on deck, it's a glorious day! We should be nearing the Straits of the Bosporus."

Like a turtle surveying the world outside its shell, Hannah stuck her head out from the berth. The smell that greeted her was rank with vomit. "Don't they ever clean down here?"

"What do you think this is, first class? Here passengers are to look after themselves."

"Only one day has passed and already it is impossible. What will it be like in a week? Who is in charge?"

"I don't know. It seems they wait for volunteers."

"We'll have to do something about that," Hannah replied and, holding her babushka over her mouth and nose, made her way to the stairway as quickly as possible.

Agreeing that the way to prevent seasickness was to stay out in the fresh air, Hannah and Lazar remained on deck, even through an afternoon shower. Hannah had draped her largest shawl around them both, and together they shivered and laughed as the rain splashed their faces and hands.

"I suppose this is the only bath I am going to get, so I might as well make the best of it," Lazar said, pretending to lather and scrub.

Hannah assisted by rubbing the raindrops into his face, and then, holding his cheeks, boldly kissed him.

"Aren't you too anxious, my little bride?"

"Aren't you?"

"I can wait . . . at least until this evening . . . no later!"

Even though they crept downstairs after midnight a voice called, "Hannah?"

"Yes, Mama."

"Good-night, Hannah. Good-night, Lazar."

"Good-night, Mama." Calling his mother-in-law "Mama" for the first time, Lazar realized his voice was more strained than sincere.

"Damn!" Hannah whispered. "She's still awake. That's why she arranged to have us sleep underneath her!"

"Hushhhh! We'll just be very quiet."

"But she'll hear something . . ."

"Then what do you want to do?"

"Wait till she's asleep."

"How will you know when that is?" Lazar asked, bumping his head on the low ceiling as he struggled to remove his trousers in the close quarters.

Hannah suppressed a giggle as he rubbed his head. "I know how she sounds when she's asleep. It's a soft whistle like this: Eeeeesshhhh, eeeeesshhhh."

"So we wait till your mama whistles?" Lazar said in a mocking tone. "If you must have it that way, but until then could we at least . . ." He continued undressing her slowly.

They took their time caressing each other, building an exquisite tension as they lay impatiently naked, listening for the signal to begin in earnest. Acutely conscious of every sound in the room, they heard snores, deep groans, baby cries, coughs, and choking noises. Wooden parts of the ship creaked with every roll, loose ropes flopped against the walls, and parcels slid back and forth along the undulating floor.

"How many are sleeping in this room?" Hannah asked.

"Let's see," Lazar said seriously, hoping the mental diversion would lessen his desire. "There are three levels; each has an average of three in a bunk, some more with young children, some less like you and me. Now, around each side of the room are twenty-five groups, times nine. So, in this compartment there must be about two hundred twenty-five people."

"And they all snore!" Hannah laughed, pressing her face into Lazar's stomach to muffle the sound.

"And your mama, is she among them yet?"

"I don't care anymore," Hannah said, easily slipping her body under his.

## · 8 ·

BY THE FIFTH MORNING conditions in steerage had deteriorated even further. There was only one washroom in Hannah's section, about seven by nine feet, containing eight faucets of cold water, four along either of its two walls, and a matching number of basins. These same basins served as dishpans for greasy tins and laundry tubs for soiled clothing and diapers.

There were six toilets for men and six for women, each but an open trough. Everything was filthy, sticky and disagreeable to the touch. Hannah witnessed people gagging as they attempted to enter the narrow spaces, even using the floor in their rush to be gone.

"How long will we have to endure this?" Hannah asked Lazar.

"Because of the various ports of call, weather conditions, and all of that, they do not promise an exact arrival date in New York. But they say approximately three weeks, though I suspect it will be longer."

"How will we survive it? The stench is worse every hour!"

"That is the least of it!"

"Why?"

"Last night on deck, I overheard some discussions. Some of the Galitzianers are upset. It seems some of their kosher food was stolen yesterday and they refuse to eat what is served by the steamship line. They plan to get even . . ."

"So what can they do? Make a pogrom? I thought we were leaving all that behind!"

"I am keeping my eyes and ears open. Maybe I can help."

"Of course you can. You speak almost everyone's language. You know how to organize people to work with you. It's not a revolution, but maybe you could prevent an uproar. The Lord in Heaven knows this is too small a ship on which to wage a war."

"Hannah, you are right! And the other problem . . . the toilets, the kosher kitchen . . . You worked in a hospital, you know the proper ways to do these things."

Lazar became their leader. It took only a few words, spoken boldly that night after the soup had been ladled from the large black kettles provided by the steamship line. Hannah would long remember his stirring speech.

"Brothers and sisters at sea," he began, demanding their attention by banging the soup ladle on his tin plate. A hush came over the room, but no one stopped eating. "Tonight we are but one body of people. We are not men or women, Litvak or Galitzianer, socialist or Zionist, not even Jew or Gentile. We are travelers sharing the same passage, all leaving behind friends and family, sorrow and pain. We all have the same uncertain future."

Hannah could sense the audience's response. He had their attention!

"In the Talmud it is written: 'When you change your habitation, you change your luck,' " he said. Then he explained the system he had devised for cooperation and sharing food.

His words made an impact on the devout, who were concerned that their kosher rations might not last the journey.

"Won't you each select someone from your group to speak with me about your needs? We will have a council to decide disagreements, committees to do the necessary work. Together we will turn this voyage around to prove we can all live together, freely, without the tyranny of the czar!"

Somewhere down in the nether reaches of the engine room, a loud clanking and hissing were heard. A moment later the whole boat trembled under the stress of a mechanical problem. The few lights swinging from the ceiling dimmed, and the crowd cringed.

Lazar raised his hands to calm the group and spoke in a loud, clear voice. "This is my wife, Mrs. Sokolovsky, a fine nurse." Lazar pushed a reluctant Hannah toward the group. The engine resumed a more natural hum and the lamps glowed brighter. The crowd's attention riveted on Hannah. "She will help with the sick, with the children. We must make this a clean and safe place for the sake of the little ones."

An old man held a bony finger in the air and asked, "What about us?"

"For everyone's sake," Lazar amended. "We must not succumb to idleness that will breed dissatisfaction and disharmony." Lazar's voice became less strident. "So, are you with me?" He lowered his head in a theatrical gesture to win them over.

Enthusiastic responses echoed in the room. "We are! Yes, yes!"

When the excitement had subsided, Hannah exclaimed, "What a gift you have! How do you know what to say?"

"I just spoke what came to mind."

"Everyone was with you; all of them want to make it work," she said, taking one of his hands in both of hers.

"Sometimes it is easier to get a hundred on your side than to convince one that you are right."

Hannah tilted her head to catch the focus of his gaze. "One man or one woman?"

"With a man I might have had a chance, but with a woman like you . . ." Lazar placed his free hand on top of hers, so all four of their hands formed a tower.

"I thought you had it very easy with me!" Hannah's eyes sparkled. She took her hand from beneath his and placed it back on top of the pile and squeezed him.

"If you call that easy, cleaning up this mess" — he gestured to the disorder in steerage — "will be nothing at all."

Lazar's plan succeeded. Crews of women cleaned the kitchen and toilet areas three times each day and were in charge of the sick and the meals. The older children and grandparents were given the task of tending to the youngest babies and children. The men kept active with study groups and deck watch, for during the roughest weather everyone had to be accounted for.

With the addition of someone's salami, another's onions, even the ship's broth became palatable. A large amount of kosher foodstuffs was uncovered, and the most devout were fed small but adequate portions each day and were allotted as much hard bread and crackers from the ship's stores as they needed. The fresh-water barrels were kept covered and water was doled out carefully to prevent contamination. The sickest passengers were segregated in the area next to the toilets and were tended by a rotating shift who emptied their bowls, wiped their brows, and fed them plain broth and sweet tea until they recovered.

The trip took longer than expected. The winds were not with them much of the time, calls at ports were delayed as freight was unloaded and loaded. Though steerage passengers were not permitted to disembark, Lazar and Hannah watched the sights and listened to the sounds of Istanbul, Athens, Palermo, Algiers, and finally Lisbon from their familiar position beside the rail. When the ship pulled out of Portugal almost three weeks from the date they had arrived on board, the Russian emigrants finally felt they were on their way.

Enchanted with the great ocean, Hannah hated to stay below. She believed there was no end to the expanse of waves or the variety of sizes and shapes they presented. While others screamed in fear at the power of the water, Hannah marveled at each new swell. As long as she watched the horizon, ate with moderation, and did not let her stomach become too empty, she felt remarkably well.

Each evening as the sun sank, Hannah would feel a wonderful surging in her heart, a tightening and drawing nearer to her new husband and new life. After dark, most everyone would appear on the small flat deck between the two belching funnels to smoke tobacco, air their clothing, and listen to the Russian folk songs filled with nostalgia and yearning. Then the others: Swedes, Norwegians, a few English and Portuguese would contribute songs of their own. The Norwegians mastered dancing on deck and their turning and bobbing transfixed Hannah. One slim blond cavalier would pound the deck in such an exuberant fashion that he took her breath away. Even Lazar noticed her absorption in the young man's performance and frowned in a definite expression of jealousy.

Each morning Olga awoke more petulant than ever, but by evening she would accept a sip of wine and then would join in all the songs. By the second week she knew every word and every melody, no matter the language, and harmonized with her surprisingly rich soprano voice.

As the deck festivities were ending on the night of October 30, Lazar and Hannah stood with arms around each other's waist.

"We should have taken a three-funnel ship!" Hannah complained.

Lazar was confused by the remark. "Why is that?"

"Well, if a journey takes two weeks in a ship with two smoke-stacks, it should take only one if it had three!"

"But Hannah," Lazar spoke sincerely, "I really don't want the voyage to end yet."

Interpreting his words to mean that their romance would somehow change when they arrived, Hannah said, "We'll still be together."

"It's not that." Lazar groped for the right words.

His hair, which gleamed like silver in the moonlight, blew across his face in the soft evening wind. Hannah held the shimmering strands back from her husband's face, noticing how the set of his protruding cheekbones matched the proud outline of his jaw.

"On this ship I am respected, I am the leader," Lazar said. "If we only had a few more weeks I could do so much with these people. We would all be united in a strong political front, we could . . ."

Lazar was interrupted as one of the ship's officers came toward them. "That's the one who helped arrange a larger food allotment in exchange for our section requiring fewer services from the crew," he said in Hannah's ear.

"Mr. Sokolovsky," First Officer Braden said, touching his hand to the brim of his stiff cap.

"Yes, sir!" Lazar responded in German, clicking his heels together with mock respect.

"Do you have any doctors among your group?"

"What kind of a doctor do you require?"

"In second class we have a couple, a Jewish couple, and the woman is going to have her baby. Upon boarding she advised us it was not expected until November, but now she thinks otherwise."

Hannah tugged at Lazar's sleeve. "A baby! My wife is a doctor, a doctor of midwifery. She studied in Moscow. I am certain she could attend the case."

"How fortunate! Is this your wife, then?"

"Hannah, will you go with him?"

"Of course," Hannah replied quietly, not wanting to reveal her excitement.

"Do you need anything?"

"My medical bag. Mama knows where everything is better than I do. Have her bring it to me and I'll go with the officer."

Turning to him, she spoke slowly in Yiddish, knowing he would understand since some of the words were almost identical with German. "Has she been in labor a long time?"

"They just wanted a doctor. That is all I know, ma'am."

Hannah followed him up the outside stairway near the forward smokestack and down the narrow passageway, which, in that part of the ship, was carpeted with a ruby wool that looked like a long tongue reaching down into an endless mouth. They made three confusing turns before reaching cabin B-56.

She knocked and the door opened immediately. Hannah stared at the strikingly handsome man who stood before her.

"I'm, I'm Mrs. Sokolovsky."

"We asked for a doctor."

Hannah spoke quickly to try to impress him with her credentials. "I'm a midwife; I've studied medicine at the Imperial College in Moscow."

"But you look so . . . so young." The man almost apologized for his doubts.

"I have much experience in both Gentile and Jewish births. I have even delivered noble ladies in Moscow," she added, sensing he was a man who wanted the best for his wife.

A tired woman, her thick wavy hair pulled back into braids, lay on a lower bunk, her face partially covered by the floral-patterned curtain that hung above the berth on a shining brass track. "What did you expect on this ship? A professor?" she asked her husband.

"This is my wife, Shifre, and I am Nahum Belinsky. We are from Nikolayev. Do you know it? My father has been in America for seven years now."

"His father is a big man with factories, buildings!" Mrs. Belinsky bragged. "Nahum! Move this thing!" she said, struggling to push the curtain from her face without sitting up. "He couldn't wait to get me to America!"

"I waited until your father said we could marry, didn't I?" Mr. Belinsky defended himself in a soft but firm voice. "Then it was your troubles, not mine, that kept us back in Russia for almost a year."

"That is too bad," Hannah commiserated.

"Terrible! My mama was dying. She took so long! We thought it would be only a week, but it took her almost a year!" she whined. "We could have been in America by now, instead of having the baby this way."

Belinsky ran his long fingers through his thick hair in an exasperated gesture.

Quietly Hannah stood aside while they bickered. Hannah felt herself unwittingly siding with the husband and not the wife, whose voice had already developed a scolding edge.

"Ahmmm . . ." Hannah interrupted. "Would you like to tell me what is happening?"

"What is happening?" Mrs. Belinsky asked, patting her belly as though it were obvious.

"Why you think the baby is coming," Hannah said in a controlled voice, which she hoped didn't reveal her impatience.

"It's tugging at me, pulling me down to the bed. You know what that means?"

"I'll have to examine you, then," Hannah said, for she knew no other way to discover what was occurring. Belinsky answered a knock on the door and in stepped Mama.

"Thank you for bringing it, Mrs. Blau," Hannah said formally, not wanting to introduce her mother.

"But . . . don't you . . . ?" Mama said as Hannah escorted her to the hall and closed the door.

"These are very odd people," Hannah said firmly. "I'll need to be alone with them."

"They must be rich to have a cabin like this! Just two beds! Their basins are china, not even tin like ours! Get some good food while you are up here, and see if you can bring down some white

bread for us. Since Lisbon everything has been stale. And with
their money they can afford to pay double your fee!"

"Yes, Mama. Tell Lazar I will be here for a while."

Knowing her stethoscope might make a good impression, Hannah unwrapped it first and checked the fetal heart tones. Gratified
to hear a loud and rapid beat, she said, "You have a strong baby in
there!"

For the first time, Mrs. Belinsky warmed. "Do you think so?"

"Do you have any other children?" asked Hannah.

"Of course not! We've been married less than a year. I got
lucky, if you call this lucky!"

"I'm certain that is in your favor," Hannah added to give her
patient confidence.

"During the last few days have there been any changes?"

"Some . . . something has come out of me."

"Blood or mucus?"

"Some of both."

"A lot of bleeding, enough for a pad?"

"No, little spots, I don't know what you call it. And my stomach
. . . lots of pains, they come, they go, they come again."

"Can you sleep through them?"

"She can sleep through anything!" Belinsky volunteered.

Hannah had almost forgotten he was in the room. Belinsky wore
an amused expression, which she blamed on her position. In order
to examine his wife Hannah was forced to kneel with her skirts
pulled up around her.

"Anything else?" Hannah asked, rising to her feet.

"Just that my bowels are very loose. So what can you expect?
The food on this ship would kill a horse."

Belinsky coughed and said, "It hasn't made me ill and we have
the same tray exactly!"

"You! Nothing would touch you!"

Hannah leaned on the ornate brass railing that ran down the
first part of the bunk to keep a passenger from falling out in a
rough sea. "Well, it could be your condition. Sometimes the baby
can make that happen. It helps to prepare you."

"I told you the baby is on its way!"

"Why shouldn't I believe you?" Belinsky retorted as he reached for a cigar. "What do I know?"

Hannah nodded to Belinsky and pointed gracefully to the door. "To be certain I will need to examine your wife. Would you . . . ?"

"Of course." He bowed as he left.

"Nahum! Don't leave me!" his wife shrieked. But he was already out the door.

The internal examination revealed that Mrs. Belinsky's cervix was thinned out but had only dilated enough to allow one finger to penetrate the opening. Hannah guessed she was probably in the very earliest phases of labor and the child would be born sometime within the next few days, but not likely that night. Unfortunately, she realized that this patient would not tolerate being left alone, so she could not return to Lazar, even for a few hours.

"So what is it?" Mrs. Belinsky asked, her voice as demanding as a razor pressed close to the midwife's cheek.

"The baby is on its way, but it is in no rush to be born."

She rose on her elbow to protest. "You're not telling me the truth!" Then she screamed for her husband. "Nahum!"

Belinsky burst into the room upon hearing the distress call. "What's the matter with you?"

"She says the baby is coming too slowly."

"No, I did not!" Hannah asserted. "First births take a long time. You should even be able to have a good sleep tonight."

"That will be impossible!"

"Just rest while I sit here on the chair. If anything happens, I'll wake you," Hannah said, hoping this strange pronouncement might be accepted even though her more cautious ones had not been.

"That's an excellent plan!" Belinsky agreed.

"And where will you be?" his wife asked with a hint of accusation in her voice.

"Right above you, my dear."

Mrs. Belinsky pouted and whimpered. "But this other woman will be in the room while you sleep!"

"And so will you, my dear, and so will you," he said, raising his eyes to the bare metal deckhead in what seemed to be a prayer for deliverance.

· 9 ·

SHIFRE BELINSKY MOANED in her sleep and cursed her condition each time she attempted to change her position in the narrow ship's bunk, waking Hannah. When the sound deepened in pitch, Hannah knelt beside the bunk and delicately placed her fingers on the abdomen to test how strongly the contractions were tightening the belly wall.

When it was almost morning, Hannah thought she heard someone calling her from beyond her half-sleep. She listened. Was it only the ocean winds howling? No, there it was again. "Han . . . nah! Han . . . nah!" Slowly she opened the iron door and saw Lazar at the far end of the passageway.

"Shhhh! Why are you calling me like that?"

"I wasn't certain which cabin you were in; your mama just told me it was on this side."

"Why are you here?"

"I missed you," he said so simply and sadly that Hannah believed he was as lonely without her as she was without him.

"They're sleeping now and I need some air. Let's go out on deck."

They stepped over the twelve-inch sill that divided the cabin area from the second-class promenade. After the night of beating wind and pounding rain, the deck was washed clean. In the first light of dawn the droplets on the brass horns and fittings sparkled like fine-cut gems. The ship glided along as though it slipped on glass. A thin vapor of sweet air rose from the distance, though Hannah could not place the almost forgotten scent in her mind.

Hannah placed her hand over her eyes to shield the glare as the sun formed a brilliant red semicircle on the horizon. "Do you think we are near land?"

"Possibly. Last evening they said it wouldn't be for a few more days."

"I wonder which will happen first, this baby or our arrival? At the rate she's going I'd say my money is safer with America."

"Can't you do something to hurry her up?"

"If I could, I would be the richest woman in the world! Only the baby decides, not the mother, nor the midwife, nor the midwife's husband!" she laughed. "Maybe we should go down to our own deck for a while?"

"The stupidity of it! Here we are all on the same ship, tossed by the same waves, going to the same place, and yet we are kept from them like caged animals."

"Do you think it will be any different in America? Won't the wealthy always have the best and the poor, like us, the worst?"

"Not if I have anything to say about it! You will always have the best!"

"So, you intend to become a rich man in America, do you? Like Belinsky's father? He came over seven years ago; already they say he lives like a king."

"I will never be a capitalist! But I have been studying American politics and I can see that it will be much simpler to introduce our socialist principles there than to overthrow the imperial government in Russia. We will lead a quiet revolution that will bring a classless society to America, a place where every man will have enough, but not so much as to make it an unfair burden on the others."

A noise rose from Belinsky's cabin. "Nahum! Help! Nahum!"

"I've got to go back." Hannah gave Lazar a quick kiss on the cheek.

"When will I see you again?"

"Don't expect me all day."

"Where is she?" called the frantic voice.

Lazar hugged Hannah one last time before she hurried to the Belinsky's cabin.

The midwife's voice was apologetic. "I'm sorry, I just needed some fresh air."

Mrs. Belinsky sulked but was silent.

"How are you feeling this morning?"

"Terrible! What do you think?"

"I thought you slept very well last night."

Belinsky straightened himself from the crouched position beside his wife. "Pardon me, I'll go freshen up." Quickly he opened the door to their private toilet.

"You are fortunate to have your own washroom!" Hannah told Mrs. Belinsky as she helped her to sit up in bed. Her words had no effect on the querulous woman.

Hannah attempted to sympathize. "It must be difficult for you."

"You don't know how miserable I've been!" She sobbed and gulped.

When Belinsky emerged dressed immaculately in a grey worsted suit, with a handsome tweed vest made from the same fabric as the inset of his fashionably wide lapels, Hannah could not help but admire him. Indeed there was something about the man that touched Hannah, and she studied his face for the answer. Thick black eyebrows had been combed into an arch over his soft brown eyes. He seemed an intense but cautious man who observed more often than acted.

Belinsky brushed back his hair, revealing a high forehead. "I'll ask the steward to send in trays for you both, but I'll take my breakfast on deck." He nodded to both women and departed from the scene with obvious relief.

Mrs. Belinsky hated getting out of bed and having her gown changed. She didn't want Hannah to help her in the bathroom, nor did she want her to leave. When the breakfast arrived her egg was too soft, and when Hannah offered hers in exchange, she only pushed it away.

Patiently, Hannah proceeded with another examination and was delighted to note that Mrs. Belinsky had made some progress during the night. Her cervix had opened to allow three fingers to pass and had done so without causing this rigid woman much discomfort.

Hannah attempted a reassuring smile. "Things are going just as expected. Your baby is very healthy and strong and so are you. You are going to be one of those fortunate women who have their babies very easily."

Mrs. Belinsky coyly accepted the remark as a compliment. "Am I really?"

"Now, let's get you dressed in something comfortable. Have you a warm robe?"

"Yes, it's hanging behind the door. The blue velvet; it was part of my trousseau."

"This is very lovely." Hannah politely admired the lace collar and cuffs. "Now then, we will go for a walk around the deck."

"Outside! I cannot!"

"It's the best thing for you and the baby!"

"I would have to get properly dressed and I cannot fit into anything I have. Even my feet are too swollen for my shoes!"

"It is still very early; hardly anyone will be out."

"Except the sailors! They look at me so . . . so strangely."

"I suppose you are right." The midwife sighed aloud. "I can see that you would rather suffer than do something you believed improper."

"Oh! Maybe a short walk this early wouldn't be too awful." Mrs. Belinsky looked up at Hannah with pleading eyes. "Would it?"

"Not at all," Hannah replied in a voice as steady as iron.

The deck steward served bouillon only to Mrs. Belinsky, ignoring Hannah because she did not belong in second class. Stimulated by the sea air, she greedily gulped two bowls, but less than twenty minutes after gorging herself, Mrs. Belinsky went to the rail and vomited into the sea. Trembling with the effort, she could stand only supported by the midwife. Hannah called the steward to summon Belinsky from his card game on the forward part of the deck. Together the three of them walked the expectant mother back to her cabin.

Suddenly contractions began to come one right after the other, less than one minute apart. In the brief interval that remained, Hannah undressed her patient and attempted to arrange her on the narrow bed.

Mrs. Belinsky refused to cooperate so Hannah could examine

her. Three times Hannah tried to slip her hand between Mrs. Belinsky's legs, but her patient pressed them closed and shrieked, "Leave me alone!"

Deciding to be firm, the midwife pulled a swollen thigh toward her with one hand and with the other pushed upward as quickly as possible. Mrs. Belinsky flexed her bent knee and firmly kicked Hannah in the breast, sending her reeling across the narrow room, where she landed on her buttocks and bumped the back of her head on a metal table leg.

Furious at the unwarranted attack, Hannah stood up shakily.

As another pain mounted, Mrs. Belinsky called, "Oiiiiiiii! Gottenyu! Loving Father!"

Once again Hannah tried to attend her, but Mrs. Belinsky thrashed so wildly she was forced to retreat and observe.

"Zoll er krenk'n un gedenk'n! May he suffer and remember! Why did he do this to *me?*" she ranted in Yiddish.

Alarmed by her anger, Hannah tried once again. "Now, now . . . I'm here to help you!"

"Oiiiiii! How can you do this to me? Let it be over! I shall die! I shall die! It's all his father's fault."

"No, no, it's no one's fault. It will be over soon. If you will only allow me . . ."

"The cholera take him!"

This was too much! In disgust, as well as confusion, Hannah stepped back and stood outside the cabin door, wondering what to do next.

"Never have I seen a more selfish and ungrateful woman!" Hannah muttered half-aloud. "Her poor husband! What kind of a life is he going to have with that shrew?"

Disturbed that her own bitterness was besting her professional attitude, Hannah didn't notice Belinsky coming toward her.

Anxiously he wrung his hands. "Is it over?"

"No, far from it!"

"Then why aren't you with her?"

"She won't, she doesn't wish . . ."

Hannah was interrupted by Mrs. Belinsky's shrieks. "Oiiiii! Help me! Eeeeeeeiiiiiiieeeeee!"

Belinsky shoved his fists into his pockets so hard the fabric began to tear. Hannah touched him gently to calm him. "I am trying everything I know. It is not a bad birth, really, but she is taking it very hard. Your wife is a very" — Hannah searched for an appropriate word — "special woman, but you know that."

"She is going to be all right, she isn't ... isn't dying?" he choked.

"Far from it. I think the baby is almost here, but she won't even allow me to examine her."

Gesturing toward the dirty heel mark on Hannah's blouse, Belinsky looked abashed.

Hannah rubbed the spot. "I don't see how I am going to finish this without some help."

"Who could you call?"

"My aunt has assisted at births ..." Hannah was interrupted by new sounds from the cabin. The high shrieks had changed to a low throaty warble.

At the same moment Belinsky and Hannah both rushed for the door and crushed each other as they attempted to press through the small frame simultaneously.

Hannah went to the foot of the bed and pushed the woman's now docile legs apart. "The baby is coming. You must help me, or I won't be able to do it in so narrow a place," she said to Belinsky.

"Just tell me what you want."

"Sit down behind her!" Hannah directed him to crouch down in the bunk. "Yes, like that! Now grasp her arms and then, if you can, hold her knees up as well. That's right!"

Hannah had Mr. Belinsky supporting his wife in a sitting position. From her sterile pack she removed the catch sheet and tucked it under the woman's straining buttocks. In a crooning voice she said, "Wait, shhhh ... shhhhh ..." Forming her hands into a cage to prevent the baby's descending head from stretching the delicate tissues, she murmured, "Good, good, good girl, good, good, that's it, good." Then with the base of her palms she pressed on the sides of the perineum, slowly opening the widening circle with a perfect sense of control.

Regretting she had not had the time to properly prepare the area with heat and mineral oil for maximum lubrication, she neverthe-less used some of the natural secretions to slip the baby's head out without the slightest tear. The moment of birth was audible in the silent room.

Belinsky had closed his eyes in fear of the unknown. At the sound, he opened them to see the amazing sight of his partially born child rotating toward him.

"Push a little!" Hannah commanded.

"Do it! Shifre, do it!" Belinsky echoed, seeing that it was neces-sary to relieve the pressure on the unborn shoulders. In an attempt to help, he pressed his wife's lower back.

"Ahhhhhh!" she cried in relief.

"A girl!" Belinsky shouted. "It's a girl! I see it for myself! It's really a girl! It's really a baby! I don't believe it!"

"Are you sure?" his wife asked. "Maybe it's a boy? You never get anything right the first time!"

"It's a girl!" Hannah agreed with the husband. "See for your-self! She's beautiful."

A whistle on the smokestack nearest their section shook their cabin. Again it screeched. And again.

"What's the matter?" Terror filled Mrs. Belinsky's face. "Some-thing is wrong with the ship! I knew I would die before seeing America! I knew it!"

"Listen!" Belinsky said. "What are they shouting?"

Since neither new parent could move, Hannah wiped her hands from the blood of the placenta, stood on her numb legs, and went to the porthole to observe the commotion on deck. Passengers swarmed at the rails, pointing and laughing. Hannah followed their eager stares until her own eyes caught the object of their ex-citement. After weeks without sight of anything except a blank horizon, something with form and substance loomed in the dis-tance.

"It's America! We're almost there!"

Looking back at the new family, she stopped. For a moment they formed the perfect tableau: the father dressed in his somber suit stroked the baby's pink shoulder while the mother, whose damp hair clung like a fine web to her face and neck, cupped the tiny buttocks.

"You couldn't wait to be born one more day!" Belinsky chided the baby gently. "Now she won't be an American, will she?"

"I don't know," Hannah responded truthfully.

Belinsky looked down at his wife in his lap. "Let's give her an American name, then."

"I promised my family I'd call it Geitel if it was a girl. Geitel after my mother!"

Belinsky sighed in resignation. "Do you need me anymore?" he asked the midwife.

"No, but thank you! I've never had a father as an assistant before, but there was no time to summon anyone else."

Belinsky extricated himself from his cramped position. "Perhaps I shouldn't have been there, but I rather enjoyed it."

"Go find out when we can get off this infernal ship!" his wife ordered. "And you, you help me get out of these clothes and take care of this baby," she commanded Hannah.

Summoning a final reserve of patience, Hannah replied, "Of course, Mrs. Belinsky, of course."

## · 10 ·

AMERICA APPEARED TO HANNAH as a massive cemetery for giants huddled at the end of a landmass too small to contain all the stones and crypts. Even the small circle of green along the quay seemed nothing more than a funeral wreath amidst the granite desolation. New York had no human proportion, and at that moment the small expanse of sea that separated them from the mainland seemed as vast as the ocean they had just crossed.

Hannah held the railing, her white knuckles betraying her excitement. "The S.S. *Haverford* must be as weary as we are," she said half-seriously to Lazar.

"What do you mean?"

Pointing to the bright red tugboats that had pulled the ship into the channel between the Statue of Liberty and Ellis Island, she laughed. "It needed the little boats to rescue it!"

Soon a small ferry with the words *George Starr* painted in blue letters on its stern pulled alongside the ship. Ladders were lowered and the passengers stood in line to disembark.

"Where do we go now?" Hannah asked her husband.

"Ellis Island, over there!" He pointed to his left.

Frowning her disappointment, Hannah said, "I thought we would stop at the statue."

"No, Officer Braden said we would be processed in that large red building. Don't you think it looks familiar? The designer must have been a Russian!" He referred to the four cupolas and spires.

The ferry took them through the narrow passage to the island, where the immigrants and their bundles spilled out onto the newly finished quay. They were escorted up the steps to the main building and into the baggage room. Mama clasped her bundles firmly. When an American officer tried to exchange them for a numbered tag, she protested. "No! Leave them be!"

The official pointed to the numeral on the tag, then to the one on the bag, to demonstrate they matched. Mama still shook her head. Then he gestured to all the guards around the room and indicated they would not allow anyone to leave with a bag without a matching number.

Lazar stepped up and put his arms around his mother-in-law's trembling shoulders. "Come now, Mama, I'm certain they won't steal anything."

Mama looked doubtful but followed Lazar to the numbering station, where they each received a large white card that was pinned to their chests. Hannah was given number 51-16.

Next they were directed to climb a wide center stairway, its treads constructed of the hardest grey slate. Eva counted aloud as she walked up the sixty-seven steps. Three doctors waited and watched from the top. Did anyone walk with a limp? Were any latent heart or respiratory problems revealed by the way they breathed at the end of the climb? If so, their backs were chalked with an *L* for limp, *H* for heart, or *R* for respiration. Finally they arrived at the vast two-tiered holding room divided by freshly painted iron pipes and stanchions. They were seated in one of the sections where long wooden benches holding fifteen people each faced two directions.

"Don't be frightened. I can tell by their faces they aren't cruel men." Lazar referred to the inspectors who sat at tables at various corners of the room.

Aunt Sonia looked concerned. "Why do you think not?"

"They don't have hard lines in their faces. Their hands are soft. They do not carry weapons."

"But what if they don't like us, don't want us?" Hannah questioned.

"I asked the officer on the ship what the regulations were. We can meet every one of them. Here, look at this," Lazar said, handing Hannah a book of instructions.

"But this is in English. How did you read it?"

"I have been translating it page by page."

Hannah pursed her lips. "So what does it say?"

"That every immigrant will be examined. If there is just cause for exclusion he may be called before the special inquiry committee. And only after a majority vote shall he be deported.

"What does 'just cause' mean?" Hannah asked.

"They have a list." Lazar translated slowly: "Feeble-minded, epileptic, pauper, those with tuberculosis and other loathsome or contagious diseases, physical and mental handicaps that might prevent one from supporting himself, anarchists, prostitutes, contract laborers, children under sixteen unless accompanied by a natural parent."

Hannah shuddered. Abraham was not with his real parent, Lazar's political activities might qualify him as an anarchist, Dora could be certified mentally incompetent, and after all they had spent on their passage, they might be considered paupers.

Pointing to peasants in their vicinity, Aunt Sonia interjected,"We look more respectable than most of those . . ."

"At least we smell better!" Hannah commented.

"We may have enough money," Mama continued, "but there is another problem. Look over there!" She pointed to a table where people were being tested.

Lazar strained his neck and noticed that an inspector with a stopwatch timed people as they placed a dozen shapes in a puzzle. "Couldn't Dora do that simple thing?"

Shaking her head, Hannah replied, "Not if she were frightened or given a time limit, certainly not under these conditions."

Lazar placed his arms around Dora's shoulders. "Stay with me and everything will be all right," he told her.

Mama looked at Hannah doubtfully, but she kept her mouth closed.

"What do you think about Olga?" Hannah pointed to where she sat nursing Abraham with a very satisfied smile on her lips. "Will she give us any trouble?"

Aunt Sonia answered with assurance. "Once she became accustomed to the idea, I don't think she resented it too much. She only wanted to be near the man she thought she loved."

"Misha." Hannah recalled the name Olga had called over and over as she boarded the ship.

Mama gasped. "That's what they called one of Zalman's younger sons! How could she ever think there was a possibility with him?"

"She only wanted to be near him; she didn't think beyond that," Aunt Sonia commiserated.

An official called from the front of the room, "Manifest page fifty-one!" Startled by the noise, which echoed through the cavernous room, Abraham began to wail. Attention was immmediately focused on their group.

"Shhh!" Mama Blau tried to silence the baby's screeching as a man with a neatly trimmed mustache carrying a clipboard pointed out their row.

When no one stood, he held up the number 51 on a card and pointed to their chests. Finally they understood his meaning. They marched in a line to a desk at the far end of the room, but the commotion made the baby even more anxious. Olga swayed her body, and he started to calm. Placing her head very close to his, she began to sing to him in Polish.

As the eloquence of her voice reverberated through the vaulted hall, the skin on Hannah's arms tingled. Looking around, she saw others in their section were also moved by Olga's song but wondered what the inspector at the head of the line would do if he knew the truth about Abraham's birth and true parentage. Now that Abie was in America, his beginnings would become as much a secret as the future that stretched before him. No one remained to tell his tale except the family, and they had conspired to never reveal the truth.

❖ ❖ ❖

"Sokolow!"

Lazar and Hannah were next in line, but they did not respond.

"Sokolow, Lazar? Sokolow, Hannah, born Blau?" he asked them again.

"Lifting his head in a gesture of recognition, Lazar corrected him. "Sokolovsky!"

"S-o-k-o-l-o-w," the officer spelled and pointed to the immigration card. "In America you are Sokolow!"

Hannah was surprised Lazar didn't complain. But he had been observing the procedures with a careful eye and knew that any deviance might mean trouble. Trouble was arguing back; trouble was not having your papers in order; trouble meant the letters *SI*, for "Special Inquiry," chalked on your back. And the ultimate trouble: deportation.

On the boat they learned why Ellis was called "the island of tears." If a child failed medical inspection, one parent had to accompany him back. Back to where? So terrible were the places from which many had come that people killed themselves rather than go home or endure steerage again. On the *Haverford* a man traveling in their section explained that his wife was in first class. Because of her humpback she had failed to pass the first time they tried to enter America four years earlier. Now, with the benefit of her expensive passage, she would be welcomed to America as a "tourist."

Hannah allowed Lazar to answer for them both, and he did so haltingly in English. The inspector seemed impressed.

"What is your profession?" he asked.

"Teacher," Lazar replied.

"And your wife?"

He puffed his chest out proudly. "Doctor!"

The inspector craned his neck to get a better look at Hannah. "Doctor?" he asked as he doubtfully surveyed the woman with the flashing green eyes. But he stamped the documents rapidly and moved on to Uncle Leyb without even asking about their financial resources.

A guard directed them to the balcony for medical examinations. Overlooking the great room, Hannah stared down at the crowd.

"I don't see the Belinskys," she whispered to Lazar.

"Those in cabin class don't come here. They are examined aboard the ship. Why do you want to find them, didn't they pay you?"

"No, they didn't. When land was sighted I just wanted to be back with you."

"And you had a chance to get something to give us a good start!" Lazar said crossly. "Now you'll never see them again!"

"I'm sorry, I didn't think!" She was silent as she realized how unprofessionally she'd behaved.

The men were sent to the north balcony, the women to the south for the genital examinations. Waiting her turn outside the curtained area, Hannah admired the building. Every surface was tiled: the floor in small white octagons, the walls in shiny white rectangles, the arched ceiling in an intricate pattern of yellow brick. Despite the huge crowds the facility handled, everything was washed and spotless. Always impressed by efficiency, Hannah felt that Americans must be fine people to keep their places so immaculate and well organized! But when it was almost her turn she noticed that the doctor did not change his rubber gloves between cases. Scrutinizing the women ahead of her in line, Hannah was grateful that none looked, at least from the exterior, too unclean.

When Lazar reappeared in the next line, he went to stand beside Dora. "Now comes the very worst part!" he told his sister-in-law with a subtle cruelty. "If you don't behave they'll deport you and you'll have to go back to Russia alone, since you are already seventeen."

Dora had the appropriate terrified response when the doctor stood in her path and moved a buttonhook in front of her eyes to get her attention. She stopped short, the doctor lifted her head with a jerk, and she opened her eyes wide. Then with a swift movement he caught her eyelash with his thumb and turned the lid back searching for encrustations or pus, which were the hallmarks of trachoma. Dora passed, but not without trembling. As they moved toward the final test, the one for mental competency, Lazar poked her ahead of him and whispered, "This is the one who will send you back!"

Dora's breath came in gasps.

In English Lazar said, "She is very frightened, Doctor, sir." Then, reaching under her shawl as if to comfort his sister-in-law, he pinched her as hard as he could, just as the puzzle was placed in front of her.

"Ei! Ei!" she screamed.

"Maybe you can wait till she calms a little?" Lazar asked sweetly.

The doctor shook his head and asked Lazar slowly, "Does she go to school?"

Lazar held up his forefinger. "Number one in her class!" He smiled so convincingly the doctor waved them both on.

Hardly believing her sister's narrow escape, Hannah stood numbly in front of the same table and paid little heed to the instructions for the test. Not realizing that the stopwatch had been set, she stared as Lazar led Dora through the final checking point and down the last flight of stairs to freedom.

The inspector coughed to get her attention. Realizing that she had only seconds left, Hannah quickly put the shapes in the puzzle, but was left holding the crescent when time was up.

"But . . . I . . ." Hannah tried to excuse herself.

The inspector reviewed her papers. "Doctor?" He raised his eyebrows in surprise before waving her on.

❖ ❖ ❖

Not one of them with a mark of chalk on his back! As the family regrouped in the baggage room, they hugged each other and celebrated their good fortune.

"Did you see the Shulmans?" Eva said, referring to the Galitzianers from Lvov. "Their daughter didn't pass the eye test. What do you think will happen?"

Mama's eyes widened. "And Olga slept with them!"

"Don't worry," Leyb said softly. "I don't think there was anything really wrong with the girl; they just want to check her more thoroughly. Did you see Rabbi Weissman? He had *H* and *SI!* We have been very fortunate!"

"To New York!" Lazar pointed to the words set in blue tiles at the end of the left-hand passage. Everyone followed him past the signs for boat trains to Weehawken and Hoboken, out to the dock, and up the gangplank of the steam ferry for the short trip to Battery Park.

At the rail their mood was one of jubilance and victory. Lazar apologized to Dora for hurting her, but she would not so much as look at him.

"Mama, Mama!" Dora shrieked in fright, pointing toward the city.

"Oh, don't be a silly goose! Lazar told you he was sorry!" Mama said without turning around.

"Mama, America is worse than Russia! We will surely be killed!" Eva joined in the hysteria.

Other passengers followed Eva's frightened gaze and began to shout. As the wharf came into view a strange sight greeted the immigrants. Men dressed in warlike costumes yelled and chased each other around the walls of a round, fortlike structure. They ripped open sacks of flour and tossed handfuls of white powder at each other, forming smoky clouds in the air. Firecrackers sounded like gunshots.

"What is going on?" Hannah asked her husband.

In a few moments Lazar found a deck hand who explained the nature of the "riots" ashore and reported, "They call it 'Halloween.' Everyone dresses in costume, goes a little crazy; it's like . . . Purim in America."

"How could it be?" Mama asked with disbelief.

"Mama, don't worry," Lazar replied with brash certainty. "Nothing can hurt us now."

## · 11 ·

THE FLAG ABOVE the octagonal dome of the Castle Garden Aquarium flapped its welcome from shore, while the torch of the Statue of Liberty glinted in the distance. When they landed at the dock in front of the red-tiled fireboat building, the costumed revelers became the object more of curiosity than of fear.

As soon as the deck hand uncoiled a thick snake of a rope and wrapped it around the first black bollard on the dock, Lazar jumped ashore and reached out to lift Hannah to the wharf. Instead of finding solid earth, Hannah felt the land shift beneath her. She leaned against Lazar for support. A silver-haired lady in a coat trimmed with curly lambskin, a representative of the Hebrew Immigrant Aid Society, walked up to Uncle Leyb, who seemed from his tailored coat and grey beard to be the head of the group, and asked politely, "Are you being met by friends or relatives? Do you have a place to live? A job?"

Uncle Leyb responded in the negative to each of these questions.

"Don't worry," soothed the woman. "Where are you from?"

"Odessa," Leyb answered.

"We were from Vitebsk. You know it?" she said pleasantly to dispel their suspicions. "We help our landsleit, because we know what it is like to come to these shores without family or friends. There is no charge for our service. Our organization is open day and night. We can help you find some rooms, a job, and warn about those who would take advantage of your ignorance."

As Mama Blau stepped forward to listen, not fully trusting the woman's words, they were interrupted by a voice calling "Mrs. Sokolovsky!" Nahum Belinsky came running toward the group. "I sent Shifre and the baby ahead, but I could not leave until I had a proper chance to thank you." He brushed the hair from his forehead, but the wind at the wharfside defied him and it blew right back across his eyes.

Lazar muttered under his breath, "You mean pay you."

The woman was surprised to see someone of such obvious means greeting the group she proposed to help. "Oh, you do have friends in America?"

Belinsky answered for her. "Of course you do! My father agreed to help you get settled. After all, you delivered his grandchild. Even Shifre sang your praises."

The Hebrew Immigrant Aid Society woman shrugged her shoulders and moved over to another group of new arrivals.

"My father." Belinsky gestured to a closed carriage where the form of a corpulent fellow chewing a long cigar could be seen through the crowd. "My father says you can have some rooms in one of his buildings with two months' free rent and he will help your husband get a job."

"That is very kind, but I am certain we can manage on our own, Mr. Belinsky," Lazar said, stepping forward.

Belinsky focused his attention on Hannah. "At least a place to stay? Where will you go? Have you family here already?"

"We have no place to go," Hannah replied simply, but with force enough to convey that she was not going to let pride stand in the way of assistance that was obviously needed.

"How many are you, then?" Belinsky asked.

"Ten."

"Ten?" said Belinsky, not concealing his shock. "Ten in your family? I hadn't thought there were that many. I'd better ask my father again. Who are they all, please?"

Hannah gestured to their group. "My husband and myself; Mama and my sisters Dora and Eva; Uncle Leyb, Aunt Sonia, and their new baby Abraham; Lazar's Uncle Moishe and . . . and his wife, Olga. Ten. I'm sorry there are so many of us."

"How fortunate you didn't have to leave anyone behind!" Belinsky said politely.

"My brother will be coming . . . later."

"Good, good. Let me see what I can do."

They watched as Belinsky walked back to the carriage shaking his head and preparing an explanation. Although they could not hear the words that passed between father and son, the meaning of the pantomime was clear. At first the father was angered by the request. Then Belinsky mollified him and pointed out Hannah and her husband while the father bit off the end of a new cigar. After throwing up his hands in a gesture of surrender, he leaned out the window and handed his son a piece of paper.

Belinsky ran back to the Blaus. "Here is the address of a larger place. Show this to the landlady; her name is Esther Sholom. Her husband is a cantor, also from Odessa."

"Do you live nearby?"

"No, no. We live in a different place."

"Where is that?"

"It's called uptown." He glanced nervously toward the carriage. "My father is getting impatient."

"Thank you for your kindness, Mr. Belinsky," Mama said, careful to recognize a new ally when she saw one.

"Yes, thank you," Hannah echoed. "If you have any problems with the baby, I will come at any hour. And for your next, I will be waiting!"

❖ ❖ ❖

One-seven-three Forsyth Street. A note for Reb Sholom. A place to begin. It was more than many who arrived that day received. And Hannah knew enough to be grateful.

It would take much longer to comprehend just how fortunate she had been, for while the rooms they were given seemed cramped, filthy, and pitiful, they could have fared much worse. In a few weeks she would realize that not every apartment had both front and back windows, and doorways placed in such a way that air could circulate from the street to the alley; that not every family could live without boarders crowding their narrow quarters; that three rooms for ten people were better than one room for the same number; and that a toilet in the hall was superior to an outhouse in the courtyard. Their front room even had a view of a narrow green ribbon of park that ran from Canal Street to East Houston Street, and the shops on Hester Street were but two blocks away! If she complained about climbing up five stories, Hannah was reminded how much better it was in the summer, because you could claim the best roof spaces for sleeping on hot nights.

But it wasn't easy to adjust to the tenement buildings that formed unnatural canyons from which there seemed no escape. From the street Hannah watched the children trapped behind high windows; from her rooms she looked down into a web of railings and wash lines. Hannah's sensitive nose was assailed by the horrid smells of the city, surpassed only by those she had encountered during the first days in steerage. So many people, so much garbage! It sickened her to watch children playing in piles of horse manure, eating peelings from rotten fruit!

And her new world was in constant motion. Hannah, who had adjusted so quickly to the sea, found that she was landsick. For the first week she continued to walk in a loping sailor's gait, and when she stood still the horizon tilted. People in the markets bobbed and swayed; stationary objects danced in front of her eyes. Just as she had been amazed that she had never suffered from the movement of the boat, she wondered why no one else shared her dizzy spells. This disequilibrium added to her distress during those first few weeks in a new land, weeks she would later remember only as a blur of indistinct shapes and feelings.

America roared. Howling babies, barking dogs, braying horses, pushcart peddlers loudly clamoring to be heard. What language did they speak? It wasn't Yiddish; it wasn't English. Hannah strained to understand the words: *whaddayamean, getdahellout, sharrup.*

Everything was a question. How much was a dollar, a quarter, a dime? Where did you buy food? Why did the water only reach the fifth floor part of the day and never at night? Why didn't the radiator work when it was cold, choosing only the moments when sun warmed the front room to hiss out its heat?

How could it be that America was worse than Odessa? More pungent! More crowded! Less of everything! How could it be that they lived on an island but never saw the sea, when every view from Odessa had contained a glimpse of the water? What had happened to birds and trees in New York? Only a few sticks without leaves remained on their street; even the grass in the park was trampled. Yet one thing she understood immediately: it wasn't so special to be Jewish. Everyone was Jewish, and it didn't seem to make a difference.

One day on their way home from the Hester Street market, Lazar carried the heaviest groceries in a burlap satchel slung across his shoulder. Hannah pointed out the girls, young as her sisters, draped along the stoops on Allen Street. "They look like Moldavanka whores!"

"That's what they are!"

"Impossible! They are Jewish girls!"

"Even a Jewish girl has to eat!"

"There is no other way?" Hannah was shocked. "They look so young!"

When they reached their rooms, Mama and Aunt Sonia fell upon them to see what their few dollars had bought.

"So much butter!" Mama exclaimed.

"Lazar found a place cheaper than Epstein's, only fifteen cents a pound."

Lazar took out two round loaves of pumpernickel bread. "One with raisins, one without."

"We could have done with one," Mama admonished.

Hannah stood between Mama and her husband. "We have to eat, and tonight is special. It's Moishe's last meal with us."

Crowding had been their first problem. Hannah and Lazar had been given the smallest, airless room, in the middle, so they would have privacy; Aunt Sonia, Uncle Leyb, Abraham, and Olga had the best room, in the front, for "the sake of the baby"; and Mama, Dora, and Eva had tolerated Uncle Moishe sharing their back room. Sensitive to the fact that he was the one who least belonged, Moishe signed up at the International Labor Agency, which offered construction jobs on the Manunka Chunk Tunnel Project of the Erie Railroad that paid two dollars and twenty cents per day plus a bonus for every month on the job.

After Mama put the butter away, she busied herself chopping onions. "A boy came today from your friend Belinsky's factory. He was looking for sewing machine operators. Sonia and I went down and signed up. We start tomorrow."

"How much?" asked Lazar.

"One seventy-five to start."

Lazar hooked his suspenders with his thumbs. "Not enough! Moishe's two-twenty includes board! How do they expect you to live?"

"We're fortunate for the chance! They'll even let Dora come with me. She can do buttons or collars."

"What about me? When can I work?" Eva begged.

"Don't be in such a rush." Hannah gave her sister's apron a tug.

Eva rushed to retie it. "I'm not a child! I can do as much as anyone else if they'd give me a chance. No one will even let me out to look!"

"So go!" Mama pointed out the window with her knife. "Start with this building. Everyone does something. You want to do piecework? In the basement they string milk tags at night and their daughter carries them to the dairy early each morning. Or maybe you'd like to work as a presser? You see how the old Litvak works, sweating eighteen hours a day on the second floor?"

Eva stood next to Hannah for support. "I met a girl named Bessie. Her mama and sisters make pillow lace. It's nice work and they already have a real iron bed and their house is very clean."

"Who is this Bessie?" Mama asked.

"She lives in the next building. She's the same age as I am!"

"If you want to learn pillow lace, Aunt Sonia can teach you. But if you work twenty-four hours a day, maybe you'll make a dollar."

The argument ended, but the next week Eva mysteriously found a job rolling cigars. Mama let her go, even though she knew the slight poison that seeped from the tobacco leaves into Eva's delicate system caused her to vomit every night until she adjusted to it.

Next Uncle Leyb started to study the stalls and carts on Hester Street and found no one selling yard goods as fine as the ones he had in Odessa. With the last of his cash reserve he bought a pushcart and stocked it with presewn collars Aunt Sonia had made from scraps. A natural businessman, he prospered from the first, and after only two months he proudly moved his family and Olga into two rooms of their own.

At first Lazar didn't even pretend to look for work. He studied English, made contacts, interpreted the city to the rest of the family. He knew where there would be free entertainment or an interesting meeting, where to buy the best herring or get stale bread at a bargain. On the streets he found treasures: a broken chair he repaired for their room, a crate he made into a serviceable table. Skillfully he bargained at the market and surprised everyone with the soups he could make. After he discovered the Rivington Street Library, the house was always filled with books, and Hannah wondered what secrets he was learning about American life from the volumes marked Verne, Dickens, Thoreau, Dumas, Hugo, and Emerson.

"There's a job for another girl at Braverman's," Eva told Hannah one evening as they sat down to supper.

Lazar was insulted by the suggestion. "That's not for Hannah!"

"I should bring home more than I do now," Hannah said slowly, referring to the few collars she trimmed for Uncle Leyb.

"You're a professional! As soon as there are babies to deliver, you'll be too busy to work in a factory."

"What should I do, wear a sign saying 'Midwife for Hire'?"

"Not a bad idea!" Lazar laughed. "I'll think of something."

The next day he brought two hot knishes from Yonah Schimmel's shop, one stuffed with potato, the other with kasha, and shared them with Hannah before anyone else arrived home.

"Why did he give them to you?" Hannah asked suspiciously.

"We're landsleit. He had family in Kishinev."

"So what good is that to us? Maybe it would be better if you asked him for a job!"

"Me, a baker?"

"A baker, a peddler — who cares? Is it so much to want a home of our own before the baby is born?"

"About babies . . . Schimmel told me about a Mrs. Moskowitz — her husband has the restaurant on the corner of Broome. She expects any day, and maybe she'll have you do the delivery. It would be a start."

"That's what I've been waiting for!" Hannah said joyfully, and put away her sewing.

❖   ❖   ❖

"Mrs. Moskowitz?" Hannah asked the woman whose protruding belly advertised her condition.

"Waddayawant?" she asked, without taking her eyes off the pot of bean and noodle soup she was stirring in the back of her restaurant.

Hannah, who understood no English, continued in Yiddish. "My name is Mrs. Blau, I mean Sokolovsky, ah . . . Sokolow," she stammered.

The potential patient put down her ladle and stared at the young woman who wasn't certain of her own name. "So?" she asked impatiently.

"I'm a midwife. My husband knows Yonah Schimmel and . . ."

"Everyone knows Yonah Schimmel," Mrs. Moskowitz replied and went back to her work.

"Yes, well, Yonah Schimmel told him that you were expecting a baby."

"Nu?" Mrs. Moskowitz said, patting her bulging apron.

Hannah struggled for the right words and finally spoke her piece in a nervous burst of words. "I have studied at the Imperial College of Medicine in Moscow and I delivered with Bubbe Schtern in Odessa for many years. None of my women has ever been hurt by me, and I'd like to deliver your baby if you'll give me a chance."

The steam from the soup blew in Hannah's direction and she was forced to change her position.

Mrs. Moskowitz didn't even turn toward her as she gave her reply. "Mrs. Fingerman does all the babies on the Lower East Side. She delivered my first, she'll deliver this one, and the next, if God wills." She sighed and lifted her sagging breasts with her reddened hands.

"But surely there are more babies than any one midwife can handle?"

"About that I don't know, but mine she will do. She's a good Jewish woman and she's treated me fair. Only three dollars for everything, and you don't have to pay right off."

"Yes, I understand. Thank you and be well, Mrs. Moskowitz," Hannah said as she retreated.

After Hannah had explained about Mrs. Fingerman to Lazar he was undaunted by the competition. "Why don't you go to this woman, see if she needs some help," he suggested. "You could apprentice with her like you did with Bubbe, and then maybe one day she will be too busy, or next time the mother will call you instead."

"I don't know what she is like."

"So find out!" he said, patting his wife on the top of her shimmering black braid. "How terrible could she be?"

# · 12 ·

EVERYONE KNEW WHERE Miriam Fingerman lived, but no one knew anything about her. Her rooms were on the first floor of the two hundred block of Rivington, far enough away from the noise of the Essex Street markets to be known as the better part of the street.

A frigid December rain pummeled Hannah as she knocked on the door. A hollow voice called from within. "Who's there?"

Hannah answered nervously. "I'm here to see the midwife."

"Yah, yah!" The door flung open to reveal a woman whose bony frame towered above Hannah. "I know you!" she said, pointing a long finger. "Don't get the floor wet, stand on the rug, and take off your shawl! You'll need a proper cloak in New York! Tell your husband you must have one!"

"I've known worse cold than this!" Hannah remembered Moscow.

"How is that? You are from Odessa, are you not?"

"Yes, how did you know?"

"Mrs. Moskowitz told me all about the little greenhorn who wanted my job!" she said, making a spitting sound with her lips. "I've been in America since eighty-one, almost twenty-four years, and I know everything that happens here. Don't you forget that."

"I wanted to meet with you, talk with you," Hannah began cautiously. "Believe me, I had no plans to take away your job. I didn't even know about you when I spoke to Mrs. Moskowitz!" she added with a touch of sincerity she thought just right.

"Yah, yah." An odd expression came into Mrs. Fingerman's eyes. The older woman took the armchair, leaving Hannah to stand awkwardly in the hall.

Hannah walked over toward the emerald green sofa, which matched not only the armchair but a side chair as well. It was the first three-piece suite of new furniture she had seen in New York. "This is very lovely," she said while she remained standing.

"You like it? I got a deal from a customer who has a store on Orchard Street," she said, running her fingers along the edge of the tufted plush trimming.

"Very much. The design is . . . Oriental?" she said to make conversation. "I like your lamp; I've never seen one quite like it before."

"It's called a banquet lamp. I took it for my fee from the Zeli-koffs. I saw one just like it for almost seven dollars! And mine has a larger globe, better flowers, and is all brass, not plated!"

Nodding to be polite, Hannah felt herself beginning to perspire. There was something in the woman's manner, the yellow cast to her skin, the multitude of liver spots on her unnaturally long arms, and the off-center gaze of her eye, that sickened the younger woman.

"Odessa is never this cold, is it?" Miriam Fingerman suddenly spoke, and her tone was not conversational but accusing.

"No, but I did my medical studies in Moscow. I was also train-ing to be a doctor there."

"Why didn't you stay?" she asked and finally beckoned Hannah to be seated.

"Yes, well," Hannah choked on the words. "We had to leave Russia, the pogroms, and . . ."

"So you are not a doctor! Then let's hear no more of that. In America they are very strict about whom they call doctors. If you do not have their certificate they will put you in jail!"

"Where did you study midwifery?" Hannah countered.

"Study? I study each time I deliver. I am the very best in New York; ask anyone who knows me!"

"Then will you deliver my baby?" Hannah said, surprising even herself with the question, for that was not at all what she had in-tended to discuss.

Mrs. Fingerman raised and lowered her head as though she were taking Hannah's measure. "Yours? How far along are you?"

"Only a few months, but I can't very well do it myself, can I?"

"I see." The older woman softened so that the bones in her face were covered with folds of flesh. Pursing her thick lips in concentration, she walked around Hannah. "If you have any problems, you can take care of them yourself, I'm sure. But when the time comes, I'll do the delivery, half-price for you."

"You are very kind. I was just hoping . . ." Hannah struggled to say why she had really come.

"What is it?"

"In Odessa I assisted Bubbe Schtern for years. If you'd allow me to help you . . . during a long labor you could get more sleep, or leave me to do the washing up," Hannah ran on anxiously.

The woman contemplated the offer while pushing back her cuticles with her thumb. "Maybe you could be useful. I might send for you sometime, but don't count on it."

"But you wouldn't have to pay me . . . not at first," Hannah added.

"You seem like a nice girl, for a greenhorn. Where do you live?"

"On Forsyth."

"Thieves and whores there. What kind of a man brings a woman to a place like that?"

"Allen Street is worse."

Mrs. Fingerman stood and walked around Hannah's chair. "Who am I to tell you how to live?"

Hannah took the other woman's actions as a sign she was expected to leave. "I must be going before the weather gets even worse."

"So what's your rush?" the older midwife asked, suddenly warming. "I have some questions for you. Did you ever have 'der ponim' first?"

"A face presentation? I never delivered one, but I watched one at the hospital. They used forceps and it came out all right."

"Let me tell you how I did my last one . . ." As the older woman spun off her tale, Hannah thought her technique sounded not only far-fetched but dangerous, but by letting her talk Hannah guessed she might gain the older woman's trust.

❖  ❖  ❖

"I went to see Miriam Fingerman," Hannah obediently reported.

"What did she say?" Mama asked.

"She may call me to assist her."

Mama shook her head. "What good is that?"

"It's the only way I'll be able to practice my profession."

A frown of disapproval crossed Mama's face. "I don't know. From what I hear she's not so wonderful."

"What?" Lazar asked in surprise.

"I mention her name, ask if she'd be good for my daughter, and some say there are doctors here who will do better, maybe a little more money, but what does that matter when it is your own?"

Hannah and Lazar looked shocked, for they had never mentioned the pregnancy.

"You thought I didn't know. A mother knows her daughter!" she said, gaily pinching Lazar on the cheek. "You're a fast worker."

Pointing to Hannah's slightly swelling abdomen, she continued, "All I can say is I hope you made it in America and not on the boat!"

"Why, Mama?" asked Hannah, relieved to know Mama didn't suspect the baby had been conceived before their marriage.

"All the evil influences you could have seen! Those people in steerage with sores and twisted bones. What kind of a monster would it have been?"

"That's superstition and you know it!" remonstrated Hannah.

"You want something to look at? Try Joey Goldstein down the corner. A perfect child, all that black hair, those curls. His eyes are like two perfect olives! Make one like that!"

"I'll try, Mama," Hannah said, hugging her to seal the announcement.

Mama reached down and patted her daughter's stomach in an unexpected gesture of intimacy. "Take care of yourself and take care of the American."

"The what?" Lazar asked.

"The American, that's what I like to call your baby."

"Do you know something else?" Lazar asked.

"What?" Hannah and Mama asked in unison, thinking he was referring to his child-to-be.

"I went to a meeting, met some good socialists, and asked them about America, about the rules, the problems. I asked about our papers."

"Which ones?"

"All of them. Our documents from Russia, the religious papers, the immigration cards, the ones from Ellis Island. I wanted to know which I had to carry, so if I got stopped by the police . . ."

Alarmed that he might already be in trouble, Hannah asked, "What are you planning?"

"Nothing, darling, nothing! But you remember how we were always being detained in Russia."

"I remember." Hannah thought about the Odessa Express.

"I asked which you carry, which you keep at home; and do you know what they said?"

"What?"

"No papers! Only the little card is saved, and you don't even need to carry it with you!" He held up the small tan paper marked with the red JJ and pointed to the phrase on the back that was written in English, Swedish, German, French, Dutch, Hungarian, and Russian. " 'Keep this card to avoid detention at quarantine and on railroads in the United States, and also for your identification in naturalization,' " he read, with more passion than the words themselves should have inspired.

"I don't understand!" Hannah said.

"That's America! You don't carry any papers! No papers! That's what is meant by freedom."

"You are sounding more and more like a capitalist!" Hannah laughed at his intensity and kissed his cheeks, which glowed in excitement.

# II

❖ ❖ ❖ ❖ ❖

# Benjamin Sokolow
## Delivered June 1, 1905

❖ ❖ ❖ ❖ ❖ ❖ ❖ ❖ ❖ ❖

## · 1 ·

HANNAH WOULD HAVE SPENT more time brooding about Lazar's recent political activities if she had not been so concerned with the basics of survival. The combined earnings of Mama and her sisters were a meager twenty-seven dollars per week. With her piecework Hannah contributed no more than five dollars to the family purse. Lazar added nothing, for hadn't he been raised to be a scholar? Even if he did not spend his days studying the Talmud, he claimed he was bettering his mind with his readings and Board of Education English classes three nights a week.

But all his intellectual activity did nothing to satisfy Hannah's hungers. From the moment she awoke in the morning, she thought of nothing else but what she might eat. She dreamed of bread so fresh that it melted on her tongue, beef with juices swimming on top, a soup made from a whole chicken instead of bones and feet. Only dimly could she remember the sweetness of cream, or fruit with flesh that needed no soaking or poaching to be palatable. Now even Mama's noodles were disappointing, for she used the minimum of eggs and butter and cheap flour. The result, though tough and pale, was filling.

Lazar tried to be good to her. He brought her treats; he bartered for special prices; but he never took the slightest interest in finding a steady job, even though he might have been able to earn twice what any of the others could.

Their rent was a bargain. Everyone told them so. Only eight-fifty a month! Why, the same rooms on the street floor were more than ten dollars. At the first of the new year Belinsky's rent collector came to their door. Although they knew they had been expected to pay after two months, they had not saved a dollar.

Mama feigned surprise. "This is a mistake. Mr. Belinsky said . . ."

"Two months, he gave you two months," the collector, a boy of no more than fifteen, said in a practiced tough voice. "Now you pay like the rest."

"But we didn't know. We don't get paid at the factory, Belinsky's factory, until next week."

"Why didn't you say you worked at Belinsky's? The rent will be deducted from your wages. Much easier on me!" He whistled as he went downstairs to collect from the family who picked nuts for a living.

The next week Mama and Dora brought home almost no money, and for the first time in her life, Hannah felt pangs of true hunger. Mama and the girls sipped weak tea, chewed stale bread, and divided a few pieces of herring without complaint. Hannah took the two slices of bread she was allotted, swallowing them as soon as they were soft; but they served only to increase her appetite. When Eva turned her head toward a noise in the street, Hannah reached for her sister's slice. Why shouldn't she have it? It was for the baby inside her, the little parasite who made her so ravenous. If it weren't for the baby she wouldn't have done it. Eva turned back and saw her sister's fingers slip around the crust.

Hannah placed her hands over her eyes and wept. "Eva, I'm sorry, I didn't know what I was doing!"

"Take it. One of the girls at the shop shared with me at lunch," she lied.

"I'll find more work this week. I'll double my piecework and I'll see that Lazar brings in some money too!"

Mama swirled her glass as though the air could add more nourishment. "He's not a worker. What will he do?"

"He eats here, he sleeps here; why shouldn't he pay?"

Eva stared at the low stool where Lazar usually sat. "He hasn't taken a meal here all week."

"Because we've had no food!" Hannah spoke before she realized what she had said. Where was her husband? What was he eating? What did she really know about his life apart from her? He went to night school, to meetings. But where did he go for food?

"I'll find him and tell him he must do something!" Hannah reached for her cloak and marched down the stairs past two half-starved shoeshine boys who huddled in the doorway.

Walking toward the Pig Market on Hester near Ludlow, where "everything but a pig" could be bought from pushcarts, she searched the streets for Lazar. A stiff wind blew sleet from the river, causing the late shoppers to hurry home and the merchants to close early. As Hannah surveyed the merchandise left in the stalls she wondered if she might find a damaged piece of fish or some overripe fruit before she realized she hadn't brought even a penny with her. She stamped her freezing feet in frustration.

A broken crate in front of the butcher's stall lay in her path. With the toe of her boot she kicked it out of her way, revealing a pile of bones. She reached down and prodded them with her fingers until she uncovered a small piece of meat that radiated like a beacon in the snow. Hannah looked left and right. No one else had spied the treasure. Grabbing at the slippery fat, she pulled the bone out from the pile, but it resisted her. Was there something on top of it, or had it frozen to the bones beneath? To loosen it, she pried at the underside with her fingertips. Something warm moved at her touch. A rat as big as a small dog lifted a bristling nose and bared yellow teeth. Gagging, Hannah stumbled back. The rodent's putrid smell filled her nostrils. Vainly she tried to eradicate it by rubbing herself with snow that left her more cold than clean. Almost frantic, Hannah searched aimlessly for her husband in doorways, down darkening streets. Where were the places he frequented? Night school on Rivington? No, that was last night. A lecture? He had a passion for lectures! But they were on Thursdays. Where else? The Monopole!

To a woman walking with a bundle of piece goods on her head, Hannah asked, "Do you know a place called The Monopole?" The woman shook her head. At the corner of Essex and Broome she saw lights burning inside a pool hall. Men! Wasting their time and money! Opening the door, she asked the first one who glanced in her direction, "Do you know where The Monopole is?"

Taking a cigar out of his mouth, he spat in the corner. "It's quite a long walk for you, missus, all the way past Houston to Second Avenue."

"How do I get there?"

"After Stanton comes your First Street." He held up a finger. "You walk to number Nine Street. It's just off the corner."

Hannah creased her brow. "Corner nine and two?"

"Think you can find it?" he said as he opened the door for her. Hannah nodded and walked resolutely in the direction his cigar pointed.

After crossing Houston Street Hannah was out of her territory. For more than two months her world had been bounded by a few blocks of New York while her husband daily ventured into unknown sectors to escape the press of the ghetto. Now she vowed to convince him to stay closer to home and take better care of her.

The Monopole might have been the Café Bessarabia in Odessa. The same atmosphere of cigar smoke and tea steam, the same bearded, thin-lipped intellectuals, their women flat-chested and sallow. Once inside the frosted glass doors, Hannah was overcome by the warmth, the laughter, the clink of glasses, the familiar babble of political debate. A waiter in a blue and white striped apron passed by with two plates of cake iced with honey and walnuts. Hannah clenched her fists. Here he comes to eat cake while I am left to break my jaw on hard bread! Resolutely she marched around the room looking for the object of her fury.

She was not disappointed. In a quiet corner Lazar sat with two other men, his back to Hannah. She listened for a moment. A man in a shabby suit was deeply engrossed in explaining a point of Marxist doctrine.

Hannah stepped from behind a post and touched his shoulder. Lazar looked bewildered. "Hannah! Is something wrong?"

"Wrong!" Hannah held her palms out. "I was so hungry I found myself scavenging in the garbage and had to fight a rat for a bit of rotten meat! The rat won! Where do you get the money for this?" She gestured to the empty plates littered with bits of fruit and cake.

"He was my guest, I assure you, Mrs. Sokolovsky," said a quiet man with a thick mustache. He was sitting in the corner.

"And who are you?" she accused.

"Please sit down; have something to eat. You'll feel better," Lazar cajoled. "These are my friends Morris Reznikoff, the socialist lecturer, and David Gruber, the Yiddish writer."

"So, Mr. Reznikoff, how is it you have so much money to buy all this for my husband?"

"This time of year everybody wants to come to a lecture to stay warm, if not to learn. I charge five dollars to an organization that sponsors me and take donations as well."

"What a life; you get paid to talk! Lazar, now there's the profession for you!"

"If only I were as great a speaker as Reznikoff," Lazar said softly.

"Don't wish my life on your husband," Reznikoff continued. "All summer I might as well starve to death."

The men's even tones so contrasted with Hannah's hysterical voice that she was ashamed. Lazar pushed his glass of tea in front of her. She took a few sips and spoke without looking up. "After the baby comes, I don't know how we'll manage."

Lazar shrugged his shoulders and grimaced at his companions. "Will you be satisfied with a man of no principle? How can I fight the system that enslaves our brothers and sisters if I become a part of it? You think only of yourself, Hannah, not of me or of the workers. I give every hour of my day to saving them from the evils of their enslavers!" Lazar pounded his fist so hard that the glasses on the table jumped.

Choking in self-defense, Hannah blurted, "Only of myself . . . It's impossible to have the energy for anything else if your belly is empty! What do you know about carrying a child, having it sap all your strength? Do you want a sick or deformed baby?"

David Gruber had been silent throughout their argument. His jaw protruded so far that his upper teeth rested behind the lower, creating a powerful simian countenance. When he spoke, Hannah was as fascinated by the mechanics of his unusual facial structure as his defense of her husband. "Socialism in America is dying; we need more dedicated men like Lazar to work for us. How many immigrants can offer a disciplined commitment if they must labor to feed themselves? Most everyone finds party work tiresome, and few bring scholarship as well as leadership to the cause as your husband does. Perhaps your husband will be part of a rebirth of American Jewish socialism."

Hannah began to cough. "I'm not saying he should stop his work with you, but what about me? I'm getting sick from all this." She turned from Gruber's expectant gaze.

Reznikoff cleared his throat. "There are things we all must do to get by, though some are less of a compromise than others. Before I could make my way by lecturing I took to peddling."

"Peddling!" Lazar looked incredulous.

Hannah touched Lazar's hand and he was quiet. "What did you sell?"

"Notions. I went to a supplier on Mulberry for a whole assortment of stockings, buttons, scissors, towels, handkerchiefs, threads, pocket knives. If you spend twelve dollars, you get a heavy strap for your basket as a premium. At least you work for yourself, not a shop steward. And you come and go as you like."

"Where would I get twelve dollars for the goods?" Lazar asked.

"You could collect papers or old clothes uptown, where they just throw everything on the street on certain days of the week, haul it downtown, and resell it in the Pig Market," Reznikoff continued. "That's probably more to your taste than knocking on doors, taking all sorts of cuffs and insults."

"But scavenging for rags, bottles . . ." Lazar implored Hannah.

"I should do the same for food? Have you ever seen a rat this close?" She held her fingers four inches from her nose.

"Enough of that! In a few days there will again be money in the house; you can borrow from Leyb until then."

"How can I ask them when Belinsky took part of Sonia's salary for our rent? You think they are so well off? Olga keeps what she earns for herself, and Uncle Leyb puts everything else back into his stock so maybe someone in our family will succeed."

"You won't be happy until we're all millionaires! If that's what you want, find yourself another man! I always told you my work would be as important in America as it was in Russia, and let's not forget which one of us wanted to come here and why!"

"Lazar!" Hannah's face grew hot with shame. Rising to stand, she knocked over an empty glass with her elbow. Gruber caught it before it slipped to the floor. Tears blinding her eyes, Hannah pushed her way out the double doors and onto the street.

Disoriented by hunger as much as anger, she began walking uptown, berating herself for her behavior in public, cursing Lazar's ability to seem right when he was the one who was wrong. Realizing nothing looked familiar, she discovered she was on Fourteenth Street. She turned around, wrapped her cloak around her more securely, and tucked her chin into the knot of her babushka. Furious at the stupidity that had led her so far from home, she began to criticize herself. Why had she expected Lazar to change his ways without thinking of doing the same herself? If she couldn't be a midwife in New York, she could get a job in a factory, take in more piecework, not just the few collars and cuffs she did for her uncle at half price. The only reason she hadn't done so in the first place was because Lazar felt she was "too good" for that kind of work, that she deserved better. And if he supported her profession, why couldn't she do the same for his?

A tightness in her chest began to grow and swell, warming her from inside. She felt calm with the knowledge that she had evidence of Lazar's love in his caring. Maybe he didn't show it by slaving as a machine operator, but he had married her, come to America for her — and what had she done for him? Demands! Curses! Threats! How many women were abandoned by the fathers of their babies? She should count her blessings!

"Hannah!" Lazar rushed toward her as she approached Ninth Street. "Where were you? I've been looking everywhere!"

"I turned the wrong way and went all the way to Fourteenth Street. Why is it wider than all the rest?"

Lazar's warm breath fogged the air in front of his nose. "It's a boulevard, like the Razamovsca, remember?" He placed his arms around Hannah and pulled her toward him.

They walked in silence until they reached Grand Street. Hannah wanted to apologize, but could find no words. "Is Fourteenth Street uptown?"

"When the numbers get higher you go uptown, lower downtown."

"Then you reach the name streets like Grand and Hester."

"That's right."

"Lazar, how far uptown have you been already?"

"All the way up First Avenue, past the big hospital, Bellevue, to the number fifties, across to Fifth Avenue down past where all the capitalist millionaires live better than the czars of Russia!" He spat on the pavement.

"I'd like to walk uptown with you."

"Why is that?"

"To see what it's like, this America. To be with you away from the house and Mama and . . ."

Lazar noticed that Hannah's eyes were filling with tears. "What is it?"

Hannah coughed and wiped her eyes on her sleeve. "We are together so little, we don't talk, we only . . ."

Lazar stopped walking, stepped back, and threw up his hands. "Now you are complaining about that!"

Hannah pulled him toward her. "No, no, I'm not!"

They pressed their cold lips together and kissed. Lazar placed his hands under her cloak and rubbed them on her hips and thighs. She wriggled away.

"But you must keep me warm! I'm freezing!"

"If it's warm you want, let's hurry home."

Even though it wasn't late, everyone was in bed, having found that sleep dulled the ache of hunger. Quietly they undressed. Lazar fell upon Hannah with a fierceness she found more exciting than frightening, and then he gave her the chance to do the same to him. When they were content, but still joined, he whispered to her, "You know when I was happy?"

"Mmmm?" she murmured, thinking it was something to do with their first lovemaking.

"That time I spoke to steerage. As a writer in Russia I never saw the effect of my words, but that night . . . even as the engines made a noise, even when the passengers were afraid, they trusted me. Sometimes I feel as though I have been given a gift, a touch, something that I must use. Do you understand?"

"I do," Hannah answered. To herself she thought she had the same feelings about midwifery . . . a gift, a touch, something she must do. How could they find a way to feed themselves, do for their child, and yet follow their innermost wishes?

Hannah felt something. At first she thought it was Lazar releasing himself from her, but then she knew the feeling came from a much deeper place. It felt like an eyelid twitching inside.

Lazar had sensed it as well. "What was that?"

Hannah smiled. "Your baby, darling, your baby."

## · 2 ·

RESOLVED TO ASSUME more responsibility for finding work, Hannah decided to visit Miriam Fingerman once again, bringing along a medical text with some photographs as an excuse.

This time Mrs. Fingerman invited Hannah in more graciously, and as soon as she was seated on the tufted green sofa, Hannah opened to the page she had marked. "Remember you mentioned the face presentation? I've brought you a book that describes a technique for that problem."

Mrs. Fingerman pulled the book from Hannah's grasp as soon as she saw the illustrations. "Such pictures of women! What kind of a person would allow it?"

Hannah smoothed her hair and apologized. "Their faces are covered; no one knows who they are."

"Tcht, tcht!" Mrs. Fingerman's tongue clicked in rhythm with the turning of the pages. "Look at this!" She stopped and pointed to a diagram illustrating styles of forceps. Her finger tapped the diagram labeled "Axis-Traction Forceps." "This is what I have!"

"You ... you have forceps?" Hannah's voice betrayed her shock.

"Why shouldn't I?"

"I was taught ..." Hannah stumbled to put her thoughts in order. "We were never permitted forceps. It was believed that they were too dangerous for midwives to use."

"That's what they always say to exclude you from their ranks. What's so special about forceps? Would you rather have a dead baby and mother?"

"But the risks!" Hannah's voice was high and thin.

Miriam Fingerman wore a gold watch chain around her neck. She lifted its circular case, clicked it open, and looked at the time. "What isn't a risk?"

Reaching for her book, Hannah said. "I'm sorry to have kept you so long."

Mrs. Fingerman didn't release the volume from her grip. "No, no. I'm pleased you came again. I would have called on you, but I couldn't remember where you lived," she replied, rubbing the insignia on the outside of the watchcase.

Hannah watched the woman's fingers stroke the engraved gold initials. "Your watch is very lovely. I've never seen colors like that," she said, pointing to the faint blue and pink that were enameled into the gold design.

"My betrothal gift," Mrs. Fingerman replied curtly.

Deciding not to pry further, Hannah waited for the older woman to speak, but she was involved in reading the text. A few minutes passed. Mrs. Fingerman checked her watch again, closed the book, and contemplated Hannah, who patiently sat with her hands folded in her lap.

"Ten hours, it's been ten hours. Don't you think I should go back now?"

Leaning forward, Hannah asked, "What?"

"To Zaretsky's! Last night the woman was in labor, nothing happening. You think I wanted to lose a whole night's sleep there?

You have to know when to stay and when to come back, or you will go crazy in this business."

"How far along was she last night?"

Mrs. Fingerman held up her thumb. "Just this," she said pointing to the tip. "But you would never know it from listening to her!"

"And it's been ten hours?"

"I told them to call me only if she feels like bearing down."

"But wouldn't that be too late?"

"If the baby comes without me, they didn't need me in the first place. Anyway, when that happens they refuse to pay my fee! I can do all the work for days, but if I am not there to catch the baby, pfffft! They're done with me!"

"Maybe you'd like me to check her, save you the trouble?" Hannah tried to control her enthusiasm.

"No, you come with me. You wanted to be my assistant, so assist!" Mrs. Fingerman stood, brushed her skirts in place, and adjusted the semicircle of lace at her bust. After buttoning her heavy overcoat, she wrapped a fur scarf around her neck and placed the matching muff over her hands.

Bustling down the hallway, Mrs. Fingerman called back to Hannah, "Bring the book!"

❖ ❖ ❖

It was obvious why Mrs. Fingerman had elected not to spend the night at Mrs. Zaretsky's bedside, for her room in a basement on Rivington Street was the most dismal Hannah had ever seen. In the dank and narrow hall, moisture oozed from the walls, creating an eerie shimmer. As soon as Mrs. Fingerman entered the patient's room, she went to the small stove fashioned from an oil drum and stirred the few remaining coals with a poker. A sudden burst of warmth blasted the room before the chill again dominated. The metal bed upon which Mrs. Zaretsky lay was twisted and broken. A ragged child sat beside her mother, scratching a scab on her arm.

Mrs. Fingerman spoke in a loud voice. "How are we doing now?"

The woman tried to slide up to the head of the bed, but slumped back into the bundle of rags that served as her pillow.

"The same; all the time they come; it never stops." She coughed.

"Did you sleep last night?"

"A little, when she'd let me." Mrs. Zaretsky elbowed her toddler.

"And Mr. Zaretsky? Where is he now?"

"He had to go to the factory; always another in line to take your place if you don't appear."

Hannah looked around the room for any sign of food. All the tin pots and bowls were empty. There wasn't a kettle or samovar in the house. A glass milk bottle lay on its side under the washbasin and an empty seltzer bottle was beside the bed. Hannah tried to find some place to sit, but the chair's cane seat was broken, so she perched on the edge of a battered steamer trunk to watch as Miriam Fingerman pushed Mrs. Zaretsky's legs apart and did a quick internal exam. Hannah noted that Mrs. Fingerman neither explained the procedure nor washed her hands.

"That's an improvement!" Mrs. Fingerman said, wiping her hand on a towel draped over the metal bedpost. To Hannah she whispered, "I don't understand it; she's fully dilated but not able to push."

"May I look?" Hannah asked warily.

Mrs. Fingerman shrugged her shoulders.

Removing the torn and dingy comforter from the woman's body, Hannah examined the external dome with gentle hands. Just above her pubis a second pouch distended forward. "Look here!" Hannah called and pointed out the hump. Her bladder is so full it's presented an obstruction."

"Let me see!" Mrs. Fingerman said, pushing on the spot. "Hmmph! I suppose you are right. There isn't even an inside toilet; they use the building in the yard."

Hannah reached for the basin, placed it under the woman's buttocks, and encouraged her to void.

Mrs. Fingerman directed Hannah to remove the slopping pan of amber liquid. "Take it out to the street and dump it."

"Where's the latrine?"

"Just toss it out the front door; no one will notice."

Reluctantly Hannah obeyed and dashed the contents out toward the street, but she immediately regretted it when she saw the evidence spattering a snowbank. As soon as Hannah returned she watched the older midwife direct the second stage of labor.

"Push, now push!"

Hannah lifted the young child out of her mother's bed and sat her on the floor among some broken crockery. The child placed a piece in her mouth. Hannah tapped her hand and took it away. "No, you'll cut yourself," she said, and looked around for something to amuse the girl. Mrs. Fingerman still wore her woolen coat, but she had unwrapped her fur scarf and placed it across the broken chair. Without thinking, Hannah handed it to the child, and she began to play with the six small fur tails that fringed the end.

A groan rose in Mrs. Zaretsky's throat. Hannah stood up and watched Mrs. Fingerman apply pressure on the mother's abdomen to squeeze the baby down. Even after the contraction was over, the older midwife continued the exertion. Deep ridges formed on Mrs. Zaretsky's forehead as she gasped at the pain. "Stop it! No!" she begged and tried to push the older midwife off her belly, but Mrs. Fingerman held the patient's arms away. "It will be over soon."

With the next contraction she moved the woman into a diagonal position on the bed and held her legs apart. Not daring to interfere, Hannah remained in the background.

As the baby's head appeared, Mrs. Fingerman permitted it to crown without assistance. At the next contraction the shoulders appeared. The midwife stepped forward, grabbed for the child, and pulled it from the woman's bulging vagina. The baby was plopped on the rubber sheet that partially covered the filthy mattress. "Hand me the scissors to help me tie the cord," she demanded. Hannah did as she was told.

The baby had not yet cried. The older midwife snapped her fingers at the baby's buttocks and clapped her hands in front of its face. Then she held the newborn girl aloft by her feet and swung her back and forth. Mucus dribbled from her mouth. Hannah stepped in and wiped it away and the child finally began to wail. Her mother looked up at the reddening child. "A girl, another girl. Mordecai will be disappointed." Then, calling to her older daughter, she said, "Look, you have a sister; isn't she pretty?"

The little girl stood and came to stand beside her mother, still trailing the fur scarf in her hand. "Poor baby, don't cry," she said in a tiny voice. "Are you cold?" Lifting the fur piece from the floor, the child placed it across the slippery newborn baby and tried to wrap her head. The fur stuck to the creamy vernix and the tails blotted a small pool of blood that formed on the mattress.

Busy with the extraction of the placenta, Mrs. Fingerman had not noticed. But after she placed the cord and placenta in a waiting bowl she caught sight of the bedecked newborn. "What are you doing, you stupid brat?" she screamed.

The child, who still held one end of the fur, looked up with surprise. When she lifted her chin, she caught the full force of Mrs. Fingerman's angry blow across her cheek, screamed in terror, and ran down the hall. Mrs. Zaretsky also realized what had happened, and she tried to sit up and unravel her newborn from the fur. "Leave it alone!" the midwife screeched. "Where's my muff? What did that little bastard do with it?"

Hannah pointed to the trunk where it lay untouched. "It's here." Her voice caught in her throat. She pointed to Mrs. Zaretsky. A fresh stream of blood issued from the woman's vagina, but the midwife continued to wipe her fur piece. Hannah stepped forward and mopped the discharge, noting that the woman's flesh had torn and required some stitching. She was sure this was because the midwife had not properly manipulated the shoulders as they emerged. "Do you plan to stitch her or shall I?"

"Why bother? She'll heal as well without."

"I'll finish the case if you'd like me to."

"Please yourself."

Hannah prepared the site by thoroughly cleaning it. Then she applied a few external sutures, and, grasping the tissues deeply at the side, brought the parts together, tying them in strands and knotting them.

Mrs. Fingerman hadn't even waited for Hannah to finish before she left. Eventually Mr. Zaretsky arrived with some bread and herring and prepared a simple supper for the family, inviting Hannah to join them. Knowing they had even less than she did, she politely excused herself and packed the needles and instruments. Mrs. Fingerman had already taken everything except the suturing materials, even, Hannah was annoyed to note, her medical textbook.

Nothing about Mrs. Fingerman pleased Hannah: neither her

voice nor her manner, and certainly not her technique! If this was the woman who delivered everyone in the neighborhood, surely they could get better service from Hannah. Perhaps Mrs. Zaretsky would recommend her to friends. But then, Hannah lamented, the word of this poverty-stricken woman wouldn't be of much value.

## · 3 ·

HANNAH WAS DETERMINED to write to Dr. Jaffe, and after much soul-searching, she finally wrote the address on the envelope on the marble counter at the post office: J. S. Bruchermann, 34 Frederrich-Hershen Strasse, Zurich, Switzerland. Handing it to the clerk, she hesitantly asked, "Please? How much?"

"Howdaya 'spect me ta read dat, lady?"

Tilting her head to one side, Hannah asked, "What?"

"English!" he shouted and pointed to the words on the envelope. "Write it in English!"

A hot flush lit her cheeks. A woman carrying a chubby baby overheard the conversation, and spoke in Yiddish. "Go to a letter writer. There's one on Canal near Orchard."

"How much?" Hannah asked.

"Ten cents for the envelope."

As the letter writer quickly copied the address, Hannah worried again if she should have revealed so much without consulting Lazar or Mama. In a short letter she had written about Chaim's arrest, the Odessa pogroms, her marriage to Lazar, and the fact she was expecting a baby (in that order).

That night she dreamt the letter was ripped from its mail sack by Scarneck in the boxcar of the Odessa Express, shredded with a knife, and sent swirling across the Ukrainian countryside. It would never reach her; Dr. Jaffe would never, never find her . . .

Hannah twisted in her blankets, and as she tried to unwrap herself Lazar stirred. "What is it?" he asked.

"Just a bad dream about Russia."

"That's what I have every night!" he said, turning his back to her.

❖ ❖ ❖

The next month, when the rent was again summarily deducted from Mama, Sonia, and Dora's wages, Lazar became irate.

"Those capitalist bastards are squeezing the life from us!" He pounded on the crate table, splitting the wood. "We won't stand for their tricks another time!"

"Lazar, you cannot fight everyone!" Hannah said, pausing to cough. "At least there are no pogroms, no papers. You said yourself . . ."

"All we have done is traded one kind of poison for another."

Hannah bowed her head so her tears would not be seen by everyone. "Lazar, please," she whispered.

Her husband went to the front window and cleaned the moist glass with his sleeve. He looked down at the street and saw the huddled, freezing tenement dwellers pushing home, market baskets filled with Sabbath treats. Pivoting on his left foot, he ignored his wife and spoke to Mama.

"I have a plan. The next rent is not due until March, right?"

"Yes, but it is so hard to save. We just finished paying Sonia back her wages from last month; now it begins again. If we moved to a smaller place perhaps there would be more left over for food."

Eva gazed at the bare walls, which had been scrubbed and decorated with the few utensils they owned. "Here we have running water and a tub in the kitchen. I don't want to go to somewhere else!" She implored first Mama and then Lazar. Brightening with an idea, she said, "If we put four boarders in the front room we could bring in sixteen more dollars a month!"

Mama was indignant. "Boarders? In my home? Never!"

"But everyone has them!"

"You don't know what you are saying!" Mama yelled. "They'll steal your food, rob you blind, and I have two daughters yet who aren't married. How could I take that chance?"

Eva blushed and Dora looked confused. "If I were married that would be one less person at home," Eva said, hoping the catch in her voice wasn't too evident.

"I won't hear of it for at least another year. Besides, your sister comes first."

"You were promised to Papa at my age and Abie's mother, Rayzel, was already . . ." She stopped and changed to an even more unfortunate line of thought. ". . . And anyway, who would want Dora?"

"Eva!" Mama stepped forward and shook her daughter so hard that hairpins fell to the floor. "Never say that again! Abie must never know! And I don't want you to talk like that about your sister! She's worth two of you and your spiteful, ungrateful mouth. No supper for you tonight! Get out of my sight!"

"Supper?" Eva pointed to the hard bread and weak soup that were being prepared. "It's not worth eating anyway." She spit out the words before running from the room and down the stairs.

Dora ran to the door and looked after her sister. "Where's she going?"

"Probably off to that friend of hers who makes the pillow lace," Mama said calmly, but she betrayed her true worries by clasping and unclasping her hands. Turning the coals to heat the soup faster, she asked Lazar, "So what is this 'plan'?"

"I want you should leave Belinsky's so he can't do this to us anymore."

"But he pays good wages . . ."

"What do you get there?"

"Sixteen-fifty for six days, and Dora makes nine dollars doing buttons."

"I know another contractor, a good socialist named Schneiderman who has a modern system." Lazar pulled a scrap of paper from his pants and found a pencil on a shelf. Gesturing to the women, he had them look over his shoulder while he did the calculations.

"First he gets the job, say for three hundred cloaks for a price of two hundred twenty-five dollars delivered, or seventy-five cents a piece. Then each of three operators gets fifteen dollars, three basters get thirteen dollars, three finishers get ten dollars, two pressers get twelve dollars, one button girl gets nine dollars, and he pays himself eighteen dollars for trimming, busheling, sales, and delivery."

"But Lazar," Hannah interrupted, "Mama makes a dollar fifty more than that already."

"Wait till you hear me out and you will see how you can beat the capitalists at their own game." He pointed to the figures, drew a line for a total, and said, "His labor costs are one hundred sixty-five dollars up front. He pays this at the end of the week. Now he has expenses: rent of six dollars, oil and repair of three dollars, and five dollars in payments on his machines, totaling fourteen dollars. Next he delivers the garments, making a profit of forty-six dollars, which he divides equally among the workers. In this case each gets a bonus of three dollars and fifty cents, so Mama would make two dollars more than at Belinsky's!"

"Really?" Mama was impressed.

"Of course if he makes a better deal with the contractor, or if the workers can finish a job in less than a week, everyone makes more money!"

"Why don't they all work that way?" Hannah asked in a high, excited voice.

"Schneiderman's idea is so new it's hardly been tried. But once the workers have a taste of his system, no one will be left to slave for misers like Belinsky. You women will be some of the first to join the ranks of the liberated American worker!"

"Lazar, this sounds like a system even you could join in good conscience," Hannah said deliberately. "Why don't you also take a job at Schneiderman's?"

"What could I do? Press pants? I will go from sweatshop to sweatshop, teaching the method, proving that it works."

"And you think it will?" Hannah asked, placing her hand on her husband's muscled shoulders.

"Of course!" he finished triumphantly.

The first order at Schneiderman's went well, but Mama and Dora returned exhausted every day after working twelve hours, rather than the nine expected at Belinsky's. On the second job their spirits waned; a presser became ill and left, so it took ten days to complete. When the expenses for the three extra days were deducted from the profit, each worker received only a three-dollar bonus, and Mama brought home eighteen dollars for ten days of work, losing eighty-five cents a day compared to what she had made at Belinsky's. The next week was not much better, but when the rent was due at least it was not deducted from their wages.

Instead the rent collector came. Lazar put him off with slippery talk about getting paid on Mondays. In the middle of the night they moved almost fifteen blocks down Delancey to 81 Willett Street. The next morning no one was surprised to find the Blaus and Sokolows had gone. It happened all the time.

## · 4 ·

THE SCHNEIDERMAN EXPERIMENT lasted but a few weeks. More and more contractors competed for the same jobs, and Schneiderman found he could not bid low enough for the work and still pay out his bonuses. Shops able to produce a thousand cloaks a week with machines that had already been paid for got all the business, so Schneiderman sold his equipment and became manager for a firm on East Broadway. Aunt Sonia went to work for Uncle Leyb, who had saved enough from his pushcart to stock a tiny storefront on Hester Street, proudly hanging up his sign, "L. Meyerov, Imported Laces and Yard Goods," next door to "S. Scharlin and Son, Manufacturers of Gambetta Snuff."

Mama found a job with the Burgenest family's children's clothing business as the first operator, making eighteen dollars. And after Dora learned smocking, she brought in an astounding fifteen dollars a week. From time to time Lazar peddled tin or copper, sometimes old rags. He brought his pack home at night looking weary and resigned, usually with empty pockets. Though he would go from street to street calling for junk, he used every opportunity to kibitz with his friends and proselytize for his latest idea. Now and then he contributed unusual items: a dented but serviceable kettle found at an uptown dump, a flank of beef traded for some old books, a warm shawl donated by an admirer of his fiery speeches. And when he had not brought anything home in several days, Lazar might relieve a melamed from teaching a flock of unruly boys for a few hours, earning a dollar while the instructor slept. Even though Lazar brought in less than any of the Blaus, he did just enough to neither inspire their criticism nor inflame Hannah's rage.

Not that Hannah had the strength for argument. In the last weeks of her pregnancy the edges of her world blurred, perhaps because life was less of a struggle in the spring. One morning, an hour after the sun rose, she gathered a few pieces of needlework and moved down to the stoop to observe the daily parade. First the bums arrived to buy buttermilk at five cents a quart from the dairy store. "Why buttermilk?" Hannah had once asked the proprietor's wife.

"Soothes their stomachs after a night of drinking," she had responded gruffly.

Diagonally across the street was a livery stable. The drivers waited outside on a bench, teasing a goat named Tammany with a bottle of beer. He lapped it up, frisked his tail, and butted the drivers who played him like a bull.

By the time more women and children made their way down to the street, the peddlers came through. As she watched the sparks fly from the ancient scissors grinder's wheel she remembered that Lazar had complained about his razor. Asking the old man to wait, she climbed the four flights, then walked down again. When she arrived panting at the bottom, another woman, draped in a poppy-studded kimono, was first in line. The girl, also expecting a baby shortly, chewed some sunflower seeds and spit the shells onto the street. While Hannah waited the girl offered her some, and she eagerly accepted. "When does your baby come?" Hannah asked, delicately removing the shell with her fingernail.

"In a few weeks; not soon enough, though! And yours?"

"Not till summer. Not soon enough!"

The young women put their heads together and laughed.

Hannah began to cough. "Shouldn't have run up those stairs. I have no breath left anymore." Then she rubbed her back.

"Does your back bother you too?" the girl asked.

"Always; it's because the ligaments are stretching to make more room for the baby."

"Liga . . . what?"

"I'm sorry, you see I'm a midwife and I forget that not everyone understands those words. My name is Hannah Sokolow, and yours?"

"Jenny," the girl said, paying the scissors grinder, who grimaced as he took her money.

Jenny stepped back while Hannah's razor was sharpened. As the noise reached its peak, she spoke close to Hannah's ear.

"Could I call you when my baby comes?"

"Of course," Hannah answered calmly.

For more than an hour they sat on Hannah's stoop while she rambled on about babies and remedies for constipation, and told successful birthing stories to ease not only Jenny's mind but her own as well. But Jenny, seeming in awe of the educated woman, spoke little about herself.

From a fruit peddler Hannah purchased two apples for them, while Jenny walked back to her home for some cheese and bread and her seven-string guitar. After they finished eating, Jenny sang songs from her native Kiev. Hannah, enjoying both the company and the music, admired the whiteness of the girl's arms and the roundness of her delicate chin.

Arriving home early that afternoon, Lazar saw them together. "Hannah! Come upstairs with me at once!" he ordered. Hannah bristled under his command, but did not argue, not wanting Jenny to overhear his harsh words.

Halfway up the stairs he asked sharply, "What are you doing with that whore?"

"What?" asked Hannah in disbelief.

"If Mama ever saw you with her, we'd never hear the end of it!"

Hannah cringed when she realized that everyone on the block had seen them together. "Maybe you are wrong. Her family's from Kiev; she hopes to bring her parents over."

Lazar placed his hands in his pockets and contemplated the

problem. "I wouldn't want anyone to say anything that might hurt you."

Hannah was more touched by his protective words than angry. Yet once she had been told, there was no denying Lazar was right. Jenny wore the bright housedress characteristic of the girls she had seen on Allen Street. And Allen Street was where she had said she was from and where she would go after the birth of the child.

❖ ❖ ❖

A few days later a child's voice aroused Hannah as she dozed in her chair. "Come for Jenny!" he called.

Lazar need never know about this case, she thought as she made her way across the street to Jenny's rooms.

Hannah's first words were an apology. "I'm sorry I haven't seen you all week. I've been very tired." She rambled on, hardly giving the girl a chance to speak.

Jenny pointed between her legs. "There's some blood and . . ." She staggered toward a mattress on the floor.

"Lie down and we'll see what is happening," Hannah said.

When Hannah examined her she was surprised, first, to find that Jenny's pubic hair had been shaved and, second, that with so little fuss she had managed to dilate within an inch of giving birth.

Through the next vigorous contractions Jenny began to sweat and clench her fists so tightly that the veins popped out on her arms.

Speaking softly, Hannah asked, "Should anyone be called?"

"I've sent the kid for Solly."

"Then Solly is the father?"

"No, I don't think so, but then you never know; it's always possible . . ." She was quiet while a pain peaked, and as it diminished she continued, "Anyway, he's made arrangements for the baby so I can go back to work."

"But why? Can't you get something in a factory or a shop?"

"Once you are in the life, you stay there. They starve you first so you know how it feels; then you never want to go back to anything else. Fifty cents ten times a night. Once you are used to it . . ."

"How do you . . . why did you?" Hannah stuttered.

"I was only ten when I came over with my sister. As soon as

Solly saw me he had his eye on me. When he thought I was ready, he sent Jimmie, the nigger, and his gang after me one night. Even Jimmie took a turn. Then they beat me and left me to suffer. Solly took care of me, fed me, taught me what to do. He promised no one would hurt me again ... ahhhh!" She gasped and began to pant and shudder.

As the contraction mounted Hannah tested its internal intensity and felt the sudden descent of the baby's head.

"Very good! This is going to be an easy birth." When she withdrew her hand she felt a sudden urge to wash again. From her kit she removed a bottle of carbolic acid and mixed the disinfectant solution with water before scrubbing her hands raw.

Hannah watched Jenny stoically submit to the final stages of labor. Unwrapping Jenny's gown, Hannah mopped the sweat that formed between her high breasts. How pretty she was: her face with the fanatical dark eyes of a prophet, her cheeks the color of ripe peaches, her brows forming a perfect arch.

The baby's head was easily delivered, but the shoulders seemed wedged. Deftly Hannah rotated the baby 180 degrees, and with the next push the little girl was born.

Jenny bent over and touched its wrinkled nose and said, "Don't cry, I'll take care of you."

A few minutes after Jenny was comfortably resting, Solly arrived. The pug-nosed pimp first lifted the blanket covering Jenny's body and examined the area between her legs. "Won't take long to get you back in shape." He turned to Hannah. "You're the midwife Jenny told me about?"

Hannah nodded slowly.

He pulled a cigar out of his pocket and began to chew the tip. "What do I owe you?"

"Five dollars," Hannah said to the wall.

Holding the cigar in his teeth, Solly reached into his vest pocket and pulled out a roll of crisp bills. "Here's fifteen. But I want you to watch her until Friday. Saturday night it's back to Allen Street."

"But Solly," Jenny protested.

"Don't worry, we'll put you on special for a few weeks." He turned his back on her and walked over to the basket where the infant was sleeping.

"Don't wake her!" Jenny whispered.

Paying no attention, Solly unwrapped the coverlet. "Too bad it's a girl." He rearranged the cigar on the other side of his face.

"You can't take her yet!"

Solly turned to the new mother, who lay quivering under the quilt. He curled his lips and snarled, "Don't start nothin'!"

Jenny tried to sit up.

Solly snatched the baby and rushed out.

"Come back!" Hannah shouted. "Bring that baby back!" But it was no use. By the time Hannah reached the curb, he was out of sight.

The next morning Hannah trudged across the street to check her patient, bringing some buttered bread and jam to share with the unhappy girl. A pair of men's suspenders hanging over a chair swayed in the breeze from the open doorway. The ragged mattress was still in the center of the room, but Jenny was nowhere in sight.

Hannah stepped over the empty bottle marked CARBOLIC ACID that she had left the day before, opened closet doors, peered out into the back alleyway, and called Jenny's name over and over. But the girl had vanished.

· 5 ·

AFTER JENNY'S DISAPPEARANCE Hannah found distraction by learning more about the neighborhood. Sometimes she ventured across the Bowery to the Italian section, daring fate by tasting pork sausages cooked on a small coal fire and served with mustard on a roll. Other times she indulged herself with a penny's worth of hot chickpeas served in a newsprint wrapper.

One day, craving something cool to drink, she searched the streets for sight of the red-fezzed lemonade peddler. Perspiration dripped down her back and thighs, causing her to stop and fan herself every few minutes. In that oppressive heat there was no escape from the reek of rotten orange peels, fish scales, and sour milk. Finally Hannah found the peddler, who had a large bronze container strapped to his back. After she paid a penny, he selected a glass from the pan of water he wore around his waist, rinsed it once, and placed it in front of the curved spout that came over his left shoulder. When he leaned forward the liquid gushed out into the glass.

After Hannah downed two large drinks, her attention was drawn to Spector, the fruit vendor, calling out in a jumble of Yiddish and English, "Gutes frucht! Metsiyes! Bargains! Dray pennies die whole lot." Hannah gave the man two cents; he argued for a moment; then, raising his hands in prayer for himself, he wrapped the purchase in newspaper and dropped it into her bag.

Too exhausted to shop any further, Hannah avoided the rest of the market street and turned right on Broome. The next block was congested by an agitated group of Orthodox Jews who gathered closely about a wagon upon which a man was beginning to speak. Hannah recognized the familiar figure of Preacher Drummond. Three policemen stood by, knowing that his appearances frequently led to trouble.

With his hand beseeching the crowd, he called in a loud voice, "There is only one God, and that God is the God of the Jews."

Instead of cheers, the words were greeted with derisive laughter.

But Drummond, his clean-shaven chin pointed toward the sky, continued firmly, "I know you think we believe that Jesus Christ is . . ."

Yeshiva boys threw bottles and fruit. Drummond expertly ducked his head, but one banana peel thrown by a street urchin who shouted "Christ the Fatherless Liar!" struck him on the cheek.

Drummond humbly hung his head and said with a theatrical whisper, "If I did not love you Jews, I would not devote my life and fortune to saving your souls. You cannot help that you were raised in this stronghold of prejudice! I do God's work among you and I leave my results only with God!"

When there was a small break in the crowd Hannah hurried through, shaking her head at the preacher's absurd calling. Week after week he was jeered and spat upon, and still he came back for more. Surely there were easier missions than this hopeless attempt to convert the most devout and entrenched Jews of New York! She considered Drummond a lunatic, but she had to admire his persistence.

By the time Hannah reached home, she was exhausted. Her legs felt too heavy to support her body. As soon as she lay down on her mattress she slipped into a deep sleep.

When Lazar arrived home and saw his wife oblivious to the usual frantic pre-Sabbath activity in the room, he knelt beside her. Stroking Hannah's damp forehead, he asked Mama Blau, "Do you think we should call a doctor?"

"Making a baby can take all one's strength. Leave her be."

Still Lazar sat beside Hannah, watching and wondering. Her swollen breasts rose and fell in a slow steady beat, but her abdomen danced with life as the active fetus within played out its own rhythms. Placing his head to the stretched belly wall, Lazar tried to separate the dull flutter of Hannah's heart beating over the quick ticking of his child.

An hour later, Hannah woke slowly. As she sat up a trickle of warmth dripped down her leg.

"Hannah, is that you?" Lazar called. "Are you all right?"

She looked out and saw he was reading the *Forward* by the light of the Shabbes candles. Before responding, Hannah felt her abdomen for any signs of tightness or contractions, as she would with any woman in labor, not realizing that if there had been pains she would have felt them herself! "Nothing, nothing," she muttered. Did she dare examine herself internally?

She had expected Miriam Fingerman to do the delivery, but now that the moment was about to become reality, the very thought of that uneducated, ill-tempered woman touching her body or baby was abhorrent.

"Lazar!"

He came quickly and sat beside his wife and held her hands.

"Do you know how to get that doctor from your Odessa Society?"

Feeling her forehead with his lips, he said, "You are ill!"

Stroking his cheek with her thumb, she tried to soothe him. "I just think the baby may be coming."

"Isn't it too soon?" He stood and began to circle their narrow room.

Hannah looked up, her eyes wide with meaning, and shook her head. "A little, but not really."

Lazar bit his lip and studied his wife. At once she seemed both strong and frail, so determined and so afraid. "Why do you need a doctor?"

"*That* woman!" Hannah emphasized the first word. "She's dirty, ignorant, and dishonest. I'd rather have a stranger, a doctor, anyone but her."

Several hours passed before Dr. Strauss could be found, and when he arrived he found Hannah slowly chewing small pieces of bread and washing them down with cold tea to quench a deep thirst.

"I'm happy to see you still have your appetite!"

"My wife's an expert at this." Lazar puffed out his chest. "She studied to be a midwife at the Imperial College in Moscow."

"But I've never had a baby of my own before!" Hannah said sweetly.

Dr. Strauss placed his spectacles on his nose and peered at her closely. "Tell me about your condition."

Hannah sighed. "Only a few pains; I wouldn't even call them that. But my water is continually leaking and I am spotting."

"It is too early for me to do anything, then. I don't normally do deliveries anymore, only in emergencies."

"Where do your patients go?" Hannah asked.

"To Bellevue. The new hospital is well equipped, and they do not charge charity patients more than they can afford. For you it would be a few dollars at most."

"I wanted to have the baby at home," Hannah protested.

"Too many problems! Not clean enough! The delivery rooms at the hospital are scientifically designed with every sanitary precaution."

"Couldn't you make an exception in my case?"

The doctor either didn't hear Hannah's question or chose to ignore it. Instead he spoke of Lazar.

"You can't imagine how much help your husband has been to the Workmen's Society of Odessa! He's one of those rare men who are able to make a disciplined commitment to the cause. Of course we have our disagreements; the young and the old are not supposed to always see eye to eye . . ."

Gripped with a slight pain, Hannah reacted strongly to draw the men away from a potential argument. Dr. Strauss stared at his watch. "It lasted more than a minute, didn't it?"

Hannah nodded.

"It will take some time to get you admitted and settled, so why don't you get ready?"

Just before the hired carriage arrived, Mama walked Hannah to the street and kissed her daughter fully on the lips. "A blessing on you." Her voice quavered.

In the early hours of the morning a slight rain was falling. Hannah was protected only by the short awning over the passenger seat. Every bump in the street could be felt through the tense springs of the squeaking carriage as they drove along the river to Bellevue Hospital. At the freshly paved emergency entrance, a nurse waited between two tubbed evergreen shrubs.

"This is Mrs. Winthrop." Dr. Strauss made the introductions. "And this is Mrs. Sokolow."

"Very good," said the nurse, whose starched uniform with a fashionably pouched chest made her look like a cockatoo trying to attract a mate.

Resisting the nurse's tug on her elbow, Hannah stopped and firmly set her feet apart. "Aren't you coming with me?" she asked both men in Yiddish. They turned and stared at her for a moment, as though they heard words from an invisible source.

The nurse patted Hannah between her shoulder blades. "You'll be fine with us."

Hannah took a few steps before glancing back to see her husband's head pressed close to the doctor's. The last words she heard were Lazar's next volley in the dispute. "You have been here so long you have become deficient in theoretical subtlety and victimized by the flatness of American polemic . . ."

Hannah was led to an examining room constructed of white octagonal tiles neatly grouted into the floor and green rectangular ones set into the walls. One end of the room was lined with steel wash-basins. Draped above on a series of hooks and holders on the op-posite wall was an alarming variety of rubber tubing. Tall glass cyl-inders on tables held every imaginable type of tool: scissors, clamps, probes. Hannah steadied herself and tried to identify the American versions of the forceps. In a locked glass cabinet on the opposite wall she recognized a quart of ether; a six-ounce jar of fluid extract of ergot; tubes of adrenalin, Pituitrin, and cam-phorated oil; jars of silver nitrate; and a working hypodermic sy-ringe with tablets of morphine and scopolamine placed nearby.

A large tub in the corner was partially prepared for a bath. Han-nah was surprised to see that so modern a room contained no shower. With all this equipment, weren't they schooled in the lat-est techniques?

Hannah heard the scraping of wheels coming closer. She grasped the round metal seat of the chair she had been ordered to sit in and stared as a long table was positioned in the center of the room. Hard and flat, without even a horsehair pad, the table looked like a slab fit only for a cadaver. Nurse Winthrop pushed it next to the washbasins and set a foot brake with the heavy thud of her heel. Then she went to the sink and began an elaborate hand-washing technique. First the nurse pared her fingernails and re-moved all traces of dirt with a dull instrument. Dutifully she con-tinued to scrub with hot water and green soap and, when satisfied with the results, soaked her hands up to the elbows in an alcohol bath for one minute. Opening a bottle marked BICHLORIDE 1:1000, she formed a solution in a smaller pan and soaked her hands another three minutes by the clock. Then she picked up a sterile towel, dried herself, neatly folded it, and began to unravel a twisted group of rubber tubes.

Hannah's professional interest became more subjective with every purposeful maneuver. What procedures were they about to perform? The image of Mrs. Winthrop working to hook up the ir-rigation device blurred through a shimmering mask of red light.

The door opened and in stepped another nurse, who waited with her arms crossed impassively in front of her chest until she was called.

"We're ready, Mrs. Barnes."

The second nurse walked directly toward Hannah and planted her thighs in front of Hannah's face. Looking up from her low stool, Hannah saw cheeks of iron, hands of steel, and eyes that betrayed no compassion. As Hannah turned toward the wall, the tiles flickered and beckoned, the stainless array on the instrument table twinkled in readiness. Placing her hands over her eyes to protect herself from the intense examining light, Nurse Winthrop positioned beside her, Hannah listened. From somewhere in the past she heard the roar of a train rumbling through the night, the screams from the Old Bazaar, the imprecations on the Razamovsca, and she knew that never before had she been more afraid.

## · 6 ·

HANNAH SUFFERED all the aseptic procedures of the newly opened Maternity Division. Immediately after admission, Hannah received a saline enema and then was douched vaginally with bichloride of mercury. Because she was a charity patient, Hannah's head was washed with a virulent mixture of kerosene, ether, and ammonia, which caused her head to sting long after the libations were over. She was even forced to disinfect her mouth with a foul-tasting rinse. Once every orifice had been decontaminated, they shaved her pubic hair and wiped her nipples and umbilicus with ether, which burned her tender skin. The intensity of Hannah's contractions began to mount, but the nurses proceeded doggedly with their routine.

For the rest of her labor, they wheeled her cart into a room with four other women. The first babbled in Polish that Hannah partially understood; the second, a black American woman, was incomprehensible; and the other two shrieked and pleaded in Italian. In order to prevent her from falling from the narrow labor cart, Hannah's hands were tied to the railings with leather cuffs; and her legs, already dressed in sterile elastic stockings, were similarly bound.

Wordlessly, a doctor with a full beard and wire-rimmed glasses pushed his hand inside to ascertain her stage of labor, sending a harsh wave of pain down Hannah's back. She submitted without complaint but, as soon as he left, regretted not having asked how much dilation she had achieved. Perhaps she was halfway along, perhaps more . . . or less. A second doctor repeated the exam an hour later. This time Hannah tried desperately to communicate with the smooth-faced young man.

"How much?"

He patted her head. "Now don't you worry."

She moved her fingers back and forth to attract his attention. In Yiddish she asked, "How many fingers?" He wrinkled his nose and tilted his head in a feigned attempt to understand her. She tried again in Russian. "How many centimeters?"

The doctor smiled and shook his head. "See you later." He strode from the room clicking his heels.

Hannah pounded on the cart in frustration, but she was stopped by an excruciating pain that felt as if a metal spike were being slowly hammered into her back. She arched herself in an attempt at a different position, but the various bindings held her fast. Furiously she tried to wriggle free, to move away from the agonizing sensation. Any conscious effort at remaining calm dissolved as she experienced a second, then a third, contraction. The pressure rose under her rib cage. From somewhere far away she heard herself screaming.

They came. Four of them buzzed above her, their chins wagging, their eyes darting, their fingers fluttering like hungry pigeons. Someone held his hand inside during a whole contraction. Hannah reached to push him away, but only her head moved forward. Mrs. Barnes snapped it back, and her ears rang with the echo of the metallic pillow. A doctor wearing boots pushed his way into the circle.

"You might as well take her to delivery."

"Of course, Dr. Harrington," Mrs. Barnes replied, releasing the brake on the cart with her hand. "She's much too active to stay in the labor ward now."

In the room with the vaulted ceiling Hannah was prodded and poked. "One more irrigation will get the head down," a male voice suggested.

From the corner of her eye Hannah watched the instruments being arranged on the table: three lengths of forceps and a variety of scissors and sutures.

Could anything be wrong? The baby was clearly in a vertex position. Her labor had been within reasonable limits for a first-time mother, and other than her back pain, everything had seemed normal. She didn't know if her urge to bear down was the result of the forceful enema or if it really was the baby's head dropping. Nevertheless, she was involuntarily beginning to press herself to the table in the first efforts of expulsion when Dr. Harrington arrived in the room, his hands held high in the air, dripping with disinfectant.

"Hello, Winnie!" he greeted Mrs. Winthrop. "Is she ready?"

The nurse pointed to Hannah's straining buttocks.

The doctor, his hands held stiff as a sleepwalker to preserve them from contamination, walked around to Hannah's head. Her face was contorted with the effort of birth as well as the frustration of being bound and tied and unable to communicate.

As Dr. Harrington bent close to Hannah's face, a lock of brown curly hair fell in front of his face, and as he spoke she smelled strong coffee on his breath. "First baby?" he asked, holding up one finger. Hannah nodded. Then, as if the volume of his voice would somehow express his meaning more clearly, he spoke even louder. "Everything will be just fine." With a satisfied smile he strode to the other end of the delivery table.

Mrs. Winthrop extended the long stirrups out and to the sides as far as they would go and lifted Hannah's legs higher and further apart. After some jerking and pulling, the doctor nodded his approval and the nurse buckled Hannah's thighs, knees, and ankles with wide leather straps.

"Lights please!"

Mrs. Winthrop used a long metal hook to adjust the fixture that looked like wide suction cups at the end of an advancing octopus. The glare of the repositioned lights forced Hannah to close her eyes for a moment, but they opened with a snap as soon as the doctor called, "Prepare a set of Simpson forceps."

Forceps! The word was similar in Russian, having been derived from the same Latin root. From the deep rectal pressure she felt, Hannah had surmised the baby was descending properly. If only she had a few more minutes, she was confident she would expel the baby herself. Hannah locked her teeth together, pressed her lips closed, and squeezed, hoping to push the infant out before the doctor could begin his work.

Like any expectant mother, Hannah had been worried about the safety of the child, but now, as she lay at the mercy of the medical staff, her only concern was for herself. She was appalled by the number of knives and needles that glimmered on the instrument table.

"Call Dr. Emmett. I'd like him to see this procedure," Dr. Harrington said as he touched the baby's advancing scalp. When the younger clean-shaven doctor appeared in the room, he continued, "No need to scrub, Lawrence, I only wanted to show you my variation on Tarnier's mediolateral episiotomy."

Mrs. Barnes stood beside him with a beaker of yellow disinfectant. "Now!" he commanded, and she poured the cold liquid across Hannah's vulva, causing her to flinch. To Dr. Emmett he said, "Notice the dislocation downward and forward." He pointed with his finger but did not touch. "Now only the resistance of the outlet remains to be overcome. Scissors!"

Hannah watched the instrument that was handed to the doctor and noticed peripherally that he had selected a rounded perineum scissors, which at least would not injure the child's scalp. The cold metal hovered, then clamped Hannah's tissues. Hannah knew just what was coming next, and her knees shook uncontrollably. Nurse Winthrop appeared at her head with a cotton pad filled with ether, which she pressed to Hannah's face. Hannah turned away, but by holding her, the nurse finally forced a few whiffs into her nose.

"Now we are ready for the delivery. Forceps!" Dr. Harrington said. He grasped the handle of the first blade and inserted it around the baby's descending head.

The nurse checked the fetus with her stethoscope.

With a snap of his wrist the doctor locked the forceps closed. "Heart tones with blades closed!"

"Normal!"

"Let's begin traction."

Dr. Harrington waited for a uterine pain and began to pull harder. "Hannah felt that the interference of instruments was merely hindering her progress, but she was powerless to do more than close her eyes and groan.

The doctor crouched down, placed his right foot at the base of the operating table, and took one final pull. "There!" he cried out. "Perfect traction!" After unlocking and removing the blades, he let them clatter to the floor. Hannah knew her baby's head must now be elongated by the forceps. Nurse Barnes pressed upon her abdomen and in a moment the shoulders were also born. Dr. Harrington lifted the child into the air, and proclaimed, "A boy!"

But Hannah couldn't look.

"Dr. Emmett, would you like to do the repair?" Dr. Harrington asked, stepping away from the foot of the table. "I'll adjust the light for you."

This time when the nurse administered more ether, Hannah did not struggle against the anesthetic. As Mrs. Barnes lifted the ether pack from her face, the room shifted and reeled. Distantly she heard Dr. Harrington congratulating his associate. "Very nice work; your crown suture is perfection."

"Doctor!" Nurse Barnes called out just as Dr. Harrington was stepping out of the room. "Look!" Hannah felt her pulse racing, her limbs shaking out of control.

"Blood pressure!"

The nurse hastened to fasten a cuff and take a reading. "Eighty over sixty, Doctor! Her color is worsening," she said as she touched Hannah's ashen face.

"Didn't think she'd lost that much blood." Dr. Emmett reached into the metal bucket beside the cart. "Let me reexamine the placenta." Lifting the slippery organ, he ran his fingers over both the maternal and fetal surfaces. "It appears to be complete."

"I'll have to do an internal examination," Dr. Harrington replied.

Dr. Emmett glanced forlornly at his handiwork. "But my sutures!"

"Damn your sutures, boy!" Dr. Harrington said as he slipped on a fresh pair of gloves. "Here's the problem," he muttered. "A cervical tear about three centimeters long."

Pointing to Nurse Winthrop, who struggled to readjust the ether mask, Dr. Emmett asked, "Shall I help get her under?"

"Right, and when she's down, I'll need you to hold the retractors so I can get a good look."

Drifting under the effects of the anesthetic, Hannah was able to hear fragments of the conversations in the room, though her mind did not register much meaning.

"What's her pulse?"

"One hundred and three," Nurse Barnes reported with a sigh of relief. "Pressure is ninety over sixty and she's warming up nicely."

Dr. Harrington turned to the younger doctor. "That woman just seemed to be fighting everything I was doing. Maybe I'll just give up this charity work and stay with my private patients."

"Do you want to do the second repair yourself, Dr. Harrington, or should I prepare a new set of gloves for Dr. Emmett?" the nurse asked.

Dr. Harrington peered at the nurse abstractedly, then glanced back at Hannah. "Better do it myself," he said, sitting on a stool that put him at eye level with the table. As he lifted the first piece of silkworm gut he muttered, "Everything ... have to do everything myself!"

## · 7 ·

DAINTY CHIMES ANNOUNCED the change of shifts in the ward. With precise movements the day nurses exchanged places with the night staff. Her clipboard poised like a shield, the nurse in charge of Postpartum Unit Six made rounds with her replacement.

The new nurse, wearing a tag identifying her as Mrs. Schindler, stopped to read Hannah's chart. "How much morphine has she had?"

"One-sixth of a grain every four hours. She gave Harrington quite a time, I hear. Her husband — handsome fellow he was —

came around earlier, but he couldn't rouse her. If she asks for him, tell her he'll return tomorrow."

Mrs. Schindler stared at the empty crib beside the bed. "The baby is all right, then?"

"A beautiful boy, but he has a few forceps bruises; better prepare her for that. Doctor wants her on lots of fluids; she lost about two liters of blood. She's got a catheter to tend and she's not to leave her bed until the packing is removed."

As Hannah listened, she understood only a few words. Every time she opened her eyes the room swam with bright colors, but when she closed them it was far worse. The discomfort, which centered below her waist, spread down her legs, across her back, and to almost every muscle in her body.

After the nurses moved away from her bed, she turned slightly on her side, hoping to relieve some of the worst pressure. The woman in the next bed was sitting up, her legs dangling off the side. In her arms she held a totally bald newborn who had just finished nursing. Seeing that Hannah was finally awake, she smiled and said in Yiddish, "Feeling better now?"

Relieved to be able to talk to someone again, Hannah said, "I think so. Is your baby a boy or girl?"

"Another boy!" she said with obvious pride. "Our third! My Samuel claims that we can only make sons."

"What will you name him?"

"Eli, but in English it will be Edward, for the king of England. We came to America through Liverpool, and I loved the pictures of the king. What did you have?"

Have? Hannah stopped. She'd had a baby! But why was the crib empty? Hannah's pulse raced and her skin became cold and clammy. Her neighbor noticed the change and called, "Nurse! Nurse!"

Mrs. Schindler saw Mrs. Rosenblum pointing to bed eleven, and fearing another hemorrhage, she ran to attend Hannah herself.

Tugging at Mrs. Schindler's apron, Hannah choked, "My baby ... my baby ..."

Stroking her arm, the nurse smiled, revealing two gold-capped teeth. "Baby's fine," she said in Yiddish.

"You are Jewish?" Hannah asked, surprised.

"No, German, so it was not hard for me to learn the language."

"You are certain my baby is all right?"

"He's in the nursery. We were going to wait until you'd had a nice supper, but if you promise me you'll eat everything on your tray after I bring him, I'll send Mrs. McGuire for him right now."

"Of course, I promise!" Hannah tried to sit up.

"Don't rush yourself. And doctor says you are to stay in bed. You understand?"

"Yes, I will, I'll do anything you say. Bring her to me!"

Mrs. Schindler patted Hannah's head and spoke close to her face. "Him! You had a little boy. Don't you remember?"

❖ ❖ ❖

Lazar went directly to the crib where his son slept on his stomach, his knees pressed up close to his chest. "My child!" he said, his hands trembling with anticipation as he wondered where to lift the tiny thing.

"Don't wake him; he's just fallen asleep," Hannah cautioned.

But Lazar paid no attention. Tangling the blankets that covered and bound him, he raised the baby and held him out from his chest to examine the wrinkled face. "Doesn't look like much yet!"

Hannah pouted. "Give him time!"

Running his fingers over the baby's dented temples, Lazar asked, "Are these bruises serious?"

"The doctor used instruments. It will take a few weeks to heal, but they say he is normal."

"They say? You're the expert; don't you know?"

"I have just begun to know him. Yesterday I slept most of the day."

"When do you get out of here?" Lazar asked, uneasy in the room filled with more than a dozen women and babies.

"I would leave right this minute if you would take me home!"

Lazar furrowed his brow and placed the baby in Hannah's arms. "Better stay as long as possible. The food is good and there is someone to care for you. With Mama and the girls working, you would be home alone, and if anything were to happen, all those stairs . . ."

"But you could be with me, bring me meals, help, just for a few days . . ."

"Normally, yes, you know I would. But this is a bad time. I've made some commitments . . ."

"What now?"

"We're working on a federation of Jewish trade unions, trying to get the ILGWU to stop its internal wrangling and begin negotiations with the Industrial Workers of the World. I'm meeting with Schlesinger and Dyche. This could be a beginning . . ."

"If you help me for a few days I am certain . . ."

"Dr. Strauss said this was the best place for you!"

Hannah sighed so loudly that the baby slipped from her grasp, startled, and began to cry, his cheeks puffing and his temples pounding. "Shhh, Shhh!" Hannah said into his ear, but he continued to scream louder. Lazar backed away slightly while Hannah lifted her gown and attempted to offer him her nipple. The infant paid no attention, tossing his head aimlessly back and forth. "Here, here, don't be so stubborn," she coaxed, allowing her nipple to rub against his cheek. Finally she lay him on his stomach and rubbed his back until he calmed before she attempted to nurse him again. Then, like a little kitten pouncing on his prey, he grabbed the nipple, and his tiny fists pounded on the breast demanding a faster flow. "In another day or so my milk will be in. Then he'll be more satisfied," Hannah explained.

Lazar placed his hands on the child's cheek and rubbed the soft skin. Distracted from his sucking, the baby turned toward his father's finger.

"Don't! You see how difficult it is to get him started!"

Lazar retracted his finger as though he had been stung and placed it behind his back. Trying to control himself, he pressed his lips into a thin line. "Have you thought of a name?"

Hannah nodded. "Your father was Benyomen. Let's call him that," she suggested, because she thought naming him for Lazar's side might strengthen his paternity.

Delighted by her suggestion, Lazar agreed. "It would be Benjamin in English, like Benjamin Schlesinger the union activist. And his other name could be after your father, Itsik. Do you prefer Isidore or Isaac or . . . ?"

"Benjamin Isidore is fine," Hannah said quickly, but as she scrutinized the child's features, she felt a pang. Little Benjamin was bruised and misshapen, his features were unformed, and she couldn't find any resemblance to Lazar no matter how hard she searched.

· 8 ·

HOW COULD ONE tiny baby take up so much space? His accouterments — blankets, diapers, wrappers — either were waiting to be washed or were dripping fresh from the laundry pot. Terrified that virulent summer fevers would breed in their tenement, Hannah demanded that everything he wore be bleached and boiled. For fresh air, Hannah nursed on the fire escape landing or on the roof, refusing to bring her son down to the street, where the rotten vegetables and manure in the gutters seemed to visibly carry disease.

Hannah's recovery was slow; her strength returned by degrees. At first she blamed the heat, then the fact she had so little help, finally the baby himself, who slept poorly by both day and night. Every noise, every vibration unnerved the infant, causing him to cry out. Calming him was another problem. Hannah paced their three cramped rooms holding him in every position, patting his back and his bottom, kissing his head, shaking him too hard in her frustration.

In her heart she wondered if the baby felt her distance from him, for although she nursed him, tended his every need, something was wrong. They opposed each other. Just as Hannah fell asleep he awoke; when her breasts were empty he wanted to eat, but when they overflowed with milk he was content to suck his fingers. To an outsider it would have seemed that Hannah showed Benny great tenderness as she kissed the back of his satin neck and rocked him in her arms. Only she knew her ugly secret: something was missing; she did not love the child as she should.

In contrast, Lazar was surprisingly devoted. In the times he was at home, Benny was content in his arms. Lazar spoke to him as if he were an adult, and Benny would seem to mimic his father's speech patterns with nonsense sounds. Soon a routine formed. Lazar would arrive home, the Yiddish paper under his arm. Reaching for the baby, he would check his diaper and, if it was wet or dirty, would change the child himself, much to the amazement of Mama Blau. "A man do such a thing?" Then he would sit by the window, settle the baby so that he could turn the pages, and begin to read aloud.

Watching father and son, Hannah was certain that Lazar accepted the child more fully than she herself had. Searching for clues to her reticent love, she decided she lacked some elemental instinct that would have made her adore Benny.

❖  ❖  ❖

Even though Mama admired her grandson, she spent little time helping with his care, grateful that she had completed the task of rearing her own children. Advice she offered without hesitation, but her hands were always too full to hold him, her eyes too tired to bathe him, her feet too sore to walk him. Distracted with her own worries, she found the child to be more of a burden than a pleasure, and Hannah wondered if Mama's reaction stemmed from a deep suspicion as to the date of his conception. Nevertheless, Benjamin came within reasonable limits for being legitimate, having been born exactly 236 days from the wedding. Another three or four weeks would have been desirable, but the science of pregnancy was not so well organized that anyone knew for certain he had come too soon. If Mama begrudged Hannah his legitimacy, there was no strong evidence other than her lack of interest in the child. But in truth Mama had other problems; she was trying to find a husband for Dora.

❖  ❖  ❖

The best shadchen, or matchmaker, they could afford was hired. Though not a rabbi, Koppel Katz dressed like one in a somber suit, a black silk skullcap, and a full beard. Prepared for the fact that Dora was "different," he decided on a home visit to check out the girl, because "I would lose my reputation if I represented someone unfairly."

"This is my daughter Dora," Mama said, pushing her forward.

"A pretty girl!" the shadchen said, clapping his hands. "Not so much of a problem as I thought! I have Russian, Lithuanian, and even American boys who would like one as sweet as you!" he said, appraising her with the eye of a skilled merchant. "I don't see any problem here."

"We have no dowry for her," Mama apologized, "but she does have a job, even if she is a bit slow . . ."

The matchmaker picked up on her words. "Does she read or write?"

"No, but she can make change, do the shopping, and cook very well. She'll make a good, obedient wife."

"But any self-respecting Jewish man will want children who are normal!"

Hannah stepped forward. "My sister's disability will not affect her children!" she said with assurance.

"What do you know?" Koppel Katz asked.

"My oldest daughter's a doctor; she studied in Moscow!" Mama defended.

"My respects." The shadchen nodded to Hannah. "But how can you prove this to the boy and his parents?"

"We have every evidence my sister was damaged during her birth, or slightly thereafter. Her children should be normal."

"Should! Aha! Can you offer proof?"

"Only God can give that," Hannah retorted.

The matchmaker folded his arms across his chest and studied the group. "If I tell them the older sister's a doctor . . . You have a baby, don't you?"

"Yes, he's asleep in the other room."

"And there is no problem with that child?"

Hannah jumped up and faced him squarely. "Of course not!"

"No offense, but everyone else in your family? There are no other . . . problems?"

Mama pushed out her chest and lowered her voice. "None at all!"

"I think I might be able to find someone willing to accept your daughter, but not from my usual group of young men. For this my fee will be higher. You understand?"

Mama nodded.

"And I want you to have a picture taken of her. I don't do this in all my cases, but for her it might be a good idea. Have her wear that pretty dress and put some rouge on her cheeks," he said, patting his own for an example. "And maybe let her hair come down more around her face," he said, tilting his head as though he were about to recreate Dora on canvas.

"We'll do as you say, Mr. Katz," Mama said. "But I won't take just anyone for my Dora. She needs someone who can earn a living, not just a scholar like some ..." She spoke in Hannah's direction.

"Of course, Mrs. Blau, America isn't Russia, is it?" Mr. Katz whined. "We can't have our men in the study house all day! Bring me the pictures next week, and we'll see what we can do."

## · 9 ·

BY THE TIME Benny was two months old the risk of summer fevers had passed and Hannah was willing to bring him down to the street. Lazar had found a serviceable wood and reed carriage. Although it lacked the original parasol and did not recline, Hannah could wrap the baby securely, buffer him with bunting and quilts, and take him for a comfortable stroll by the river or through the less crowded residential streets.

While protesting that the baby should not be exposed to diseases that incubated in hot weather, Hannah had also avoided the issue of her own exercise. Unwilling to admit that her body had not yet recovered from the onslaught of medical interference, Hannah hid the unpleasant aspects of her convalescence.

After two weeks in the hospital, her bowel and bladder functions had returned to a state that the medical staff had considered normal, and so she was released, though she continued to bleed for two more months as well as suffer pain during elimination. Walking just one flight of stairs, sitting on a hard chair, even lifting the baby into his bath could bring tears to her eyes. Finally, after twelve weeks, she could get down to the street or lie on her bed without wincing in pain. With sweetness and teasing she had artfully put off Lazar's advances, but once she began to go outdoors and take a more active part in housekeeping, he hinted that it was time to renew their lovemaking.

On a night so oppressively hot that everyone else had dragged their bedding out to the roof, Lazar seized the opportunity to be completely alone with his little family. To spare Hannah the chore, he sponged Benny down, dusted him with cornstarch, and laid him on his stomach. Immediately the baby curled up, tucked his hands between his knees, and pushed his diapered buttocks in the air. Patting him gently, Lazar hummed a little before sliding beside Hannah. "He'll sleep for a while," he said, fingering the buttons on the front of her transparent camisole.

"On a night like this he's sure to wake several times to nurse," she corrected.

"Can you blame him? He feels the heat as much as you or I and needs a drink!"

"Just once I'd like to sleep through a whole night!"

Lazar placed his arms around Hannah's shoulders and pulled the thin ribbon woven into the bodice of her camisole. "You've had a rough time with him, haven't you?" he said, kissing her neck. "I've missed you!"

"It's you who go away. I'm always here with Benny."

"I meant that I've wanted you for so long. I've tried to be patient."

Pushing him aside, Hannah said, "We can't, not yet."

"You said . . . when the bleeding stopped . . . and it's been several weeks already!"

Hannah leaned toward him, her knees wide apart to cool herself. "How did you know?"

Lazar didn't answer, but his eyes were riveted to her abdomen and below.

Hannah modestly pressed her legs together. "You check my undergarments?"

"I knew it would take time for you to heal, but I didn't think it would be this long!"

"If the delivery had been normal, if the doctors hadn't ..." Tears streamed down Hannah's cheeks. "I've wanted you too, but I've been afraid it would hurt. You can't know how badly I've felt ..."

Lazar sat beside her and drew her into his arms, kissing her cheeks and neck. Undoing the strings at the neck and waist, he slipped the camisole over Hannah's head and reached over to kiss her breasts.

Pushing him away, she said, "Those are Benny's now!"

Lazar looked up to see if she was serious and, noting the wry lilt of her mouth, went to work with his tongue.

A tingling in her chest forewarned Hannah that the milk was about to let down, surprising Lazar with a spray of warmth across his face.

"Hey! Why did you do that?" he laughed, wiping himself with a cover from the bed.

"It just happens!" Hannah apologized.

"Let me try something else," he said, lowering his face to her thighs.

"Lazar don't! I'm not ready. It will hurt! I can't!"

"I won't do anything that you don't want. I promise, my darling. I'll be very gentle with you. I just need to be close to you, near you, with you." He pushed Hannah on her back and fully undressed her. "You're as beautiful as ever, more so." He kissed her abdomen. "May I just do this?" he asked, rubbing his pelvis across her leg.

"Yes, that's fine."

Confident that she could trust her husband, Hannah relaxed and enjoyed the familiar sensation of having Lazar touch and excite her. And even though Lazar kept his word and did not attempt penetration, she was able to climax in his arms.

As soon as they were apart, Benny began to scream. Lazar brought the child and arranged him beside Hannah's breast. "Your turn!" he said, before falling asleep on his side of the bed.

After that Lazar was anxious to try positions and methods that would satisfy them both, always mindful not to force Hannah. For

the first time Hannah began to feel more than a generalized pleasure from Lazar's caresses. As he licked her ear or stroked her
thighs she concentrated on sensations, marveling at all the places
on her body that were receptive to his touch. In gratitude she
reciprocated. Never before had she allowed herself to touch or kiss
him so intimately. But once she had begun to learn his body with
her hands and mouth she was astonished at the fresh feelings that
were awakened by a man she thought she had known so well.

❖ ❖ ❖

It was almost September before Hannah strolled Benny over to
their old building on Forsyth Street. She wanted to introduce him
to Mrs. Sholom, the cantor's wife, as well as learn if there had been
a letter for her, although she had relinquished hope that her message had ever reached Dr. Jaffe.

Mrs. Sholom was at the market, but Reb Sholom sat on the
stoop picking green grapes off a bunch and spitting the seeds into
the gutter. He made the appropriate noises when Hannah showed
him the child. "You should have had me at the circumcision! For
you I would have sung without a fee!"

Hannah flushed. "Next baby, for sure!" she said in a cheery
voice. "Have there been any letters for me? I was expecting one
from Europe."

"Nothing at all! Some people inquired for you. Fanna didn't tell
them where you were, thought you might not want them to
know."

"Who was it?"

"One was the Belinsky boy. Said something about wanting to
see you, not your husband, but you never know, might be some
sort of a trick."

"Did he say anything else?" Hannah wondered if Belinsky's wife
might be expecting again. If Hannah delivered their baby in
America, she would finally have a birth worth talking about, since
she had only a pauper and a prostitute to her credit so far.

"He said he wasn't concerned about the back rent, that it had
been an error to take it out of the wages, that he wanted to apologize."

Benny began to stir and Hannah rocked the carriage.

"He lives at Six East Sixtieth Street. Very easy to remember a fancy address like that," he said, offering Hannah some grapes.

Politely refusing, Hannah asked, "Do you think I should visit him there?"

"Ask your husband; the man always knows best!"

Annoyed by his words, Hannah pretended to rearrange Benny's blankets. "I'll come back in a few days to see Mrs. Sholom. Please give her my regards," she said, starting down the block.

"Likewise to your mama!" the cantor called.

After a few steps, Hannah turned on her heel. "You said 'some people' had asked for us? Who else?"

"Oh, yes!" The cantor lowered his eyebrows in concentration. "It was a woman, very tall, very unusual, spoke Russian like an aristocrat."

"Did she leave her name?" Hannah said, trying to summon a picture to fit his description.

"No, no . . . I'll have to ask Fanna." He twirled a lock of his beard. "Didn't seem very important, probably someone wanting your services. That's it, she probably needed a midwife!"

"I'm sorry I missed her," Hannah sighed. "If she comes again, please give her my new address."

"Of course. Take care of the boy; be well." The cantor stood and ambled back into his basement rooms.

All the way home Hannah wondered who the tall woman who spoke in Russian could have been and who had recommended her for the job. Perhaps it was Mrs. Belinsky and that was why Mr. Belinsky had also been by? If she spoke in Russian it could have been any one of Lazar's intellectual associates. Or Dr. Strauss could have made the referral . . . No, she discarded that theory when she remembered that the doctor knew their present address. She pondered the identity of the mysterious stranger until Benny began to fuss louder and louder, distracting her completely.

## · 10 ·

AS TIME PASSED, Hannah began to feel more like she thought a mother should feel. When he nursed at her breast, Benny turned his head so he could watch his mother's face, reaching with his palm to pat her cheeks and coo his appreciation for her sustenance. His flesh filled out and it looked as if he were being plumped with daily doses of goose down.

After his bath, Hannah would stretch him out on a thin towel, rubbing his body until it glowed. Ready for the routine as soon as he was dry, Benny would lift his arms and grasp his mother's thumbs; then Hannah would lift him toward her in an exercise to strengthen his back and neck muscles. Next she would form his little arms into an X across his chest and stretch them down to his sides and out as far as they could go. Finally, she would encourage him to kick at her hands and push his little legs to remove any kinks or curves remaining from the fetal position. Hannah giggled and mimicked his expressions, kissing his feet, tummy, and the special sweet place behind his ears before wrapping him in a loose kimono.

Now when she picked him up she gave him an additional squeeze and kiss, even when no one was around to observe her. Why did he suddenly seem so perfect, so precious?

❖ ❖ ❖

On the street or in the marketplace, Benny was good publicity. Hannah never ignored comments about his health and beauty, always aware that the stranger, or her daughter or sister, might someday be having a baby.

In early September Hannah fell upon a wealth of possibilities as she passed P.S. 4 on Rivington Street, where cautious mothers, many of them large with child, waited to escort their young children home. With great deliberation, Hannah parked her carriage in front of a group of pregnant women. One woman, draped in a loose cotton gown and wrapped in a thin Russian shawl, immediately began to stare at Benny and commented, "Ohhh, a little prince! Such fat little hands and feet!" She nudged the woman next to her. "Kayn ayen hore! Don't let the evil eye get that one."

Hannah abruptly asked the woman beside her, "Who helped you deliver your last child?"

"Hilda was born in Cracow. I've lost three in this country. They came too soon."

"How sad!" Hannah sympathized. "But you are so far along now; surely you will have good luck!"

"That's what my mama says as well! Now that I've stopped pressing pants I can breathe better, maybe . . . Shymara wants a son, of course."

"From the way you are carrying, so forward, it looks like you will have one!"

"An expert?" One woman elbowed the other woman's side.

"About boys and girls, no one ever knows," Hannah admitted. "But I am a midwife, trained in Odessa and Moscow, and I would be happy to deliver you . . . half price now that we are friends!" she said, attempting to sound as sincere as possible. "I live at number Eighty-one Willett, fourth floor, rear. You can call for me day or night if you have any questions or problems. Also, unless I do the delivery, there is no charge at all."

The women in the school yard looked suspicious for a moment, but then the first lady spoke again. "Maybe I can ask you a question?"

"Yes . . ." Hannah waited.

"My husband says he must . . . but I say he mustn't. Which one of us is right?"

The other women pressed closer, giggling and waiting for Hannah's response. "I cannot comment on the religious aspects," Hannah hedged, "but I was taught in Moscow that it can certainly be a cause of miscarriage."

The woman nodded. "I thought so!"

Standing in the background, another spoke in so soft a voice

Hannah had to bend toward her to hear the question. "But what if you do not have a miscarriage problem, could you then?"

Hannah sucked in her breath. Although she had learned many reasons for avoiding sexual penetration during pregnancy, she had not practiced what she had been taught. "The doctors tell us many things, that it aggravates the sickness which accompanies pregnancy, causes infection, or makes the wife lose respect for her husband, since she herself rarely wishes to participate. Also I have heard it said that since animals do not . . . ah . . . copulate when the female is with child, it would be wise for man to follow their cautious instincts."

The woman's voice became bolder and she challenged Hannah further. "But what do you think?"

Hannah scraped her feet on the pavement and thought of her own life with Lazar. "Unless there are problems like miscarriage, pain, or infection, and if the woman wishes as well as the man, and if it is in the middle months of the pregnancy, then once in a great while . . ." She stumbled and recovered with a better rationale. "It is too much of a hardship to make the man wait the entire time and the months afterward as well; I think that is why so many men end up on Allen Street."

The women gasped. Perhaps Hannah's words had been too strong for them. Wasn't there any way she would ever become accepted as a midwife?

Hannah decided to visit the Belinskys, hoping that Mrs. Belinsky might be expecting again. Why else would they have inquired for her? And wasn't it a well-known fact that a woman always preferred the same birth attendant for every delivery? Since Mrs. Belinsky's first child was almost a year old, another could be well on its way. A delivery of someone of her position would bring Hannah more customers who could well afford to pay for her services, maybe as much as twenty dollars, not to mention the pleasure it would be to work in clean airy rooms and to wrap an infant in expensive garments instead of rags.

She draped Benny in the shawl that Aunt Sonia had embroidered with a silk flowered design and placed a knitted bonnet on his head, fluffing the bow under his neck. Without telling the family where she was going, she took a streetcar uptown for the first time.

Without a doubt, Hannah decided, the New York trolleys were neither as well padded nor as attractive as the Odessa ones, further evidence that nothing in America was as well made or kept. Arriving at 6 East Sixtieth Street, Hannah was greeted by a portly doorman in black and white livery that made him look like a penguin. Even though Hannah had worn her best blouse, with bone stays at the collar and cuffs to keep it as crisp as possible, she still trembled under his gaze.

"Is Mrs. Belinsky in?" she asked in her halting English.

"Is she expecting you?"

"Not today, but she knows me. I am Mrs. Sokolow, the midwife who delivered her baby."

"Then I must ask you to go to the service entrance," he said, pointing to a door beneath the stairs.

Although Hannah did not understand every word, his meaning was clear. Taken aback, she nevertheless followed his pointing finger, and in a moment the lower door was opened by a maid dressed in a black uniform with a white lace apron. "Come in," she said. "Frederick has gone to find the missus." She reached for the baby, but Hannah held Benny close.

Hannah waited. A half-hour must have passed. Benny stirred and needed nursing, but Hannah tried to jostle him back to sleep instead, for if she were called upstairs she would have to stop the feeding and that would make him furious. When he could wait no longer, Hannah relented.

Finally, the maid reappeared. "Mrs. Belinsky is resting, but she said you may visit with Gertrude."

"Gertrude?" Hannah asked as she took Benny off her breast.

"The baby! Didn't you want to see the child?"

"Oh!" Hannah had remembered the child was named Geitel. "No, I want Mrs. Belinsky, or Mister," she added slowly.

"Mister?" the maid inquired. "I'm sorry I did not know; I'll be back."

"Mrs. Sokolovsky!" Mr. Belinsky appeared at the kitchen door.

"My name is Sokolow now, Mr. Belinsky," Hannah began to chatter in Yiddish. "So sorry to have bothered you."

"Come upstairs with me. I'd like you to see Gertrude." Then, peeking at her baby, he asked, "It's a boy, isn't it?"

"Yes, his name is Benjamin. But I thought your baby was to be Geitel?"

"What a good memory you have! That is her Jewish name, of course, but my father thought we all should have American names. He decided on Gertrude for her, Sondra for Mrs. Belinsky, and I am Nathaniel. What do you think about that?"

Hannah nodded politely. "Very nice, very American."

On the way upstairs, Hannah passed through reception rooms filled to overflowing with expensive objects that seemed to have been selected for no other reason than their large size. The nursery, painted simply in yellow with white trim, was a refreshing change from the dark public rooms. Little Gertrude stumbled about holding the windowsills for balance while a starched nursemaid applauded her efforts. Belinsky lowered himself on one knee and said in Yiddish, "Come to me, come to Papa!"

Gertrude let go for a moment and took a few hesitant steps but, annoyed at her slow progress, slipped down on all fours, crawled to her father, and placed her arms around his neck. As she smiled, Hannah saw she was just cutting her front teeth. Belinsky wiped the child's saliva from his beard and stood up. In English he asked, "Mrs. Dopple, would you take care of Benjamin for a few minutes while Mrs. Sokolovsky, I mean Sokolow, and I talk?"

The nurse took Hannah's bundle of baby and blanket, nodding her agreement. Gertrude reached up fascinated with Benny, but the nurse wouldn't let her touch. "Shhh, don't wake baby, shhhh."

Hannah followed Belinsky down two flights into a large library that smelled of fresh varnish and wax. An ornate silver teapot was placed beside dainty English cups painted with violets.

"Shifre, I mean Sondra, must do everything properly. My father even had her learn about American sugar," he said, passing the silver bowl in which the sugar was mounded like a snowball. "And

American milk and American clothing ..." he said, pouring enough sweet cream into her cup to suppress any bitter flavor. "He wouldn't let any greenhorns in his family!"

"You look very American to me," Hannah said as she stared at the gentleman who wore the most fashionable cut of worsted trousers, a crisp stiff collar without buttons, and a wide silk tie knotted precisely at his throat. His hair had been parted in the middle and slicked back on the sides to reveal an even higher forehead than Hannah had remembered.

She felt his eyes upon her and hoped he hadn't noticed the nervous manner she had of twisting her hands in her lap. Finally she had the courage to break the silence. "I heard you had asked about me and I wondered if ..."

"Yes, I was surprised you had moved without a word to us."

"We were ... my husband ... you see ..."

Belinsky pushed his hand out in front of him. "Stop, please, that was not my concern. My father said there could be no exceptions to his policies, but I believe he acted too harshly. Let's not talk of that again. Are you doing well? The *Times* says that the birthrate on the Lower East Side is the highest in the city." He paused, realizing his comment might be taken as an insult.

"Now that Benny is older I expect to deliver more babies, uptown as well as down." Hannah hoped her meaning was clear.

"Most of our neighbors have doctors in and some have been going to a clinic that gives the twilight sleep, but Shifre, I mean Sondra, will have none of that!"

"When are you expecting? Do you have a date?"

Belinsky looked confused.

"Isn't that why you wanted me, another baby is coming?"

"No, no! Far from it!" Belinsky paused.

Hannah looked at the floor; the colors of the Oriental rug blurred in front of her eyes. Hearing Benny cry from a distance, she blinked quickly and stood up. "I must go to him."

"Just another minute ..." Mr. Belinsky reached for her arm. "Your eyes are so unusual, green like emeralds."

Hannah trembled.

Belinsky spoke in a wistful voice. "My father used to say I should marry a girl from Odessa."

"Why?"

"Odessa girls . . . so much warmer, kinder, sweeter than the ones in our village. An Odessa girl wasn't out for every kopeck; she wanted music and dance, to enjoy life more."

"Then why didn't you find one?"

"I don't know, but since I met you, I have regretted it even more."

"But you don't really know me!"

"You are right, of course. Perhaps that is why I always ask for you on Forsyth Street when I make my inspections for my father. I wanted to see you again."

Benny's wailing increased and Hannah became agitated. The door to the central hall was cracked slightly and Hannah moved to push it open so she could step outside. Anticipating her move, Belinsky reached around and pulled it closed. At the click of the latch, Hannah sucked in her breath.

Belinsky's eyes darted back and forth and then came to focus above Hannah's bosom. There was no mistaking his glance. Feeling as though she had turned to stone, Hannah did not move. Benny's noises faded from her mind as she tried to grasp the extent of Belinsky's intentions. He placed one hand on Hannah's shoulder and allowed it to trail across her breast. As though wracked by a sudden chill, Belinsky stopped. Hannah could not help realize that she had excited him.

"Now it will be better," he said obtusely and opened the door. Feeling both perplexed and stimulated, she turned toward the nursemaid who, standing in the hallway, vainly attempted to settle Benny by bouncing him on her shoulder. As soon as he saw his mother he was quiet.

"You like your mama, don't you baby?" Belinsky said in the child's ear. "It's good that you admire beauty when you are young!"

Hannah turned the child away from Belinsky and said, "Thank you for letting me see Gertrude. And please give Mrs. Belinsky my respects."

"Will you come again?" he asked quickly as she headed toward the massive front door that the liveried doorman held open. "Maybe our children could be friends?"

"Do you think your father would approve of that?" Hannah snapped.

Belinsky frowned. "I see whom I wish!"

Hannah tried to adjust the baby's bonnet, but her hands fumbled. "I meant that I don't get uptown very often."

"But I get downtown almost every day. My job is to collect the rents from the managers and handle repairs."

"Repairs! There was never one while we lived at Forsyth Street!"

Belinsky ignored her comment. "Where do you reside now?"

Hannah was silent.

"I won't make any trouble for you. If I know of a family needing the services of a midwife, where would I send for you?"

"To Eighty-one Willett Street, fourth floor." She paused, not wanting him to know they still didn't have a whole floor to themselves. "Rear."

"I'll remember," he said, smiling. "Frederick, will you call my carriage for Mrs. Sokolow?"

"Yes, sir!" he said before helping Hannah down the steep front steps and across the small garden where yellow mums winked in the late afternoon sun.

# · 11 ·

BENNY SLEPT. The rhythm of the horses, the jostling of the carriage lulled him while Hannah remained bolt upright. The smell of the animal, the feel of the leather seats, the slap of the reins revived memories and dreams long ago buried by her present struggle for survival.

If only she had stayed in Moscow she might have had a life of ease, as comfortable as that of Shifre Belinsky. Certainly the Meyerovs lived with as many amenities as they had, as did Petrograv, and others of his class. Not that she had been so poor in

Odessa. If she and Lazar could even have a home as comfortable as the one on Melnitsky Square, with a garden, flowers, fresh sea air . . .

How unfair it was for a woman, a mean and selfish woman like Shifre Belinsky, to have such leisure, such comforts! Her daughter would only know the best . . . food, doctors, schools. Little things, too, like a smooth banister to rest her hand on, a clean floor on which to crawl, a healthy well-rested mother with time to play games and sing nonsense songs, and a father devoted to her up-bringing and support.

At Thirty-sixth Street they turned west. "Look at that!" The driver tried to get Hannah's attention as he pointed toward Madison Avenue, where she got a glimpse of a dark stone house with an impressive wing in a contrasting lighter stone. "That's where Mr. J. P. Morgan lives and has his own private art museum!"

What did a man do with his own museum? Hannah needed less. Less than Belinsky, but certainly more than she had so far been able to acquire. Belinsky had come to America and had been handed his home, his job, everything! What did he have to do for it? Walk around like a big man inspecting everything! "Now that's something even Lazar could do," she thought maliciously.

The carriage slowed at Herald Square and Broadway as they waited to cross the trolley tracks. A train whistled into the elevated station at Thirty-third Street. Hannah wondered if they were going the right way and asked the driver, "Aren't we on the wrong side of town?"

"Yes, but I am supposed to pick up a package for the missus at R. H. Macy. I didn't think you would mind waiting."

"No, of course not," Hannah said, perfectly happy for the diversion of riding about the city in a comfortable carriage.

All too soon the streets became more familiar. Children carried bundles on their heads, vendors jostled for space on a corner, boys played ball with sticks, people filled the streets so full that the carriage could hardly pass. Thousands lived on each narrow block, crammed like insects caught in jars, squirming, crawling, climbing on each other's heads to escape. As they moved closer to Willett Street, Hannah felt stifled. The idea of climbing up the rotten planks to her rooms, of sleeping on her lumpy mat, of eating what-

ever little had been purchased with their meager dollars, or subjecting Benny and herself to the torment of their daily life without
a possibility or hope of bettering themselves, choked her further.

How could she escape? How could she return to the pristine,
spacious world of the Belinskys? She resolved to make more money
on her own, save every possible penny, and slowly move out from
the rear flat to a whole floor again, to a better neighborhood, then
uptown. Slowly, step by step, if she put her mind to it she was certain she could succeed.

Just then they passed The Monopole on Second Avenue. Hannah noticed a woman wearing a long black cape in a Russian style
who turned slightly on her heel. Her silhouette revealed that she
was expecting a child! Hannah's mind raced to remember the description of the woman Reb Sholom had mentioned who needed
her services. When she looked back toward the café she saw the
face of the tall woman and gasped.

"Stop the carriage! Stop here! Please!"

"But you are to go to Willett. It's too far to walk with the
baby," he said, slackening the reins.

"I must get out here!" Hannah shouted.

"Whoa!" The driver stopped the carriage and went around to
help Hannah down.

"Thank you!" she said as she ran back toward the café, clutching Benny in her arms.

The woman had disappeared. Hannah looked in vain to the
right and the left. Then she noticed the double doors in front of
the building were swinging as though someone had just entered
the café. Cautiously Hannah backed through the door, holding
Benny close.

As soon as she stepped inside the smoke-filled room, Benny
reacted to the clatter of china and the loud hum of excited voices.
Hannah pressed him closer to her chest to muffle the sound as she
went from room to room. When she entered the main dining
room, Benny wailed once again, and everyone, including the
woman in the cape, turned toward the sound of the angry child. As
soon as Hannah had a good look at her face she handed Benny to a
surprised waiter, stretched out her arms, and ran to greet the
woman.

"Rachael! Is it really you?" she gasped.

Dr. Jaffe had changed. Her once angular form had filled out and softened; the sharp bones of her cheeks and jaw were blunted by her pregnancy. Though her expression was less intense than Hannah had remembered, her face was still surrounded by the familiar electric burst of coppery hair.

Benny stubbornly resisted relinquishing his mother's attention and wailed to be fed and fondled. The waiter gave the baby back and settled them at a corner table. Hannah rocked Benny on her knee and asked, "How long have you been here?"

"Almost ten weeks. I've been to your old address several times . . ."

"So you are the Russian lady the cantor told me about!"

"I don't know why he was so suspicious, but he wouldn't tell me where you had moved. I'd almost given up hope, but yesterday I was introduced to a Dr. Strauss, who said he knew your husband."

"Where did you meet him?"

"At the hospital. I have a job!"

"Already! For almost a year I have been trying to establish myself and you find a position in only a few weeks," Hannah said with jealousy slipping into her voice.

"Dr. Harrington had studied with Bruchermann and my husband in Vienna, so I was very fortunate to have their recommendations."

"Dr. Harrington of Bellevue?" Hannah asked in a hoarse voice.

"You know him too?" asked Dr. Jaffe, surprised that Hannah would already have encountered the esteemed obstetrician professionally.

"He delivered Benny," Hannah said in a hesitant voice as she considered describing the hideous details of her confinement. Shifting Benny to another position, she steered the conversation back to her friend. "You are at Bellevue?"

"Not exactly. I'm on the house staff of Gouverneur Hospital, at the edge of the river on Water Street. It's the downtown branch of Bellevue and Allied Hospitals and serves emergency patients from the Lower East Side. Most of our cases are either Jewish or Italian."

"Which division?"

"General Emergency Care. I live in rooms they provide, as I am on call for ambulance duty round the clock."

"But they don't do normal births, have a nursery, or even a research facility. I thought you wanted to . . ."

Brushing back her hair with a careless gesture of her long tapered hands, Dr. Jaffe interrupted. "One can't always have one's own way! Haven't you at least learned that by now?"

Hannah's heart jumped at the censure. Sensitive to Hannah's change of mood, Dr. Jaffe waved her hand toward the table where her other friends were sipping a thick soup. "Won't you join me for supper?"

"But I . . ." Hannah didn't know how to explain that she had but a few cents in her pocket.

"As my guest, of course. They make a wonderful version of karnetzlach; you remember that type of Hungarian sausage I love served with mameliga."

"I adore cornmeal pudding!" Hannah brightened. "But I don't know about sausage."

"Are you still kosher?"

"No, my husband is not observant. You would never guess that when I first met him he was a yeshiva boy with earlocks almost to his shoulders! But I still would prefer something else."

"Have some goulash instead!" Dr. Jaffe suggested before she hailed the waiter by confidently calling to him in Roumanian.

Benny demanded to be nursed, a task Hannah managed discreetly by lifting her shirtwaist from the bottom, then draping his mouth with her shawl. A plate of sour pickles and tomatoes was placed in front of the women. Without realizing how much witness she was giving to her everlasting hunger, Hannah crunched one after another. Pretending not to notice, Dr. Jaffe launched on her tale of leaving Russia and coming to work in New York, explaining that she had not been expected to last in her staff position very long.

"America is very backward about women as physicians. You can't imagine how poorly I, and the nice American girl, Emily Stimson, are treated. The very first night I was on duty I was assigned the routine catheterizations on the male surgical ward!"

Hannah gasped at the idea. "What did you do?"

"What could I say? They were obviously testing me." Rachael stopped to bite into a small green tomato. "I knew I could handle the procedure, but the delicate instrumentation requires the patient have complete confidence in his physician, and I worried most that I would get a jittery old fellow who would make the job impossible."

"What did you do?"

Rachael wiped her chin. "At first I was certain that the assignment would be withdrawn, that it was merely a capricious whim, so I waited for further orders; but as soon as I realized they were serious, I also understood they were hoping I would create an erotic response in the patients, making the job impossible, and thereby proving that a young woman physician had no business on their service. Little did they know that in Russia I was well schooled in treating male as well as female patients and developed more than an average skill at the procedure." Dr. Jaffe hesitated while she snapped a celery stalk in half, buttered and salted both narrow depressions, and took a defiant bite.

"So you were a success!"

"Of course! Now eat your goulash!" the doctor replied, anxious to begin the main course that had just been served. Confidently she bit a hunk of mottled sausage, then chewed it more elaborately than necessary. "Delicious! Are you certain you won't try a taste?"

Hannah shook her head and stirred her goulash into its deep nest of egg noodles, savoring the sheer quantity of meat that was hers to eat.

As soon as they had wiped their plates clean with the last crust of bread, Benny wriggled and fussed with such determination that it became obvious he would not relax any longer.

Outside, Dr. Jaffe reached for the bundle of squirming baby. "May I hold him?" she asked as she took him in her arms and pressed his thick head of coal black curls to her shoulder. "He's really quite the most handsome young boy I've ever seen. But he would be beautiful; he looks exactly like you."

Hannah startled. "Do you think so? I always thought he looked like his father."

"Not knowing your husband, it would be difficult for me to agree. But I've never seen a child whose facial structure, hair coloring, skin tone were so much the mother's. It looks as though a part of you were cut off and grew into a new child. Wouldn't it be wonderful if we could all reproduce that way? Then we wouldn't have to bother with men."

"Rachael! You don't mean that!"

The doctor buried her face in Benny's curls. "Herzog has been away so long, I suppose I've forgotten how useful they can be."

Hannah barely heard Rachael, for as she stared at her son in the other woman's arms, she knew her friend had made her see something she had never before realized. Except for his eyes, which showed no sign of changing color from their neonatal blue to Hannah's brilliant green or Petrograv's somber brown, he appeared the very image of her. For four months Hannah had scrutinized his features for some resemblance to Lazar, but Benny had stubbornly remained darker in complexion and smaller in frame, so much more the image of the Russian doctor that Hannah had almost accepted that he had been conceived at the Hotel Richelieu. Never before had she even searched for her own features in the child, and this blindness had cost her many hours of agony.

With a happier step, Hannah led the way to her home, following for as long as possible those streets lit by city lamps and trolley lines until there was no other course than to wind through the littered back alleys with studied swiftness and caution.

❖ ❖ ❖

They arrived at Willett Street long after Hannah was expected, and she knew she would have been questioned if it had not been for the immediate assurance Dr. Jaffe's presence would give.

Noticing Hannah's nervousness as they ascended the creaking stairway, Rachael asked, "Tell me, what is your husband's political position?"

"Why?"

"I wouldn't want to insult him the first time I meet him."

"I think Lazar would call himself a Yiddishist, although he is actively becoming a socialist . . . in the American sense."

"As long as he's not a Zionist he'll get on with my husband."

"Your husband! I've forgotten about him!" Hannah stopped on

the second-floor landing and looked directly at Dr. Jaffe's abdomen with embarrassment. "How stupid of me!"

"I thought you were very tactful not to ask. These days one does better not to surmise about such things, for you are bound to be as wrong as right. Ezekiel Herzog was released from prison a little less than a year ago. We still keep different names for both political and practical reasons. He summoned me to meet him in Kiev, where we lived for several months before we went together to Hamburg. But the rest I'll tell you together with your family, for I am certain they will also be interested in my story."

❖   ❖   ❖

Hannah was pleased by her family's transfixed response to this impressive woman who was as tall as Lazar and able to match his knowledge of politics point for point. By the end of the simple introductions they had already discovered the drift of each other's political leanings and were launched on discovering how many people they knew in common. Dr. Jaffe was able to reveal what had happened to most of them.

After several minutes of spirited talk, Lazar was silent. There was only one more name to go and no one in the room dared to speak it.

"What about my brother?" Eva asked boldly.

"You mean Chaim Blau?" queried Dr. Jaffe.

Dr. Jaffe went to stand beside Mama in a gesture that Hannah interpreted as indicating the worst possible news. But the doctor understood that good news sometimes had an even more devastating effect than expected tragedy. "If everything goes according to our plans, Chaim Blau will be arriving in America before the end of the year," she said, leaving a long pause between each word so that her meaning would be clear.

Mama cried, "Gottenyu! Is it true?"

A full half-hour passed before the family calmed to a point where Dr. Jaffe could explain. "I received your letter, Hannah, when we were already in Hamburg. Herzog and I were working for the Hebrew Immigrant Aid Society. Routinely I showed your letter to everyone coming out of Russia, trying to get information on your brother for you, and finally one of our patients directed us to a young man with a raging case of trachoma who went by the name of Illya Swerdlow. At first he thought I might be an agent for the authorities and admitted nothing, but after a few days I won his trust and he revealed that he was your brother."

"But his eyes, are they cured?" demanded Hannah. "I thought it was almost impossible to ever be rid of the disease or its signs."

"The treatments are not very pleasant. Pus must be squeezed out from under the eyelids. Sometimes the sores must be lanced, and the whole area bandaged and kept cool with ice during the healing. Your brother bravely withstood the worst pain. When I left Hamburg he had demonstrated such great progress that my husband felt he would be able to pass inspection as soon as the residual swellings were healed."

Lazar paced the room, rubbing his hands together in a gesture of excitement and anticipation. "How long will that take?"

"Only a few months; surely by November he'll be able to cross."

Mama looked confused. "Other than the trachoma, there is nothing else wrong with him?"

"When he arrived in Hamburg he was very thin and weak, but when I last saw him I thought he was quite the most delightfully healthy specimen it had ever been my pleasure to care for, and as I knew who he was, his excellent progress was even more special to me."

Mama's stern composure had broken completely. She hugged the strange woman to her as though she were her own and babbled her gratitude in three languages.

# BOOK THREE

* * * * * * * * * * * *

## *America*

# I

❖ ❖ ❖ ❖ ❖

# *Nora Herzog*
## Delivered January 15, 1906

❖ ❖ ❖ ❖ ❖ ❖ ❖ ❖ ❖ ❖ ❖ ❖

## · 1 ·

HANNAH BELIEVED THAT Dr. Jaffe brought them all good fortune, for as soon as she brought word of Chaim's impending return, everyone's luck improved. First the matchmaker, Koppel Katz, announced that he had found Dora a husband.

The man was Daniel Greenbaum. At twenty-four he was six years older than Dora, with the maturity to aid his acceptance of his bride's mental weakness. His face was attractive enough for any mother-in-law to adore, with large black eyes made even more pronounced by thick bushy eyebrows. Clean-shaven, he appeared much younger than his years, and his lips were so soft and pink that his virtue seemed impeccable. Shyly he sat with eyes downcast while he answered the questions put to him. They learned that he was an orphan raised by an uncle and sent to America when he was sixteen. He worked as the manager of a stable on Delancey Street.

After the first interview, Lazar walked the young candidate outside while Mama and the matchmaker negotiated.

"What did I tell you?" Katz smiled and licked his lips. "Isn't he a gem! A more attractive pair I've never put together! And smart!

Did you hear him speaking the English with your daughter's husband?"

Mama nodded, but she did not speak.

As Koppel Katz waited for her response he twirled the fringes of his tallis that peeked out from beneath his long gabardine coat. "Maybe a man who works around horses is not suitable for your daughter?"

Mama sniffed and sighed. "No, no. He's more than we ever hoped to find. Only . . ." She tried to phrase her words so as not to offend the shadchen. "Why is he so willing to accept our Dora?"

"A beautiful girl like your daughter is one in a million!"

Hannah interrupted. "Then why has it taken so many months to find even one willing to talk with us about my sister?"

"Ah . . ." The matchmaker paused to straighten his skullcap, which had slipped sideways on his slick mop of hair. "The boy is an epileptic."

Mama gasped and reached out for Hannah's hand.

"He has fits, but not very often, and afterward he is absolutely normal. His mind is perfect, and you can see for yourselves that his appearance is perfectly ordinary. The boy will be a credit to your family.'"

"How often are his seizures?" Hannah asked.

"Maybe two or three times a year."

Mama looked away from the matchmaker and asked Hannah, "Do you think Dora could manage if he had an attack?"

"I don't know much about it, Mama."

Mama contemplated the problems with her head bowed. Suddenly she stood up and walked across the room to rearrange a lace cover on the back of the green upholstered chair. "It's time for me to move in any case. I will live with Dora and Daniel after the wedding."

Koppel Katz clapped his hands together and bowed to her. "Mazel tov!" he cried. "May they have a hundred years of health and happiness!"

❖   ❖   ❖

Hannah's second piece of luck came only a few days later. As she examined the oranges at Spector's stall, Hannah's mouth watered with the expectation of their sweetness. She was about to bargain for three instead of the two she could afford when Pearla Spector asked in a whisper, "Are you still a midwife?"

Hannah bristled at the word *still.* It pointed up the sorry fact that she had not been able to practice her profession since becoming a mother herself. "Yes, I am!"

"I'm going to have a baby!" the obese woman announced.

"Wonderful!" Hannah exclaimed. "When?"

"I must be crazy, but I think I am going to have it right this minute!" she said, dramatically clutching her abdomen.

"That's unlikely," Hannah said kindly. "I couldn't even tell that you were with child!" Hannah stopped. The merchant had turned so pale that it looked as though her features had been crudely molded in fresh dough. "You certainly aren't feeling very well. Let's get you home."

Mr. Spector stopped piling apples in a ruby pyramid and asked, "Shall I come with you?"

"No, no, I'll be fine," his wife demurred.

But he trailed after his wife and Hannah.

"Help me get her on the bed," Hannah said, puffing and sweating with the exertion of maneuvering the corpulent woman.

In a few seconds, Mrs. Spector thrashed her legs and lifted her hips, forcing Hannah to move away to protect herself from injury. It seemed almost as though the woman really was having contractions.

"Please don't cut me open!" She screamed so loudly that Spector rushed into the room.

"What's the matter?"

"Go downstairs and get my sister Lilly," Pearla begged.

Spector rubbed his forehead. "The baby is coming now?"

"I doubt that," Hannah said. "Usually it's not until many months after a woman discovers she is expecting that the baby comes. I'll know more after I examine her."

"Pearla, Pearla darling, are you all right?" her sister called as she flew into the room, dropping her shawl on the floor. Hannah couldn't believe the two women were related. The older sister was so thin that the bones in her elbows came to sharp points that had worn through the fabric of the sleeves.

"Lilly, Lilly, stay with me," Pearla moaned. She gave such an intense shudder that the bed danced on all four metal feet.

Hannah could wait no longer to find out what was happening. With great effort the two women lifted the massive bloomers off Mrs. Spector. "Hold her knees apart for me," Hannah said. Once the legs were in position, the thick rolls of flesh almost closed the midwife's access to the vagina. Fearful that her arm would be caught in the blubbery vise, Hannah hurried to perform the examination.

Withdrawing her hand as though she were being chased by an unseen viper, she gulped and shook her head in surprise. The cervix was fully dilated and Hannah had felt the head already crowning. "Can you find me some clean linens, a shoelace or ribbon, scissors, blankets, anything?" Hannah ran into the small kitchen area where Spector sat drinking tea. "Is the water still hot?"

"Do you want a glass?" he offered.

Hannah grabbed the iron kettle and poured its contents into a nearby basin. "Boil some more!" she demanded.

The two women pushed and dragged Pearla to the bottom edge of the bed, but even when they had her in position, Hannah realized it would be impossible to deliver her there, for her hips sunk into the feather mattress so deeply that Hannah could not begin to get to the perineal area.

Her voice rising in panic, Hannah shouted, "I can't do it here. We'll have to move her . . ." She glanced toward the front room. "She'll have to sit there!" Hannah pointed to a stuffed Morris chair with a matching fringed ottoman pushed into the corner and covered with a sheet.

"That's our wedding chair!" Spector protested. "We only use it for special occasions."

"What's more special than this?"

Hannah arranged Pearla's legs to rest on the sides of the ottoman and then sat between them and below her on the floor so she could have direct access to the area where the baby's head was already making an appearance. Without time to gently ease the tissues around the child, Hannah worried about lacerations, but was gratified to learn that the woman's flesh was not only generous but elastic. After a few short bursts of pushing, the baby was born and he lay on Hannah's lap crying mightily. As soon as she cut the cord, Hannah stood up and handed the infant to his mother. "He's beautiful, a fully grown child. I was worried he might be too early, but you can tell from his creases and his long fingernails that he came right on time!"

As Pearla held her child her obvious pleasure radiated to everyone in the room. Spector shyly stood in the doorway before Hannah gestured for him to join his wife. "Lilly," Pearla said to her sister, "you always said it was so horrible to have a baby. I myself remember hearing you scream for hours. Now wasn't that unnecessary? This was the easiest thing I ever did! It never hurt for a moment, it was only strong, like this . . ." She reached over and clamped her hand on her sister's arm and made a fist.

Lilly pulled her slender arm away, revealing red dents. "Perhaps you had a better midwife."

"I don't know that I had anything to do with it," Hannah replied modestly.

"But you did!" Pearla turned toward her husband. "Mrs. Sokolow didn't get her oranges, did she? Give her a dozen, at least!"


· 2 ·


DORA'S WEDDING was planned for after Chaim's arrival. And true to Dr. Jaffe's prediction, he descended the gangplank of the steamship *America* along with fifteen hundred other steerage passengers on the last day of November 1906.

His trachoma had healed to the point where even the medical examiners at Ellis Island had not detained him. Within a few hours he was processed and on the same evening was feted by his family in their two small rooms on Willett Street. Dutifully Chaim admired his nephew Benny, congratulated his prospective brother-in-law, Mr. Greenbaum, and credited Dr. Jaffe with his good fortune. In their great joy, everyone tried to overlook the changes imprisonment had worked on him. Hannah could only mourn the disappearance of his pink and white cheeks, the thick black ring-lets, the sturdy broad frame that she had loved. In place of the bright-eyed student she had left in Odessa the day she departed for midwifery school, Hannah saw a very different, much older man. The surgery on his eyes had left them weak and watering. Poor nutrition and suffering had robbed his hair of all its luster. He had begun to grow a mustache, but even it looked unfinished and unkempt. His clothing sagged on his sallow frame, and when he walked he avoided standing straight because of an obscure pain in his lower back.

Finally, Lazar decided the time had come to ask questions. "You escaped? It's unheard of these days! How did you do it?"

Chaim leaned back and closed his eyes to focus on the recollection. "I was incarcerated in the Kresty for almost four months before they moved me secretly to Moscow. There I was lodged in the Butyrky prison, the clearinghouse through which political prisoners pass on their first stage of exile to Turkistan, Siberia, or the Arctic. Gershuni, who had been Sazonov's most intimate friend, was there at the same time. They kept him in the Pugachev Tower, but we were able to stay in contact."

"How did you do that?" Lazar asked.

"We devised a language and system of taps and passing on of phrases ... You have no idea what you can do if you ..." His voice trailed off as his eyes focused on some far-off point.

"Later Gershuni and I traveled together on the Trans-Siberian Railroad on our way to Arkatui."

"But that's almost on the Mongolian border!" Lazar exclaimed.

"That's right, and it was over two hundred miles from Serensky, the nearest railhead, from where we were forced to march."

"But how did you escape?" Mama asked impatiently.

"Shhhh! I want to hear it all!" Hannah said.

Chaim inhaled deeply and waited until everyone was quiet. "After the Butyrky and the Kresty I thought I had reached heaven. The skies of Arkatui were bright blue, the steppes stretched out endlessly in every direction, there was so much space, so many flowers, little groves of beeches and white birches. Some of the inmates lectured in law, history, medicine, music, and literature for both the villagers and the prisoners."

"Sounds more like a university than a prison," Hannah commented. "Must have been a simple thing to escape."

"Hardly." His voice swelled with emotion. "Many attempted, but they were always brought back. Gershuni led a crew digging a tunnel, but before it was complete, a guard tripped over the soft earth where it was coming to the surface, and he was caught. The only other tunnel in the place was the one leading to the prison governor's cabbage cellar. In order to get into it, I contrived to be placed inside a brine-filled cabbage cask."

"Didn't they check those barrels?" Mama pondered aloud.

"Yes, they would pierce the top with bayonets, but I was protected by a metal helmet."

Eva gasped. "How did you breathe?"

"I had two rubber tubes held in my mouth, which led to small holes at the bottom of the cask."

Eva's face became animated with the vision of her brother in the barrel. "But weren't you miserable in that cramped position?"

"I willed myself to think of everything else," Chaim said in a righteous tone. "I recited the Talmud and tried to stay awake so I would remember to breathe through the tubes."

"What a religious pickle!" Lazar punned. The unexpected comment made everyone laugh.

"Now, now!" Mama said, holding her hands up. "I want to know what happened!"

"Well," continued Chaim seriously, "when I estimated that it was the middle of the night, I emerged from the cellar. But I was wrong, the time was much earlier than I had guessed. Still, I was able to slip into the forest. As soon as I met up with my rescuers, a snowstorm began raging. We were so delayed by the weather that I thought the authorities would have telegraphed ahead and all would be lost, but the storm also knocked out most of the wires. A month later I reached Switzerland, where the Bund supported me until I was well enough to go to Bremen."

As the final details of Chaim's story were told, Hannah observed a wistful glimmer in her husband's eyes. It was almost as though he wished he could have been the one telling the tale.

Chaim coughed and suddenly his face looked more grey than white. "I regret one thing only . . . that . . . that . . ." He choked.

"Because of my escape . . . the others . . . my comrades were made to suffer."

Hannah poured Lazar a glass of tea from the samovar. He picked it up and sipped before forcefully spitting it out. "Ach! Too cold!" he said peevishly. "How many times do I have to tell you I like it steaming or not at all?"

"It's a wonder you haven't scalded your tongue a thousand times!" she retorted. "How can you be so ungrateful about something so petty when you hear all Chaim's been through?" she said in a false whisper.

"So that is it! Perhaps I would have been better off exiled to Siberia than here in America with a lifetime sentence!" he shouted.

Chaim started. "What is the matter?"

"Nothing for you to worry about!" Lazar said, storming from the room and out of the house."

"Why is he upset?" Chaim asked, shocked by the domestic quarrel on his first day home.

"Lazar's very sensitive," Hannah said, holding her head in her hands as she rested her elbows on the table. "It hasn't been easy for him . . . Your disappearance, coming to America . . ." Hannah stopped herself. "No more of that," she said, brightening. "He'll be back shortly and then we can celebrate."

But Hannah was wrong. For the first time, Lazar stayed out all night.

· 3 ·

DURING HER SECOND WINTER in New York Hannah was more grateful for the warmth of Dr. Jaffe than anything else, for it was that friendship which kept her from a desperate struggle with Lazar. Her husband's complex response to Chaim had taken the form of a fierce protective attachment to his old comrade.

For a few weeks Chaim lived with them, sleeping on the sofa

that Mama had relinquished after Dora's wedding. Soon Chaim chafed at Hannah's desire to know his whereabouts at every hour, so at the first opportunity, he moved to a communal house on Essex Street that was formed by some Jewish radicals from the Am Olam movement in Kiev. Though Hannah had been pleased to see Chaim living with others of similar philosophy, Lazar still seemed to spend more time with her brother than with her.

Night after night Hannah's only company was Eva, who was too tired to help with either Benny or the housework. Unable to hide the fact that she was disgusted by her sister's lazy behavior, Hannah criticized constantly, causing a perpetual round of abusive words, and the two sisters quarreled incessantly.

Eva's only interest seemed to be the care and cleaning of her one dress outfit, a pink silk shirtwaist and long black satin skirt, which did the most to highlight her figure and rosy-cheeked health without emphasizing her awkward posture and very plain features. It was her preoccupation with these clothes that worried Hannah the most. She noticed how the blouse was always hung on a hanger and stuffed with rags to keep the sleeves puffed and the collar crisp. A white handkerchief was bleached, ironed, and tied around her waist so that her partner's sweating palms would not mark the satin skirt at a ball at the Pythagoras Hall. If Hannah dared question her sister about her evenings out, Eva responded with a petulant pout, "I contribute more money than any of you, so I'm entitled to my privacy."

To that Hannah had no quick response. Lazar's peddling and junk sales were irregular, though every now and then he brought in a reasonable sum by trading and selling old books, for which it seemed he had a certain knack.

Fortunately Mrs. Spector, the fruit seller, had given Hannah a fine reference in the marketplace after her precipitous delivery, and the publicity had its effect. Hannah was rewarded with as many births as she could handle and would have contributed a substantial sum each month if she had been paid promptly and in cash. Instead, she often had to take goods in trade for services. Though the Spectors still provided her with a regular supply of fresh fruit and the Honigmans delivered seltzer weekly, not all the bartered items were as useful. Hannah could hardly demand cash from a family that had none to give, and so reluctantly she began her collection of broken jewelry, secondhand furniture, table linens, candlesticks, copper pots, comforters, handmade lace, as well as services from grinders and window washers, laundresses and florists. While hoarding some of the items that she might later need to trade if times grew worse, she could not help but see the irony in sometimes having a bouquet on the Sabbath table instead of a plump chicken. Grateful to have the business, as well as the reputation of providing gentle and safe births, she rarely complained and accepted Eva's regular salary for the rent and other necessities.

Dr. Jaffe's baby was due early in the spring. With Hannah on standby to perform the delivery, the doctor had agreed not to go to a hospital, even though she had argued that it might be injudicious to overlook her colleagues and have her baby at home. Hannah pointed out that although Rachael had already attended many emergency deliveries, the births had occurred either at home or en route to the hospital, and so she had never witnessed the full medical regalia of one of Dr. Harrington's productions. In the end Hannah had prevailed, because Dr. Jaffe knew that together they would be able to decide wisely should any complications arise.

As the time drew near, Dr. Jaffe began to spend her nights sharing Eva's room "just in case." Hannah rejoiced in Rachael's constant company. Once Benny had settled down for the night, the two women would begin hours of conversation that would end only when one of them, usually the very tired and pregnant doctor, could stay awake no longer. Although Hannah knew that Rachael was anxious for her husband to finally join her, selfishly she hoped it would not be too soon.

At first Dr. Herzog had been expected on the same ship as Chaim, but when he had not appeared, Rachael had shrugged it off, saying that something of great importance must have detained him. Hannah wondered how her friend so blithely accepted her husband's absence when she herself took offense for every hour Lazar did not appear home after he was expected.

"I suppose I have a completely different view of it from you," Dr. Jaffe had replied.

"Could you explain it to me?" Hannah asked. "I fear I am becoming the wife I vowed I would never be."

"When Ezekiel was imprisoned I could have wailed and moaned. Certainly that is what I wanted to do, but I told myself that it could have been worse, he could have been killed or maimed . . . or even have taken another woman."

"Is it enough to be thankful for what you have?"

"Not always, but it helps me to remember the plight of others in relation to my own. For a long time I resented the emergency duty at Bellevue, always wishing I had one of the research positions. Then, when I realized how few women in America have medical careers, I became more content."

Hannah shook her head and sighed. "I wish I could be more like you."

"Nonsense, you are perfect just as you are! Don't you know how many women envy you your rich black hair and stunning eyes, the way you capture the interest of every man in the room?"

"But I don't . . ." Hannah protested.

"Then you aren't paying attention!"

"If that is true, why can't I have the same effect on my own husband?" Hannah quavered.

"I've never seen a man more loving toward his wife, when he is here."

"That's just it, *when* he is here! How often have you seen him come in before you have gone to sleep? He has time for everything else . . . everyone else besides me."

"I think you are wrong!" Dr. Jaffe protested. "He tries to escape this . . ." Her arm gestured to the bleak room. "Your husband has a brilliant mind that craves stimulation from lectures and discussions. Do I like being confined either? No! But after the baby comes I'll resume most of my normal activities."

"You'll soon learn how impossible it is!"

"Nothing is impossible with planning. What if we made an agreement between us? I would supervise your baby one evening, the next you would do the same for mine."

"I don't know if I would want that," Hannah demurred.

"That is a separate issue," Dr. Jaffe finished and yawned. "One we will take up tomorrow evening."

Their nightly discussions were soon interrupted by a series of false alarms. For the better part of two weeks, Dr. Jaffe was certain she was in labor. Just as soon as her rhythmic contractions became closer together and more severe, they would end. After the fifth evening of pains Hannah was full of mirth, while Rachael was disgusted with her progress.

"Better check in at the hospital . . . This will be a difficult birth . . . Something must be going wrong . . . or I'm losing my mind . . ." she mumbled during the endless hours of pacing the small rooms of Hannah's apartment.

"I cannot watch you fidget any longer!" Hannah said. "Let's not stay home this evening!"

"What do you suggest?"

"The theater! I've never been, though I know Lazar goes all the time. I was given a pass by Bertha Kalish when I delivered her child last month."

"What is playing?"

"Wouldn't a terrible story be better than sitting here all night watching the minute hand on the clock going round and round?"

Reluctantly Dr. Jaffe agreed. Slowly she moved her massive form down the stairs and the few short blocks to the Belt Line Trolley, which took them to the Grand Theater, where there was a Yiddish production of *A Doll's House*.

Whatever Hannah expected, she was not prepared for the raucous informal atmosphere of the Yiddish theater. Certainly the crowd was not the staid audience she had encountered at the Rialto in Odessa. The women in simple day dresses changing sleepy babies mingling with the sellers of candy, fruit, and soda gave the impression of an indoor carnival rather than a house of sophisticated culture. But as soon as the curtain went up, a hush fell over the audience like a blanket, and no one dared interrupt with more than a cough.

Bertha Kalish's playful femininity seemed to epitomize Nora, and in a few moments Hannah became mesmerized by every word, gesture, and motion of her beautifully pointed jaw. By the beginning of the third act, Dr. Jaffe's contractions became so intense that she involuntarily half stood up from her seat. The ladies behind them began to complain. She clenched her teeth to control an outcry.

"Rachael, should we leave now?" Hannah whispered.

"Not yet. I can't remember how Nora persuaded Torvald not to go to the mailbox; besides, this is probably just another false alarm."

Suddenly her face turned ashen.

"Put your head down and take a few deep breaths," Hannah encouraged. In a few minutes, much to Hannah's relief, Rachael was able to sit up. "Now, if you can stand, we'll go home."

"No! No!" Rachael hissed. "The play distracts me. I'm sure we have plenty of time," she said and turned toward the stage to prove she could concentrate on the action.

Though David Kessler neither looked nor spoke like Lazar, Hannah kept comparing him with her husband and herself with Nora. She clutched at Rachael's hand as Kessler suddenly walked across the stage and stared vacantly into the audience. "Empty. She is gone." A flash of hope momentarily crossed the actor's face before he finished saying, "The most wonderful thing of all . . . ?" A door slammed in the distance as the curtain came down. The audience broke into a ringing, stamping applause over which Hannah said, "I think we'd better be going now to get ahead of the crowd. I have enough money for a carriage."

"But no one else is leaving. Check the program," the doctor said without moving.

Hannah pointed to the word *Intermission* after the third act. "You're right! There's another act!"

"A fourth act to *A Doll's House?* You must be mistaken. I've seen the play several times in Moscow, and that has always been the end."

"What shall we do?" Hannah asked, anxious to be away from the crowd but interested to know the end of the play.

"We'll have to stay. I can't imagine what they've added to the production."

"But Rachael, it might take an hour and you don't look well now!"

"My last contraction was seven minutes ago, and since this is

my first baby, you know I have more than enough time." Rachael
sniffed and settled her spectacles in place as the curtain went up.

The fourth act was quite a surprise. Nora returned to her husband, and cheerfully at that, for the conventions of the Yiddish
theater demanded that a family be kept intact and that every play
must have a happy ending. Dr. Jaffe was more satisfied than Hannah, who thought the adapter had tampered with Ibsen's meaning.

All the way home Hannah fretted, but soon Rachael was safely
in bed. As the night wore on, Dr. Jaffe made slow yet steady
progress, and Hannah knew the birth was drawing nearer when
Rachael began to agree with everything she said.

But by dawn Hannah suspected a complication. When Rachael
was almost fully dilated, Hannah confirmed her diagnosis that the
baby, although coming in the normal head-down position, was pos-
terior, with its face pointing upward rather than down.

Hannah discussed the possibilities with her friend.

"What would you do without my opinion, Hannah?" Dr. Jaffe
asked, her voice becoming higher as another pain began to mount.

With her fist pushed into her patient's lower back exerting a
steady counterpressure to ease the pain, Hannah deliberated.
When Dr. Jaffe was again in control she answered. "I'd like to attempt a digital rotation."

"Then that's what you will do," Dr. Jaffe said with such great
trust and warmth that Hannah felt confident in her abilities.

As soon as Hannah touched the ridgelike seam on the baby's
descending head, she pushed its scalp with her finger. It cooper-
ated by spinning like a top and rotating 180 degrees. Now the baby
was in the perfect anterior position, and within minutes the birth
was complete.

Dr. Jaffe held her little daughter in her arms, remarking on every
feature of her perfect body.

"What will you name her?" Hannah asked.

"I was just thinking of Nora. It's a soft and gentle name, but I'd
hope she'd be able to stand on her own, not to depend on a man
for everything, as you and I have done."

"But Rachael . . ." Hannah protested. "You, of all the women I
have ever known, are the most independent!"

A deep furrow formed across Rachael's forehead as she sucked in her cheeks and said in a plaintive voice, "That is my pretense. Inside I think I am more like you than I dare admit. At least you are honest about your feelings; I am nothing but a sham."

Clicking her tongue, Hannah said, "You are only saying those things because you are so tired.'

Rachael leaned back against her pillow and closed her eyes. "Maybe that is why I can finally speak the truth. What good is my husband to me? From the time we were married we have spent at best a few days a month together, and now I haven't seen him in almost half a year. Who knows what will happen once he gets here?"

Just then Nora began to squirm, and Hannah arranged her at Dr. Jaffe's side. "Nurse your baby," she commanded.

Rachael turned toward little Nora, who peered at her mother with wide eyes and a mouth that was formed into a perfect waiting oval. Stiffening as Hannah undid her gown, Rachael allowed Hannah to lead her through the motions of putting a child to the breast. Any stranger who chanced to view this scene would never have guessed that this new mother already had a vast professional knowledge of babies, for Dr. Jaffe trembled so profoundly that it appeared as though she had never held a child in her arms.

# · 4 ·

BECAUSE SHE COULD hardly take her newborn child to live in her sparse quarters at the hospital, Rachael remained with Hannah after the baby was born. The arrangement suited everyone but Eva, who felt that Hannah had spitefully imposed the doctor and her squalling baby on her.

At age sixteen Eva had already risen to be the manager of her division at the cigar factory because of her abilities at calculations as well as the fact that the owner, Noah Braverman, had taken a personal interest in her. Many times when Mama or Hannah met

Eva at the factory, the bloated man, whose oleaginous form added ten years to his appearance, spoke well of her. "A smart little mind, a bright flower, she blooms in my shop . . . She's like my own daughter!" he'd finish, patting Eva on the head like a puppy. Embarrassed by the attention, Eva would pull away, but she was not ashamed to brag about her latest raise, which made her salary the equivalent of a senior operator's in Mama's shop.

But her high wages, coupled with the authority she wielded over those many times her age, served to exaggerate the unpleasant characteristics in her personality. Whenever she was at home Eva voiced a series of harangues and complaints about their crowded conditions, made even more intolerable by Dr. Jaffe and Nora's use of her valuable space.

In exchange for Hannah's caring for Nora when Dr. Jaffe was on duty, the doctor did the same for Benny on her off hours, allowing both women time to pursue their medical careers. Rachael also encouraged Hannah and Eva to attend the same night school on Rivington Street from which Lazar had graduated a year before. While Hannah reluctantly agreed, Eva complained she was too exhausted from work to consider school and felt she had a right to some amusement in the evenings.

The form of this amusement was not clear. Several times a week Bessie, the lace maker from Forsyth Street, and Eva attended a workmen's society ball; being well chaperoned, these innocent events were preferable to other unknown possibilities. Still, Hannah worried excessively that harm would come to Eva.

Not unaware of her youngest daughter's tendencies, Mama discussed the matter with Hannah. "The time has come to find Eva a husband, but after Dora's wedding and matchmaking fees it will be six months at least before I can afford to make another celebration!" she said in a resigned voice. "And who knows, some girls bloom later than others . . ." she mused. Without beauty, education, or a dowry, the only offering Eva could bring to a marriage was the wages from her job, and although that alone might purchase her a husband, she could hardly expect one as bright or handsome as even Dora had found.

Hannah remained watchful, but when she saw Eva primping for

another evening out she could not restrain herself. "Maybe you should find other friends besides Bessie," she suggested.

Eva stopped tucking her hair back with an army of pins and snapped, "What do you have against Bessie? She's a good worker, she's devoted to her mother."

"I've seen her prancing down the street, the boys buzzing about her like flies on an exposed piece of orange. And I've seen the way you admire everything she does. Look at you now, trying to roll your hair in her style when it doesn't suit you one bit!"

When Eva broke into sobs, Hannah felt a catch in her throat.

"What have I done that is so terrible? I work hard, make a living for all of us, and all you ever do is scream at me! Do you think I like stuffing tobacco into those stinking molds or having to protect Braverman from the union organizers? Every time I go out with Bessie everyone looks at her, not me! Bessie merely puts her head out in the air shaft to dry her hair and men open their windows to talk to her. One of them sent her love poems and begged to be allowed to call on her at home, but her mama won't permit it."

While Hannah was full of sympathy for Bessie's struggle to get out from under the tyranny of her mother, she also understood what it meant to lose a contributing member of the household. Later, when Eva reported that Bessie was blissfully engaged to Mr. Steinberg, a cutter in a pants shop, Hannah tried to make up for her past distrust of the girl by inviting the engaged couple to supper. After the wedding took place, Eva missed her companion so acutely that she pouted until spring.

❖  ❖  ❖

Dr. Ezekiel Herzog finally arrived to claim his wife, Rachael, and baby, Nora, the same week the last of the soot-blackened piles of snow were washed down the gutters by the March rains. Within a few days of clearing immigration, he moved his family nearer the hospital, to Cherry Street.

Just as Eva had felt the loss of Bessie's company, Hannah was bereft at the absence of her friend. After moping every evening Lazar was out, she needed to escape the close rooms as well as avoid Eva's nasty mouth and belligerent moods. So Hannah began to frequent the lecture and meeting halls with Lazar, who gladly introduced her to all his friends. Their evenings out would usually end back at The Monopole, which thrived by appealing to every faction. The café had added a gaming room to accommodate card and chess players, a front dining room for ladies, and partitioned areas so that doctors or actors, radicals or poets could gather together in select groups. For Hannah it became a place where she and Lazar could finally share something besides complaints about their shabby existence.

Invariably, after an evening away from home together, Lazar would want her. Now he understood how she liked him to stroke her breasts and touch her, just so. And she knew when to press him and where he wanted to be squeezed, when to wait and when to drive on. Willingly, happily, they pleasured each other in a less selfish and yet more satisfying manner than they ever had before. And because of what she felt was happening between them, Hannah came to believe that everything else might also change for the better.

## · 5 ·

MANY OF THE CASES on Hannah's busy schedule came from another Monopole regular: Dr. Strauss. He referred to Hannah those women who were, in his opinion, too obstinate to accept the hospital. In rare cases when risk factors were present, Hannah consulted with the doctor during the course of the labor and, if complications developed, would transport a patient to the hospital, even over her protests, for Hannah was quick to acknowledge where her skill and equipment were insufficient.

Dr. Strauss had asked her to make frequent prenatal visits to a Mrs. Feigenbaum, who had swelled so quickly that Dr. Strauss had suspected a tumor, and now, in her last trimester, was so huge that she could barely climb the stairs.

Hannah was concerned that Mrs. Feigenbaum had miscalcu-
lated her dates and might be delivering early, until she heard two
distinct heartbeats and a multiple pregnancy was confirmed. Finding even the simplest activity too exhausting by the following
week, Mrs. Feigenbaum took to her bed. On the next examination
Hannah pulled out her stethoscope and listened for the dual beats
with pleasure, but her excitement increased when she thought she
had heard a third. Hannah practiced external maneuvers in an attempt to separate the various heads and buttocks she thought she
felt. Although she could identify at least three polar points, she
needed five to be certain about triplets, so she called in the doctor
for his opinion.

After the examination, Dr. Strauss became quite excited as he
told Mrs. Feigenbaum, "There is a fair chance you will have three
babies, and since they are bound to come early, you must let everyone treat you as a princess. Call me or Mrs. Sokolow at the slightest sign and we will take you to the hospital."

"Every time I go to a hospital someone dies! You'll never get me
there!"

"Don't you want your babies to have the best possible chance?
With a multiple birth there can be so many complications . . ." he
protested.

Mrs. Feigenbaum was adamant. Dr. Strauss spoke privately to
Hannah. "When the time comes she'll be more receptive. When a
woman's really in labor she'll do anything I say to get the baby
out!"

As much as Hannah wanted to object to his unfair manipulation, she bit her tongue, as she didn't dare risk offending the source
of most of her referrals. "I'll come by daily, Doctor, and I'll summon you if she goes into labor. If she lasts the full term there
might be a chance for a safe delivery at home . . ."

"That would be unwise, but we shall see," he said, and descended the worn stairs four flights to the street.

In the middle of that same night, Hannah was awakened by a
knock on the door. Feigenbaum himself had come because his wife
thought the babies were on their way. Although Hannah doubted
she was due that soon, she was unwilling to take any risks with this
important case

Mrs. Feigenbaum was already straining and within less than ten minutes of Hannah's arrival delivered a tiny little girl into her hands. The second child presented in frank breech, but was so small that the delivery posed no problem; the third appeared only five minutes later. By the time Dr. Strauss arrived, Hannah was attempting to care for three premature baby girls, whom she had lined up on a mattress beside the stove for warmth and observation. The first child, named Ruth, was having respiratory problems, and the doctor went to work on her immediately. The second was the smallest of the group, but seemed remarkably strong, her hands balled in tight little fists that waved as she demonstrated a fearsome cry. "That one's a fighter," the doctor said. "A little mass of blood and iron."

Mrs. Feigenbaum lay exhausted in her bed, watching the infants she had just produced while Dr. Strauss listened to the last daughter's heartbeat with a stethoscope. "I want to call her Naomi!" Mrs. Feigenbaum announced.

"And what will you name this last little one?" he asked to keep the mother from inquiring too quickly about her health, for the sounds in her chest were so weak and irregular he believed she would not last very long.

"Ruth, Naomi . . . I'm too tired to think of another."

"Esther," Hannah suggested.

"Yes, call her Esther." Mrs. Feigenbaum closed her eyes and repeated the names of her tiny children over and over as if the words were a potent incantation that would help to keep them from harm. But little Esther's condition was grave and in a few hours she was gone.

Although Hannah and Dr. Strauss worked on the remaining two children, suctioning their secretions and stimulating their breathing, Ruth also succumbed in the first twelve hours and the fate of the tiny Naomi appeared hopeless as well. The child weighed less than three pounds and was so weak she could not suck the breast. Hannah fed her every hour by expressing colostrum, the golden fluid that precedes a mother's milk; yet the baby took less than an ounce at a time with an eyedropper.

Before leaving Hannah in charge of the fading child and her postpartum mother, Dr. Strauss signed the first two death certificates and filled out a third with Naomi's name to save himself additional paperwork. Speaking to Hannah privately on the street, he said, "Go home and get your own rest now."

"But the baby will need to be fed and watched around the clock. Her mother is too weak for the chore."

"What does it matter?"

"But you said yourself that she was the strongest . . . blood and iron . . ."

"Don't be foolish!" Dr. Strauss interrupted. "I've never seen one that small live, and to pretend otherwise is a delusion. If you want to do the mother a favor, you could begin to sympathize with her for her terrible loss."

"Dr. Strauss!" The hours without sleep had made Hannah short-tempered. "No wonder you are just a 'society' doctor! You'd be better off wasting your time at The Monopole than giving out such bad advice! Don't you think this baby is worth the extra time it would take . . . ?" Hannah's voice trailed off as she realized her angry words might ruin her reputation as a sensible midwife.

The doctor merely stared at the pavement, his hat in his hand, until she was finished. Placing it back on his head, he spoke with an even voice. "You see how exhausted you are? You can't be expected to work without sleep. If you must continue with this thankless case, so be it. Call me when you need the death certificate signed."

"That won't be necessary, Doctor," Hannah responded with more control in her voice. Turning from him she hurried to prove him wrong.

❖  ❖  ❖

If Hannah had known the grueling hours of tedious care that lay ahead, she might have become discouraged. But her naive optimism carried her through the first difficult days.

Because Naomi had to be kept at a constant temperature, as her little body could not regulate itself, Hannah found a small wooden box that had held cherries and lined the inside with thick layers of flannel and cotton wool, which could be changed if the baby soiled them. So that Hannah could observe the child's color and respiration without undue handling, the naked baby was covered with only a thin piece of muslin, for the midwife intuitively felt that the child should be treated as though she were still in the womb. In her diligence to maintain something close to an interuterine environment, Hannah went so far as to keep the child in semi-darkness and reduce the noise level.

From the beginning the baby had severe lapses in breathing. One moment she'd be pink and lively, the next she would gag and turn blue. The only warning was an almost inaudible catch in her throat and a minute jerk of her doll-like limbs. Hannah hovered over her like a sparrow nestling her chick, to be certain she would catch the child within the first seconds of cessation of breathing. When Naomi's vital signs faltered, Hannah would lift the child onto a towel on her lap and began a delicate massage of all her limbs with warm mineral oil, which also served as her bath, since Hannah believed the child's skin was too fragile to be touched with the harshness of soap or water.

But the task of observing the baby round the clock with total vigilance was impossible, and by the second night, Hannah was alarmed to realize how often she had dozed off in her chair. Shaken by the thought of losing the child, Hannah made herself a strong glass of tea. As she pondered how to remain alert for a longer period of time, her mind wandered back to when Bubbe Schtern would leave a new mother alone for the first time, tying a piece of string around the mother's wrist, then fastening the other end to the center of the infant's cradle, saying, "You must rest. If the baby wakes, you have only to pull the string a few times. The rocking should put him back to sleep, but if that doesn't do it, you will know you must feed him."

The memory provided a clue to solve Hannah's current dilemma. She found a piece of fine suture thread and tied it around Naomi's delicate wrist and then wound the other end around her own finger. In less than an hour, the child tested her by stopping breathing so silently it was as though a snuffer had blotted out the flame of a candle. But the resulting jerk of Naomi's arm had been enough to set the thread in motion, and all Hannah needed to do was snap the line twice to activate the child's system once again. Soon the crisis passed and Hannah was able to sleep.

At first Hannah claimed she didn't mind the awkward pattern of resting no more than two hours at a stretch, but by the second week exhaustion was beginning to dominate, and the only way she could stay awake was to be eating or drinking constantly.

"You must allow me to do more," Mrs. Feigenbaum said, after relieving Hannah of the chore of feeding Naomi and then writing down the number of ounces she appeared to have swallowed.

"I don't mind at all," Hannah insisted, though her drooping lids spoke more eloquently than her words.

Mrs. Feigenbaum had to persist to wrest from the midwife more responsibility for her own child. "Look how much stronger she is already!" The mother placed her forefinger in the baby's mouth to show how well the child could suck. Without asking permission, Mrs. Feigenbaum lifted her blouse, loosened her corset, and placed the child at her breast. Hannah began to protest, but then stood back to watch the tender struggle. After the fifth attempt, the baby latched on and began the slow sucking and gulping that indicated she was able to feed herself. Mrs. Feigenbaum leaned back on her pillows exultant with her victory.

Later she told Hannah, "There is nothing I love more than holding a baby. I lost three before this, and now I mourn for five, so I know what a tragedy it is to lose a baby. But when your child lives and grows up you forget the baby he was in the next age that comes along. The baby who dies is your baby forever."

Naomi didn't die. She defied every medical statistic, and by some miracle, not to mention the meticulous care she received, she flourished. When Dr. Strauss examined the child at three months of age he could not help but compliment Hannah on her achievement, and again Hannah's reputation soared.

No one was more grateful than the Feigenbaums. Although they were not among the most destitute of the population, they could not afford to fully pay for Hannah's work, nor could Hannah use enough of Mr. Feigenbaum's plumbing services to offset the debt. Though Mrs. Feigenbaum had pledged to help Hannah in any possible way, it was not until Hannah had been back in her own home for several weeks that an idea occurred to her.

Eva was more tyrannical than ever, having been forced to be

with Benny while Hannah nursed Naomi. Denied weeks of parties and time on her own, she was utterly obstinate. A certain pucker of her mouth, the slight way she pushed her hip to the side when she walked, the fastidiousness with which she groomed herself and fussed with her corsets made it all too clear to Hannah that a husband had better be found before she got into trouble.

When living at the Feigenbaums' Hannah had been privy to an interesting development in their family. Mrs. Feigenbaum's brother, Napthali Margolis, had come to America several years before, leaving his betrothed behind. At first he worked on the railroads, ending up in the oil fields of Pennsylvania. There he lived in a camp in order to save almost every penny he earned, for he was determined to bring his bride to a life of comfort in America. With $300 down he purchased a five-year lease on a tenement building of his own. Taking only one back cellar room for himself, he let out the rest of the apartments by the week, acting as handyman, janitor, painter, carpenter, plumber, and rent collector. When the lease ran out, he had saved enough to make a down payment on the purchase of the building as well as to acquire a second lease on one across the street. "Soon my brother will own half the Lower East Side!" Mrs. Feigenbaum had bragged.

While Hannah was caring for Naomi, tragic news arrived. Minna, the girl who was expected to marry Napthali that summer, had been the victim of a Passover pogrom in her small Polish village. Cossacks had driven the Jews into a flooding river, shooting those who clung to its banks and letting the ones who floated downstream drown in the raging currents.

"We knew nothing about the girl, but my brother always said she was the most beautiful thing he'd ever seen — eyes like a doe, skin like velvet," Mrs. Feigenbaum had said. "When he is ready we'll send for a shadchen. Surely with his future he will attract another beauty!"

Eva was not a beauty. But the Feigenbaums owed Hannah a great debt, and on the strength of that, as well as the impossibility of a peaceful life with her sister under the same roof, Hannah went to negotiate a match. Without even asking to see Eva, the Feigenbaums tentatively approved, especially after hearing that she was already a factory manager at her young age. Together the young couple would certainly prosper, and everyone agreed it would do Napthali good to be married as soon as possible.

Only Lazar had suggested that the young couple be given a chance to be alone for a while, to talk and eventually decide for themselves. At their first meeting Eva was so gay and excited, her clothing and bearing so immaculate in contrast to Napthali's disheveled and sullen state, that she actually appeared more attractive than they had hoped. Within a few weeks the wedding date was set, Liberty Hall on Houston Street was hired for the party, and Aunt Sonia volunteered to make the wedding dress herself.

It was after Eva refused to go through with a fitting that the trouble started. Aunt Sonia whispered something to Mama, and Mama came to Hannah with the startling news that Eva had changed her mind, adamantly refusing to say anything more than that the marriage would not take place.

# · 6 ·

MAMA WENT DIRECTLY to Mrs. Feigenbaum to learn what her brother had said or done, but Mrs. Feigenbaum denied any knowledge of the disaster that had befallen the families.

"Something must be wrong with your daughter for her to act so foolishly!" she said in anger. "If it weren't for the great service Mrs. Sokolow did us, we never would have considered her!" Mrs. Feigenbaum had not meant her words to turn into so deep an insult and immediately apologized by taking Mama's hand and leading her over to where the infant Naomi slept. "Would you like to hold her?"

"Could I?" Mama asked, lifting the baby in her arms. "She's like a feather!" Mama melted and said, "I'll talk to Eva. Maybe it's nerves . . . Even Hannah almost fainted at her own wedding."

"I'm certain Napthali will be the most gentle of husbands," Mrs. Feigenbaum replied earnestly. "I'll have Murray talk to him."

❖ ❖ ❖

No one could get Eva to explain until, exasperated by the situation, Hannah asked Dr. Jaffe to speak with her sister. After that meeting, Hannah met Rachael at Moskowitz's restaurant.

"Your sister is pregnant, almost three months along," Dr. Jaffe said immediately as she took her seat at the narrow table by the window.

Hannah gasped. "I should have known! Three months! How could she do this to us?"

"Can't you see that she was too frightened to tell anyone?" replied Dr. Jaffe with great sympathy in her voice.

"She's been asking for this for some time with her parties, her dresses, and her jealousy of that vacant-headed Bessie!"

"Hannah!" Dr. Jaffe shook her mass of wiry red hair. "Eva is not responsible for this! Your sister has been caught in one of the most despicable traps that a man could have set! Bastards!" She spoke with such force that heads turned in the restaurant, bringing a crimson rush to Hannah's face.

"Shhhh!" Hannah leaned forward. "What do you mean?"

"At the cigar factory . . . the owner, that disgusting pig of a man . . . Braverman . . . has been having his way with her for months. That's why she received so many raises and bonuses . . ."

"She sold herself to him!" Hannah sputtered.

"At first he took her by force. Later she submitted because he threatened to ruin her, make certain she would never work again."

"He couldn't do that!"

"Remember how young Eva is. She's lived in the hope that she'd attract a boy at one of these dances who would marry her and then she'd be safe from the old drunkard, may they sew shrouds for him!"

"What can we do now?" Hannah asked.

"There's only one thing to do."

"Braverman is already married, and we cannot deceive the Feigenbaums . . ." Hannah said, blindly avoiding the intent of the doctor's words.

"Eva says she will kill herself if she must have the baby, and after talking to her, I think I believe her."

"What are you saying?" Hannah choked on the possibility.

"If we don't do the job, there are others who will. I can give you a bloody list of failures that I am called upon to save," Dr. Jaffe replied slowly. "Most times I am too late."

Hannah squeezed and unsqueezed her fists. "There must be another way . . ."

"Eva says she won't have this child and you know as well as I that you can't force her to do anything she doesn't want to do. This boy, Napthali, seems an unusually good chance for her, doesn't he? And while I don't approve of all this matching of children, your sister may come to feel very deeply for him once this has passed."

"If you do it, I don't want to know about it . . ." Hannah said, looking away from her friend.

"I'm willing to perform the operation, but I will need your help."

Hannah's voice was accusing. "Do you do this very often?"

"No! But I have much experience in dilation and curettage, as I am so often called in to repair the damage from less skilled operators. You've had everything so easy that you can't imagine the suffering of others."

Hannah thought uneasily of the unresolved question concerning Benny's paternity and what she might have endured if it had not been for Lazar. All at once the resentment she felt at her sister's morose moods and belligerent words dissolved. Poor Eva! No wonder she had been so impossible lately! How had she been so blind and selfish not to have seen the girl's misery?

"You are right," Hannah conceded. She longed to tell her friend more of the truth about herself as well, but there was time only to think of Eva. If Rachael was surprised at how quickly Hannah had turned agreeable, she made no comment. Together they planned Eva's surgery for the next afternoon.

❖   ❖   ❖

It was feared that Eva might prove a difficult case, but the procedure went swiftly and without event in Dr. Herzog's examining room. Hannah's hands were far too unsteady and her experience in such cases was so limited that Rachael handled the entire procedure herself, with her husband administering enough ether to keep Eva relaxed. Hannah held her hand, doing what little she could to make up for her former insensitivity to her younger sister.

Once Eva understood that Hannah took her side, she apologized for all the difficulties she had caused at home. Together the sisters decided that the fewer people who knew the better, and so they told everyone that Eva was suffering from a nervous stomach condition that only rest and a tranquilizing medicine prescribed by Dr. Jaffe would cure. The wedding was delayed for only a month, and though Eva had been expected to return to Braverman's after her recovery, Dr. Jaffe explained that working with tobacco had contributed to the illness. Although Eva sacrificed her manager's income by quitting her job, Napthali and the Feigenbaum family could hardly fault her for obeying "doctor's orders" and arranged for her to take over the management of Napthali's accounts.

The idea to have a quiet ceremony out of respect for Napthali's loss was Eva's, but Mama and the Feigenbaums worked together to prepare a bountiful feast, while Uncle Leyb hired the musicians and entertainers. Relieved to be away from the cigar factory and to be marrying a young man with excellent prospects, Eva blossomed into a beautiful and contented bride. Hannah's misgivings about the abortion were utterly dispelled by Eva's glowing face under the marriage canopy.

❖   ❖   ❖

Even though the earnings from Hannah's deliveries and aftercare were now substantial, there was never enough to properly feed or clothe the three of them, let alone support Lazar's continual purchase of old books, meals away from home, or dues for the various societies and clubs he joined. Whenever Hannah broached the subject of their dwindling resources, Lazar avoided the issue with an excuse. The day following Eva's wedding, Hannah could wait no longer.

After supper she cleared the table, poured Lazar a second glass of boiling tea, handed him a list of their expenses, and said as quietly as possible, "Eva contributed over thirty dollars a month, which paid for the rent plus much of our food. Now how shall we manage . . . ?"

"Three or four more deliveries would do it!" Lazar said abstractedly. "What are you so excited about?"

Hannah checked her tone of voice, for if she became excited Lazar would take his usual course and storm out of the room. She folded her hands on the table to demonstrate that she was calm. "I never turn away work. I am doing every birth in the neighborhood and then some. Last week I went up to Eighteenth Street on a recommendation."

"Perhaps now that it is summer more will be expecting?"

"Lazar! This is not the fruit business! Women don't suddenly ripen in hot weather!"

"Why not? Wouldn't you think more would be planted in the cold and harvested in the summer?" He laughed.

Hannah shook her head and tried to be serious, but she began to giggle. "We must find a way to make up the difference . . ." She stopped while Lazar covered her protesting mouth with kisses.

"I've looked forward to this for so long . . ." he said, caressing her more strongly.

"To what?" Hannah said without pulling away from his tight grasp.

"To being alone with you, finally alone. They are all gone, your mama, your sisters, your aunt and uncle and Abraham" — he kissed her again before continuing his chant — "that friend of yours and her baby . . . Uncle Moishe . . . Do you realize we have never been together without anyone else? Never! Never! Coming home I'd always dream that only you and Benny would be here. Finally it's come true. Don't spoil it by complaining," he said as he unbuttoned her dress.

"But . . . Benny is not asleep . . ."

Lazar glanced over to the kitchen floor where Benny was sitting contentedly arranging spoons in one bowl and forks in another, chortling at his proficiency. "He can do that for hours . . . This will only take minutes." Lazar pulled Hannah toward their small back bedroom and drew the lace curtain to give them a semblance of privacy. Reluctantly she acquiesced, realizing once again how skill-fully Lazar had avoided their financial problem.

❖ ❖ ❖

Hannah hoped her business would increase. When it didn't, she began to raise her fees slightly to close the gap between their spendings and her earnings. Everything seemed in balance for a few months. Then a series of small reversals drained all their resources. By the end of August, Hannah was without funds to pay either the rent or her butcher bill. Lazar still shrugged off the problem.

Then, for the first time, Aunt Sonia found it necessary to refuse Hannah. "I'm sorry," she said, arranging bolts of fabric so she would not have to look into her niece's pleading eyes. "This has been a bad month," she said, wiping perspiration from her brow.

The small narrow room was unbearably hot, and Hannah could see for herself why no one wanted to enter the shop. "Maybe you should move some of your remnants out onto the street," Hannah suggested.

"I would, but I can't watch Abie outside. He's too fast for me to catch, I'll tell you."

"And Olga, she can't watch him for you?"

"I thought you knew . . . Olga has left us."

Hannah's mouth dropped in surprise, for she had seen Olga dancing and singing merrily at Eva's wedding. "Where has she gone?"

"She's working uptown in a café where she serves the tables and sings afterward. American songs she is learning!"

"I didn't think she'd last as long as she did," Hannah said under her breath.

"What?" Sonia asked.

"Nothing . . . I'm sorry to have bothered you," she said, leaving the steaming shop for the comparative cool of the street.

When Hannah returned home, Lazar was bathing Benny in the sink. "He already had a bath this morning!" she snapped.

"He woke completely drenched and stinking," he shouted. "You should be grateful I stayed with him all morning."

"Grateful! I was trying to borrow some money to hold us over until I can get some more work."

"If you could only collect on some of your old cases, we'd be fine. Doesn't that lady over on Delancey still owe you, and what about . . . ?"

"I can't squeeze it out of them any more than I can squeeze it out of you! And as for being grateful that you are willing to spend a few hours with your own child . . . it is the only useful thing you ever do!" she finished and stormed from the house. Burdened with their wet and squealing son, Lazar could not chase after her.

At first she did not think of where she was going, but the breezes from the East River drew her. She sat on the stone bulkhead and observed the gulls circling and diving in the distance, heard their raucous calls in counterpoint with the yells and whoops of the splashing boys who jumped from the splintered pilings into the murky river. In a far corner of the park someone was playing an accordion, and the sound of clapping children against the hum of the music reminded Hannah how Lazar adored dancing with his child, singing comic songs to make him laugh.

If nothing else, Lazar was good to his son and a far better parent than any other man she knew, even her own papa, who had spent much less time with her than with her brother. In her mind's eye, she could see Chaim and Papa hand in hand, walking away, leaving her to cry on the steps.

"That's only for the men . . ." Mama had insisted, as though that explanation would quell Hannah's hurt.

Papa and Chaim . . . now she was abandoned by Lazar and Chaim . . .

Reaching up with her right hand, Hannah rubbed her eyes to blot out the painful vision, and in so doing, brought another image to mind. Chaim! The small boy with the enviable curls and dimpled cheeks, his bright eyes and eager mind captivating all who knew him. Competing with Chaim for every scrap of attention had been Hannah's childish occupation, and even now as a grown woman she was still fighting the same battle, but this time the prize was not her parent's or teacher's approval but her husband's! Was her marriage the final victory over her older brother? Was she

allowing the vestiges of childish anger to creep forward and under-
mine her present life? After all, what terrible acts had Lazar com-
mitted against her?

Agitated, Hannah stood and began to pace along the edge of the
pier. She should be grateful that Lazar was so happy with his son,
and in most ways content with her as well. The breeze nearer the
water whipped her skirt around her ankles. With her fingers she
lifted her damp shirtwaist and tried to bring some cooling air to
her bosom, which, even after suckling a baby for almost a year, was
as high and firm as it had always been.

Two gentlemen strolled by and took a long look at her. With
some pride she realized she was still considered a handsome
woman, probably the most attractive one in the park that day.
Lately she had begun silently to compare herself with other ladies
she saw on the street, in pictures, or newspapers. Her complexion
was still perfect. Her figure was thin and her waist could be
cinched almost as tightly as before her marriage. With slim wrists,
long arms, and a swanlike neck, she wore her few decent clothes
with style, although she still wished herself a few inches taller, at
least for the sake of better proportion. Vanity! "What good is
beauty," she thought, "if it can't buy enough food to eat?"

A jeering laugh caught her attention. She turned to watch two
boys perched on the pilings, the older one taunting the younger to
jump from a great height.

"Dope!" the taller boy said and pushed. But the younger child
reached out, grabbing the other's arm, and together they tumbled
into the water. It was Hannah who saw the bigger boy hit his head
on the base of the piling while the smaller one fell into the water
with a funnel-shaped splash.

"Get him! Get him!" she screamed.

"Aw, he's all right!" his friends shouted and pointed to the wild
thrashing of his arms and legs.

Hannah would not be mollified even though the boy seemed to
be swimming back to the quay. Two boys swam over and helped
him out, while the younger boy who had been pushed said, "Serves
Mike right . . ."

Hannah reached to grasp the child's limp form as he was prodded onto the dock next to a cluster of oaken casks. Thinking

quickly, Hannah pushed one of the larger barrels over on its side and directed the boys to lay Mike across its curvature.

"Put him here," she pointed. "With his stomach down!"

Hannah turned the boy's head to the side and checked his throat with her finger. After clearing his tongue so he could breathe, she pressed on the small of his back just below the rib cage with a forceful downward and forward motion. River water gushed from his mouth, and the resulting sputter and gag was further evidence that his breathing had resumed.

"Go to the hospital for a doctor!" Hannah pointed to the boy nearest her. "You! Run!"

As Hannah continued to push the injured boy's legs forward, the barrel rolled back beneath his chest and he expelled another rush of water. Back and forth she pumped his body, until the boy was so empty he began to protest the treatment. By the time the emergency physician arrived, Mike was able to give a full account of his adventure.

"The boy says he almost drowned!" the doctor reported to Hannah after he made his assessment. "Lucky you were there, miss."

"I did nothing at all," Hannah demurred. "His friends pulled him from the water; all I did was massage him until he was better . . ."

"There is no evidence of injury except a slight swelling and a laceration that will need a suture or two. But I think we'll keep him in the hospital overnight. Can't be too careful with a boy from a family like his."

"Is he someone special?" Hannah asked, shading her eyes from the sun.

"He says he's Michael Tremain, Jr., son of the chairman of the Board of Supervisors."

Although Hannah did not have the sense to be sufficiently impressed by the child's antecedents, the young doctor, always sensitive to a human interest story that might be good for the image of his institution, released the story to the papers.

By the next day, Hannah's name and picture had appeared in a dozen English and Yiddish columns under headlines such as MID-WIFE SAVES POLITICIAN'S SON. The stories went on to describe

Hannah as "Mrs. H. Sokolow of 81 Willett Street," who undertook the "daring rescue of Michael Tremain, Jr.," and finished by saying that the "professional midwife and masseuse modestly said, 'I only helped the boy recover his breathing and took no extraordinary measures.' But the Tremain family believes they owe their son's life to the brave woman who, by God's good graces, was at the right place at the right time."

After several days had passed Hannah thought the attention had ceased. However, the story was kept alive by a series of articles on proposed legislation to prohibit river swimming and the letters of agreement and protest that followed. Lazar rejoiced in the publicity, expecting that it would bring a new flock of expectant mothers to Hannah's doorstep. Instead she began to receive queries about the fee she charged for a massage. Before she understood what was happening, she had developed a roster of clients who would give her business every few weeks instead of once a year at best.

Elsewhere in the city, Hannah's notoriety was having a different effect on a certain Inspector Noyes. In checking her name against his list of midwives licensed to practice in New York City, he found that she had never applied for, nor had she ever been granted, the required certificate. Tracking down illegal midwives was his sole responsibility, but since the "ignorant women" who patronized the immigrant caregivers protected their own, he busied himself writing monographs with such titles as "The Position of the New York State Department of Health Relative to the Control of Midwives" more often than going out in the field to enforce the statutes he had helped to draft.

After looking up Willett Street on his map, he was gratified when he saw it was in the jurisdiction of his Centre and Walker streets office. He pulled out a crisp field report form, dipped his pen in ink, and filled in the space marked "Suspected Midwife" with the words "H. Sokolow," barely controlling his satisfaction at having initiated a brand new case.

## · 7 ·

CLARENCE NOYES had been a minor statistician with the Health Department in charge of compiling figures on maternal mortality until his work had come to the attention of Dr. Linsly Williams, deputy commissioner of health, who had used Noyes's charts and tables in preparing the medical society's position papers on the regulation of midwifery. The helpful young Noyes was promoted to oversee the new department that would license the best of the midwives as well as drive the incompetents out of business. His energetic response to the job resulted in gratifying statistics during the first two years of service: 31 fines, 3 imprisonments for "gross violations" by illegal midwives, and 1,344 licenses granted to qualifying midwives. If he could increase the arrests, Noyes guessed he might have a chance to be appointed assistant commissioner when Ernst Lederle retired the following year.

The inspector prided himself on his appearance. His fingernails were trimmed to the quick and buffed with a soft rag. His crisp charcoal uniform featured shining silver buttons with the raised initials HD, and he proudly wore his engraved name shield over his left breast. Perhaps it was the newspaper clipping with the photograph of the attractive and tidy young Mrs. Sokolow that made him snap the wrinkles from his jacket and run a slick of fresh polish over his boots. This midwife was something of a heroine. He would have to do everything exactly by the regulations so as not to risk having his recommendations altered because of some laxity in procedure. Since he had helped to draft these very rules, he was confident he could handle the inspection.

❖ ❖ ❖

With Benny visiting Eva, Hannah and Lazar were relieved to have the afternoon free to attend a lecture. But as they climbed down the stairs together, a uniformed gentleman wearing military boots asked if they were the Sokolows and explained he had come from the Department of Health. A shiver of terror shook Hannah's composure. She knew why he had come! Somehow he had been informed about Eva's abortion. But who could have told?

After awkwardly following the Sokolows as they backed up a flight of stairs, Inspector Noyes spoke clearly and calmly to Lazar, explaining that this was but a routine call. "Would you please ask your wife to bring me her instruments, so I may ascertain the number and quality of the tools she has at her disposal."

"Her equipment is privately owned and should be of no interest to you, sir," Lazar responded crisply.

"I realize that, but the Department of Health will give midwives under their jurisdiction additional supplies as part of the program to aid mothers and babies."

"Is that so?" Lazar asked both the inspector and Hannah.

"Dr. Jaffe has brought me some already from the hospital," Hannah replied.

"Dr. Jaffe?" The inspector raised his thin eyebrows.

"My wife studied medicine with the doctor in Moscow!" Lazar replied with a smirk.

"You say you studied in Moscow? Do you have a certificate?"

"Hannah, get your papers!" Lazar said.

Hannah brought out her box and laid the documents on the table, but the inspector could not read the Russian. "I will have these checked by the authorities, but if you hold a degree from a recognized medical institution, either American or European, there should be no trouble in granting you a permanent license to practice midwifery in the state of New York," he said very rapidly to Hannah. Turning to Lazar, he continued, "You must understand that I have not come to harass you, but I am obligated to be certain that no one delivers babies who is not completely competent. The statistics of infant and maternal deaths in this city have been shocking, and it is my responsibility to protect the lives of innocent families who unknowingly accept the services of uneducated practitioners."

"What difference does it make if she is licensed or not?"

"It is illegal for a midwife to practice without a license, and she would be subject to arrest, imprisonment, and fines if she is not. But since she claims to have a degree, the requirements should not be difficult to fulfill."

Lazar studied the inspector's face, searching for a twist. Finding him to be sincere from all outward signs, he offered the inspector a seat and took one opposite him. "Hannah, let's find out what this is all about," he said in Yiddish. Then he asked the inspector, "What are these requirements?"

The inspector pulled out a large folder and began reading pages of technical jargon. Hannah became agitated as she listened to the list of procedures midwives could and could not perform.

". . . The lawful practice of midwifery does not include the use of any instrument, nor the assisting of childbirth by any artificial, forcible, or mechanical means, nor the performance of any version, nor the removal of adherent placenta, nor the administering, prescribing, advising, or employing of any drug other than a disinfectant."

Pushing the application form toward Hannah, the inspector continued, "If you will sign your name in the three places I have marked, I will immediately set up an appointment for your written examination and process your preliminary license. Until it is issued I must caution you that you would be performing an illegal act in delivering a child."

"But I have some women expecting quite soon. I cannot refuse to attend them. What would you have me do with them, take them to the hospital?"

"Even when you are fully licensed you will be required to refer some of your patients," Inspector Noyes responded. "Section Eleven of the Act requires that a midwife refer complications such as a contracted pelvis, bleeding, and prolonged labor. I will leave with you a list of these conditions. And again I must remind you not to attend a confinement case until I bring you your documents. Do you understand?"

"I think we will need time to learn exactly what we must do," Lazar said politely.

"It is not our intention to be unfair," Noyes said, clearing his throat. Placing his body so that his back was to Lazar, he said to Hannah, "Thank you very much for your time," and turned on his heel. "Ah" — he paused — "one more item ... I still must inspect your instruments to be certain you have a kit that qualifies ..."

Hannah became suspicious. So far the inspector had restricted his comments to midwifery and had said nothing about abortion; perhaps the moment she feared had come. In the brightest voice she could summon, Hannah replied, "Please come this way."

Which tools might be considered illegal? Forceps? Dilators? Her speculum? Hannah was extremely proud of her equipment, which she kept wrapped in sterile towels and readied for a delivery at any hour. Lifting her bag onto the bed, she first pulled out a drape sheet and laid it across the comforter. She removed a pair of rubber gloves and fitted them to her hands. "If you don't mind, sir, I would prefer to handle the equipment myself and rewrap it as we go, to save the trouble of disinfecting everything once again."

"May I ask what you use for that purpose?"

"For my own hands I use green soap for five minutes and then a solution of Lysol two percent. For my instruments I prefer carbolic acid, two percent, and for the patient I prepare a solution of bichloride of mercury one to five thousand."

Obviously impressed, Inspector Noyes nodded. "That follows the department's recommendations exactly."

Without Lazar to speak for her, Hannah became bolder. "I can see that you are only doing your job, sir, but I think you will find I am a highly qualified member of my profession. I have personally delivered more than three hundred women and have assisted and observed more than a thousand cases, including Caesarean section."

"How is that possible?" Noyes stammered. "You're a very young woman!"

Hannah's smile beguiled him and he was charmed by her pleasant manner and the amused twinkling of her emerald eyes. Hannah was not unaware of the effect her close presence in the darkened bedroom was having on the gentleman. "Now to my kit!" she announced in a loud voice.

"Ah ... I don't think it will be necessary for you to undo all your work here. I ... I just need to make certain that you have the one percent solution of silver nitrate required for the baby's eyes."

"I have some from the clinic."

"And that you do not have any illegal tools . . ."

"Why would I have them?"

"You must swear you have no syringes, wire catheters, dressing forceps, uterine sounds or applicators . . ."

Deliberately Hannah put away the few items she had already laid out, then stood at attention.

"We must be certain that you neither perform abortions nor do instrument deliveries . . . With your background you must know the danger."

Hannah stood serenely in wide-eyed innocence. She did not know if Inspector Noyes was more impressed with her military posture or the forward thrust of her bosom; but he did not press her further.

"Thank you again for your time and cooperation, Mr. and Mrs. Sokolow," he said, closing the door softly behind him.

They waited until the echo of his footsteps had completely receded. Hannah ran and threw her arms around Lazar's neck. "If I don't get the papers to practice what I will do?"

"There is always well-baby care and massage. And Benny and . . ." He patted her stomach. "Have I guessed your secret?"

She answered without enthusiasm. "It is very early yet, but yes, I think I am pregnant. Another baby won't make me happy if I'm forced to stop practicing midwifery!" she added with vehemence.

"That bureaucrat didn't expect you to have so many qualifications . . . he's after women like . . ."

"Fingerman! She does everything against the rules, not only of 'the state of New York' " — she mimicked Noyes's officious tone — "but of correct obstetrical practice. He should try searching her house for illegal tools!"

"Do you have anything he should not have seen?"

"I diverted him before I had to take out every piece, but some of my instruments could have been construed as such."

"I think you had better take them to your sister's house, at least until they have finished with their investigations."

"Still, he may have seen something that will disqualify me."

Preoccupied with his watch, Lazar said, "I suppose we have missed Zhitlovsky's lecture. What shall we do instead?" he said, cupping her breast in his hand.

Hannah looked from one side of the room to the other. "Nothing seems right around here!" She lifted a pillow from the sofa and tried to plump its matted feathers. In a moment of surprising rage, she threw it across the room. "All I've ever wanted is to be a midwife! I'm a good one too! Why is it so difficult? Why does everyone stand in my way? Can't they see . . . ?"

Lazar picked up the pillow, dusted it off, and held it out to Hannah. "It's not the end of the world," he said to calm her. "He's only one petty bureaucrat."

Pushing the pillow aside, Hannah said, "No, you don't understand how important this is to me. Finally I'm achieving something. Just when I have begun to earn the respect of so many new mothers . . ."

Lazar tilted his head, smiled sweetly, and threw the pillow down to the floor. "You are the best!" he said, pulling her down beneath him and covering her with kisses. Hannah did not resist. She wrapped her arms around his neck while he struggled with the fastenings on their clothing, mumbling the words of endearment that usually soothed Hannah's doubts.

## · 8 ·

BY ROSH HASHANAH, the New Year, each of Mama Blau's daughters had announced she was expecting a baby. Mama prayed for three healthy and whole babies, adding that she would die a satisfied woman if God should be so good as to grant her a wife and child for Chaim as well.

Though Chaim was in New York, he appeared only sporadically at his mother's table for a few unexpected minutes before going off again. He was still secretive and even more circumspect and surly than before his imprisonment. Yet his insolent remarks or thoughtless late appearances drew neither scoldings nor admonitions, so grateful were they to have him back. One glance at his gaunt face, the haunted stare of his large luminous black eyes, or the slight tremor in his left hand, and all was forgiven.

There was no doubt he was making a new life for himself without his family. Once Chaim had found a group that was politically to his taste, even Lazar was brushed aside, though from time to time they would meet at The Monopole. When Lazar and Chaim had no real issues to fuel their arguments, they continued to hone their rhetoric and firm their individual stances by debating each other, spewing out quotations from Aristotle, Spinoza, Darwin, Marx, Kropotkin, and Hegel like geysers of intellectual pretension in preparation for encounters with more difficult foes.

One afternoon when Lazar appeared indifferent to his challenges, Chaim said to his sister, "You have no true religious sentiments, Hannah; you're merely following the prescriptions for the sake of tradition."

Hannah shrugged her shoulders, pretending to be disinterested, though she could not help feeling wounded, as she had as a child when Chaim had criticized her.

Insensitive to her reaction, Chaim continued with a particularly vicious attack. Hannah searched the café room for a familiar face, looking for a way to escape his barbs. Thankfully, Dr. Herzog was just entering with a Dr. Bauman, who, it was rumored, had been on the personal staff of Emperor Franz Joseph. Hannah rushed to join them.

Herzog kissed her on both cheeks. "My dear, you are looking more beautiful than ever," he said in a proprietary fashion.

Hannah enjoyed his cosmopolitan charm, and graciously replied that she was delighted to see him. "Will Rachael be joining you?"

"Not today, I'm afraid. She has some typhoid cases she wanted to follow up with home visits to educate them on sanitary conditions." He turned to Dr. Bauman. "Imagine that, Victor!"

Dr. Bauman sniffed and puffed out his chest, exposing an ample midriff beneath his unbuttoned vest. "Ridiculous. It's against my principles ever to visit a walk-up tenement above the second floor." Bending his head to flirt with Hannah, he continued, "Don't you know that almost everything a doctor need examine can be delivered in a basket?"

"Except perhaps for the tongue," Hannah acerbically replied.

Although Lazar was watching Hannah's encounter with the medical professionals out of the corner of his eye, he was more attentive to one of Chaim's wilder schemes for a fund-raising event. Apparently their discussions were not going well, as Hannah observed Lazar's face becoming flushed with rage.

"This atheistic nonsense has gone too far! How do you expect to convert anyone to your extremist cause with this rubbish?" he said, crumpling a handbill in his fist. Hannah had already seen the offensive announcement. It was a statement by the "War Against God" group, which purposely was holding its annual fund-raising banquet on Yom Kippur.

"You are making a tremendous mistake in pursuing these tactics, for you will lose your ability to stir Jewish workers. They will distrust you at precisely the moment that you might assist them in their fight for fair wages and conditions."

"The pious have always dragged us down," Chaim retorted. "If they still believe that Joshua caused the heavens to stand still or that Moses wrote the laws, I have no use for them!"

"It appears you have no use for anything of value anymore. You think only of yourself, not the worker, not the Jew, least of all your family or mother," he said with bitterness creeping into his voice. "Be thankful that you have a mother," he said uncharacteristically, before shredding the invitation. "Hannah!" he called. "We're leaving!" Before Hannah could say a proper farewell to the doctors, Lazar had marched to the back of the café.

Although Hannah followed him almost immediately through the swinging doors that led to the gaming room, she could not find him. As her eyes adjusted to the darker smoke-filled room, she could feel the men staring at her. Indeed she knew there was something compelling about the simplicity of her cotton dress, with its neckline created by rows and rows of simple fagoting that perfectly offset her tiny waist and the curve of her neck. The door to the kitchens was opened by Herman the headwaiter, and for a moment, Hannah stood — highlighted in the aisle — frozen like a startled doe.

Herman broke the silence. "Your husband is in the kitchen. I'll get him for you."

Trapped until Lazar returned, she demonstrated her nervousness by rewinding a tendril of hair that she had twisted for decoration at her cheek. "Won't you keep me company for a moment, Mrs. Sokolovsky," a voice called from a dim spot at the far end of the room. Hannah turned to see Nathaniel Belinsky gesturing toward a small corner table. Hannah eased her way past two chess players and took a seat. "What a pleasure to see you again!" he said, wetting his lips with his tongue.

"My husband . . . he's in the kitchen . . ." Hannah stammered.

"Do you come here often?"

"More so now that my baby is older. Lazar and my brother are here almost every day, so it's convenient to have a place to meet."

"Then your brother finally is in America!"

"You remembered that!" Hannah said with genuine surprise.

"I'm known, particularly to my father, as a very poor student of detail. But there are some things I never forget."

"Yes?" Hannah queried vaguely to make polite conversation.

Belinsky leaned forward and Hannah could smell his sweet breath, which revealed he had been drinking mint tea in the Oriental fashion. "Everything you have ever said to me remains in my mind, ready for recall at any moment I feel the need for refreshment. I've even saved this," he said, reaching into his breast pocket to pull out a creased clipping with the headline MIDWIFE SAVES TREMAIN BOY.

"That really isn't true!" Hannah said. "I did very little. The boy hadn't drowned. But it has been good for my business. Now that I am doing so many massages I wonder if anyone remembers I am a midwife." Hannah spoke rapidly so that Belinsky would not be able to interrupt. Looking over her shoulder for any sign of Lazar, she said, "I was wondering if you might be needing my services again shortly. Gertrude must be adorable, but children need a sister or brother . . ."

"That's what her mother says; that's what my father commands!" Belinsky sadly answered. "We have not yet been fortunate enough to be blessed with another child."

Hannah placed her hand at her throat and straightened her high collar as an excuse to avoid the intensity of his stare. "When you consider the adjustment to a new country, different water and foods, it is very understandable that it might take your wife some time . . ."

"That is not the problem . . ." Belinsky's voice suddenly fell. "Couldn't we talk sometime about it, in private? I think you might be able to help us."

Hannah was confused, but there was something about his urgency that appealed to her altruistic nature. "It is probably something simple . . ."

"I'd rather not say more now, but could you meet me at my offices . . . No, of course not . . . Could we have lunch somewhere?"

Hannah saw Lazar standing beside the double doors that led from the kitchen. Herman was pointing out Belinsky's table and Lazar was coming toward them. Quickly Hannah asked, "Where?"

Belinsky realized there was no more time to speak, "I'll meet you here, outside, tomorrow at noon."

"But everyone knows me here!"

"We'll go somewhere else," he finished as he stood to greet Lazar, who merely nodded before ushering his wife from the room.

As soon as they were outside Hannah asked, "Why were you in the kitchen?"

"Herman knows how much I love Hungarian food and always saves me a plate of goulash and noodles. He doesn't dare serve me in the front, or too many of the other regulars who linger and never order would expect the same."

"Why does he do it for you?" Hannah interrogated.

"Let us just say I have done him many favors," Lazar said in his silkiest voice.

"You should have done more," Hannah said darkly.

"No man wants to get into more debt than necessary with characters like Herman."

Hannah stopped and turned, hardly believing Lazar's indifference to her. "You go off to your goulash and leave me hungry!"

"You seem to do very well for youself! First you flirt at the doctors' table, then I find you with that capitalist landlord who sucks the blood from our people! One button off his precious waistcoat would have bought dinner for twenty!"

"Lazar! I was merely inquiring after his family . . . His wife may be expecting again, and it would be a very handsome job for me to have!"

Lazar relented. "Let's buy you a knish! They always bring us luck! Remember the first job I got you from Yona Schimmel?"

Hannah shook her head and laughed up at Lazar. "You twist everything around. I never did the Moskowitz delivery!"

He blinked. "Didn't you?" He was genuinely confused.

Hannah held his hand as they walked on together, reconciled for the moment, thinking how wonderful it would be if she could convince herself that the way she wanted it to be was the way it would be, even if it meant rearranging the past or present to suit the image. Lazar never meant to be cruel or irresponsible; it was just that some part of him was unable to view life as it was. There was a beauty to his blindness, for it protected him from believing he hurt others and also shielded him from the disappointments that people with more normal sensibilities seemed to feel.

She held Lazar's arm tightly for balance as they stepped up onto the steep curb at the corner where Canal Street met Division. They always walked this block of Yiddish and Hebrew bookstores more slowly so that Lazar could browse through the bargain stalls on the street. As usual, Hannah paid little attention to the books, but a small sign in the window of the second establishment, called The Gate, said BOOKSHOP FOR SALE, INQUIRE WITHIN.

"I wonder how much it costs?" Hannah asked Lazar, whose interest was diverted by a slim volume of verses.

"What?" Lazar asked.

"To own a bookstore."

"Who wants a bookstore?"

"You do!" Hannah answered impulsively. "It's perfect for you!" she continued, pulling him inside.

## · 9 ·

THE ELDERLY COUPLE, Sam and Lena Lipsky, who ran the book-store that featured all the works of Chaim Nachman Bialik in their window, claimed to have known the poet in Russia. After talking with them a few minutes Lazar ascertained they knew him even less than he had. Yet the fact that Lazar could discuss the revered Bialik with such intimacy immediately placed him in a favorable light with the Lipskys.

"Why are you selling such a thriving business?" Lazar asked.

"Our sons are living uptown. One teaches in the university, the other in the yeshiva. They want their mama and papa should live beside them and they think we could do a good business in their neighborhood," Mr. Lipsky answered.

Hannah walked around touching a book here, opening one there. Though dusty and poorly lit, the store seemed to be very well stocked in Hebrew books, yet lacking in the Yiddish titles she knew Lazar preferred, particularly those by modern political writers. "How much are you selling for?" she asked lightly.

"Three hundred dollars for the stock and the lease."

Astonished by the price, Lazar started toward the street. Hannah blanched but continued, "How many books do you have in all?"

"Over a thousand on the shelves and almost that many in the basement. Not to mention our fine collection of unpublished manuscripts, any one of which might some day be worth a fortune," Mrs. Lipsky said. "We've always dreamed of discovering another Bialik here in America."

Mr. Lipsky saw his opportunity to encourage the young couple's interest. "It's a wonderful life for a husband and wife. We brought our boys up right here in the store, and both are now scholars. How could they help it?"

"My wife is a doctor," Lazar bragged as usual.

Mrs. Lipsky almost bowed to Hannah. "For you we might make a special exception, wouldn't we, Sam?"

"Why not? You wouldn't need any cash at all. You could pay . . . let's say fifty percent of the receipts until the debt is finished. I don't see any reason why that should take more than a year or so," he said, going on to describe an elaborate deal that included their taking all the duplicate stock uptown, holding the lease in their names, and writing out notes and legal releases.

Lazar barely listened to the negotiations, as a small, privately published volume had arrested his interest. "How much for this?" he asked, holding up the faded book.

"Ah, a man of rare taste!" chortled Lipsky. "One of my favorites. With one page in Russian and the next in Hebrew you really see the workings of a brilliant mind. I couldn't let it go for less than two dollars, but if you want the shop, it comes as part of the deal."

And so The Gate became Lazar's store. Hannah hoped it would bring in enough additional income to allow them to keep their heads above water, as well as quench Lazar's thirst for books and written material. Beyond that, her expectations were few, although she did think that if he spent only half as many hours in the store as he had in the cafés, some profit was sure to be made without a strain on her husband's good humor. Yet Hannah knew she must not anticipate too much, for there was no doubt in her mind that the real reason Lazar decided to attempt to run the establishment was so he could have the cherished volume without paying the two dollars.

❖   ❖   ❖

Belinsky waited for Hannah at The Monopole the next day for over an hour and, when she didn't appear, left a message with Herman. Hannah had not forgotten the appointment, but Lazar had requested her help in taking inventory of the bookstore before they signed the agreement; she had so desperately hoped he would find this work interesting, she would have done anything he asked.

The message Herman carried for Hannah had been discreetly worded to avoid suspicion, because no one knew better than Belinsky that the headwaiter, with his smooth face and knowing eye,

on the side was a moneylender who liked to receive his install-
ments and interest on time. The more he knew about a man, the
greater leverage he would have to make certain that if anyone was
paid it would be he.

Herman delivered the note to Hannah the next evening as she
sat with Dr. Jaffe. Without apologies she silently read it: "Mrs.
Belinsky has asked me to once again thank you for your ministrations on her behalf and has requested you meet me at The Monopole at one in the afternoon any day this week that suits your convenience to collect your fee. I was sorry to have missed you today,
but understand that your services may be required at unpredictable
times. Kindest regards, Nathaniel Belinsky."

"What's that all about?" Rachael asked, reaching for the folded
piece of paper.

"A client attempting to pay an old bill." Hannah tucked the
note into her skirt with a yawn. "I was at The Gate when he came
by yesterday," she said, launching into the tale of the bookstore.

Rachael was enchanted with the plan. "Let's have a bottle of
wine to celebrate!" She clapped her hands and ordered before
Hannah could protest.

When it arrived the two women clinked glasses. "Here's to
keeping our husbands so busy they won't have time for real trouble . . ." Rachael laughed and added, ". . . so we'll have time for
more of our own!"

Hannah took a sip and put her glass down. The cheap wine
burned her throat. Thinking over Rachael's toast, she first wondered how much her perceptive friend had guessed. Then a certain
bold angle of the doctor's shoulder made Hannah aware that she
was speaking more about herself than Hannah.

Rachael's amber eyes sparkled like glowing coals. "I'm back on
duty at the hospital. Every third night Herzog stays home with
Nora."

"You are on duty nights?" she questioned. "And you are looking for trouble?"

"Don't be such a silly child! Herzog and I have been apart more
than we've been together. We've had agreements about this sort of
thing. Matter of fact, it has made our union stronger, more vibrant
than . . ." Dr. Jaffe stopped as she surveyed the dismal reaction her

confession was having on Hannah. Although Hannah refused to acknowledge or discuss the issue, it was not, as Rachael supposed, because she rejected it as too immoral to consider; rather she saw Rachael's predicament mirroring her own strong attraction to Belinsky.

"No more of that now ... some other time ... when you are ready ... we'll talk then ..." Rachael finished her wine in two long swallows, buttered a thick slice of black bread from a basket on the table, and passed it to Hannah. "Besides, I have some news that should prove more interesting."

"What is that?" Hannah said, barely listening, for she was watching a giant of a gentleman who had clattered into the main dining room, kissing and embracing everyone from the bar girl to Herman and half the crowd in between. "That's Chaliapin, the great baritone. Lazar took me to hear him a few weeks ago."

Dr. Jaffe buttered herself another slice of bread without looking up. "Yah! Yah! So?" she said with studied indifference. "I don't believe in encouraging that kind of a show. He's not onstage here, and he shouldn't expect everyone to applaud and admire him wherever he goes."

"I suppose you are right," Hannah said, reluctantly turning her eyes away from his entourage of women in lacy shawls and iridescent gowns. "What did you say was so interesting?" she said, doubting that the doctor's gossip could be as enthralling as the theatrics behind her.

"I've been corresponding with Moscow on some medical matters. Along with the tables and statistics I requested has come some fascinating news ..." She stopped and munched her crust, deliberately chewing slowly to keep Hannah in suspense. Finally she swallowed. "Dr. Speransky has been given a promotion and is now the directress of the entire college. Chernyshevsky has taken an appointment in St. Petersburg and ..."

"Petrograv!" Hannah filled in the silence as Dr. Jaffe had anticipated.

Aware of Hannah's sensitivity toward her former professor, Rachael said softly, "Petrograv has become the minister of health, due in part, I am certain, to his fortunate marriage to a high-placed young woman."

"Marriage?" Hannah tried not to choke on the lump of bread she had stored in her cheek. "So soon?"

"Hannah! You are expecting your second child already! Did you think he would wait forever?"

"Then you know?" Hannah said, thinking Rachael referred to Petrograv's visit to Odessa, their meeting at the Hotel Richelieu, and possibly Benny's paternity as well.

"Only that the professor followed you to Odessa and returned like a wounded soldier. It was Lazar who made you refuse to see him, wasn't it?"

"Refuse to see him?" Hannah asked with surprise. "Is that what he told you?"

"Petrograv said that your parents would not allow him to call on you, but since I knew your father was dead, I assumed that was the excuse you made because you didn't want him to know you were already promised to Lazar."

Hannah sighed deeply, wishing she had the courage to unravel the past and explain the true circumstances of their brief relationship, but said only, "It was more complicated than that."

"At least the Yakovlevs will see he lacks nothing, especially since their daughter had been so terribly afflicted with a joint disorder that they despaired of her ever marrying."

"The Princess Olimpiada had rheumatism!" Hannah exclaimed.

"How did you know that?" Dr. Jaffe inquired.

"I introduced the doctor and the princess!" Hannah said excitedly. "Petrograv helped her through a violent attack when he was in Odessa!"

"It seems he did more than that, for he apparently cured the girl, though remissions do occur in young adults. But" — she paused — "if you introduced them . . ." she finished, shaking her head in confusion. "I don't understand . . . how did you come to know someone like the princess?"

"I'll tell you the whole story, later, some evening when it is quiet . . ." Hannah promised. For the moment she wanted to be left alone to think about Petrograv and wonder at the turns fate had handed each of them — and to mull over, for the last time, the possibility that everything might have been different.

## · 10 ·

THE NEXT AFTERNOON Belinsky waited in his landau in front of The Monopole. As soon as he saw Hannah he alighted from his carriage to greet her, and then, to ensure discretion, he bustled her inside, signaling the driver to move forward. Carriages of all types formed processional lines up Broadway, the backbone of Manhattan. Victorias, broughams, road wagons mingled with the motorbuses, cruising cabs, shining automobiles, delivery wagons, short-haul trucks, and ordinary bicycles. Policemen, both mounted and standing, dotted the center of the avenue, attempting to direct the unending stream of traffic.

"I've arranged a private room at the Café Martin; it's on the site of the old Delmonico's on Twenty-sixth Street. Have you ever been there?" Belinsky asked Hannah.

"No, never," Hannah replied. "Even The Monopole is beyond our means. And though Herman considers us among his regulars we are always seated in the section reserved for the 'lingerers,' not the 'orderers' like you." Hannah continued to prattle on about Lazar and his acquisition of The Gate to convince Belinsky that her loyalties were firmly set with her husband.

"Whoa!" their driver shouted as he pulled his horse to the curb to let a four-in-hand with blowing horns pass. As the carriage swerved, Belinsky caught her hand in his. Hannah pretended not to notice. "Look!" She pointed with her free hand. "It's just a bunch of children begging their driver to race an automobile!"

Belinsky didn't look up. His eyes were riveted to her bosom, where soot from the departing vehicle had landed. Hannah slipped her hand from under his, lifted the specks with the edge of her tapered fingernail, and then clasped her own two hands together firmly in her lap.

Before meeting Belinsky she had resolved she would merely listen to his problem, offer the appropriate advice, and refer him to a
physician if there was the slightest medical difficulty. If the gentleman had anything else in mind, she had rehearsed a firm case for
marital fidelity and was determined not to stray from her prepared
script. Still, she could not suppress the fantasies of him that had
been stirred during her conversation with Rachael.

As they rounded a steep corner, Belinsky squeezed even closer to
her, and she had to remind herself to be sensible. Don't forget Petrograv, she warned herself. All that remained from that foolhardy
experience were a few distasteful memories and a lingering distress.

When the carriage slowed at the approach to the restaurant,
Hannah brushed a loose strand of hair back from her face. Seizing
the opportunity, Belinsky clasped her hand in his and kissed it with
more tenderness than passion. "You look so lovely this afternoon!"
Hannah accepted the compliment silently. The sheer, embroidered blouse she had selected for the occasion had been fashioned
years before in Odessa, and Hannah had had to squeeze her figure,
now bloated with her early pregnancy, into the narrow shape. The
moment she took her seat in the restaurant's booth, the tightness
of the corset was acutely evident. She shifted uneasily to find a
comfortable position.

Belinsky inquired solicitously, "You aren't at ease here?"

"It's very . . . lovely . . ." Hannah said, pretending to admire the
pigeon-blood damask curtains that could be closed to ensure privacy. "I just cannot imagine what I would like to order."

"I've taken the liberty of selecting for you in advance. I hope
you don't mind."

"Not at all, that saves me the trouble of a decision."

"I would think you are a woman who finds it simple to make up
her mind. After all, your medical training prepares you for such
work, while an uneducated woman is the one who leaves everything up to the man."

The waiter bowed and inquired whether he could begin service.
Belinsky nodded and a silver trolley was wheeled between the
draped columns and placed alongside their elaborately decorated
table set with four different wine glasses as well as an alarming

array of cutlery. Hannah followed Belinsky's lead in unraveling the intricately folded napkin and placed it on her lap. A deep bowl filled with a pink and white soup was placed atop the vermeil service plate. Belinsky lifted his spoon, but it hovered in midair while he attempted to dissolve Hannah's resistance to his seductive glances.

To avoid his stare, Hannah dipped her spoon into the rosy liquid, tasting the delicate cream and pepper stock. Not knowing how to respond to the unusual combination of flavors, she watched Belinsky's reaction. She noticed he had used a spoon of a very different shape, and while he was diverted by the wine steward pouring the Montilla, she discreetly searched for one that matched, wiped the soiled one with her napkin, replaced it, and began again.

"The crab bisque is superb, don't you think?" Belinsky inquired politely.

Hannah dropped her spoon into the bowl with a clatter. "I've never had shellfish before . . ."

"Let me order something else."

"No, I don't keep kosher. Well I do . . . it's just that I don't know any other way to manage a kitchen . . ." Hannah stammered. To prove it didn't matter, she took another sip and said, "It's very delicious."

As the waiter boned the whole poached fish decorated with slivers of almonds, the wine steward appeared and poured from a bottle of Scharzhofberger 1893 into the second glass. Hannah had not touched the first, but felt obligated to taste the second.

Belinsky chattered amicably about his work — the problems of being a landlord with a social conscience, his difficulties with his father — pausing in his monologue to allow the headwaiter to carve the two delicate squab and set the disjointed birds in a nest of rice and green grapes.

Noticing that Hannah had barely touched her wine, the steward commented, "Perhaps madame would prefer some champagne with this course?" He removed her glasses and filled a third one shaped like a perfect tulip. "It's a Perrier-Jouët 1889." Dutifully she took a sip, and nodded her approval, thinking that it really was an improvement over the other bottle.

Belinsky seemed pleased. "You like champagne?"

"Yes, I think I do," Hannah laughed aloud. "Very much!" The wine steward bowed and backed from the room.

When they were alone once again, Belinsky continued his tale. "Whenever I follow my father's orders precisely, he finds something wrong with what I have done, though it may mean forgetting what he told me or changing his mind. Since I am his only son, he says he will consider me a complete failure until I have sons of my own."

At first Hannah found it difficult to be sympathetic to Belinsky. His economic advantages seemed obvious and it was clear that his father had showered him with gifts: an elegant home, beautiful furnishings, more money than he needed so that he was able to freely gamble his earnings away. His problems were clearly not financial, but in the more delicate area of family and sexual relations.

Here was a couple who obviously could produce children, as they had immediately conceived one after their marriage, but for some reason found it impossible to have another. From her knowledge of Mrs. Belinsky, Hannah could see no apparent reason for her to be infertile, except perhaps her difficult and demanding temperament caused her to refuse her husband too often. Was Belinsky going to request that she counsel his wife on the importance of frequent sexual relations?

Still, there was another possibility. Might Mrs. Belinsky have become pregnant with Gertrude by a man other than Belinsky? This was not an implausible situation, as Hannah well knew. If she herself had not conceived another child by Lazar, the truth about Petrograv could have become evident.

Hannah picked at the squab with her fork, not daring to lift the tiny bones in her fingers and gnaw at them in the same aggressive manner as her partner, and waited for him to broach his questions directly.

Belinsky refilled both their glasses. "So you can see the importance of having more children as soon as possible. With sons running around the house, I will be more free to follow my own pursuits, to work for philanthropic causes to aid our people. If you can help me find a solution to this problem, many others, yourself included, will be helped as well!" He asked, glancing quickly to read her expression before lowering his eyes to his plate, "May I count on you?"

How well he played her, Hannah thought. No matter that his argument made no real sense. She wanted to do something for this man.

"I'd be pleased to be of help to you," Hannah said slowly. "But I am confused as to the nature of your request."

Belinsky was momentarily spared his explanation while the table was cleared, a silver bowl filled with lemon sorbet was placed before them, and the waiter brought their tea and a silver platter of frosted cakes.

When the final service was complete, Belinsky lifted his hand to shade his face. "The sun is too bright for my eyes," he said, closing the drapes that not only covered the window but the restaurant corridor as well. Then, instead of returning to his seat opposite Hannah, Belinsky slid alongside the banquette and took Hannah's hand. She caught her breath and turned aside demurely.

Belinsky pressed his thigh against hers and squeezed her hand so tightly he pinched her wedding ring. "Do you know what torture it has been to have you so close and yet so far away, my darling?"

Hannah drew back and tried to suppress her panic. "This will hardly achieve the goal you have set for yourself, Mr. Belinsky. I am certain your father has in mind a legitimate heir," she said in what she hoped was a stern voice.

"You've misunderstood me, Hannah. It is so difficult to explain . . . I am a man in feelings only and then . . . I have the desire, but as soon as we . . ." In all her imaginings about this meeting Hannah had not made allowances for this development. At one moment Belinsky was the aggressive seducer she had feared, and the next he was a timid boy who openly wrung his hands and sobbed out the tale of his inadequacies.

He explained that since Gertrude's birth he had been welcome in his wife's bed, but everything went wrong at the last and most important moment. His failure to father a child had disappointed his domineering father, and his wife had become exasperated to the point of openly ridiculing him and threatening to expose his weakness publicly. No wonder the man who seemed to have everything found ease in his wines and games and looked for solace to a sympathetic woman!

"Have you seen a doctor about this?" Hannah spoke diffidently.

"Several. They all have the same suggestion."

"Then you must do as they say," Hannah replied energetically, for she was relieved to be done with the role of his counselor.

Belinsky placed his hands, palms up, in her lap, sighed, and said in an anguished voice, "That is what I am attempting to do!"

Hannah began dimly to comprehend. "How can I . . . ? There are women who know what to do . . . Allen Street . . ." she stammered.

"I've tried that and everything else, but the doctors tell me I must find someone for whom I have strong feelings. From the moment I met you on the ship, and after, when you came to see Gertrude, and every time since . . . I've known you are the only one."

As Hannah listened she was not without sympathy. "If you were successful with this other woman, do the doctors feel you could repeat it with your wife?"

"That is precisely their prescription, though there are no guarantees. It would be a great service, and not so far removed from your profession as to be totally out of line. I would be willing to pay highly; anything you would need would be yours . . ."

Belinsky had made an unfortunate mistake. Hannah saw in a flash how the man must have made similar bungles with his father, even his wife: at one moment almost attaining his goal, and the next dashing his hopes by poor timing and carelessness. Hannah was appalled by his suggestion.

"I beg you not to be angry with me. Perhaps I used the wrong words." He stumbled with apologies. "Payment is not what I had in mind, but I could help your career, recommend you to influential families . . . You are a good, honest, talented woman . . . Perhaps you could just instruct me on how I could proceed with my wife, teach me the art of massage, something . . . anything . . ." He pleaded so desperately that Hannah was sickened.

Her corset dug deep into her pelvis, causing acute discomfort. She groped for the proper words that would end the confrontation. "Perhaps I could find some books for you to read," she suggested.

Her voice was so subdued that Belinsky straightened up and

mopped his brow with the napkin he discovered he had been clutching in Hannah's lap. Hannah waited until he had composed himself. She reached over and tenderly smoothed his hair. Speaking as she would to a child, she said, "Now go sit in your own seat, and after I have had a few minutes to myself, I will answer you."

Startled by the possibility of an affirmative response, Belinsky allowed Hannah to leave. As soon as she was outside the curtain, a woman with lace collar and cuffs directed Hannah to the lounge and stood by to hand her towels, tie her sash, and primp her hair.

Hannah searched for the words to refuse his impossible request without further wounding his pride. Imagine a man such as Belinsky having such a problem! Rarely had she ever seen, let alone been with, a more apparently virile man. Though he was a totally different, more compact physical type than Lazar, she had to admit that Belinsky was just as attractive as her husband. And he was a great deal richer. No, she would not regret leaving Willett Street to live in luxury half as fine as the Belinskys'. No matter how much he whined about his difficult father and demanding wife, she might be willing to pay a similar price to trade positions.

Although the powder-room matron had finished straightening her hair, Hannah continued to be transfixed by her own appearance. The mirror showed her excited reflection and she saw for herself the effect she must be having on Nathaniel Belinsky.

"Nathaniel." She tried the word on her tongue and it rolled off as though she had said it a thousand times. "Nathaniel . . . I cannot . . . I will not . . . Perhaps if circumstances had been different . . . I'm very sorry, Nathaniel, but . . ." she murmured to herself.

Finally Hannah was ready to return. Approaching the table, she saw that Belinsky was attempting to light a cigar, but his hand trembled so badly he placed his match down in disgust.

Hannah opened her mouth to speak, but when she glimpsed the feverish expectation in his eyes, she caught her breath. Instead of the words of refusal she had rehearsed, she found herself saying "I think I can help you, but you will have to allow me to select the proper time and place."

Belinsky was so stunned by her answer that shock contorted his handsome face. And as he embraced her, his passionate kisses overcame whatever rational thoughts she might have had.

# II

❖ ❖ ❖ ❖ ❖

# *Solomon Karp*
## Delivered July 3, 1907

❖ ❖ ❖ ❖ ❖ ❖ ❖ ❖ ❖ ❖

## · 1 ·

WHY HAD SHE CHANGED her mind? Hannah searched for the answer the entire carriage ride back to Willett Street. She was consoled in her predicament only by the fact that she might still refuse at any time. But she could not deny that she felt stirred by the prospect of intimacy and would not be content until her curiosity and — yes, she admitted — her desire were satisfied.

To quiet her conscience, Hannah privately blamed the bleakness of her days, the poverty of her existence, the few challenges in her career. Though Belinsky had tried to suggest that he would gratefully help her become established as a society midwife, this larger goal was obscured by the admission that her own perverse nature sought not only excitement and gratification but also the powerful feeling of being needed by a man the world respected far more than it did her.

Arriving home, her head spinning with reasons for her absence, Hannah was relieved to find no one to listen to her labored excuses. A note from Lazar said that he had taken Benny to the bookstore and she could meet them there. Hannah sat at the

kitchen table and ran her hand over the splintered surface. Still
dizzy with the effect of the champagne and the rich meal, which,
instead of satisfying her hunger, had only made her uncomfortable,
Hannah unlaced the gored batiste corset that had heroically held
her figure erect. The two side panels, reinforced with ten-inch steel
bones, had created welts in her flesh. As soon as she was undone,
her distended abdomen relaxed. Hannah gave a long sigh of relief
and slipped down to her mattress. Although she did not appear
pregnant once she was fully bound and dressed, the inevitable effects of her condition had begun to mark her body with the map of
reproduction. How foolish she had been to try to hide the truth
from Belinsky! If she finally succumbed to his wishes, he would
discover her secret after one glance at the prominent blue veins
displayed on her fuller breasts, the darkening brown circles around
her nipples, not to mention the hard mound of her uterus that ex-
panded a bit more each day.

Another baby! Another mouth to feed, another responsibility! It
was all too much to contemplate, so Hannah pulled the quilt over
her naked body, luxuriating in the feel of her skin against the cool
covers, and submitted to an indulgent half-sleep, pondering the
pleasurable possibilities with Belinsky.

When the official notice of the midwifery examination arrived by
mail, Hannah was made to sign a piece of paper saying it had been
delivered before the postman would turn over the large white envelope with the blue and gold seal of the Department of Health.
Hannah ripped it open and read the document that set forth the
conditions of the test.

After several attempts to decipher the bureaucratic English,
Hannah threw the sheaf of paper down in disgust. All the rules and
restrictions, though necessary perhaps to rule out the Fingermans,
were also cleverly designed to harass the competent. Why should
she have to conform to an American official's concept of hygiene
and medical standard when her own, though slightly different, was
just as stringent? If it hadn't been for that persistent reporter and
his article about the drowning, she could have gone on just as she
had without interference!

When her initial anger had abated, Hannah looked for something to occupy herself and, noticing how tarnished her brass mortar and pestle was, she set to work polishing it. As her fingers
pressed the metal paste into nicks and grooves, she reviewed all the
reasons she was discouraged. Nothing was going as she would have
liked! The Gate would never do more than give Lazar a modest
wage. Although Hannah was in demand as a midwife, her work
now could be curtailed by this official whim. If she failed the
exams, she would be forced to work illegally and would have to
charge even less than she did now to get anyone to use her services.
Yet there would be a certain prestige value in obtaining a bona fide
license. It would set her apart from the likes of Fingerman, and
some doors that seemed closed to her now might magically open.
She could even have little cards printed, like the ones she had noticed on the marble hall table at the Belinskys', with her name and
title in engraved letters announcing: "H. Sokolow, Licensed Midwife"!

With that optimistic image before her, Hannah put down her
polishing and opened a textbook to prepare for the examination,
which was set for the following Monday.

The regulations for the licensing exam permitted Hannah to bring
an unrelated interpreter, and Dr. Jaffe was the only person as clever
with languages as Lazar.

When they appeared before Inspector Noyes, Rachael was
dressed in a peasant's long black skirt and flowered shawl, and her
unruly hair was braided tightly and wrapped around her head. She
even brought her knitting and attempted to work on a garment of
indeterminate shape while Hannah breezed through the simple yes
or no answers on the written examination. After it was completed,
the inspector checked the paper in front of Hannah, who, thinking
she had gotten every answer correct, was dismayed to see him mark
the ninth question with a red X.

"But why?" Hannah asked, incensed that she had not received a
perfect score on so simple a test.

Inspector Noyes pointed to the question and read it aloud in English. " 'After a baby is born the child's eyelids should be separated

and one drop of a two percent solution of silver nitrate placed in each eye.' The answer should have been no."

Hannah belligerently tapped the page. "How can you mark my answer wrong when that is exactly the recommendation in the papers you sent out?"

"I beg to differ with you, Mrs. Sokolow," the inspector said, calmly opening the pamphlet to the exact page. "You did not read the words correctly. It says 'two drops of a one percent solution'! The confusion of the numbers is quite common, I assure you, but it helps weed out the careful students from the careless."

"I don't see the difference! One drop of two percent or two drops of one percent should have the same effect! No baby has been harmed by this mistake!"

"The department specifically issues the one percent solution. If you gave only one drop you would lose half the prophylactic powers of the silver nitrate; if you used more than two you might damage a child's eyes. We need to be certain that licensed midwives are qualified to handle our directives, which are designed to further the cause of hygienic measures for mothers and infants." Inspector Noyes stiffened and made a soft noise in the back of his throat. "In any case, Mrs. Sokolow, you have passed the written exam, as only seven correct answers were needed. Are you ready for the second half of the examination?"

Hannah's cheeks burned at his pettiness, but she steeled herself to swallow the insult and nodded.

"Very good. Will you be so kind as to sit across from me at this table," he said, removing some charts from a large yellow envelope. "I see you have brought along your own interpreter. For the record I need her name."

Totally unprepared for this formality, Hannah shot Dr. Jaffe a terrified look. She needn't have panicked. Dr. Jaffe tightened her shawl around her shoulders and replied, "My name is Rucheleh Herzog," using the diminutive of her Yiddish name and her married surname. Hannah swallowed in relief.

"Sometimes the technical translation is difficult for someone not schooled in medical terms; therefore you will be permitted three passes if the question or answer cannot be translated to your satisfaction. Are you ready now?" the inspector asked.

"Yes," Hannah replied, folding her hands in her grey serge skirt.

The inspector propped a chart in front of Hannah and began to ask questions centered on female anatomy, using a foot-long wand to point to the specific parts of a diagram marked "Vulva." Hannah responded in a flat, professional tone of voice, "Clitoris, vestibule, labium minus, labium majus . . ." and finished with "anus." Though Hannah concentrated so that she would not make an error, Rachael was kept amused by the examiner's uneasy manner.

Inspector Noyes swallowed hard and quickly hid the diagram back in its envelope. The rest of the questions took on a more clinical nature, and Hannah speedily answered them all, impressing the examiner with the thoroughness of her education in obstetrics. Nearing the end of the page the inspector asked, "At how many weeks gestation will the mother experience quickening?"

Dr. Jaffe translated and Hannah quickly answered, "Sixteen weeks."

"I think you should reconsider," the doctor said before translating her answer.

"But why? That is correct!"

"I think the question refers to a primipara, not one who has already had a child, since all his other questions, unless specifically phrased for a multipara, have been like that."

"So you think I should answer eighteen weeks?"

"I would if I were you."

"If you are having difficulty with the translation, ladies, you may elect your first pass."

"I don't wish to pass," Hannah said stubbornly.

"Then I must inform you your time to answer this question is up."

"Sixteen weeks!" Hannah said in English. "For a multipara, that is, and eighteen weeks for a primipara," she added to be certain she was correct.

"A very complete answer, though I only need the eighteen weeks for the test."

Dr. Jaffe turned her head so the inspector would not catch her smile.

After Hannah had answered the optional advanced section of the exam with an almost perfect score, the inspector finished

marking his papers, added his totals, and announced, "On the oral
and written examinations you have scored ninety-seven percent.
One of the best I have ever seen! However, with your optional
credits you receive one hundred and nine points, entitling you to a
special Meritorious License, which only needs renewing every two
years. Congratulations!"

Hannah hugged Dr. Jaffe and shook the inspector's hand, noting
the faint disappointment that crossed his face as he handed her the
papers to take down the hall for processing. When they were out in
the corridor Hannah asked Rachael, "Why do you think he didn't
want me to succeed?"

"Don't you realize that the purpose of this procedure is to weed
out midwives so that the doctors will have more patients for their
clinics and hospitals?"

"Why can we not work in concert? You know how many of my
patients would never set foot in a hospital even if they were dying,
let alone in normal childbirth! Would it be better if they were left
to fend for themselves?"

"Try to explain that to them! They feel that no woman can ever
know as much as a man. These Americans are just as superstitious
as our Jewish fathers." Rachael's voice became militant. Clenching
her fists and shaking them in the air, she continued, "They still
think I know less than they do on every subject; so they assume
that a midwife, even one as well prepared as you, must be even
more ignorant. If they gave that same exam at the door of the medical schools to every American doctor who walked out with a fresh
M.D. painted after his name, not one would achieve as high a
score as you did. Some of them arrive at Bellevue authorized by the
state of New York to render service to women without ever once
having delivered a child on their own!"

"How is that possible?" Hannah asked in alarm.

"It is an optional part of their course!" Rachael spat out. "I
could tell you tales that would make a radical out of you! But
enough! Let's go somewhere to celebrate."

"Where?"

"The Monopole, where else? Maybe Lazar or your brother will
be there."

As Hannah followed Rachael down the long granite stairs leading away from the imposing Department of Health Building, with
her freshly stamped license clasped in her hand, all her worries dissolved.

"The Monopole it is!" Hannah sang out, oblivious to the disapproving heads that turned to stare because she skipped down the
street.

## · 2 ·

LAZAR WAS NOT at the café and Hannah was disappointed not to
be able to share her moment of glory with him. She sat at Dr. Herzog's table with Rachael. Except for sudden bursts of laughter
from the back room, the restaurant was peculiarly quiet. Hannah
strained to listen for a hint of Belinsky's voice and started every
time the door that separated the brighter front dining areas from
the gaming room opened and closed.

"Relax! It's all over!" Rachael said, patting Hannah's arm.
Turning to her husband, she continued, "You should have seen
the examiner, a pathetic man! His cheeks were all pushed in and
his eyes popped out." She grimaced an imitation.

"Probably a thyroid condition," Dr. Herzog diagnosed in a
hoarse voice. "Maybe you should have examined him!"

"Whatever would he have done if he had found out you were a
doctor?" Hannah asked with a shiver.

"Would a doctor have brought knitting?" Rachael chuckled.

"Knitting! Do you even know how to make a single stitch?"

Rachael pulled the needles and yarn from her bag and began to
tangle the wool so severely that she soon threw it to the floor in
disgust. "Well, I *am* out of practice!"

Hannah buttered a piece of bread and lathered it with chopped
eggplant.

"After pointing at those charts all day" — Dr. Jaffe paused while she poured herself a second glass of wine — "I'm sure the fellow would be useless to his wife."

"Somehow he didn't look like a married man to me," Hannah said thoughtfully.

"Ah!" Rachael clapped her hands. "So that was his problem!"

"Probably still lives with his mother," Dr. Herzog interjected.

"What makes you think so?"

"From the way you describe him he fits right into the type I've been studying."

"I thought you were interested in general medicine."

"Herzog has met several students of Freud and he is considering becoming one himself, if only by correspondence."

"Have you read very much about male psychology?" Hannah asked Herzog directly.

"I've just recently finished three of Freud's essays on sexuality. Why?"

"I've been wondering . . ." Hannah paused and began her question again. "A patient whom I once delivered has been having difficulty conceiving a second time. It seems the problem may be solely the man's. Apparently he desires to have relations with her, but when the moment approaches, he cannot. She asked me for some remedies and I was at a loss as to how to help her." Hannah hoped her delicate phrasing would be understood.

Dr. Herzog answered slowly and deliberately. "As much as I know you might wish to help this woman, the man himself must first desire and then seek out the cure if it is to be any success. How are we to know the root of his problem? He probably does not know it himself! Only after years of exploration into his childhood, rattling all the dark corners of his past, can we begin to unravel the mystery of his ailment."

"Surely there is a simpler solution," Hannah interrupted. "Something medical or practical."

Closing his eyes for a moment, Herzog sighed. "Some quackery might work for a brief time, further suppressing the problem and in the end aggravating it to the point of madness."

"Don't be so dramatic, darling!" Rachael arched her eyebrows. "There are many known physical causes for impotence. I remember the case of a young army officer we treated at the Medical College, who, on the eve of his marriage, received a blow to the occiput falling from a horse. He became impotent without any other derangement of his bodily or mental functions."

"Ah, but the blow to his head may have only been a trigger, the perfect excuse. Notice that the fall did not take place at an ordinary time, but the day before he was to be married, the last possible moment before he would be forced to prove himself a man! I hardly think that was merely a coincidence." Herzog's beard bobbed with authority.

"But the soldier was cured after several weeks of rest and therapy," Rachael replied smugly.

"What kind of therapy?" her husband asked with disbelief.

"It was the British cure suggested by a Professor Eaton, who wrote that the proper communication between the cerebellum and the organs of procreation could be restimulated with the aid of electricity."

"Are you saying you shocked the poor fellow?" Herzog removed his glasses and wiped his brow.

Dr. Jaffe nodded confidently. "After a few weeks of treatments he was cured and the wedding took place."

"Was this case followed afterward to see if the result was permanent or temporary?"

"I don't know; until now it was not a cure that held much interest for me."

"It hardly does credit to you as a physician, my dear, to recommend such a drastic and unscientific treatment now."

Rachael clenched her fists. "I was merely stating a possible disagreement with your argument. Don't twist every word of mine to suit yourself!"

Acutely embarrassed at having provoked harsh words between her friends, Hannah hunched her shoulders forward and buttered her last piece of crust.

❖   ❖   ❖

Marital dissension was not a stranger to her household either. Whatever gains she and Lazar had made had begun to dissipate as he developed an interest in his bookstore or, more accurately, the

people it attracted. Whenever Hannah visited The Gate she noticed the central point of interest was the samovar and not the
books. Lecturers and lingerers mingled at all hours, and Lazar obviously found more satisfaction in holding court than in returning
home to his family.

If Hannah hinted that he should spend more time with her, her
husband was quick to mention that the store had been her idea. At
first she attempted to participate in his new life, but Lazar made it
clear that she was an intruder.

As a result Hannah generally avoided the shop, but one afternoon she had arranged to meet Lazar there at the end of the day
before going to Dora's home for dinner. When she arrived, Lazar
was taking inventory and was not yet ready to leave. While waiting, she discovered some general health books tucked on a back
shelf, and without knowing why, she thumbed through a health
text written by a Dr. Gustav Ney. Her eyes widened when a subject of particular interest appeared in black and white. Although
Dr. Ney euphemistically referred to the "organ of philoprogeni-
tiveness" in his discussion of "the problem," he went on to explain
and diagram the most complete explanation of impotence she had
ever read.

Hannah shut the book quickly when Lazar turned her way.

"Anything the matter?"

"No, no . . . not exactly what I was looking for," Hannah said in
a shaking voice.

As she thought about Belinsky she tried to imagine him undressed, but the only male figure she could summon was that of
Lazar. How would he differ? Would his wavy dark hair extend to
thick mats on his chest and thighs? Would his pubic area be more
hidden than her husband's blond one? Would his organs be a different shape or size? Hannah leaned back against a bookshelf and
closed her eyes. A shiver of emotion coursed through her as she remembered Belinsky's firm kiss in the Café Martin. What would
they do if they were again alone and had more time?

Suddenly Hannah guessed Belinsky's true motive. What a devil!
How well he understood that she was a woman ruled more by her
head than her heart! He had fabricated the entire difficulty just to
have his way with her!

Hannah envisioned the scene. They were lovers. Belinsky was even more attuned to her every wish and far more virile than she had expected. Afterward he would tell her that she had cured him, for how could she prove otherwise? What cleverness! And to think she had almost believed him!

But then, he did exhibit some of the symptoms Dr. Ney described . . . Could he be telling some part of the truth? What happened when a man wanted a woman . . . or for that matter, when a woman wanted a man? Who could describe why anyone felt the way they did or why Hannah couldn't shake the immense attraction that she was feeling for someone she knew she mustn't have? If the doctors, if the books could not provide the answer, who would?

Lazar noticed a strange expression on his wife's face and asked, "Are you feeling ill?"

Hannah linked her elbow under his, looked up at his rugged face, made even more interesting by its concern and confusion. "Not at all! Let me explain . . ."

❖  ❖  ❖

"What kind of a question is that?" Lazar asked, hesitating in the middle of Hester Street. Wagon wheels screeched and an angry driver hurrying home from the market cursed at the distracted couple. Hannah pulled Lazar back to the curb to let him pass.

"I've been asked to counsel this patient and I haven't the slightest idea what to say to her," she said, brushing the buzzing flies from her hair.

"Maybe he doesn't want his wife; have you thought of that? Maybe he was saddled with some dumpy old bag with a molding wig and two prunes for a chest. There's no cure for that!"

"She's not unattractive. She says that her husband tries, but fails just at the moment most men would be delighted to commence."

"You can't turn a fish into a stone, Hannah. Not every man has the ability, the stamina, the strength." Lazar pointed, with more contempt than pity, at several men who shuffled across the market square. "These men are slaves by day; how can you expect them to be masters by night? Not until all men have a fair wage, decent hours and conditions, not until the pharaohs of the sweatshop are forced to bend to the will of the unions, will they become free men in their own beds as well!" he finished, raising his fists in the air.

Realizing that Lazar always found a political rationale for every difficulty, she only said, "Come, we'll be late for dinner."

As soon as they arrived at the stable Dora's husband managed, Lazar went from stall to stall, handing up a bit of fresh straw from the bale in the center aisle to the horses he knew by name while Hannah climbed the two flights to her sister's rooms.

It was the smell that assailed her first. If it had been less acrid, more tinged with metal and steam, she might have guessed that Dora was in labor. But the groans were too husky to have come from a female. Hannah stood in the hall and stared through the archway. She saw Daniel on the floor, his legs jerking wildly. From her work with eclampsia of pregnancy, Hannah knew how to handle a seizure. She rushed forward and wiped Daniel's purple face until she could see what needed to be done.

His tongue was grossly swollen and it was necessary to push it forward and clear the bright pink mucus from his throat. After a few minutes he breathed heavily; his color slipped back to a livid pink and slowly blanched to a normal hue. Instead of regaining consciousness he fell into a deep sleep. As soon as the crisis had passed, Hannah called Lazar to help her undress him. Mama brought basins of hot water and a strong soap and stood by to assist. Then the three of them managed to lift Daniel to the sofa, where he slept the rest of the afternoon.

"There was no warning, nothing!" Mama recalled the first minutes of the attack. "He looked straight ahead as though there was someone at the door. The next second he bent forward and fell on his face."

Dora had barely moved through the whole attack. She clutched her abdomen and stared blankly at the wall. Hannah stroked her hair. "How are you feeling? Is the baby very active?" Dora didn't respond.

"Maybe you should have something to eat?" Mama cajoled. "Come taste my broth."

Together Hannah and Mama walked Dora to the table. Mama spoke to Hannah as though her other daughter were not present.

"Will he do it again . . . soon?"

"I doubt it. I'm more worried about Dora. She's due any time now, and if she reacts as badly to her labor as this, she might have a difficult time."

"I could stay here and you could take Dora home with you. That way it would be more convenient if she labors at night."

"Good. It will be better if she doesn't have to be with Daniel for a few days. I think she was terribly frightened," Hannah said and then convinced Dora to sip the soup.

· 3 ·

WITHOUT ANY CURIOSITY as to why Hannah suddenly developed an unusually amorous appetite, Lazar was more than happy to submit to her whims. Hannah began suggesting early bedtimes and Lazar responded willingly.

Though she daydreamed continually about Belinsky, Hannah still relied on her husband for gratification. At first she convinced herself that she really wanted Lazar, but after he had thoroughly satisfied her, Hannah would awake in the middle of the night, burning with desire for her fantasy of someone darker, deeper-voiced, more carnal than her intellectual husband.

One night the image of Belinsky beside her was so vivid she turned on her stomach, pressed her fingers between her legs, and tried to still the throbbing slickness. Unsuccessful, she watched Lazar toss and turn. How poorly he slept! She remembered how often in the past he had waked her, not out of sexual desire, but for comfort. Most times she would hold him willingly, but there were moments when she resented the disturbance. For once she would wake him! Gently she stroked between his legs and kissed his ear. He rolled over and blinked. "Again?" he asked in a sleep-sodden voice.

"Do you mind?" Hannah asked.

"I suppose not," he said somewhat uncertainly. Instead of

reaching to stimulate her breasts, as was his usual first step, he lay with his hands behind his head and did not touch her.

She reached over and kissed his lips, forcing them apart with her tongue. Would Belinsky want her to do this? Or would he pounce eagerly on her and expect her to merely submit to his entry? Lazar responded momentarily, but then relaxed. Fearing he was slipping back into his dreams, Hannah quickly nuzzled and bit his tiny raspberry nipples. Remembering the weeks after Benny's birth when she would not allow Lazar to penetrate her, she inched her mouth downward and caressed his organ. Still Lazar was inert. She might have been working on a corpse until his hand brushed her hair and urged her on. He guided her and showed her what he wanted her to do, how to stroke him, how to hold him. Is that what Belinsky would like? She felt Lazar becoming larger and fuller. He moaned softly, pushed her face away, and pulled her on top of him. "Is this what you wanted?" he asked as she spread her legs across his hips.

❖　❖　❖

Hannah was sinking into a deep satisfied slumber when she heard Dora calling from the front room in a hoarse voice. "Hannah!"

Surprisingly, Dora had gone well into labor before summoning help. Hannah set about to prepare her bedroom for delivery, urging Lazar out from beneath the covers. "Won't I ever get any sleep tonight?" he groaned in protest.

Handing him his pants and suspenders, Hannah implored him to go for Daniel and Mama. When he was gone she swiftly made up their large bed with a rubber catch sheet and freshly sterilized linens.

Once the house had filled with anxious family, Lazar quickly made himself some breakfast and then, before dawn, set off for his store, pleased he had a place to escape the confusion. Hannah sat with Dora, rubbing powder into her abdomen and back, crooning to her during contractions, and trying everything she knew to keep the girl calm. Despite all her efforts, Dora was wracked with in-consolable pains and cried out for them to be over.

Mama was alarmed. "It might not be so simple! Maybe you

should send for a doctor. Dora's always had problems; why should this be any different?"

"It's a first baby; it will take a while, but everything is absolutely normal. My major concern is to keep her from lacerating during the delivery, because I don't think she will have enough control to cooperate in the final stages. I want to make certain everything will stretch without having to cut her. In the last hour I will need lots of hot strips of linen ready."

Hannah unrolled her instruments and laid them out. With a pair of tongs she placed ripped pieces of sheeting in a pot of water and brought them to a boil on the stove. As soon as she felt the second stage, the point at which Dora would push the baby out, was imminent, she began to drape her sister with the warm cloths, finally laying the hottest ones on the top. With her gloved hands she continued to massage the entire circle around the gaping vulva, pushing the flesh back, making the edge of the hole as elastic as possible.

Watching her work Daniel peeked from the doorway, curious but afraid to step across the sill. "Do you want to be with us?" Hannah asked calmly.

"Is it permitted?" the shy man queried, looking away from the women who worked between the legs of his wife.

"Come in and sit by her head," Hannah invited. "Now talk to her, anything to distract her."

Daniel leaned over and began to whisper to Dora, stroking the damp tendrils of hair that fastened themselves to her forehead back away from her flushed face.

"Could you hold her up more, so her head is against you, here?" Hannah demonstrated by tapping her own breast.

As he pulled his wife into his lap, Dora complained that she could not move, but as soon as she was positioned with her husband bracing her back, she sighed and said, "It's better, it's better."

"The head is coming!" Hannah said, barely able to contain her own excitement. "Mama, pour the oil now," she ordered as she pulled off her gloves to better get the feel of the birth and thus control it more accurately.

Mama dripped warm mineral oil onto her hands as Hannah manipulated the folds of skin back over the emerging head. The midwife used her left hand to ease the upper tissues over the bulge, then twisted her right palm so that the space between the thumb and forefinger was as wide an L as possible; the heel of her hand supported the perineum while the thumb stroked the spot where the forehead, the first part of the child to actually enter the world outside the mother, slipped forward. Dora gasped at the release and then reached down between her legs to try to rid herself of the remaining unborn obstruction.

"Wait, wait," warned Hannah as she watched the child slide to the side so the shoulder could be born amidst a gush of watery fluid.

Dora's hands fluttered in front of the child, desperate to touch her newborn. Hannah cupped her sister's hands around the baby and assisted her as she lifted him into her cradling arms.

Then his father reached around with hovering fingers. "May I touch him?" Daniel asked so softly that only Hannah heard him.

"He's yours," she said simply and turned to look at Mama, who cried silently at the first sight of her own newborn grandson.

## · 4 ·

HANNAH HAD LITTLE TIME for The Monopole during the busy period after Dora's child was born. But the first day she had time to meet her friends she hurried to the café. Immediately she noticed Belinsky's carriage waiting by the curb, and she could hardly contain her excitement.

She went directly to the gaming room and blinked a few times as she tried to focus on the faces in the shadows. Belinsky was nowhere in sight. Hannah inched back to the door, closed it firmly, and spun around toward a room on the right reserved for special guests of the manager. Sitting at the table usually occupied by the dance master Fokine and his retinue, Belinsky was entertaining a lady. Although Hannah could only see the woman's back, she admired her elaborate upswept hairdo as well as the long flowing folds of her silk skirt, which draped around the legs of the French provincial chair. Without saying a word Hannah caught Belinsky's attention. At first his eyes registered a pleasant flicker of surprise, though he managed gracefully not to miss a beat in his conversation. His apologetic expression strained to convey he would explain everything later. Nodding that she understood, Hannah retreated to the more familiar and less pretentious front room, anxious to take her usual anonymous seat at the doctors' table.

But because she did not look where she was heading, Hannah bumped into a waiter carrying a full tray of pastries. The clatter caused Belinsky's companion to start and turn in her direction. Surprisingly, the gentleman was dining with his wife! If Hannah had been quick-witted enough to recover from the situation, she would have walked into the room and reintroduced herself to Mrs. Belinsky. Instead she rejected a confrontation and hurried away.

With great relief she saw that Rachael was just arriving. "I'm so glad you're here!" Hannah said in a rush.

As soon as the ladies reached their seats Herman asked, "Would you like your usual tea, Doctors?"

"I wouldn't," Hannah said with some force. "I'd prefer beer."

Dr. Jaffe raised her eyebrows at her friend's unusual request. "The same," she said quickly.

Hannah stared into a mirror across the room, which reflected the scene from the elegant front dining room clearly enough so she could see that the Belinskys were leaving.

"How's Benny?" Rachael asked, but Hannah was too distracted to answer.

"That's the end of my dilemma," Hannah thought to herself. "Now he won't dare ask me again."

"Is something the matter?" Rachael asked softly.

"What?"

"You are acting so strangely."

"No . . . no . . ."

"I heard Dora had her baby!" Rachael said, ignoring Hannah's mood. "How are they doing?"

"Beautifully. He was large, over eight pounds, really quite a surprise for only thirty-four weeks."

"Do you suppose . . . ?"

"Dora and Daniel! How could they?"

Dr. Jaffe was amused by Hannah's momentary innocence. "Men and women together, it's always the same. They had enough opportunities to be alone before the wedding, didn't they?"

"We never thought . . ."

Herman brought the beers. Though Hannah took a hearty swallow, she could not help but frown at the sour taste.

"Why did you order it if you didn't want it?" Rachael laughed.

"You never know when something different might be something better!"

Rachael changed the subject. "Remember that case you discussed with Herzog and me?"

"Which one was that?"

"About the woman whose husband is impotent." She spoke more loudly than necessary. Heads turned in their direction.

"Rachael!" Hannah muffled a laugh.

"I was reading some monographs Herzog was translating and found a reference in one by a Hungarian, Ferenczi, which claimed that the problem is usually of psychogenic origin."

"Herzog was right?"

"I'd hate to admit he was correct, because the case could have a medical basis as well as a psychological one, but I thought you'd be interested in Ferenczi's conclusions."

"What did he say?"

"In coitus," Rachael said, careful to divide the word into three distinct syllables, "complete potency is only possible when all of the libido trends are fused on a real, constructive love object."

"It doesn't take a genius to know that a man isn't interested in a woman he doesn't love, Rachael," Hannah said caustically.

"It's not as simple as that. It is my guess that your patient's husband might suffer a pollution resulting from a repressed wish of a culturally forbidden nature."

"The theory is interesting," Hannah replied. "You seem to be more tolerant of Herzog's newest intellectual passion these days."

"If I am not, he will continue in any case. At least it gives us something potentially benign to discuss."

Hannah made her beer last as long as possible and half-listened to Rachael's discourse. It was relaxing to hear her postulate on the psychological aspects of sexuality while she ruminated on more concrete problems of her own.

❖ ❖ ❖

When she left the café hours later, Herman slipped a note into her hand before he opened the door to the street.

"I must explain . . . tomorrow at 1:00 . . . N.B." She read the hastily written message as she walked home. Something in the tense scrawl suggested to Hannah that Belinsky was more distraught than she. If she did not go to meet him, it would end the possibility of an alliance. A simple, inoffensive solution. Yet she could not leave it that way. Everything must be finished, must have an end. She felt compelled beyond basic sense to arrange her schedule the next day to meet him one last time.

# · 5 ·

As SHE APPROACHED the café the next afternoon, a good-natured crowd of people filled the sidewalks, as the early November day was as warm as any in midsummer. Because she could not risk meeting friends who might expect her to join them, Hannah watched for Belinsky's landau at a trolley stop a block away from The Monopole. The crowd seemed an unending, interminable mass of unknown faces. Carriage wheels kicked up dust, and an occasional automobile passed, belching smoke. The great noise of the midday throng welled up from the narrow side streets and reverberated along the walls of the tenement rows. Hannah winced at each siren or squeaking wheel, every wail of a child or mother's guttural call across an alley. The noise! Never before had she been so sensitive to it, but now Hannah thought if it did not diminish she would lose her mind from the aural assault.

A shattering honk from the curb caused Hannah to flinch. There, sitting like a prince behind the tiller of an automobile, was Belinsky. He helped Hannah into the black vehicle with distinguished red trim.

He spoke in a matter-of-fact voice. "Better that we leave this neighborhood before we are noticed."

Hannah ran her hands across the red tufted-leather seats. "I think anyone who looks in this direction will be more interested in the vehicle than its occupants."

"Do you like it? It's a curved-dash Oldsmobile. My father doesn't even know I have it."

"Then how did you buy it?"

"I won it!" he said with glee. "I had planned to sell it after a few days, but I just couldn't. It has a two-speed Leland engine and a Briscoe body!"

Hannah bit her tongue and looked away from Belinsky. She did not want to hear him prattle about his expensive new toy. He didn't notice the tight expression on her face because a break in the line of traffic had occurred above Thirty-fourth Street and he was more intent on steering his way up the avenue past the Altman store, the public library, St. Patrick's Cathedral, and the imposing Vanderbilt house. In front of the University Club, he slowed to allow a throng of pedestrians to cross.

"Where are we going?" Hannah shouted over the ticking sound of the car's idling engine.

"That depends on you. We could ride about all day if you'd like, or if you'd prefer . . ." he said. The meaning was clear even though his voice had dropped to where it was drowned out by the chugging of the exhaust.

"Today!" Hannah said, flustered. "I expected we would talk again . . . You said you wanted to explain. When I saw you and your wife together . . ."

Belinsky pulled up beside a curb. "My wife has been anxious to see where I go and what I do," he began to explain as he used the hand lever to brake the car in three uncertain jerks. "She doesn't understand that a man needs time away from his home," he said, wiping the steering tiller with a soft cloth he had tucked under the seat for that purpose. "She'd heard some unpleasant rumors about The Monopole, so I agreed to take her and show her what a decent establishment it really is."

"You were wise to keep her in the front dining room! What did she think?"

"She was quite relieved by the atmosphere: intellectual, refined, and not too ..." The exact word wouldn't come, so he spun his hands in the air to explain what he meant.

"... too pretentious?"

"Yes, perhaps, though no one is more pretentious than my wife. She would prefer everyone else, including her husband, to live modestly so she may shine in the dark."

Hannah phrased her words precisely. "Did she recognize me?"

"Not at first. Later she continued to ask why you looked so familiar and I ..." Belinsky hesitated.

"You told her!"

"What could I do? I thought it best not to hide that I knew you, so I told her that you were the midwife who had delivered Gertrude on the ship and that I had seen you several times when I collected rents. Finally she recalled your visit to see Gertrude again and wondered why you didn't approach us at the table. Then she suggested ..."

Hannah turned toward Belinsky rigid with anxiety. "What?"

"Only that we invite you to the house to see how well Gertrude is developing."

"Nahum! I cannot do that. How could I sit in your parlor and sip tea, pretending that nothing is between us!"

"There *is* nothing between us," he said flatly. Then he brightened. "Yet!" He placed his hand over Hannah's own, which lay demurely clasped in her lap. "Until today, until now. If you could come one Wednesday for only an hour, if you could talk with Sondra about ... Gertrude, and babies, and such, all her fears will be allayed."

"She suspects something!"

"There is no reason, only . . ."

"You did say something!" Hannah rose in her seat, but Belinsky pushed her back down.

"No, not with words. But when I saw you standing there I tried to say so much to you with my glance, I think she may have sensed what I was feeling, though she has no proof. Don't you see that if you came to our home she would know there was nothing, for if you were guilty you would not dare?"

Hannah pulled away from his grasp and pressed her hands to her face. "I could never be so devious! You have asked far too much of me! I would like to help you, in some other way, but not this . . ."

Instead of responding, Belinsky attempted to move forward by pulling a lever back and forth, but the car stopped humming altogether. With a deep sigh, Belinsky stepped to the street and cranked the starter with several forceful turns. As he pulled himself back up to his seat, he said very softly, "You will still take lunch with me, won't you?"

Thinking he had capitulated, Hannah did not have the heart to refuse. Besides, she wanted to be near him a little longer. "I would like that very much."

The Oldsmobile sputtered and coughed, releasing a small cloud of black smoke that the obstinate wind blew back across their laps. Hannah buried her nose and mouth in the cloth Belinsky handed her. The smell of the man's handkerchief clearly hinted at an expensive cologne mingled with tobacco, and Hannah found herself pleased to be breathing in the scent. Her heartbeat quickened. She knew she must keep him away, yet after weeks of longing to be near him, it seemed so senseless. Before she could decide, Belinsky steered the contraption around the curving drive of the Hotel Plaza. A young carriage boy, thrilled with the opportunity of parking the Oldsmobile, tipped his hat to Belinsky in gratitude.

Without turning her head to the right or left, Hannah glimpsed the elegant ladies and gentlemen who strolled across the main lobby. A small orchestra played in a pavilion at the far end of the room. The atmosphere was so much more open and public than even the Café Martin, Hannah visibly relaxed and took Belinsky's arm as they walked toward the restaurant.

Suddenly she froze and wouldn't walk forward. Belinsky felt her resistance. "What is it?"

"I cannot go in there with you!"

"Of course you can't," he said as he steered her away from it and down the thickly carpeted side hall to the bank of elevators.

As she stared at her slightly distorted image in the ornate polished brass panel of the elevator door, Hannah began to wonder exactly what he had planned.

Snap! The doors were parted by a liveried operator. Belinsky steered Hannah into the mahogany interior. "Seven, please."

"Yes, sir!" the operator answered, nodding his head with the proper degree of deference.

As soon as they were on the seventh floor, Hannah was certain that its hallways did not lead to another restaurant or roof garden. She hesitated and glanced back to the elevator, where the operator waited before shutting the doors. Though this was the moment to refuse, it would require a public explanation.

Without a wasted movement, Belinsky pulled out the key and opened the door to room 701 and allowed Hannah to enter first. Everything was prepared. The room had a view of the park below, where each tiny tree looked like the tip of a freshly dipped paintbrush. A small lake crossed by an arched bridge sparkled in the sunshine, and people linked together like chains weaved in and out of the greenery. In front of the large semicircular window a small table had been covered with a pink cloth and set with rose-patterned china. Three shapes of wine glasses were readied, while two silver urns held iced bottles draped in pink napkins. Crimson roses, baby's-breath, and small sprigs of miniature pink carnations were massed with ferns in crystal vases on the table, on the mantle, and beside the bed.

Even her fantasies had not been as elaborate as this enchanting scene. Avoiding the sleeping area, Hannah walked in a wide circle until she arrived at the trolley and began to lift the silver domes that protected the food. One platter held thin slices of rare roast beef, tongue, and lamb decorated with tomato halves filled with a creamy mixture of cold vegetables and topped with alternating black and green olives. The next cover hid a tureen filled with a delicate broth, kept warm by a small candle that burned beneath the chafing dish, and the last revealed a whole stuffed pheasant decorated by the bird's own plumage.

Belinsky stepped beside Hannah and pulled out the chair next to where she was standing. "I told you I was inviting you to luncheon. Please, let me serve you."

Numbly Hannah did as she was told and allowed her soup bowl to be filled by Belinsky. He passed the bread basket across to her and watched as she obediently broke a roll in half and lavishly spread it with three iced butter curls. Without looking directly at him, Hannah alternately sipped at the soup and stared out at the passing scene on the avenue.

After she had finished, Belinsky jumped up and prepared her a plate with a sample of each delicacy and poured the wine. "I remembered how much you enjoyed the champagne at the Café Martin."

"Yes, I did," Hannah said, the edges of her lips softening despite herself. The warm soup, as well as the wine, relaxed her further. Motioning out the window as a bolt of lightning snapped across the park, she said, "Look, Nahum! If that hit one of those buildings would the people inside have been hurt?"

"I like you to call me Nahum; no one else does anymore. My mother would have hated Nathaniel, but my father wishes to forget the past entirely. And no, the lightning will not hurt anyone, it just goes through the pipes, then harmlessly into the ground."

"Still, I don't think it is safe to construct such tall buildings. Anything over six stories must be unwise. I can't imagine why they do it."

Belinsky leaned back in his chair. "There is a story about the rabbi of Vilna, who had a little walled garden behind the shul so small that his students laughed at the folly of having such a tiny enclosure. 'Yes,' agreed the rabbi, 'my garden is not very long nor again very wide, but do you not see how deep down it goes or what wonderful height it has?' So it is in New York. We may own very little ground, but we still have the earth beneath and the sky above to call our own. To make use of this previously unconsidered space all future buildings will have to be skyscrapers." Belinsky's eyes flickered with excitement. "Skyscraper!" he said reverently. "Such a perfect word, don't you think?"

Then Belinsky pointed to the highest buildings in sight. "Do you know what has made them possible?"

"What?" asked Hannah, enjoying the break from the intensity of their encounter.

"The elevator! Before eighteen eighty-seven apartments above the eighth floor were impractical, but now in buildings with electrification, higher rents are paid for the top floors, where the air and light are better."

"Why do you seem so interested in skyscrapers when all your work is among the tenements in our neighborhood?"

"I have some capital of my own and I am investing it in skyscrapers now that there is no limit to what can be built. All the new construction is going to be in steel, which can carry hundreds of feet if necessary. Have you ever seen the Tower Building on Lower Broadway?"

"Yes, I think so."

"That was the first steel-skeleton building in New York. Do you realize that on a plot of land a mere twenty-one-and-a-half-feet wide they have managed to erect a building over one hundred sixty feet in height? The thirteen stories yield a fantastic ten thousand dollars a year in rentals alone!"

"I didn't know that," Hannah said quietly.

In order to postpone the inevitable confrontation, Hannah allowed him to continue, though the subject had begun to lose its fascination. Hannah lifted a cream-filled pastry from a platter and slowly picked at a swirl of chocolate icing with her fork.

When Belinsky finished his discourse, Hannah knew the time had come to speak. "I'm expecting another child," she said as though it offered a perfect excuse.

"So I guessed; yet it is still very early, isn't it?"

"About four months."

"You are having no discomfort?"

Hannah moved the flakes of pastry about but did not eat it. "None."

Belinsky pushed his chair back from the table. "If I were worried about the possibility of a child, it would be much more difficult. This way I shall have more confidence."

Hannah watched as he took two steps to her side. "I would

never want to hurt you . . ." All his movements seemed to be slow-
ing down; his body swayed in front of her, his breath ruffled the
top of her hair. Placing his hands on her shoulders he reached
across the plates and glasses to kiss her forehead; then he bent his
knees and kissed her neck. Finally he kneeled and rested his head
in her lap. "Please . . ." he whispered. "Please . . ."

## · 6 ·

HANNAH LOOSENED Belinsky's tie and unfastened the stiff line of
buttons on his shirt, but its removal was complicated by a sliding
buckle that prevented the shirt from bulging out over his vest.
While Belinsky took over the task of undressing himself down to
his shorts, Hannah did the same, leaving only her camisole and
muslin drawers in place. As she backed away from the table, she
stepped over the small piles of clothing and sat on the edge of the
wide bed.

When Belinsky followed her, Hannah allowed herself one
glance at the site of his supposed affliction. Since he was obviously as stimulated as any man could be, Hannah was now certain that his excuse was but an elaborate fabrication.

His kisses were gentle at first, but then his pink tongue pressed
her mouth open to explore the edges of her lips. His competent
hands untied her bloomers and stroked the hard mound of her
belly before reaching for her blossoming breasts. How had Belinsky
known that this was the precise gesture that would arouse her the
most quickly? Hannah leaned back on the tufted bolsters and
stroked his neck to encourage him. As her hands guided Belinsky's
back to urge him forward, her mind struggled to make sense of
what was happening, what she wanted to happen . . . now . . .
sooner, faster . . . now.

At last he slipped his shorts over his thin hips and kicked them off the bed. Though Hannah shivered at his approach, she steeled herself to remain quiet so that he would have no difficulty with his entrance. As soon as he was safely inside she felt a spark of triumph. She held him tightly with her arms and legs and slowly exhaled a sigh of pleasure.

She wanted him to thrust toward her, but he was still, very still. She raised her hips, but he pressed her down by fully laying his weight across her. Without any external movement, she squeezed him with a secret inner grasp, yet as she used her hidden muscles she felt him soften and diminish until there was nothing left to hold. How could he do this to her when she wanted him so completely?

Belinsky's arms clutched at Hannah's shoulders, his chin dug into her collarbone, and with a massive shudder of defeat, he rolled onto his side. It was so quiet Hannah could hear muffled sounds from the street, but the dominant noise was the uncontrollable thumping of her own heart. Wasn't there anything more she could do? She reached for Belinsky and touched his genitals; he pushed her hand away. Suddenly she felt more anger than sympathy for this pathetic man. Turning away from him she stared out the window and tried to summon her sensible self.

Rain was falling in heavy grey sheets, obscuring all but the most impressive buildings. Her breathing became slower and the tensions subsided slightly. If only she could divert him from his failure, if only he'd relax again, pay more attention to how she was feeling . . .

"I still wouldn't feel safe in a skyscraper in a storm such as this," she said to break the wall of silence.

Belinsky rolled toward the view. "That's nonsense. You're safer fifty stories up than on the street!"

"How can that be?" she asked, turning to face him.

"The architects compile strain reports showing the wind bracings from the cellar to roof." Belinsky seemed relieved to have his attention distracted by a practical subject.

"How do you know all this?"

"Because I am planning to build one myself at the corner of Fourth Avenue and Seventeenth Street." He waited to see if Hannah was impressed with his plans, but she was much more intent on following through with their original goal. Without his being fully aware of it, her hands had gently maneuvered him to the point where he could once again attempt penetration. Sadly he puckered his mouth and shook his head. "It's no use . . ."

"Nahum," her voice was hoarse, but compelling. "Please . . ."

"You want me?"

"I do . . . please . . ." This time she did not wait for him to advance first. Hannah slid atop him. A shimmering feeling shot through her and she pressed him deeper, closer, without pausing to see how he was reacting. It was like her dream of him. She rubbed her breasts across his face until he could not resist taking her brown nipples in his mouth. Arching her neck back, she hummed with pleasure.

After her own orgasm mounted and subsided she noticed that he had shut his eyes and his face wore a mask of frozen tension. Veins pulsed in his brow while his hands began to move across her flanks, coming to rest on her smooth buttocks.

She kissed him over and over again as she rolled over on her back. Still piercing her firmly, Belinsky had the freedom to move at his own pace. His face looked threatening as he lunged toward her over and over; then he stopped. Hannah opened her eyes and stared at him. His eyelids fluttered wildly, his teeth scraped together, and this time his shudder was victorious.

"I will be devoted to you forever," he crooned. "Devoted, forever . . ."

❖　❖　❖

Hannah pretended to sleep at Lazar's side later that night, though she was filled with a current of shame that kept her awake the entire night. She was mortified by how easily she had deceived her husband, and even more, she worried that she had not begun to suppress the feeling that she wanted to be with Belinsky again.

Why was he so different from Lazar? As she watched her husband's body rising and falling in his sleep, she knew she did not really wish to live with anyone else, though she would not have minded living someplace else. But Belinsky, with his dark flashing eyes, muscular loins, had wanted her so desperately, had needed her in a way more basic than her husband ever had. And there was something in the sincerity of Belinsky's admiration for her that she did not want to relinquish.

❖ ❖ ❖

The next day Hannah checked Dora, who had been complaining of breast pains. Upon examination she found that Dora's right breast was hot and swollen. Large lumps had formed around the clogged ducts. As Hannah had suspected, her sister was not nursing consistently from both breasts. Hannah advised both Mama and Daniel how to observe the feedings and attached a safety pin above Dora's right breast after it had just been emptied. "Now when you nurse at the left breast, move the safety pin to the other side. That will remind you to use the other breast the time after that. It is important you switch back and forth. Do you understand?"

When Dora nodded that she did, Hannah left to make a call at the Health Department office, where she was required to register the babies in her care, and returned home early to take Benny for a walk in the park.

Turning down Willett Street, she heard the fire alarm from the station on Clinton Street. The clangs came even louder in her direction, and fearing that some neighbor's house might be affected, she quickened her step.

All of a sudden something darted from the gutter. An object? No, a child! Benny!

"Benny! Benny!" she screamed and raced toward him in vain, for, before she could reach her child, he had dashed out to the center of the street.

In the second that Benny saw the oncoming horses advancing in his direction, he became transfixed with terror and froze to the spot. Though the driver had spied the child, he could not possibly check the great hose truck in so short a distance, and there was no room to swerve to the right or left, since Benny was standing in the very center of the narrow street. From her perspective Hannah saw it all: the smashing hooves, the crushing wheels heading straight toward him.

"Benny! Benny!" She closed her eyes.

The child could not hear her over the pounding of the hooves and the noise of the bell, though if he could he probably would not have known which way to move, as the undercarriage was almost upon him. The driver called his horses to pull wide on either side and went on at full speed. With perfect precision timing, over they went and slowed halfway down the street.

Benny remained standing, his hands covering his eyes. Hannah ran over to him and crushed him in her arms sobbing, "I'm sorry, I'm sorry, Benny, forgive your mama, forgive me."

The driver walked back toward the hysterical woman while his companion took the wagon on to the unseen fire. "I couldn't stop in time; I did my best, took a risk. Is he all right?"

Hannah released her tight grasp so the driver could see that Benny was not harmed. "How did you get the horses to go off on either side like that? What magnificent driving!"

"Thank you, ma'am. The chief is talking about changing the trucks over to those gasoline-powered monsters, but I think that would be a mistake. Give me a good horse anytime!"

Hannah thanked the man again and again before carrying Benny to the sidewalk where Mrs. Friedlander, his babysitter, was wailing. "I'm sorry, I only went inside for a moment. I've never left him alone before!" Mrs. Friedlander protested so strongly that the child himself began to cry. Grabbing him from Hannah, Mrs. Friedlander kissed and felt him all over to convince herself he was all right.

"I'd better take him up now and put him to sleep," Hannah said, reaching for him.

"I'll do it; he's too heavy for you."

Hannah didn't protest, but followed the babysitter upstairs and allowed her to help undress him, understanding how responsible she still felt for the near tragic incident.

"Don't tell your husband; it will only drive him crazy when he thinks what might have happened. Never have I seen a man who loves his boy so much!" Mrs. Friedlander pinched Benny's cheek affectionately. "Papa's boy!" she said, before leaving Hannah alone with him.

All Benny wanted to do was nurse. He clutched at Hannah and sucked so hard that tears burned in her eyes. As the immediate shock faded, Hannah felt her skin begin to tingle with a frightening sensation. Revealed to her, as plain as a printed document, was the reason for the scare: she was being warned about her own selfish behavior. Warned, but not punished. In all her deliberations about Belinsky, the smallest of her concerns had been the rightness or wrongness of the action. Everything revolved around how she felt, what she wanted, how to deceive others, how to make everything work for her benefit alone. Her own son and his welfare had been pushed in the background so she might follow her midwifery, spend time with her friends and Lazar, go off riding in noisy automobiles, dine at the Plaza, and find pleasure in the arms of another man.

"I will be better, I must be better," Hannah thought as she rocked Benny in her arms, kissing the tender nape of his neck and rubbing his soft cheek with her thumb. "I'll be a good mother; I'll never do it again; please keep him safe," she whispered in the closest thing she knew to a prayer.

· 7 ·

KEEPING HIS PROMISE, Belinsky recommended Hannah's midwifery services to Mr. Golden, of the railway family, and when their first son, after three daughters, was born in their Seventy-second Street town house without even a tiny laceration to the mother, Mrs. Golden referred Hannah to her sister, Mrs. Edelman, who seemed to know every socially prominent mother in the Jewish community.

Because Hannah's dress and decorum were more than proper enough for the wealthy ladies who required her services, she found a modest acceptance among them at afternoon teas, as long as the topics of conversation revolved around their babies. When the subject turned to dressmakers, charity balls, country homes, and the like, Hannah knew how to step back or move to another circle so as not to distress any of the privileged ladies who did not care to be reminded that their origins were so similar to Hannah's.

One of the most gracious of the women Hannah met at the Edelmans' was Beatrice Karp, whose husband, Mortimer Karp, had astonished the financial world with his daring investments. While the Belinskys' uneasiness with sudden wealth was revealed in their pretensions, the Karps' similar rise to power was marked by humbleness. Instead of being aloof and snobbish, Mrs. Karp treated everyone, Hannah included, with kindness.

When Hannah arrived for Mrs. Karp's regular massage appointment a few days before Christmas, Mrs. Karp requested that the midwife be shown to her private sitting room, where Mrs. Karp leaned back against the bolsters on the curved velvet divan. "I apologize for bringing you out on such a cold afternoon, but I do not want a massage today. I am just too tired and unwell."

"I'm sorry to hear that," Hannah said, sitting on the edge of a green leather chair studded with large brass tacks that appeared to be the eyes of a flock of unblinking frogs. "I'll be happy to come back some other day."

"It has started to snow already, hasn't it?"

Hannah nodded. "That doesn't matter . . ."

"I can't ask you to go right back out in this weather," she apologized.

"It is no trouble, really!" Hannah said as brightly as possible so Mrs. Karp wouldn't feel unduly obligated. "You must take your rest."

"I'd really enjoy your company, though. I've no one to talk with all day until Mortimer comes home . . . and who knows what time that will be!"

"I'd be pleased to remain as long as you like . . . My baby is with my husband at his bookstore and he'll be quite content all afternoon."

"How does his father look after him?"

"Not in the same way a mother would! He keeps a large stack of old newspapers and lets Benny tear them into pieces. Benny calls the pile his 'snow place'!"

"How adorable! I would like you to bring your son with you

some afternoon. My greatest regret is that we were never blessed with children. Everything else . . . but not the one thing in the world we wanted most," she said, wiping her lips with a lace handkerchief. Suddenly her voice changed as she asked, "Do you know how I met Mortimer?"

"No, I don't," Hannah responded quietly.

"Everyone supposes we were an arranged marriage, but it was really quite a different tale. My father had agreed I should be wed to a boy who also lived in our town of Zvihil. The boy was well known for his angelic voice; they said he was destined to become a great cantor. Though I tried my best to like the young man, I could not overcome the fact that I was repulsed by the sight of his face."

"Why?" Hannah asked.

"Now that I think about it, the mark wasn't so bad, but to me then . . . I was so young . . ." Mrs. Karp said, her voice drifting back to the past. "Across one cheek and eye he had a large red patch, larger than this!" She demonstrated, almost covering her own face with her hand. "The boy's family maintained that the birthmark resulted from his mother's having watched a cow being butchered while she was expecting him. They said it was the sight of the pools of fresh blood imprinted on the baby, but I worried that it might be transferred to my own children and, with that argument, won my mother to my side. Finally my father could not take both our protests and called off the marriage, but furious at my disobedience, he ordered me to marry the very next stranger who appeared in the town who would have me."

"And the next man was Mr. Karp?" Hannah asked in amazement.

"Actually it was Mortimer's uncle, a tax collector, who made an arrangement for me to marry his nephew over a bottle of slivovitz. I never saw Mortimer before the wedding and didn't care what he was like as long as his face was not deformed!"

"If you had only known that in a few years you would be here!" Hannah gestured across the room.

"I knew my young husband was a genius; everyone said he had a brilliant mind for figures, but he could not get into any Russian school of higher education because of the quotas. So his father sent him to study in America. Instead of enrolling in college, he invested his tuition and our first year's board, and this is the result."

Mrs. Karp began to perspire heavily.

"Do you want me to call someone?" Hannah asked too late. Mrs. Karp turned her head to avoid the upholstery, vomiting onto the highly polished floor. As soon as Hannah pulled the call tassel, the butler stepped inside. Seeing the difficulty, he summoned Mrs. Karp's private maid as well as the scullery maid and inquired if he should send for the doctor.

"No, no ... I already have my medicine," Mrs. Karp said weakly. "I'll just go back to bed."

"You should never have gotten up at all this morning, ma'am," her red-headed maid admonished as she led her to the bedroom.

"I thought I'd feel better after breakfast, Mamie."

Hannah helped Mrs. Karp undress and slipped her arms into a long cotton gown. "Are you certain the doctor shouldn't be called again?" Hannah asked as she combed back the lady's hair and tied it in a ribbon.

"I don't know what more he can do for me. I am rarely ill, but lately every little thing bothers me. Pains in my back and side, my breasts, always dizzy. The doctor thought it would pass in a few days, but since it hasn't I'm afraid that it could be something more serious ... something ..." She drifted for a moment and then asked clearly, "Do you think it is normal for a woman my age to go through the change?"

"I do not know how old you are, Mrs. Karp, but I would think you are far too young for that!"

"I'm thirty-seven, but with no one to look after but myself, most would think me younger, wouldn't they?"

"By ten years at least!" Hannah confirmed politely. "Have you stopped altogether?"

"The last two months were hardly anything ... a few drops ... this month nothing at all."

Hannah sat quietly and observed the woman propped up in bed. She looked very ill indeed: her eyes surrounded by dark circles, her long nose made more prominent by the pinched skin around her cheeks. Grey hairs flecked a luxuriant expanse of rich black hair. People aged differently and disease could hasten such a process.

Perhaps the woman had a tumor of some kind. Hannah could tell from the nervous tremor in her cheek that she was deathly afraid.

"What has the doctor given you?"

"Only the herbal remedy he says everyone is taking."

"You have not had a complete examination?"

Mrs. Karp shook her head.

Though she knew she was unqualified to make a medical diagnosis, Hannah could possibly discover a breast lump, note any unusual vaginal discharge, even palpate a tumor.

"Sometimes it is easier to be examined by another woman. I would be very gentle, and if you do have a female complaint I will refer you to a physician."

"If you would be so kind!" Mrs. Karp said with relief.

Hannah always carried her medical kit. She thought it might inspire confidence in the ladies who planned to hire her for their deliveries. She removed her speculum from her bag and showed it to the woman so as not to frighten her. "I will need to use this to visualize you internally," she said after washing her hands. "Now draw your legs up . . . good . . . like that . . . And could you slide down to the bottom of the bed? Now I will be as quick as possible." She talked almost continuously to keep Mrs. Karp relaxed. First she felt with her sensitive fingers for any signs of abnormal growths; then she inserted the speculum and peered at the cervix, which looked a dusky purple in color instead of the expected pink. Hannah swallowed hard but tried to keep her face a mask of unconcern. After withdrawing the speculum, she used her left hand to press on the abdomen while the right felt from within to determine the size and shape of the enlarged uterus. Hannah wiped her hands and then untied the dressing gown at the neck. She massaged each breast with her fingertips. When she pressed under Mrs. Karp's arms, the woman winced.

"It hurts there?" Hannah acknowledged. More gently the midwife squeezed the nipples with her fingers and a drop of fluid dampened her fingers. "Are your waists tight?"

"Yes, they are, but I have lost weight, not gained!"

Hannah felt around the circumference of Mrs. Karp's throat. "You've been sick for several weeks, is that right?"

"Yes . . . I can hardly keep anything down."

Hannah sat on the bed and took Mrs. Karp's hand in hers. With the other she stroked the frightened woman's arm. "I believe I now know exactly what the difficulty is, Beatrice," she said, using the woman's first name to make the pronouncement more personal. "Unless I have totally wasted my entire education and experience, you are going to have a baby in less than six months."

Mrs. Karp's eyes nearly exploded from her head. She opened her mouth and shrieked so loud that her maid, Mamie, ran into the room. "God in Heaven! How can it be true after all these years? I thought it was impossible for me . . . to ever have a child!"

Mrs. Karp embraced Hannah with all her might.

## · 8 ·

EVERYTHING WAS ALMOST PERFECT. Lazar was content with The Gate, spending most of his hours there each day selling a few books, entertaining his friends. Benny was talking like an American, had stopped wetting his pants during the day, but still wanted the breast before bedtime. Eva and Napthali had purchased an even bigger building on Stanton Street, directly across from Public School 91, and were willing to let Hannah and Lazar have the middle apartment for a reasonable rent so they would have more space when the next baby arrived. Dora's Jacob seemed absolutely normal, even a bit advanced, as he was sitting up and clapping his hands at only five months. And Hannah was doing more and more work for wealthy uptown Jewish women.

During the month of February she brought in an astonishing forty-five dollars from deliveries and another fifty-five from massages. For the move to the new apartment she splurged and ordered a brand new Fairmount wood stove with shiny nickel trim and a hot-water reservoir on the side. Gossips at the Karp salon had also spread the word that Mrs. Belinsky was expecting her second child, and Hannah looked forward to doing both society births.

During the last weeks of her second pregnancy, Hannah felt remarkably happy and well. As she planned the birth, there was no possibility of her agreeing to go to a hospital, and she prevailed upon Rachael, the one person she most trusted, to deliver her at home. Dr. Jaffe had been surprisingly concerned that something might go wrong and pointed out that Hannah had far more experience with actual births than she did. But Hannah was so adamant that Rachael could not refuse.

And so Hannah's daughter, named Emma Leonia, was born at noon in the brightly lit bedroom of Hannah and Lazar's new apartment. Dr. Jaffe worried that Hannah might rip at the site of her previous scar, but all their preparations had been successful, including having Hannah deliver in almost a squatting position to minimize stress on her tissues. Less than an hour after the birth, Hannah was up and walking about showing off her exquisite and delicate daughter to the neighbors down the hall.

Emma was Hannah's idea of a perfect baby. Indeed the child was radiant. She never cried, for the moment she might have thought to she was lifted up to be kissed or carried or fed. She napped in the crook of Hannah's arm and only had to be repositioned slightly if she needed the breast. Hannah managed to sleep and nurse her at the same time, and so felt well rested in the mornings. Benny had to be watched so he didn't kiss his sister too hard or attempt to lift her from the cradle that had been a gift from the Edelmans, but for the most part he saw the baby as an added amusement in his life.

As she handled and loved her daughter, Hannah felt a tightening in her chest, a regret that she had never really known how to touch a baby before. Compared to the gentle ways she discovered to hold Emma, she had been too brisk with every other child she had taken into her care. If she had only known how her arms could be fluid like water, her hands buoyant instead of grasping, her fingers featherlike extensions for support and stimulation, she might have given so much more to her first child and the others she had helped bring into the world.

When she permitted herself to recall how she had mothered Benny, Hannah cringed with the memory of the uncertainties she had transferred to the innocent boy. With him she had felt an ambivalence that she feared had scarred him in some invisible way, while Emma was the recipient of a boundless love. Milk flowed from her breasts when she even thought of Emma flicking open her eyes and looking for her mother. To Hannah her daughter was an angel sent as a sign of forgiveness, and she did not forget to be thankful for her every single day.

## · 9 ·

"NEVER IN A THOUSAND YEARS would I have thought anything like this could have happened!" Mrs. Feigenbaum said, breaking the news to Hannah first.

"But you told us Minna was killed in a pogrom!" Hannah was incredulous. "How can she appear suddenly in America?"

"She held on to a log and floated downstream, where some peasants took pity and rescued her. They nursed her for three months, then helped her to cross the border. It took her six months to earn her passage!"

"If she had only written Napthali this tragedy could have been prevented!" Hannah pounded on the table in a rage.

Eva and Napthali had been so happy. At first from gratitude, then slowly with love, Eva helped her husband manage his properties, quick to paint a wall or repair a window herself if necessary to keep up his buildings, their buildings. She was proud that they now either owned or held the lease on seventy-four separate flats! And so excited that they were going to move uptown to West End Avenue as soon as their baby was born!

"Does Eva know yet?" Hannah asked.

"No, but as soon as Minna arrived we called Napthali. How were we to know whether it was the same woman or not?"

"Maybe all she wants is the money?"

"No! She says she will not rest until she has him back!"

Hannah sighed deeply. "What is she like?"

Mrs. Feigenbaum shook her head sadly. "A miserable, scrawny thing . . . though Napthali says she must have suffered greatly to have changed so much."

"What do you want me to do about it?" Hannah asked uncertainly.

"We think you should be the one to tell your sister."

"And what should I say? That her husband is not her husband and that her baby will be a bastard?"

"We told Minna she must take the issue to the rabbis, let them decide."

Confused as to where she should turn for help, Hannah went to The Monopole hoping to find Lazar or Dr. Jaffe. She was surprised to see Chaim, who, instead of arguing as usual, was having his portrait sketched by a little man with a mustache.

Her brother listened with great sympathy to the tale. "What shall we tell Eva and Mama?" Hannah moaned at the end.

"Where will she sleep? Does she have any money? How is her health?" was his response.

"She's strong as a horse; the baby isn't expected for many more weeks," Hannah answered.

"Not Eva! The girl, Minna! Poor woman comes to this country expecting to be protected by her fiancé, only to find he is married and his wife's family is ready to persecute her!"

"Nobody wishes to harm her!"

"Then how do you expect to get rid of her? Push her in the Hudson instead of the Dniester?" Chaim said with great feeling. "We must help her, not drive her from our homes and hearts!"

Though shocked at first by Chaim's sympathetic attitude, Hannah recalled how often he had championed the cause of the loser. "Will you be able to tell Eva that she has married someone she cannot have?"

"The Feigenbaums were wise to select the Rabbinical Court. Even if there is no possible way to please both parties, at least the decision will not be a personal one. If they divorce, the child will still be legitimate; and with her settlement Eva will find someone else willing to have her."

"Do you think that might happen?"

"I don't know, but she should be prepared. I will go talk with this . . . this Minna. Maybe I can help her. At the Am Olam there are women who have also endured terrible hardships. They will befriend her, help her find work. The trouble with you, Hannah, is that you have had everything so easy. Your education was handed to you like a gift, you have a chosen husband, two healthy children, so you forget about those less fortunate. Life is worthless unless you give back more than you take." Chaim trailed off, his voice becoming hoarse. He cleared his throat. "I'll go to the Feigenbaums' now, so this Minna won't be alone tonight."

"Wait, I'm not finished!" The artist waved his pencil in the air as Chaim departed without looking back.

❖ ❖ ❖

While they waited for the decision from the Rabbinical Court, Mama and Hannah took turns making certain Eva wasn't alone.

After the initial shock, Eva's attitude was so positive that everyone feared a great depression if she lost. Anxious to do even more to help her own case, she wrote a plaintive letter and posted it to the editor of the *Jewish Daily Forward*, who ran an advice column called "A Bintel Brief."

Subsequently her letter was printed among other tragic tales of ghetto life. It concluded:

> Tell me, Mister Editor, what should I do? Do I give my dear husband, whom I have come to love better than life itself, back to his betrothed, or do I fight to keep him for myself?

The editor responded in bold black letters:

> Though the unfortunate lady from Europe has reason to be distraught, for fate has handed her a terrible turn, she never actually was married. Therefore, by the laws of God and the state of New York, you are the only lawful wife. Perhaps you and your friends can find it in your heart to forgive her and help her make an adjustment to this land.

It was almost as though the rabbis had read the same newspaper, for in a few weeks they had decided much the same, suggesting that Napthali give Minna enough money to help her through her first months in America. Minna refused the payment.

Only three days after the final pronouncement, Hannah delivered Eva of a girl named Isabel after Napthali's father, Israel, and, conveniently, after Eva's father, Itsik. Although Hannah had feared that Eva might have difficulty because of her abortion, her anxiety was unfounded and her sister suffered less than the usual first-time mother.

At the family celebration, which Mama suggested because "a girl is also a gift from God," Chaim was asked to hold the child. Mama paraded all her grandchildren — Benny, Emma, Jacob, and tiny Isabel — in front of her acquaintances, bragging that Benny was so smart, Emma so beautiful, Jacob so advanced for his age, and the infant the most lively she had ever seen. Quietly at first, then more loudly after the toasts had been sipped, she declared once and for all that the time had come for her son to produce a child as well. Disgusted by the fuss and attention, Chaim left the party without saying farewell to anyone. He was not seen again for months.

❖   ❖   ❖

Because Hannah felt so secure with her own earnings and because her calendar was dotted with due dates for which she had been hired months in advance, she paid little attention to the economic status of The Gate. If she had watched the business with any interest, she might have known that Lazar's payments to the Lipskys amounted to so little that they could worry they were being cheated out of their percentage, though that was not the case.

In the beginning Lazar had developed a fluid pricing structure, so that the same book might be sold above what it should have cost to a patron he suspected could afford it and way below the wholesale value to friends and political allies. For a while Lazar deluded himself into thinking that this precarious system was balancing itself so that the richer patrons were supporting not only the poorer ones but himself. Whenever he had less money at the end of the week as well as fewer books, he brushed away any sense of failure, confident he had made a great contribution to "the cause."

Everyone he wanted to see eventually stopped by The Gate. It was so convenient. Lazar could arrive each morning, read his paper in silence, and then wait for his friends and associates to arrive.

When serious customers asked for a specific title, paid, and left immediately, Lazar might complain they made him feel like a grocer. There were even books that Lazar would not sell at all. One had a particularly lovely binding, another had scholarly notes of imagined importance in the margins. These were his babies, his children, his people, and for him to sell them would be akin to dealing in slaves.

Not only did The Gate attract socialists, Bundists, and Zionists, but also a group of unrecognized writers whose acceptance at the store amounted to belonging to a fraternity. One knew seven languages, but on principle spoke only Yiddish; another, with a large goatee and loose cape, wrote his manuscripts at Lazar's wrapping table and stored them in the basement, where they were not to be read until his death.

Hannah's ignorance of the store's management was shattered one morning when Lazar arrived and found the door padlocked by the sheriff. The contents were to be sold at auction to pay Lazar's debt to the Lipskys, and no amount of maneuvering or hysterical rantings would change the official's mind.

After a Bundist attorney interceded in his behalf, Lazar was able to recover his "personal belongings," which to him included a hundred or so of his most cherished books and manuscripts, his tea kettle and blue sweater, and Benny's blankets and toys. From then on Lazar never again went past The Gate, walking blocks out of his way to avoid it.

## · 10 ·

THOUGH HE HAD ALWAYS lived with the terrifying uncertainty of his affliction, Daniel Greenbaum was, outwardly at least, a calm, kind man. Never once did he hint that he was unsatisfied with the burden of his illness or his slow wife. He made certain that Dora was always neatly dressed, tucking her bodice in, pinning a loose hem, and centering the part in her hair. There was no question that he loved her just as he adored his infant son. And his reward was that both wife and child returned his lavish affection.

Daniel had worked their life into a series of familiar patterns and systems, and as long as they were followed, Dora functioned quite adequately. It had been his idea to arrange everything in terms of three: one for today, one for tomorrow, and an extra "in case." Three onions on the window ledge, three carrots in a basket, three oranges in a bowl. When only one remained, Dora would purchase two more. He planned three rotating meals: beef flanken for Monday and Tuesday, fish for Wednesday and Thursday, chicken boiled on Friday, served cold on Saturday, finally appearing as soup on Sunday. Dora did laundry every first day, ironed on the next, and shopped on the last. All very orderly, very rigid, yet the structure allowed Dora to relax and believe that she was just like everyone else: a wife, the mother of a precious boy, someone important.

There was no way of knowing when Daniel's seizures might recur. After consulting with Dr. Jaffe, Hannah made a tongue saver by padding a small wooden spoon and convinced Daniel to keep it in his pocket along with a vial of ammonia to revive him. Moe at the stables, Cantor Persky at the synagogue, Mama, and Dora were all shown what to do for him; but he did not have another attack. Dr. Jaffe guessed that marriage had a healing effect on him, explaining that epileptics were thought to benefit from an unstressful life as well as regular sexual activity.

Every evening at sundown Daniel took part in the minyan at the synagogue, where they could count on him to be one of the requisite ten men to say prayers at the close of the day, on the Sabbath, and for any funeral in the congregation. Understanding it was probably the fear he wore so close to his heart that kept him devout, even Lazar never chided his scrupulous obeisance to the old scriptures.

A few hours before Friday night prayers, Daniel would arrive home for a clean bundle of clothes. Dora had learned how he wanted everything arranged: his prayer shawl folded on top of his silken Sabbath caftan with his small velvet cap placed in the center. Then he would trudge to the public bathhouse, where he would first take his soaking bath, then join the men in the Turkish steam room to chat and stimulate his skin with a special type of twig broom.

That Friday in late spring was not particularly special. Only afterward did everyone wonder if the icy rain had made the difference, for in order to protect his dry clothes from the moisture, Daniel had taken off his warm coat and wrapped it around his bundle. Then, chilled by the soaking shirt on his back, he had entered the fragrant fog of the bathhouse, quickly stripped, and hurried to his bath because the hour for the Sabbath was drawing quickly upon him. A quarter of an hour earlier there might have been more men in the room, and the tragedy might have been forestalled. But as it was, Daniel entered the tiled room alone and adjusted the water to his satisfaction before climbing into the tub.

At some point after the warmth of the water began to drain the bitter cold from his bones, the delicate balance of his brain was shattered. The attendant said he never heard a cry or a splash. In the violent first seconds of a seizure, Daniel had become unconscious and drowned.

Dora could not be consoled and the only solution to her grief was large doses of medication to keep her calm, if not asleep. She could not be trusted even to nurse her child, so Jacob was hastily weaned to bottles and porridge, a much more complex affair than breastfeeding.

In her heart Eva supposed she should volunteer to take the child and Dora in, but her own world was too fresh, too precarious after the shattering episode with Minna. How could her family expect her new husband to accept the responsibility of a retarded sister and another infant child? Instead she offered Dora a small flat in one of their buildings and felt she had done her duty.

So Hannah ran between her home and Dora's when she was not delivering babies, which now were coming several times a week. One of Hannah's greatest worries was that there would not be time enough to do all the births that dotted her calendar. Though there never had been a direct conflict of cases, there were days when she was required to attend one confinement in an airless tenement and another in a fifteen-room town house, giving a full twenty-four hours of service.

Although it was never discussed, Lazar knew Hannah paid all the bills. His contribution was to take over when Hannah was not in the house, prepare breakfast for the family, and shop for their meals. Hannah paid Dora a few dollars a week to do her ironing, knowing that her sister needed both the money and the regular, undemanding work. The days worked out with everything just barely getting done, but Hannah was so pleased to be an active midwife she was rarely heard to complain.

Chaim had sat with the family when they mourned for Daniel, staying a few hours in the evening as was expected, but he remained so silent and secretive that Hannah was frightened. When she confided her fears to Lazar, he said, "Don't worry yourself over him. Right now he is organizing a parade for May Day. Everything is so legal he even has a permit to march! He wants it to be the biggest organized socialist event in New York!"

The threatening May Day weather did not deter the socialists, who turned out in force with lanterns, banners, and marching bands. When paraders and curiosity seekers assembled in front of the small cottage in Union Square, there were between six and seven thousand people organized into four divisions.

Hannah brought Benny out to watch, holding tightly to his hand so he would not be lost in the crowd. She had strapped Emma to her chest with a large shawl, knowing that the child would sleep as long as she rocked her body from side to side if she stirred.

"Look, Benny!" she said as a company of police bore the American flag between two blood red socialist flags.

Benny jumped up and down at the procession of banners with brightly painted inscriptions. He shouted "Hurrah!" at the blacksmiths who carried large hammers across their shoulders, marched in step to a boys' fife and drum corps, and whimpered when the mill workers with large painted spools had passed him by.

Though Hannah searched for Lazar in the crowd, she couldn't find him before Benny, exhausted by all the excitement, began to kick at the forest of feet in front of him so furiously that Hannah knew she had to take him home. Weaving her way through the tightly packed clusters around the speakers' platform, Hannah thought she saw someone who might help her carry her son at least to the edge of the throng.

"Chaim!" she called and waved. Her brother and his companion, a girl in a black cloche with a white egret plume, turned toward her voice. Hannah's eyes widened at the sight of the beautifully dressed woman. She tried to say "Minna!" but the word caught in her throat.

From the proprietary manner of the girl's walk as well as the way she kept close to Chaim's side, Hannah instinctively knew why her brother had been even more secretive than usual.

"Minna!" she repeated while she groped for a polite phrase. "I haven't seen you since . . ."

Minna's delicate hands lay limp at her sides as she waited for Hannah to say what she meant.

Benny reached his hands up to his uncle and Chaim lifted him onto his shoulders.

"I need to get the children home. Could you help me to the street?" Hannah asked nervously.

Minna tried to communicate something to Chaim with her eyes, and though Hannah noticed the flick of her lashes, she could not decipher their private message. When they were finally out of the crush, Hannah unwrapped Emma and changed her position. Minna peeked over the shawl and said softly, "She's very pretty!"

Although Hannah would normally have smiled at the compliment, she drew her lips back and merely nodded. Just having Minna hovering around her reminded her of the threat she had posed to the security of the family.

When they reached a quiet corner Chaim lifted Benny down. The boy began to scream and kick. "Up! Up! I want to see!"

Hannah apologized, "He's just so tired and excited."

"I'll walk you all the way home, then," Chaim said.

"But you'll miss the speeches. Cahan, Jonas, Saniel all haven't been on yet."

"They'll go on all night. We can get back in an hour or so. Besides, Minna could use something to warm her. I told her not to wear so thin a dress, but she wanted to look her best for today."

As Hannah turned and stared at Minna's elegant jade green jumper and white blouse with tapered wrists, the girl's flickering lashes now signaled he had her approval to speak.

"Since May Day is so special to both of us, we decided it was the perfect time to be married," he said as though he were reciting a memorized speech.

"Married! When?"

"This morning, at City Hall," Minna whispered.

"You didn't have a rabbi? It will kill Mama!" Hannah said the first words that came into her mind. Her pounding heart and shaking shoulders had been too much for even the docile Emma, who began to scream; and seeing that his sister was somehow usurping his circle of attention, Benny began to whimper that his stomach hurt.

Without another word, they hurried to Hannah's apartment to settle the children. After Benny collapsed in bed and Emma began to nurse greedily, they discussed, as quietly as they could, the impact the wedding would have on the family.

## · 11 ·

MAMA SURPRISED EVERYONE with her reaction. It was as though Minna had been a perfectly acceptable candidate to become her son's wife all along! If the wedding hadn't already taken place, she might have shown her true feelings, but since it was over she felt she no longer had the authority to disapprove. Chaim must have known it would be that way, Hannah thought; that's why he did it in secret. Always the clever one! Always the winner! If she or any of her sisters had done such a thing, Mama would not have been so supportive. An old bitterness rose to choke her. She didn't wish to have anything to do with her brother or his woman ever again!

Mama pulled her daughters together, persuading them to make the best of it. To smooth everything over Minna convinced Chaim to go through with a small religious ceremony and reception in Liberty Hall, which Hannah and her sisters attended with great reluctance.

After the blessings on the wedding feast, Hannah had just placed her spoon in the soup when a message came that she was to attend a birth uptown. Ordinarily she would have resented being called away, but she was not at all sorry to leave this party, for she had no interest in celebrating what she thought was a disastrous alliance. And when she heard the name of the client she was overjoyed, for her favorite case was about to deliver.

Beatrice Karp had made elaborate arrangements for her home confinement. A vast quantity of sweaters and blankets, tiny gowns, and embroidered pillows had been ordered weeks in advance. Seeing in a gallery an impressionist painting by Mary Cassatt of a mother tenderly caressing a plump child, Mortimer Karp had brought it home and placed it over the mantel to further inspire his wife.

Hannah had agreed that a doctor should check Mrs. Karp on the days she did not visit, though Beatrice had pleaded that Hannah should do the delivery, for she trusted the midwife far more than the doctor her husband preferred. To ease Mr. Karp's mind, however, Hannah met with Dr. Williamson and discussed every aspect of the case, promising to call him in at the slightest provocation.

But the labor was blissfully normal. Mrs. Karp seemed to welcome the early contractions. With each pain she clasped her hands in joy and paced the room, for she was too excited to even get into bed to rest. Hannah examined her every hour, noting with great satisfaction that her progress was steady.

"Your wife has the constitution of a much younger woman. Some women hold back, try to restrain the feeling, thus delaying the inevitable and making it more difficult for themselves. But Mrs. Karp is so ready to receive her child that I suspect we will have it here before morning," Hannah reported to Mr. Karp, who occupied his time by filling out financial forms. Though he thought he was doing the work with great precision, he would later find that the long columns he totaled that night did not balance.

The baby was a big one. Once Hannah had eased it out, she was not unduly alarmed that the child was not immediately crying. She showed Mrs. Karp that her baby was indeed a son before pounding between his tiny shoulder blades to startle him into taking his first breath. Nothing.

Wiping the mucus from his nose and throat did not help either, nor did a forceful pressure as she milked his neck to clear it further. Quickly she reached for her De Lee suction bottle, threaded the thin rubber tubing down his throat, and sucked out a few large globs of mucus into the glass interior with the second tube in her mouth. But the baby remained flaccid and blue.

A feeling crept up Hannah's back, like a cold knife ripping at her spine. The baby was dead! It had not moved at all. Not a sound had issued from his mouth. Mrs. Karp and the nursemaid stared without speaking, while Mamie in the doorway placed her hand over her mouth to silence the scream that rose in her throat. Holding the baby's feet, Hannah spun around, hoping the force of the movement would jerk some life into the stubborn, inanimate thing. As she did so, the corner of her eye caught sight of two silver bath pitchers in the corner: one filled with cold water, the other with hot.

"Mamie, pour the cold water into the basin!" she yelled like a Prussian officer. "And you," she ordered the nursemaid, "bring Mrs. Karp's bowl and fill it with the hot!"

Before Mamie had finished, Hannah held the baby in the ice water and let the final drops from the pitcher bounce off his belly. Then she reached across to the other tub and lowered him into the hot water. Next she went back to the cold, and once more to the hot. Something in her arms moved. At first she thought it was the swish of the water on her wrists, but then she saw the child was turning pinker. Perhaps he was just stimulated by the temperature of the water, but Hannah did not stop to consider all the possibilities. Back and forth, back and forth: a few seconds in the hot, a few seconds in the cold. Again and again she dunked the child, rubbing his limbs, smacking his cheeks, pleading with him to respond. "Ahhhhh!" It wasn't actually a cry, more a shiver or a mutter, but it came from within the child. "Ehhhhhhhh!" The sound was more high-pitched. And then it rang out like the most perfect of chimes: "Aiiiiii-eiiiii!"

His fingers and toes blossomed like roses, his brow wrinkled in the painful process of expression, but he was alive. So startled was the nursemaid that she dropped the china basin she had been holding, shattering it and spilling the contents on the rug, but no one cared in the least.

The commotion brought Mr. Karp bounding up the stairs still clutching his green accounting sheets. Oblivious to the disarray of the room when he saw his child, he ran about kissing each of the women in turn, finally daring to lean over and do the same for the woman who after twenty years of marriage had given him his son.

❖ ❖ ❖

The eighth day after the Karp's son had survived his birth was, by Hebraic law, the time for his bris. Because Hannah was credited with saving the precious child, she was not only invited to the ceremony but was also asked to take the honored role of the kva-terin, or godmother. Lazar, too, was invited to join the festivities.

"You must go, I suppose," he sulked, looking up from a volume of Damon Runyon stories. "All your fancy customers will be there. But you cannot expect me to debase myself by pretending to ap-prove of either the barbaric ritual or their capitalistic excesses." He pretended to continue his reading.

"Barbaric ritual!" she said, slamming his book. "Didn't you have the same done to your own son?"

Lazar reached for the book, but Hannah took it to the other side of the kitchen. "Perhaps it was seeing it done to Benny that changed my mind. You can't tell me that he didn't feel the pain."

"Do you think you can change thousands of years of tradition because your child was made to suffer for a few minutes?"

Lazar walked over to his wife, retrieved the volume, and searched for his place.

"Even if I didn't disapprove of the ceremony itself, I wouldn't want to set foot in a place like the Karp palace, for to do so I would be spitting in the face of my brothers who are fighting for a more equal share of the wealth."

"No one need know where you have been" Hannah said sweetly, returning to her chair at the table. Picking up a piece of cold toast, she took a small bite and considered what words might sway him to her side. From experience she knew it was useless to argue or plead with him.

She placed her palms flat on the table and leaned back resolutely in the chair. "In a war, what elements are important to victory?"

Diverted by something he was reading, Lazar had lost the thread of the conversation. "What?" he asked, and then considered. "Guns, ammunition, I suppose!"

"What good are weapons if the enemy cannot be found?"

"I don't see what this is all about," Lazar said impatiently.

"Don't you need information about your opponents? Don't you ever try to infiltrate their meetings and establishments?"

"Yes, but . . ."

"You are always condemning capitalists like Karp and his cronies. But how much do you really know about these men? Do you know what their homes are like, who their friends and associates are, what they read or eat? Don't you think it would be of some value to have access to such a home by invitation instead of by force?"

Lazar stroked his thumb across his cheek in a gesture that told Hannah he had capitulated.

❖ ❖ ❖

"Lazar, please hurry!" Hannah called, pacing back and forth in the front room. "Their carriage is waiting!"

"In a moment!" he called in a vexed voice. "I don't know how to manage all these buttons."

When he emerged dressed like a gentleman, Hannah gasped. She had never seen her husband look so elegant. He had borrowed a summer-weight cutaway and a five-button vest. Underneath a crisp monarch-wing collar was a black satin bow tie that matched the band on the stiff derby he had set on his head at a jaunty angle.

Hannah took his arm. "You look wonderful!"

"So do you!" he admitted as they walked down the dusty tenement stairs to the street.

Tubs of orange marigolds flanked the doorway to the Karps' residence. As Hannah and Lazar waited their turn in line with the dozens of carriages pulling through the front gates, she glanced across the street to where a guard watched over the few automobiles that had been driven to the affair. Noticing her quickened breathing, Lazar asked, "Is something the matter?"

"I was just admiring that black auto with the red trim."

"The curved-dash Oldsmobile?" Lazar responded smugly.

"How did you know what it was?" Hannah asked.

"I read the papers, so I think I know a bit about what goes on in this world! Those cars will be the ruination of this country!"

"Why? Think of all the problems they will eliminate: feeding, stabling, veterinary treatments, and the massive cleaning of the streets and gutters!"

Lazar saw that the doorman had arrived to help them down. "This is hardly the time to argue the evils of progress, Hannah."

The butler recognized Hannah immediately, for the midwife had been back every day that week to supervise the mother and baby's welfare. "Mrs. Karp is in the drawing room, Mrs. Sokolow. Would you join her there?"

"Of course," Hannah said with deference. "Lazar, why don't you have a look around."

Nothing was spared for the bris of the Karps' baby. Every influential Jewish family in New York had been invited, and knowing the importance of this baby to Mortimer and Beatrice, almost everyone had come to share their joy. Though the Karps had moved away from their formal religion, they were determined to do everything for their child with both correctness and style. The Karp baby, Solomon, was not only being introduced to the beliefs of his forefathers but to the society in which he would hold an illustrious position as well.

The Karps had even chosen Ben Ezra Weiderman, the most orthodox and devout ritual circumsciser, or moyl, they could find; he would perform a flawless ceremony and also had great skill with the knife.

When Hannah entered the drawing room, Mrs. Karp graciously stood to greet her. "You look lovely, Mrs. Sokolow!"

"Thank you," Hannah replied. "It was quite an unexpected honor to be selected."

"It is you who do us the honor," Beatrice replied.

In a few minutes the ladies who wished to witness the event were escorted to the ballroom. Then Hannah quietly took the child from his mother, so as not to disturb his sleep until the last possible moment. As ritual dictated, the mother was to stay in another room so she would not be anxious during the surgery.

At the door of the vast ballroom, Hannah handed the baby over to the gentleman designated as the kvater, or godfather, whom Hannah recognized as Mortimer Karp's partner, Isaac Lowenthal. As soon as the child was placed on the specially embroidered satin pillow, he startled. Hannah soothed him before Lowenthal took the child to an elaborately carved gilt chair that stood on a little platform in full view of all the standing guests.

The moyl, decked in flowing black robes and wearing the beard and earlocks of a pious East European Jew, stepped forward. He spoke so loudly that his voice echoed in the vast room. "This chair is devoted to Elijah the prophet, may his remembrance be for the good."

The baby made a vivid contrast to the man who stood over him: white lace next to black linen, innocence beside worldliness, the past receiving the future. Everything and everyone appeared withered and pallid next to the child's radiant freshness. Although she had heard the words many times before, there was something about the majesty of the ceremony and the surroundings that caused Hannah to reflect on the great emotional importance of the event.

The baby woke and began to fret as he was lifted from the chair and handed to the sandik, the man given the highest honor of holding the child while the rite was performed. The more illustrious the sandik, the more propitious for the child's future. Hannah stared at the man who had been selected. Even with his prayer shawl draped over his shoulders he did not look particularly pious; rather, he appeared bored by the whole event. Yet there was something about his thick head of white hair, the curve of the bristles of his mustache, and the intense look in his coal black eyes that seemed familiar. When he bent toward the child, Hannah realized that the sandik was Belinsky's father! Mortimer Karp had craftily selected the one man in the room who might have been, by a fraction of accounting, more powerful than he. Perhaps anticipating some future business dealings, he undoubtedly thought it wise to bind the families together with a concern over an infant, so that later feuds might be settled with less enmity and cost.

After allowing the infant to suck on a wine-soaked cloth, the elder Belinsky firmly held the baby's legs while the moyl immersed his own hands in a disinfectant solution. As he lifted the double-edged knife in his right hand, he recited loud enough for all to hear: "Praised be Thou, O Lord our God, King of the Universe, who hast sanctified us with Thy commandments, and commanded us concerning the rite of circumcision." With great deftness he performed the ritual. As Hannah observed this procedure she could not help but wince, and to spare herself the sight of the suction, she turned away. The Karps apparently wanted everything done by the strictest tradition.

"Praised be Thou, O Lord our God, King of the Universe, who has sanctified us by Thy commandments, and has bidden us to make him enter into the covenant of Abraham our father," the moyl recited.

Then the men present responded, "As he has been entered into the covenant, so may he be introduced to the study of the Law, to the nuptial canopy, and to good deeds."

After prayers over the wine, a few drops were put into the baby's mouth. "And Thou, in Thy abundant mercy, through Thy holy angels, give a pure and holy heart to Solomon Moses Karp. May his heart be wide open to comprehend Thy holy laws ..." The moyl finished the final prayers before giving the benediction over the bread so the feast could commence.

Solomon had calmed after being reswaddled, though clumsily, by his sandik, Belinsky. Hannah stepped forward to receive the child and quickly rearranged him on the pillow to make him more comfortable. As she began to lift the infant in her arms to take him back to his mother, her face was momentarily bent close to Belinsky's. Was it her imagination that the old man looked at her with some recognition? His eyes, black jets set deeply into their sockets, reflected only her own image, but something about his immobility, the set of his jaw, seemed disapproving.

Although anxious to taste the smoked salmon, chopped liver, fish balls, and thin slices of beef, Hannah stood nervously behind Mrs. Karp in case she or the baby needed some assistance. At some point she would have to join Lazar, if only to keep him from saying anything foolish. She only hoped he would be so hungry for the luncheon that his mouth would be too full to speak. Also, she knew Nathaniel Belinsky and his wife were somewhere in the crowd. She hadn't seen Belinsky since their affair at the hotel, and she trembled at the idea of a reunion.

Mrs. Karp placed her sleeping baby in his cradle and gently rocked him.

"Come, Mrs. Sokolow, let's take this opportunity to eat while Solomon is quiet," she said, leading the way toward the buffet table.

With a studied unassuming manner, Hannah murmured her greetings to everyone who came up to congratulate Solomon's mother. Lazar was nowhere in sight.

"Mr. and Mrs. Nathaniel Belinsky, I'm sure you know Mrs. Sokolow already!" Mrs. Karp beamed.

"Of course," Nathaniel said, bowing deeply. "And we have heard about your valiant efforts on behalf of Solomon Karp." The way he used the child's name, so formally, it sounded as though he were talking about a business associate.

Hannah felt a tingling in her hands and toes as she groped for the appropriate response.

Mortimer Karp waved toward his wife from across the room and she signaled back that she was on her way. "I'm certain you three have much to reminisce about. If you will excuse me, then ..." she said, gliding away.

Turning back to the Belinskys, Hannah noticed how carefully Mrs. Belinsky had dressed herself to hide the effects of her pregnancy. Belinsky said blandly, "I understand that your husband is here, but I have not seen him in several years, so I don't know if I would recognize him."

"I don't see him now," Hannah said, "but I'll make it a point to reintroduce you."

Speaking directly to Belinsky took a great effort and Hannah could think of nothing to say, so she pivoted slightly and asked his wife, "How is Gertrude? The last time I saw her she was just beginning to walk."

"Gertrude," she said, searching for a way to describe her daughter. "She's quite a pretty girl, but she has a terrible temper and her nurse is always filled with complaints." The irritation in her voice gave Hannah the distinct feeling that this mother had little time or patience for her child.

Hannah decided to agree with her for the sake of conversation. "My son is a bit younger, but I know how you feel. He's always doing naughty things like running out into the street ..." She stopped. Why had she thought of that now? Belinsky, Benny's near accident, all tied together, entangling her in a guilty web.

"Nat!" a voice called to Belinsky. He turned toward an immaculately dressed man in a grey silk suit with a modern plaid bow tie.

"It's Zuckerman again!" Sondra said under her breath. "You'd better see what he wants now!"

"Excuse me, ladies," Belinsky said, walking toward the voice.

"Just because Zuckerman's company, Germania Life Insurance, is financing the construction of Nathaniel's latest project he thinks he owns him!" Sondra said, puckering her mouth as though something tasted sour. As she spoke her eyes searched the room for anyone else she knew.

"I hope you are feeling well," Hannah said in a weak attempt to get her attention.

"This has been an unbearable summer already! Thank goodness we are spending long weekends in the mountains, though my husband keeps rushing back to check on his steel girders! Well, at least it isn't another woman!" she said with a throaty laugh that made Hannah's skin prickle.

Hannah shifted her weight from one foot to another. A waiter carrying a tray of champagne passed by on Mrs. Belinsky's side. Mrs. Belinsky took a glass but totally ignored Hannah as she sipped. The waiter also seemed not to care if Hannah was served, but she reached for one so she would have something to hold.

After quickly finishing her drink, Mrs. Belinsky licked her lips

"That's better. Don't you think it's hot in here?" And then she said, without any introduction, "I have these cramps . . ."

Hannah looked puzzled. "In your stomach?"

"No, no, in my leg! What do I do about them?" she demanded.

Hannah nodded that she understood. "Your heavy uterus is probably pinching some nerves that are sending signals of pain down to your leg. It's quite normal between the fifth and seventh months. How far along are you?"

"Exactly six months. To the day. It wasn't hard to figure out!" she said with a giggle.

"Try elevating the leg when you are in bed, take hot baths, and use compresses. It should subside in a few weeks when the baby's position changes. If not, call me and we'll see what we can do."

Suddenly Mrs. Belinsky's voice became quite shrill. "By the way, didn't you ever get invited to my Wednesday tea . . . after I saw you downtown at that place where Nathaniel used to go?"

Hannah stood still, bent her head slightly, and hoped the rush of blood to her face wouldn't be too visible.

"I though I had asked Nat to invite you to see Gertrude again."

Hannah could think of no response.

"Must have slipped his mind . . ." Mrs. Belinsky said before she was distracted by a friend who waved in her direction. "Oh there's Mrs. Rosenzweig. I must go and give her my regards." She turned her back to Hannah without another word.

Though Hannah was uncomfortable by herself, she was grateful that the confrontation had ended. She searched for her husband among the small groups that seemed to bob and sway in the pools of bright yellow sunshine pouring in from the high side windows. Where was Lazar? She couldn't remember seeing him in the room during the ceremony. Perhaps he had taken her point about "getting information on the enemy" too seriously! Hannah eyed the buffet and wondered if she could stop to help herself first, but some protective instinct urged her to find her husband immediately.

As she passed the drawing room door she overheard Beatrice Karp retelling her birth story to a new, fascinated group of women. How close Hannah was to becoming the most sought-after midwife in New York! She searched for Lazar in the front meeting room, the drawing room, the downstairs study, even the coat rooms flanking either side of the ballroom. She peeked into the green-tiled solarium that featured a fountain where porcelain fishes and frogs spouted water onto real lily pads, and opened doors that led down passageways to the servants' areas. Then she continued out to a glass-walled porch that ran along the back side of the house. Shrill voices of children playing among the greenery rang out against the hard panes of glass. Although Hannah could see that Lazar was not there, the fresh flowery smell of the room arrested her momentarily. How beautiful! Summer flowers bloomed in carved stone pots and hung in moss-draped cages from the rafters. She sucked in the clove sharpness of the pink and white carnations, the spicy scent of the enormous red geraniums, and the sweetness of the miniature rose trees that were pruned to perfection.

Looking out toward the manicured gardens, she noticed a geometric privet hedge and five graduated pools of water, each on a terrace slightly higher than the first. The voices in the room echoed in a polyglot of Yiddish, English, German, and Russian. She closed her eyes and listened. From the sounds she could have been anywhere that Jews congregated: at Uncle Velvel's in Moscow, at the theater in Odessa, in steerage, or in Liberty Hall! All the same people, some with more, some with less. For a moment she allowed herself to feel some of the same anger that motivated Lazar and Chaim. The unfairness of it all! Why should Karp, a boy from a small Russian village not that far from where Lazar had grown up, have all this while they still worried about making ends meet?

Hannah opened her eyes, but they refused to focus. The overpowering fragrance of the flowers, the heat of the day, the glass of champagne, coupled with the fact that she had not yet eaten, overcame her. She found a small stone bench beside a large Boston fern, sat down, closed her eyes, and waited for the dizziness to pass.

# · 12 ·

"ARE YOU FEELING all right?" a familiar voice asked.

Hannah opened her eyes and saw Nathaniel Belinsky bowing before her.

"I must apologize for leaving you with Sondra . . ." Belinsky said softly. "Was it difficult for you?"

"I didn't mind," Hannah said with dignity. "Apparently things went well with you."

Belinsky straightened his back and took her moist hands in his. "I suppose . . . The end was achieved . . . but . . . it's not as you might think."

"What do you mean?"

"If you believe that we were totally reconciled or that my feelings for her returned as well, you are wrong."

Hannah's eyes filled with tears. "Then how could you?"

Belinsky tried to answer but could only utter a choked cough. After taking a deep breath he began again. "I would close my eyes and think of you."

Hannah remained silent.

"I'm grateful for the memory and the hope," Belinsky continued.

"The hope?"

"That someday again . . ." He pulled her close to him and rekindled a spark she thought had been quenched.

Hannah knew she should retract her hands from his grasp, but she could not move away. Did she want him because he adored her or because there was something about the dichotomy of his position that was fascinating? All his wealth and the backing of his powerful family did not bring him any happiness. But there was something else: a basic physical attraction she could neither deny nor explain.

Just then his wife appeared in the doorway.

Hannah and Belinsky jumped apart abruptly. She began to flush; Belinsky was obviously perspiring.

He walked over to his wife as casually as possible. "There you are!" Seeing that his wife's face was frozen in a frightful grimace, he asked, "Aren't you feeling well, my dear?"

Suddenly Mrs. Belinsky began to rip at her hair. Pins and combs hurtled to the floor and she continued flailing her arms so wildly that a seam in her straining bodice split wide open with an audible rip. "What an idiot I've been!"

"Please don't get so upset . . ." Belinsky importuned.

The noise had attracted a great deal of attention. Belinsky's father burst into the room. His face almost matched his white shock of hair as he grabbed his son and shook him. "What is the meaning of this?"

"Shifre had too much to drink already. She imagines that . . ." He fumbled for words in the glare of his father's disapproval.

Drawing herself to her fullest height, Hannah made a great effort to speak calmly and precisely. "Mr. Belinsky!" she said, pushing between the father and son. "A terrible mistake has been made!"

"It has?" He raised his eyebrows at the young woman's affrontery. "Mr. Belinsky and I were only discussing the health of his wife," Hannah hurried without taking a breath. "At the buffet she confessed she was having some pains and other symptoms, which, quite frankly, I found worrisome. I didn't want to alarm her, so I took this opportunity to advise Mr. Belinsky of my diagnosis."

Because Hannah appeared to be speaking as a professional, Belinsky's father seemed to soften.

"Perhaps it was unwise to speak to your son alone at a gathering such as this, but I felt it was my only opportunity to see him quickly and avoid a possible . . ." She tried to indicate by a drop in her voice that the rest might be too personal to reveal in the crowd.

During the silence Mrs. Edelman stepped forward in Hannah's defense. "I saw Mrs. Sokolow conferring with Mrs. Belinsky in the ballroom. Mrs. Belinsky did seem very agitated about something, and she did drink several glasses of champagne very quickly. I know for a fact that wine affects me . . ."

"Sondra." The father-in-law turned and confronted the accuser. "Did you hear the words they were speaking?"

"No ... I ... I ..." she said, shivering. "I saw the way she looked at Nahum ... I only thought ... Perhaps I did drink too much ... I wasn't feeling well today ..." she said, beginning to sob. Two friends took her arms, helped her lie down on a wicker sofa, and fanned her face.

The elder Belinsky, wishing everything would be over as soon as possible, quickly apologized. "This must be very upsetting for you. If there is anything we can do ..."

Hannah interrupted kindly. "If you will only tend to her health and follow my suggestions, I will be rewarded by seeing you enjoy your newest grandchild this winter!"

"My grandchild!" His face illuminated with pleasure. "So that is what all this fuss is about!"

As he turned to embrace his son, Hannah took the opportunity to continue her search for Lazar. Now she was more anxious than ever to return home.

Mrs. Karp stopped Hannah at the door of the drawing room. "I met your husband, Mrs. Sokolow. He's such a scholar!"

"I've been looking for him everywhere!" she said, quite relieved. "Where is he now?"

"I think he may still be with Mortimer in his study on the second floor. Do you know where that is?"

"Yes, I'll find the way myself," Hannah said and hurried up the wide curving marble staircase. As soon as she reached the first landing, she heard her husband's agitated voice from the next room. "You are just another black-hearted plutocrat whose soft and flabby hands carry no standard but greed! Don't you see what damage you and your friends are doing to your own people?"

"How many do you expect me to feed?" Mr. Karp said slowly. "A hundred, a thousand, a million? When will you be satisfied? When I am reduced to living in the ghetto once more? Don't you realize that I can do far more for our people here? It's not only money; influence, politics, prestige get the job done. These things move slowly ... you must be patient ..."

"Patient! When was the last time you saw a baby frozen to

death because the landlord was too cheap to buy enough oil? Or children maimed by machines in the factories . . . or . . ."

"Enough! One man cannot change the whole system. But in America there are opportunities. There are no educational quotas, no limits to where a man may go or live, and in this possibility is our salvation. I am on the board of three hospitals that provide services to our people. I am the trustee of two universities and can see that qualified students receive full scholarships. I have influence with manufacturers. The unions, if they are patient, will win their battles one by one over the next few years!"

"I don't believe you!" Lazar said, not even noticing his wife standing in the doorway.

Karp put his arm around Lazar's shoulders. "You are young; you cannot be expected to wait. But listen to me: you will not win by starting a conflagration. If you do, the other side will consolidate their forces and trample you. You aren't entirely wrong, but you aren't entirely right either. If you don't allow the landlords and the factory owners to make a profit, they will have no incentive to go on and you will lose all your housing, all your jobs . . . everything!"

In an effort to prove he hadn't been won over, Lazar pushed the man's arm away. Mortimer Karp attempted to steady himself by reaching toward the edge of a glass-topped case that protected a collection of rare books. Although he broke his fall, he grazed his forehead on the edge.

Hannah rushed forward and mopped the blood from his brow. The wound was very superficial. "I'm sorry; my husband is very volatile. He didn't mean to hurt you . . ."

"I know, I know . . ." Mr. Karp said, taking the handkerchief from her hand.

Lazar backed from the room, leaving Hannah to finish the apologies. And, as quickly as possible, the honored godmother said her farewells and hurried to her husband.

"Hannah!" Lazar called as soon as he saw her. "I'm so sorry. I know what these people mean to you. I was only admiring his books. He has two of Shakespeare's first folios and an illuminated Gutenberg Bible in those cases! Imagine owning some of the world's rarest volumes! When he found me looking at them we got to talking. I didn't plan it that way . . . I didn't!" Hannah was so surprised to hear Lazar contrite, she did not wish to add to his misery.

"I know, I know," she said, patting his hand. "I only wish . . ."

Lazar tried to complete her sentence. ". . . that it never happened . . ."

"No, that I had more time there. With all that glorious food I didn't have a chance to eat a thing!"

"Neither did I!" Lazar remembered. "I'm starving!"

"How about the Hungarian place on East Broadway?"

"Wonderful idea!" Lazar said, placing his arm around her waist and pulling her close.

They walked down Fifth Avenue looking for a trolley stop. When Hannah caught sight of the Belinskys heading home in the Oldsmobile, she sighed. She knew she had just lost the chance to do the one delivery she most desired and only hoped the incident would not ruin the unblemished professional reputation she had so far achieved.

# III

❖  ❖  ❖  ❖  ❖

# Mary and Catherine West
## Delivered June 3, 1908

❖  ❖  ❖  ❖  ❖  ❖  ❖  ❖  ❖  ❖  ❖

## · 1 ·

THE PATTERN OF HER MARRIAGE would have been obvious to Hannah if she had studied it as closely as she did some of the relationships around her. Lazar was mercurial and ineffectual; Hannah was the steady provider, both emotionally and financially. On a daily basis much could be ignored, but there were portents of a deeper disturbance, the most obvious being Lazar's inability to sleep soundly.

After they were married, Hannah had taken the muffled sounds she heard in the middle of the heaviest, darkest part of the night as a sort of cough, a clearing of the throat. Eventually she became so accustomed to the tossings, the blanket pullings, even the muted cries, that she was uncertain whether it happened every night, only after a spicy meal, or during especially humid weather. Sometimes he'd call out so fiercely that someone on the street might have thought the man was suffering an unspeakable pain. If Lazar's cries also disturbed Benny or Emma's slumber, the rest of the night would be ruined. Hannah would spend the next day shaking with fatigue.

It was a horrible summer. The days of heat and foul air were unrelenting, while the nights offered no solace or rest. In spite of Hannah's scrupulous hygiene, Emma eventually succumbed to a mild case of summer fever. Knowing how quickly a baby could dehydrate, Hannah dripped boiled sugar water into her mouth and fastidiously cleaned every mess she made to prevent reinfection. One night Hannah was pulled almost hourly from her bed by her daughter's wails. Each time Emma had to be bathed, changed, and forced to accept a small amount of liquid. And just as the baby succumbed to a deep sleep that permitted Hannah a true dream-filled slumber of her own, a fearsome groan rose from deep within Lazar's chest, shaking her awake. With her heart pounding and her head aching, Hannah reached across to him and pummeled his back.

"What is it? Why are you doing this to me?"

Lazar raised himself on one arm, blinked open his eyes, and stared at her as though she were crazy.

"Why can't you sleep like a normal man?"

Lazar's throat quavered. "My dreams, it must be my dreams."

"What do you dream?" Hannah asked more softly. "Can't you tell me about it?"

"I don't remember them, just the feeling after . . ."

"And what is that?"

For a long while Lazar didn't answer, and by the time he did, the words did not tell as much as the distortions of his broad Slavic face. "It's here," he said, grasping the base of his throat. "It's heavy and thick and it won't let me breathe . . ."

The only way Hannah knew to comfort him was with her body. She kissed him sweetly and then more passionately. Lazar groped for her, unsure that was what he wanted, but hoping the contact would subdue the source of his anguish. Hannah was relieved when Lazar responded to her. This was something she knew, something she could work with; the other was too elusive to be explored. At that moment, it was his need for her that quickened her breath and caused her to open her thighs and press him closer, faster, sooner than she was usually ready. With her arms, with her legs, she encompassed him, held him, urged him on. But Emma's cries shattered the moment. They stopped. Lazar rolled away without a word. As quickly as possible Hannah took care of the child, and when she returned to bed, Lazar had fallen asleep.

❖ ❖ ❖

The next day when Dr. Jaffe arrived to check Emma, she placed a prescription for tincture of opium on the center of the round kitchen table and said, "Try two drops before bedtime and go to three only if the symptoms persist. I don't like to give this to children unless it is absolutely necessary. Have you tried the limewater and chalk?"

"Yes, but it doesn't help," Hannah yawned.

"Poor dear," Rachael murmured.

"She's so young . . ."

"No, it's you I am pitying. You can't go on like this, running to deliveries at all hours, tending the children, not getting your rest."

"If only . . ." Hannah started, but stopped, not knowing how to explain about Lazar.

Rachael probed Emma gently, testing the doughy texture of her skin to evaluate whether the child might need additional fluids and waited for Hannah to continue. She knew her friend well, for if she had questioned Hannah, she might have received a polite denial of any difficulties.

Hannah's voice was hesitant. "Something has always been wrong with Lazar. Something at night . . ."

"What does he do?"

"It sounded like coughing in the beginning; now I'd call it . . . screaming. Sometimes it even wakes the children."

"He does this every night?"

"At first I thought it was infrequent, but now . . ."

"Suddenly it is worse?"

"It is louder, more violent. It is some sort of dream that he says strangles his throat. I think he'd be better without me!" Hannah blurted out the last words without really thinking.

"How can that be true? Since you say he's been doing it since you first knew him, it must have been caused by something before you ever met."

"It was all my fault, right from the first. He never wanted to marry me, to come to this country."

Dr. Jaffe spoke in a soothing voice. "You didn't hold a gun to his head. He came to be with you!"

Pretending to be deeply interested in the curve of her daughter's toes so she would not have to look up when she spoke, Hannah finally confided, "Lazar didn't love me as much as he didn't want to shame me."

"I don't understand . . ." Rachael hesitated. Then she thought she knew. "But you are a modern woman! You mustn't regret a little indiscretion!"

"I deceived him. He must know or have guessed!"

Rachael sniffed the air as though she might smell the answer to the riddle. "So you told him you were going to have a child, but it wasn't the truth. It's not terrible to have used that to bring him here with you. As it turned out Benny came so quickly that Lazar is probably still counting on his fingers."

Even though there might have been some safety in letting the doctor establish her own conclusions, Hannah wanted to unburden herself completely. "No. Lazar may have guessed that he might not be the child's father."

The ringlets framing Rachael's face seemed to stand to attention as she exclaimed, "He isn't Benny's father?"

"Might not be . . ."

"Then who . . .?" Her startled eyes blinked in surprise and she stammered only the first syllables. "P . . . P . . . Petro . . ."

Hannah acknowledged her guess with a guilty bite of her lower lip.

Rachael flung her head back and shook out her fiery crown of curls. "Hannah! Hannah! What a devil you are!" she said, more amused than upset. "I never would have suspected! You always did everything so perfectly that I envied your consistency!"

"And I've envied your spirit. You have done whatever you wished, honestly and openly, not caring what others thought."

"I speak more boldly than I act," the doctor said obscurely.

"What do you mean?"

"My ideals are far ahead of my experiences."

"But you and Herzog . . . when you are on duty nights . . . while he was in prison . . ."

"Only Herzog, only after our marriage, and not very often at that. We seem to be more suited as intellectual partners than as lovers. We met in the movement, that was our bond, so I don't know why I expected it would be different afterward. Herzog has great human understanding about others, but not of himself. For instance, he has told me that Lazar has a mental scar as visible as a physical wound, so I wasn't surprised to learn he has terrors in the night. But the other . . ."

"That's not everything . . ." Hannah blurted. "Do you know Belinsky?"

"The elder megalomaniac or the insipid son?" Rachael answered coarsely.

"Nathaniel has his invisible scars as well," Hannah defended.

"Nathaniel!" Now her voice was incredulous. "What could you possibly have seen in him?"

"He's very . . ." Hannah searched for a word to justify her attraction.

". . . Rich!" Rachael finished bitterly.

"No, I was about to say that he is worthy of some sympathy. Remember my interest in men with physical problems? I took your advice, sparingly, and we were successful."

"You allowed yourself to be used by him in that way?"

Hannah's emerald eyes flashed with anger at the unfair condemnation. "At least I don't brag or hint at things I never have done!" she said before regretting the words. Emma stirred in her arms, but did not awaken. "I'm sorry, I didn't mean that any more than I meant to become involved with Petrograv, or Belinsky, or even Lazar when I did." Hannah smoothed her daughter's hair with her fingers. "Those opportunities appeared like . . . like tempting feasts. It's impossible to resist a little bite, then another, until you regret everything the next morning and then for the rest of your life."

"She who has regrets is a fool twice!" Rachael replied forcefully and picked up her shawl and medical bag. "Only two drops of the medicine at first and definitely no more than three!" she admonished in a firm voice before she propelled herself out the door and down the stairs with so purposeful a maneuver Hannah had no chance to reply.

## · 2 ·

JACOB WAS AHEAD of himself when he began to walk at ten months of age. With his fat little body hurtling unsteadily to the right and the left without warning, he left Dora far behind. It had been so much easier to look after a helpless child who needed everything done for him and who didn't mind his mother's tedious ministrations. But as soon as he learned resolutely to shake his head when offered yet another serving of mashed banana or precociously to untwist the nipple from his bottle and pour the contents out, Dora had no quick skills for diversions or admonishments.

Mama came home too late in the evening to do more than elevate her feet after assisting with meal preparations. The strain of Daniel's death had affected her deeply, and Hannah noticed that old physical problems she had once made light of were beginning to affect her severely. Veins in her legs swelled, a shoulder could no longer bear weight without pain, and arthritis was beginning to knot her once flexible fingers. Jacob exhausted her with his activity; Dora's dullness disheartened her. The only solution was for Hannah to care for Jacob more frequently, but the strain of her own active toddler and nursing baby made it too difficult to provide more than a few hours of relief a week. Yet there was something in the child's dark eyes so reminiscent of Papa the struggle seemed worthwhile.

Now that Dora was living with Mama in one of Napthali's smaller, shabbier buildings, Dora was expected to attend to some custodial duties in exchange for the minuscule rent they paid. She swept the steps and walk, polished the brass-plated gas lamps, and reported maintenance problems to her brother-in-law. When the nights turned unexpectedly chilly in September, Mrs. Kirsch on the first floor began complaining that the heat was not on yet. With a misguided sense of duty, Dora took it upon herself to light the furnace.

As best as they could later determine, she was dressed only in the loose silk nightgown Aunt Sonia had given her for her wedding night. She carried a lit tapered candle because she never had much success striking long matches. Thinking she remembered how Napthali turned the valve, Dora placed the candle on the floor, and with two hands working together, she was able to open it enough to release a small hiss of gas. When she reached for the candle, it licked at the hem of the flimsy shift. Probably she turned as soon as she felt something stinging at her legs, but the draft that was stirred by her movements did nothing more than feed the flames faster.

No one saw her bathed in fire from her toes to the ends of her thick dark hair: a twirling torch. Yet, if it had not been for the invisible vapor that moments later ignited and exploded, she might have been saved. Once found, Dora was not only dead, she had been burned almost beyond recognition.

❖ ❖ ❖

Hannah moved the orphaned baby into her house, and during the first nights when he needed comforting constantly, she tucked him into her bed. No matter what Lazar or anyone else said, the child needed to be held.

There was not as much hysterical mourning at Dora's death as there had been at her husband's. Though Mama Blau anguished over the horror her daughter had endured in her last lucid moments, she felt as though a burden had been lifted from them all. Attention was focused on Jacob.

"He's so young, he'll not remember," everyone said to console themselves, though no one believed it.

Lazar was impatient after a few weeks. One evening when Hannah, already exhausted by the demands of the three children, was called out to do a delivery and expected him to take care of the brood by feeding them supper and putting them to bed, he spoke his mind. "Go, go, have a good baby . . ." he said, pushing her out the door. "But this is the last time I'll take care of your sister's boy."

"Lazar!" Hannah stopped and placed her instrument bag in the hall.

"You can't expect me to be responsible for him forever! I can't handle him."

"You'll learn, as you did with our own. He's no different."

"Isn't he? How do you know that, considering both his parents were defective?"

"How can you say such a thing about such a beautiful child? Why, he's more advanced than either of ours was at his age!"

Lazar looked at her searchingly. "We'll see how it goes," he said and closed the door in her face.

From then on Lazar could only find fault with Jacob. He criticized that the child drooled too frequently, ate the wrong foods, drank too much milk, was costing too much to feed. When Jacob poked a spoon toward Emma's face, Lazar became fierce with protectiveness for his daughter and spanked the confused baby as though his intent had been malicious.

Though Hannah wanted to keep Jacob, she didn't want the child to suffer in her home, and so she mildly suggested that Mama keep the child with her at night and she would mind him during the day. They tried this alternative for less than a month before realizing that the disruption caused Jacob too many problems. Next Eva was asked, and though it still embarrassed her to refuse, she protested that she "thought" she might be expecting again.

The burden was accepted by Hannah. Although the work was grinding, she would not even discuss the matter with Lazar, and her refusal to do so rankled him. Then, exactly two months after Dora's funeral, Lazar brought home a prim lady dressed in black with only a proper strip of lace on her collar and cuffs.

"This is Mrs. Wilson," Lazar introduced. "From the Hebrew Immigrant Aid Society."

"From Hebrew Aid?" Hannah asked. Wilson didn't sound like a Jewish name.

"She's here about Jacob."

Hannah stood and faced the woman squarely, wishing her gaze could cause her to dissolve. "Jacob! He's our child!"

"He is not! Mrs. Wilson knows many Jewish families who want babies but cannot have their own. She has found a wonderful one for Jacob, a family who can do more for him than we ever could."

"No one can do more for him than his own family!" Hannah said, guarding the doorway to the room where the child was napping.

Lazar shook his head slowly and a long wisp of his unruly hair slipped over his eyes, a gesture Hannah remembered was once fascinating, but at that moment it seemed distasteful. "His own family!" he said, mocking her exact intonation. "His grandmother can't care for him, his other aunt who could well afford to raise him properly won't be bothered, and you are so busy with your own two and your work that he receives less than perfect devotion. Can't you see how well he would do with people who had all the money and time for him? He's so young that he'll never remember the past." Lazar's voice was becoming higher in pitch as he faltered for words. "Will he?" he asked Mrs. Wilson.

The woman, who first appeared as timid as a sparrow, spoke in a strong voice and was intelligent enough to use Yiddish to soften the blow. "We have found Jacob an excellent placement with a family living in a small city in the South. They are prominent merchants and the child will have every advantage. They have even agreed that his Hebrew name shall remain Jacob," she said, as if that would make the whole situation agreeable.

"I'd never let my sister's child be raised by strangers!" Hannah spoke with less force than she had before.

Mrs. Wilson walked to the door, turned, and spoke the powerful words she had rehearsed. "I must inform you, Mrs. Sokolow, that you have no legal right to the child and that an adoption by you could be blocked by the courts." Without explaining further she departed quickly.

"How dare she say we have no legal right?"

"I won't support you in this," Lazar replied, his voice as cold as steel.

"You would go against me?" she shouted.

"We'll have more of our own one day soon," he muttered to ease the tension that gathered between them.

"I don't want more children! I want Jacob!" Hannah screamed and ran from the room.

## · 3 ·

FINALLY, HANNAH had to accept the truth. No one really wanted Jacob. The actuality of his care and raising for years to come was another thing altogether. Without the assistance of her family Hannah lost the fight with Lazar. With great reluctance, Hannah packed the child's few clothes and wrote out a detailed schedule of his day, his idiosyncratic sleeping patterns, his tastes in food, the ratio of milk to water in his bottles, and an explanation of what his baby words meant.

When Jacob was gone from her arms, she cursed not only Lazar but the insensitivity of everyone who insisted it was "for the best." In her mind she pictured the family that would receive Jacob. She painted a warm maternal smile on the woman who would devote herself to his care and saw the father as a prosperous version of Daniel who lovingly would applaud the child's progress. She tried to imagine them cheerfully waking at night when he cried, splashing him during his bath, and kissing his bruises; but even the most perfect images seemed so unreal that Hannah knew she had done something both irrevocable and wrong.

At first she blamed herself, Mama, and Eva, but eventually transferred all her rage to Lazar. If it had not been for his demands, if he had not found Mrs. Wilson, if he had been willing to help for a while, to work so she could stay home!

Now she no longer felt pity at his night terrors, only fury if he disturbed her rest. She would choose to sleep on the sofa of a patient in early labor over coming home to be agitated by her husband. Worse, Lazar hardly noticed the changes in her feelings. Something was absorbing his time and interest. Since there was no more money in the house than usual, Hannah knew he had certainly not found a job.

To further punish her husband, Hannah failed to disclose the exact amounts of her own earnings. Extra fees, bonuses, even some large payments were never mentioned. As her account approached six hundred dollars, she secreted the bankbook. With her savings they could easily move uptown if Lazar would allow it. Or she might purchase some furniture: a separate bed for each of the children, the oak pillar table she had admired on East Broadway, a curved glass china closet, or a set of matching dishes. She imagined Benny pulling a little steel wagon with the word *Express* printed on its side or discovering a china doll for Emma to love. For herself she wanted some new dresses, fine enough to look right in the Karps' drawing room should she be invited there again. All these things were affordable if she was willing to admit the existence of her fund, but an elusive "something" convinced her to resist anything they didn't absolutely need.

More and more of Lazar's old friends and one-time rivals from his Bundist days in Russia were arriving on American shores. After the collapse of the 1905 revolution, they either had become disgusted or feared for their lives; and until they found their new niche and cause, they rambled from cafés to union-hall meetings along with Lazar. Though her visits to The Monopole to meet Rachael were infrequent because her days were filled with prenatal and postnatal visits, Hannah kept track of the new names that Lazar tossed out like crumbs to a bird — Vladeck, Chanin, Dubinsky, Hillman — and listened for clues as to what influence their ideas might be having on her husband.

Lazar's theoretical debates had been part of her life for so long that Hannah accepted them in the same way she allowed Benny his tantrums and Emma her inconsolable hour from seven to eight each evening. She saw his illusory causes, with their subsequent marches and speeches, as transient weather systems. Though Hannah admitted the necessity of the storms to nourish the parched land, she thought she understood better than Lazar the tremendous amounts of time and nurture each change would require. He expected miracles. "A seed doesn't become a tree overnight," she told him often, but it was not the kind of analogy he either believed or adopted, and he treated her convictions with scorn.

Hannah and Lazar had begun to lead very separate lives. When she would arrive home, he would depart, as though each were only punching a time clock to mind the children. They were like boarders in the same house who discussed only mealtimes or the need for certain supplies, unless either one had news about Minna and Chaim, for they both had developed a riveting interest in the minutiae of Hannah's brother's marriage and manner of life.

At first Chaim had become involved with one of the more loosely organized Am Olam groups, until Minna, whose own disordered plans and dreams were magnified in the chaos of the Kiev group's communal house, appeared on the scene. After a brief attempt to work reforms on the regular members, she convinced Chaim to help organize a different branch by arguing that order would yield productivity.

Minna had been right. Instead of working for wages, a fact that had frustrated every group member forced to do a share of the labor, they organized their own laundry on Henry Street. Her reforms also included eliminating all meats from the kitchen, a political code that embraced atheism and anarchy, and new-found feminism. She even went so far as to proclaim that she had obtained and was using a birth-control device from a clinic on Amboy Street in Brooklyn.

Although Lazar denounced his brother-in-law's association with anarchists like Katz and Zolatoroff, he could not hide his admiration for Chaim's freedom from any conventions of habitat, diet, or marriage. And while Minna was younger than Hannah, her sister-in-law made her feel inexperienced and backward. In fact, Hannah had no idea what birth-control device Minna could possibly be using, but her curiosity about it was dimmed by the lack of time she had for a day-long trip to the Brooklyn clinic, doubts about both its effectiveness and safety, and the disturbing admission that she herself hardly needed such a thing, since the other conflicts in her marriage had virtually ended any lovemaking.

Yet, with all the difficulties, Hannah had made an effort to maintain a certain warmth in their home. Even when they disagreed with each other, they both attempted to remain constant and sunny when the children were around. But after Jacob was given away, it became more difficult for Hannah to hold her tongue, and even when she did, Lazar caught the restrained bitterness and was quick to find the precise words to undo her further.

Knowing that Hannah felt guilty when her work took her away from the children, he would point out a bruise she hadn't noticed, that the baby's shoes were too tight, or the fact he had washed out a soiled pair of panties when she hadn't been home. In defense Hannah remained away as long as possible. Every additional dollar earned was put away. Hoarding her money, her time, and affections, Hannah moved further and further apart from her husband.

Until Jacob left their home, no quarrel had been severe enough to keep her separated from Lazar in bed. Even if Hannah began the night precariously balancing herself at the edge to avoid touching him, by morning she would find her arms around his shoulders, her ankles entwined with his. Now she was so often thoroughly repelled that the gulf between them remained all night, though neither slept as well as they pretended they had.

One morning a particularly vehement argument started because Hannah had allowed Benny to cut a picture from a newspaper that Lazar wanted to save. Thus they began their day as unpleasantly as they had finished the last one.

"You must be kinder to Benny today," Hannah hissed. "I had to take him to the toilet twice last night and you know how sound a sleeper he usually is. Poor thing probably thinks you are still angry with him when he wasn't doing anything wrong."

"Why is it always something I did?"

"Lazar, he's just a small boy, but he understands more than you think!"

"More than his mother . . ." Lazar muttered.

"What?" she said, unwilling to let the remark go unchallenged.

Lazar swung his legs over the bed and turned his back to Hannah. "He understands more about me than you do. He knows I wasn't angry with him. It's your lack of interest that frustrates me. You knew I was saving that paper and you deliberately let him have it!"

"It was with the others you had already read!"

"Hadn't I pointed out the article by Berkman?"

"We've been over that already. How many times more . . . ?"

"Useless! Useless to continue with you. You only hear what you want. Nothing I do makes any difference to you, to anyone here. Why am I wasting my time when there is so much to be done?"

Hannah began slowly to unbraid her hair, combing out the larger knots with her fingers. The long black strips fell down her back and shoulders. "I'm not exactly content either. Do you think I want to spend the rest of my life in these close, dark rooms?"

"What you want and what I want are entirely different. There's a glint of gold behind those green eyes of yours! You want to be like Eva and your Aunt Sonia. Move uptown! More rooms, more windows, higher rents! A new sofa would make you happy, wouldn't it? A green one. And when you grew tired of that you'd want a red one. First in velvet, then . . . brocade. Isn't that what those fancy Karps have? You wouldn't stop until you had what they have. And they aren't stopping until they have more. You only look forward, never back. You don't see the heads you are climbing over, pushing further into the dust."

"No one harms anyone intentionally. We wouldn't have to be like the Karps to do better for the children!"

"The children! We will do more for them by leaving the world a better place. Let the revolution come while they are still young enough to reap the rewards of the stable productive society that will follow! You and I want very different lives; you want to better yourself, but I want to better the world!"

"Everything isn't perfect in America, but look how quickly progress can be made. Why would anyone fight against the system that has been so kind already?"

"Exactly! Even your brother, with all his talk and ideals, has fallen prey to the false prophets. But I have not been deceived! All over the world a movement is taking place that we can join. Vienna! Moscow! London! These are the progressive cities! That is where history will be made in the next decade!"

Until Lazar mentioned Europe, Hannah had felt he was just off on another of his endless arguments, but something about the intensity and clarity of his speech made her tremble. She walked around the bed and faced the intensity of his gaze. "You are but one man. Do you think you can fight the whole world?"

"Someone must make a stand. One man. Then another. That's how it begins." He stared out across the room as though a horizon were in sight. "I won't be alone, I assure you."

Slowly Hannah approached Lazar and knelt before him, her nightdresss tangling under her knees. "Everyone thinks they are strong, invincible. But every man, even the bravest, the tallest, the most finely equipped soldier, has but a human body filled with blood and bones. One blow, one bullet . . . You've seen for yourself how little it can take to destroy life."

Seeing Hannah at his feet, Lazar felt he could be kind. He raised her up and pulled her onto his knee. "I know what I must do; I must finish the work I began in Odessa!"

"You would go back there?"

"That is where my people still need me the most!"

"You'd be arrested within a week of your return."

"There have been reforms. Stolypin . . . the Duma . . . all have more authority. Now workers are able to form legal trade unions, true political parties are permitted to exist, a strong undercurrent is forming. I want to be there when it all comes together to form the united party we have been creating."

"United party? What is this nonsense?"

"You'd know everything if you had been listening to me for the last few months."

He was right. It had always been there, seething under the surface like a rising bowl of dough. No matter how often she pushed it, kneaded it back down, it always rose again.

"Perhaps afterward you will understand," he was saying with condescension in his voice.

"Afterward?" Hannah whispered.

"I am going back, Hannah. There is nothing you can do to keep me here a day longer than I want to stay."

Hannah jumped off his lap and whirled across the room. Agitated, she paced from one corner to the other trying to respond quickly to his insane ideas. "No one goes back! All the leaders are here!" She stopped and reconsidered her last sentence. So, that was it! He would take the place of those who had departed, fill vacated seats, become important more quickly. She could beg him to stay, plead with him, protest that his children needed their father.

For a moment she stared at him and then walked purposefully into the kitchen, put a kettle on to boil, found some eggs and cracked them very slowly into a cup and mixed in some stale bread to make Benny's favorite breakfast. Her knees felt sore from the hard floor. She had been down on her knees almost begging him to stay with her! Hadn't she suffered enough since he had agreed to marry her because of Benny?

From the open doorway she could hear Lazar dressing. He was waiting for her pleas, but she would give him no such satisfaction. She poured a glass of boiling tea and slammed it on the table. Lazar sauntered in and sat down.

Hannah stood in front of him, her eyes slightly above the level of his forehead. "Go then! Do what you must! I won't stand in your way! But" — she turned and walked back to the stove and spoke as she ladled the beaten eggs into the hot pan, her words sizzling as well — "don't come to me for your fare! I've paid for everything else, but I won't support your self-destruction!"

Lazar had taken a slow sip of the boiling liquid, holding it in his mouth till it cooled, but the impact of her words forced him to swallow and burn his throat. He opened his mouth in a gasp and then recovered. "Don't worry. The return ticket is less than a third of the crossing. The boats go back so empty they are happy to have any paying passengers."

For a moment Hannah could see nothing but blackness. "One-third of the fare!" Her ears rang with the impact of his words. Perhaps he was serious if he had already checked the price of a ticket! Impossible! Lazar was a talker, not a doer. Everyone knew that. Everyone said that. Didn't they?

## · 4 ·

AFTER SHE RECOVERED from her shock at Lazar's wild plan, she knew he had been bluffing. She had not argued further, she had not capitulated, so she thought she had won. The assumption of victory allowed Hannah to rise from her gloomy state without rancor. Lazar was no longer the villain, the opponent; he needed sympathy. To make amends Hannah spent the morning rolling paper-thin strudel leaves, preparing a spicy meat filling, then stuffing flag-folded triangles and baking each with an extra painting of melted butter. Though Lazar didn't mention that this was the first time in more than a year she had prepared his favorite dish, he didn't hesitate to eat seven and visibly enjoy every mouthful.

During their reunion in the center of the bed later that evening, Hannah thought she understood even more about Lazar, for he was the opposite of the docile forfeiter of the morning, taking his wife with more force and more imagination than usual. He began by deliberately stroking her to melt any reserve that had grown between them during their estrangement. When she was thoroughly suffused with a burning heat, he poised himself like an archer, bowed her thighs, and entered her swiftly.

Through experience he knew exactly what Hannah was feeling, but just as he guessed she was about to climax, Lazar made a point of withdrawing. He paused a few savage seconds, waiting for her to beg him with thrusting hips to come back within. Then he complied, expertly bringing her back to the same precarious place. Again and again he would start her, stop her, turning her from front to back, from side to side. Then, when his own fever could no longer be suppressed, he stayed with her, pounding wildly, since she did not beg him to stop. At the clutch of her first spasm, he shuddered violently and plunged more deeply than he had ever dared before. Without regret Hannah had assented to his every demand and followed his lead completely. Between that morning and that evening, Hannah believed they had truly found a balance.

They slept entwined. Curiously, neither was disturbed the whole night, not by a child, not by a patient, and not by one of Lazar's terrors. Hannah's dreams tumbled together without interruption, and in the morning she felt so heavy and peaceful she could hardly rouse herself at the usual time though Lazar had already left their bed. Hannah slipped over to his place, still warm and indented from his body. "He must be down the hall in the toilet room," she silently mused. "He likes to get there early before too many people come knocking on the door. He'll probably come back to bed," she thought languidly before she slipped back to sleep.

"Mama, Emma's pishy." Benny squirmed next to his mother and held his nose.

Hannah turned toward him, ruffled his curls, and kissed the nape of his neck. Emma was calling, but not yet crying, so she hugged her boy for an extra moment to forestall leaving the warm bed. Just like Lazar not to change her if he could avoid it. The space beside her was cold. "Lazar!"

"Papa's out," Benny said, idly patting his mother's face in a gesture identical to the one she sometimes used to stroke him awake.

"Must have gone for the papers," Hannah mumbled, curling her toes in search of her slippers.

There was no soiled glass on the table or in the sink. Hannah felt the kettle. Cold. The coals in the stove hadn't yet been turned and there was only the barest glow left from the night before, so Hannah tended the fire. She'd make an especially large breakfast: oatmeal with butter and raisins, a fresh pot of tea, and two of the pastries she had managed to reserve from the night before. Lazar would bring back the papers and read them all before noon. She'd stay home, tell some stories to Benny during Emma's nap, start a vegetable soup. Only Mrs. Ginzburg at two and Mrs. Sachs at three were scheduled for massages.

Benny ate his oatmeal, plopping in extra raisins when his mother wasn't paying attention. Emma was washed and nursed. She even accepted a few spoons of cereal without protest. Such a good baby, always happy to please. When Emma became occupied with the effort of rolling herself first to the left and then to the right, Hannah allowed herself to wonder where Lazar had gone so early.

The tea grew cold in her glass. Emma had fallen back to sleep and Benny tugged at her sleeve wanting to be amused. "Not now!" she said hoarsely and pushed him aside. She went to the closet. Anything missing? Only Lazar's woolen jacket, but he probably would have worn it anyway. Her eye fixed on a pile of books he had been studying. Was it somehow shorter? Had he taken a few volumes back to the library? Hard to tell; she rarely paid attention to his voracious reading.

The edge of a brown strap peeked out from under their bed. "Oh! Oh, no!" she shouted and fell to her knees. The strap fastened the wicker case that held their official documents, the papers they so rarely needed in America. On top of the pile lay Hannah's license to practice midwifery; then came their immigration documents and applications for naturalization and the children's birth certificates. Hannah found her fading yellow inspection card marked with the big red letters JJ. She rifled the papers a second and third time. Lazar's inspection card was gone, as were his Russian documents and the certificate he had received from the night school on Rivington Street.

Too dizzy to stand, Hannah eased herself up onto the edge of their mattress. How could he leave without saying anything to her or the children? How could he have been so loving last night when all the while he had been planning this? He must have at least written something down, but where was it? As though her hand were being guided, it slipped under her pillow and grasped the folded piece of paper she had sensed might be there. She held it in her hand a long while before daring to open it.

He had ripped the last page from a book of Bialik's poetry, a desecration almost as shocking as the words.

> What is thy business here, O son of man?
> Rise, to the desert flee!
> The cup of affliction thither bear with thee!
> Take thou thy soul, rend it in many a shred!
> With impotent rage, thy heart deform!
> Thy tear upon the barren boulders shed!
> And send thy bitter cry into the storm!

"Damn him!" she shouted aloud before crumbling the paper and tossing it at the wall. "He leaves his wife, his children and begs for pity!" She shouted so loudly that Benny came running and buried his head in her lap to be consoled in case he had done something to warrant her fury.

"Don't worry, Benny, don't worry."

Anxious to keep busy, she ripped the blanket from the bed and shook it out the air shaft until her arms ached and then remade the bed with painstaking precision. After she had fluffed each wrinkle from the pillows, she replaced the lumpier, thicker one on Lazar's side, the thinner one on hers. Useless! Lazar would never again lay his head there! Her fingers reached for the pillow's center and dented it slightly. Never again? Impossible! Though she knew that Lazar could leave her after all the bitterness between them, she did not believe he could forsake his children. They would draw him back eventually. Once he overcame this passion to do something, once his illusions had been shattered . . .

From the closeness of their bedroom Hannah rushed into the front parlor. Everything looked wrong! Frantically she began to clean. After hours of rearranging the apartment, she was finally hungry. She found two potatoes and put them on to boil. Potatoes would be enough for her and Benny. Hannah checked her watch. Almost four o'clock. She had forgotten her massage appointments! Her head broke out in a fierce pounding. When she closed her eyes internal sparks threatened her; when she opened them they blurred. No! She would not allow herself to cry about this! What had Lazar really contributed? Certainly no money! If he had been home they would have needed four potatoes, some herring or cheese, sour pickles, a fresh pot of tea. For herself she could get by with much less. Now they'd have the same income and need less food. It made so much sense Hannah wondered why she could not accept her own arguments.

It was many hours later when she was exhausted enough from a last attempt at rearranging the furniture to go to bed. Finally she was too tired to think and tried to surrender to the numbness of the night.

What had the poem meant? "With impotent rage, thy heart deform . . . And send thy bitter cry into the storm." How could she have given him more, prevented this? Rachael would know what to do . . . I'll ask Rachael . . . And with that small hopeful thought, she fell asleep.

## · 5 ·

THERE WAS A FEELING of pressure, something pushing her shoulders downward, like a roosting bird that would not be shooed away. Comfort. She craved it as much as her children did, and for a moment she was more sympathetic to their nightly wanderings.

As though she expected something to happen, she sat up in bed and waited. In a remarkably short time she heard footsteps in the hallway. Probably someone using the toilet. No. They stopped in front of her door and someone tapped lightly. Someone having a baby? The children! How could she go out now and leave them?

It sounded as though the door was opening slightly. She was thankful she had bolted it from the inside with the chain lock. She wrapped herself in her shawl and stumbled to the kitchen. "I'm coming!" she called in a loud whisper.

The only light in the room was a faint glow from the coals in the stove that danced on the ceiling and was reflected in the nickel trim along the top of the warming oven. In the dimness she saw a familiar boot in the door. "Aye!" she cried as soon as she saw the face.

"Won't you let me in?"

Though her fingers felt thick and clumsy, Hannah finally unlatched the chain and pulled Lazar inside. On the floor he placed a small canvas sack containing the few items he had selected for his journey. Then he reached around Hannah with his strong arms and lifted her as though she were a precious bundle. He carried her over to a kitchen chair and arranged her on his lap, kissing and stroking her head with his lips while his hands renewed their memory of her body.

For a long while all Hannah heard was the sound of his breath like a hot wind across her ears. "I was on the *Carpathia* by seven this morning," he finally said with great reluctance. "I watched them load the cargo all morning. We were set to sail at two with the tide. Suddenly all my secret plans seemed ridiculous. I could think of nothing but you. I tried to convince myself that it would be for the best; you and I . . . we've had our troubles. Then I knew that everything was my fault . . . I created them to have an excuse to return to Russia, yet once it was within my reach, I didn't want it . . ."

". . .The children. You came back for them, didn't you?" Hannah said, holding herself perfectly still so she might feel his slightest reaction to her words.

"Think that if you must, but the truth is that I love you beyond them and everything else. As I watched the freight being loaded into the hold, I remembered how frightened you were when I came to you in steerage. You hadn't trusted me to be there then . . ." Lazar's voice began to shatter and he coughed to regain control.

There was nothing she could say. He said he had come back because of her, though in her heart she believed something else: he had been too afraid to leave, too unsure of where he would go or what he would find. Yet his actions revealed more sense than cowardice.

"Where have you been all day?" Hannah inquired with a false casualness.

"Waiting. Walking. Wondering . . . wondering what to do to make you forgive me so we could begin again."

"There's one thing . . ." Hannah said, kissing his cheek and winding her arms around his neck. "No, two . . ." She smiled to take the sting away from the requests. "You need work; not for me, not for money, but for yourself. I was thinking you might teach."

"Who would want me?"

"Maybe a university?" she said suddenly, for the idea had just begun to form and she hadn't considered all the possibilities.

"I don't know if I'd qualify!"

"If doctors teach obstetrics who have never delivered a baby," Hannah said quickly, "there must be a place for Professor Sokolow, the esteemed linguist!"

From the way Lazar clasped her hand, she thought he was accepting the idea very well. Teaching would give him a special status, a place to go, a small income that would seem respectable even to the most socialistic of his compatriots.

"And?" Lazar asked expectantly.

"What?"

"You said there were two favors."

"I need to know why." She hesitated. "Why the nightmares, why you needed to go back, why you never explained it to me!"

"You never asked!"

"Until . . . until I read the poem I didn't know the question."

"If you thought the Odessa pogrom was the worst . . . if you had seen . . ."

"Kishinev!" Hannah said aloud.

Lazar's hands tightened on her wrists and his palms suddenly felt moist and cold. He nodded.

"You thought that if you hadn't been in Odessa, you might have been able to prevent it? Or . . ." Hannah had a second guess that seemed more pointed toward the truth. "Or that if you had been there you might have died with them?"

At first Hannah thought her gropings had finally penetrated the mystery, until Lazar vehemently shook his head.

"No . . . you don't understand . . ."

"Then tell me!" Her voice was shrill with impatience.

Lazar's lips moved, but the words would not come. A spasm cracked his cheeks as his breath was pulled inside and held there for a long moment. "I've left a mark in the book for you for years. You've never found it," he accused.

Hannah held her head in her hands and slipped off his lap. "Riddles, games . . . What mark, what book?"

"Bialik. Kishinev. Didn't you find the page I left for you? 'The City of Slaughter.' You've read it. Don't you know?"

Hannah had read the whole poem once, but had been too disturbed by the graphic brutality to read it again.

Lazar walked into the front parlor, starting to sit in his armchair, but bumped into a table instead. "Where's my . . . ?"

"I've rearranged the furniture," she said impatiently. "Everything will be different now." She was still waiting . . . waiting . . .

He settled back in his favorite chair. "I was in Kishinev for Passover. I had gone home to show my parents how I had changed; to tell them I was dedicating my life to the Bund. That was when I had shaved my beard, cut my payess, abandoned the yeshiva. No longer would I be their prodigy, their wonder!

"My mother didn't recognize me at first and my father would not sit beside me. I wasn't ashamed of the effect I was having on them; I was pleased that they so clearly saw my defection.

"We were to have the seder that night at my uncle's in the town. The whole family, except Uncle Moishe, had gathered and the women were finishing the preparations for the meal," he continued without stopping. "The organized bands were preceded by urchins throwing stones at the windows. I ran out the back, down the alleys, trying to find some of the boys I knew from school to help me, but no one would listen. They said the bishop had promised there would be no difficulties, but there was something different in the air. I could smell it!"

"You were there?" Hannah said under her breath. "I never knew!"

Lost in the world of his own memories, Lazar didn't hear or respond. "No one recognized me for a Jew. In my student cap and trousers I could walk the streets as freely as the others while the 'work' was going on."

Hannah nodded, remembering her first glimpse of his youthful Slavic features: the high cheekbones and eyes the color of the sky, his Russian hair style and height. The fact that he was a Jew but didn't look a Jew had not only made him so attractive to her but had saved his life.

"The pogrom began like all the rest: looting, riots, broken windows. No one suspected the butchery that would come. I followed the bands ... watching, once having to throw a few rocks with them to save revealing myself. No one noticed how badly I aimed. Then when I heard about some brutalities in our quarter I ran through the back streets ..."

Lazar didn't continue and Hannah didn't ask. She sat on the edge of his chair and touched his arm. A long time passed before he said two incongruous statements, the last she would ever hear on either subject. "I don't like the parlor this way." Then, "There were fourteen of us in town for the seder, all gone. Three sisters, four brothers, cousins, my father, and ... when I found my mother, she had spikes driven into her head."

Once the words had been spoken, once the image had been formed in her mind, she only wished the secret had been kept. Now she knew that concealment could be a gift instead of a deception. Hannah would rather not have known, not have understood so acutely.

At least Lazar had returned to her and the children. She admitted her relief in having him back. He was familiar, comfortable, and, most important, he was hers because he had come home for her. In the few short hours she had believed him gone Hannah had realized exactly what it was she wanted from him: to stay with her as a "husband" because that was what made her "a wife"; to help raise their children so they would know their own benevolent intellectual father; to be beside her in the night. Not so much to do, to earn, to give as to be — to be there. Everything else she could do for herself.

## · 6 ·

IT TOOK BUT A WORD to Beatrice Karp to secure a teaching position for Lazar. Mortimer Karp had served on several university committees, and although he had not given a substantial sum to New York University, he felt it was time he did so. It gave him more pleasure to give money in direct association with a return on his investment. Hospitals that cared for friends and family were more likely to receive donations than those that merely courted his pocketbook, and so a school that agreed to employ the husband of a woman who had done so much for him would enjoy his attention to its financial needs for many years to come.

Within a few weeks it was arranged. There was a position open for an associate professor of German at New York University's men's campus in the Bronx. With his knowledge of literature far outranking his sense of grammar, Lazar was given all the courses on the history of German literature, and he began to develop an esoteric specialty: the Gothic period to the time of Klopstock.

The salary was minimal, but with his new professorial status Lazar received benefits: he was welcome at faculty meetings and lectures, could purchase books and supplies at reduced costs, could use the library and research facilities, and even became eligible for subsidized housing in the neighborhood.

More than that, Lazar had a title, a profession, and a purpose. Students felt welcomed in his presence. They listened attentively to his discourses on politics and literature, amazed at the proliferation of quotes he had ready for every argument. He challenged their perceptions of literature by denying ready interpretations of Lessing, Gleim, Ut, and the later Prussian poets. He uncovered new shades of meaning for words and phrases, making language more than a grammatical collection of nouns and verbs, but a melodious form of expression that reflected history and culture with every newly memorized word. Utilizing all the persuasive skills that had won him a place in the revolutionary movement, Lazar began to find the respect for which he had always searched developing among his students. Though he still wore the same battered comfortable clothes, Hannah noticed that he polished his shoes, whistled as he arrived home, and more often than not, slept soundly at night.

❖　❖　❖

Chanukah came early that year, and though the family usually only celebrated with sweets for the children and a heaping plate of potato pancakes, they had been invited to the Karps' to share the holiday with six-month-old Solomon. Now that he had a child, Mortimer Karp was tempted by the array of things he could shower upon his "little miracle," and a party was the ideal excuse. Beatrice had suggested that the Sokolows join them, first so Hannah could see how well Solomon was growing, so proud was she that the child's rich plumpness had come solely from the breast milk she alone provided, and second because she knew that Mortimer's generosity was bound to extend to Hannah's less fortunate children.

Beatrice had arranged the dining room so that the children could eat with the family. Even the infant Solomon was propped on cushions at the table. The centerpiece was a pyramid of brightly colored boxes that were opened as soon as everyone was seated, totally disrupting the service of the hot cherry soup with tiny egg drops. Although the kitchen girls fluttered about removing ribbons and box lids, everyone seemed more entranced with the fascinating assortment of playthings than with the traditional meal.

Hannah assisted Beatrice in opening the baby's gifts, beginning with a sensible group of celluloid chime rattles. Next there was a metal canary whistle that Benny appropriated. When Lazar tried to take it away, Mortimer insisted the boy keep it. Then Hannah unwrapped a brass drum, which Emma pounded in delight with two wooden sticks. Benny howled so loudly he also wanted a drum that Mortimer helped him open a Rubenstein toy piano finished in rosewood. With his plump fingers Benny began to plunk out a tune while Emma pummeled the drum and Solomon tried to shake his noisiest rattle.

Beatrice held her ears and laughed, "Geniuses, musical prodigies all of them!" But she did not ask them to stop. Instead the nurse and her assistant carried them off to the parlor while the adults enjoyed the meal.

When Emma and Solomon required feeding, Hannah and Beatrice went up to the nursery to attend the babies; Benny was permitted back in the dining room with the men. As soon as the infants were greedily sucking, Beatrice remarked, "You remember Sondra Belinsky? She is due very soon!"

"I've not been asked to check on her, so I've lost track of her dates."

"I told her that it was ridiculous for her not to have the best when the time came, but she . . . she said she was too embarrassed by the terrible scene she made at Solomon's bris to ever ask you to attend her again."

"When women are pregnant they may act quite differently than they would otherwise." Hannah worked on her phrasing. "If she is not comfortable with me, it is best she select someone else."

"You are so understanding," Beatrice said with a warm gush of words. "Your patience, your kindness . . . I don't see how you can be so gracious."

Though Hannah smiled demurely, her thoughts were quite different. "I delivered Gertrude and I would dearly love to deliver the next one as well, so it's a pity she feels as she does. I suppose she'll be going to a hospital for twilight sleep."

"No. Sondra wants a midwife, to spite her father-in-law, who thinks she should go to the hospital. One thing he cannot dictate is how she will have the child!"

"You've seen her lately?"

"Yes, often. She won't be confined! Not that I believe that a woman in her advanced condition should hide in closets, but until last week she attended every party and tea."

"Then she must be feeling very well!"

"Not to hear her tell it! She is filled with complaints, though I don't doubt she is miserable, for I've never seen anyone so enormous. Even her face is bloated. And her clothing! She had some velvet shifts made up especially, quite original . . . and . . . Well, I would never wear them out in public . . . but a Belinsky can do as she wishes!"

"If she is as large as you say, perhaps she will have twins," Hannah said wistfully.

"You would still like to deliver her, wouldn't you?"

"Of course!"

"Then I'll speak to her about it again. I've never heard of the woman she's selected."

"Who is that?"

"Klingerman? Fingerhut? I don't remember for certain."

"Fingerman?"

"That sounds like the name. Do you know her?"

"Yes, I worked with her when I first began in New York."

"Then she must be very good!"

Better not criticize another midwife openly, Hannah decided, for even if the words were true it might sound as though she were jealous of the competition. "She's very experienced."

"But not as proficient as you are, I am certain!" Mrs. Karp said sweetly.

Hannah tilted her head. "I've had more formal training, perhaps, but I am certain Mrs. Belinsky will have an easy time. Even her first delivery was uneventful."

"That is what she fully expects!" Beatrice said in a throaty voice. "How that woman can plan! She's already ordered the food for the bris!"

"Then I hope she also arranged to give birth to a boy!" Hannah said as she buttoned her blouse and tucked her sleeping baby into the waiting crib.

During the party, a heavy snow had fallen. When Mortimer finally asked that the carriage be prepared, the driver explained how slippery the streets had become and wondered if it might not be better to wait until morning, when a journey with tiny children might be less precarious.

Even Lazar did not resist the offer to stay the night. They were treated to delicate smoked salmon at midnight and given an elegant guest room in which a blazing fire had been lit. Benny and Emma were welcomed into Solomon's nursery, and Hannah was told they would be tended all evening and she would only be disturbed in case of emergency. With the special gift of not having to be vigilant through the night, as well as being sated by the fine food and drink, Hannah tumbled between the Karps' silken sheets with Lazar, who happily refrained from political comments regarding their decadent evening.

❖   ❖   ❖

In the morning the snow continued to fall as they were driven home by sleigh. Even the ugly streets of the Lower East Side were blanketed under twelve inches of fresh white powder that made the dowdiest buildings seem beautiful. Footprints and wagon tracks were almost instantly filled in, freshening the streets; and as soon as the drifts reached the windowsills, children began tunneling through the packing snow rather than trying to walk over it. Lazar's classes were canceled, or so he assumed, for it was impossible to travel by trolley.

With nothing else to do, Hannah mounded flour in a bowl, broke a few eggs in the center well, added spoonfuls of water, and began to make a rich noodle dough. By the time Lazar and Benny returned from playing in the street, she was shaking loose the fine-cut noodles and spreading the long strips on a floured cloth to dry before cooking. The late afternoon light cast long purple shadows over the street; the shouts of mothers calling their children in were muffled by insulating snow. The world was softer, gentler. She hugged Benny close and gave him a loud kiss on the cheek.

A jingling sound outside the window caused Benny to push away from his mother. "Look, Papa, another sleigh!"

Lazar went to see what had excited the child. "It's stopping here! Maybe the Karps are having another party tonight!"

"Hurray!" Benny chimed.

A knock on the door confirmed that the driver had been sent to the Sokolows, but he wanted only the midwife. Benny moaned his disappointment and buried his face in Lazar's lap.

"Who is it?" Hannah asked as she dusted flour from her hands.

"Mr. Belinsky asked if you would come as a favor to him."

Hannah looked to Lazar for an explanation. He shrugged his shoulders. "Maybe she couldn't find anyone else?"

"If I know Mrs. Belinsky, it's probably only a false alarm, and I'll be back to have a late supper with you," she said as she bundled out into the cold.

· 7 ·

THE CONTINUOUS SNOW had transformed the city. Everything moved more slowly and the only brightness was dots of colorful woolens worn by those adventuresome or desperate enough to venture outdoors. As the sleigh glided uptown, the setting sun appeared at eye level, causing the ice-encrusted trees to sparkle as Hannah was whisked by.

The sleigh's runners sang out when they scraped frozen patches, but they were hardly detained by even small mountains of drifting snow. Hannah wished she could slow her uptown journey to give her more time to prepare mentally for the case. Why had she been called? A hundred reasons presented themselves, and she began to narrow her theories to the possibility that, once in labor, Mrs. Belinsky had sought the familiar care of the midwife who had delivered her first child under unusual circumstances. Or, just as likely, Mrs. Fingerman had been sent for first but could not be found, since many people had been displaced by the blizzard. No matter whether she was the first or second choice midwife, she had the job just as she was meant to from the beginning! No birth was more desired, no baby was more "hers," and to deliver the Belinsky heir would be the final jewel in her crown! The Karp child, the Belinsky baby; together they would make her the most sought-after midwife in New York!

In her mind Hannah tried to picture Mrs. Belinsky. Hadn't Mrs. Karp suggested that she had grown uncommonly large in her last weeks. Twins! It still could be possible. Twin sons! What a triumph that would be for Nathaniel!

By the time the sleigh glided up to the front door of the Belinsky mansion, Hannah was glowing with the fantasy of delivering two healthy male children in a few short hours. Without waiting for help from the driver, she tossed the fur covers from her lap and stepped out onto the swept curb, but the leather of her boot slipped on a small patch of ice and she fell backward into a stone balustrade. Though the back of her head stung as she was helped up by the Belinskys' butler and driver, she protested that she was not hurt.

The two men half carried, half walked her into the front hall, dusting her cloak and fussing at her until she convinced them she was unharmed. Instead of being directed to Mrs. Belinsky's chambers as she had expected, she was ushered into Mr. Belinsky's study on the second floor.

The shades were drawn and only a small lamp burned on the desk, casting gloomy shadows onto the ceiling. In a few seconds a wooden door opened at the far side of the room near the bay windows and Belinsky appeared. Even the dim light could not be blamed for the odd color of his skin. The once aristocratic pallor that offset his oiled mustache had turned bilious. Large grey pouches sagged under his eyes, and Hannah perceived how the man would look thirty years hence.

"Thank you for coming," he said solemnly. "I wasn't certain you would."

Hannah stepped in front of his desk. "How could I refuse to help you?"

"I didn't know what else to do. Shifre is too weak to decide anything for herself, and Mrs. Fingerman says she doesn't need to go to the hospital. Shifre didn't want to leave home either, but now . . ." he said, shrinking into the chair beside his desk. Then he sighed, reached for a silver letter opener, and rubbed the blade in his hands.

Like a mother protecting a child from harm, Hannah took it from him and replaced it in its leather holder. "When did it begin?"

"What?" he asked.

"The labor."

Nathaniel bent his head and rubbed the back of his neck. He was almost too exhausted to explain. "Before the snow began, that afternoon."

"Wednesday night was the first night of Chanukah," Hannah tried to clarify. "There was a light snow before sundown and then it became worse. This is Thursday afternoon. Was it Wednesday?"

"Before that. Tuesday. I had gone to the site, checked the girders for the upper stories, and came home to have lunch with Shifre. She's been in bed for over a week now."

Hannah tried to define the situation further. "So you came home Tuesday and she was in labor?"

"I asked if she had pains and she said she thought so, but she wasn't certain. She was very confused. So I sent for Mrs. Fingerman. But the midwife didn't arrive until later that evening."

"Did she think your wife was in labor?"

"Not at first. But when she saw how bloated she had become and heard her complaints she said she could do something to bring it on faster."

"Break the waters?" Hannah asked.

"Something that wouldn't hurt her or the baby, that is all I know. Apparently it worked because that night . . ."

Hannah interrupted, "Tuesday night?"

"Yes, Tuesday, before midnight, the pains began. I heard her crying out all night long. Mrs. Fingerman said it would be better if I stayed away. I told her I had been with my wife when Gertrude was born, but she said it was woman's work . . . I didn't want to be in the way . . . but still I couldn't sleep. Awful sounds! Well, you know that Shifre isn't the strongest, bravest . . ."

"So she has been laboring almost forty-eight hours and the child has not been delivered?"

"Mrs. Fingerman said that sometimes it can take this long, particularly when the mother becomes overtired and cannot sleep."

Hannah's breath came in rapid little bursts as she tried to think of what might be happening without indicting the other woman too harshly.

"Does Mrs. Fingerman know you've called me?"

"No! There is something about that woman I didn't like from the first. She's like one of the old witches who were paid to mourn beside my mother's coffin!" He groaned.

"Maybe you didn't like her because she wasn't me!" Hannah said to tease him out of his pessimism.

When he stared at her directly, she thought he was going to smile; instead his black eyes shimmered with tears and he covered his face with his hands in shame. "What have I done to her?"

In a vague effort to pacify him Hannah handed back the letter opener before abruptly heading for Mrs. Belinsky's chambers on the floor above.

Nothing Belinsky said had prepared her for what she was about to see.

Mrs. Belinsky lay flat on her back, her feet poking through a haphazard tangle of bedclothes. She was grossly swollen; her skin was the color of flour paste. Hannah gasped and, without a moment's hesitation, tossed the remaining covers to the floor to see if the bloated corpselike body was even alive. Placing her hand next to the woman's mouth, Hannah was rewarded by short pants of fetid breath. Mrs. Belinsky's tongue appeared coated, and her pulse was rapid with an accentuated second heart sound. With the side of her hand, Hannah checked Mrs. Belinsky's reflexes at the kneecap and was unsurprised to find them exaggerated.

Rapidly she began to give orders. "Bring me my instruments! Get me a chair!"

Servants appeared. Hannah knelt on the chair to better examine the woman, who was lying on a high four-poster bed. "When did she urinate last?"

"Not since yesterday," a frightened maid replied.

Hannah placed her stethoscope in her ears and listened to Mrs. Belinsky's chest. "Gottenyu!" Hannah said aloud, then clamped her mouth shut. Never had she heard such marked degeneration!

She turned to the servant who stood beside her stiffly holding Hannah's instrument bag. "Has she had any seizures?"

The girl looked blankly at Hannah.

"Has she had any convulsions?" Hannah said louder to make herself understood.

Still no response.

Grabbing the girl's shoulders, Hannah shook her. "Any tremors? Attacks? Tell me!"

Hannah was shocked by her own vehemence and let her go. Why wouldn't the girl answer? She spoke more slowly, and then as the words formed she realized she had been screaming at the maid in Yiddish. "Has ... she ... been ... shaking?" she repeated slowly in English.

The girl nodded.

"Elsa, you may go now," a stern voice said. "Now, Mrs. Sokolow, may I answer some questions for you?"

From her awkward kneeling position, Hannah glanced over her shoulder and saw Mrs. Fingerman standing at the far side of the room. The other midwife had dressed immaculately for a delivery in a wealthy man's home. She wore a fine beaded waist and a sateen skirt with matching fitted jacket; her gold watch was prominently displayed upon her heavy bosom. Mrs. Fingerman walked with such stiff authority that, if it hadn't been for the obvious distress of the patient, Hannah might have been deluded into thinking Mrs. Fingerman knew what was best.

Before speaking, Hannah returned to Mrs. Belinsky's rigid form, placed the bell of her stethoscope firmly above the navel, and listened. Moving it across the great mound she made several other soundings. What she had immediately guessed was now proven. With a peremptory sweep of her hand she shooed the two remaining servants from the room. Then, stepping off the chair, she walked across to Mrs. Fingerman and slapped the rubber tubing of the instrument into her open hand.

"Listen to the fetus!"

"I don't know why you were called!" Mrs. Fingerman whined. "That Belinsky fellow is certainly quick to make a tumult! But of course, all fathers-to-be are nervous, aren't they?" she said with an uncertain laugh.

"I'm a friend of the family," Hannah asserted.

"Then why didn't they call you first?" she asked in a singsong voice.

"I am supposed to consult you about the condition of the mother and the baby. Let's begin with the baby."

Although Mrs. Fingerman was clumsy with the stethoscope, she did manage to insert it in her ears, untwist the tubing, and listen. "These things never work right!" she complained as she fumbled with the earpieces.

"The baby is dead!" Hannah said flatly.

"But I hear a rumbling. I haven't found a beat yet, but she is so swollen it muffles the sound."

With a rough pull, Hannah yanked the stethoscope from Fingerman's head. "Dead! For how long? Did you hear fetal sounds when you first examined her? Why isn't she hospitalized? What were you planning to do, wait until *she* died as well? How many convulsions has she had? Why didn't you call a doctor?" Hannah raged on, her fists raised in the air, unable to stop until Mrs. Belinsky reacted by turning her head to one side and opening her mouth.

"What?" Hannah asked, thinking the patient was going to speak. Instead she sighed, her body became rigid and her features distorted, and her arms flopped backward. Her hands clenched and her naked toes flexed, drawing her whole body to the left side in a tonic spasm.

It reminded Hannah of Daniel's epileptic fit, but she was spared a full clonic convulsion. After only a few twitches, Mrs. Belinsky lay quite still, though her eyes were bloodshot and protruding, her lips purple. With her body now completely exposed, Mrs. Belinsky's heart, thumping violently against her chest wall, was clearly visible. Hannah held her wrist until the respirations quieted down.

"That was the worst one yet," Mrs. Fingerman said, surrendering to the truth. "Her labor was making progress until this morning. I thought she would deliver soon."

"But the swellings, the decrease in her urine. You must have recognized that she was a potential eclamptic. If she had been taken to a hospital . . ."

"It wasn't so obvious then as it is now. It happened slowly. I've been here more than two days . . . no sleep. You can't expect one woman to do everything!"

While Mrs. Fingerman defended herself Hannah took Mrs. Belinsky's temperature under her armpit and read it aloud. "One hundred two point six! When did you break the water?"

"How did you know that?"

"When did *you* break the water?" she shouted.

"Tuesday night."

"You'll have to take her to a hospital right now. Explain everything. Maybe they can save this from becoming an even worse disaster. I've never seen one get better unless the whole stinking uterus is removed."

"But no more children . . . She is a young woman!"

"Better to be barren than dead!" Hannah's voice had deepened. "Do you want her life on your conscience as well?"

"I have done nothing . . ."

Hannah pointed her finger at Mrs. Fingerman's face. The woman's loose jowls quivered at the attack and her thinly protected lids fluttered their innocence. "You must transfer her to the hospital; it's the only course left."

"Belinsky called you to relieve me; now she's your responsibility," Mrs. Fingerman said under her breath.

Hannah stopped. She turned her back on the older midwife and looked down at the thick Chinese rug emblazoned with mythical tigers and dragons. Numbly she walked the red flowering trail back to the brass legs of the bed and pulled the covers up over Mrs. Belinsky's deformed body. The pathetic woman was awake, blankly staring at them.

For the first time Hannah spoke directly to Mrs. Belinsky. "I'm here to help you." As Hannah took the frigid hand in hers and stroked her arm she was uncertain whether or not Shifre recognized her. "I'll be with you now. We're going to need more help; that's why you'll come with me to the hospital."

Mrs. Belinsky's dry cracked lips moved painfully. "No, they promised . . ."

"I know, but I will stay with you. I won't let anyone hurt you." Hannah's liquid voice soothed her as well as the patient. "It is for the best, I promise."

Toward the doorway she called, "Tell Mr. Belinsky to prepare the sleigh. We're going to Gouverneur's right now! Have blankets ready, and put all my things back in the bag," Hannah said in one breath, and in the next she crooned to the weak, disheartened woman in her arms. "The snow, have you ever seen snow so high?"

The butler and the sleigh driver carried Mrs. Belinsky, swathed in sheeting and lap robes, while Hannah walked alongside, never letting go of her hand. Belinsky walked downstairs behind the disheveled procession.

"Will she be all right?" His voice was so thin she could barely hear him.

"Just a precaution . . . because of the weather. I need to have a doctor's help with this. Don't worry, she'll be in good hands. I'll stay with her!" Hannah said in a litany. "Don't worry, I'll be with her."

"Shall I come?" he asked as they started out the front door.

Hannah didn't answer because another small attack was occurring that required all her attention. Without even taking his cloak, Belinsky hopped in next to the driver and shouted at him to be off.

Even as she attended to Mrs. Belinsky's seizure in the sleigh, Hannah was able to glimpse something from the corner of her eye. The figure of Mrs. Fingerman, swathed in brown fur and bent against the wind and churning snow, slipped around the opposite corner, fleeing the scene.

As the driver cracked the whip to spur the horses over a slight drift, Belinsky turned back to view Shifre lying in the midwife's lap. His breath and Hannah's and his wife's all visibly mingled in the space over the fur robes and tangled bedclothes. Hannah's presence placated him.

Was his wife conscious of what was happening? The red stare in her eyes led him to believe she was not. Would she be all right?

No, he thought, as he saw Hannah's strained effort to keep every-one calm. This was not merely a precaution. The young midwife was holding something back from him, just as she should, for to destroy his hope would have been like murdering him at that moment. If Shifre should die, he thought, *he* would never forgive himself . . . He would do anything . . . he would take back everything . . . or if she must go . . . at least he would have the baby! Hannah would see to it; Hannah was the best. As the sleigh whipped around a corner, a runner rested on its edge and caused it to tilt. Belinsky's heart jumped, then pounded again: at least he'd have the baby.

## · 8 ·

THE SLEIGH DRIVER had only heard "hospital" and, guessing the seriousness of Mrs. Belinsky's condition, headed directly for the Sloane Hospital for Women only a few blocks away. Though Hannah would have preferred Gouverneur Hospital, where she was known and respected, she dared not protest, for they arrived quite swiftly at the emergency entrance. Four attendants whisked Mrs. Belinsky onto a stretcher and into the green-tiled corridor of the private facility. Immediately a nurse began to unwrap the shivering woman, whose bloated face and purple lips signaled great distress.

Keeping her promise to stay with Mrs. Belinsky, Hannah ran alongside holding onto the covers. As soon as she was wheeled into a treatment room, a doctor appeared and commenced his examination.

To save time, Hannah began quickly to list the patient's symptoms. "This is Sondra Belinsky. She's a multipara two, laboring for forty-eight hours plus. Waters manually broken thirty-six hours plus. Several seizures in the last four hours though she hasn't lost consciousness completely. No urine has been passed in approximately twenty-four hours and the baby . . ."

The doctor, who had been performing his own rapid exams, barely appeared to pay attention to Hannah. He stopped listening to Mrs. Belinsky's heart, turned, and asked perfunctorily, "Who are you?"

"I'm Mrs. Sokolow, a licensed midwife," she said, sounding steadier than she felt.

"And you have been handling this case?"

Hannah paused. How could she explain about Mrs. Fingerman? The permutations and implications of the various answers possible at that moment were too tedious to contemplate. Though later Hannah would remember the moment over and over, wondering how better she might have responded, she simply didn't answer at all.

"You seem to know the case, so you must be aware of the gravity of her situation."

Hannah nodded. "Yes, Doctor . . ."

"Jenks," he said with an edge of contempt. "And that manual rupture of membranes is beyond the authority of your license?"

"I . . ." Hannah could barely express her confused thoughts. She knew she wasn't to blame, but the truth might not seem believable. "It was someone else, before I arrived . . . not my responsibility . . . I only . . ." Hannah fumbled.

Dr. Jenks saw her discomfort as further evidence of her inadequacies. "What you have brought us, then, is the sum total of your failure!" he said, his deep black pupils staring out from the thin slits of his eyes. "For heaven's sake, when will the authorities see the light and outlaw these ignorant women?" he muttered as though she weren't there. Still holding onto Mrs. Belinsky's limp wrist, he performed all the very same tests on it Hannah had when she first appeared at the bedside. Although Hannah was distraught at both the severe nature of the case and her own predicament, she noticed an agitation in the doctor that suggested he also was uncertain of the best course of treatment.

The charge nurse, alerted by the elaborate sleigh and the information taken from Belinsky for the admitting papers, had also summoned the chief of staff, Dr. Campbell, to consult on the case.

"This is an atrocious piece of work!" Dr. Jenks said to brief the administrator. "What do we have here? A rotting fetus, an eclamptic woman who might have had a hundred percent better chance had she been brought to us sooner. If she had been under medical treatment, any doctor would have seen this coming weeks ago and could have begun proper measures!" he railed. "You and your kind," he said to shame Hannah, "have long enslaved women with your superstitious nonsense! But until this moment I've never seen such a clinically pathetic case of neglect and abuse!"

Again Hannah tried to explain. "Another woman, another midwife was there before me . . . I was called too late. As soon as I realized . . ."

Dr. Jenks ran his fingers through his silver hair with one hand and spoke more calmly. "I don't blame you for trying whatever you thought was best. Even though you are not technically permitted, trying to induce labor in a pre-eclamptic woman is a correct procedure if done hygienically and properly." He paused and turned to his colleague. "Of course we have evidence here of sepsis; therefore we cannot rule out the improper technique as well."

"It wasn't I who broke the waters . . . I know better, I was trained at the Imperial College in Moscow . . . I have a certificate . . ."

Taking no interest in her qualifications or denial, the rotund chief of staff, dressed in a pinstripe suit that was too tight, roughly pushed her aside. He lifted Mrs. Belinsky's eyelids with his fingers. "Albert, I think we must go full speed ahead. The girl can be dealt with later."

"Dr. Campbell, are you suggesting we should empty the uterus immediately?" Dr. Jenks replied, arching his craggy brows.

"That would ease the symptoms, but her vital signs are so erratic I think we must deal harshly with the attacking toxins before removing the cause of the affliction."

The two men continued to work together, obviously stimulated and perplexed by the case.

Although Hannah did not leave the room, she tried to be as inconspicuous as possible. All the treatments the doctors suggested were of the most radical nature, but Hannah could see that they had no other course. The mortality rate from eclampsia was at least 20 to 30 percent, and rarely had cases as severe as Mrs. Belinsky's ever resulted in both a living mother and baby. The fact that the child had died gave Hannah some hope for the mother's survival, since the doctors could now proceed without concern for the passenger.

The nurse and doctors worked with bleedings and respiratory equipment while discussing the origins of toxemia. "It must be in the placenta. Why else would all mammals be prey to such a paradox: that a woman can be murdered by the pregnancy formed from her own body?" continued Dr. Jenks as he injected a subdermal solution of 0.7 percent salt into Mrs. Belinsky's leg.

Hannah barely listened to the academic discussion. Instead she intently observed Mrs. Belinsky's worsening color and tone.

"We've got to purge her if we are going to do any surgery!" Dr. Jenks announced.

Though Mrs. Belinsky was conscious part of the time, she barely protested, moaning only as she was turned and wiped and poked. There was something so pathetic about the once vibrant and impossible woman's inability to remonstrate that Hannah truly wished she would respond to the treatments so she might hear her sputter and curse again.

After the first hour of intensive care, she did seem to improve slightly. There were no further seizures and the doctors had begun to talk about the best way to remove the baby, weighing vaginal Caesarean section against the merits of destructive surgery on the baby, which would save the uterus and cause less bleeding, but could risk further infection in an already septic environment.

While they debated, Hannah slipped outside to find Belinsky and explain what was happening.

Belinsky waited on a wooden bench where several other assorted relatives of patients seemed equally agitated. Taking his hand she led him to a more private corner of the large room and spoke gently.

"We did the right thing by bringing her here. She is getting wonderful care."

"Will the baby come soon now?"

"No," Hannah said aloud, then pleaded silently: Don't ask anything else.

Belinsky observed Hannah's face, which she tried to keep immobile so as not to reveal her panic. "Shifre is dying, isn't she?"

"It is very serious, but there is much they can try. She has been responding progressively . . ."

"Why don't they ask me what to do?" he interrupted. "It's for me to decide, isn't it?"

"Since when did you become a doctor, Nathaniel?" Hannah asked without recrimination.

"But it's my wife, my child!"

Hannah watched him grapple with an imaginary decision, though she knew there was none to be made. But if there had been, she thought she guessed what he would have chosen. She felt as though she could not have hurt him more by plunging a knife into his heart. "The baby is gone. A long time now, even before you sent for me."

Reeling back, Belinsky clutched at the straight hard sides of the wall. His fingers scraped the tiles. "There was a baby when you got there!" he accused. "What did you do to her? What did you do?"

"Nothing . . . I arrived too late for the baby!"

"Liar! After all I did for you . . ."

Hearing the commotion, two nurses ran to calm Belinsky, and believing Hannah was aggravating his grief, they called a guard who firmly escorted the midwife outside the hospital.

Hannah looked out across the desolate white landscape. In the lamplight the length of her shadow extended fully across the avenue. Nothing was moving. A brisk wind shot up from between the canyons of buildings and bit at her heels. She had promised she wouldn't leave Mrs. Belinsky, but how could she demand to stay when even the husband didn't wish her there? He had been upset; she couldn't blame his irrational actions. A great feeling of weariness pressed her down. Where would she go that time of night without trolleys or transportation of her own? Only the Karps lived within walking distance. Holding her head down to protect against the howling snow that stung her cheeks with purposeful lashes, Hannah made her way back to the same doorstep she had left that morning, carrying her bundled children and their glorious gifts.

What would happen if all those doctors could not save Mrs. Belinsky? The same delicate flakes that twelve hours before had glistened and smiled at her now rebuked her. She trudged on weary and bereft. By the time Hannah stumbled into the Karp mansion she could not stop shivering, not so much from the cold as from unrelenting terror.

❖   ❖   ❖

For two more days Mrs. Belinsky suffered the massive effects of the eclamptic condition. Though the doctors methodically employed every technique from bleedings to hysterectomy, her pulse remained weak and compressible, her fever elevated daily, her seizures became more frequent and prolonged. In the last hours her lungs swelled, an eerie rattling developed in her chest, and finally the bloody froth that issued from her mouth and nose was the definitive precursor of the end.

Because the exact cause of death was in dispute, a review meeting was called by Dr. Campbell, who requested that all three physicians who had tended the patient be present. As soon as they were assembled around the oval boardroom table, Dr. Campbell began to list the facts of the case. "Dr. Jenks, who was on call when the patient finally expired, wrote out the preliminary cause of death as 'aspiration pneumonia.' Now, I do not want to disagree completely, for I do believe that the actual cause was the result of blood and slime being drawn into her lungs by her deep stertorous respirations. We also know she had such a raging infection that even the hysterectomy did not cure it."

Dr. Jenks leaned forward. "I think we should list the fact that she died from an actual disease, eclampsia. This will make the case more readily available for further research, and it may point up the fact that the death might have been preventable if she had been seen earlier by a reputable obstetrical specialist."

"Now we are getting to the point, aren't we?" Dr. Campbell interjected. "Why did a woman with her financial resources turn to an immigrant scrubwoman? This is a perfect case to further dramatize the severity of the midwife question!"

"What are you proposing?" the third doctor inquired.

"We must be certain that the documents of record, namely the death certificate and other official papers, clearly direct the blame toward the woman responsible for the sad outcome. Theoretically," he told his colleagues in his most persuasive voice, "midwifery is useless, just like osteopathy and Christian Science. But we are faced with the unfortunate fact that these things do exist, and further, that the community demands them."

Dr. Jenks pounded the table with his fist. "Gentlemen, look what has happened in Massachusetts, where the law pronounced an ultimatum that the midwife shall not exist, and yet, in spite of legal prohibition, she continues her work in collusion with physicians who charge the midwives to sign their birth certificates."

"Yes, well, that is a separate issue to be dealt with," replied the chief of staff. "If the women demanding midwifery could be attracted to a maternity hospital, the question would be solved. I think we are doing admirably with our native population, but we have a continuous influx of foreigners who have been in the habit from time immemorial of employing their own kind."

"So now we must control immigration as well as the midwives?" the third doctor recapitulated.

"I didn't say that entirely. I think we should move in two ways: first to educate the clientele and second to improve our maternities so that they will be cheerful, attractive places, offering the best services. Let the newly delivered women be the heralds of our ministering. I propose that all patients, even those in the charity wings, be offered twilight sleep to lessen or eliminate their pains. The nursing staff should be encouraged to be cheerful and pleasant, even under provocation. The hallways, examining rooms, and nurseries could be brightened with paint and modern cots. In time, when the sisters and daughters of these women believe that they can find more comfort and safety in the hospital than they ever could at home, we can rigorously attack the midwife problem!"

"That's very well said, but what would you do about the present issue, the cause of death?" asked Dr. Campbell.

Dr. Jenks stood, removed a piece of paper from his breast pocket, and read aloud. "Official cause of death: 'Improper manipulation by unprofessional methods and criminal neglect by a midwife, namely Mrs. H. Sokolow, with the result being infection and aspiration pneumonia.' "

"You realize, Doctor, that a certificate such as that would have to be forwarded to the coroner's office," the chief of staff commented.

"If you and my colleagues do not believe that violators of the statutes regarding midwifery in the state of New York should be brought to justice I am willing to reconsider my words."

Dr. Campbell stood and placed his immaculate palms down on the conference table. "I see no reason not to pursue the Belinsky matter." He leaned toward the other men. "Considering the illustrious name involved, the case should receive some notoriety. I've already spoken to the coroner, and he feels there may be enough evidence to indict on manslaughter. With any luck, we could have this one behind bars!"

"Then we are in agreement!" Dr. Jenks said, unwrapping a specially blended cigar he had been saving for a worthwhile occasion.

## · 9 ·

THE WORDING OF Mrs. Belinsky's death certificate was suspicious enough for the coroner to contact the district attorney's office, but before an assistant district attorney was assigned to pursue the matter, the agency demanded a written complaint charging the midwife with specific crimes. Though Dr. Jenks privately remembered Hannah's protestations that another woman had actually ruptured the membranes, he chose to officially ignore it, believing, for the most part, that the frightened midwife had been lying. As soon as the words of the complaint were composed by the panel of doctors and duly signed by the next of kin, Nathaniel Belinsky (who had dismayed the administrator with his initial reluctance to press charges), a magistrate's warrant was issued for Hannah Sokolow's arrest.

They came for Hannah when Lazar was away from home. A neighbor summoned him from The Monopole and gave him Hannah's hastily written note that begged him to go to the Karps for advice. Mortimer Karp immediately contacted the prestigious law firm that handled his business interests, but the attorney actually assigned the matter was but the senior partner's untried son, Wade L. Roberts III.

The case was to be conducted discreetly and expediently to save the lawyers and Karp any embarrassment, and no fees were to be charged, Roberts Jr. explained to his son. "For when you consider the volume of business we handle for Karp, Lowenthal and Company, that hardly would be proper. Better to leave it a favor among gentlemen, a chip to be cashed later if necessary."

Before proceeding to have Mrs. Sokolow released from jail, young Roberts studied the wording of the complaint and wondered how the Karps could have become involved with the unsavory person it so graphically described.

It read in part:

> That the said Hannah Sokolow is directly responsible for the death of Mrs. Sondra Belinsky and her infant son on the twentieth of December, 1907, at Sloane Hospital of this City, due to the filthy condition of her hands and arms.
>
> That her treatment of the mother and child was so grossly negligent that it resulted first in the death of the child and then in that of the mother.
>
> That by practicing illegal maneuvers she is guilty of gross violations of her privileges to practice as a midwife, and that Dr. Jenks and Dr. Campbell have severely denounced the treatments and practices of this woman and hold her utterly unfit to practice as a midwife.
>
> For these reasons this complainant respectfully asks that said midwife be bound over for the next session of the grand jury to be indicted for manslaughter.

But as soon as Roberts met Hannah, he knew that the lovely raven-haired woman who held her back so erect in spite of the frightening events of the day and spoke an intelligent and precise, although accented, English was very different from the ignorant hag he had pictured from the documents. His immediate assumption was that no judge would insist that this wife of a respected professor, with degrees of her own from foreign universities, remain in jail. And even though they had the bad luck to have the arraignment heard by the formidable Judge Carlson, the lawyer had guessed correctly. Hannah was freed after a bond was posted by the Karps. This little victory gave Roberts great confidence, for although his client would never know it, this was to be his very first criminal case.

❖   ❖   ❖

Young Roberts, as he was called around the Maiden Lane offices, had literally been twiddling his thumbs for almost two years since he graduated from Yale Law School. Although he was invited to sit in on all the firm's trials, he was given no more than a clerical position in preparing briefs. Not once had he been allowed to speak directly to a client or a judge, except during the social gatherings that were as much a requirement for his job as appearing at the office at eight sharp each morning. Two years, even five, was not too long to wait his turn, considering that he would be moving right up into a partnership, following the path his father had set for him from birth. No need to be anxious, just plod along, do what was expected, and everything else would come, his parents reminded him over and over again. As long as he met a few minor expectations, he was clear to pursue life as he saw it.

The difficulty for Wade Roberts III was that, almost despite himself, he had become inordinately fond of the law and wanted nothing more than to have a free rein in its practice. Not one of the suitable young ladies who had been dangled in front of him by his mother or her friends had sufficiently excited him to warrant more than an evening's attention, no sport since crew had inspired him to exercise, and no particular intellectual interest held as much fascination as reading current issues of the *Law Review*.

To almost anyone else the case of *The People* v. *Sokolow* might have been seen as a distasteful lump of work to be brushed out of sight as quickly as possible. Words such as *incompetent, filthy, illiterate, puncture of bag of waters, eclampsia,* and *illegal operations* that dotted the complaint had unpleasant connotations. But no matter who she was or what the case was about, it was his and his alone, for no one else in the firm had either the time or the slightest interest to be concerned with how it was handled. Roberts was allowed to prepare as he chose, and as long as the outcome was as favorable as possible considering the circumstances, he would eventually be rewarded for his judicious and discreet attention to the matter.

Without much practical experience, Roberts decided to approach the case in a textbook manner. He conscientiously worked with a medical dictionary, writing out the definitions of unfamiliar terms. He reviewed the rules and regulations regarding the licensing of midwives as set down by the Department of Health, noting the inconsistencies and vagaries of their definition of what was and was not permitted. Then, with plenty of time to work on the case, he proceeded to the most enjoyable aspect of the job: the intensive preparation of his client for the grand jury inquest.

❖   ❖   ❖

After her initial rage at the unjust accusations had dissipated, Hannah had almost convinced herself that the whole episode was a mistake, for how could she have been charged with any crime whatsoever when all she had done was seek prompt help for her patient within the shortest possible span of time after making a diagnosis? The first error had been Mrs. Belinsky's own. Some combination of her own vanity, modesty, and fears had prevented her from seeking medical attention during the last difficult days of her pregnancy. Then Mrs. Fingerman's inept recognition of the early symptoms of eclampsia, combined with her poor technique, aggravated the infection and caused the death of the fetus. Hannah was confident that when all was explained to the authorities, everything would be over.

Lazar saw it quite differently. Without a current cause of his own, he saw this as a classic attack by the bureaucratic element he took a particular delight in resisting. Hannah was too personally involved with the death of Belinsky's wife and child, too worried about her professionalism being tested, to see the real issues at stake. He felt the doctors in America were a true representation of the sins of capitalism, and even the Doctors Jaffe, Herzog, and their coterie who should, with their socialist backgrounds, have known better, had begun to mouth the rhetoric of medical politics, condemning as "quackery" every type of practice that did not fit their rigid standards! To aid his wife, Lazar began to read everything he could find on the American judicial system and to discuss with her attorney every aspect of the case.

One morning when Hannah returned home from the market,

she found Roberts and Lazar again discussing incomprehensible subjects such as arraignments, inquests, and the like. But as she looked at the young attorney she felt buoyed with hope. The Karps had come to her rescue with a bright, sweet-faced young man who would certainly be the person to prove how sorely she had been wronged! When she had first heard that an attorney had taken her case, she had worried that he would be a grim fellow who would condemn her privately while defending her publicly. But this one! Though his Prince Albert coat looked woefully out of place in her tenement parlor, his easy manner and delightful smile reassured her.

Hannah busied herself making tea in a samovar the way Lazar preferred. She listened, but didn't understand what they were talking about. Just to have Roberts there, working on her behalf, gave Hannah a feeling of comfort she had not felt since she heard of Mrs. Belinsky's death. It will only be a matter of time now, she droned to herself as the water began to boil in the central cylindrical tank of the urn. Then it will be over and everything will fall back as it should. After the infusion was strong enough, she placed the earthenware teapot containing the essence on a tray and showed the young attorney how to mix water from the spigot with the brewed tea to make a perfect glass. Roberts's hand shook slightly as he took the richly colored liquid from Hannah. He stirred in plenty of sugar and took a taste. "I never knew tea could have so much flavor!" he said, impressed. "At home it tastes like slightly soiled water!"

Both delighted to have pleased him and relieved to have something not so serious to talk about, Hannah threw her head back and laughed. Too soon he began his questions, the same questions as the day before. It was as though he believed that this time she would have a different version to tell or some new information, but unfortunately Hannah disappointed him with the same steady recounting of the events leading up to Mrs. Belinsky's transfer to the hospital.

Yet, the more often they talked, the quicker the whole episode was becoming a separate thing from Hannah herself. Now it was something with numbers and files, notations and folders; it became less a part of her and more a circumscribed impersonal activity.

When Roberts was either satisfied or exhausted, he left to continue his research in his firm's law library. Every day he searched for statutes that might prove relevant. Roberts guessed that the assistant district attorney would not have as much time as he did for background study; and he believed his father's maxim that the best lawyer was the best law clerk, ever attentive to details that the other side might overlook.

A few weeks before the grand jury hearing, Roberts met Hannah and Lazar in his offices. "I've asked you to come here so that we might talk in an atmosphere not quite as comfortable as your home and yet not quite as severe as a courtroom," Roberts said as he seated himself across from Hannah.

She glanced around the impressive room — paneled in imported oak and with brass sconces on the wall matching the fixture over his desk — and shifted from one foot to the other. Lazar pulled out a chair for her and when she was seated continued to stand behind her and rest his hands on the carved back. "I've already explained that to Hannah. Now may we begin?" Lazar asked with assurance.

"Of course," Roberts replied. "Now, Mrs. Sokolow, is it not true that you knew the deceased for many years before her latest confinement?" he said in a formal voice.

"Yes, I delivered her first child."

"Don't offer information, just answer the question," Lazar instructed.

"Sorry," Hannah said, twisting a lace edge on her sleeve.

"And did you not have a social relationship with the family?" Roberts continued.

"No, I did not." Hannah answered the way she thought the lawyer wanted her to.

"But Mrs. Sokolow," he said in his regular tone, "we discussed the fact that you had met Mrs. Belinsky at various afternoon teas, that you had visited their daughter at their home. Your answer might be interpreted as deceptive."

"I thought ... well, it wasn't social, we just met a few times ..." Hannah swallowed hard.

"How do you expect her to answer you?" Lazar rushed to his

wife's defense. "These questions are not black and white, just shades of grey."

"Indeed! That is what we must demonstrate to the panel at the inquest. If they see too dark a shade of grey, the case will go to trial."

Hannah sighed and closed her eyes. "If I tell the truth it will be suspicious; if I lie, I might be found out. They can prove that I did know the Belinskys, but that doesn't mean that I would have harmed the woman."

Roberts spread his fingers and raked them through the tight curls on his head. "They are more interested in proving harm by neglect, not malicious intent."

"I didn't neglect her! Not for two extra minutes! If you could only find Mrs. Fingerman and force her to come and . . . What's the word?"

"Testify?" Lazar volunteered.

"Yes, testify! Did you send someone to the address I gave you?"

"She hasn't been home since the incident. We're trying to learn if she had any children, close relatives, but for the moment she has just vanished. In any case we have plenty of time to find her, for she won't be needed until after the inquest."

"Then how will we prove my innocence?"

Roberts sighed and locked his fingers together on top of his polished desk. "I thought you understood. The inquest is not an adversary proceeding. The assistant district attorney will try to provide enough evidence to warrant a trial. Until there are charges, we cannot defend you with witnesses."

"Won't the doctors be at the inquest?" Lazar asked.

"That's different," Roberts replied.

Lazar spoke very seriously. "Isn't it likely the inquest will rule that Hannah must stand trial?"

Roberts grasped his baby-soft chin with his right hand and stroked it downward. "I'm of that opinion. That is why I would like your permission to file an 'Information Against You,' which will allow us to skip the inquest and move swiftly to trial. Then, when we can bring our own witnesses, you will certainly be vindicated."

"Just think of all the good that could come of a trial!" Lazar said, his blue eyes flickering with enthusiasm.

Hannah stared at her husband and then at her attorney. Roberts was smiling, as though he were about to receive a gift he had wanted for a long time. "You *want* a trial?" Hannah choked. I thought you were going to help me get away from this . . . this terrible mistake. I've done nothing wrong! As soon as I attended Mrs. Belinsky, I had her brought to the hospital. The baby was gone already! Explain it to the judge, the court, whomever you must, and let me be done with it!"

"That might solve your particular case, Mrs. Sokolow, but think of all the other women who practice legal midwifery who are also being unfairly harassed. I've taken it upon myself to read what the medical practitioners are saying in this matter, and believe me, you are not the only one they are going after," he said, searching through some publications on his desk. "Here's one in the *New York State Journal of Medicine* that concludes, 'Midwives must be eliminated if obstetricians are to be recognized as the best choice for patients and if they are to wipe out economic competition'!"

Hannah stood and walked around the room, fingering the brown and gold morocco bindings on the law books without reading their titles. Lazar sat down in her chair.

Roberts read on, " 'Some thirty thousand women have taken enough practice away from the physicians to obtain an excellent livelihood, unquestionably invading the field of the doctor and making the community the loser because these females are incapable of coping with the abnormalities of the . . . puer . . . per . . . ium.' " He struggled with the medical term. "Our case could be the ideal mechanism to demonstrate the unfairness of the charges against not only one midwife but of a whole system of health care that is threatened by the doctors who have organized to rid themselves of an economic threat!"

"Don't you see how much you could do for other women by allowing this to come to trial?" Lazar continued.

Hannah whipped around and stared at him with such fierceness that he slumped back in his chair. "And what if it doesn't? What if they prove I did something wrong?"

Lazar walked over to Hannah and placed his arms around her

shoulders. "That's impossible. How can they prove you did something when you did not?"

"They can twist the facts, they can lie; who knows what can happen? The innocent are sometimes proven guilty!" she said, unaware that she had been shrieking her last few sentences.

Roberts spoke to Lazar in a deliberate voice. "I think your wife remembers Russia and their harsh system of justice. In America you are innocent until proven guilty. The burden of proof is not on us, but on them."

Hannah shook her head. "I don't want to go through with it a second longer than necessary. I can't sleep at night, I can't work! With a trial it could go on for months, years! I heard you two talking. I know it could take that long!"

Lazar pressed Hannah back into her seat and pulled a chair up beside her. "Won't you look beyond yourself to the larger issues, the anti-Semitic aspects? Why, this very much parallels the Dreyfus case!"

"No one has said anything about me being Jewish!"

"Are you so naive as to believe that a Christian woman would have received a charge of manslaughter? Do you not want to be completely exonerated?"

"Like Dreyfus?" Hannah asked.

"Exactly!" replied Lazar, pleased that she was swinging to his side.

"Lazar, how can you suggest that I be like poor Alfred Dreyfus? Has there ever been a man more wrongly accused? How many years did it take to free him from the irons on Devil's Island? Almost five! Even then it was years and years before he was completely absolved of a crime!"

"And now?" Lazar said with veneration, ". . . Now the name Dreyfus stands for everyone who has been unfairly maligned." As he finished his eyes were wild and shining.

"Then you go to the courtroom and place yourself up for trial!" Hannah shouted. "I'm not a soldier, nor a revolutionary! I am only a midwife; that's all I ever wanted to be!"

Roberts shrugged his shoulders. "We cannot force you to do anything that you do not want to do. Let us rest a few minutes and then we will continue our preparations."

"Then you see it my way? I won't have to go to trial?"

"Now, we will only know that after the inquest," he said to mollify her. "In any case the issue of the revocation of your license has been placed in the hands of the Department of Health. If you are convicted of a felony it will automatically be terminated, but if not, that will be an entirely separate issue, which we will address when the time comes," Roberts droned on, but Hannah wasn't listening.

Although the three of them should have been united, Hannah's worries revolved around an issue the attorney and her husband had not given the slightest attention. At the arraignment Hannah had been quick to memorize the police detective's phrase, "The defendant had considerable prior knowledge of the deceased." Was he already hinting that Hannah might have had some reason for wishing the woman dead? Wouldn't a love affair with her husband constitute vivid evidence if it were brought out in court? Lazar had made so light of the accusations Mrs. Belinsky made at the Karps' circumcision party in describing it to Roberts, the attorney had already decided the incident was of little consequence to the case.

On the other hand, Hannah worried that someone might have actually overheard the words she had spoken to Belinsky and made a more accurate assumption as to their relationship. Considering that she and Belinsky were now in opposition, the witnesses would more likely side with the man than the midwife.

And what about the truth of the matter? Someone could implicate Hannah in the affair. Faces of those she once thought inconsequential suddenly loomed before her as potential tormenters: Herman at The Monopole; the powder-room attendant at the Café Martin; the doorman, elevator operator, or carriage boy at the Hotel Plaza. If located, any of them could present evidence that Hannah and Belinsky had probably been lovers. And Belinsky himself! Would he actually testify against her? He, of all people, knew that nothing had been her fault. But then, if she had not seen it herself, she never would have believed he could have signed his name to the complaint! What had possessed him to do such a despicable thing? Hurting her would not bring back his wife or child!

For herself she had little pity. She saw the course of events like an arrow that had been released long before, but destined for its target nonetheless. If she hadn't been so deceptive so many times this might never have happened. She had lied to Mama, to Lazar, to herself. For everything she had done wrong, she had never been punished; for something she had not done, she received the blame. With her own convoluted reasoning, she accepted it all. In the evenings she reread Dreyfus's journal. No wonder he was so courageous! He knew he was perfectly innocent; he knew that eventually the culprit would be found.

But she could not see this to the end, for she had done far too much wrong. Now her greatest fear was that the manslaughter charge would be upgraded if they ever suspected she had been trying to get Belinsky for herself, something that was totally untrue either in the past or present.

Then what had she wanted? At the time she had hardly reasoned out her actions; she had only followed her desires down a winding road without a beginning or end. He had seemed so charming, so needful, and if she had not been so blinded by Lazar's obvious faults, perhaps she might have realized sooner what a weak character Belinsky truly was.

She had never really planned to do what she had; it had happened. Yet both men had been forced to make conscious decisions concerning her. The moment Lazar had stepped off the *Carpathia,* he had decided for her; the moment Belinsky had signed the complaint, he had decided against her. Did he hope to win vengeance against some formless fate by pointing a finger at her? Could he assuage his debilitating guilt by passing on the blame? Then why had he done it? The question blazed in her mind. Why?

In the end she had been tested as well. When she had seen Mrs. Belinsky's condition she could have fled; she could have insisted that Mrs. Fingerman handle the case, or forced the family to transport her without medical attention en route. Instead she had done exactly what was necessary, without even considering the consequences for herself. About that she could still be proud.

If a trial was the only alternative, Hannah would steel herself and survive it, for she retained a sense of righteousness that ultimately would lead to victory. But the risks were so great that as she listened to her two defenders, Lazar and Roberts, make their battle plans, she decided to grasp the one last chance she had to protect herself.

## · 10 ·

THE MELTING ICE and snow revealed remnants of horse manure and garbage frozen in hidden layers weeks before. The sewers could barely contain the flowing refuse that gurgled through the gutters. Pedestrians had to be alert to avoid a disastrous step in the blackening slush.

To escape soaking her feet, Hannah decided to take the Third Avenue Trolley from the Bowery to Fourth Avenue and East Seventeenth Street, an address she had fortuitously been able to remember. She knew Belinsky well enough to suppose he might find distraction, if not solace, in the building of his skyscraper.

There was no mistaking the corner. A large sign that could be read from both streets proclaimed: FUTURE HOME OF THE GERMANIA LIFE INSURANCE COMPANY, ASSETS OVER $50,000,000. Underneath, a smaller one read: N. BELINSKY AND COMPANY, GENERAL CONTRACTORS. Hannah stood across the street studying the construction. She counted twenty-two floors, all but the last six already faced in stone. The entire structure was dotted with men in overalls and caps; the ones on the highest floors seemed to disappear into the mist. Cranes lifted beams; hooks dangled in the air waiting for something to be detached; a solitary worker on a high deck gestured eloquently to someone on the street below. The framework echoed with the vibrations from the riveters, but the loudest sound Hannah heard was the fearful pounding in her own head.

"Is Mr. Belinsky here today?" she asked the first man who turned in her direction after she walked onto the site.

"What?" he asked, unable to hear her thin voice above the grating of cables.

"Belinsky!" she shouted.

"He's in his office!" the burly man said, pointing upward with his forefinger before his wide smile demonstrated how few teeth he had.

Seeing that Hannah was confused, he called, "Hey! Marty! Take this lady to Belinsky! And don't lose her, ya'hear!"

Marty silently led the way up a crude staircase to the platform that would eventually be the second floor. In the very center of the structure a roughhewn set of partitions had been knocked into place, and a stovepipe vent protruded out, giving off long wisps of smoke that the poor draft inside the building could not ventilate adequately.

A tall man carrying a clipboard of jumbled papers and receipts exited and doffed his cap to Hannah as she entered the room. Hannah closed the door behind her and stood waiting for Belinsky to look up from the figures he was trying to balance. He muttered a few words under his breath, crumbled the work in front of him, and tossed it into the open door of the wood stove without paying any attention to his visitor. "Claude, this won't work. See if you can get a better bid out of J and L in Pittsburgh."

Hearing no response, he placed his pen down and raised his head. Through the changing mirror of his eyes, Hannah was able to read his thoughts: surprise, fright, then shame. He closed his eyelids but still said nothing.

"Nahum, I've come because I wanted you to know that I am not angry with you," Hannah began quickly. Without remembering her prepared plea, she improvised, and as she did, a fresh understanding of what had happened made itself visible. "I know you never wanted to hurt me, for you knew better than anyone that I had nothing to do with the unfortunate . . . that I would have done anything I could have . . . that I *did* do what had to be done!"

"It's just that . . ." He tried to interrupt, but Hannah stopped him.

"The doctors and your father forced you to sign, didn't they? And because you didn't dare risk them discovering what happened between us, you thought that signing the complaint proved you couldn't have cared for me."

"Yes," he nodded. "How did you know?"

How did she know? Hannah reflected. It had just come to her, and now that she believed she understood, the knowledge might help her win her way.

"The Karps found me a lawyer; my husband wants me to fight back, but I'm afraid . . . for both of us. Do you think that someone won't be found who might try to prove that you and I together . . . or that I wanted you . . . or . . . ?"

"It was that other woman! Why did I ever let her into my home? The filthy, ignorant old fool! She's the one at fault, not you!" Belinsky's voice was so agitated that Marty poked his head inside to see if he was needed. Immediately sensing that he should not have done so, he backed away.

Hannah had remained against the wall at the far side of the room, but she took two tiny steps closer and spoke in Yiddish. "Nahum, listen to me. Fingerman has been away for weeks, no one can find her."

"I'll hire detectives . . . she will show up!"

"Even if she were found, she can't speak at the inquest. There still will be a trial and we can't take that risk!"

"Then what can we do?"

"My husband, my lawyer, they all know I have been unfairly charged by you and the hospital. They understand why the doctors are trying to eliminate midwives, but they don't know why you would be against me."

"It's not me . . . You must believe that. My father must have someone to blame . . . Better . . ."

". . . Better me than you!" Hannah finished the sentence. "So you would take everything: my work, my husband's belief in me, even perhaps my freedom, so you can have this!" she said, pointing to the rugged walls of the construction shack but meaning the sky-scraper and the world at large. Her words became ponderously slow and a fresh vehemence deepened her voice. "I have never felt such pity as I feel for you. To think how much I believed in you . . . in your abilities . . . to think I once wanted you!" she said, stepping backward again.

Belinsky, thinking Hannah was leaving, jumped up and pushed his way past a metal can of oversized bolts to stand by her side. Awkwardly he grabbed her wrists to hold her there another minute. "I've made a dreadful mistake. I didn't know what I was doing. They told me to sign the papers! How could I have thought about what was right when I had just seen Shifre for the last time? They had taken the baby out to try to save her . . . in pieces . . . It was a boy . . . I saw that much under the blanket . . ."

Hannah lifted his hands that still held onto her wrists. "Then you will tell them that you have reconsidered, that you do not wish the painful episode to be prolonged by a trial, that nothing can bring your loved ones back. I overheard my lawyer saying that if you withdrew the charges and refused to cooperate there wouldn't even be an inquest."

"But the hospital?"

"The hospital and doctors are also attempting to have my license revoked through the Department of Health. If you drop your criminal charges, perhaps they will drop theirs."

"How can I do that now? I don't want to hurt you but . . ."

Hannah's lips drew back tensely and she spoke from a place deep in her throat. "You may be willing to lie in court about how long I attended your wife and what services I performed, but what if they ask about my . . . what do they call it? . . . my motives? Are you ready to explain about the Hotel Plaza?" Although she attempted to keep her voice under control, her face contorted and her words were garbled.

Belinsky closed his eyes to block out the images that swam before him. "I never thought they would ask those things. Hannah, you must believe I never wanted to hurt you, believe me . . ." He faltered and released Hannah's wrists.

His quivering and whimpering were repulsive. "I must go home . . . my children . . . must leave . . ." she said, opening the door.

"I . . . there's so much more . . ."

Hannah stopped and turned. Belinsky's eyes widened. He looked as though he believed she was going to come back to comfort him. He half-smiled expectantly.

"Do it today, won't you?" Hannah said so lightly it almost didn't sound like the command it really was.

# · 11 ·

THE DEPARTMENT OF HEALTH, upon reviewing the petition from Sloane Hospital, revoked Hannah's license to practice midwifery. The hospital administrators had been openly disappointed that the manslaughter charge had been dropped, but the assistant district attorney had said that there was no case once Belinsky refused to testify against the defendant. So the doctors had acted swiftly to win their round and rid themselves of one more midwife by whatever legal means they had.

Roberts had not been deterred by their expected victory and had filed a plea in the New York Supreme Court to set aside the revocation, stating that Hannah had been denied due process because "said Department of Health had not notified her of the proceedings in which her license was revoked."

The court ruled that she was entitled to a hearing, and for weeks Lazar and Roberts carried reams of paper in and out of meeting rooms and up and down long staircases, waited in lines, made the necessary arguments, and answered questions. Eventually Hannah was sworn in and allowed to give, by means of transcribed testimony, her version of the licensing case. Testimony under oath was also given by Dr. Jaffe, Inspector Noyes, and the Sloane Hospital doctors. Mrs. Fingerman was never located.

In the end, the Department of Health ruled against Hannah again, saying that the powers to both grant and revoke licenses clearly were held by the department, which retained the sole discretion to decide, by whatever standard they chose, who should be licensed to practice midwifery.

"They giveth, they taketh away . . ." Roberts said, finally admitting defeat to the Sokolows as they sat in his office wondering where to appeal next. "There is nothing more we can do in this case. However, just because one license has been revoked does not mean you cannot meet the requirements for another, especially since you weren't convicted of any crime!" He beamed as though the news would be received as a gift. "I haven't acquired my own samovar yet, but won't you have some coffee with me?" he asked, ringing for his secretary.

"They have proven themselves to be arbitrary and unfair and I will no longer bow to their ridiculous demands," Hannah railed. "Besides, much of what they insist midwives do is unnecessary, and much of what they forbid is not medically, but economically, biased!"

"Hurrah!" Lazar cheered so loudly that Roberts's male secretary, an older gentleman Roberts had inherited with the office, almost dropped his silver coffee platter. "Now you are sounding like a proper revolutionary!"

"Me?" Hannah said in surprise.

"All socialists are simply frustrated capitalists!" He mocked himself, not really believing the words though they sounded witty and fresh.

Lazar poured Hannah a cup, adding almost half again as much cream as coffee to take away the bitter taste she had never learned to appreciate.

"As your attorney I cannot advise you to flout the rules and regulations of the state of New York," Roberts said soberly, ignoring the cup his assistant had left on his desk.

"But . . . you told me . . ." Lazar scolded his friend.

Roberts quickly added two lumps of sugar to his coffee and shook his head. "About that you must make your own decisions. As for this case, I cannot help you further. I still don't understand why that scoundrel Belinsky dropped his charges. It would have been such an excellent case to try!" he said, stirring so fast that the brown liquid dripped down the sides of the gold-banded cup.

"Perhaps he didn't wish to be publicly reminded of his sorrows," Hannah said cautiously.

"More likely he finally realized that he would have lost the case as well as his wife!" Lazar finished.

"I suppose," Roberts said amicably. "Mrs. Sokolow, I want you to give some thought to reapplying for a license. Maybe not now, but in a year or two. It would be so much easier, so much less of a worry, to work legally. I understand that to qualify you would need to attend further instruction here in New York, but only for six months or so."

"Never! Why, in Europe I was almost a doctor!"

"In any case, you can always work as a masseuse," Lazar added brightly. He looked at Hannah's barely touched coffee. "If you are finished with that, I have something to show you!"

"Ah yes, don't let me keep you," Roberts said, obviously privy to the secret.

As her husband steered her toward the door, Hannah turned and asked Roberts, "Will I like it?"

Roberts shrugged his shoulders. "I'd be surprised if you didn't!" He winked just before he lifted the cup to his lips.

When they were out in the hallway Lazar said, "I don't understand how anyone, let alone an intelligent man like that, can take his coffee once it has cooled. The whole purpose is to have it hot!" he said, exaggerating the *h* dramatically.

❖ ❖ ❖

From Roberts's office, Lazar took Hannah up to University Heights. She thought she was to see his office and classrooms, but instead he showed her the new apartment he had rented for his family. Later Hannah wondered if the idea had been Lazar's own or if Roberts had been the one to suggest and arrange it, but she wasn't sufficiently curious to press the point. It was enough that he had done it without pestering and persuasion from her; he had done it to please her and to help her forget the wretched weeks since Mrs. Belinsky died.

Lazar had chosen a clean and cheerful apartment only seven blocks away from his classroom at the University Heights campus, one block from the Aqueduct Avenue Trolley and only three from the Broadway Elevated, making it accessible to all parts of the city. There were five large, sun-filled rooms, a private toilet, a bathtub in its own little room rather than in the kitchen, central heating, and hot water. The rent was partially subsidized by the university.

In gratitude Hannah admitted the existence of her secret savings and decided to use them to furnish their new home. Though Lazar thought it unnecessary, he did not restrain her from ordering a matching upholstered parlor suite with a rocker, sofa, armchair, and side chair; a set of dishes in the Glenmore Rose pattern; and assorted linens and bric-a-brac. In fact, he encouraged her budding domestic interest because he hoped it would help her relinquish midwifery more gracefully.

If Lazar wasn't teaching, he was in his office, or at the library several blocks closer to his house. He'd found a new café, frequented by faculty members who discussed politics in softer tones and with longer words than Hannah recalled hearing at the more boisterous Monopole. Lazar's books, his notes, his newspapers suddenly seemed less of a distraction, for they were now a respectable adjunct to his job, so Hannah stopped resenting and began to enjoy tidying the table where "the professor" corrected examinations in the evening.

Because she thought she had everything she had ever wanted (except her midwifery, which she believed was lost forever), Hannah tried to forget how listless she felt, how uninterested in achieving anything. Sometimes a whole day went by without her getting dressed in street clothing. She'd wash a pot, sit down and think; pick up a paper, sigh, and put it down. Lazar didn't notice. The children didn't notice. Hannah hoped the tiredness would go away.

Hoping that a structured week with places to go each day might be the cure for her loneliness, Hannah planned a very busy schedule for herself and the children, filled with outings to the library and the park, lessons for Benny, games for Emma. The children might have been content, but Hannah craved the unexpected events that each birth would bring and the challenge and companionship she received from her patients. Wednesday evenings, when Lazar taught late, Hannah gathered the children and took them to Aunt Sonia's for supper, because after a long day alone with them she needed adult conversation.

One such night in May it was warm enough so that the children didn't even need sweaters. The air was damp and sweet. The trolley windows were open. Benny rushed for the window seat and smiled and waved to everyone. Emma didn't cry or beg to nurse. Hannah was content. Nothing had gone wrong all day. Aunt Sonia had promised to make spiced herring balls, sweet and sour meat-

loaf, and potato pudding. Best of all, Abraham would amuse both
the children so she could sit and rest.

"I have a customer for you!" Aunt Sonia announced before
Hannah walked across the doorsill.

"For a massage?" Hannah asked casually.

"Of course not. For a baby," Aunt Sonia said.

"Does she know about my license?"

"No, but this one won't mind in the least!"

"You sound so confident. Do I know her?"

"Here," Aunt Sonia said, handing her a printed calling card.
"Mrs. Franklin W. West, Fifty-four East Sixty-first Street. Nice
lady," she finished and turned quickly toward the kitchen. "Go see
her tomorrow and make your arrangements," she called back to
Hannah without turning around because she didn't want her niece
to see her mischievous smile.

During dinner Uncle Leyb described the opening of the seventh
of his fabric shops in a country town called New Rochelle. "Maybe
we will move there if it is successful. Houses, big houses, are not
unreasonable. They remind me of the country homes in Russia,
like the dacha Velvel had outside Moscow."

"Have you heard from Uncle Velvel?" Hannah asked.

"Yes, he hears," Aunt Sonia said, putting some meat on Benny's
plate even though he pushed it onto the tablecloth, kicked his feet,
and screamed, "No! No meat!"

Aunt Sonia ignored the child's protests and tried to feed him.
"Velvel should emigrate now! Leyb offers to send for him, but his
wife doesn't want to leave their home. Maybe they could send the
little girls here until Toibe can be convinced to leave her precious
furniture."

Leyb studied a glistening piece of beef as though with enough
patience it would reveal some secret. "I cannot tell my brother
what to do. But if he comes, there's enough here for him and his
girls as well. In a few more years there will be ten, maybe fifteen,
stores," he said without a hint of pride in his weary voice.

# · 12 ·

"YES, MRS. WEST is expecting you," the butler said with an exaggerated British accent as he escorted Hannah into the most extraordinary home she had yet seen.

From the street the house appeared to be but a modest family dwelling with the only unusual feature being a private stable attached to its left side, but once inside, the guest felt she was in another world. Every square foot of wall and ceiling in the vestibule was mirrored. Even the floors were of a richly polished metal, so the one piece of furniture, a jade-encrusted Chinese cabinet, was reflected a thousand times.

In contrast, the parlor walls were muted by dark teak panels and lit by large candelabra attached to silver-plated wall sconces, which, even at eleven in the morning, burned brightly. The effect caused one to immediately stare at the ceiling, where intricately carved moldings that had been freshly gilded were used as a glittering frame for a fresco of plump cherubs floating among luminous clouds. The two sideboards and twelve formal chairs were cast in heavy bronze and could barely be moved. Hannah sat uncomfortably on a tapestry-covered seat, wondering who could possibly live in this unique home.

The door opened and a woman entered, preceded by so huge an expectant abdomen that layers of lace and egret feathers could not camouflage it. "Hannah! Now that you are here I can relax and leave it all to you!" she said, rushing forward to greet the midwife. Hannah was perplexed by the stranger, whose hair was tied with half a dozen black velvet bows and whose swollen arms were decked with a myriad of tinkling gold bracelets.

"You do not recognize me!" she said in a thick accent. Then her whole face became quite petulant.

"Olga!" Hannah clapped her hands. "You ... here! Isn't this ...?"

"Wonderful?" She rippled with laughter. "I thought Mrs. Meyerov would have told you. Ah, but she wanted to make it a surprise! I'll tell you everything," she said like a child about to show off her new toys.

For an hour Hannah sat without moving as Olga explained how she had sung in cafés until she met Mr. West, which she pronounced "Vesht." "He came every night and requested the same song each time. 'A Bird in a Gilded Cage,' you know it? He said he made Emma Carus famous by giving her the chance to sing it on stage and would do the same for me. But then he whisked me off to this house and made me too happy to bother with work. Now — " she patted her abdomen — "I will be too busy to give more than a few private recitals for our friends. My husband runs a music publishing company and has songs written just for me! All the best writers he finds. You must know Von Tilzer, Charles K. Harris?"

Hannah shook her head.

"Perhaps not the names, but you know the songs: 'Hello Central, Give me Heaven,' 'In My Merry Oldsmobile'?"

"Oldsmobile," Hannah stammered.

"Then you know!" Olga said, misunderstanding Hannah's recognition of the car name.

Olga observed Hannah as she rubbed her hand across a bronze statue of a bear beside her. "You like it? For my birthday my Frankie gave it to me. He gives me anything I want and more. So lucky am I! Who would have thought . . . ?"

"Who would have thought . . ." Hannah echoed. "And now a baby! It looks like it will be soon."

"Very. The doctor I went to last week says I am doing well. But it is you I want to deliver me."

"And your husband, doesn't he want you to go to a hospital?"

"No, he wants what I want. Hannah, Mrs. Sokolow . . . you must do this for me!" Olga's voice changed from the imperious to the solicitous. "Last time you came too late; I don't want anything to happen now."

"You look very healthy, the doctor said . . ."

"I know, but you remember, so long ago now . . . Odessa. I want you should come to stay here. Then you can't possibly be delayed."

"Olga, I have two children . . ."

"Bring them to live here!"

"Let me give you a thorough examination and then we'll decide."

Under all the layers of silk and lace, behind the perfumed handmade undergarments, Hannah discovered a delightfully healthy expectant mother. At twenty-one Olga was perfectly suited to childbearing. The breasts that once nurtured Abraham had swollen in readiness for the next child. The skin on her abdomen had stretched to cover the almost pointed mound without any noticeable marks. Olga tensely awaited the verdict as Hannah listened with her stethoscope to the child's heartbeat. When the midwife did not look up immediately to reassure her that everything was normal, she pushed Hannah's shoulder to gain her attention.

Lifting her head, Hannah said, "Everything's fine! Don't worry!" before remembering giving the girl very different news in a grim attic room many years before. Her tone softened. "You want to hear your baby?" she asked, giving Olga the earpiece and letting her listen to the vibrant, reassuring thump.

"Ticka-tacka-ticka-tacka! Is that it? It's so much faster than I thought it would be."

"Yes, now let me try over here," Hannah said, replacing the stethoscope on her head. She kept her left hand on the spot just to the left of Olga's navel where the beats had been heard and moved the metal circle higher, just under her right breast, and listened for a strong placental rush. Instead she was greeted by a heart beating at a slightly different pace. "Ticketa-tacketa, ticketa-tacketa!" Back to the first spot, she listened again. Then under the breast. "Listen here." She passed the earpieces back without revealing her excitement. "Can you hear it? A little more quickly this time?"

"What is it? Does the baby feel how happy I am, is that why it goes like that, like a song to me! Di . . . ti . . . ti, dot . . . ti . . . ti, Mamalah's sweet ba . . . a . . . by!" she sang out in her clear soprano voice.

"Babies!"

"La, la, la . . ." Olga murmured. "What?"

"Two babies. I hear two very different, distinct heartbeats!"

"Twins! Everything my Frankie does turns to gold! Every song he picks is a winner! Now he makes a baby and it turns into two! Even the doctor didn't discover this!"

"It isn't always possible to hear two babies. Even a few days ago they may have been in different positions blocking each other. But now that we know we can make some plans."

"What shall I do?"

"The most important thing is to rest, for we want the twins to be born as close to term as possible."

"We go to the theater or to a concert every night. It's how my husband finds new talent for his business."

"Until the twins are born you must stay home!" Hannah ordered.

"Of course, I will! What else?"

"I want you to eat four eggs every day, a quart of milk either in a pudding or with your meals, and fresh fruit in between. You will have to build yourself up if you are to provide enough milk for two, though I doubt you will have any problems there."

"I forgot to tell you that my husband wants to hire a nurse. He doesn't want to tire me with the feedings!"

"He doesn't know?"

"He thinks I came to America to find my fortune as a singer."

"I will never tell anyone our secret." Hannah took Olga's hand in hers. "But I cannot believe you do not want to feed your own baby."

"You know I *will*, but wasn't he sweet to worry? Wait till you meet him; he's quite an exceptional man!"

Franklin West was one of the most generous and original people Hannah ever met. When he attended the theater, the columnists reported what he had worn as dutifully as they described the actors upon the stage. His crushed velvet and satin suits, ivory walking sticks, high hats made from exotic furs were the focal point of many photographs as well as caricatures. Not that it mattered to him, for "Mr. W.," as he was called in Tin Pan Alley, blossomed with any type of attention, be it flattery or parody.

Olga's announcement of twins was welcomed by her husband not only for the news itself but also for the opportunity to prepare for the event with great style. In lieu of moving her family into the confusing, unorthodox household, Hannah agreed to check Olga two times a day and to stay when any true sign of imminence appeared.

For three weeks she never once examined Olga without encountering evidence of the massive preparations that were taking place in her household. The nursery was being custom designed for two children instead of one, with every possible convenience. Each side of the room was a mirror image of the other, containing a wooden rocking cradle, a stationary metal crib, a washstand with running water and baby bath, and a wardrobe stocked with flannels, pinning blankets, silk bonnets, rubber diaper drawers, and silken christening robes. A folding bed for a nurse was placed on each side of the room and a partition erected between them to give the ladies privacy. When Hannah mentioned casually that the babies might be more comfortable if they slept where they could see each other, the rooms were rearranged the following day.

During the last week, while they were all in a state of nervous expectancy, Olga decided to purchase a duplicate of everything on Hannah's list of supplies for the delivery. After Hannah surveyed the quantities of pads and pans, she exclaimed, "I know we are having two babies, but they are still coming from only one mother!" and suggested that the additional items be removed so they would not clutter the room.

Although Hannah made light of the situation, she fastidiously kept a chart on Mrs. West's condition, listing her vital signs and the exact heartbeat of the babies, listed as A for above and B for below. She also kept a small drawing of the positions she thought the babies were in and rechecked daily to reassure herself that they had not moved. Only 47 percent of twins both presented in the cephalic, or head-down, position, the ideal situation for an uncomplicated delivery, but Hannah was certain that one of Olga's babies had its head well engaged in the pelvis, while the second floated just above and would probably slip into place during the birth.

There were to be no startling changes. Although Olga had not yet complained of pains, a morning examination approximately one week before she was due indicated that the cervix had opened wide enough to admit two fingers. Hannah remained in residence and left word that Dr. Jaffe was to be summoned to help with the two infants. To keep Olga calm through the early contractions, Hannah supervised her during a long bath and had a hairdresser in for a coiffure to keep her occupied. Then the three women spent several hours in Olga's back garden, admiring the oversized azalea plants that Mr. West had purchased as a border for a concert stage several weeks before and shipped home immediately after the engagement.

Most everything in the Wests' household, including the staff, seemed to be leftovers from one performance or another. The mirrored foyer had once been part of a vaudeville set; the fresco on the parlor ceiling had been a background for a performance of *Peter Pan*. Even the butler was a tenor recovering from tuberculosis.

Though Olga claimed she was too excited to eat, Hannah forced her to sip hot bouillon in the morning, liquid gelatin in the afternoon, and a syrup of honey and tea in the early evening to keep up her strength. Olga had wisely not sent a message about the impending birth to Mr. West, who might have done something as ridiculous as ordering a brass band to rush the event along; so he went to see Anna Held, the coquettish French musical comedy star who was causing a sensation with her provocative performances, as planned.

By the time Olga had taken to bed, Hannah and Dr. Jaffe had agreed that everything was going quite normally, but just to be certain, they compared notes on how to deliver interlocked twins either if the heads attempted to enter the pelvis simultaneously or if the second head caught in the neck of the first twin. Hannah listened attentively as Rachael described a delivery where the second child, coming as a breech, straddled the first in shoulder presentation, and another where four extremities presented themselves breech and she had to sort out which leg belonged to what twin before pulling them downward.

Olga's luck held out, and just a few minutes before Mr. West returned from a late supper at Delmonico's, Hannah delivered first one little girl, named Mary, and then, three minutes later, a second almost identical in size and appearance, called Catherine. Under Dr. Jaffe's direction, two nurses bathed and dressed the robust infants and laid them across their mother, who seemed more interested in having her new hair style perfected before her husband was admitted to the room than in having the opposite end tended and cleaned.

When Mr. West was finally permitted in, Hannah proudly stood beside the bed to assist with the babies should she be needed. They were already sucking at their designated breasts with heads touching in Olga's lap. At the sight of the new mother propped up with pillows, feeding the two perfect children, the new father gasped, recovered, then shouted, "Bravo!" so emphatically that he caused his daughters to startle and his wife to laugh aloud.

# · 13 ·

"Now you know you cannot abandon your career!" Rachael urged several days after Olga's delivery.

"How many more families like the Wests do you suppose will call me?" Hannah sighed despondently. "There will always be those repeat customers who will have me despite everything, but for the most part women either want the hospitals or someone with a license. I've delivered gutter babies in the past, and I'm not about to do it again, for those are precisely the women who benefit most from the clinics."

"But I haven't seen you as happy as you were when you delivered Catherine and Mary since . . . since the Karp child was born. You even enjoyed the weeks of preparation for the twins, the prenatal visits, the organization of it all. How can you give up everything you have studied and worked for? For you the twins were a simple delivery, but don't think I didn't notice how skillfully you were able to handle the twisted cords."

"It was just a simple over and under, like undoing yarn!" Hannah demurred.

Rachael shook her head. "Tell me you don't want to deliver babies anymore."

"Of course I do!" Hannah stamped her foot. "But I don't want to fear recrimination each time or, worse, worry that I can't transfer a patient to a hospital without ending up in jail myself. That's one reason I asked your help with the West case, so that you could take Olga if she bled too much or if something else occurred."

"But if someone asks you to undertake a perfectly normal delivery?"

"I might do it."

"And you would love every minute of it!"

"Yes."

"Then you must remain a midwife!"

Hannah's heart pounded as she thought about becoming active again. "And go against the law, every time?"

"Hannah!" Dr. Jaffe shook her head so hard it seemed that sparks were shooting from her red cap of curls. "I feel as though we are back in Moscow and I am trying to push you into the Medical Section."

Hannah's thin mouth twitched with the memory. "You want me to go to Bellevue, back to school, to start all over again. That's like trying to send Lazar to kindergarten!"

"Compared to you, he'd be easy to convince, and we all know how stubborn he can be! Their program only lasts six months and you would deliver babies or assist every day. The doctors are very good and the facilities excellent."

"I heard that everything is in English, and you know even Benny writes his letters better than I do. I'd be so ashamed if I did anything wrong!"

"You'll distinguish yourself in the delivery room. And the mothers, so many of whom speak Russian or Yiddish, would find you a great comfort. I've seen them screaming and frightened because no one understands them or takes the time to explain what is happening."

"But it is all the way downtown. We are so settled here now!"

"When you lived downtown you delivered uptown. What is the difference?"

"I should stay home with the children; they need me there," Hannah argued, all the while concealing her budding excitement.

Rachael had almost lost her patience, so she only handed Hannah a slip of paper. "Mrs. Julian is in charge of the program. Talk it over with your brother before you decide."

"With Chaim?" How well Rachael understood her! Chaim would not be defeated by judges and courts and official pieces of paper. Chaim would pretend to join the ranks outwardly and then fight to change everything that was wrong within, as he was doing that very moment in the cloakmakers' union. What was it Papa had said? "There's always another way."

The next afternoon Hannah found herself inquiring at the Bellevue School of Midwifery.

"The best way to explain our program," said the directress, "is to give you a short tour of our facility."

As they walked up to the obstetrical floors of the sprawling red brick building, she began a memorized description of the training program in a voice that retained an aristocratic ring even though it was permanently hoarse.

"Did you know that Bellevue is now the only regular institution in America incorporated for the purpose of conferring a licensed diploma in midwifery?" she asked but did not wait for a reply. "Here we are, Mrs. Sokolow." She opened the double doors onto the ward. "This new wing is laid out in the most progressive design, with a mop sterilizer and utility room for every twenty-five patients. We are proud to have electricity, which allows us to heat a nursing bottle, to have hot water on hand for instruments, and to prepare the infant linens by ironing safely right in the nursery."

Though impressed by the white metal furniture, the immaculate hallways, and the familiar rows of mothers and babies being tended by a friendly staff, Hannah willed her expression to remain bland and disinterested.

"I expect you'd like to see labor and delivery, wouldn't you?" Mrs. Julian led the way into a large operating theater with fifty observation seats bolted to the floor. Hannah was shocked to see two delivery tables set up side by side but did not comment.

"This is the main obstetrical operating room," she said, pronouncing each *t* crisply. "We can handle two cases at the same time, which makes the teaching program even more efficient, as no one need miss either delivery. I believe we learn first by observation and second by participation. Our goal is to graduate technically educated midwives who will be as proficient as any physician in the area of confinements. Dr. Brannon, president of our Board of Trustees, has seen that our beds have been increased so that every midwife will be able to observe more than one hundred deliveries and attend almost half again as many before she graduates."

Hannah's mind raced with the essential calculations. "In six months I could do fifty births!" Hannah exclaimed. "That's at least two per week! And if I observed four or five more, I would have a chance, statistically, to see a breech once a month!"

"At least!" her guide said, slightly puzzled at what had aroused the young woman, who had seemed quite bored. "Any special case — breech, Caesarean, even a hemorrhage — is brought to the operating theater for demonstration purposes, and if possible, the teaching bell is rung to summon all available students to observe the procedures."

". . . the teaching bell is rung . . ." was the only part of that sentence Hannah heard. What would it be like to again respond to the call of a bell for classes, surgery, and meals; to walk down long passageways among doctors, nurses, midwives, and patients every day; to deliver baby after baby all in the same convenient place; to once again use and perfect her skills?

Mrs. Julian prattled on about how certified midwives were going to be organized in the future while Hannah hurried as far ahead as was polite to peek into the labor rooms. An Italian woman cried out every few seconds while her midwife impassively attended her. In another cubicle Hannah noticed a woman shivering with fright.

Silently she shook her head. I could show them a few things around here!

"... Dr. Mary Putnam Jacobi placed her stamp of approval upon this venture in her address to the American Medical Association in June ... Very gratifying after all our work ... Suitable education for the midwife is finally at hand ..." Mrs. Julian droned on.

They were in front of a smaller delivery room. A bound and drugged mother was hardly aware as her wet and naked baby lay mewing in the arms of a midwife who looked too young to know what she was doing. The baby seemed to understand and didn't cry too loudly.

"... more women coming voluntarily to our clinics ... an asset to the city ... a wise economy to centralize maternity care ... scientific data can be collected more efficiently."

Hannah paid no attention to Mrs. Julian's practiced prattle as she tried to control the anxious feeling that almost compelled her to burst into the room to remove the leather straps from the mother's wrists. Inhuman practice! Who ever thought such a treatment would be necessary? She wished there was not a minute more she would have to wait before she could enter the program. All these women ... all these babies! Prenatal, postnatal, deliveries... What had the director said? ... one an hour ... twenty-four babies a day!

"Do you think you might want to join us?" she asked Hannah.

Lost in a world of her own, Hannah missed the question. Could she permit herself to go through the ignominy of starting over from the beginning after all she had already learned and accomplished?

Despite Hannah's reticence, Mrs. Julian must have sensed the spark of interest Hannah was attempting to restrain. Now the directress used her most persuasive arguments. "Some of our more distinguished graduates have had the good fortune of going on to study at the Medical College of the New York Infirmary just across the street. Of course, a woman physician must still battle the great odds of public opinion and practical obstacles, but someone with determination, talent, and courage could succeed."

She opened a door to a small room just off the main corridor, which was empty except for a large wicker cradle in the center. "I've saved this for last. Do you know what they call this place?"

Hannah shook her head.

"The saddest room in New York. It is readied day and night to receive any baby whose mother cannot support it. When a mother leaving the ward lays her child there, she parts with it for all time and cannot reclaim her baby. But we promise them the babies will be cared for with love until the right family can be found. Some of our midwives rotate through here to care for our foundlings as well. Maybe you'd like to try that program too?"

A sob caught in Hannah's throat. Babies given away, mothers making such sorrowful decisions. "I'm primarily interested in delivery, but I've handled many babies and have training in pediatrics as well," she said solemnly.

"Many of our midwives find their most rewarding work here," Mrs. Julian said, confident she had snagged another serious applicant. "I'll give you the forms. You may fill them out at your leisure."

Still reluctant to proclaim her enthusiasm, Hannah politely took the papers and thanked Mrs. Julian for her kindness, but did not give her the satisfaction of a commitment. A residual nugget of anger at the way the medical establishment had treated her in the Belinsky matter restrained Hannah from embracing their rules and systems too quickly.

As soon as she was out on the sidewalk, she turned the corner and walked to the back of the hospital, which faced the river. She looked up at the imposing red flank of the building and noticed an outside iron stairway that led to the patients' veranda on the obstetrical floor. What a marvelous place for laboring women to walk during labor, Hannah decided. They could promenade all around the veranda without being out of sight of the delivery suites. And those large windows must be opened, for the view across the river would do wonders for those restless to give birth. "Must do something about that," she said half-aloud before realizing she had still not consciously made her decision to enroll.

Slowly she walked back toward the front of the hospital, reluctant to even lose sight of the birthing areas. Upstairs there were half a dozen expectant mothers who all carried their own little mysteries. What presentation, what size, what sex baby would they have? What would each need from Hannah and what could she do for them? How had she even considered forever refraining from this most exciting of ventures, when even if she had done a hundred or a thousand births it would not have been enough?

"Courage and determination"! Mrs. Julian's words suffused her completely. Dreams that had been dashed after leaving Moscow, after the Belinsky case, might still come true. Her license to practice could be restored, and there was still the possibility of becoming a doctor . . .

For a long moment Hannah studied the bleak escarpment of the hospital building. Maybe it was only a change in the angle of the sunlight reflected from the ribbon of river, but the dozens of windows seemed transformed from a blank, institutional stare to a benevolent gaze. A gust of air off the water ruffled the enrollment forms she clasped in her hand. She pressed them to her more closely. "Better not take them home, they might be lost," Hannah thought and turned back toward the cascade of front steps.

Inside the entranceway, she had the sense of something wonderfully familiar. Far away on one of the upper floors a bell tolled three times. Whether it was announcing the time of day or calling a midwife Hannah wasn't certain, but without another thought, she hurried to find Mrs. Julian. Maybe it wasn't too late to begin, to begin again, that very day.